BY TERRY BROOKS

Shannara

First King of Shannara

The Sword of Shannara

The Elfstones of Shannara

The Wishsong of Shannara

The Heritage of Shannara

The Scions of Shannara

The Druid of Shannara

The Elf Queen of Shannara

The Talismans of Shannara

The Voyage of the *Jerle Shannara*

Ilse Witch

Antrax

Morgawr

High Druid of Shannara

Jarka Ruus

Tanequil

Straken

Genesis of Shannara

Armageddon's Children

The Elves of Cintra

The Gypsy Morph

The World of Shannara

The Magic Kingdom of Landover

Magic Kingdom for Sale—Sold!

The Black Unicorn

Wizard at Large

The Tangle Box

Witches' Brew

A Princess of Landover

The Word and the Void

Running with the Demon

A Knight of the Word

Angel Fire East

Sometimes the Magic Works: Lessons from a Writing Life

THE MAGIC KINGDOM OF LANDOVER

VOLUME 1

THE MAGIC KINGDOM OF LANDOVER

VOLUME 1

TERRY BROOKS

BALLANTINE BOOKS DEL REY NEW YORK

The Magic Kingdom of Landover, volume 1 is a work of fiction. Names, characters, places, and incidents are the products of the author's imagination or are used fictitiously. Any resemblance to actual events, locales, or persons, living or dead, is entirely coincidental.

2009 Del Rey Trade Paperback Edition

Published in the United States by Del Rey, an imprint of
The Random House Publishing Group,
a division of Random House, Inc., New York.

DEL REY is a registered trademark and the Del Rey colophon
is a trademark of Random House, Inc.

Originally published in three separate volumes in the United States by Del Rey, an imprint of The Random House Publishing Group, a division of Random House, Inc., as *Magic Kingdom for Sale—Sold!* in 1986, *The Black Unicorn* in 1987, and *Wizard at Large* in 1988.

This book contains an excerpt from the forthcoming book *A Princess of Landover* by Terry Brooks. This excerpt has been set for this edition only and may not reflect the final content of the forthcoming edition.

Map by Russ Charpentier

ISBN 978-0-345-51352-6

Printed in the United States of America

www.delreybooks.com

2 4 6 8 9 7 5 3 1

Book design by Liz Cosgrove

CONTENTS

MISTS and the FAIRY WORLD
Melchor
Deep Fell
Rhyndweir
THE GREENSWARD
The Heart
Sterling Silver
LAKE COUNTRY
Lake Irrylyn
MISTS and the FAIRY WORLD

MISTS and the FAIRY WORLD
Fire Springs
EASTERN WASTELANDS
The MAGIC KINGDOM of LANDOVER
ew
Libiris
MISTS and the FAIRY WORLD
R. CHARPENTIER '09

MAGIC KINGDOM FOR SALE—SOLD!

For Kennard, Vernon, Bill, John and Mike
It happened something like this . . .

The Witch of the North seemed to think for a time, with her head bowed and her eyes upon the ground. Then she looked up and said, "I do not know where Kansas is, for I have never heard that country mentioned before. But tell me, is it a civilized country?"

"Oh, yes," replied Dorothy.

"Then that accounts for it. In the civilized countries I believe there are no witches left, nor wizards, nor sorceresses, nor magicians. But, you see, the Land of Oz has never been civilized, for we are cut off from all the rest of the world. There we still have witches and wizards amongst us."

—L. Frank Baum, *The Wizard of Oz*

CONTENTS

BEN

The catalogue was from Rosen's, Ltd. It was the department store's annual Christmas Wishbook.

It was addressed to Annie.

Ben Holiday stood frozen before the open cubicle of his mailbox, eyes slipping across the gaily decorated cover of the catalogue to the white address label and the name of his dead wife. The lobby of the Chicago high rise seemed oddly still in the graying dusk of the late afternoon rush hour, empty of everyone but the security guard and himself. Outside, past the line of floor-to-ceiling windows that fronted the building entry, the autumn wind blew in chill gusts down the canyon of Michigan Avenue and whispered of winter's coming.

He ran his thumb over the smooth surface of the Wishbook. Annie had loved to shop, even when the shopping had only been through the mail-order catalogues. Rosen's had been one of her favorite stores.

Sudden tears filled his eyes. He hadn't gotten over losing her, even after two years. Sometimes it seemed to him that losing her was nothing more than a trick of his imagination—that when he came home she would still be there waiting for him.

He took a deep breath, fighting back against the emotions that were aroused in him simply by seeing her name on that catalogue cover. It was silly to feel like this. Nothing could bring her back to him. Nothing could change what had happened.

His eyes lifted to stare into the dark square of the now-empty mailbox. He remembered what it had been like when he had first learned that she had been killed. He had just returned from court, a pre-trial on the Microlab case with old Wilson Frink and his sons. Ben was in his office, thinking of ways to persuade his opposition, a lawyer named Bates, that his latest offer of settlement would serve everyone's best interests, when the call had come in. Annie had been in an accident on the Kennedy. She was at St. Jude's in critical condition. Could he come right over . . . ?

He shook his head. He could still hear the voice of the doctor telling him what had happened. The voice had sounded so calm and rational. He had known at once that Annie was dying. He had known instantly. By the time he had gotten to the hospital, she was dead. The baby was dead, too. Annie had been only three months pregnant.

"Mr. Holiday?"

He looked about sharply, startled by the voice. George, the security guard, was looking over at him from behind the lobby desk.

"Everything all right, sir?"

He nodded and forced a quick smile. "Yes—just thinking about something."

He closed the mailbox door, shoved everything he had taken from it save the catalogue into one coat pocket and, still gripping the Wishbook in both hands, moved to the ground-floor elevators. He didn't care for being caught off balance like that. Maybe it was the lawyer in him.

"Cold day out there," George offered, glancing out into the gray. "Going to be a tough winter. Lot of snow, they say. Like it was a couple of years ago."

"Looks that way." Ben barely heard him as he glanced down again at the catalogue. Annie always enjoyed the Christmas Wishbook. She used to read him promos from some of its more bizarre items. She used to make up stories about the kind of people who might purchase such things.

He pushed the elevator call button and the doors opened immediately.

"Have a nice evening, sir," George called after him.

He rode the elevator to his penthouse suite, shucked off his topcoat, and walked into the front room, still clutching the catalogue. Shadows draped the furnishings and dappled the carpeting and walls, but he left the lights off and stood motionless before the bank of windows that looked out over the sunroof and the buildings of the city beyond. Lights glimmered through the evening gray, distant and solitary, each a source of life separate and apart from the thousands of others.

We are so much of the time alone, he thought. Wasn't it strange?

He looked down again at the catalogue. Why do you suppose they had sent it to Annie? Why were companies always sending mailers and flyers and free samples and God-knew-what-all to people long after they were dead and buried? It was an intrusion on their privacy. It was an affront. Didn't these companies update their mailing lists? Or was it simply that they refused ever to give up on a customer?

He checked his anger and, instead, smiled, bitter, ironic. Maybe he should phone it all in to Andy Rooney. Let him write about it.

He turned on the lights then and walked over to the wall bar to make himself a scotch, Glenlivet on the rocks with a splash of water; he measured it out and sipped at it experimentally. There was a bar meeting in a little less than two hours, and he had promised Miles that he would make this one. Miles Bennett was not only his partner, but he was probably his only real friend since Annie's death. All of the others had drifted away somehow, lost in the shufflings and rearrangings of life's social order. Couples and singles made a poor mix, and most of their friends had been couples. He hadn't done much to foster continuing friendships in any case, spending most of his time involved with his work and with his private, inviolate grief. He was not such good company anymore, and only Miles had had the patience and the perseverance to stay with him.

He drank some more of the scotch and wandered back again to the open windows. The lights of the city winked back at him. Being alone wasn't so bad, he reasoned. That was just the way of things. He frowned. Well, that was his way, in any case. It was his choice to be alone. He could have found companionship again from any one of a number of sources; he could have reintegrated himself into almost any of the city's myriad social circles. He had the necessary attributes. He was young still and successful; he was even wealthy, if money counted for anything—and in this world it almost always did. No, he didn't have to be alone.

And yet he did, because the problem was that he really didn't belong anyway.

He thought about that for a moment—forced himself to think about it. It wasn't simply his choosing to be alone that kept him that way; it was almost a condition of his existence. The feeling that he was an outsider had always been there. Becoming a lawyer had helped him deal with that feeling, giving him a place in life, giving him a ground upon which he might firmly stand. But the sense of not belonging had persisted, however diminished its intensity—a nagging certainty. Losing Annie had simply given it new life, emphasizing the transiency of any ties that bound him to whom and what he had let himself become. He often wondered if others felt as he did. He supposed they must; he supposed that to some extent everyone felt something of the same displacement. But not as strongly as he, he suspected. Never that strongly.

He knew Miles understood something of it—or at least something of Ben's sense of it. Miles didn't feel about it as Ben did, of course. Miles was the quintessential people person, always at home with others, always comfortable with his surroundings. He wanted Ben to be that way; he wanted to bring him out of that self-imposed shell and back into the mainstream of life. He viewed his friend as some sort of challenge in that regard. That was why Miles was so persistent about these damn bar meetings. That was why he kept after Ben to forget about Annie and get on with his life.

He finished the scotch and made himself another. He was drinking a lot lately, he knew—maybe more than was good for him. He glanced down at his watch. Forty-five minutes had gone by. Another forty-five and Miles would be there, his chaperone for the evening. He shook his head distastefully. Miles didn't understand nearly as much as he thought he did about some things.

Carrying his drink, he walked back across the room to the windows, stared out a moment, and turned away, closing the drapes against the night. He moved back to the couch, debating on whether to check the answerphone, and saw the catalogue again. He must have put it down without realizing it. It was lying with the other mail on the coffee table in front of the sectional sofa, its glossy cover reflecting sharply in the lamplight.

Rosen's, Ltd.—Christmas Wishbook.

He sat down slowly in front of it and picked it up. A Christmas catalogue of wishes and dreams—he had seen the kind before. An annual release from a department store that ostensibly offered something for everyone, this particular catalogue was for the select few only—the wealthy few.

Annie had always liked it, though.

Slowly, he began to page through it. The offerings jumped out at him, a collection of gifts for the hard-to-please, an assortment of oddities that were essentially one-of-a-kind and could be found nowhere but in the Wishbook. Dinner for two in the private California home of a famous movie star, transportation included. A ten-day cruise for sixty on a yacht, fully crewed and catered to order. A week on a privately owned Caribbean island, including the use of wine cellar and fully stocked larder. A bottle of one-hundred-and-fifty-year-old wine. Hand-blown glass and diamond creations, designed per request. A gold toothpick. Sable coats for little girls' dolls. A collector's chess set of science fiction film characters carved from ebony. A hand-woven tapestry of the signing of the Declaration of Independence.

The list of offerings went on, item after item, each more exotic and strange than the one before. Ben took a strong pull on his scotch, almost repulsed by the extravagance of it all, but fascinated nevertheless. Then he thumbed ahead into the center of the catalogue. There was a transparent bathtub with live goldfish encased in the framework. There was a silver shaving kit with your initials inlaid in gold. Why in God's name would anyone . . . ?

He caught himself midway through the thought, his eyes drawn instantly to an artist's rendering of the item being offered on the pages that lay open before him.

The promo of the item read as follows:

MAGIC KINGDOM FOR SALE

Landover—island of enchantment and adventure rescued from the mists of time, home of knights and knaves, of dragons and damsels, of wizards and warlocks. Magic mixes with iron, and chivalry is the code of life for the true hero. All of your fantasies become real in this kingdom from another world. Only one thread to this whole cloth is lacking—you, to rule over all as King and High Lord. Escape into your dreams, and be born again.

Price: $1,000,000.
Personal interview and financial disclosure.
Inquire of Meeks, home office.

That was all it read. The artist's colorful rendering depicted a knight on horseback engaged in battle with a fire-breathing dragon, a beautiful and rather thinly clad damsel shrinking from the conflict before a tower wall, and a dark-robed wizard lifting his hands as if to cast an awesome and life-stealing spell. Some creatures that might have been Elves or Gnomes or some such scampered about in the background, and the towers and parapets of great castles loomed against a gathering of hills and mists.

It had the look of something out of King Arthur and the Knights of the Round Table.

"This is nuts!" he muttered almost without thinking.

He stared at the item in disbelief, certain that he must be mistaken. Then he read it again. He read it a third time. It read the same. He finished his scotch in a single gulp and chewed on the ice, irritated with the nonsensicality of the offering. A million dollars for a fairy-tale kingdom? It was ridiculous. It had to be some kind of joke.

He threw down the catalogue, jumped to his feet, and crossed to the bar to mix himself a fresh drink. He stared momentarily at his reflection in the mirrored cabinet—a man of medium height, lean, trim, and athletic-looking, his face rather drawn, with high cheekbones and forehead, slightly receding hairline, hawk nose and piercing blue eyes. He was a man of thirty-nine going on fifty, a man on the verge of passing into middle age too young.

Escape into your dreams . . .

He crossed back to the couch, placed the drink on the coffee table and picked up the Wishbook once more. Again he read the item on Landover. He shook his head. No such place could possibly exist. The promo was a tease, a hype—what the car business called puffing. The truth was masked in the rhetoric. He chewed gingerly at the inside of his lip. Still, there wasn't all that much rhetoric being used to promote the item. And Rosen's was a highly respected department store; they were not likely to offer anything that they could not deliver, should a buyer appear.

He grinned. What was he thinking? What buyer? Who in his right mind would even consider . . . ? But of course he was questioning himself now. He was the one considering. He had been standing there, drinking his drink and thinking about how he didn't belong; and when he had picked up the Wishbook, the item on Landover had caught his attention right away. He was the one who felt himself the outsider in his own world, who had always felt himself the outsider, who was seeking always a way to escape what he was.

And now here was his chance.

His grin broadened. This was crazy! He was actually contemplating doing something that no sane man would even think twice about!

The scotch was working its way to his head now, and he got up again to walk it off. He looked at his watch, thinking of Miles, and suddenly he didn't want to go to that bar meeting. He didn't want to go anywhere.

He walked to the phone and dialed his friend.

"Bennett," the familiar voice answered.

"Miles, I've decided not to go tonight. Hope you don't mind."

There was a pause. "Doc, is that you?"

"Yeah, it's me." Miles loved to call him Doc, ever since the early days when they went up against Wells-Fargo on that corporate buy-out. Doc Holiday, courtroom gunfighter. It drove Ben nuts. "Look, you go on without me."

"You're going." Miles was unflappable. "You said you were going and you're going. You promised."

"So I take it back. Lawyers do it all the time—you read the papers."

"Ben, you need to get out. You need to see something of the world besides your office and your apartment—however lavish the two may be. You need to let your colleagues in the profession know that you're still alive!"

"You tell them I'm alive. Tell them I'll make the next meeting for sure. Tell them anything. But forget about me for tonight."

There was another pause, this one longer. "Are you all right?"

"Fine. But I'm in the midst of something. I want to stay with it."

"You work too hard, Ben."

"Don't we all? See you tomorrow."

He placed the receiver back on the cradle before Miles could say anything further. He stood staring down at the phone. At least he hadn't lied. He was in the midst of something, and he did want to stay with it—however crazy it might be. He took a drink of the scotch. If Annie were there, she would understand. She had always understood his fascination with puzzles and with challenges that others might simply step around. She had shared so much of that with him.

He shook his head. Of course, if Annie were there, none of this would be happening. He wouldn't be thinking about escaping into a dream that couldn't possibly be.

He paused, struck by the implications of that thought. Then holding his drink in his hand, he crossed back to the sofa, picked up the catalogue, and began reading once more.

Ben was late getting to the offices of Holiday and Bennett, Ltd. the next morning, and by the time he arrived his disposition was less than agreeable. He had scheduled an early appearance on a merger contest and gone straight to the Courts Building from home, only to discover that somehow his setting had been removed from the docket. The clerks had no idea how this had happened, opposing counsel was nowhere to be found, and the judge presiding simply advised him that a resetting would be the best solution to the dilemma. Since time was of the essence in the case in question, he requested an early setting—only to be told that the earliest setting possible was in thirty days. Things were always busiest with the approach of the holiday season, the motions clerk announced unsympathetically. Unimpressed with an explanation that he had heard at least twenty times already that November, he requested a setting for a preliminary injunction—only to be told that the judge hearing stays and pleas for temporary relief was vacationing for the next thirty days at some ski resort in Colorado, and it hadn't been decided yet who would bear his docket load while he was gone. A decision on that would probably be made by the end of the week and he should check back then.

The looks directed at him by clerks and judge alike suggested that this was the way of things in the practice of law and that he, of all people, ought to realize it by now. He ought, in fact, simply to accept it.

He did not choose to accept it, however, did not care in the least to accept it, and was, by God, sick and tired of the whole business. On the other hand, there was not very much he could do about it. So, frustrated and angered, he went on to work, greeted the girls in the reception area with a mumbled good morning, picked up his phone messages, and retired to the confines of his office to fume. He had enjoyed less than five minutes of that when Miles appeared through the doorway.

"Well, well, just a little ray of sunshine this morning, aren't we?" his friend needled cheerfully.

"Yeah, that's me," he agreed rocking back in his desk chair. "Joy to the world."

"Hearing didn't go so well, I gather?"

"Hearing didn't go at all. Some incompetent took it off the call. Now I'm told it can't be put back on until hell freezes over and cows fly." He shook his head. "What a life."

"Hey, it's a living. Besides, that's the way it all works—hurry up and wait, time is all we've got."

"Well, I'm fed up to the teeth with it!"

Miles moved over to occupy one of the client chairs that fronted the long oak desk. He was a big man, heavy through the middle, thick dark hair and mustache lending maturity to an almost cherubic face.

His eyes, perpetually lidded at half-mast, blinked slowly. "Know what your problem is, Ben?"

"I ought to. You've told me often enough."

"Then why don't you listen? Quit spending all of your time trying to change the things you can't!"

"Miles . . ."

"Annie's death and the way the legal system works—you can't change those kinds of things, Ben. Not now, not ever. You're like Don Quixote tilting with windmills! You're ruining your life, do you know that?"

Ben brushed Miles aside with a wave of his hand. "I do not know that, as a matter of fact. Besides, your equation doesn't balance. I know that nothing will bring Annie back—I've accepted that. But maybe it's not too late for the legal system—the system of justice that we used to know, the one we both went into the practice of law to uphold."

"You ought to listen to yourself sometime," Miles sighed. "There's nothing wrong with my equation, chief. My equation is painfully accurate. You have never accepted Annie's death. You live your life in a goddamned shell, because you won't accept what's happened—as if living like that is somehow going to change things! I'm your friend, Ben—maybe the only one you've got left. That's why I can talk to you like this—because you can't afford to lose me!"

The big man leaned forward. "And all of this crap about the way things used to be in the practice of law sounds like my father telling me how he used to walk five miles through the snow to get to school. What am I supposed to do—sell my car and walk to work from Barrington? You can't turn back the clock, no matter how much you might like to. You have to accept things as you find them."

Ben let Miles finish without interruption. Miles was right about one thing—only he could talk to him like this, and it was because he was his best friend. But Miles had always approached life differently than he, always preferring to blend in with his surroundings rather than to shape them, always preferring to make do. He just didn't understand that there were some things in life a man simply should not accept.

"Forget about Annie for the moment." Ben paused meaningfully before continuing. "Let me suggest that change is a fact of life, that it is a process brought about by the efforts of men and women dissatisfied with the status quo, and that it is essentially a good thing. Let me also suggest that change is frequently the result of what we have learned, not simply what we have envisioned. History plays a part in change. Therefore, what once was and was good ought not to be cast aside as being simply wishful reminiscence."

Miles brought up one hand. "Look, I'm not saying . . ."

"Can you honestly sit there, Miles, and tell me that you are satisfied with the direction that the practice of law in this country is taking? Can you even tell me that it is as good and true as it was fifteen years ago when we entered the profession? Look at what's happened, for Christ's sake! We are bogged down in a morass of legislation and regulation that reaches from here to China, and even the judges and lawyers don't understand half of it. We used to be able to call ourselves general practitioners—now we are lucky to be competent in one or two fields, simply because of the updating we must constantly do in order to keep ourselves current. The courts are slow and overburdened. The judges are all too often mediocre lawyers put on the bench through politics. The lawyers coming out of law school view their occupation as a way to make big bucks and get their names in the paper—forget the part about helping people. The whole profession has the worst press this side of Nazi Germany. We have advertising—advertising! Like used-car salesmen, or furniture-store dealers! We don't adequately educate ourselves. We don't adequately police ourselves. We just go through the motions and try to get by!"

Miles stared at him, his head cocked appraisingly. "Are you about finished?"

He nodded, slightly flushed. "Yeah, I suppose so. Did I leave anything out?"

Miles shook his head. "I think you covered the whole nine yards. Feel any better?"

"Much, thanks."

"Good. One final comment, then. I heard everything you said, I duly recorded every word, and I happen to agree with most of it. And I say to you nevertheless, so what? There have been thousands of speeches given, thousands of committee meetings held, thousands of articles written addressing the very problems you so eloquently outline in your tirade—and how much difference has any of it made?"

Ben sighed. "Not much."

"That is understating it. Since this is so, what difference do you think you are going to make?"

"I don't know. But that's not the point."

"No, I don't suppose it is for you. So, what the hell? If you want to enter into a one-man war with the system in an effort to change it, fine and dandy. But a little moderation in your commitment wouldn't hurt. A day off now and then for some of life's less pressing matters might give you some perspective and keep you from burning out completely. Okay?"

Ben nodded. "Okay. Yeah, okay. But I'm not good at moderation."

Miles grinned. "Tell me about it. Now let's talk about something else. Let's talk about last night. Believe it or not, a few people asked about you at the bar meeting—said they missed seeing you."

"They must be desperate for companionship, then."

Miles shrugged. "Maybe. What was so important that you had to cancel out? New case?"

Ben thought about it a moment, then shook his head. "No, nothing new. Just something I wanted to follow up on." He hesitated. Then impulsively he reached down into his briefcase and pulled out the Wishbook. "Miles, want to see something really odd? Take a look at this."

He thumbed the catalogue open to the item about Landover and passed it across the desk. His friend shifted forward to take it from him and then settled back again in the chair.

"Magic kingdom for sale . . . Landover—island of enchantment and adventure . . . Hey, what is this?" Miles fumbled to find the cover.

"It's a Christmas catalogue," Ben explained to the big man quickly. "From Rosen's, Ltd. out of New York. A Wishbook. You've seen the type—full of one of a kind gifts."

Miles started reading again, finished, and looked up. "Only a million dollars, huh? What a bargain! Let's fly right to New York and apply—beat the rush."

"What do you make of it?"

Miles stared at him. "Same as you, I hope. Someone is nuts!"

He nodded slowly. "That's what I thought, too. But Rosen's wouldn't put an advertisement in a catalogue like this if they couldn't produce."

"Then it must be staged. The dragons must be overgrown lizards or something. The magic must be sleight of hand." Miles laughed. "Knights and damsels courtesy of Central Casting, dragons courtesy of the San Diego Zoo! Johnny Carson will have the whole menagerie on sometime next week!"

Ben waited for the big man's laughter to die away. "Think so?"

"Of course, I think so! Don't you?"

"I'm not sure."

Miles frowned, then read the advertisement one time more. When he was done, he passed the catalogue back across the desk. "Is this what kept you home last night?"

"In part, yes."

There was a long silence. Miles cleared his throat. "Ben, don't tell me that you're thinking of . . ."

The phone rang. Ben picked it up, listened for a moment and looked across the desk at his friend. "Mrs. Lang is here."

Miles glanced at his watch and rose. "Needs a new will drafted, I think." He hesitated, looked for a moment as if he might say something more, then jammed his hands in his pants pockets and turned for the door. "Well, enough of this. I've got to get some work done. Catch you later."

He left the room frowning. Ben let him go.

Ben left work early that afternoon and went to the health club to work out. He spent an hour in the weight room, then spent another hour on the light and heavy fighter's bags he had persuaded them to install several years back. He had been a boxer in his teens—fought out of Northside for the better part of five years. He had been a silver glover and could have been a gold, but other interests had taken him away and then he had gone east to school. But he still kept his hand in—even sparring a couple of rounds now and then back at Northside when he found the time. For the most part, he simply worked out, staying fit, keeping himself sharp. He had done so religiously since Annie died. It had helped him to release some of the frustration and anger. It had helped him to fill the time.

It was true that he had not been able to accept her death, he thought as his cab worked its way through the rush hour traffic from the health club to the high rise. He could admit it to himself if not to Miles. The truth was that he didn't know how to accept it. He had loved her with an intensity that was frightening, and she him. They never spoke of it; they never had to. But it was always there. When she died, he had thought of killing himself. He had not done so only because he had known deep inside that he should not, that he should never give in to anything so obviously wrong, that Annie would not want him to. So he had gone on with his life in the best way that he could, but he had never found a way to accept that she was really gone. Perhaps he never would.

Frankly, he wasn't sure that it mattered all that much whether he did.

He paid the cabdriver at the curb, walked into the lobby of the high rise, greeted George, and boarded the elevator for his penthouse suite.

Miles saw him as a grief-stricken recluse, hiding from the world while he mourned his dead wife. Maybe that was the way everyone saw him. But Annie's death had not created the condition; it had merely emphasized it. He had been slipping back into himself more and more in recent years, dissatisfied with what he viewed as the continuing deterioration of his profession, frustrated with the way in which it seemed to sink down upon itself until it no longer served the purposes for which it had been created. Miles would think it odd that he should feel that way—Doc Holiday, the corporate trial lawyer who had slain more Goliaths than any David had ever dreamed of facing. What did he have to feel frustrated about when the system had worked so effectively for him? But of course one's personal successes sometimes only served to point up the inequities worked on others. It was that way with him.

He mixed a Glenlivet and water in his apartment and retired to the front room, seating himself on the sofa and staring out the window into the lights of the city. After a time, he pulled the Christmas Wishbook from Rosen's from his briefcase and opened it to the item on Landover. He had been thinking about it all day; he had been thinking of nothing else since he had first laid eyes on it last night.

What if it were real?

He sat there for a long time, the glass in his hand, the catalogue open before him, thinking about the possibility.

His present life, he felt, was at a standstill. Annie was dead. The profession of law—for him, at least—was just as dead. There were more cases to be taken, more courtroom battles to be won, more Goliaths for David to slay. But the excesses and deficiencies of the legal system would still be there. In the end, he would simply be going through the same ritual with its frustrations and disappointments, and it would all be meaningless. There had to be more for him in this life.

There had to be.

He looked at the colorful rendering of the knight in battle with the dragon, the damsel in the castle keep, the wizard casting his spell, the fairy folk looking on. Landover. A dream out of a Wishbook.

Escape into your dreams . . .

For one million dollars, of course. But he had the money. He had money enough to buy it three times over. His father and mother had both been wealthy and he had enjoyed a lucrative practice. The million dollars was there—if that was the way he chose to spend it.

And there was the interview with this fellow Meeks. That puzzled him. What was the purpose of the interview—to screen applicants? Did they anticipate there would be that many and was there some reason to choose among them? Perhaps, where a King was to be selected, there was.

He took a deep breath. What sort of King would he make? He had the price of the kingship—but so would others have it. He was physically and mentally fit—but others would be, too. He was experienced in dealing with people and with laws—others might not be. He was compassionate. He was honorable. He was farsighted.

He was crazy.

He finished off the drink, closed the Wishbook, and went into the kitchen to make dinner. He took his time about it, preparing a rather extravagant beef and vegetable dish, and served it to himself with wine. When the meal was finished, he moved back to the front room again and reseated himself on the sofa before the Wishbook.

He already knew what he was going to do. Perhaps he had known all along. He needed something to believe in again. He needed to recapture the magic that had first drawn him to the practice of law—the sense of wonder and excitement it had brought to his life. Most of all, he needed a challenge—because that was what gave life meaning.

Landover *could* offer him that.

He was not yet certain that it would, of course. Perhaps it was all an elaborate charade of the sort envisioned by Miles, where the dragons were large iguanas and the knights and wizards were all supplied by Central Casting. Perhaps the dream was a sham, an imitation of what the imagination would have it truly be. Even if it were all real—if it were all as described, all as the artist had rendered it to be—still it might be less than the dream. It might be as ordinary in truth as his present life.

Yet the gamble was worth it, because he had seen the parameters of his present life and there were no unknowns left in it. And somehow, in some unexplainable way, he knew that whatever choices he might make now, with Annie gone the only wrong choice he might make was to make no choice at all.

He crossed back to the bar and made himself an Irish Mist. He toasted himself solemnly in the mirror and drank.

He felt exhilarated.

The following morning, Ben went down to the office only long enough to cancel his appointments for the remainder of that week and the next and to wrap up a few small matters that needed immediate attention. He was taking a short vacation, he told the girls and the law student who clerked for them part-time, doing research. Everything could wait until he returned. Miles was in court in Crystal Lake, so there were no questions asked. It was just as well.

He called O'Hare then and booked a flight.

By noon, he was on his way to New York.

MEEKS

New York City was cold, gray, and alien, the jagged edges of its bones cutting into a sky masked in clouds and mist, the flat planes of its skin glistening through a steady downpour. Ben watched it materialize beneath him as if by magic as the 727 slipped over the waters of the East River and settled down toward the empty runway. Traffic jammed the distant freeways, lifeblood flowing through arteries and veins, but the city had the feel of a corpse.

He took a cab from LaGuardia to the Waldorf, settled back in silence as the driver played reggae, and ignored him. He booked a single at the Waldorf, resisting the temptation of requesting a suite. There would be no such modern suites in Landover. It was a meaningless concession perhaps, but he had to start somewhere, and this was as good a place as any. One step at a time, as the saying went.

In his room, he took five minutes to unpack, then picked up the Manhattan phone directory and looked up the number to Rosen's. He found it in bold print, dialed and waited. When the department store switchboard answered, he asked for Customer Service and was transferred. He indicated to the new voice that he was interested in an item in the Christmas Wishbook and needed to make an appointment with Mr. Meeks. There was a pause, a request for the item number, and again he was transferred.

This time he was kept waiting for several minutes. Then a third voice came on the line, a woman's also, this one soft and graveled. Could he give her his name, address and the number of a major credit card? He could. When did he wish to see Mr. Meeks? Tomorrow morning, if possible. He was visiting from Chicago for a few days only. Would tomorrow morning at ten o'clock be satisfactory? That would be fine. Ten o'clock sharp, then? Fine.

The line went dead. He stared at it for a moment, then hung up.

He went down to the lobby, bought a *Times,* drank several scotches—Glenlivet and water over ice, as usual—and went in to dinner. He ate with the paper before him, scanning its sections without interest, his mind elsewhere. He was back in his room by seven. He watched a news special on El Salvador, and wondered how after so many years people could continue to kill each other so casually. A variety hour special followed, but he let it play without watching, distracted by a sudden need to analyze the particulars of what he was about. He had thought it through at least a dozen times already that day, but there was always the same nagging uncertainty.

Did he really know what he was doing? Did he really appreciate what he was getting into?

The answers this time were the same as they had been each time before. Yes, he knew what he was doing. Yes, he appreciated what he was getting into. At least, as far as he was able to, he did. One step at a time, remember. He knew he would be leaving a lot behind him if he went and if this Kingdom of Landover proved to be real, but most of it would be in the nature of material possessions and creature comforts, and those really didn't matter to him anymore. Cars and trains and airplanes, refrigerators and stoves and dishwashers, indoor toilets and electric shavers—all the modern things that were left behind to go fishing in Canada. Except that on a fishing trip, such things were left behind for only a few weeks. That wouldn't be the case here. This would be for much longer than a few weeks, and it wouldn't be like any camping trip he had ever heard about—or at least he didn't think it would.

What would it be like, he wondered suddenly? What would it be like in this fairy-tale kingdom called Landover—this kingdom that had somehow come to be offered for sale in a department store catalogue? Would it be like the land of Oz with Munchkins and witches and a tin man who talked? Would there be a yellow brick road to follow?

He resisted a sudden urge to pack up his suitcase and get the hell out of New York before going any further with the whole business. When you got right down to it, what mattered was not the sanity of his inquiry or the future into which he might choose to step. What mattered was the conscious decision to make some change in his life and in making that change to find something that would offer him the purpose of being that he had lost. When you held your ground, the old saying went, you stopped moving. When you stopped moving, everything about you would eventually pass you by.

He sighed. Trouble was, those old bromides always sounded truer than they were.

The variety show gave way to the late news, weather, and sports. Ben undressed and put on pajamas (did people wear pajamas in Landover?), brushed his teeth (did people brush their teeth in Landover?), shut off the television, and went to bed.

He was awake early the next morning, having slept poorly as he always did the first night away from home on a trip. He showered, shaved, dressed in a dark blue business suit, caught the elevator to the lobby where he purchased an early edition of the *Times,* and went into Oscar's for breakfast.

By nine o'clock, he was on his way to Rosen's.

He chose to walk. The decision was a perverse mix of stubbornness and wariness. The store was only half a dozen blocks from the hotel on Lexington, and anything that close ought to be walked. The day was iron gray and chill, but the rains had moved northeast into New England. A cab was a waste of money. Furthermore, by walking he could approach the store at his own pace and on his own terms—kind of work up to what he was going to do. The trial lawyer in him always appreciated the advantage of being able to orchestrate one's own entrance.

He took his time, letting the feel of the autumn morning bring him fully awake, but he was there by nine-forty anyway. Rosen's was a fifteen-storey chrome-and-glass cornerstone to two thirty-plus-storey skyscrapers that ran half a block on Lexington and the better part of a short block on the cross street west. An old establishment, the store had obviously been remodeled when the skyscrapers had gone in, the aged stone facade giving way to a more modern look. Plate-glass display windows lined the walkway along Lexington, filled with fashions displayed on mannequins with frozen smiles and empty stares. The late morning rush hour traffic passed them by unsmiling, unseeing. Ben followed the line of windows south to a recessed entry and passed through two sets of double doors sandwiching a weather foyer to the store within.

The ground floor of Rosen's opened out before him, cavernous, polished, sterile. Rows of metal-and-glass display cases filled with jewelry, cosmetics, and silver filled the hall, gleaming and shining beneath a flood of fluorescent light. A handful of shoppers browsed the aisles that ran between the display cases while store personnel looked on. No one seemed much interested in generating sales. It all had the appearance of some arcane ritual. He glanced about. To his right, an escalator climbed through the ceiling to the floor above. To his left, a bank of elevators lined a distant wall. Straight ahead, where even the most bewildered shopper could not fail to see it, a glass-encased directory announced the departments and the floors on which they could be found.

He took a moment to read the directory. There was no listing for Meeks. He hadn't really expected that there would be. The departments were listed alphabetically. Under the letter C he found the heading, Customer Service, special ordering—eleventh floor. Fair enough, he thought—he would try that. He angled his way through the maze of cases to the elevators, caught one standing open and took it to the eleventh floor.

He stepped from the elevator into a reception area comfortably furnished with overstuffed chairs and couches and fronted by a broad, wraparound desk and typing station. An attractive, thirtyish woman sat behind the desk, absorbed in a phone conversation. Rows of lighted buttons blinked on and off on her console.

She finished her conversation, hung up the phone and smiled pleasantly. "Good morning. May I help you?"

He nodded. "My name is Holiday. I have an appointment at ten with Mr. Meeks."

He might have imagined it, but he thought her smile faded slightly. "Yes, sir. Mr. Meeks does not use offices on this floor. Mr. Meeks uses offices on the penthouse level."

"The penthouse level?"

"Yes, sir." She pointed to another elevator in an alcove to Ben's right. "Simply press the button labeled PL. That will take you to Mr. Meeks. I will telephone to let his receptionist know that you are coming."

"Thank you." He hesitated. "This is the Mr. Meeks who is in charge of special ordering, isn't it?"

"Yes, sir. Mr. Meeks."

"The reason I ask is that your directory lists Customer Service, special ordering, on this floor."

The receptionist brushed nervously at her hair. "Sir, we post no listing for Mr. Meeks. He prefers that his clients come through us." She tried a quick smile. "Mr. Meeks handles only our specialty items—a very select collection of merchandise."

"The items in the Christmas Wishbook?"

"Oh, no. Most of those are handled by regular personnel. Mr. Meeks is not in the employ of Rosen's. Mr. Meeks is a privately employed sales specialist who acts as our agent in certain sales transactions. Mr. Meeks handles only the most exotic and unusual of the items offered in the Wishbook, Mr. Holiday." She leaned forward slightly. "He designates his own line of sales items, I understand."

Ben lifted his eyebrows in response. "Quite talented at his work, then, is he?"

She looked away again suddenly. "Yes, very." She reached for the phone. "I will call up for you, Mr. Holiday." She pointed to the second elevator. "They will be expecting you when you arrive. Good-bye."

He said good-bye in response, walked into the designated elevator and punched PL. The doors closed with the receptionist glancing covertly after him as she held the phone receiver to her ear.

He rode the elevator in silence, listening to the sound of the machinery. There were only four buttons on the panels above and next to the doors, numbered 1, 2, 3, and PL. They stayed dark for a time as the elevator rose, then began to light in sequence. The elevator did not stop for anyone else along the way. Ben almost wished that it had done so. He was beginning to feel as if he had stepped into the Twilight Zone.

The elevator stopped, the doors opened and he found himself back in a reception area almost identical to the one he had just left. This time the receptionist was an older woman, in her fifties perhaps, diligently engaged in sorting through a raft of papers stacked in piles on her desk while a harried-looking man of like age stood before her, his back to the elevator, his voice high-pitched and angry.

". . . don't have to do everything that old bastard tells us, and someday he's going to hear about it! Thinks every last one of us is at his beck and call! If he doesn't quit treating us like lackeys, then, damn it, I'll take this to . . ."

He cut himself short as the receptionist caught sight of Ben. Hesitating, he turned and stalked quickly into the open elevator. A moment later, the doors slid shut.

"Mr. Holiday?" the receptionist inquired, her voice soft and graveled. It was the woman he had spoken to on the phone the previous afternoon.

"Yes," he acknowledged. "I have an appointment with Mr. Meeks."

She picked up the phone and waited. "Mr. Holiday, sir. Yes. Yes, I will."

She placed the receiver back in its cradle and looked up. "It will only be a few moments, Mr. Holiday. Would you have a seat, please?"

He glanced about, then took a seat at one end of a sofa. There were magazines and newspapers on a table beside him, but he ignored them. His gaze wandered idly about the reception area, a well-lighted, cheerful center with solid wood desks and cabinets and cool colors on the walls and floors.

A few minutes passed and the phone on the receptionist's desk rang. She picked up the receiver, listened momentarily, and hung up.

"Mr. Holiday?" She rose and beckoned. "This way, please."

She led him into a corridor that opened up behind her work area. The corridor ran past a series of closed doors and branched left and right. That was all the farther Ben could see.

"Follow the hallway back, left up the stairs to the door at its end. Mr. Meeks will be expecting you."

She turned and walked back to her desk. Ben Holiday stood where he was for a moment, glancing first at the empty corridor, then at the retreating figure of the receptionist, then back again at the corridor.

So what are you waiting for? he asked himself admonishingly.

He went along the corridor to where it branched and turned left. The doors he passed were closed and bore no title designation or number. Fluorescent ceiling lights seemed pale against the pastel greens and blues of the corridor walls. Thick pile carpet absorbed the sound of his shoes as he walked. It was very still.

He hummed the theme from *The Twilight Zone* under his breath as he reached the staircase and began to climb.

The staircase ended at a heavy oak door with raised panels and the name "Meeks" stamped on a brass back plate screwed into the wood. He stopped before the door, knocked, turned the sculpted metal handle and stepped inside.

Meeks was standing directly in front of him.

He was very tall, well over six feet, old and bent, his face craggy, his hair white and grizzled. He wore a black leather glove on his left hand. His right hand and arm were missing completely, the empty sleeve of his corduroy jacket tucked into a lower pocket. Pale blue eyes that were hard and steady met Ben's. Meeks looked as if he had fought and survived more than a few battles.

"Mr. Holiday?" he asked, his voice almost a whisper. He sounded a good deal like his receptionist. Ben nodded. "I'm Meeks." The head dipped slightly. He didn't offer his hand and neither did Ben. "Please come in and have a chair."

He turned and shuffled away, hunching as he went as if his legs no longer worked properly. Ben followed him wordlessly, glancing about as he went. The office was elegant, a richly appointed room furnished with a massive old desk of scrolled oak, matching chairs with stuffed leather seats and backs, and workbenches and endtables covered with charts and magazines and what appeared to be work files. Floor-to-ceiling bookcases lined three walls, filled with ancient tomes and artifacts of all kinds. A bank of windows comprised the fourth wall, but the curtains were drawn tight across them and there were only the ceiling lamps to give the room its oddly muted light. Deep pile carpet of earthen brown sprouted from the floor like dried saw grass. The room smelled faintly of furniture polish and old leather.

"Sit down, Mr. Holiday." Meeks beckoned to a chair drawn up before the desk, then shuffled his way around to the overstuffed swivel chair on the other side, easing himself down into the worn leather gingerly. "Can't move like I used to. Weather tightens the bones. Age and weather. How old are you, Mr. Holiday?"

Ben glanced up, midway through the process of seating himself. The sharp, old eyes were fixed on him. "Forty, come January," he answered.

"A good age." Meeks smiled faintly, but without humor. "A man's still got his strength at forty. He knows most of what he's going to learn, and he's got the strength to put it to good use. Is that so with you, Mr. Holiday?"

Ben hesitated. "I guess so."

"That's what your eyes say. Eyes tell more about a man than anything he says. Eyes reflect a man's soul. They reflect a man's heart. Sometimes they even tell the truths a man wants to keep hidden." He paused. "Can I offer you something to drink? Coffee, a cocktail, perhaps?"

"No, nothing, thank you." Ben shifted in his chair impatiently.

"You don't believe that it's possible, do you?" Meeks' brows furrowed deeply, his voice soft. "Landover. You don't believe it exists."

Ben studied the other man thoughtfully. "I'm not sure."

"You appreciate the possibilities, but you question them, too. You seek the challenges that are promised, but you fear they may be only paper windmills. Think of it—a world like nothing anyone on this earth has ever seen! But it sounds impossible. If I might invoke a time-honored cliché, it sounds too good to be true."

"It does."

"Like a man walking on the moon?"

Ben thought a moment. "More like truth in lending. Or full faith and credit between sister states. Or perhaps consumer protection against false advertising."

Meeks stared at him. "You are a lawyer, Mr. Holiday?"

"I am."

"And you believe in our system of justice, then?"

"I do."

"You do, but you know as well that it doesn't always work, don't you? You want to believe in it, but it disappoints you much too often."

He waited. "That's a fair statement, I suppose," Ben admitted.

"And you think it might be that way with Landover as well." Meeks made it a statement of fact, not a question. He leaned forward, his craggy face intense. "Well, it isn't. Landover is exactly what the advertisement promises. It has everything that the advertisement says that it has and much more—things that are only myth in this world, things only barely imagined. But real in Landover, Mr. Holiday. Real!"

"Dragons, Mr. Meeks?"

"All of the mythical fairy creatures, Mr. Holiday—exactly as promised."

Ben folded his hands before him. "I'd like to believe you, Mr. Meeks. I came to New York to inquire about this . . . catalogue item because I want to believe it exists. Can you show me anything that would help prove what you say?"

"You mean flyers, color brochures, pictures of the land, references?" His face tightened. "They don't exist, Mr. Holiday. This item is a carefully protected treasure. The specifics of where it lies, what it looks like, what it offers—that is all privileged information which can be released only to the buyer whom I, as the seller's designated agent, ultimately select. As a lawyer, I am sure that you can appreciate the limitations imposed upon me by the word 'privileged,' Mr. Holiday."

"Is the identity of the seller privileged as well, Mr. Meeks?"

"It is."

"And the reason that this item is being offered for sale in the first place?"

"Privileged, Mr. Holiday."

"Why would anyone sell something as marvelous as this fantasy kingdom, Mr. Meeks? I keep asking myself that question. I keep asking myself if I'm not somehow buying a piece of the Brooklyn Bridge. How do I know that your seller even has the authority to sell Landover?"

Meeks smiled, an attempt at reassurance. "That was all checked carefully prior to listing. I supervised the inquiry myself."

Ben nodded. "So it all comes down to your word, doesn't it?"

Meeks sat back again. "No, Mr. Holiday. It comes down to the worldwide reputation of Rosen's as a department store that always delivers what it offers exactly as promised in its catalogues and advertisements. It comes down to the terms of the contract the store offers to the buyer on specialty items such as this one—a contract that permits recovery of the entire purchase price less a small handling fee should the item fail to prove satisfactory. It comes down to the way we do business."

"Could I see a copy of this contract?"

Meeks bridged the fingers of his gloved hand against his chin and stroked the ridges and lines of his face. "Mr. Holiday, I wonder if we might first back this conversation up a bit to permit me to fulfill the terms of my consignment of this specialty item. You are here to decide whether or not you wish to purchase Landover. But you are also here so that I might decide whether or not you qualify as a purchaser. Would a few questions to that end be an imposition?"

Ben shook his head. "I wouldn't think so. But I'll tell you if they are."

Meeks smiled like the Cheshire Cat and nodded his understanding.

For the next thirty minutes or so, he asked his questions. He asked them very much the way a skilled attorney would ask them of a witness at an oral deposition in pre-trial discovery—with tact, with brevity, and with purpose. Meeks knew what he was looking for, and he probed for it with the experienced touch of a surgeon. Ben Holiday had seen a good many trial lawyers in his years of practice, some of them more accomplished than he. But he had never seen anyone as good as Meeks.

In the end, a lot of ground was covered. Ben had graduated fifteen years earlier from Chicago University's School of Law, Order of the Coif, *summa cum laude*. He had gone into practice immediately with one of the larger firms, then left after five years to form his own firm with Miles, specializing in litigation. He had won a number of nationally reported corporate law cases as a plaintiff's attorney and settled dozens more. He was respected by his fellow attorneys as one of the best in his field. He had served as president of the Chicago Bar Association and as chairman of a number of committees on the Illinois State Bar. There was talk of running him for president of the American Trial Lawyers Association.

He came from a very wealthy family. His mother had been born into money; his father had made his in futures. Both were dead. He had no brothers or sisters. With Annie's death, he had been left essentially alone. There were some distaff cousins on the West Coast and an uncle in Virginia, but he hadn't seen any of them for better than five years. He had few close friends—in truth, he had only Miles. His colleagues respected him, but he kept them at a distance. His life in the past few years revolved almost exclusively around his work.

"Have you any administrative experience, Mr. Holiday?" Meeks asked him at one point, a rather veiled look to the hard, old eyes that suggested the question asked something more.

"No."

"Any hobbies?"

"None," he answered, thinking as he did that it was true, that he in fact had no hobbies nor personal pastimes save for the time he spent in training at Northside. He almost amended his answer, then decided it did not matter.

He gave to Meeks the financial statement he had prepared in response to the catalogue advertisement, detailing his net worth. Meeks examined it wordlessly, nodded in satisfaction and set it on the desk before him.

"You are an ideal candidate, Mr. Holiday," he said softly, the whisper quality of his voice becoming almost a hiss. "You are a man whose roots can be easily severed—a man who will not have to worry about leaving family or friends who will inquire too closely of his whereabouts. Because, you see, you will not be able to communicate with anyone but myself during your first year away. That is one of the conditions of acceptance. This should pose no problem for you. You are also a man with sufficient assets to make the purchase—hard assets, not paper assets. You can appreciate the difference. But most importantly, perhaps, you are a man who has something to offer as King of Landover. I don't suppose you've thought much of that, but it is something that matters a great deal to those for whom we act as agent. You have something very special to offer."

He paused. "Which is?" Ben asked.

"Your professional background, Mr. Holiday. You are a lawyer. Think of the good that you can do as not simply one who interprets the law but as one who makes it. A king needs a sense of justice to reign. Your intelligence and your education should serve you well."

"You mean that I shall have need of them in Landover, Mr. Meeks?"

"Certainly." The other's face was expressionless. "A king always has need of intelligence and education."

For an instant Ben thought he detected something in the other's voice that made the statement almost a private joke. "You have personal knowledge of what a king needs, Mr. Meeks?"

Meeks smiled, hard and quick. "If you mean, do I have personal knowledge of what a King of Landover needs, the answer is yes. Background is required of our clients in a listing such as this, and the background provided me suggests that Landover's ruler will have need of the qualities that you possess."

Ben nodded slowly. "Does this mean that my application has been accepted?"

The old man leaned back again in his chair. "What of your own questions, Mr. Holiday? Hadn't we better address those first?"

Ben shrugged. "I'll want them addressed sometime. It might as well be now. Why don't we begin with the contract—the one that's guaranteed to protect me from making what most people would consider a foolish investment."

"You are not most people, Mr. Holiday." The craggy face dropped a shade, changing the configuration of lines and hollows like a twisted rubber mask. "The agreement is this. You will have ten days to examine your purchase with no obligation. If at the end of that time you find it not to be as advertised or to be otherwise unsatisfactory, you may return here for a full refund of your purchase price less a handling fee of five percent. A reasonable charge, I'm sure you'll agree."

"That's it? That's the whole contract?" Ben was incredulous. "All it takes is my decision to back out?"

"That's all it takes." Meeks smiled. "Of course, the decision must be made in the first ten days, you understand."

Ben stared at him. "And everything that's been advertised in the catalogue will be there as promised? All of it? The dragons and knights and witches and warlocks and fairy creatures?"

"And you will be their King, Mr. Holiday. You will be the man to whom all must answer. A great deal of power—but also a great deal of responsibility. Do you think that you are equal to the challenge?"

The room went still as Ben sat before old Meeks and thought of the roads in his life that had led down to this moment. Except for Annie, he had lost little on his journey. He had taken the opportunities that mattered and made the most of them. Now he was presented with an opportunity greater than any previously offered and in taking it he would be leaving nothing of consequence behind. With Annie gone, everything that mattered lay ahead.

Nevertheless, he hesitated. "Could I see a copy of that contract now, Mr. Meeks?"

The old man reached into his center desk drawer and withdrew a single sheet of paper backed in triplicate. He passed it across the desk to Ben. Ben picked up the contract and read it through carefully. It was exactly as the old man had promised. The Kingship of Landover was to be sold to him for a price of one million dollars. The language of the catalogue promo was repeated with appropriate warranties. The closing paragraphs provided for a full refund of the purchase price less the handling charge if within ten days of arrival in Landover the purchaser chose to return the specialty item and withdraw from the Kingdom. A key for such withdrawal would be provided at time of purchase.

Ben paused on reading the final lines. The purchaser agreed on forfeiture of the full purchase price if he or she returned the item anytime after the first ten days *or* if he or she chose to abandon Landover for any reason during the first year of Kingship.

"What is the point of this final covenant?" he asked, glancing back again at Meeks. "Why can't I leave for a visit back?"

Meeks smiled—a rather poor attempt. "My client is concerned that the purchaser of Landover appreciate the responsibilities that Kingship entails. A man not willing to—what is the saying?—'stick it out' for at least a year is not a worthy candidate for the job. The agreement assures that you will not wander off and leave the duties of the throne unattended—at least for that first year."

Ben frowned. "I guess I can understand your client's concern." He placed the contract back on the desk, one hand resting on it lightly. "But I'm still a bit skeptical about the offer in general, Mr. Meeks. I think I should be candid. It all seems a bit too easy. A mythical kingdom with fairy creatures that no one has ever seen or heard about before? A place no one has ever been to, that no one has ever come across? And all I have to do is to give Rosen's one million dollars and I own it?"

Meeks said nothing. His aged, craggy face was expressionless.

"Is this kingdom in North America?" Ben pressed.

Meeks said nothing.

"Do I need a passport to reach it? Or medical protection from its diseases?"

Meeks shook his head slowly. "You need no passport or immunization. You need only courage, Mr. Holiday."

Ben flushed slightly. "I think some common sense might be called for as well, Mr. Meeks."

"A purchase such as the one you propose to make, Mr. Holiday, requires least of all common sense. If common sense were the basis of the sale, neither one of us would be having this conversation, would we?" The old man's smile was cold. "Let us be candid, as you suggest. You are a man seeking something that is not available to you in the world you know. You are a man who is tired of his life and all of its trappings. If you were not, you would not be here. I am a man who specializes in selling specialty items—items that are bizarre, that appeal to a limited market, that are invariably difficult to merchandise. I am a man who cannot afford to jeopardize his reputation by selling something that is in any way counterfeit. If I did so, I would not have lasted long in this business. I play no games with you, and I sense that you play none with me.

"Nevertheless, there are certain things that both of us must accept on faith. I must accept you as a potential ruler of Landover basically on faith, knowing little of your real character, but only so much as I have surmised from our short interview. And you must accept much of what I tell you of Landover on faith as well, because there is no meaningful way to show it to you. You must experience it, Mr. Holiday. You must go there and learn of it for yourself."

"In ten days, Mr. Meeks?"

"Time enough, believe me, Mr. Holiday. If you find otherwise, simply use the key provided you to return."

There was a long silence. "Does this mean that you have decided to offer me the purchase?" Ben asked.

Meeks nodded. "I have. I think you are eminently qualified. What do you say to that, Mr. Holiday?"

Ben looked down at the contract. "I'd like to think about it a bit."

Meeks chuckled dryly. "The caution of a lawyer—well and good. I can give you twenty-four hours before the item becomes available to the open market once more, Mr. Holiday. My next appointment is scheduled at one o'clock tomorrow. Take longer if you wish, but I can promise nothing after one day's time."

Ben nodded. "Twenty-four hours should be enough."

He reached for the contract, but Meeks slipped it quickly back. "My policy—and the store's—is not to allow copies of our contracts out of the office prior to signing. You may, of course, examine it again tomorrow at your convenience if you decide to buy."

Ben climbed to his feet and Meeks rose with him, tall and stooped. "You should make the purchase, Mr. Holiday," the old man's whispered voice encouraged. "You are the man for the job, I think."

Ben pursed his lips. "Maybe."

"If you decide to make the purchase, the contract will be waiting for you at the receptionist's desk. Thirty days will be allowed to complete arrangements for payment of the list price. Upon receiving payment in full, I will make available to you instructions for undertaking the journey to Landover and assuming the throne."

He walked Ben to the office door and opened it. "Do yourself a favor. Make the purchase, Mr. Holiday."

The door swung closed again, and Ben stood alone.

He walked back to the Waldorf through the noonday rush, had a leisurely lunch and retired to the lounge just off the lobby. With a yellow pad and pen in hand, he began to make notes about his interview with Meeks.

A number of things still troubled him. One of them was Meeks himself. There was something odd about that old man—something that went beyond his rough appearance. He had the instincts of a seasoned trial lawyer—hard-nosed and predatory. He was pleasant enough, but beneath the surface was a shell of armor two inches thick. The bits and pieces of conversation Ben had overheard in the reception areas and the looks he had seen in the receptionists' faces suggested that Meeks was not the easiest man to work with.

Yet it was more than that. Ben just couldn't seem to put his finger on what it was.

There was the problem, too, of still not having learned much of anything about Landover. No pictures, no flyers, no brochures—nothing. Too difficult to describe, Meeks had hedged. You have to see it. You have to accept the sale on faith. Ben grimaced. If their roles were switched and Meeks were the purchaser, he didn't think for one minute that that old man would settle for what he had been told!

He hadn't really learned anything about Landover in the interview that he hadn't known going into it. He didn't know where it was or what it looked like. He didn't know anything other than what had been described in the brochure.

Escape into your dreams . . .

Maybe.

And maybe he would be escaping into his nightmares.

All he had to fall back on was the clause in the contract that let him out of the purchase if he chose to rescind within ten days. That was fair enough. More than fair, really. He would lose only the fifty-thousand-dollar handling fee—an expensive, but not unbearable loss. He could journey to this magical kingdom with its fairy folk, with its dragons and damsel and all, and if he found it to be any sort of ripoff, he could journey back again and reclaim his money.

Guaranteed.

He scribbled notes hastily on the pad for a moment, and then looked up suddenly and stared out across the empty lounge.

The truth was that none of that mattered a whit. The truth was that he was prepared to make the purchase just as things stood.

And that was the real problem. That was the thing that bothered him the most. He was prepared to spend a million dollars on a dream because his life had reached a point where nothing that he was or had mattered to him anymore. Anything was preferable to that—even something as wild as what he was considering, a fantasy like Landover with iguanas and Hollywood make-believe. Miles would say he needed help if he were even considering this ridiculous purchase—serious, professional help. Miles would be right, too.

So why was it that none of that made any difference to him? Why was it that he was probably going to make the purchase nevertheless?

His lean frame stretched in the cushioned easy chair. Because, he answered himself. Because I want to try something that other men just dream about. Because I don't know if I can do it, and I want to find out. Because this is the first real challenge that I have come across since losing Annie, and without that challenge, without something to pull me from the mire of my present existence . . .

He took a deep breath, the sentence left unfinished in his mind. Because life is a series of chances, he thought instead, and the bigger the chance, the greater the satisfaction if he were to succeed.

And he would succeed. He knew he would.

He tore the notes from his yellow pad and shredded them.

He slept on the matter as he had promised himself that he would, but his mind was already made up. At ten o'clock the next morning he was back at Rosen's, back in the penthouse at the receptionist's desk fronting the corridor that led to Meeks' secluded office. The receptionist did not seem at all surprised to see him. She handed him the contract with its triplicate carbons together with a statement of Rosen's payment policy allowing thirty days same as cash on all specialty items purchased. He read the contract once again, saw that it was the same, and signed it. With a carbon copy tucked into his suit pocket, he departed the building and caught a cab to LaGuardia.

By noon, he was on his way back to Chicago. He felt better than he had felt in a very long time.

LANDOVER

The good feeling lasted until the next morning when he began to discover that no one else was quite as keen as he was on this proposed change in his life.

He called his accountant first. He had known Ed Samuelson for better than ten years; while they were not close friends, they were nevertheless close business associates who respected each other's advice. Ben had served as attorney for the accountancy firm of Haines, Samuelson and Roper, Inc. for almost the whole of that time. Ed Samuelson had been his accountant from the beginning. Ed was probably the only man alive who knew the full extent of his holdings. Ed had worked with him when his parents had passed away. He had suggested most of the investments that Ben had bought into. He knew Ben to be a shrewd and astute businessman.

But when Ben called him that morning and told him—*told* him, not asked him—to sell bonds and securities valued at almost one million dollars and to do so within the next ten days, it was clear to him that Ben had lost his mind. He exploded through the phone receiver. A sale such as that was unadulterated madness! Bonds and CDs could be liquidated only at a loss, because the penalty for early withdrawal was severe. Stocks would have to be sold at market value and in many cases the market was down. Ben would lose money all the way around. Even the tax deductions available from such a rash act couldn't begin to compensate him for the losses he would suffer! Why, in God's name, was it necessary to do this? Why did he suddenly need a million dollars in cash?

Patiently, if somewhat evasively, Ben explained that he had decided to complete purchase of an item that required cash up front and no delay. The tone of his voice made it clear that he was not prepared to reveal the nature of the item. Ed hesitated. Was Ben in some kind of trouble? Ben assured him that he was not. This was simply a decision that he had come to after some extended thought and he would appreciate Ed's help in securing the capital needed.

There wasn't much more to discuss. Reluctantly, Ed Samuelson agreed to do as he was asked. Ben hung up.

Things were even worse at the law office. He called Miles in first; when his friend had seated himself, coffee in hand, Ben told him that he had decided to take a leave of absence from the firm. Miles almost dropped the coffee.

"A leave of absence? What in the hell are you talking about, Doc? This law firm's your whole life! Practicing law is your whole life—has been since Annie died!"

"Maybe that's some of the problem, Miles. Maybe I need to get away from everything for a time—get a fresh perspective on things." Ben shrugged. "You're the one who's been telling me how I need to get out more, see something of the world besides this office and my apartment."

"Yeah, sure, but I don't see . . . Wait a minute, what kind of a leave of absence are you talking about? How long are you planning to be gone? A couple of weeks? A month?"

"A year."

Miles stared at him.

"At least," Ben added. "Maybe more."

"A year? A whole goddamn year? At least?" Miles was flushed with anger. "That's not a leave of absence, Doc—that's retirement! What are we supposed to do with the practice while you're gone? What about your clients? They're not going to sit around a whole year waiting for you to come back! They'll pack it in and find another firm! And what about the trials you've scheduled? What about the cases you've got pending? For Christ's sake, you can't just . . ."

"Calm down a minute, will you?" Ben interrupted quickly. "I'm not bailing out and leaving the ship to sink. I've thought it all through. I'll notify all of my clients personally. Cases pending will be disposed of or reassigned. If anyone's unhappy, I'll refer them to another firm. I think most will stay with you."

Miles shifted his bulky frame forward against the desk. "Doc, let's be honest here. Maybe what you say is true—for the most part, at least. Maybe you can satisfy most of your clients. Maybe they'll accept your taking a leave of absence from the firm. But for a year? Or longer? They'll drift, Doc. And what about the trial work you do? No one can just step in and handle that. We'll lose those clients for sure."

"We can stand to lose a few if that's the way it has to be."

"But that's the point. That's not the way it has to be."

"What if I died, Miles? Tonight, just like that. Dead and buried. What would you do then? You'd have the same problem, basically. How would you solve it?"

"It's not the same thing, damn it, and you know it! The analogy stinks!" Miles came to his feet and leaned forward abruptly, arms braced on the desk. "I don't understand what in the hell has gotten into you, Doc. I don't understand at all. You've always been so damn dependable! A bit unorthodox in the courtroom, sure—but always level-headed, always under control. And a really brilliant trial lawyer. Hell, if I had half of your talent . . ."

"Miles, will you give me a break . . . ?"

The big man brushed the comment aside with a shake of his head. "A whole goddamn year you want to go trooping about? Just like that? First you fly off to New York without a word of explanation, chasing after God knows what, leaving the same day you decide to go, not even talking with me about it, not a word since we sat here and talked about that crazy item in that catalogue, whatever the name of it was, Ross, or Rosenberg's or whatever the hell, and now off again, just like . . ."

He stopped suddenly, the words dying away in his throat. His face froze in stunned recognition. "Oh, my God!" he whispered softly. His head shook slowly from side to side. "Oh, my God! It's that damn catalogue fantasyland, isn't it?"

Ben didn't answer him for a moment, undecided as to whether he should. He had intended to keep Landover a secret. He had intended to say nothing of it to anyone.

"Miles, sit back down, will you?" he said finally.

"Sit down? How in God's name do you expect me to sit down after . . . ?

"Just sit the hell down, Miles!" Ben cut his friend short.

Miles went still, held his position a moment longer, then sank slowly back into his chair. The stunned look stayed on his florid face.

Now it was Ben who leaned forward. His face was hard. "We've been together a long time, Miles—as friends and partners both. We know a lot about each other. Most of it we've learned from experiences shared. But we don't know everything about each other because that's not possible. No two human beings can know everything about each other, even under the best of circumstances. That's why certain things we do always remain a mystery to everyone else."

He cocked his head. "Remember the times you've warned me about backing away from a case because there was something not quite right about it? Remember, Miles? Drop that case, you'd tell me. It's bad news. It's a loser. Drop it. Sometimes I'd do it. I'd agree with you and I'd drop it. But sometimes I wouldn't. Sometimes I'd take the case anyway, and I'd tell you I was taking it because it felt right to me. You'd go along with that decision—even though you didn't agree with it and you really didn't understand it. But you trusted me to take the chance, didn't you?"

He paused. "Well, that's what I'm asking you to do now. You can't understand and you won't agree. So just put all that aside and trust me."

Miles' eyes shifted to the desk top and up again, "Doc, you're talking a million dollars here!"

Ben shook his head slowly. "No, I'm not. I'm talking about saving myself, Miles. I'm talking about something that doesn't have a price tag."

"But this is . . . crazy!" Miles' hands gripped the edge of the desk top until the knuckles were white. "This is irresponsible! It's just plain stupid, damn it!"

"I don't see it that way."

"You don't? Shucking off your professional responsibilities, your life's work? Going off to live in a castle and fight dragons—assuming there are any and you're not simply getting fleeced? No TV, no Bears games, no Wrigley Field, no cold beer, no goddamn electricity or showers with hot water or indoor toilets or anything? Leaving behind your home and your friends and . . . Jesus Christ, Doc!"

"Just think of it as an extended camping trip—the kind where you get away from it all."

"Great! A million-dollar camping trip!"

"My mind is made up on this, Miles."

"Off to some godforsaken . . ."

"My mind is made up!"

The hard edge to his voice left them both shaken. They stared at each other in silence for a moment, feeling the distance between them widening as if a chasm had opened. Then Ben rose and came quickly around the desk. Miles rose as well. Ben put a hand on his shoulder and gripped it.

"If I don't do something, Miles, I'm going to lose myself," he whispered. "It may take a few months or even a year, but in the end I'm going to slip into the cracks and be gone. I can't let that happen."

His friend looked at him wordlessly, sighed and nodded. "It's your life, Doc. I can't tell you how to live it. I never could." He squared himself. "Will you at least take a few days to think about this some more? That's not asking too much, is it?"

Ben smiled wearily. "I've already thought it through a hundred different ways. That's enough. I'm all done thinking."

Miles shook his head. "Guess a blind man could tell that, couldn't he?"

"I'm going to tell the others now. I'd appreciate it if you'd keep what you know to yourself."

"Sure. Why not? Why let anybody else know that the leading light of the firm is deranged?" He gave Ben a final glance, shrugged and turned toward the office door. "You're nuts, Doc."

Ben followed him out. "Yeah, I'll miss you, too, Miles."

He called the staff together then and told them of his plans for a leave of absence from the firm. He told them of his need to get away from his present life, the city, the practice, everything familiar; he told them that he would be leaving in the next few weeks and that he might be gone for better than a year. There was stunned silence and then a flurry of questions. He answered them all patiently. Then he left and went home.

He never mentioned Landover to any of them. Neither did Miles.

It took him the better part of three weeks to put his affairs in order. Most of that time was spent in tying up the loose ends of his law practice—communicating with clients, clearing his court calendar, and reassigning his case load. The transition was difficult. The staff had accepted his decision with stoic resolve, but there was an undercurrent of dissatisfaction in their looks and conversation that he could not mistake. They felt that he was deserting them, bailing out. And truth be told, he was feeling a bit ambivalent about that possibility himself. On the one hand, the loosening of ties with the firm and his profession gave him a newfound sense of freedom and relief. He felt as if he were escaping a trap—as if he were beginning his life all over again with a chance to discover things he had missed the first time around. On the other hand, there were undeniable twinges of uncertainty and regret at letting go of what he had spent the better part of his adult life building for himself. There was that sense of abandoning the familiar for the unknown that characterizes all journeys made for the first time.

Still, he could come back whenever he chose, he reminded himself. There was really nothing permanent in any of this—at least, not yet.

So he went about the business at hand and tried not to think about the ambivalent feelings, but the more he tried not to think about them, the more he did, and in the end he gave up on it altogether and accepted that it was inevitable. He let the feelings buffet and rage within him, let the doubts and the uncertainties gnaw, and found that he gained a certain measure of strength by being able to withstand them. He had made his decision; he found now that he could live with it.

The three weeks came to an end and he had completed the transition at the firm. He was free of his professional obligations, free to pursue whatever other paths he might choose to follow. In this instance, the path he had chosen led to a mythical kingdom called Landover. Only Miles knew the truth, and Miles wasn't talking. Not to him, not to anyone. Miles was in a determined funk. Miles was convinced he was crazy.

"There will come a time, Doc—a time in the not-too-distant future, unless I miss my guess—when a lightbulb will click on inside your muddled head and you will realize in a flash of belated wisdom that you made a huge mistake. When that happens, you'll come slinking back to the firm, feeling a bit sheepish and a lot poorer, and I will take enormous pleasure in saying 'I told you so' at least half a dozen times. But that hasn't anything to do with anyone but you and me. So we'll just keep this bit of middle-aged foolishness between ourselves. No point in embarrassing the entire firm."

That was the last comment Miles had made with regard to his decision to purchase Landover. He had made it the day after Ben had announced his decision to take a leave of absence to the partners and staff. Since then, he had kept his conversations with Ben confined strictly to business matters. Three weeks later, he had not said another word to his friend about Landover. He had contented himself instead with meaningful glances and a condescending manner suggestive of a shrink trying to glean some insight into the mind of his prize lunatic.

Ben tried to ignore this behavior, but his patience wore thin. The days dragged past, and he grew anxious to end the waiting. Ed Samuelson called to announce that the stocks and bonds had been liquidated and the money was available for the investment—if Ben was still certain that this was something that he wanted to do without further consultation. It was, Ben assured him as if missing the pointed suggestion, and wired the purchase price of Landover to Rosen's in New York, attention Meeks. He made arrangements with Samuelson to manage his financial affairs for an indefinite period of time, preparing suitable powers-of-attorney and supplemental authorizations. The accountant accepted them with a look that was suspiciously similar to the one recently adopted by Miles. Ben's patience ebbed some more. He paid his rent at the Towers for twelve months in advance and arranged for cleaning and security checks. He told George to keep an eye on things, and George seemed genuinely anxious that he have a good trip and a pleasant stay at wherever it was that he was going. George was probably the only one who felt that way, he decided. He prepared an update of his last will and testament, cancelled magazine and newspaper subscriptions, called the health club to advise them he would not be coming in for a time, but to keep the boxing facilities intact, put a hold on his mail at the post office effective the first of next month and deposited the key to his bank lockbox with Ed Samuelson.

Then he sat back to wait some more.

The waiting ended in the fourth week, three days before the end of the month. Snow flurries spit and swirled in the graying afternoon, the post-Thanksgiving pre-Christmas holiday weekend flooding the city with eager shoppers dying to celebrate Christ's birth with an exchange of cash for goods. His discontent with the waiting was breeding a rather nasty cynicism. He was watching the madness from the confines of his ivory tower when George called up to announce that a special delivery envelope had arrived from New York.

It was from Meeks. There was a letter, airline tickets, a roadmap of the state of Virginia and an odd-looking receipt. The letter read as follows:

Dear Mr. Holiday,

I write to confirm your acquisition of the specialty item known as Landover, as listed in our most recent holiday catalogue. Your payment in full of the requisite purchase price has been received and escrowed, pending the passage of ten days per our contractual agreement.

I enclose airline tickets which will convey you from Chicago to Charlottesville, Virginia. The tickets will be honored on presentation to representatives of the appropriate carriers at any time during the next seven days.

Upon arrival at the Charlottesville Allegheny terminal, please present the enclosed receipt at the courtesy desk. An automobile has been reserved in your name and will be made available upon your arrival. A package and written instructions will be waiting for you as well. Read the instructions carefully and keep safe the contents of the package.

The roadmap of the state of Virginia is marked in detail to enable you successfully to complete the final leg of your journey to Landover. At its end, you will be met.

On behalf of Rosen's, Ltd., I wish you a pleasant journey.

Meeks

He read the letter through several times, glanced at the airline tickets and the receipt, then examined the roadmap. A red pen line traced a passage on the roadways leading west of the city of Charlottesville to a small "x" in the midst of the Blue Ridge Mountains just south of Waynesboro. There were cursory instructions printed in the margins of the map, numbered in consecutive paragraphs. He read them through, read the letter once more, then folded the entire packet up again and slipped it back into the envelope.

He sat there for a time on the sofa, staring out at the gray day with its flurry of white snowflakes and the distant sounds of the holiday rush. Then he walked into the bedroom, packed a small overnight bag and called down to George for a taxi.

He was at O'Hare by five o'clock.

It was beginning to snow harder.

It was not snowing in Virginia. It was cool and clear, the sky filled with sunlight that streaked a backdrop of forested mountains glimmering crystalline with morning dew. Ben eased the steel-blue New Yorker into the right lane of Interstate 64 traveling west out of Charlottesville toward Waynesboro.

It was midmorning of the following day. He had flown to Washington National, stayed overnight at the Marriott across from the airport, then caught Allegheny's 7:00 A.M. flight to Charlottesville. Once there, he had presented the odd-looking receipt at the terminal courtesy desk and received in exchange the keys to the New Yorker and a small box wrapped in plain brown paper addressed to him. In the box was a brief letter from Meeks and a medallion. The letter read:

> The medallion is your key into and out of Landover. Wear it, and you will be recognized as the rightful heir to the throne. Remove it, and you will be returned to the place marked "x" on the map. Only you can remove it. No one can take it from you. Lose it at your own peril.
>
> Meeks

The medallion was an aged, tarnished piece of metal, its face engraved with a mounted knight in battle harness advancing out of a morning sun that rose over a castle encircled by a lake. A double-link chain was fastened at its apex. It was an exquisite piece of workmanship, but badly worn. The tarnish would not come clean, even with rubbing. He had slipped it around his neck, picked up the car reserved in his name and turned south out of Charlottesville onto Interstate 64.

So far, so good, he thought to himself as he drove west toward the Blue Ridge. Everything had gone according to script.

The map supplied by Meeks lay open on the seat beside him. He had memorized the instructions written on it. He was to follow 64 west almost to Waynesboro and exit the Skyline Drive on the road south toward Lynchburg. Twenty miles in, he would come upon a wayside turn-around on a promontory overlooking a stretch of mountains and valleys within the George Washington National Forest. It would be marked with a small green sign with the number 13 in black. There would be a courtesy phone and a weather shelter. He was to pull over, park, and lock the car with the keys inside, and cross the roadway to the nature path on the opposite side. He was to follow the path into the mountains for approximately two miles. At that point, he would be met.

The map didn't say by whom. Neither did the letter.

The map did say that someone would come later to pick up the car. The phone could be used to arrange for transportation back again, should he decide later to return. A telephone number was provided.

A twinge of doubt tugged suddenly at him. He was a long way out in the middle of nowhere, and no one but Meeks knew exactly where he was. If he were simply to drop from sight, Meeks might suddenly be a million dollars richer—supposing for the sake of argument that this was all an elaborate hoax. Stranger things had happened and for much less.

He thought about it for a moment and then shook his head. It didn't make sense. Meeks was an agent for Rosen's, and a man in his position would have been thoroughly checked. Besides, there were too many ways that Meeks could be caught in such a thing. Miles knew of Ben's contact with the store and the reason for that contact. The funds he had cabled could be traced. Copies of the confirmation letter from Meeks were with his safe papers. And the ad for Landover's sale was public knowledge.

He forced the doubts from his mind and concentrated on the drive ahead. His anticipation of what lay ahead had been working on him for weeks. He was so keyed up that he could barely contain himself. He had slept poorly last night. He had been awake before sunrise. He was susceptible to all sorts of half-baked ideas.

He reached the entrance to Skyline Drive in a little more than thirty minutes and turned south onto it. The two lane highway wound steadily upward into the Blue Ridge, weaving through the tangle of forest and mountain rock, rising into the late November sunlight. Panoramic views spread away to either side, the sweep of the national forestlands and parkways slipping past in breathtaking still life. Traffic was light. He encountered three cars traveling in the opposite direction, families with camping gear and luggage, one pulling a fold-up trailer. He came across no one driving south.

Twenty minutes later, he caught sight of the turn-around with its green sign stenciled with the number 13 in black. Easing off the gas pedal, he pulled the New Yorker off the parkway onto the gravel wayside and came to a stop before the courtesy phone and weather shelter. He climbed out of the car and looked about. To his right, the wayside ran several dozen feet to a chain and post guard rail and a promontory that overlooked miles of forestland and mountain ridges comprising a small part of the national park. To his left, across the deserted roadway, the mountainside lifted into the morning sunlight, a maze of trees and rocks wrapped in thin trailers of mist. He stared upward toward the mountain's summit, watching the mist swirl and stir like ribbons drawn through the air. The day was still and empty, and even the passing of the wind made no sound.

He turned, reached into the car and took out his overnight case. It was really little more than a glorified duffel bag filled with a few odd possessions he had thought to bring—a bottle of his beloved Glenlivet to be saved for a special occasion, toiletries, paper and pens, several books, a couple sets of boxing gloves, recent copies of magazines he was still reading, tape, antiseptic, an old sweatsuit, and running shoes. He hadn't bothered with much in the way of clothing. He knew that he would probably be better off wearing whatever they wore in Landover.

He closed the car and locked it, the keys inside. He slipped his billfold into his duffel, glanced about once again, and crossed the roadway. He was dressed in a light sweatsuit of navy blue with red and white piping and navy blue Nikes. He had brought the Nikes and the running shoes because he couldn't decide what better to wear on a journey such as this and because he doubted that there would be anything more comfortable in shoes once he got where he was going. It was odd, he reflected, that Meeks hadn't bothered with any instructions about clothing or personals.

He stopped at the far side of the roadway and scanned the forested slope before him. A small stream ran down off the rocks through a series of rapids that flashed silver in the dappled sunlight. A pathway crisscrossed the stream's banks and disappeared into the trees. Ben hitched the duffel over one shoulder and started up.

The pathway wound in a series of twists and turns along the stream, leveling off at intervals in small clearings where wooden benches provided a resting place for the weary hiker. The stream gurgled and lapped against the earthen banks and over rock falls, the only sound in the late November morning. The parkway and the car disappeared behind him as he climbed, and soon there was only the forest to be seen. The climb grew less steep, but the forest closed about on either side, and the pathway became more difficult to discern. Eventually, the stream branched away into a cliff side that dropped from a great height, and the pathway ran on alone.

Slowly a mist began to settle in about him.

He stopped then and again looked about. There was nothing to see. He listened. There was nothing to hear. Nevertheless, he had the unpleasant sensation of being followed. Momentary doubt tugged at his resolve; perhaps this whole business was one big, fat mistake. But he shoved the doubt aside quickly and started again along the trail. He had made the commitment weeks ago. He was determined to see it through.

The forest deepened and the mist grew thicker. Trees loomed tightly all about him, dark, skeletal sentries with their dying leaves and evergreen boughs, their trailers of vine and scrub and swatches of saw grass. He was having to push his way past the pine and spruce to keep on the trail, and the mist lent a hazy cast to a morning that had begun with sunshine. Pine needles and fallen leaves crunched underfoot; from beyond where he could see, small animals darted through the carpet.

At least he wasn't entirely alone, he thought.

He was growing extremely thirsty, but he hadn't thought to pack a water container. He could go back and try the stream water, but he was reluctant to lose time doing so. He turned his thoughts momentarily to Miles to take his mind off his thirst. He tried to picture Miles out here in the woods with him, trudging through the forest and the mist, huffing and grunting. He smiled. Miles hated all forms of exercise that did not involve beer cans and tableware. He thought Ben was crazy for continuing his boxing workouts so many years after he had ceased to box competitively. He thought athletes were basically little boys who had never grown up.

Ben shook his head. Miles thought a lot of things that didn't make much sense.

He slowed as the pathway ahead petered out into tall grass. A deep cluster of pine barred his passage forward. He pushed his way through and stopped.

"Uh-oh," he whispered.

A wall of towering, rugged oak rose before him, shrouded in layers of shadow. A tunnel had been cut through its center, hollowed out as if by a giant's hands. The tunnel was dark and empty, a black hole with no end, a burrow that ran on into trailers of mist, stirred by invisible hands. Sounds drifted from out of the black, distant and unidentifiable.

Ben stood at the tunnel's entrance and stared into the mist and the dark. The tunnel was two dozen feet across and twice as high. He had never seen anything like it. He knew at once that nothing in his world had made it. He knew as well exactly where it led. Nevertheless, he hesitated. There was something about the tunnel that made him uneasy—something beyond the fact that it was an unnatural creation. There was a look and feel to it that bothered him.

He peered about warily. There was nothing to be seen. He might have been the only living thing in the forest—except that he could hear the sounds from somewhere ahead, like voices, only . . .

He experienced a sudden, violent urge to turn about and go straight back the way he had come. It was so powerful that he actually took a step backward before he could catch himself. The air from the tunnel seemed to reach out to him in a velvet touch that trailed moisture against his skin. He tightened his arm about the duffel and straightened, bracing himself against what he was feeling. He took a deep breath and exhaled slowly. Did he go on or did he turn back? Which choice for intrepid adventurer, Doc Holiday?

"Well," he said softly.

He started forward. The tunnel seemed to open before him, the darkness drawing back at precisely the rate at which he advanced. The mist caressed him, a lover's hands tender and eager in their touch. He walked steadily, purposefully, letting his eyes sweep briefly right and left, seeing nothing. The sounds continued to stray from out of the invisible distance, still unrecognizable. The forest earth had a soft, spongy feel to it, giving with the weight of his body as he trod upon it. Dark trunks and limbs wrapped about, walls and ceiling that locked away all but the faintest light, a web of damp bark and drying leaves.

Ben risked a quick glance back. The forest from which he had come was gone. The tunnel entrance was gone. It was the same distance back as forward, the same look either way.

"Special effects are pretty good." He forced a quick smile, thinking of Miles, thinking of how ridiculous it was to feel what he was feeling, thinking that he was liking this whole business less and less . . .

Then he heard the scream.

It lifted from out of the dark and the mist from somewhere behind him. He glanced back once more, still walking. There was movement in the tunnel dark. Figures darted from the trees—human in appearance, but so slight and willowy as to be almost ethereal. Faces appeared, thin and angular with sharp eyes that peered from beneath thatches of moss-hair and corn-silk brows.

The scream sounded again. He blinked. A monstrous, black apparition hung upon the misted air, a thing of scales and leathered wings, of claws and spines. The scream had come from it.

Ben quit walking altogether and stared. The special effects were getting better and better. This one looked almost real. He dropped his duffel on the trail, put his hands on his hips and watched it assume three-dimensional proportions. It was an ugly thing, as big as a house and as frightening as the worst of his dreams. Still, he could tell illusion from reality. Meeks would have to do better than this if he expected Ben to . . .

He terminated the thought abruptly. The apparition was coming directly for him—and it didn't look quite so fake any longer. It was beginning to look decidedly real. He picked up the duffel and backed away. The thing screamed. Even the scream sounded real now.

Ben swallowed hard. Maybe that was because the thing *was* real.

He quit being rational and started to run. The apparition came on, the scream sounding once more. It was close to him now, a nightmare that could not be shaken out of sleep. It settled down upon the tunnel floor and ran upon four legs, the wings pulled back against it, the body compacted and steaming as if heated by an inner fire. And there was something on its back—a figure as dark as it, armored and misshapen, clawed hands grasping reins to guide the thing it rode.

Ben ran faster, his breathing labored and sounding of fear. He was in good condition, but the fear was eroding his strength quickly, and he could make no headway on the creature trailing. All about him he watched the strange faces materialize and then vanish, spirits wandered from the mists, lost in the trees—spectators to the chase taking place within the tunnel. He thought momentarily to break from the pathway and force his way into the forest with the gathering of faces. Perhaps the thing chasing him could not follow. It was so big that, even if he tried, the trees would at least slow its pursuit. But then he would be lost in the dark and the mist and might never find his way back. He stayed on the trail.

The apparition chasing him screamed again, and he could feel the tunnel floor shake with its approach.

"Meeks, damn you!" he cried desperately.

He could feel the medallion rub against his chest within the confines of his running suit. He clutched at it instinctively, the talisman he had been given to bring him safely into and—if need be—safely out of Landover. Maybe the medallion could dispell this thing . . .

Then a rider appeared suddenly at the edge of the darkness ahead, a ragged, hazy form. It was a knight, his armor battered and chipped, lance lowered until it almost rested upon the ground before it. Both rider and horse were soiled and unkempt, apparitions as unfriendly in their appearance as the thing that thundered toward Ben from behind. The rider's head lifted at his approach, and the lance came up. Behind it, there was a sudden trace of daylight.

Ben ran faster still. The tunnel was ending. He had to get clear of it; he had to escape.

The monster that pursued screamed, the sound dying into a frightening hiss. "Stay away from me, damn you!" Ben cried frantically.

Then the horse and rider loomed suddenly before him, grown huge and strangely awesome beneath their covering of dirt. An exclamation of surprise broke from Ben's lips. He had seen this knight before. He had seen his image engraved upon the medallion that he wore!

The breath of the black thing burned against the back of his neck, fetid and raw. Terror streaked through him, and there was the cold touch of something inhuman in his chest. The knight spurred his horse from the blaze of sunlight that marked the tunnel's end, and the faces in the forest whirled as if disembodied ghosts. Ben screamed. Black thing and knight closed at him from either direction, bearing down on him as if he were not there.

The knight reached him first, racing past at a full gallop, the flanks of the charging horse knocking him sprawling from the pathway. He tumbled headlong into the shadows, and his eyes closed tightly against a sudden explosion of light.

Blackness engulfed him, and everything spun wildly. The breath had been knocked from his body, and he was having trouble catching it again. He lay face downward against the earth, the feel of grass and leaves damp against his cheek. He kept his eyes tightly shut and waited for the spinning sensation to cease.

When at last it did, he opened his eyes cautiously. He was in a clearing. The forest rose up all about him, misted and dark, but he could still glimpse traces of daylight beyond its screen. He started to his feet.

It was then that he saw the dragon.

He froze in disbelief. The dragon lay sleeping several dozen yards to his left, curled in a ball against a row of dark trunks. It was a monstrous thing, all scales, spikes, claws, and spines, its wings folded against its body, its snout tucked down into its forelegs. Steam puffed in ragged geysers from its nostrils as it snored contentedly. The raw, white bones of something recently eaten were scattered all about.

Ben sucked in his breath slowly, certain for an instant that this was the black thing that had chased him through the tunnel. But, no, the black thing had been something different altogether . . .

He quit worrying about what it was and started worrying about how to get away from it. He wished he knew if any of this was real, but there was no time to debate the matter now.

Cautiously, he began to slip through the trees, edging his way past the sleeping dragon in the direction of the light. He had his duffel looped over one shoulder and clamped tightly against his side. The dragon appeared to be sleeping soundly. It would only take a few moments to get clear of it. Ben held his breath and continued to place one foot silently in front of the other. He was almost clear of the beast when one lidded eye suddenly slipped open.

Ben froze a second time. The dragon regarded him balefully, the single eye fixed on him as he stood there amid the trees. Ben held his ground a moment longer, then slowly began to back away.

The dragon's horn-crusted head swung quickly about, lowering against the forest earth. Ben back-pedalled faster, seeing the forest trees thin about him, sensing the light grow brighter behind. The dragon's lip curled back almost disdainfully to reveal row upon row of blackened teeth.

Then the dragon blew at him as a sleeping man might blow at a bothersome fly. The odorous breath picked Ben up and flung him like a rag doll through the forest mist. He closed his eyes, tucked into a ball, and braced himself. He struck the earth roughly, bounced a few times, and rolled to a stop.

When he opened his eyes again, he sat alone in a clover meadow.

QUESTOR THEWS

Sunshine seeped down through rifts in a clouded sky, bathing the meadow with bits and pieces of its warmth. Ben blinked and squinted through its brightness. The misted forest with its shadowed tunnel was gone. The apparitions were gone as well—that black thing, the battered knight, even the dragon.

Ben straightened. What in the hell had happened to them? He brushed at the sheen of sweat on his forehead. Hadn't they been real after all?

He swallowed hard. No, of course they weren't real! They couldn't have been! They were just some sort of mirage!

He glanced about quickly. The meadow in which he sat spread away before him in a carpet of muted greens, blues and pinks, a mix of colors he had never seen in grasses. The clover was white, but touched with crimson spots. The meadow dropped downward into a sprawling valley which rose again miles distant in a wall of mountains that formed a dark barrier against the skyline. Behind him, the trees of a forest loomed blackly against a mountain slope. Trailers of mist hung over everything.

The apparitions had been somewhere in the trees behind him, he thought suddenly. Where had they disappeared to?

And where was he?

He took a moment to collect his thoughts. He was still shaken from his ordeal in the forest tunnel, frightened by the dark things that had come at him, bewildered that he was sitting here in this meadow. He took several deep breaths to steady himself. Whatever it was that had seemed to threaten him in that forest, he was all right now. He was back in the Blue Ridge. He was in Virginia, some twenty miles or so below Waynesboro, a few miles in from the parkway that ran through the George Washington National Forest.

Except that . . .

He glanced about once again, more carefully this time. Something wasn't quite right. The weather was wrong, for one thing. It was too warm for late November in the Virginia mountains. He was sweating beneath his running suit and he shouldn't have been doing that, even with the scare he had just experienced. The air had been cooler than this by at least thirty degrees before he had entered that tunnel in the forest.

The clover was wrong, too. There shouldn't be clover blooming in November—especially clover that looked like this, white with crimson spots, like a polka-dot flower. He looked back at the forest. Why were there still leaves as green as summer's new growth on the trees? The leaves should be colored with autumn's touch. The only green should be on the pines and spruce.

He shoved himself hurriedly to one knee. A mix of panic and excitement crept through him. The sun was directly overhead, exactly where it ought to be. But in the distant skies two spheres hung low against the horizon—one faintly peach, the other a sort of washed-out mauve. Ben started. Moons? Two of them? No, they had to be planets. But when had the planets of his solar system ever been so clearly visible to the naked eye?

What in the hell was going on?

He sat back slowly, forcing himself to remain calm. There was a logical explanation for all of this, he reasoned, fighting back against a mix of panic and excitement. The explanation was simple. This was what he had been promised. This was Landover. He glanced about at the green meadow with its spotted clover, at the summer trees of the forest, at the odd-looking spheres hanging above the horizon, and he nodded sagely. There was nothing to worry about. This was just more of the special effects he had experienced in the forest tunnel. This was only a broader projection of such effects within a pocket of land hidden away in the Blue Ridge Mountains of Virginia. He wasn't sure how it had been managed—especially in the middle of a national forest—but he was sure of what it was. He had to admit that it was pretty amazing. The valley with its summer temperatures could have been a lucky discovery, but the odd flowers, the spheres that looked like planets or moons, and the apparitions in the forest tunnel must have taken some effort and scientific know-how to create.

He came to his feet, slowly rebuilding his confidence. His experience in the forest had unnerved him badly. That black thing and the knight had seemed almost real. The knight's horse had felt very real when it galloped past, knocking him from the trail into the shadows. And he could still feel the breath of the dragon on his face. He might almost have believed . . .

He stopped short. His gaze, wandering across the floor of the valley below as he puzzled matters through, had caught sight of something.

It was a castle.

Ben stared. A huge swatch of green dominated the central portion of the valley, a checkerboard of meadows and fields dissected by meandering rivers. The castle stood at the near end of that checkerboard. An odd haze that hung over the whole of the valley had obscured his vision at first. But now he was beginning to pick things out, to see things clearly.

One of those things was the castle.

The castle was some miles distant from where he stood, swathed in mist and shadows beyond a deep forest. It sat upon an island in the middle of a lake, forest and hills all about, patches of mist floating past like clouds dropped down to earth. It was a dark and forbidding citadel, appearing almost ghostlike within the swirling haze.

He squinted against the muted light of the sun to see more clearly. But the mist closed suddenly, and the castle was gone.

"Damn!" he muttered softly.

Had that been an apparition as well—another of Landover's special effects? A faint suspicion was beginning to gnaw at him. Was it possible that all of these special effects were not special effects at all? He felt a twinge of the panic and excitement return. What if everything he was seeing was real?

A voice boomed out behind him, and he jumped a foot.

"Well, then, here you are, wandering about in this meadow—not at all where you were supposed to be. Did you stray from the pathway? You look a bit fatigued, if you don't mind my saying so. Are you all right?"

Ben turned at once. The speaker stood about ten feet behind him—a bizarre caricature of some pop artist's gypsy. He was a tall man, well over six feet, but so lean as to be almost sticklike. A mop of curling white hair hung down over large ears, wisps of it mingling with beard and brows of the same color and kind. Gray robes cloaked the scarecrow form, but they were decorated with an array of brilliant sashes, cloth pouches, and jewelry that left the wearer looking something like a fragmented rainbow pinned against a departing thunderstorm. Soft leather boots too big for the feet curled up slightly at the toes and a hawklike nose dominated a pinched and owlish face. A gnarled walking stick guided the way as he came a step closer.

"You are Ben Holiday, aren't you?" the fellow asked, a sudden glint of suspicion in his eyes. A massive crystal dangled from a chain about his throat, and he stuffed it rather self-consciously into the recesses of his robes. "You do have the medallion?"

Ben didn't care for the look. "Who are you?" he replied, trying to put the other man on the defensive.

"Ah, I asked you first." The other smiled amiably. "Courtesy dictates that you answer first."

Ben stiffened, a touch of impatience in his voice at being forced to play this cat-and-mouse game. "Okay. I'm Ben Holiday. Now who are you?"

"Yes, well, I will have to see the medallion." The smile broadened slightly. "You could be anyone, after all. Saying that you are Ben Holiday doesn't necessarily make it so."

"You could be anyone, too, couldn't you?" Ben asked in reply. "What gives you the right to ask me anything without first telling me who you are?"

"I am the one sent to meet you, as it happens—assuming, of course, that you are who you claim. Could I see the medallion?"

Ben hesitated, then pulled the medallion from beneath his clothing and, without removing it, held it out for examination. The tall man leaned forward, peered momentarily at the medallion and nodded.

"You are indeed who you claim. I apologize for questioning you, but caution is always well advised in these matters. And now for my own introduction." He bowed deeply from the waist. "Questor Thews, wizard of the court, chief advisor to the throne of Landover, your obedient servant."

"Wizard of the . . ." Ben glanced sharply about one time more. "Then this *is* Landover!"

"Landover and nowhere else. Welcome, High Lord Ben Holiday."

"So this is it," Ben murmured, his mind racing suddenly. He looked again at the other. "Where are we exactly?"

Questor Thews seemed puzzled. "Landover, High Lord."

"Yes, but where is Landover? I mean, where is Landover in the Blue Ridge? It must be close to Waynesboro, am I right?"

The wizard smiled. "Oh, well, you are no longer in your world. I thought you understood that. Landover bridges any number of worlds—a kind of gateway, you might say. The mists of the fairy realm connect her to your world and the others. Some bridge closer, of course, and some don't even have the barrier of the mists. But you will learn all that soon enough."

Ben stared. "I'm not in my world? This isn't Virginia?"

Questor Thews shook his head.

"Or the United States or North America or Earth? None of it?"

"No, High Lord. Did you think that the fairy-tale kingdom you bought would be in your world?"

Ben didn't hear him, a desperate obstinacy seizing hold. "I suppose that those planets in the sky over there aren't fake, either? I suppose that they're real?"

Questor turned. "Those are moons, not planets. Landover has eight of them. Only two are visible in the daylight hours, but the other six can be seen as well after dusk during most of the year."

Ben stared. Then he shook his head slowly. "I don't believe any of this. I don't believe one word of it."

Questor Thews looked at him curiously. "Why do you not believe, High Lord?"

"Because a place like this can't exist, damn it!"

"But you chose to come here, didn't you? Why would you come to Landover in the first place, if you did not believe that it could exist?"

Ben had no idea. He was no longer certain why it was that he had come. He was certain of only one thing—that he could not bring himself to accept what the other man was saying. Panic flooded through him at the very thought that Landover could be somewhere other than on Earth. He had never dreamed that it would be anywhere else. It meant that all of his ties with his old life were truly severed, that everything he had once known was really gone. It meant that he was alone in an alien world . . .

"High Lord, would you mind if we walked while we carry on this conversation?" the wizard interrupted his thoughts. "We have a good distance to cover before nightfall."

"We do? Where are we going?"

"To your castle, High Lord."

"My castle? Wait a minute—do you mean that castle that I saw just before you appeared, the one in the middle of the lake on an island?"

The other nodded. "The very place, High Lord. Shall we be on our way?"

Ben shook his head stubbornly. "Not a chance. I'm not going anywhere until I find out exactly what's going on. What about what happened to me in the forest! Are you telling me all that was real? Are you telling me there actually was a dragon sleeping back there in the trees?"

Questor shrugged nonchalantly. "There could have been. There is a dragon in the valley—and he often naps at the fringes of the mists. The mists were his home once."

Ben frowned. "His home, huh? Well, what about that black, winged thing and its rider?"

The wizard's shaggy brows lifted slightly. "A black, winged thing, you say? A thing that seemed a nightmare, perhaps?"

Ben nodded his head anxiously. "Yes—that was what it seemed."

"That was the Iron Mark." The other pursed his lips. "The Mark is a demon lord. I am surprised he would come after you there in the mists. I would have thought . . ." He stopped, smiled a quick smile of reassurance and shrugged. "A demon strays into Landover now and again. You happened to come across one of the worst."

"Come across it, my aunt Agatha!" Ben flared. "It was hunting me! It chased me down that forest tunnel and would have had me if not for that knight!"

This time Questor Thews' brows lifted a good deal further. "Knight? What knight?" he demanded quickly.

"The knight—the one on the medallion!"

"You saw the knight on the medallion, Ben Holiday?"

Ben hesitated, surprised at the other's sharp interest. "I saw him in the forest, after the black thing came at me. He appeared in front of me and rode at the black thing. I was caught between them, but the knight's horse sideswiped me and knocked me from the trail. The next thing I knew I was sitting here in this meadow."

Questor Thews frowned thoughtfully. "Yes, the horse knocking you from the pathway would account for your appearance here rather than at your appointed destination . . ." He trailed off, then came slowly forward, bending close to look into Ben's eyes. "You might have imagined the knight, High Lord. You might have only thought to see him. Were you to think back on it, you might see something entirely different."

Ben flushed. "Were I to think back on it, I would see exactly the same thing exactly." He kept his gaze steady. "I would see the knight on the medallion."

There was a long moment of silence. Then Questor Thews stepped back again, one hand rubbing at his ear thoughtfully. "Well," he said. "Well, indeed." He looked surprised. More than that, he looked pleased. He pursed his lips once again, shifted his weight from one foot to the other and hunched his shoulders. "Well," he said a third time.

Then the look was gone as quickly as it had come. "We really do have to start walking now, High Lord," he said quickly. "The day is getting on and it would be best if we were to reach the castle before nightfall. Come along, please. It is a good distance off."

He shambled down through the meadow, a tall, ragtag, slightly stooped figure, his robes dragging through the grasses. Ben watched dumbly for a moment, glanced hastily about, then hitched up the duffel over one shoulder and followed reluctantly after.

They passed from the high meadow and began their descent toward the distant bowl of the valley. The valley stretched away below them, a patchwork quilt of farmlands, meadows, forests, lakes and rivers, and swatches of marsh and desert. Mountains ringed the valley tightly, forested and dark, awash in a sea of deep mist that strung its trailers down into the valley and cast its shadow over everything.

Ben Holiday's mind raced. He kept trying to fit what he was seeing into his mental picture of the Blue Ridge. But none of it worked. His eyes wandered across the slopes they were descending, seeing orchard groves, seeking out familiar fruit trees, finding apple, cherry, peach, and plum, but a dozen other fruits as well, many of a color and size completely unfamiliar to him. Grasses were varied shades of green, but also crimson, lavender, and turquoise. Scattered through the whole of the strange collection of vegetation were large clumps of trees that vaguely resembled half-grown pin oaks except that they were colored trunk to leaf a brilliant blue.

None of it looked anything at all like the Blue Ridge Mountains of Virginia or the mountains of any other part of the United States that he had ever heard about.

Even the cast of the day was strange. The mist lent a shadowed look to the whole of the valley, and it reflected in the color tones of the earth. Everything seemed to have developed a somewhat wintry look—though the air was warm like a midsummer's day and the sun shone down through the clouds in the sky.

Ben savored cautiously the look, smell, and feel of the land, and he discovered in doing so that he could almost believe that Landover was exactly what Questor Thews had said that it was—another world completely.

He mulled this prospect over in his mind as he kept pace with his guide. This was no small concession that he was being asked to make. Every shred of logic and every bit of common sense that he could muster in his lawyer's mind argued that Landover was some sort of trick, that fairy worlds were writer's dreams and that what he was seeing was a pocket of merry old England tucked away in the Blue Ridge, castles and knights-in-armor included. Logic and common sense said that the existence of a world such as this, a world outside but somehow linked to his own, a world that no one had ever seen, was so far-fetched as to be one step short of impossible: Twilight Zone; Outer Limits. And one step short only because it could be argued that anything after all was *theoretically* possible.

Yet here he was, and there it was, and what was the explanation for it, if it wasn't what Questor Thews said it was? It looked, smelled, and felt real. It had the look of something real—but at the same time it had the look of something completely foreign to his world, something beyond anything he had ever known or even heard about this side of King Arthur. This land *was* a fantasy, a mix of color and shape and being that surprised and bewildered him at every turn—and frightened him, as well.

But already his initial skepticism had begun to erode. What if Landover truly was another world? What if it was exactly what Meeks had promised?

The thought exhilarated him. It left him stunned.

He glanced surreptitiously at Questor. The tall, stooped figure marched dutifully next to him, gray robes dragging through the grasses, patched with the scarfs and sashes and pouches of gaily colored silk, his whitish hair and beard fringing the owlish face. Questor certainly seemed to feel at home.

His gaze wandered back over the sweep of the valley, and he consciously opened a few heretofore padlocked doors in the deep recesses of his mind. Perhaps logic and common sense ought to take a backseat to instinct for a while, he decided.

Still, a few discreet questions wouldn't hurt.

"How is that you and I happen to speak the same language?" he asked his guide suddenly. "Where did you learn to speak English?"

"Hmmmmm?" The wizard glanced over, preoccupied with something else.

"If Landover is in another world, how does it happen that you speak English so well?"

Questor shook his head. "I don't speak English at all. I speak the language of my country—at least, I speak the language used by humans."

Ben frowned. "But you're speaking English right now, damn it! How else could we communicate?"

"Oh, I see what you mean." Questor smiled. "I am not speaking your language, High Lord—you are speaking mine."

"Yours?"

"Yes, the magic properties of the medallion that permit you passage into Landover also give you the ability to communicate instantly with its inhabitants, either by spoken word or in writing." He fumbled through one of the pouches momentarily and withdrew a faded map. "Here, read something of this."

Ben took the map from him and studied the details. The names of towns, rivers, mountain ranges and lakes were all in English.

"These are written in English!" he insisted, handing the map back again.

Questor shook his head. "No, High Lord, they are written in Landoverian—the language of the country. They only appear to be written in English—and only to you. I speak to you now in Landoverian as well; but it seems to you as if your own language. The medallion's fairy magic permits this."

Ben thought it through for a moment, trying to decide what else he should ask on the matter of language and communication, but decided in the end that there really was nothing further to ask. He changed subjects.

"I've never seen anything like those trees," he informed his guide, pointing to the odd-looking blue pin oaks. "What are they?"

"Those are Bonnie Blues." Questor slowed and stopped. "They grow only in Landover as far as I know. They were created of the fairy magic thousands of years ago and given to us. They keep back the mists and feed life into the soil."

Ben frowned dubiously. "I thought sun and rain did that."

"Sun and rain? No, sun and rain only help the process. But magic is the life source of Landover, and the Bonnie Blues are a very strong magic indeed."

"Fairy magic, you said—like the magic that enables us to communicate?"

"The same, High Lord. The fairies gave the magic to the land when they created it. They live now in the mists about us."

"The mists?"

"There." Questor pointed in a sweeping motion to the mountains that ringed the valley, their peaks and forests shrouded in gray. "The fairies live there." He glanced once more at Ben. "Did you see faces in the mist when you passed through the forest from your world to ours?" Ben nodded. "Those were the faces of the fairies. Only the pathway you walked upon belongs to both worlds. That was why I was concerned that you had strayed too far from it."

There was a moment's silence. "What if I had?" Ben asked finally.

The stooped figure pulled the gray robes free from a trailer of scrub on which they had caught. "Why, then you might have wandered too deep into the fairy world and been lost forever." He paused. "Are you hungry, High Lord?"

"What?" The question startled Ben. He was still thinking about his brush with the fairy world and the possibility that one could wander lost in it forever. Until now, this world into which he had come had seemed fairly safe.

"Food and drink—it occurs to me that you may not have had either for some time."

Ben hesitated. "Not since this morning, as a matter of fact."

"Good. Come this way."

Questor walked past him down the slope to a small cluster of Bonnie Blues at the edge of an oak grove. He waited for Ben to join him, then reached up and tore free a branch from one of the trees. The branch broke cleanly and soundlessly. The wizard knelt, grasped the base of the branch with one hand, and with the other stripped it of its leaves. The leaves tumbled into the lap of his robe.

"Here, try one," he offered, holding out one of the leaves. "Take a bite of it."

Ben took the leaf, examined it, then cautiously bit into it and chewed. His face brightened with surprise. "It tastes like . . . like melon."

The other nodded, smiling. "Now the stalk. Hold it like this." He held the broken end upright. "Now suck on it—there, at the break."

Ben did as he was told. "Well, I'll be damned!" he whispered. "It tastes like milk!"

"It is the staple of human existence in the valley," Questor explained, chewing a leaf himself. "One can live on only the Bonnie Blues and a small amount of drinking water, if one has nothing else—and there are those who do not. It wasn't always so, but times have changed . . ."

He trailed off, distracted. Then he glanced at Ben. "The Bonnie Blues grow wild everywhere in the valley. Their reproductive capacity is amazing—even now. Look there—look at what has happened."

He pointed to the tree where the limb had been broken off. Already, the break was healing over and beginning to bud anew.

"By morning, a new limb will have begun to grow. In a week's time, it will be exactly as we found it—or should be."

Ben nodded without comment. He was thinking about Questor's carefully phrased qualifications. "Times have changed . . . Their reproductive capacity is amazing—even now . . . In a week's time, it will be exactly as we found it—or should be." He studied the Bonnie Blues behind the one the wizard had chosen. They seemed to be flourishing less successfully, signs of wilt on their leaves and a drooping to their limbs. Something was distressing them.

Questor interrupted his thoughts. "Well, now that we have sampled the Bonnie Blues, perhaps something a bit more substantial would be in order." He rubbed his hands together briskly. "How would you like some ham and eggs, some fresh bread, and a glass of ale?"

Ben turned. "Are you hiding a picnic basket in one of those pouches?"

"A what? Oh, no, High Lord. I will simply conjure up our meal."

"Conjure . . . ?" Ben frowned. "You mean use magic?"

"Exactly! After all, I am a wizard. Now, let me see."

The owlish face screwed up, the shaggy brows narrowing. Ben leaned forward. He had eaten nothing since breakfast, but he was more curious than hungry. Could this odd-looking fellow really do magic?

"A bit of concentrated thought, fingers extended so, a quick motion thus, and . . . hah!"

There was a flash of light, a quick puff of smoke, and on the ground before them lay half a dozen scatter pillows, tasseled and embroidered. Ben stared in amazement.

"Oh, well, we will need something to sit upon while we eat, I suppose." The wizard brushed the matter aside as if it were of no consequence. "Must have turned the fingers a bit too far right . . . Now let me see, once again, a bit of thought, fingers, a quick motion . . ."

Again the light flashed, the smoke puffed, and on the ground before them appeared a crate of eggs and an entire pig dressed out and resplendent with an apple in its mouth.

Questor glanced hurriedly at Ben. "The magic is fickle on occasion. But one simply tries harder." He stretched forth his sticklike arms from his robes. "Here, now, watch closely. Thoughts concentrated, fingers turned, a quick motion, and . . ."

The light flashed brighter, the smoke puffed higher, and from out of nowhere a massive tressel table laden with food enough for an army materialized before them. Ben jumped back in surprise. Questor Thews could certainly do magic as he claimed, but it appeared his control of it was rather limited.

"Drat, that is not what I . . . the thing of it is, that . . ." Questor was thoroughly agitated. He glared at the table of food. "I am simply tired, I imagine. I will try once again . . ."

"Never mind," Ben interrupted quickly. He had seen enough of the magic for one sitting. The wizard looked over, displeased. "I mean, I'm really not that hungry after all. Maybe we should just go on."

Questor hesitated, then nodded curtly. "If that is your wish, High Lord—very well." He gave a quick motion with one hand, and the pillows, the pig, the crate of eggs and the entire tressel table with its meal disappeared into air. "You see that I have the magic at my command when I wish it," he announced stiffly.

"Yes, I see that."

"You must understand that the magic I wield is most important, High Lord." Questor was determined to make his point. "You will have need of my magic if you are to be King. There have always been wizards to stand behind the Kings of Landover."

"I understand."

Questor stared at him. He stared back. What he understood above everything, he thought to himself, was that, except for this half-baked wizard, he was all alone in a land he knew almost nothing at all about and he had no desire to alienate his one companion.

"Well, then." Questor's ruffled feathers seemed suddenly back in place. He looked almost sheepish. "I suppose that we should continue on to the castle, High Lord."

Ben nodded. "I suppose we should."

Wordlessly, they resumed their journey.

The afternoon wore on; as it did so, the mists seemed to thicken across the land. The cast of the day dimmed, shadows gathered in dark pools, and the color of the fields, meadows, forests and the lakes and rivers scattered through them lost all hint of vibrancy. There was a sullen feel to the air as if a storm might be approaching, though clearly none was. The sun still shone, and no wind stirred the leaves of the trees. Another moon hung suspended against the skyline, newly risen from beneath the mists.

Ben was still wondering what he had gotten himself into.

It was becoming increasingly apparent to him that Landover was nothing of the sham that Miles Bennett had envisioned. The creatures were not courtesy of the San Diego Zoo and the inhabitants were not supplied by Central Casting. The magic that Questor had performed was not the old rabbit-in-the-hat variety, but magic of a sort imagined in newsstand pulp fantasy. By God, would Miles have been astonished by that table and twenty-course dinner trick! How could anyone possibly conjure something like that up so quickly unless they truly were in a fantasy world where magic was real?

That was the other side of the coin he toyed with, unfortunately. Landover was really not a part of Virginia or the United States or North America or anywhere else on Earth. Landover was a whole other world entirely, and he had somehow stepped through a time zone to reach it.

Damn, it was exciting and terrifying all at once!

He had wanted this, of course. He had made the purchase understanding that he was going to a fantasy world, that he was buying the throne to a fantasy kingdom. But he had never imagined that it could actually be. He had never thought that it would turn out to be just exactly what the promo and old Meeks had said it would be.

He thought suddenly of Annie and wished she were here with him. She would have been able to help him accept what was happening, he thought. But Annie was not here, and it was because he had lost her that he had come in the first place. Landover was his escape from what her loss had cost him.

He shook his head admonishingly. He must remember that he had come to this world to renew his life, to leave behind the old, to find a different existence from what he had known. He had intended to cut all of his ties; he had wanted to begin again. That being so, it was foolish to bemoan the fact that he might have gotten exactly what he had wanted.

Besides, the challenge it presented intrigued him beyond anything he had ever known.

He mulled matters over in silence, letting Questor lead the way. The wizard had not volunteered any further information since the aborted luncheon, and Ben thought that he might be well advised not to ask any more questions of the man for the time being. He concentrated instead on studying the land about them; first, what was visible from the high slope during their descent and, later, what could be seen more closely from the valley floor. They were traveling east, he concluded, if the sun's passage through the skies was an accurate compass. Mountains ringed the valley and the mist lay over everything. Lake and river country comprised the south end of the valley, desert and scrubland the east, hills the north and heavy woods the west. The center of the valley was a green flatland of fields and meadows. There were castles in the central plains; he had glimpsed their towers through the mist. There was a very dark, very unpleasant-looking hollows north and west, a deep bowl that seemed to gather mist and shadows until they stirred like steaming soup. He viewed all this during their descent from the meadow where Questor had found him; when they reached the valley floor he saw his first people. They were an unimpressive bunch—farmers with their families, woodsmen and hunters, a few stray traders with their wares, and a single rider bearing an heraldic banner of some sort. Except for the rider, the rest looked rather downtrodden. Their clothes were poor, their tools and wagons battered, and their stock worn. The homes of the farmers had seen better days and lacked any decent upkeep. Everyone seemed tired.

Ben saw all of this from some distance off, including the people, so he could not be entirely certain that he was seeing it accurately. Nevertheless, he didn't think he was mistaken.

Questor Thews said nothing about any of it.

It was mid-afternoon when he turned Ben suddenly north. A stretch of wooded hills lay before them, shrouded in trailers of mist that hung across the trees like factory smoke. They passed through in silence, picking their way cautiously where limbs and leaves left the pathway in shadow. They were well north of the lake and river country Ben had seen earlier, yet a sudden cluster of lakes and ponds came into view through the trees, bits of dark water mirroring the muted sunlight in bright splashes. Trailers of mist hung over these as well. Ben glanced about uneasily. There was in these woods a hint of the look and feel that had been present in the fairy world.

They climbed a high ridgeline that rose above the forest trees, and Questor brought Ben to a halt. "Look down there, High Lord," he said and pointed.

Ben looked. Several miles off, ringed in a gathering of trees, mist and shadows was a clearing that shimmered with sunlight. Colors reflected brightly, a rainbow's mix, and there seemed to be flags waving softly in a forest breeze that did not reach to the ridge on which Ben stood.

Questor's arm swept down again. "That is the Heart, High Lord. There you will be crowned King of Landover several days hence when the proclamation of your coming has been sent. Every King that Landover has ever had has been crowned there—every King since Landover came into being."

They stood on the ridgeline a moment longer, staring downward into that single spot of brightness amid the haze of mist and shadows. Neither spoke.

Then Questor turned away. "Come, High Lord. Your castle lies just ahead."

Ben followed dutifully after.

STERLING SILVER

The trees closed about, the mists came up, and Questor Thews and Ben Holiday were back within the forest. Shadows darkened the pathway anew, and the colors and feel of the Heart were gone. Ben pushed his way resolutely forward, keeping pace with the shambling figure of the wizard. It was not easy, for Questor covered ground rapidly despite his odd gait. Ben shifted the duffel from one arm to the other, feeling the muscles cramping with stiffness. He rubbed at his shoulders with his free hand and pushed up the sleeves of the running suit. There was sweat soaking through the back of his pullover.

One would think they could free up an escort and carriage for their new King, instead of making him hike it in, he groused inwardly. On the other hand, maybe they didn't use carriages in Landover. Maybe they flew on winged horses. Maybe Questor Thews should have conjured up a couple of those.

He chewed thoughtfully at his lower lip, remembering Questor's attempts at providing lunch. Maybe he was better off hiking.

They climbed toward a new ridgeline of blue spruce grown so thick that pine needles formed a carpet on the forest earth. Boughs pushed and slapped at their faces, and they bent their heads against them. Then the trees broke apart, the far side of the ridgeline dropped away into meadow, and the castle stood before them.

Ben Holiday stared. It was the same castle he had seen before—only now he could see it clearly. It sat half a mile distant within a lake upon an island just large enough to support it. The lake was iron gray, the island bare of everything but wintry scrub. The castle was a maze of stone and wood and metal towers, parapets, causeways, and walks that thrust into the sky like the fingers of a broken hand. A shroud of mist hung across the whole of the island and the waters of the lake and stirred thickly in a sunless cauldron. There was no color anywhere—no flags, no standards, no banners, nothing. The stone and wood had a soiled look, and the metal appeared to have discolored. Though the mortar and block seemed sound and the bulwarks did not crumble, still the castle had the look of a lifeless shell.

It had the look of something out of *Dracula*.

"This is the castle of the Kings of Landover?" Ben asked incredulously.

"Hmmmmm?" Questor was preoccupied again. "Oh, yes, this is it. This is Sterling Silver."

Ben dropped his duffel with a thud. "Sterling Silver?"

"That is her name."

"Sterling Silver—as in bright and polished?"

Questor's eyebrows lifted. "She was that once, High Lord."

"She was, was she? Once upon a time, a very long time ago, I'll bet." A well of disappointment opened in the pit of his stomach. "She looks more like Dingy Dungeon than Sterling Silver."

"That is the result of the Tarnish." The wizard folded his arms over his chest and looked out across the meadow. "Twenty years she has been like this, High Lord—not so long, really. The Tarnish has done it. Before, she was bright and polished as the name implies. The stone was white, the wood clean and the metal shining. There were no mists to block the sun. The island was alive with flowers of every color and the lake was crystal blue. It was the most beautiful place in the land."

Ben followed his gaze back to the nightmare that waited below. "So what happened to change all that?"

"The Tarnish. When the last true King of Landover died twenty years ago and no heir ascended to the throne, the discoloration began. It was gradual at first, but quickened as time passed and no King ruled. The life goes out of Sterling Silver, and the Tarnish marks her failing. No amount of cleaning or scrubbing or polishing of stone, wood, and metal can restore her." He glanced over. "She dies, High Lord. She follows her Lord to the grave."

Ben blinked. "You speak of her as if she were alive."

The owlish face nodded. "So she is, High Lord—as alive as you or I."

"But she's dying?"

"Slowly and painfully."

"And that is where you want me to live—in a dying castle?"

Questor smiled. "You must. You are the only one who can heal her." He took Ben's arm and propelled him ahead. "Come along now, High Lord. You will find her quite pleasant on the inside, where her heart is still warm and her life still strong. Things are not really so bad as they might seem. Come, now. You will find her very much a home. Come."

They descended the ridgeline through the meadow to where the waters of the lake lapped softly against a bank of marshy grasses. Weeds grew in thick tufts where the shoreline had eroded and stagnant pools had formed. Frogs croaked and insects hummed, and the lake smelled faintly fishy.

There was a long boat with a curved prow and knight's head, low gunwales, and rudderless stern pulled up upon the banks. Questor motioned, and they climbed aboard. Ben moved to a forward seat while Questor sat in the stern. They had just settled themselves when the boat began to move. It lurched free of the lake shore and slipped quietly into its waters. Ben looked about curiously. He could discover no source of propulsion for the boat.

"The touch of your hands lends it direction," Questor said suddenly.

Ben stared down at his hands as they gripped the gunnels. "My hands?"

"The boat, like the castle, is alive. It is called a lake skimmer. It responds to the touch of those it serves. You are now foremost of those. Will it to carry you and it shall do so."

"Where shall I will it to carry me?"

Questor laughed gently. "Why, to the front door, High Lord."

Ben gripped the gunnels and conveyed the thought silently. The lake skimmer sped swiftly across the dark waters, leaving a white swale in the wake of its passing.

"Slowly, High Lord, slowly," Questor admonished. "You convey your thoughts too urgently."

Ben relaxed his grip and his thoughts, and the lake skimmer slowed. It was exciting, having use of this small magic. He let his fingers brush softly across the smooth wood of the gunwales. It was warm and vibrant. It had the feel of a living thing.

"Questor?" He turned back to the wizard. The sense of life in the lake skimmer bothered him, but he kept his hands in place. "What was it you said before about my healing the castle?"

The fingers of one hand came up to rub the owlish face. "Sterling Silver, like Landover, is in need of a King. The castle fails without one. Your presence within the castle renews her life. When you make her your home, that life will be fully sustained once more."

Ben glanced ahead to the spectral apparition with its dark towers and battlements, its discolored stone walls and vacant eyes. "What if I don't want to make her my home?"

"Oh, I think you will," the wizard replied enigmatically.

Think whatever you want, Ben thought without saying it. His eyes stayed on the approaching castle, on the mist and shadows that shrouded it. He expected at any moment to see something with fangs appear at the windows of the highest tower and to see bats circling watchfully.

He saw, however, nothing.

The lake skimmer grounded gently on the island banks, and Ben and Questor disembarked. An arched entry with raised portcullis stood before them, an open invitation to be swallowed whole. Ben shifted the duffel from one hand to the other, hesitating. If anything, the castle looked worse close up than it had from the ridge crest.

"Questor, I'm not sure about . . ."

"Come, High Lord," the wizard interrupted, again taking his arm, again propelling him ahead. "You cannot see anything worthwhile from out here. Besides, the others will be waiting."

Ben stumbled forward, eyes shifting nervously upward along the parapets and towers; the stone was damp and the corners and crevices a maze of spider webs. "Others? What others?"

"Why, the others who stand in service to the throne—your staff, High Lord. Not all have left the service of the King."

"Not all?"

But Questor either didn't hear him or simply ignored him, hurrying ahead, forcing Ben to walk more quickly to keep pace. They passed from the entry through a narrow court as dark and dingy in appearance as the rest of the castle and from there through a second entry, smaller than the first, down a short hall and into a foyer. Misty light slipped through high, arched windows, mixing with the gloom and shadows. Ben glanced about. The wood of the supports and stays was polished and clean, the stone scrubbed, and the walls and floors covered in rugs and tapestries that had retained some of their original color. There were even a few pieces of stiff-looking furniture. Had it not been for the gray cast that seemed to permeate everything, the room would have been almost cheerful.

"You see, things are much better inside," Questor insisted.

Ben nodded without enthusiasm. "Lovely."

They crossed to a door that opened into a cavernous dining hall with a huge tressel table and high-backed chairs cushioned in scarlet silk. Chandeliers of tarnished silver hung from the ceiling; despite the summer weather, a fire burned in a hearth at the far end of the hall. Ben followed Questor into the hall and stopped.

Three figures stood in a line to the right of the dining table. Their eyes met his.

"Your personal staff, High Lord," Questor announced.

Ben stared. The staff consisted of a dog and two large-eared monkeys—or at least two creatures very like monkeys. The dog stood upright on its hind legs and wore breeches with suspenders, a tunic with heraldic insignia, and glasses. Its coat was golden in color, and it had small flaps for ears that looked as if they might have been tacked on as an afterthought. The hair on its head and muzzle made it appear as if it were half porcupine. The creatures that looked like monkeys wore short pants and leather cross-belts from waist to shoulder. One was taller and spindle-legged. The other was heavy and wore a cook's apron. Both had ears like Dumbo and prehensile toes.

Questor motioned to Ben, and they moved forward to stop before the dog. "This is Abernathy, court scribe and your personal attendant."

The dog bowed slightly and looked at him over the rims of the glasses. "Welcome, High Lord," the dog said.

Ben jumped back in surprise. "Questor, he talks!"

"As well as you do, High Lord," the dog replied stiffly.

"Abernathy is a soft-coated Wheaten Terrier—a breed that has produced a good many champion hunting dogs," Questor interjected. "He was not always a dog, however. He was a man before he was a dog. He became a dog through a rather unfortunate accident."

"I became a dog through your stupidity." Abernathy's voice was very close to a canine growl. "I have remained a dog through your stupidity."

Questor shrugged. "Well, yes, it was my fault in a way, I suppose." He sighed, glancing at Ben. "I was trying to disguise him and the magic made him thus. Unfortunately, I have not as yet discovered a way to change him back again. But he does quite well as a dog, don't you, Abernathy?"

"I did better as a man."

Questor frowned. "I would have to dispute that, I think."

"That is because you must find some way to justify what you did, Questor Thews. Had I not retained my intelligence—which, fortunately, is considerably higher than your own—I would undoubtedly have been placed in some kennel and forgotten!"

"That is most unkind." The frown deepened. "Perhaps you would have preferred it if I had changed you into a cat!"

Abernathy's reply came out a bark. Questor started and flushed. "I understood that, Abernathy, and I want you to know that I don't appreciate it. Remember where you are. Remember that this is the King you stand before."

Abernathy's shaggy face regarded Ben solemnly. "So much the worse for him."

Questor shot him a dark look, then turned to the creatures standing next to him. "These are kobolds," Questor advised Ben, who was still struggling with the idea that his personal attendant was a talking dog. "They speak their own language and will have nothing to do with ours, though they understand it well enough. They have names in their own language, but the names would mean nothing to you. I have therefore given them names of my own, which they have agreed to accept. The taller is Bunion, the court runner. The heavier is Parsnip, the court chef." He motioned to the two. "Give greeting to the High Lord, kobolds."

The kobolds bowed. When they straightened, their mouths parted to reveal rows of sharpened teeth behind frightening smiles. They hissed softly.

"Parsnip is a true kobold," Questor said. "He is a fairy creature who has chosen open service to the household of a human rather than a haunting. His tribe is one of those that drifted out of the fairy world and stayed. Bunion is a wight, more a woods creature than a domestic. Generically, he is a kobold, but he retains characteristics of other fairy creatures as well. He can pass through the mists as they, though he cannot remain. He can cross through Landover with the swiftness of the fairies as well. But he is bound to Sterling Silver in the same fashion as Parsnip and must always return."

"For reasons that man and dog can only surmise," Abernathy interjected.

Bunion grinned at him blackly and hissed.

Ben pulled Questor Thews aside. It was with some effort that he managed to conceal his irritation. "Exactly what is going on here?"

"Hmmmmm?" Questor stared back at him blankly.

"Read my lips. If I'm understanding all of this correctly, the King of Landover lives in a dungeon and is attended by a menagerie. Are there any more surprises in store for me? What have I got for an army—a herd of cattle?"

The wizard looked slightly embarrassed. "Well, as a matter of fact, High Lord, you don't have any kind of army at all."

"No army? Why is that?"

"It disbanded—more than a dozen years ago, I'm afraid."

"Disbanded? Well, what about retainers—workers, servants, people to look after things in general? Who does that?"

"We do—the four of us." Questor Thews made a sweeping gesture back to Abernathy and the two kobolds.

Ben stared. "No wonder the castle is dying. Why don't you bring in some more help, for God's sake?"

"We have no money to pay them."

"What do you mean, you don't have any money? Don't you have a royal treasury or whatever?"

"The treasury is empty. There isn't a coin in it."

"Well, doesn't the throne tax in some fashion so that there should be money?" Ben's voice was getting louder. "How did Kings pay for anything in the past?"

"They taxed." Questor glanced angrily at Abernathy, who was shaking his head in amusement. "Unfortunately, the taxing system broke down some years ago. Nothing has been paid into the treasury since."

Ben dropped his duffel and put his hands on his hips. "Let me get this straight. I bought a kingdom where the King has no army, no staff but the four of you, and no money? I paid a million dollars for that?"

"You are being unreasonable, Ben Holiday."

"That depends on whose shoes you're standing in, I'd say!"

"You must be patient. You have not yet seen all that there is to see nor learned all that there is to learn of Landover. The immediate problems of taxes and retainers and an army can be solved once proper attention is given to the finding of the solutions. You must remember that there has been no King in Landover for more than twenty years. Since that is so, you must expect that not all will be as it should."

Ben laughed without humor. "There's the understatement of the year. Look, Questor, let's get to the heart of the matter. What else should I know about being King of Landover? What other bad news have you got to tell?"

"Oh, I think that is about the worst of it, High Lord." The wizard smiled disarmingly. "We will have time enough to discuss it all later, but I think a bit of dinner is in order first. It has been a long day, a long journey, and I know that you are tired and hungry both."

Ben cut him short. "I am not that tired or that hungry, damn it! I want to know what else you've been . . ."

"All in good time, all in good order—you have your health to consider, High Lord," Questor intoned, ignoring him. "Parsnip will prepare our meal—the castle's magic still keeps her larder well stocked—and while he is doing so, Abernathy will show you to your rooms where you may wash, take a change of clothes, and rest a bit. Abernathy, please escort the High Lord to his bedchamber and see that he has what he needs. I will be along in a while."

He turned and strode from the room before Ben had a chance to object further. Parsnip and Bunion exited as well. Ben was left staring at Abernathy.

"High Lord?" The dog beckoned to a spiral staircase that wound upward into the castle dark.

Ben nodded wordlessly. He was obviously not going to learn anything more for the moment.

"Lay on, Macduff," he sighed.

Together, they began to climb.

It proved to be a rather healthy trek. They climbed numerous stairs and followed half a dozen shadowed halls before reaching the appointed rooms. Ben spent most of the time lost in thought, pondering the unpleasant news that he was a King without any of the trappings, that he was Lord over Castle Dracula and not much else. He should have been paying closer attention to where he was going, he chided himself when they finally arrived, if for no other reason than to be able to find his way back again without help. He had a faint recollection of stone-block floors and wooden-beamed ceilings, of oak doors and iron fastenings, of tapestries and coats of arms, of muted colors and the discoloration of the Tarnish—but not much more than that.

"Your bath chamber, High Lord," Abernathy announced, halting before a heavy wooden door carved in scroll.

Ben peered inside. There was an iron tub with clawed feet and scrolled sides filled with steaming water, a tray with soaps, a pile of linen towels, with a change of clothing and a pair of boots stacked on a stool.

The bath looked inviting. "How did you manage to keep the water hot all this time?" he asked, wondering suddenly at the steam.

"The castle, High Lord. She still retains something of her magic. Food for the larder, hot water for baths—that is about all she has strength enough left for." Abernathy cut himself short and started to leave.

"Wait!" Ben called suddenly. The dog stopped. "I, uh . . . I just want to tell you that I'm sorry that I acted so surprised that you could talk. I didn't mean to be rude."

"I am quite accustomed to it, High Lord," Abernathy replied, and Ben didn't know if he meant the rudeness or the surprise. The dog peered at him from over the rims of his glasses. "In any case, though I am recognized everywhere within Landover as a major curiosity, I doubt that I will prove to be the biggest surprise that you will encounter."

Ben frowned. "Meaning what?"

"Meaning that you have a lot to learn, and the lessons are likely to be rather astonishing."

He bowed perfunctorily, backed through the door and closed it silently behind him. Ben's frown deepened. That last comment sounded almost like a warning, he thought. It sounded as if Abernathy was advising him that the worst was yet to come.

He brushed the matter from his mind, stripped off his clothes, lowered himself into the tub of water and lay back blissfully to soak. He remained in the tub for the better part of the hour that followed, thinking over all that had happened to him. Oddly enough, the focus of his concern had shifted completely since his arrival in Landover. Then, his concern had been with whether or not what he was seeing and experiencing was real or induced by clever special effects and the ingenuity of modern science. Now, his concern was with whether or not he should be here at all. Questor's revelations about the condition of the kingship were disheartening at best. He had paid a million dollars for a throne that commanded no retainers, no army, no treasury, and no taxing program. He found himself more inclined to accept that Landover was indeed a world apart from his own, a world in which magic really *did* function, than to accept that he had purchased a throne that commanded nothing.

Still, he wasn't being entirely fair, he chided. He had paid for a throne, but he had also paid for the land—and the land seemed to be exactly as advertised. Moreover, he had to expect that after twenty years with no King sitting on the throne, Landover's monarchy was likely to be floundering somewhat. He couldn't reasonably expect that a working tax system, a standing army, a body of retainers, and a full treasury would survive twenty years of no King. Matters would quite naturally get out of hand after a while. It was logical that there should be some work required of him to get things moving again.

So what was he worried about? When measured against his initial expectations, Landover was far more than he could ever have hoped for, wasn't it?

But Abernathy's veiled warning and his own doubts nagged at him nevertheless, and he could not seem to set the matter to rest. He finished his bath and climbed from the tub, toweling dry. The water in the tub had stayed an even temperature the entire time he was bathing. The room felt comfortable as well—even the stone of the floor was warm against the soles of his bare feet. There was an odd sense of vibrancy in the air, as if the castle were breathing . . .

He cut short the thought, unwilling to pursue it further just then, and began to dress. He pulled on stockings, some loose undergarments that fastened together with stays, a pair of forest green breeches with ties and a belt, and a loose fitting cream tunic with loops that slipped over metal hooks. The makeup of the ensemble seemed strange to him—the whole of it free of the buttons, zippers, Velcro fastenings and elastic bands that he was accustomed to—but the fit was good and he felt comfortable dressed in it.

He had just finished pulling on the pair of soft leather boots and was wondering what had become of Abernathy when the door opened and Questor appeared.

"Well, you seem rested and refreshed, High Lord." The wizard smiled—rather too broadly, Ben thought. "Was the bath satisfactory?"

"Quite." Ben smiled back. "Questor, why don't we cut through all this bull, and get . . ."

"This what?"

"Bull." Ben hesitated, searching for a better word. "Smokescreen."

"Smokescreen?"

"The social amenities of Kingship, damn it! I want to know what I've gotten myself into!"

Questor cocked his head thoughtfully. "Oh, I see. How would it be if I were to show you exactly that?"

Ben nodded at once. "That would be fine. That would be wonderful, in fact."

"Very well." The wizard turned and started from the room. "Come with me, please."

They exited the bath chamber and passed back into the hall. Questor took Ben deep into the castle where a pair of massive scrolled doors opened into a tower well with a staircase that spiraled upward into shadow. Wordlessly, they began to climb. When they had reached the landing at the head of the stairs,

Questor had Ben press his palms firmly against a crest of the medallion's image of castle and knight that was graven into a massive oak and metal-bound door seated in the tower wall. The door opened soundlessly, and they stepped inside.

They were in a small, circular room. The wall before them opened halfway around from floor to ceiling into clouds of mist that swirled past the towers of the castle as they rose darkly against the coming night. A silver guardrail on stanchions curved at waist height across the opening. A silver lectern was fastened at its midpoint. Ben looked at it momentarily, then looked at Questor. The room had the appearance of a speaker's platform designed to permit royal addresses to whatever audience could be found in the clouds.

"This is the Landsview," Questor said. "Step over to the rail, please."

Ben did as directed. The silver of the rail and lectern was stained with the Tarnish, but, beneath the discoloring, Ben could see thousands of tiny characters scrolled into the metal, etched by the hand of some enormously patient craftsman. Questor fumbled through the pouches he wore strapped about his waist and after a moment produced the same worn map that he had shown Ben earlier when explaining why it was that Ben could speak and read Landoverian.

He unfolded the map carefully and placed it on the lectern.

"Place your hands upon the railing before you, High Lord," he said.

Ben did so. Questor put his hands upon the railing as well. They stood together that way for a moment, staring out into the darkening mist. It was almost dusk.

Then a sudden warmth spread through the metal, a vibrancy of the sort that Ben had experienced in the bath chamber.

"Keep your hands firmly fixed upon the railing," Questor admonished suddenly. "Look at the map before you and select anything drawn upon it that you wish to see. The Landsview will show it to you."

Ben glanced over at him doubtfully, then looked down at the map. The whole of the valley was inscribed on the parchment, inked in various colors to designate forests, rivers, lakes, mountains, plains, valleys, deserts, towns, territories, and castle keeps, the names of all meticulously marked throughout. The colors were faded, the parchment worn. Ben squinted. His eyes came to rest after a moment on Sterling Silver and then on the dark and forbidding hollows he had seen earlier from the heights. The name of the hollows was smudged and illegible.

"There," he indicated, inclining his head. "That hollows north of here. Show me that."

"The Deep Fell." Questor spoke softly. "Very well. Grip the railing tightly, High Lord. Take a deep breath. Concentrate on the map."

Ben's hands tightened. His eyes locked on the map and the hollows marked upon it. The mists that shrouded Sterling Silver swirled in murky trailers before him, and the darkness of coming night slipped across the land. Time froze. He glanced curiously at Questor.

"Concentrate on the map, High Lord."

He looked back at the map, concentrating.

Then the whole of the castle fell away beneath him, stone block walls, towers, and battlements dissipating into empty air, the mists faded and the night sky shone clear and starlit all about him. He was flying through space with only the silver railing and lectern wrapped about him for support. His eyes widened in shock, and he stared downward. Below, the valley sped away in a void of shadows and moonlight.

"Questor!" he cried out in terror, arms stiffening to brace his fall.

The wizard was next to him. One hand slid across to squeeze his.

"Do not be frightened, High Lord," he said. His voice was calm and reassuring, so normal in tone that they might still have been standing within the tower. "It is only the magic at work," he continued. "You are in no danger while you hold fast to the railing."

Ben was holding on so tightly that his knuckles had turned white. He was firmly anchored, he discovered. While there was the sensation of movement, he could neither feel nor hear the wind rush past and no air stirred the parchment map. He held his breath and watched the land sweep away hundreds of feet below, a panorama of shadowed forests, jutting mountains and shimmering lakes. Landover's moons had all risen into view now, a gathering of colored spheres dotting the heavens—peach, burnt rose, jade, beryl, sea green, a sort of washed-out mauve, turquoise, and the largest of all, a brilliant white. It was the strangest display that Ben had ever witnessed, a kind of still life fourth-of-July.

He relaxed a bit now, beginning to feel more at ease with what was happening to him. He had ridden in a hot air balloon once. This flight had something of the feel of that.

They circled the valley's mountains in a slow arc, crossing above the mists of the fairy world.

"There is where Landover's magic is born, High Lord." Questor spoke suddenly. "The fairy world is the source of her magic—a place of timelessness and infinite being, of everywhere and always. It borders on all worlds and has access to all. Corridors pass through it, linking the worlds without. Time passages, they are called—pathways that lead from one world to another. You took one of those pathways when you passed from your world into Landover."

"Do you mean that the fairy world lies *between* my world and Landover?" Ben asked, realizing suddenly that he was shouting to be heard and that it was quite unnecessary.

Questor shook his head. "Not exactly. The fairy world is an ephemeral place of non-being, High Lord. It is and at the same time it isn't, being both everywhere and nowhere all at once. It cannot be self-contained nor is it the final source of all things. Do you understand?"

Ben smiled. "Not a word."

"Think of it in this way, then. It is closer to Landover than to any of the other worlds it touches upon. Landover is a sort of stepchild."

An odd comparison, Ben thought and watched the mists slip away. Then they were descending, dropping swiftly toward the Deep Fell. The hollows lay directly below them, a tangled stretch of wilderness forest nestled close to the high mountains that formed the northwest corner of the valley's perimeter, a dismal and forbidding wood that light could not seem to penetrate. Shadows lay over everything, and the mists of the fairy world that ringed the valley seemed to reach downward and drape across it like the corner of a blanket.

"There dwells the witch Nightshade." Questor spoke again. "It is said that she crossed over from the fairy world in a time so distant it has been forgotten by all but her. It is said that she came into the world of mortals to take a lover and that, having done so, she can never go back again."

Ben stared downward into the black. It had the look of a pit that bored all the way to hell.

Once more, they swept away across the land. They sped from horizon to horizon, Ben's eyes picking out names inscribed upon the parchment map, one landmark after the other. He found the country of the River Master, another creature of the fairy world, a spirit who had assimilated into human form and adopted as his home the lakes and rivers that dominated the southern half of the valley, ruling over the sprites and nymphs that dwelt within their waters. Ben explored the hills and steeps north above the smudge of the Deep Fell, where lived numerous tribes of gnomes, trolls, and kobolds. Some were miners, farmers, hunters, and tradesmen, some thieves and cutthroats; some were industrious and honest, some shiftless and malicious; some were friendly and some not. Questor was speaking now. The Lords of the Greensward laid claim to the whole of the central valley, their vast holdings of farmland and stock the wealth of a few families whose lineage could be traced back generations, feudal barons whose subjects were thralls working the crops and animals for their masters.

"Slaves?" Ben interrupted sharply, appalled.

"Thralls!" Questor repeated, emphasizing the word. "These are men and women of free will; but they receive of the land and its bounty only what is allocated to them by the barons."

Slaves, Ben thought to himself. A rose by any other name . . .

Questor's voice droned on, but Ben missed the rest of what he was saying, his attention diverted suddenly to something new. He thought it at first to be nothing more than a peculiar speck of darkness against the silhouette of one of Landover's moons. Then he realized that the speck was moving.

It was moving toward them.

It flew out of the south, a huge, winged shadow that grew in size against the horizon. Featureless when Ben caught sight of it, it began to take more definite shape as it approached. Leathered wings flared, spined and arched like the struts of a monstrous kite stretched to its breaking point. A barrel-shaped body undulated like a serpent's with the flying motion, its hide covered with scales and plates. Great, clawed feet tucked against its body, and its neck arched snakelike above it, flared behind a head so odious to look upon that Ben flinched in spite of himself.

It was the dragon.

"Questor!" Ben whispered hoarsely, afraid to shout.

The wizard turned, and his head lifted toward the great beast. "Strabo!" he whispered in reply, and there was something almost like reverence in his voice.

They ceased to move then, frozen suddenly in midair. The dragon flew past them, so close that it seemed it would brush against them. It did not see them, for they were not truly to be seen—but it appeared to Ben as if it sensed their presence. The crusted head swept over so that its blooded eyes fixed on them, and its jagged snout split wide. A sharp, frightening hiss ripped through the stillness of the night, lingering and dying slowly into silence.

But the dragon did not slow or change course. Northeast it flew until it had become a distant speck once more. They stared after it until it was gone.

"My God!" Ben said finally, his voice still a whisper. His thirst for adventure was suddenly quenched. He stared down wildly at the empty space that spread away beneath him, the space in which they still hung, unmoving. "Damn it, I've had enough of this, Questor! Take us back to where we came from!"

"The map, High Lord," the wizard said calmly. "Fix your eyes upon the map and seek out Sterling Silver."

Ben did so at once, almost frantic to have his feet back upon solid stone. He found the designation for the castle and concentrated his thoughts upon it. Almost instantly he was back within the tower, standing before the open wall, staring out into the mists.

He released the railing as if it burned him and stepped quickly back. "That beast . . . that was the dragon that I stumbled on in the forest!" he snapped.

"Yes, High Lord, it was," the other agreed, turning away from the railing with him. The owlish face was contemplative. "Strabo is his name. He lives east where the valley is a wasteland of desert, marsh and scrub. He lives alone there, the last of his kind."

Ben folded his arms into his chest, suddenly cold. "He was close enough to touch."

"It only seemed so." Questor's smile was wry. "The magic made it appear that way. In truth, we never left this room."

"Never left?"

"You may try it yourself sometime, High Lord. The magic of the Landsview is yours to wield—and you have seen for yourself how it works."

"All too well, thank you."

"Have you learned enough about Landover for tonight, then? Would you like to have dinner now?"

Ben had regained his composure. "Dinner would be fine." He took a deep breath. "Are there any surprises that go with it? If there are, I would like to know about them now—not after the fact."

The wizard pushed his way back through the tower door. "No, High Lord. There should be no surprises with dinner. It should be quite pleasant. Come along."

They trekked back through the corridors and stairwells of the castle until they had again reached the dining hall. Ben still had questions that needed answers, but he was weary and he was hungry and the questions could wait. He let himself be led to the head of the tressel table and seated. His stomach was beginning to settle again, the chill to leave his body. He had survived after all, with no apparent damage. So if that was the worst that he was to endure . . .

"Would you care for some wine, High Lord?" Questor interrupted his thoughts. The day was gone, and the darkness of the castle was deepening. The wizard lifted his hand and pointed, and the chandeliers came alive with light, a soft golden glow that was flameless and smokeless, yet had no apparent power source. "Another little touch of the magic." The other smiled. "Did you say you wanted wine?"

Ben slumped back in his chair. "Yes—and leave the bottle."

Questor gestured, and the wine appeared at his elbow. The wizard had taken a seat on his right. Abernathy and Bunion appeared and sat on his left. Parsnip would undoubtedly join them after bringing out the dinner. They were just one, big, happy family.

Ben faced the wizard. "I'll say it once more, Questor—no more surprises. I want to know everything. I want to know about the medallion. I want to know about Meeks. I want to know who sold Landover and why. I want to know all of it."

Abernathy put his paws on the table and looked at Ben from over the rims of his glasses. "I would drink the wine first, High Lord, if I were you."

The shaggy face glanced knowingly at Bunion seated next to him. The kobold smiled and hissed and showed all of his teeth.

Ben reached for the wine.

He had consumed a good portion of the bottle before Parsnip reappeared with dinner. The kobold brought a stew made of beef and vegetables, fresh-baked bread, cheeses and pastries. Whatever else was wrong, no one was starving to death, he thought.

He ate a bowl of the stew with pieces of bread and cheese, drank several glasses of wine and thought about Annie and Miles and what he had left behind. Questor and Abernathy argued about everything from the nature of a balanced meal to the role of magic in health care. The kobolds grinned and ate everything in sight. When it came time for seconds, Questor found the stew too cold and suggested it be reheated. Parsnip hissed and showed his teeth, and Abernathy suggested it was better served cold. Questor disagreed. The argument was resolved when Questor used the magic to reheat it where it cooled in its kettle, and the kettle exploded in flames setting fire to the whole of the tressel table and the linen service set upon it. Everyone jumped up, yelling, hissing and barking all at once. Questor used the magic again, and this time it rained inside the dining hall for fifteen minutes.

That was enough for Ben. Wineglass in hand, Abernathy leading, he retired to the royal sleeping quarters, scorched and soaked and woozy. Tomorrow, he decided as he lay back within the coverings of his bed, would be a better day.

CORONATION

Tomorrow might indeed have been a better day, but Ben Holiday never had a chance to find out.

He dreamed as he slept, dreams of truth and fantasy. He dreamed of Annie and of finding her alive again, his exhilaration at being with her and loving her blunted by a pervasive sense that she could not stay and he must lose her once more. He dreamed of Miles, bluff and cynical as he reminded Ben at every turn on a journey through a Chicago filled with Bonnie Blues that he had told him so. He dreamed of lawyers and courtrooms in which kobolds hissed from jury boxes and judges had the look of shaggy dogs. He dreamed of high rises and concrete parkways and soaring over all a dragon as black as night. He dreamed of demons and knights, of faces in the mist, and of castles that shone like the sun.

He dreamed, and the world slipped away from him.

When he came awake again, it was morning. He lay within his sleeping quarters, a vast chamber of tapestries and silken hangings, of polished oak and heraldic stone sculptures. He lay within his bed, a great canopied sarcophagus of oak and iron that looked as if it might successfully double as a barge. He knew it was morning by the slant of the light through the high arched windows, though the light remained gray and hazy as the mist without screened away its color. It was quiet within his room and quiet in the rooms without. The castle was like a stone shell.

Yet there was warmth in that castle. Sterling Silver was a dungeon to look upon and it lacked the visual appeal of even the most spartan, avant-garde, chrome-and-steel Chicago high rise, but it had the feel of a home. It was warm to the touch, from the floors that he had walked upon to the walls that he had brushed against. The warmth was in the air, despite the mist and the gray; it flowed through her like a life blood. She was what Questor Thews had called her. She was a living thing.

Waking up inside of her felt right. It felt secure and comforting, the way it was supposed to feel when one woke within one's own home.

He stretched and glanced over to the nightstand on which he had placed his duffel and found Questor Thews sitting on a high-backed chair, looking at him.

"Good morrow, Ben Holiday," the wizard greeted him.

"Good morning," he replied. The good feelings evaporated in a rush as he remembered the wizard's gloomy revelation of the night before—that he was a King without retainers, army, or treasury.

"You rested well, I trust?" Questor asked.

"Quite well, thank you."

"Wonderful. You have a busy day before you."

"I do?"

"Yes, High Lord." Questor was beaming. "Today is your coronation. Today you shall be crowned King of Landover."

Ben blinked. "Today?" He blinked again. There was a sinking feeling in the pit of his stomach. "Wait a minute, Questor. What do you mean, *today* is the coronation? Wasn't it just yesterday that you were telling me that the coronation would not take place for at least *several* days because you needed time to inform all those that needed informing?"

"Well, ah . . . yes, I did say that, I admit." The wizard screwed up his owlish face like a guilty child. "The trouble is, it wasn't yesterday that I said that."

"It wasn't yester . . . ?"

"Because this isn't tomorrow."

Ben flushed and sat up quickly in the bed. "Just what in the hell are you talking about?"

Questor Thews smiled. "High Lord, you have been asleep for a week."

Ben stared at him in silence. The wizard stared back. It was so quiet in the room that Ben could hear the sound of his own breathing in his ears.

"How could I have slept for a week?" he asked finally.

Questor steepled his hands before his face. "Do you remember the wine that you drank—the wine I provided?" Ben nodded. "Well, I added a dash of sleeping tonic to its content so that you would be assured of a good night's rest." He gestured with his hands. "It was in the magic I used, just an inflection of the voice and a twist." He demonstrated. "The trouble was, I overdid it. The dash became a thimbleful. So you have been asleep for a week."

"Just a little mistake of the magic, is that it?" Ben was flushed with anger.

Questor fidgeted uneasily. "I am afraid so."

"Well, I am afraid not! What sort of fool do you take me for? You did it on purpose, didn't you? You put me asleep to keep me here!" Ben was shaking, he was so mad. "Did you think I had forgotten the ten-day withdrawal clause in my contract? Ten days were allotted me to return to my own world if I wanted my money back, less the handling fee. Don't tell me you didn't know that! Now eight of those ten days are gone! It's all rather convenient, don't you think?"

"One minute, please." Questor had gone stiff with indignation. "If it were truly my intention to keep you in Landover, High Lord, I would not have bothered to tell you about the sleeping potion or the lost days of sleep *at all*! I would simply have let you think it was still only your second day in Landover and all *ten* days would have passed before you realized differently!"

Ben regarded him silently for a moment and then sat back. "I guess you're right about that." He shook his head in disbelief. "I suppose I owe you an apology, but frankly I'm too mad to apologize. I've lost a whole damn week because of you! And while I've been sleeping, you've gone right ahead with the plans for making me King—sent out the invitations and everything! Good thing I woke up on time, isn't it, or you would have been faced with a bedside coronation!"

"Oh, I knew you would awake on time after I discovered the problem," Questor hastened to assure him.

"You mean you *hoped* you knew," Abernathy interjected, appearing through the bedroom door with a tray. "Breakfast, High Lord?"

He brought the tray over and set it on the nightstand. "Thank you," Ben muttered, his eyes still fixed on Questor.

"I knew," the wizard said pointedly.

"Beautiful day for a coronation," Abernathy said. He looked at Ben over the rims of his glasses. "I have your robes of office ready. They have been altered to fit exactly as they ought to." He paused. "I had plenty of time to measure you while you slept."

"I'll bet." Ben chewed angrily on a piece of bread. "A whole week's worth of time, it appears."

Abernathy shrugged. "Not quite. The rest of us drank the wine as well, High Lord."

"It was an honest mistake," Questor insisted, brows knitting.

"You make a lot of those," Abernathy sniffed.

"Perhaps it would please you if I simply quit trying to help at all!"

"Nothing would please me more!"

Ben held up his hands pleadingly. "Hold it! Enough, already!" He looked from one to the other. "I don't need another argument. As a lawyer, I got my fill of arguments. I need answers. I said last night that I wanted to know the whole story behind the sale of this Kingdom—well, not last night, but the last time we talked, anyway. So maybe this is the time for it, Questor."

The wizard rose, cast a dark glance at Abernathy, and looked back again at Ben. "You shall have your explanation, High Lord. But you must settle for hearing it as we travel to the Heart. The coronation must take place at noon, and we must leave at once in order to be there on time."

Abernathy headed for the door. "His anticipation knows no bounds, I'm sure, wizard. High Lord, I will return with your robes shortly. Meanwhile, try eating a bit more of the breakfast. The castle's magic continues to fail, and we may all soon be foraging the countryside for sustenance."

He left. Questor glared after him, then turned hastily to Ben. "I will only add, High Lord, that, with two days remaining, you have sufficient time to use the medallion to return to your own world—if that should be your wish."

He hesitated, then followed Abernathy out. Ben watched them go. "A whole week," he muttered, shoved the breakfast tray aside, and climbed from the bed.

They set out within the hour—Ben, Questor, Abernathy, and the two kobolds. They left Sterling Silver and her barren island on the lake skimmer, slipping silently through the murky lake waters to the meadow beyond. From there, they passed back into the forests and the mist.

"It would be best to start at the beginning, I suppose," Questor said to Ben after they had entered the forest trees. They walked a step ahead of the others, shoulder to shoulder, the wizard with the studied, swinging gait, shoulders stooped and head lowered. "The problem with the throne began after the death of the old King more than twenty years ago. Things were much different then. The old King had the respect of all of the people of Landover. Five generations of his family had ruled in succession, and all had ruled well. No one challenged the old King's rule—not Nightshade, not even the Mark. There was an army then and retainers and laws to govern all. The treasury was full, and the magic protected the throne. Sterling Silver was not under the Tarnish; she was polished and gleaming like something just crafted, and the island on which she sits was the most beautiful spot in the land. There were flowers and there was sunshine—and no mists or clouds."

Ben glanced over. He was dressed in a red silk tunic and pants with knee-high boots and silver stays. Abernathy carried his ceremonial robes, crown and chains of office. "Questor, I hate to have to tell you this but your explanation is beginning to sound like a bad fairy tale."

"It grows worse, High Lord. The old King died and left but a single son, still a youth, as heir to the throne. The son's guardian was a wizard of great power but dubious principle. The wizard was more father to the son than the old King, having cared for the boy after his mother's death and during the old King's frequent absences from court. The son was a mean-spirited boy, bored with Landover and displeased with the responsibilities his birthright demanded of him, and the wizard played upon this weakness. The wizard had been looking for a way to escape what he viewed as his own limited existence in Landover for some time; he was court wizard then—the position that I now hold—and he thought himself destined for greater things. But a court wizard is bound to the throne and the land by an oath of magic; he could not leave if the throne did not release him. So he employed his considerable skill with words and convinced the boy that they should both leave Landover."

He paused, and his owlish face turned slightly toward Ben. "The wizard is my half-brother, High Lord. You know him better as Meeks."

"Oh-oh." Ben shook his head slowly. "I begin to see the light."

"Hmmmmm?"

"Just an expression. And will you quit saying *hmmmmmm* like that? My grandmother in her dotage used to do that every time I said something to her, and it damn near drove me crazy!"

"Sorry. Well, the trouble with leaving Landover is that when you go, you take nothing with you. The magic won't allow it. Neither my half-brother nor the old King's son could stomach that! So they devised a scheme to sell the throne to someone from another world. If someone from another world were to buy Landover, then my half-brother and the old King's son could collect the proceeds in that other world and thwart the laws of this one which would prohibit them from taking anything out. That way, they could live comfortably wherever they were to go."

"How did they decide on my world?" Ben asked.

"Research." Questor smiled. "Yours was a world in which the inhabitants were most likely to be attracted to life here. Landover was the fantasy that they dreamed about."

Ben nodded. "Except that it really isn't."

"Yes, well." Questor cleared his throat. "Time passed while my half-brother subverted the old King's son, while the son grew to manhood, and while they schemed to break their ties with the land. The son never really wanted the throne in any case; he would abandon it quickly enough, whatever the conditions imposed, so long as he could be assured that he would be well looked after. It became the responsibility of my half-brother to find a way to make that happen. That took some thinking and some maneuvering. While all this was happening, the kingdom was falling apart. The magic works on strength of commitment, and there was precious little of that. The treasury emptied. The army disbanded. The laws broke down. The population began to lose its sense of unity and to drift into armed camps. Trade between them all but ceased. Sterling Silver had no master and no retainers to look after her, and she began to fall under the Tarnish. The land was affected as well, withering and turning foul. My half-brother and the old King's son were left with the problem of selling a, ah . . . how do you put it in your world, High Lord? . . . oh, yes, a 'pig in a poke' . . . to some unsuspecting customer."

Ben stared upward into the trees beseechingly. "You have such a way with words, Questor."

"Yes, but you see, High Lord, it doesn't have to be that way—that's what I have been trying to explain to you. A King of strength and wisdom can restore Landover to the way it once was. The laws can be put back—especially by someone like you, who understands the nature of laws. The treasury can be replenished, the army can be restored, and the Tarnish can be cleansed. That is why I donned the mantle of court wizard when it was discarded by my half-brother. That is why I agreed to help my half-brother seek a buyer for the throne. I even wrote the words for the notice of sale."

"You wrote that pack of lies for the sale item in the catalogue?" Ben asked in astonishment.

"I wrote it to attract the right kind of person—one with vision and courage!" A bony finger jabbed at Ben. "And it is not a pack of lies!" The finger dropped away and the lean face tightened. "I did what was necessary, High Lord. Landover must be made new again. She has been allowed to waste away with the fragmenting of the old King's rule, and a loss of the magic will destroy her completely."

"We have heard this speech before, Questor," Abernathy muttered from behind them. "Kindly put it to rest."

The wizard shot him an irritated look. "I am speaking only what needs to be spoken. If you are weary of the speech, close your ears."

"Questor, I'm not following your part in all of this." Ben brought the conversation back around to the subject at hand. "If you feel so strongly about what Landover needs, then why did you let your half-brother and the old King's son run it into the ground in the first place? What were you doing all those years that followed the death of the old King? Where were you while the throne of Landover sat vacant?"

Questor Thews held up his hands imploringly. "Please, High Lord—one question at a time!" He rubbed at his bearded chin fretfully. "You must understand that I was not court wizard then. My half-brother was. And while I don't like to admit it, I am not the wizard that my half-brother is. I am a poor second to him and always have been."

"Where is my quill and scroll," Abernathy exclaimed. "I must have this in writing!"

"I am improving, however, now that I have *become* court wizard," Questor went on, ignoring the other. "I was without position at the court while my half-brother was in service—an apprentice grown too old to stay on, yet unable to find other work in the Kingdom. I traveled quite a bit, trying to learn something of the magics of the fairies, trying to find work to occupy my time. Some years after the old King died, my half-brother called me home again to help with the administration of the court. He advised me of his intention to leave the Kingdom and not return. He advised me that the old King's son had decided to sell the throne and go with him. He appointed me to act as court wizard and advisor to the new King."

He stopped, turning to face Ben. "He thought, you see, that I would cause him little trouble since I was a poor wizard to begin with and something of a failure in life. He thought that I would be so happy to have the position of court wizard that I would acquiesce to anything he wished. I let him believe that, High Lord. I pretended cooperation, because it was the only way I could aid the land. A new King was needed, if matters were to ever be set right again. I was determined to find that King. I even persuaded my half-brother to let me write the words in his sale notice that would bring that King to Landover."

"And here I am," Ben finished.

"Here you are," Questor agreed.

"A million dollars light."

"And a Kingdom richer."

"But my money is gone, isn't it? The contract I signed was a fraud from the beginning? Meeks and the son have walked off with the money, and I'm stuck here for the rest of my life?"

Questor looked at him for a long time, and then he shook his head. "No, High Lord, you are not stuck here for any longer than you choose to be. The contract was valid, the escape clause was valid, and the money awaits you, if you return within ten days."

Now it was Ben's turn to stare. "I'll be damned," he whispered. He studied Questor wordlessly for a moment. "You didn't have to tell me this, you know. You could have let me think the money was gone and that I must stay."

The wizard seemed sad. "No, I could never do that, High Lord."

"Yes, he could," Abernathy chimed in. "And he would, too, if he thought he could get away with it." He squatted and scratched at his neck with his hind leg. "Do you think there are ticks in these woods?" he asked. "I hate ticks."

They walked on in silence. Ben thought through all that Questor had told him. Old Meeks and the dead King's son conspiring to make a quick killing by selling the throne to the Kingdom and setting themselves up in a new world with the money—it made sense, he guessed. But there was a piece to this puzzle that was still missing. The trouble was, he couldn't figure out what that piece was. He knew it was there somewhere, but he couldn't quite manage to put his finger on it. He exercised his lawyer's skills in an effort to solve the problem, but the missing piece kept eluding him.

He gave up looking for it after a time. He would stumble across it sooner or later and he had a bigger problem just now, in any case. Eight of the ten days allotted him under the terms of the contract had already expired. That left him exactly today and tomorrow to decide whether or not he was going to back out of his purchase and head home again. He could do that, Questor had assured him. He believed Questor. The question was not so much whether or not he could, but whether or not he wanted to. Nothing of Landover had turned out to be the way it was advertised in the catalogue—except, of course, in the very broadest sense. There were dragons and damsels and all of that, there was magic, and he was King over all—or about to be. But the fantasy was not what he had expected it to be; it wasn't even close. The money he had paid seemed far too much for what he had gotten.

And yet . . . the plaintiff gave way to the defendant . . . and yet there was something indefinable about Landover that appealed to him. Most probably, it was the challenge. He hated to admit it; but if he were to be honest with himself, he had better admit it here and now. He did not like to back away from anything. He did not like to lose. Admitting that he had made a mistake in coming here, in paying one million dollars for a fantasy that truly *was* a fantasy, though not the fantasy he wished, rankled him. He was a trial lawyer with a trial lawyer's instincts and bullheadedness, and he did not like to walk away from any kind of fight. There was surely a fight ahead for him in Landover, for the sovereignty of the throne was in shambles, and it would take one hell of an effort to restore it. Didn't he think that he could do that? Wasn't he capable of matching his skills against those of any of the subjects that he was expected to rule?

Miles would have told him it wasn't worth it. Miles would have thrown up his hands and gone to civilization—to Soldier Field and elevators and taxis. His associates in the profession would have done the same.

Annie would not. Annie would have told him to tough it out and she would have stood with him. But Annie was dead.

He tightened his jaw, frowning. When he got right down to it, he was dead, too, if he gave it up now and went back. That was why he had taken the gamble in the first place and come—to give himself back his life. He still thought he could do that here; he still believed that Landover could be his home. Besides, money was only money . . .

But a million dollars? He could hear Miles' exclamation of disbelief. He could see Miles throwing up his hands in disgust.

He was surprised to discover that he was smiling at the idea.

It was exactly noon when the mist and trees parted almost without warning, and the little company entered a clearing bright with sunshine, its grasses a glimmer of green, gold, and crimson. Bonnie Blues grew all about the edges of the clearing, evenly spaced and perfectly formed, and only those that nestled close against the forest beyond showed signs of the wilt that Ben had observed on his journey in. Burnished timbers of white oak formed a dais and throne at the clearing's center. Polished silver stanchions were anchored at the corners of the dais, and in their holders were tall white candles, their wicks new. Flags of varying colors and insignia lifted from behind the dais, and all about were white velvet kneeling pads and rests.

Questor's arm swept across the sunlit clearing. "This is the Heart, High Lord," he said softly. "Here you shall be crowned King of Landover."

Ben stared at the gleaming oak and silver of the throne and dais, the flags and candles, and the clipped grasses and Bonnie Blues. "It shows nothing of the Tarnish, Questor. It all looks as if it were . . . new."

"The Tarnish has not yet reached the Heart, High Lord. The magic is strongest here. Come."

They crossed in silence, slipping between the lines of velvet kneeling pads and armrests to where the throne and dais waited at the clearing's center. Fragrant smells filled the warm midday air, and the colors of the grasses and trees seemed to shimmer and mix with liquid ease. Ben felt a sense of peace and reverence within the clearing that reminded him of the church sanctuary on Sunday morning when he had been brought to it as a boy. He was surprised to discover that he still remembered.

They reached the dais and stopped. Ben glanced slowly about. The Heart was all but deserted. A few worn-looking herdsmen and farmers, with their wives and children in tow, stood hesitantly at the edges of the clearing, whispering together and looking uncertainly at Ben. Half a dozen hunters in woodsman's garb clustered in a knot in the shadows of the forest, where the sunlight did not reach. A beggar, ragged in fraying leather pants and tunic, sat cross-legged at the base of an oak riddled with wilt.

Other than those few, there was no one.

Ben frowned. There was a hunted, almost desperate look in the eyes of those few that was troubling.

"Who are they?" he asked Questor quietly.

Questor looked out at the ragged gathering and turned away. "Spectators."

"Spectators?"

"To the coronation."

"Well, where is everybody else?"

"Fashionably late, perhaps," Abernathy deadpanned. Behind him, the kobolds hissed softly and showed their teeth.

Ben put his hand on Questor's shoulder and brought him about. "What's going on, Questor? Where is everyone?"

The wizard rubbed his chin nervously. "It *is* possible that those who are coming are simply a bit late arriving, detained perhaps by something that they had not foreseen when they . . ."

"Wait a minute." Ben cut him short. "Run that by me once more—'those who are coming' did you say? Does that mean that some don't intend to come?"

"Oh, well, I was simply using a figure of speech, High Lord. Certainly all who can come will."

Ben folded his arms across his chest and faced the other squarely. "And I'm Santa Claus. Look, Questor, I've been around long enough to know a fox from a hole in the ground. Now, what's going on here?"

The wizard shifted his feet awkwardly. "Ah . . . well, you see, the truth of the matter is that very few will be coming."

"How few is very few?"

"Perhaps only a couple."

Abernathy edged forward. "He means just the four of us, High Lord—and those poor souls standing out there in the shadows."

"Just the four of us?" Ben stared at Questor in disbelief. "The four of us? That's all? The coronation of the first King of Landover in more than twenty years, and no one is coming . . ."

"You are not the first, High Lord," Questor said softly.

". . . but the four of us?"

"You are not the first," the wizard repeated.

There was a long moment of silence. "What did you say?" Ben asked.

"There have been others before you, High Lord—other Kings of Landover since the death of the Old King. You are simply the latest of these to ascend the throne. I am sorry that you have to hear this now. I would have preferred that you heard it later when the coronation ceremony was . . ."

"How many others?" Ben's face was flushed with anger.

". . . completed, and we had . . . What did you say?"

"Kings, damn it! How many others have there been?"

Questor Thews squirmed. "Several dozen, perhaps. Frankly, I have lost count."

The sound of thunder rolled from somewhere distant through the forest trees and mist. Abernathy's ears pricked sharply.

"Several dozen?" Ben did not yet hear it. His arms dropped to his sides and the muscles of his neck corded. "I can understand why you might have lost count! I can understand as well why no one bothers to come anymore!"

"They came at first, of course," the other continued, his voice irritatingly calm and his gaze steady. "They came because they believed. Even after they quit believing, they came for a time because they were curious. But eventually they were no longer even curious. We have had too many Kings, High Lord, who were not real."

He gestured roughly toward the few who had assembled at the forest's edge. "Those who come now come only because they are desperate."

The thunder sounded again, louder this time and closer, a deep, sustained rumble that echoed through the forest and shook the earth. The kobolds hissed and their ears flattened back against their heads. Ben looked about sharply. Abernathy was growling.

Questor seized Ben's arm. "Climb onto the dais, High Lord! Go, quickly!" Ben hesitated, frowning. "Go!" the wizard snapped, shoving. "Those are demons that come!"

That was reason enough for Ben. The kobolds were already scampering ahead, and he went after them. The thunder reverberated all about them, shaking trees and earth.

"It appears that you will have your audience after all, High Lord," Abernathy said as he bounded up the dais steps on all fours, nearly losing the ceremonial robes and chains of office.

Ben went up the steps behind him, glancing back over his shoulder anxiously. The Heart was deserted save for the four of the little company. The farmers, herdsmen, their families, the hunters, and the beggar had all scattered into the concealing shadows of the forest. The mist and gloom of the surrounding trees seemed to press in tightly against the sunlit clearing.

"Help the High Lord on with his robes and chains," Questor Thews directed Abernathy, hastening onto the dais to stand with them. "Quickly!"

Abernathy rose up again on his hind legs and began fitting the robes and chains of office about Ben. "Wait a minute, Questor," Ben objected, his eyes darting apprehensively to the black tunnel entrance across from them. "I'm not sure I want to do this anymore."

"It is too late, High Lord—you must!" The other's owlish face was suddenly hard with purpose. "Trust me. You will be safe."

Ben thought that he had ample reason to question that assertion, but Abernathy was already fastening the clasps to the robes and chains. The scribe was surprisingly dexterous for a dog, and Ben found himself glancing downward in spite of the situation. He started. Abernathy's paws had blunted fingers with joints.

"He failed to get even that part right," the scribe muttered on seeing the look on Ben's face. "Let us hope he does better with you."

Shadows and mist joined and swirled like stirred ink at the far side of the clearing, and the stillness turned suddenly to a howling wind. The thunder of the demon approach peaked in a harsh rumble that shook the forest earth. Ben turned, the wind whipping his robes until they threatened to break loose. Abernathy stepped away, growling deep in his throat, and the kobolds hissed like snakes and showed their teeth to the black.

Then the demons broke from the mist and dark, materializing as if a hole had opened in the empty air, an army of lean, armored forms as shadowy as night. Weapons and plating clanked, and the hooves of monstrous, serpentine mounts thudded from rock to earth, reverberated, and died. The army slowed and clattered to a halt. White teeth and red eyes gleamed from the mists, and claws and spines jutted from the mass, as if the whole were tangled into one. The army faced the dais in a ragged line, hundreds strong, pressed between the forest trees and the kneeling pads and rests, the sound of their breathing filling the void left by the passing of the thunder. The wind howled once more and died away.

The clearing was filled with the sound of heavy, clotted breathing. "Questor . . . ?" Ben called softly, frozen where he stood.

"Stand, High Lord," the wizard whispered softly.

The demon horde stirred, weapons lifted as one, and a maddened howl broke from the army's collective throat. Abernathy stepped back, jaws snapping. The kobolds seemed to go mad, hissing and shrieking in fury, crouching to either side of where Ben stood.

"Questor . . . ?" Ben tried again, a bit more urgently this time.

Then the Mark appeared. The demons parted suddenly at their center, and he came from out of their midst. He sat astride his winged serpent, a thing that was half snake and half wolf, a thing out of the foulest nightmare. The Mark was all in black armor, opaque and worn with use, bristling with weapons and serrated spines. A helmet with a death's head sat on his shoulders, the visor down.

Ben Holiday wished he were practically anywhere other than where he was.

Questor Thews stepped forward. "Kneel, High Lord!" His voice was a hiss.

"What?"

"Kneel! You are to be King! The demons have come to see you made so, and we must not keep them waiting." The owlish face crinkled with urgency. "Kneel, so you may be sworn!"

Ben knelt, eyes locked on the demons.

"Place your hands upon the medallion," Questor ordered. Ben lifted it from beneath his tunic and did so. "Now repeat these words: 'I shall be one with the land and her people, faithful to all and disloyal to none, bound to the laws of throne and magic, pledged to the world to which I have come—King, hereafter.' Say it."

Ben hesitated. "Questor, I don't like . . ."

"Say it, Ben Holiday, if you would truly be the King you have said you would be!"

The admonishment was hard and certain, almost as if come from someone other than Questor Thews. Ben met the other's eyes steadily. He could sense a restless movement from the ranks of the demons.

Ben lifted the medallion until it could be seen clearly by all. His eyes never left Questor's. "I shall be one with the land and her people, faithful to all and disloyal to none, bound to the laws of throne and magic, pledged to the world to which I have come—King, hereafter!"

He spoke the words clearly and boldly. He was mildly surprised that he had remembered them all so easily—almost as if he had known them before. The clearing was still. He let the medallion fall back upon his chest.

Questor Thews nodded, and his hand passed through the air immediately above Ben's head. "Rise, Your Majesty," he said softly. "Ben Holiday, King of Landover, High Lord and Liege."

Ben rose, and the sunlight broke over him as it slipped suddenly through the ceiling of mist. The silence of the clearing deepened. Questor Thews bent slowly and dropped to one knee. Abernathy followed him down and the kobolds knelt with him.

But the demons held their place. The Mark stayed mounted, and none about him moved.

"Show them the medallion one time more!" Questor hissed beneath his breath.

Ben turned and held forth in his right hand the medallion, feeling with his fingers the outline of the mounted knight, the lake, castle, and rising sun. Demons cried softly in the ranks of black forms, and a few dropped down. But the Mark brought his arm back swiftly, beckoning all to stand where they were, to keep their feet. The death's head turned back to Ben defiantly.

"Questor, it isn't working!" Ben breathed from out of the side of his mouth.

There was sudden movement in the demon ranks. Astride his monstrous, winged carrier, the Mark was advancing through the screen of mist and shadows. The demons he led were coming with him.

Ben went cold. "Questor!"

But then there was a flare of light from across the Heart, as if something bright had caught the reflection of the sun. It broke from the edge of the forest shadows between the advancing demons and the dais on which Ben and his companions stood. The demons slowed, eyes shifting. Ben and his friends turned.

A horse and rider appeared from out of the mists.

Ben Holiday started. It was the knight he had encountered in the time passage between his world and this, the knight whose image was graven on the medallion, a battered and soiled-iron statue as he sat astride his wearied horse. His lance rested upright in its boot cradle and his armored form was still. He might have been chiseled from stone.

"The Paladin!" Questor whispered in disbelief. "He has come back!"

The Mark rose in the harness that bound him to his mount, death's head facing toward the knight. Demons shrank back within the mist and shadows all about him, and there were whimpers of uncertainty. Still the knight did not move.

"Questor, what's happening?" Ben demanded, but the wizard shook his head wordlessly.

A moment longer the demons and the knight faced each other across the sunlit span of the Heart, poised like creatures at hunt. Then the Mark brought one arm upward, fist clenched, and the death's head inclined, if only barely, toward Ben. Wheeling his mount, he turned back into the dark, the army he led turning with him. Shrieks and cries broke the stillness, the wind howled and hooves and boots thundered once more. The demons disappeared back into the air out of which they had come.

The mist and the gloom drew back again, and the sunlight returned. Ben blinked in disbelief. When he turned back once more to find the knight and his war horse, they had disappeared as well. The clearing was empty but for the five who stood upon the dais.

Then there was new movement in the shadows. The few farmers and herdsmen and their families, the hunters and the lone beggar slipped back into view, gathering hesitantly at the fringe of the trees. There was fear and wonder in their eyes. They came no further, but one by one they knelt in the forest earth.

Ben's heart was pounding, and he was damp with sweat. He took a deep breath and wheeled on Questor. "I want to know what in the hell is going on, and I want to know right now!"

Questor Thews seemed genuinely at a loss for words for the first time since they had met. He started to say something, stopped, tried again, and shook his head. Ben glanced at the others. Abernathy was panting as if he had been run. The kobolds were crouched close, ears laid back, eyes slitted.

Ben seized Questor's arm. "Answer me, damn it!"

"High Lord, I don't . . . I am at a loss to explain . . ." The owlish face twisted as if caught in a vise. "I would never have believed . . ."

Ben brought his hand up quickly to cut him off. "For God's sake, Questor, get hold of yourself, will you?"

The other nodded, straightening. "Yes, High Lord."

"And answer the question!"

"High Lord, I . . ." He stopped again.

Abernathy's shaggy head craned forward over one shoulder. "This should be interesting," he offered. He appeared to have regained control of himself more quickly than the wizard.

Questor shot him a dark look. "I should have made you a cat!" he snapped.

"Questor!" Ben pressed impatiently.

The wizard turned, took a deep breath, cocked his head reflectively and shrugged. "High Lord, I don't quite know how to tell you this." He smiled weakly. "That knight, the one that appears on the medallion you wear, the one that confronted the Mark—he doesn't exist."

The smile disappeared. "High Lord, we have just seen a ghost!"

PALADIN

Miles used to say that there were lawyers and then there were *lawyers;* trouble was, there were too many of the former and not enough of the latter. He used to say that when he was steamed by some act of incompetence visited upon him by a fellow practitioner of the arts.

Ben Holiday ran that saying through his mind on and off during the hike back to Sterling Silver, altering the words a bit to fit the circumstances of his present dilemma. There were ghosts and then there were *ghosts,* he corrected. There are imagined ghosts and real ghosts, phantoms of the mind and sure-enough live spooks that went bump in the night. He supposed one could safely say that there were indeed too many of the former and not enough of the latter—although maybe everyone was better off that way.

Whatever the case, the knight graven on the medallion he wore, the knight who had twice come between him and the Mark, the knight who materialized and then disappeared as if made of smoke, was certainly one of the latter and not some chemically induced distortion that was the result of eating the food or drinking the water in a strange land. He knew that as surely as he knew that Questor Thews was still holding out on him about the circumstances surrounding the sale of the throne of Landover.

And he meant to learn the truth about both.

But he was not going to learn much of anything right away, it appeared. For Questor, after proclaiming the knight a ghost that no longer existed, refused to say anything more about the matter until they were safely returned to Sterling Silver. Ben protested vehemently, Abernathy tossed off a few barbs about cold feet, the kobolds hissed and showed their teeth to the vanished demons, but the wizard remained firm. Ben Holiday had a right to know the whole story behind the appearance of the ghost—what was it he had called it, the Paladin?—but he would have to wait until they were again within the walls of the castle. The owlish face set itself, the stooped figure turned, and Questor Thews stalked off into the forest without a backward glance. Since Ben had no intention of remaining in that clearing by himself after what had just happened, he hastened after like an obedient duckling following its mother.

Some posture for a King, he chided himself. But then who was he kidding? He was about as much King of Landover as he was President of the United States. He might have been proclaimed King by an inept wizard, a converted dog, and a couple of hissing monkeys and he might have paid a million dollars for the privilege—he set his teeth, thinking of that—but he was still just an outsider who had wandered into a foreign country and who didn't yet know the customs and could barely speak the language.

But that would change, he promised. He would see it change or know the reason why.

It took them the better part of the afternoon to complete the journey back again, and dusk was settling over the misted valley and waterways when they again came in sight of Sterling Silver. The dreary, hollow cast of the fortress dampened Ben Holiday's spirits further, and they scarcely needed that. He thought again about the ten days allotted him to return to his own world under the terms of the contract he had signed—and for the first time the wisdom of doing so seemed clear to him.

Once back within the castle, Questor dispatched Parsnip to prepare dinner and Bunion to lay out a fresh set of clothing for Ben. Then taking Ben and Abernathy in tow, he set out on an expedition that took them deep into the bowels of the castle. They passed down numerous corridors and through countless halls, all musted and stained by the Tarnish, but lit with the smokeless lights and warmed by the life of the castle. Colors shimmered weakly in the gray, and touches of polished wood and stone glimmered. There was a sense of something grand and elegant passing away in the wake of the Tarnish, and Ben was bothered by it. He should not have been, he thought, as he trailed silently after Questor. He had slept only a single time within these walls, and the castle held no special meaning for him. In fact, if it hadn't been for Questor telling him that she was a living thing . . .

He shoved his thoughts aside as they stepped through a massive oak and iron-pinioned door into a small courtyard with a chapel set at its center. The chapel was as dingy and discolored as the rest of Sterling Silver, yet the mists gathered less thickly here, and traces of sunlight still fell upon the stone and wood of roof and walls and the stained glass of high, arched windows. They crossed the courtyard to the chapel steps, climbed to scrolled oak doors that were matched and pegged in iron pins and pushed their way inside.

Ben peered through the failing light. Floors, ceiling, and walls were trimmed in white and scarlet, the colors faded, the whole of the chapel's dim interior musted and gray. There was no altar; there were no pews. Coats of arms hung upon the walls with shields and weapons propped below, and a single kneeling pad and arm rest faced forward toward a dais that occupied the very center of the room. A solitary figure stood upon the dais. It was the knight on the medallion.

Ben started. He thought for an instant that the knight was alive and at watch. Then he realized that it was only an armored shell occupying the dais and that nothing living was kept within.

Questor started forward into the chapel. "Come, High Lord."

Ben followed, eyes fixed on the figure on the dais. Abernathy trailed them. The suit of armor was chipped and battered as if from many battles, the polish gone, the metal stained almost black by the Tarnish. A huge broadsword was sheathed in a scabbard at one hip, and a mace with a wedge-shaped head hung from its leather harness at the other. A great iron-tipped lance rested butt downward from the grip of one metal hand. All three weapons were as debilitated as the armor and crusted over with dirt and grime. There was a crest on the metal breastplate and on the shield that rested beside the lance—an emblem that depicted the sun rising over Sterling Silver.

Ben took a deep breath. He could be certain as he stood before it that the armor was only a shell. Yet he was certain, too, that this was the same armor that had been worn by the knight who had twice now intervened in his encounters with the Mark.

"He was called the Paladin," Questor said at his elbow. "He was the King's champion."

Ben looked over. "He was, was he? What happened to him?"

"He disappeared after the death of the old King, and no one has seen him since." The sharp eyes met Ben's. "Until now, that is."

"It seems, then, that you no longer think I was imagining things when I came through the time passage."

"I never thought that, High Lord. I simply feared that you had been deceived."

"Deceived? By whom?"

They faced each other in silence. Abernathy scratched at one ear.

"This pregnant pause in your digression suggests that some vast and terrible secret is about to be revealed," Ben said finally. "Does this mean I am about to learn the rest of what you still haven't told me?"

Questor Thews nodded. "It does."

Ben folded his arms across his chest. "Fine. But let's have all of it this time, Questor—not just part of all of it like before. No more surprises saved for later, okay?"

The other nodded one time more. "No more surprises, High Lord. In fact, it was your mistrust of me that prompted my request that Abernathy join us. Abernathy is court historian as well as court scribe. He will be quick enough to correct me if I should misspeak myself." He sighed. "Perhaps you will have more faith in his word than in mine."

Ben waited. Questor Thews glanced momentarily at the suit of armor and then looked slowly about the empty chapel. He seemed lost within himself. The silence deepened as the seconds slipped away, and the haze of twilight spread its shadows further into the failing light.

"You may begin whenever you are ready," Abernathy growled impatiently. "Dinner cools on the table while we stand about."

"I find it difficult to know where to begin," Questor snapped. He turned to Ben once more. "It was a different time, you know—twenty years ago. The old King ruled and the Paladin was his champion, as he had been champion of the Kings of Landover since the dawn of her creation. He was born of the magic, created by the fairy people as Landover herself was created, drawn from the mists of their world to become a part of this. No one has ever seen his face. No one has ever seen him other than like this—clad in the suit of armor you see before you, metal head to foot, visor drawn and closed. He was an enigma to all. Even my half-brother found him a puzzle with no solution."

He paused. "Landover is more than just another world that borders on the fairy world—she is the gateway to the fairy world. She was created for that purpose. But where the fairy world is timeless and everywhere at once, Landover is a fixed point in time and place both. She is the end point of the time passages from all of the other worlds. Some worlds she joins more closely than others. Some worlds are but a step through the mists where others, like your own, are a distant passage. The closer worlds have always been those where the magic was real and its use most prevalent. The inhabitants are frequently descendants of creatures of the fairy world who migrated or strayed or were simply driven out. Once gone from the fairy world, they could never return. Few have been happy in exile. Most have sought a way back again. For all, Landover has always been the key."

"I hope all this is taking us somewhere," Ben interjected pointedly.

"It depends on how far you like to travel," Abernathy groused.

Questor hunched his shoulders, arms folding into his robes. "The Paladin was the protector of the King, who in his turn was the protector of the land. There was need for that protector. There were those both within Landover and without who would use her for their own purposes if her King and her protector should falter. But the magic that guarded her was formidable. There was no one who could stand against the Paladin."

Ben frowned, suddenly suspicious. "Questor, you're not going to tell me that . . ."

"I will tell you, High Lord, only what is," the other interrupted quickly. "You wished to be told the whole story, and I am about to accommodate you. When the old King died and his son did not assume the throne, but sought instead for a way to abandon Landover, those who have always laid wait without began to sniff about the gates. The Paladin was gone, disappeared with the passing of the old King, and none could find a way to bring him back again. Months drifted into years as the son grew older and plotted with my half-brother to leave the land, and still no King ruled and the Paladin stayed gone. My half-brother used all of his considerable magic to seek out the absent knight-errant, but all of his considerable magic was not enough. The Paladin was gone, and it seemed unlikely that he would come again.

"Naturally, this encouraged the ones who prowled at Landover's borders. If the Paladin were indeed gone, if the magic were weakened, Landover could be theirs. Remember, High Lord—the gateway to the world of fairy was a prize that some would give anything to own. My half-brother saw this and he knew that he must act quickly or Landover would fall from his control."

The owlish face tightened. "So he devised a plan. The throne of the Kingdom would be sold to a buyer from a very distant world, giving Landover a King and extricating both the son and my half-brother from the laws that bound them to her. But they would sell the throne to a buyer for a limited period of time only—say, six months or a year. That way the throne would revert back to them and they could sell it again. By doing so, they would steadily increase their personal fortune, enabling the son to live as he chose and my half-brother to enhance his opportunities to gain power in other worlds. The difficulty with all of this was in finding interested buyers."

"So he contacted Rosen's?" Ben interjected.

"Not at first. He began by making the sales independently. His customers were mostly unsavory sorts, wealthy but with principles as dubious as his own. Frequently they were men needing to escape temporarily from their own world. Landover was a perfect shelter for them; they could play at being King, live rather well off the comforts of Sterling Silver, and then return to their own world when their tenure was ended."

"Criminals," Ben whispered softly. "He sent you criminals." He shook his head in disbelief, then looked up sharply. "What about the ones who got here and didn't want to leave? Didn't that ever happen?"

"Yes, it happened from time to time," Questor acknowledged. "But I was always there to be certain that they left on time—whether they were ready to do so or not. I had magic enough to accomplish that." He frowned. "I have often wondered, though, how my half-brother got the medallion back from such troublemakers once they had returned home again. His magic would advise him of their presence, but how could he have known where to find and how to secure the medallion again . . . ?"

He trailed off thoughtfully, then shrugged. "Never mind. The fact remains that for quite some time he successfully sold Kingships for limited periods and made a good deal of money. But his customers were an unpredictable lot, and the state of affairs in Landover was worsening in the wake of this succession of would-be Kings. More to the point, the money wasn't coming in fast enough. So finally he decided to offer the throne for sale outright—not to the unreliable sorts of people he had been dealing with in the past, but to the general public. He contacted Rosen's, Ltd. He told them that he was a procurer of rare artifacts and unusual service items. He convinced them of his worth by locating through the use of his magic a few treasures and curiosities thought lost. When he was accepted as a legitimate source of such items, he offered them the sale of Landover. I think they must have disbelieved at first, but he found a way to convince them finally. He sent one of them over for a look."

He grinned fiercely. Then his eyes narrowed. "But there was more to this sale than Rosen's imagined, High Lord. My half-brother and the old King's son had no intention of giving up for good something as valuable as the Kingship of Landover. A pre-condition to the offering gave them exclusive control over the selection of buyers. That way they could sell the throne to someone too weak to hold it, so that it would revert back to them, and they could sell it again. They could even sell options on the side—moving preferred customers to the head of an imaginary list. Rosen's would never know the difference. The difficulty now was not in finding interested customers, but in finding interested customers who possessed both the means of purchase and the requisite lack of character to succeed in staying on as King!"

Ben flushed. "Like me, I gather?"

The other shrugged. "You asked earlier how many Kings of Landover there have been since the old King. There have been more than thirty."

"Thirty-two, to be exact," Abernathy interjected. "Two already this year. You are the third."

Ben stared. "Good God, that many?"

Questor nodded. "My half-brother's plan has worked perfectly—until now." He paused. "I believe he may have made a mistake with you."

"I would withhold judgment on that, if I were you, High Lord," Abernathy spoke up quickly. "Things are more complicated than you perceive. Tell him the rest, wizard."

The owlish face tightened. "I shall, if given half a chance!" He faced Ben. "This last plan was a good one, but there were two problems with it. First, it was obvious to my half-brother that not every buyer would lack sufficient character to overcome the difficulties of governing Landover. Even though he would interview each personally, he might still mistakenly choose one who would not back away from the challenges that the Kingship offered. Should that happen, he might not get Landover back again for sale. The second problem was more serious. The longer the Kingdom languished without a strong King or with a succession of failures, the more disorganized matters would become and the more difficult it would be for any new King to succeed. He wanted that. But he also knew that the more disorganized things became, the greater the chances for usurpation of the crown from those who prowled without. He did not want that."

Questor paused. "So he found a single solution to both problems. He goaded the Mark into challenging for the throne."

"Uh-oh." Ben was beginning to get an inkling of what was to come.

"The Mark rules Abaddon, the netherworld that lies beneath Landover. Abaddon is a demon world, a black pit of exile for the worst of those driven from the fairy world since the dawn of time. The demons exiled there would like nothing better than to get back into the fairy world, and the only way back is through Landover. When my half-brother extended the challenge to the Mark and the Mark became convinced that the Paladin was no longer protector of Landover, the demon lord came out of Abaddon and proclaimed himself King."

The brows of the wizard knit above the sharp, old eyes. "There was a catch to this, of course—and my half-brother knew it. The Mark could not truly be King while another ruled under color of law and while the magic of the medallion gave its protection to the wearer. He could only claim to be King and challenge for the right. So each midwinter, when the Bonnie Blues turn white, the Mark comes out of Abaddon into Landover and asks challenge of the King. As yet, no one has accepted."

"I can imagine," Ben breathed softly. "Just to make certain that I understand all this, Questor, what form does this challenge take?"

The heavy brows lifted. "Strength of arms, High Lord."

"You mean, jousting with lances or something?"

Abernathy touched him on the shoulder. "He means, mortal combat with weapons of choice—a battle to the death."

There was an endless moment of silence. Ben took a deep breath. "That's what I have to look forward to—a fight to the death with this demon?" He shook his head in disbelief. "No wonder no one lasts very long in this position. Even if they wanted to, even if they were willing to try to straighten things out, sooner or later they would have to face the Mark. What's the point of even trying?" He was growing angry all over again. "So what do you expect of me, Questor? Do you expect me to accept a challenge that no one else would? I'd have to be out of my mind!"

The stooped figure shifted from one foot to the other. "Perhaps. But it might be different with you. None of the others had help. Yet twice now after twenty years of absence, the Paladin has come to you."

Ben wheeled at once on Abernathy. "Is he telling me the truth—the Paladin has never come to anyone before?"

Abernathy shook his head solemnly. "Never, High Lord." He cleared his throat. "It grieves me to admit it, but the wizard may have a point. It might indeed be different with you."

"But I had nothing to do with the Paladin's appearance," Ben insisted. "And I don't know that he came to me necessarily. He was simply there. Besides, you said yourself it was a ghost we were seeing. And even if he wasn't a ghost, he looked wrecked to me. The Mark looked the stronger of the two and not in the least intimidated by this so-called champion that the King is supposed to rely upon to protect him. Frankly, I can't believe any of this. And I don't know that I understand it yet. Let's back up a minute. Questor, your half-brother Meeks sells the throne to an outsider like me for a big price, choosing someone who won't last. Even if he mistakenly chooses someone who might tough it out, the Mark is on hand to make sure he doesn't. But the Mark can't be King while someone else holds the medallion—am I right? So what does the Mark get out of all this? Doesn't Meeks keep bringing other candidates in month after month, year after year?"

Questor nodded. "But the Mark is a demon, and the demons live long lives, High Lord. Time is less meaningful when you can afford to wait, and the Mark can afford to wait a long, long time. Eventually, my half-brother and the old King's son will tire of the game and will have accumulated enough riches and power to divert their interest from Landover's throne. When that happens, they will cease bothering with the matter and abandon Landover to her fate."

"Oh." Ben understood now. "And when that happens, the Mark will gain Landover by default."

"That is one possibility. Another is that the demon will find a way in the interim to gain control of the medallion. He cannot seize it by force from the wearer; but sooner or later, one of Landover's succession of Kings will grow careless and lose it—or one will accept the Mark's challenge and be . . ."

Ben held up his hands quickly. "Don't say it." He hesitated. "What about the other predators—the ones whose worlds border on Landover? What are they doing while all this is going on?"

The wizard shrugged. "They are not strong enough as yet to stand against the Mark and the demons of Abaddon. One day, perhaps they will be. Only the Paladin had ever possessed such strength."

Ben frowned. "What I don't understand is why this Paladin simply disappeared after the death of the old King. If he were truly protector of the land and the throne, why would he disappear just because there was a change of Kings? And what's become of the fairies? Didn't you say that they created Landover as a gateway to their world? Why don't they protect it, then?"

Questor shook his head and said nothing. Abernathy was quiet as well. Ben studied them wordlessly a moment, then turned back again to the suit of armor on the dais. It was tarnished and rusted, battered and worn, a shell that resembled nothing so much as the discarded body of a junk car shipped to the salvage yard for scrap. This was all that remained of Landover's protector—of the King's protector. He walked to the kneeling pad and stared up at the metal shell wordlessly. This was what he had seen in the mists of the time passage and again in the mists of the forest that ringed the Heart. Had it been but a part of those mists? He had not thought so, but he was less certain now. This was a land of magic, not exact science. Dreams and visions might seem more real here.

"Questor, you called the Paladin a ghost," he said finally, not turning to look at the other. "How can a ghost be of any help to me?"

There was a long pause. "He was not always a ghost. Perhaps he need not remain one."

"Life after death, is that it?"

"He was a thing created of the magic," Questor answered quietly. "Perhaps life and death have no meaning for him."

"Do you have any idea at all how we can go about finding that out?"

"No."

"Do you have any suggestions for finding a way to get him back again?"

"No."

"That's what I thought. All we can do is hope he shows up before the Mark issues his next challenge and turns me into the latest of a long line of kingly failures!"

"You have another choice. You can use the medallion. The medallion can take you back to your own world whenever you choose to go. The Mark cannot stop you. You need only wish for it, and you will be gone."

Ben grimaced. Wonderful. Just tap the red shoes together three times and repeat, "There's no place like home." Off he would go, back to Kansas. Just wonderful. He had to do it within the next twenty-four hours, of course, if he didn't want to return a million dollars lighter. And whether he chose to do it within the next twenty-four hours or whether he waited until the Mark came riding for him out of the black pit, he would be running in either case, leaving Landover exactly as he had described himself—the latest in a long line of Kingly failures.

His jaw set. He didn't like losing. He didn't like giving up.

On the other hand, he wasn't particularly keen on dying.

"How did I ever get myself into this?" he muttered under his breath.

"Did you say something?" Questor asked.

He turned away from the dais and the shell of armor, his eyes searching out the stooped figures of the wizard and the scribe through the lengthening shadows of twilight. "No," he sighed. "I was just mumbling."

They nodded and said nothing.

"I was just thinking to myself."

They nodded again.

"I was just . . ."

He trailed off hopelessly. The three of them stared at one another in silence and no one said anything more.

It was almost completely dark out when they left the chapel to retrace their steps through the corridors and halls of the castle. The smokeless lamps spread their glow through the shadows. The flooring and walls were vibrant with warmth.

"What do you gain from all of this?" Ben asked Questor at one point.

"Hmmmmm?" The stooped figure turned.

"Do you get a share of the profits on all these sales of the throne?"

"High Lord!"

"Well, you did say you helped write the sales pitch, didn't you?"

The other was flushed and agitated. "I receive no part of any monies spent to acquire Landover!" he snapped.

Ben shrugged and glanced over at Abernathy. But for once the scribe made no comment. "Sorry," Ben apologized. "I just wondered why you were involved in all of this."

The other man said nothing, and Ben let the subject drop. He thought about it as they walked, though, and decided finally that what Questor gained from these sales was what he had probably wanted all along—the position and title of court wizard. His half-brother had held both before him, and Questor Thews had been a man without any real direction in his life. Now he had found that direction, and it probably made him happy enough just to be able to point to that.

And shouldn't it be like that for me as well, he wondered suddenly?

He was struck by the thought. Why was it that he had purchased the throne of Landover in the first place? He hadn't purchased it with the thought that it would become some other-world version of Sun City where he might retire, play golf and meditate on the purpose of man's existence, had he? He had purchased the throne to escape a world and a life he no longer found challenging. He was the wanderer that Questor Thews had once been. Landover's Kingship offered him direction. It offered him the challenge he had sought.

So what was he griping about?

Easy, he answered himself. He was griping because this kind of challenge could kill him—literally. This wasn't a court of law with a judge and jury and rules that he was talking about here. This was a battlefield with armor and weapons and only one rule—survival of the fittest. He was a King without a court, without an army, without a treasury, and without subjects interested in obeying a sovereign they refused to recognize. He was a King with a castle that was slowly passing into dust, four retainers straight out of the brothers Grimm and a protector that was nine-tenths ghost. He might not have been looking for Sun City, but he sure as hell hadn't bargained for this, either!

Had he?

He carried the debate with him to dinner.

He ate again in the great hall. Questor, Abernathy and the two kobolds kept him company. He would have eaten alone if he had not insisted that the others join him. They were retainers to the King of Landover now, Questor pointed out, and retainers did not eat with the High Lord unless they were invited to do so. Ben announced that until further notice they all had a standing invitation.

Dinner was less eventful than the previous night. There were candles and good china place settings. The food was excellent, and no one felt compelled to improve on its service. Conversation was kept to a minimum; Bunion and Parsnip ate in silence, and Questor and Abernathy exchanged only mild barbs on the eating habits of men and dogs. Ben sampled everything on the table, more hungry than he had a right to be, stayed clear of the wine, and kept his thoughts to himself. No one said anything about the coronation. No one said anything about the Mark or the Paladin.

It was all very civilized. It was also endless.

Ben finally sent everyone from the table and sat there alone in the candlelight. His thoughts remained fixed on Landover. Should he stay or should he go? How sturdy was this wall of seemingly unsolvable problems that he was butting his head against? How much sense did it make for him to keep trying?

How many angels could pass through the eye of a needle?

The answers to all of these questions eluded him entirely. He went to bed still seeking them out.

He woke the next morning shortly after sunrise, washed in the basin placed next to his bed, dressed in his running sweats and Nikes, and slipped quietly through the halls of Sterling Silver for the front entry. He was soundless in his movements, but Abernathy had good ears and was waiting for him at the portcullis.

"Breakfast, High Lord?" he asked, his glasses inching down over his furry nose as he looked Ben over.

Ben shook his head. "Not yet. I want to run first."

"Run?"

"That's right—run. I did it all the time before I came to Landover and I miss it. I miss the workouts at the Northside Health Club. I miss the sparring and the speed work and the heavy bag. Boxing, we call it. I guess that doesn't mean anything to you."

"It is true that dogs do not box," Abernathy replied. "Dogs do run, however. Where is it that you plan to run this morning, High Lord?"

Ben hesitated. "I don't know yet. Probably at the valley's rim where there's some sun."

Abernathy nodded. "I'll send someone to accompany you."

Ben shook his head. "I don't need anyone, thanks."

The other turned away. "I wouldn't be too sure of that if I were you," he said and disappeared down the hallway.

Ben stared after him momentarily, then wheeled without waiting and strode through the portcullis and gates to the lake skimmer. He boarded and his thoughts sent the skiff leaping recklessly ahead through the gray waters. He did not need someone with him everywhere he went, he thought stubbornly. He was not some helpless child.

He grounded the lake skimmer on the far shore, turned, and jogged ahead through the gloom. He worked his way slowly to the valley slope, then started up. When he reached the rim, he turned right and began to follow the forest's edge. Below him, the valley lay wrapped in shadows. Above, the pale golden light of the sun washed the new day in trailers of mist.

He ran easily, his thoughts drifting with the soft padding of his running shoes on the damp earth. His head felt clear and alert, and his muscles felt strong. He hadn't felt like that since he had arrived in Landover, and the feeling was a good one. Trees slipped rapidly away beside him, and the ground passed smoothly beneath. He breathed the air and let the stiffness in his body slowly work itself out.

Last night's questions were still with him, and the search for their answers went on. This was the final day of the ten days allotted him for rescission under the terms of his contract with Meeks. If he didn't rescind now, he would lose the million dollars paid for the purchase of Landover's Kingship. He might also lose his life—although Questor Thews had assured him that the medallion would take him back again at any time with but a moment's thought. In any case, the choices were clear. He could stay and attempt to straighten out the morass of problems he would face as King of Landover, risk a confrontation with the Mark and give up the million dollars, or he could leave, admit that the purchase was the dog that Miles had warned, return to his old life and world, and get back most of the million dollars he had spent. Neither choice held much appeal. Neither choice held much hope.

He was breathing more quickly now, feeling the strain of running begin to wear pleasingly on his muscles. He pushed himself, picking up the pace slightly, working to pass through the wall of his resistance. A flash of something dark caught his eye—something moving through the forest. He glanced over sharply, searching. There was nothing now—only the trees. He kept moving. He must have imagined it.

He thought again about the Paladin, knight-errant of the realm. He sensed somehow that the Paladin was the key to everything that was wrong with Landover's throne. It was too large a coincidence that, with the old King's death, the Paladin had disappeared as well and everything had started to go wrong with the Kingship. There was a link between them that he needed to understand. It might be possible for him to do so, he reasoned, if it were true as Questor had thought that the Paladin had indeed appeared twice now because of him. Perhaps he could find a way to bring the Paladin back yet a third time—and this time discover if he were indeed but a ghost.

The sun rose higher as he ran on, and it was approaching midmorning when he started back down the valley slope for the lake skimmer. Twice more he thought he caught sight of something moving in the trees, but each time he looked there was nothing there. He recalled Abernathy's veiled warning, but dismissed it summarily. They were always telling you to stay off the streets of Chicago, too, but you didn't live life shut away in a box.

He thought about that as he took the lake skimmer back across to Sterling Silver. There were always risks in life. Life was meant to be lived like that because if it wasn't, then what was the purpose of living it at all? Measuring the risks was important, of course, but experiencing them was necessary. It was the same thing he was always trying to explain to Miles. Sometimes you did things because they felt right. Sometimes you did things because . . .

He thought suddenly of the faces of those farmers and herdsmen and their families, those hunters and that beggar who had traveled to the Heart for his coronation. There had been a sort of desperate hope in those faces—as if those people *wanted* to believe that he could be King. There had been only a few, of course, and he was hardly responsible to them, yet . . .

His thinking faltered as the lake skimmer grounded at the front gates of the castle. He stood up slowly, recapturing the thoughts, losing himself in them. He barely saw Abernathy appear in the shadow of the portcullis.

"Breakfast, High Lord?"

"What?" Ben was almost startled. "Oh, yes—that would be fine." He climbed from the boat and moved quickly into the castle. "And send Questor to me right away."

"Yes, High Lord." The dog trailed after, nails clicking on the stone. "Did you enjoy your run?"

"Yes, I did—very much. Sorry I didn't wait, but I didn't think I needed anyone to go along just for that."

There was a moment's silence. Ben sensed the dog looking at him and glanced back. "I think I should tell you, High Lord, that Bunion was with you every step of the way. I sent him to make sure that you were properly looked after."

Ben grinned. "I thought I saw something. But it wasn't necessary for him to be there, was it?"

Abernathy shrugged. "That depends on how well you could have handled by yourself the timber wolf, the cave wight, and the bog wump that he dispatched when he caught them stalking after you in search of breakfast." He turned off into an adjoining corridor. "And speaking of breakfast, yours is waiting in the dining hall. I will send for the wizard."

Ben stared after him. Bog wump? Cave wight? Sweat beaded on his forehead suddenly. For Christ's sake, he hadn't seen or heard a thing! Was Abernathy trying to be funny?

He hesitated, then hurried on. He didn't think Abernathy was the sort to make jokes about something like this. Apparently he had been in danger out there and hadn't even known it.

He ate breakfast alone. Parsnip brought it to him and left. Abernathy did not reappear. Once, halfway through the meal, he caught sight of Bunion standing in the shadows of an entry off to one side. The kobold grinned so that all of his teeth showed like whitened spikes and disappeared. Ben did not grin back.

He was almost finished when Questor finally appeared. He shoved his plate aside and told the wizard to sit down with him.

"Questor, I want to know exactly how things are now compared to how they were when the old King was alive. I want to know what worked then and what doesn't work now. I want to figure out what has to be done to get things back to where they were."

Questor Thews nodded slowly, brows knitting over his sharp eyes. His hands folded on the table. "I will try, High Lord, though some things may escape my immediate memory. Some of it, you already know. There was an army that served the King of Landover; that is gone. There was a court with retainers; only Abernathy, Parsnip, Bunion and myself remain. There was a treasury; it is depleted. There was a system of taxes and yearly gifts; it has broken down. There were programs for public works, social reforms and land preservation; they no longer exist. There were laws and the laws were enforced; now they are ignored or enforced selectively. There were accords and alliances and pacts of understanding between the peoples of the land; most have lapsed or been openly repudiated."

"Stop right there." Ben rubbed at his chin thoughtfully. "Who among the King's subjects stands allied with whom at this point?"

"No one stands allied with anyone, so far as I can tell. Humans, half-humans, fairy creatures—no one trusts anyone."

Ben frowned. "And none of them has much use for the King, I gather? No, you needn't answer that. I can answer it for myself." He paused "Is there any one of them strong enough to stand up to the Mark?"

The wizard hesitated. "Nightshade, perhaps. Her magic is very powerful. But even she would be hard pressed to survive a duel with the Mark. Only the Paladin possessed strength enough to defeat the demon."

"What if everyone were to band together?"

Questor Thews hesitated longer this time. "Yes, the Mark and his demons might be successfully challenged then."

"But it would take someone to unite them first."

"Yes, it would take that."

"The King of Landover could be that someone."

"He could."

"But just at the moment the King of Landover can't even draw a crowd for his own coronation, can he?"

Questor said nothing. Ben and the wizard stared at each other across the table.

"Questor, what's a bog wump?" Ben asked finally.

The other frowned. "A bog wump, High Lord?" Ben nodded. "A bog wump is a variety of forest wight, a spiny, flesh-eating creature that burrows in marshy earth and paralyzes its victims with its tongue."

"Does it hunt in the early morning?"

"It does."

"Does it hunt humans?"

"It might. High Lord, what . . . ?"

"And Bunion—would he be a match for one of these bog wumps?"

Questor's mouth snapped shut on the rest of whatever it was he was going to say. His owlish face crinkled. "A kobold is a match for almost anything alive. They are ferocious fighters."

"Why are Bunion and Parsnip still here at Sterling Silver when everyone else in the court is gone?"

The owlish face crinkled into a complete knot. "They are here because they have pledged themselves to the service of the throne and its King. Kobolds do not take their pledges lightly. Once made, a pledge is never broken. So long as there is a King of Landover, Bunion and Parsnip will stay on."

"Is it the same with Abernathy?"

"It is. This is his chosen service."

"And you?"

There was a long pause. "Yes, High Lord, it is the same with me."

Ben sat back. He didn't say anything for a moment, his eyes locking on Questor's, his arms folding loosely across his chest. He listened in the silence for the whisper of the other's thoughts and spun the webbing of his own.

Then he smiled reluctantly. "I have decided to stay on as Landover's King."

Questor Thews smiled back. "I see." He seemed genuinely pleased. "I thought that you might."

"Did you?" Ben laughed. "Then you were more certain than I. I only now made the choice."

"If I might ask, Ben Holiday—what was it that decided you?"

The smile disappeared from Ben's face. He hesitated, thinking momentarily of those few who had come to the Heart to witness his coronation. They were not so different, really, from the clients he had taken an oath to represent, and he not so different from the lawyer who had taken that oath. Perhaps he did owe them something after all.

He said nothing of that to Questor, though. He merely shrugged. "It was a balancing of the equities, I suppose. If I stay, it will cost me a million dollars—presuming, of course, that I can find a way to stay alive. If I go, it will cost me my self-respect. I would like to think that my self-respect is worth a million dollars."

The wizard nodded. "Perhaps it is."

"Besides, I don't like quitting in the middle of something. It grates on me to think that Meeks chose me because he expected that I would do exactly that. I want very badly to disappoint him in his expectation. We have a saying where I come from, Questor: Don't get mad, get even. The longer I stay, the better chance I have of finding a way to do that. It's worth the risks involved."

"The risks *are* substantial."

"I know. And I don't suppose anyone besides me would even think twice about taking them."

Questor thought a moment. "Maybe not. But no one else stands in your shoes, High Lord."

Ben sighed. "Well, in any case, the matter's settled. I'm staying and that's that." He straightened slowly. "What I have to do now is to concentrate on finding ways of dealing with Landover's problems before they bury me."

Questor nodded.

"And the first of those problems is the refusal of any of the King's subjects to recognize me as King. Or themselves as subjects. They have to be made to pledge to the throne."

The other nodded one time more. "How will you do that?"

"I don't know yet. But I do know one thing. No one is going to come here to make that pledge. The coronation would have brought them, were they at all willing. Since they refuse to come here, we'll have to go there—there being wherever they are."

Questor frowned. "I have reservations about such a plan, High Lord. It could prove very dangerous."

Ben shrugged. "Maybe, but I don't see that we have much choice in the matter." He stood up. "Care to make a suggestion as to where we should start?"

The wizard sighed and stood up with him. "I suggest, High Lord, that we start at the beginning."

LORDS OF THE GREENSWARD

There had been many who had pledged service to the Kings of Landover—families who for generations had fought in the armies of the High Lords and stood beside their thrones. There had been many who could point with pride to their record of loyal and faithful service. But none had served so well or so long as the Lords of the Greensward, and it was to them that Ben Holiday was advised he should go first.

"The barons trace their bloodlines back thousands of years—some to the time that Landover came into being," Questor Thews explained. "They have always stood with the King. They formed the backbone of his army; they comprised the core of his advisors and court. Some of them were Kings of Landover themselves—though none in the last several hundred years. They were always the first to offer service. When the old King died, they were the last to depart. If you are to gain support anywhere, High Lord, it would be from them."

Ben accepted the suggestion—although it was really less a suggestion than a caution, he thought—and departed Sterling Silver at dawn of the following day for the estates of the land barons. Questor Thews, Abernathy and the two kobolds went with him once again. Ben, the wizard and the scribe rode horseback because the journey to the Greensward was a long one. The kobolds could have ridden, too, had they chosen to do so, but kobolds in general had little use for horses, being quicker of foot and stronger of wind than the best racer that had ever run, and so almost always traveled afoot. Besides, horses were unusually skittish when ridden by kobolds. Ben had no trouble understanding that. Anything that could dispatch a timber wolf, a cave wight, and a bog wump with such ease made him skittish, too.

It was a peculiar-looking group that departed that morning. Questor led the way, his tall, brightly cloaked figure slouched across an old gray that must have been ready for pasture years ago. Ben followed on Wishbone, a sorrel with the oddly shaped white blaze that gave him his name and a propensity for seizing the bit and bolting. He did that twice with Ben hanging on for dear life each time. Questor, after the second incident, whacked him hard across the nose and threatened magic in horse tongue. That seemed to bring Wishbone to his senses. Abernathy followed atop a white-faced bay gelding and carried the King's standard with its by-now familiar insignia of the Paladin riding out from the castle at sunrise embroidered in scarlet on a field of white. It was strange indeed to see a soft-coated Wheaten Terrier with glasses and tunic riding a horse and holding a flag, but Ben kept the smile from his face, because Abernathy obviously saw nothing at all funny about it. Parsnip trailed, leading on a long set of guide ropes a pack train of donkeys with food, clothing, and bedding. Bunion had gone on ahead, sent by Questor to advise the land barons that the King of Landover wished a meeting.

"They will have no choice; they will have to receive you," Questor declared. "Courtesy dictates that they not turn away a Lord whose stature is equal to or higher than their own. Of course, they would have to receive you if you were simply a traveler seeking shelter and food, too, but that is beneath you as King."

"Very little is beneath me at this point," Ben replied.

They rode out through the mists and shadows of the early morning, skirted the shores of the lake until they were turned east, then wound slowly to the valley rim. Several times Ben Holiday glanced back through the gray, watching the stark, colorless projection of Sterling Silver against the dawn sky, her towers, battlements, and walls ravaged as if by some nameless disease. He was surprised to discover that it was hard for him to leave her. She might appear as Castle Dracula to the naked eye, and he might find her loathsome to look upon, but he had felt the warmth of her and he had touched the life within. She had been kind to him. She had made him feel welcome. He found himself wishing that he could do something to help her.

He consoled himself with the thought that one day he would.

Then the castle, the mists, and the valley disappeared behind them as the company rode east through forest and hill country toward Landover's heartland. They traveled steadily for the better part of the day, stopping once for a midday meal and several times to rest, and by dusk they were within sight of the broad sweep of fields, pastures, and farmland that comprised the Greensward.

They made camp that night within a copse of fir on a knoll overlooking pastureland given over to cattle and goats and a cluster of small huts and wooden houses some miles further east. Ben swung down gratefully from Wishbone's back when Questor brought them to a halt. It had been some time since he had ridden a horse. It had been, in truth, the better part of twenty years—and that last time had been on a date in college that he would just as soon have forgotten. Now, a world and a lifetime away, he recalled the feeling that came with a long ride—his body stiff, the land still moving about him as he tried to walk, the sensation of the horse still locked between his knees, though he was dismounted. He knew that by tomorrow he would be sore from the shoulders down.

"Would you walk with me a moment, High Lord?" Questor asked and beckoned to him. Ben wanted to throttle the wizard for even suggesting the idea, but he forced his irritation aside and went.

They walked only a short distance to the edge of the knoll and stood shoulder to shoulder staring out across the flatlands below.

Questor's arm swept the horizon. "The Greensward, High Lord—the estates of the old families, the baronies of Landover. Their domain encompasses more than half of the kingdom. There were but twenty families at last count, and those twenty rule all of the land, its thralls, their villages and families and stock—subject to the King's will, of course."

"Of course." Ben looked out over the valley. "You said twenty families at last count. What do you mean, 'at last count'?"

The wizard shrugged. "Families merge through marriage. Families accept wardship from stronger families. Families die out—sometimes with a little help."

Ben glanced at him from the corner of one eye. "Charming. They don't all get along so well, then, I gather?"

"Just so. United under the old King, they were less disposed to take advantage of one another. Divided under no monarch, they are a suspicious and at times scheming lot."

"A circumstance that I might be able to use to my advantage, you think?"

The owlish face glanced over. "There is that possibility."

Ben nodded. "There is also the possibility that their suspicions and schemes might result in them trying to do away with me."

"Tch-tch," Questor clucked. "I will be with you, High Lord. Besides, they are unlikely to waste time and effort trying to do away with a King that they regard as essentially worthless. They refused, after all, even to attend your coronation."

"You are a wellspring of inspiration," Ben admonished dryly. "Whatever would I do without your support?"

"Oh, well, that is all part of my service to the throne." Questor either missed the dig entirely or was ignoring it.

"So tell me what else I should know."

"Just this." Questor faced him. "In better times, these lands were fertile, the stock fatted, and there were willing thralls enough to make up a dozen armies to serve Landover's King. Much has changed for the worse, as you will see on tomorrow's journey in. But what has changed can be put right again—if you can find a way to secure the pledge of the Greensward's Lords."

He glanced over once more, turned, and walked back toward the camp. Ben watched him go and shook his head in disbelief. "I'll work on it," he muttered.

It took an hour longer than it should have done to set camp. There were tents to be put up, and Questor took it upon himself to aid the process through use of his magic. The magic inflated the tents like balloons and sent them floating skyward to lodge in the highest tree limbs, and it required all of Parsnip's considerable athletic skill to bring them down once more. The horses bolted from their tether when Abernathy barked—to his acute embarrassment—after catching sight of a stray farm cat, and it was another hour until they could be caught and brought back around. Then supplies were unloaded, the King's standards set, the stock fed and watered, and the bedding placed—all without incident.

Dinner, however, was a disaster. There was a stew with beef and vegetables which smelled delicious while cooking, but lost some of its flavor after Questor fueled the cooking fire with a touch of quickening which created a miniature inferno that left the kettle and its contents black and crusted. The fruit of the Bonnie Blues was moderately satisfying, but Ben would have preferred at least one plate of the stew. Questor and Abernathy carped about the behavior of men and dogs, and Parsnip hissed at them both. Ben began to consider rescinding his standing invitation to have them join him for his meals.

It was nearing bedtime when Bunion returned from his journey to the Greensward to advise them that the land barons would be waiting to receive Landover's new King on his arrival at Rhyndweir. Ben didn't know what Rhyndweir was and he didn't care. He was too tired and fed up to care and he went to sleep without worrying about it.

They reached Rhyndweir by mid-afternoon of the following day, and Ben had an opportunity to see for himself exactly what it was. Rhyndweir was a monstrous, sprawling castle seated atop a broad plateau at the joining of two rivers. Towers and parapets lifted skyward out of fortress walls more than a hundred feet high to lance into the mist-shrouded blue of the mid-afternoon skies. They had been traveling east in the Greensward since sunrise, following the labyrinth roadways that wound down through the valley's lowlands past fields and villages, past farmers' cottages and herdsmen's huts. Once or twice there had been the sight of castle walls in the distance, far from where they traveled and almost miragelike in the shimmer of Landover's sun. But none had been as grand and awesome as Rhyndweir.

Ben shook his head. Sterling Silver was so much the worse by comparison that he hated to think about it.

The homesteads and villages of the common people of the Greensward did not compare favorably either. The fields looked seedy and the crops appeared to be afflicted with various forms of blight. The cottages and huts of the farmers and herdsmen looked ill-kept, as if their owners no longer took pride in them. The shops and stands of the villages looked dingy and weathered. Everything seemed to be falling apart. Questor nodded knowingly at Ben's glance. The Lords of the Greensward spent too much time at each other's throats.

Ben turned his attention back again to Rhyndweir. He studied the castle in silence as the little company approached from the valley it commanded on a roadway running parallel to the northernmost of the rivers. A scattering of village shops and cottages lined the juncture of the rivers in the broad shadow of the castle, forming a threshold to its gates. Thralls watched curiously as the company crossed a wooden bridge spanning to the castle approach, their tools lowered, their heads lifted in silent contemplation. Many had the same worn but expectant look on their faces as those who had come to the Heart.

"They have not seen a King of Landover make this journey to their master's castle in twenty years, High Lord," Questor spoke softly at his elbow. "You are the first."

"No one else made the effort?" Ben asked.

"No one else," Questor replied.

Their horses' hooves clumped off the bridge planks and thudded softly in the dusty earth. Ahead, the roadway lifted toward the walls of the castle and the open gates. Pennants flew from the parapets at every turn, brilliant silks fluttering in the wind. Banners hung from stanchions above the gates, and heralds stepped forward to sound their trumpets in shrill blasts that shattered the afternoon quiet. Lines of knights on horseback formed an honor guard on either side of the gateway, lances lifted in salute.

"This seems a little much, given everyone's attitude about the coronation, don't you think?" Ben muttered. His stomach had the same hollow feeling it always developed before major court appearances.

Questor's owlish face was screwed into a knot. "Yes, this does appear to be a bit overdone."

"When anyone's this overly friendly in my world, it's time to watch your backside."

"You are in no danger, High Lord," the wizard responded quickly.

Ben smiled and said nothing. They had reached the gates, passing down the corridor formed by the honor guard, the blare of the trumpets still ringing across the valley. Ben took a quick count. There were at least a hundred knights in the guard. Armor and weapons glistened brightly. Visored helmets stared straight ahead. The knights were iron statues that kept their place and did not stir. Ben sat rigid atop his mount. Every muscle in his body ached from yesterday's ride, but he refused to let the pain show. This wasn't just a reception line—this was a show of strength. This looked to be a case of who could impress whom. He glanced back at his little entourage of Questor, Abernathy and the kobolds and wished he had a bit more to work with.

They rode into the shadow of the gateway through the towering walls and the great woven banners. A delegation waited in the court ahead, a gathering of men afoot, robed and jeweled.

"The Lords of the Greensward," Questor breathed softly to Ben. "The tall one, the one who stands foremost, is Kallendbor, master of Rhyndweir. His is the largest of the estates, and he the most powerful of the Lords. Look for him to take the lead in what is to follow."

Ben nodded and said nothing. He had forgotten the ache in his body, and his stomach had settled. Already, he was considering what he would say—very much as if he were about to argue a case in court. He supposed that was what he was going to have to do, in a sense. It was going to be interesting.

Questor brought the company to a halt a dozen yards from the assembly of Lords and looked at Ben. Together, they dismounted. Pages came forward to take the reins. Abernathy remained on his horse, the King's banner hanging limp from its staff. Parsnip and Bunion stood to either side, crouched expectantly. No one looked very comfortable.

Kallendbor detached himself from the assemblage and came forward. Ignoring Ben, he addressed himself to Questor, inclining his head briefly. "Well met, Questor Thews. I see that you have brought our newest King to visit us."

Ben stepped in front of the wizard at once. "It was my decision to come here, Lord Kallendbor. I thought it would be quicker to visit you than to wait for you to visit me."

There was a moment of silence as the two faced each other. Kallendbor's eyes narrowed slightly, but his face remained expressionless. He was taller than Ben by several inches, heavier by twenty pounds, red-haired and bearded, and heavily muscled. He held himself erect, conveying the impression that he was looking down on Ben.

"Coronations occur so frequently these days in Landover that it is difficult to attend them all," he said pointedly.

"I expect the number to undergo a sharp decline," Ben replied. "Mine will be the last for some time."

"The last, you believe?" The other's smile was sardonic. "That may prove a difficult expectation to fulfill."

"Perhaps. But I intend to fulfill it, nevertheless. Please understand this, Lord Kallendbor. I am not like the others who came into Landover and left again at the first hint of trouble. I came here to be King, and King is what I will be."

"The purchase of a crown does not necessarily make one a King," one of the others muttered from the cluster behind Kallendbor.

"Nor does being born into the right family necessarily make one a Lord," Ben shot back quickly. "Nor purchase of an estate, nor marriage into one, nor theft by deception, nor conquest by arms, nor any of a dozen other available schemes and artifices used since the dawn of time—none of these make either Lords or Kings. Laws make Lords and Kings, if there is to be any order in life. Your laws, Lords of the Greensward, have made me King of Landover."

"Laws older than we and not of our making," Kallendbor growled.

"Laws to which, nevertheless, you are bound," Ben answered.

There was a quick murmur of voices and angry looks. Kallendbor studied him wordlessly. Then he bowed, his face still expressionless. "You show initiative in coming here to meet with us, High Lord. Be welcome, then. There is no need for us to stand further in this court. Come into the hall and share dinner. Bathe first, if you wish. Rest a bit—you look tired. Rooms have been set aside for you. We can talk later."

Ben nodded in reply, beckoned to the others of the little company, and together they followed the Lords of the Greensward across the courtyard and into the great hall beyond. Light from high, arched windows that were glassed and latticed flooded the passageways they followed, lending a bright and airy feel to the castle.

Ben leaned close to Questor. "How do you think we are doing so far?"

"They have agreed to board us," the other whispered back. "That is more than I expected them to do."

"It is? That's not what you said earlier!"

"I know. But I saw no reason to worry you."

Ben stared at him momentarily, then shook his head. "You never cease to amaze me, Questor."

"Hmmmmm?"

"Never mind. How far can we trust these people?"

The wizard slouched ahead, smiling. "About as far as piglets hop. I would keep my wits about me at dinner, if I were you."

What followed was a leisurely period of rest and relaxation in the rooms appointed for Landover's King and his entourage. There were sleeping rooms for all, baths with hot water and sweet soaps, fresh clothing, and bottles of wine. Ben took advantage of all but the wine. His experiences with wine thus far had been less than rewarding. Besides, he trusted Kallendbor and the others no farther than Questor, and he wanted a sharp wit about him when it came time to state his case. He left the wine unopened on the serving tray and noticed that the others did the same.

The call to dinner came at sunset. Dinner was a sumptuous affair served in the castle's great hall at a long tressel table filled with foodstuffs and dozens of additional bottles of wine. Ben left the wine alone once more. He was beginning to feel paranoid about it, but that couldn't be helped. He sat at the center of the long dinner table with Kallendbor on his right and a Lord named Strehan on his left. Questor had been placed at one end of the table, Abernathy and the kobolds at another, smaller table. Ben saw at once that he was being deliberately isolated. He thought briefly about arguing the placement, but then decided to let the matter pass. He would be tested sooner or later, and it might as well begin here. It was important that he convince the Lords of the Greensward that he was capable of standing alone.

Conversation was pleasant, but minimal for the first part of the meal, and it was not until the main course of pork roast and young pheasant was nearly gone that the subject of the Kingship was broached once more. Ben was wondering idly if the Lords of the Greensward always ate so well or if this was a deliberate effort to impress him, when Kallendbor spoke.

"You seem a man of some determination, High Lord," the other complimented and lifted his glass in salute.

Ben nodded in response, but left his glass on the table.

Kallendbor drank and set the glass carefully down before him. "We would not poison a King of Landover if we wanted him dead, you know. We would simply wait for the Mark to dispatch him for us."

Ben smiled disarmingly. "Is that what you have planned for me?"

The weathered face creased with amusement. Scars showed white against the tan. "We have nothing bad planned for you. We have nothing planned at all. We are here to listen to what you have planned for us, High Lord."

"We are loyal subjects to the throne, and we stand always with the King," Strehan added from the other side. "But there has been a problem of late knowing just who that King is to be."

"We would serve loyally if we could determine that the King we are asked to serve is a true King and not simply a play King whose interests are his own and not in keeping with ours," Kallendbor continued. "Since the death of the old King and the exile of his son, we have been subjected to a barrage of false Kings who last months or weeks or even days and are gone before we can even learn their names. Pledging loyalty to such as these serves no one's interests."

"Pledging loyalty to such as these is a betrayal of those Kings that have protected the realm since time began," Strehan said. "What purpose is served in pledging to a King who can do nothing for us?"

Ben looked at him wordlessly and thought, Here comes the pitch.

"You could be another of those Kings," Strehan said.

Ben smiled. Strehan was a thin-faced, angular man, taller even than Kallendbor. "But I'm not," Ben answered.

"Then you must explain what you have planned for us, High Lord," Kallendbor insisted. "You must explain what advantage you have set aside so that we may know our pledge is well given."

Oh-ho, Ben thought. "It seems to me that the advantages of pledging ought to be obvious," he replied. "A King is a figure of central authority who governs over the whole of the land. He gives and enforces laws that are applied fairly to all. He protects against the injustices that would otherwise flourish."

"There are no injustices here in the Greensward!" Strehan snapped.

"None at all?" Ben shook his head wonderingly. "I had been given to understand that even among equals there is always dissension; and quite often, in the absence of central authority, it takes the form of violence."

Kallendbor frowned. "You think that we quarrel among ourselves?"

"I think that, if the opportunity presented itself, you might be tempted to do away with each other like that!" Ben let the shock register in their faces a moment, then bent forward. "Let's get right to the point, shall we? You need a King in Landover. There has always been a King, and there always shall be a King. It is the form of rule that the people recognize and the laws support. If you let the throne remain vacant, or if you continue to refuse to recognize whoever rightfully sits upon it, you risk everything. You are a land of diverse peoples and mounting problems. Those problems need resolution, and you cannot resolve them alone. You do not get along well with each other in the absence of the old King, and you need someone to replace him. I'm the one you need, and I will tell you why."

The rest of the table had gone quiet as the conversation between Ben and the two Lords grew more heated, and now everyone was listening. Ben came slowly to his feet.

"I came here because the Lords of the Greensward have always been the first to pledge their loyalty to Landover's throne. Questor told me that. He said it was here that I should begin, if the loose threads of the Kingship were to be pulled back together again. And it is *your* Kingship. The throne and the laws promulgated by it belong to you and to all of the people of this valley. You have lost both and you need them back before Landover splinters so far apart that, like a broken board, it will never be made whole again. I can do that. I can do that because I do not come from Landover; I come from another world entirely. I have no prejudices to hinder me, no predetermined obligations to honor, no favorites to which I must cater. I can be honest and fair. I gave up everything I had to come here, so you may be certain that I am serious in my intentions. I have a background in the laws of my world that will allow me to interpret yours fairly.

"You need those laws to be in force, Lords of the Greensward. You need them so there can be stability in your lives beyond that brought about by force of arms. Trust comes with mutual reliance and faith—not with threats. I know that all is not tranquil between the estates. I know that all is not tranquil between the peoples of Landover. It will never be so until you agree to stand once more behind a King. History and the law require it."

"We have managed well enough up until now without a King to rule over us," one Lord interjected irritably.

"Have you, then?" Ben shook his head. "I don't think so. The Tarnish that drains the life from Sterling Silver ravages the Greensward as well. I've seen the blighted condition of your crops and the dissatisfied faces of the thralls who work them. The entire valley decays; you need a King! Look at yourselves! You don't begin to feel comfortable with one another—I can sense that much, and I'm an outsider! You are threatened by demons and by others who covet this land. Divided, you won't be able to hold on to what you have for very long, I think."

Another came to his feet. "Even if what you say is so, why should we pledge to you as High Lord? What makes you think you can do better than your predecessors?"

"Because I can!" Ben took a deep breath, and his eyes found Questor's. "Because I am stronger than they were."

"I want nothing to do with this," another Lord growled from across the table. "A pledge to you puts us at risk against the Mark and the demons that serve him!"

"You are already at risk," Ben pointed out. "If no King comes to stand against the Mark, then one day he will come into the land and claim it all. Join with me and we can stop that."

"*We* can stop that?" Strehan was on his feet, towering over Ben. "What hope do *we* have, High Lord? Have you fought in battle against demons such as the Mark? Where are your battle scars?"

Ben flushed. "If we stand together, then . . ."

"If we stand together, then it seems we are no better than if we stand alone!" Strehan snapped. "What use do you serve if you have no battle worth? What you ask is that the Lords of the Greensward put their own lives forward for yours!"

Voices raised loudly in agreement. Ben felt his control over the situation begin to slip.

"I ask no one to risk themselves for me," he said quickly. "I ask for an alliance with the throne, the same alliance that you had with the old King. I will ask such an alliance from all of Landover's subjects. But I ask it first of you."

"Bravely spoken, High Lord! But what if we were to ask an alliance from *you*?"

The speaker was Kallendbor. He came slowly to his feet, standing next to Ben, his red-bearded face hard. Strehan slipped back into his seat. The other Lords went silent.

Ben glanced quickly at Questor for help, saw confusion mirrored in the wizard's owlish face, and gave up looking. He turned back to Kallendbor. "What sort of alliance did you have in mind?"

"A marriage," the other said quietly.

"A marriage?"

"Yours, High Lord—to the daughter of any house you choose. Take for a wife the child of one of us, a wife to give you children, a wife to bind you to us with blood ties." Kallendbor smiled faintly. "Then we will pledge to you. Then we will acknowledge you as Landover's King!"

There was an endless moment of silence. Ben was so stunned that for a moment he could not even comprehend what was being asked. When he managed to accept the whole of what Kallendbor had requested of him, he saw as well the truth that lay behind it. He was being asked to provide to the Lords of the Greensward a legitimate heir to the throne of Landover—one that would rule after him. He thought that, once produced, such an heir would not likely have long to wait to ascend to the throne.

"I cannot accept," he said finally. He could see in his mind's eye Annie's youthful face, and the memory of it caused him new pain. "I cannot accept because I have recently lost my own wife, and I cannot take another so soon. I cannot do it."

He saw at once that not one of them understood what he was saying. Angry looks appeared instantly on the faces of all. It might be that in Landover's baronies, as in the baronies of medieval history in his own world, marriage was mostly for convenience. He didn't know, and it was too late now to find out. He had made the wrong decision in the minds of the Lords of the Greensward.

"You are not even a whole man!" Kallendbor sneered suddenly. Shouts rang out from the other Lords in approval.

Ben stood his ground. "I am King by law."

"You are a play-King like the others! You are a fraud!"

"He wears the medallion, Lord Kallendbor!" Questor shouted out from the far end of the table, shuffling away from his seat to come around.

"He may wear it, but it does him little good!" The red-bearded Lord had his eyes fixed on Ben. The shouts from the others continued. Kallendbor played to them, his voice rising. "He does not command the Paladin, does he? He has no champion to fight for him against man or demon! He has no one but you, Questor Thews. You had best come and get him now!"

"I need no one to stand up for me!" Ben stepped between Kallendbor and the approaching wizard. "I can stand for myself against anyone!"

The instant he had said it he wished that he hadn't. The room went still. He saw the smile come immediately to Kallendbor's hard face, the glint to his eye. "Would you care to test your strength against mine, High Lord?" the other asked softly.

Ben felt the dampness of sweat beneath his arms and along the crease of his back. He recognized the trap he had stepped into, but there seemed no way out of it now. "A test of strength seldom proves anything, Lord Kallendbor," he replied, his gaze kept steady on the other.

Kallendbor's smile turned unpleasant. "I would expect a man who relies solely on laws for his protection to say that."

Anger flooded through Ben. "Very well. How would you suggest that I test my strength against yours?"

"High Lord, you cannot allow . . ." Questor began, but was silenced by the shouts of the others gathered about the table.

Kallendbor rubbed his bearded face slowly, considering. "Well, now, there are any number of possibilities, all of them . . ."

He was cut short by a sharp bark from the far end of the table. It was Abernathy who, in his excitement to be heard, had lapsed back momentarily into the form of communication basic to this breed. "Forgive me," he said quickly as the snickers began to rise. "Lord Kallendbor, you seem to have forgotten the etiquette this situation demands. You were the one to issue the challenge to a contest. It is your opponent's right, therefore, to select the game."

Kallendbor frowned. "I assumed that because he was from another world he did not know the games of this one."

"He need only know a variation of them," Abernathy replied, peering at the other over his glasses. "Excuse me for one moment, please."

He left the table walking upright, head erect. Veiled laughter rose from the gathered Lords as the dog left the room. Ben glanced quickly at Questor, who shrugged and shook his head. The wizard had no idea what the scribe was about either.

A few moments later, Abernathy was back. He carried in his hands two pairs of eight ounce boxing gloves—the ones that Ben had brought with him into Landover to keep in training. "Fisticuffs, Lord Kallendbor," the soft-coated Wheaten Terrier announced.

Kallendbor threw back his head and laughed. "Fisticuffs? With those? I would prefer bare knuckles to leather socks filled with stuffing!"

Abernathy brought the gloves about the table to where the combatants stood. "High Lord," he bowed deeply, his soft eyes on Ben. "Perhaps it would be best if you forgave Lord Kallendbor his rash challenge. It would not do to see him injured because of his inability to master your weapons."

"No! I do not withdraw the challenge!" Kallendbor snatched one pair of gloves from the scribe and began to pull them on. Strehan turned to help him.

Abernathy passed the second pair to Ben. "He is very strong, High Lord. Watch yourself."

"I thought that you knew nothing of boxing," Ben whispered, working one glove on. Questor appeared at his side, helping him tighten the laces. "How did you know to find these?"

"I was responsible for the unpacking of your possessions when you arrived at Sterling Silver," Abernathy answered, giving Ben what might have been a smile coming from anyone else. "These gloves were there along with a magazine that demonstrated your game. I studied the pictures and drawings in the magazine. Our games are much the same. You call yours boxing. We call ours fisticuffs."

"I'll be damned!" Ben breathed.

Kallendbor had his gloves in place and was stripped to the waist. Ben glanced past Questor as he worked. Kallendbor's chest and arms rippled with muscle, and scars from battle wounds criss-crossed his body. He looked like a gladiator from the cast of *Spartacus.*

A space was being cleared at the center of the room, ringed by thralls in service to the castle proper and by the other Lords of the Greensward. The space was a little more than twice the size of a normal boxing ring.

"Any rules to this game?" Ben asked, taking deep breaths to calm himself.

Questor nodded. "Just one. Whoever is still standing at the end of the fight is the winner."

Ben slapped his gloves together to test the tightness of the laces and shrugged the tunic from his back. "That's it, huh? I guess I won't have any trouble remembering, will I?"

He went around the dinner table and into the makeshift ring. Kallendbor was waiting. Ben stopped momentarily at the edge of the crowd; Questor, Abernathy, and the two kobolds crowded in close beside him.

"So much for the lawyer's approach to things," he sighed.

"I will look after you, High Lord," Questor whispered hurriedly.

Ben turned. "No magic, Questor."

"But, High Lord, you cannot . . ."

"No magic. That's final."

The wizard grimaced and nodded reluctantly. "The medallion will protect you anyway," he muttered. But he did not sound all that sure that it would.

Ben shrugged the matter aside and stepped out into the ring. Kallendbor came at him at once, hands cocked, arms spread wide as if he intended to grapple. Ben hit him once with the left jab and sidestepped. The big man turned, grunting, and Ben hit him again, once, twice, a third time. The jabs were sharp and quick, snapping Kallendbor's head back. Ben danced away, moving smoothly, feeling the adrenaline begin to flow through his body. Kallendbor roared with fury and came at him with both arms flailing. Ben ducked, caught the blows on his arms and shoulders, then burrowed into the other's body with a flurry of quick punches, stepped away, jabbed and caught Kallendbor flush on the jaw with a full right hook.

Kallendbor went straight to the floor, a dazed look on his face. Ben danced away. He could hear Questor yelling encouragement. He could hear the oaths and shouts of the Lords of the Greensward. The blood pumped through him, and it seemed to him that he could hear the sound of his heartbeat throbbing in his ears.

Kallendbor climbed slowly back to his feet, eyes glinting with fury. He was as strong as Abernathy had warned. He would not be taken out easily.

He came at Ben once more, cautiously this time, fists held protectively before his face. The fighters feinted and jabbed, circling. Kallendbor's bearded face was flushed and angry. He pushed his gloves into Ben's, knocking them back, looking for an opening.

Then, suddenly, he charged. He was quick, and he caught Ben off balance with his rush. The blows rained into Ben, thrusting through his guard, catching him in the face. Ben danced away, his own fists jabbing back. But Kallendbor never slowed. He bore into Ben like a juggernaut, knocking him to the floor. Ben struggled back to his feet, but Kallendbor's wild blows caught him twice on the side of the head and down he went again.

The shouts of the Lords of the Greensward became a roar in Ben's ears, and there were colored lights dancing before his eyes. Kallendbor was standing over him, hitting at him with both hands, the smell of his sweat heavy in the air. Ben rolled away, careening into the ring of onlookers. Hands shoved him back. Kallendbor's boots and knees struck out at him, and he felt the pain of the blows lance through his body. He curled into a ball, his gloves tight against his face, his forearms against his chest.

He could feel the medallion he wore about his neck pressed against him.

The pain was becoming unbearable. He knew he was going to lose consciousness if he did not do something quickly. He rolled to his knees, bracing. When Kallendbor rushed at him again, he grappled desperately at the other's legs, pulled him off balance and tumbled him to the floor.

Ben came back to his feet at once, shaking the dizziness from his head, gloves cocked before his face. Kallendbor was up as well, his breath hissing from between his teeth. A strange light had appeared from behind the big man and the crowd of onlookers. It was a light that seemed to be growing brighter. Ben shook his head, trying to concentrate on the advancing Kallendbor. But now others were aware of the light as well. Heads had begun to turn and the crowd to part as the light advanced toward them. There was a figure within the light, a knight in battered, worn armor, helmet visor closed.

There was an audible gasp from the crowd of Lords and thralls.

The knight was the Paladin.

The assemblage stared, murmurs rippling through the sudden silence as the figure shimmered in the light. Some dropped to their knees, crying out in the same manner as had the demons when the Paladin had appeared to them in the Heart. Kallendbor stood uncertainly at the center of the circle, hands lowered, eyes turned away now from Ben to view the specter.

The Paladin shimmered a moment longer in the light, and then he faded back again and was gone. The light died away into evening dark.

Kallendbor wheeled at once on Ben. "What trickery is this, play-King? Why do you bring that ghost into Rhyndweir?"

Ben shook his head angrily. "I brought nothing but . . ."

Questor cut the rest of what he was going to say short. "Lord Kallendbor, you mistake what has happened here. Twice before, the Paladin has appeared when the High Lord's safety was threatened. You are being warned, Lords of the Greensward, that this man, Ben Holiday, is the true King of Landover!"

"We are warned by a ghost in a light?" Kallendbor laughed, spitting blood from his cracked lips. "You have used your magic to try to frighten us, Questor Thews, and you have failed!"

He looked at Ben with disdain. "This game is finished. I want no more of you or your traveling circus. I want no part of you as my King!"

The shouts of the other Lords echoed his declaration. Ben stood where he was. "Whether you want any part of me or not, I am King nevertheless!" he snapped. "You may ignore me as you would ignore any truth, but I will remain a fact of your life! You think to ignore the laws that made me King, Kallendbor, but you will not be able to do so forever! I will find a way to see that you cannot!"

"You need not look far, play-King!" Kallendbor was beside himself with fury. He shrugged out of the boxing gloves and threw them at Ben. "You claim to be King of Landover? You claim to command the services of the Paladin? Very well, prove that you truly are what you claim by ridding us of the one plague on our existence that we cannot ourselves dismiss! Rid us of Strabo! Rid us of the dragon!"

He stalked forward until he was almost on top of Ben. "Twenty years now the dragon has raided our stock and destroyed our property. We have hunted him from one end of Landover to the other, but he has the magic of the old world and we cannot kill him. You are heir to the old magic, too—if you are who you claim! So rid us of the dragon, play-King, and then I will bow to you as High Lord and pledge you my life!"

A roar of approval rose from the throats of all assembled. "Rid us of the dragon!" they cried as one. Ben's eyes remained locked on Kallendbor's.

"Until then, I will ignore you as I would ignore the ants that crawl beneath my feet!" Kallendbor whispered in his face.

He wheeled and stalked from the circle, the other Lords following after. Slowly, the room began to empty. Ben was left alone with Questor, Abernathy, and the kobolds. The four came forward to remove his gloves and to clean the blood and sweat from his face and body.

"What's all this about the dragon?" Ben demanded immediately.

"Later, High Lord," Questor answered, dabbing at a mouse already beginning to form under one eye. "A bath and a night's sleep are in order first."

Ben shook his head. "Not in this place! I wouldn't spend another moment here if it meant hiking out across a damn desert! Pack everything. We're leaving right now. We'll talk about the dragon on the way."

"But, High Lord . . ."

"Now, Questor!"

No one chose to argue the point further. An hour later their little company was back on the road traveling west out of Rhyndweir into the night.

WILLOW

Ben's decision to leave Rhyndweir so abruptly proved to be a poor one. The company had barely cleared the outskirts of the village shops and cottages lining the castle's approach when it began to rain. The rain came slowly at first, a spattering of drops against their faces, light and teasing. Then the drops became a shower, and the shower became a downpour. Clouds blocked away the land's moons and the distant stars, and everything turned as black as pitch. Wind howled across the flat, empty pastures and fields of the Greensward, thrusting at the travelers like a giant's breath. It took only moments for the company to decide to seek immediate shelter, but they were already soaked to the bone by then.

They spent the night in a dilapidated, empty barn in which stock had once been housed. Rain blew through holes in the walls and roofing, and there were few dry spots to be found. The air turned chill, and the damp clothing seemed colder than before. Ben and his companions huddled together in the dark in a large horse stall at one end of the barn. It was dryer there than anywhere else in the building, and there was straw on which to bed. A fire was out of the question, so everyone had to make do with a quick change of clothing and a sharing of the blankets from their bedding. Questor offered to try his magic on a flameless warming device he had once successfully conjured up, but Ben would not allow it. Questor's magic evidenced an unpleasant propensity for backfiring, and their barn was the only shelter in sight. Besides, Ben reasoned obstinately, weathering out the storm in such poor surroundings seemed appropriate punishment for the way he had botched things at Rhyndweir.

"I blew it, Questor," he said to the other as they huddled in the dark and listened to the rainfall drum on the old barn's roof.

"Hmmmmm?" Questor's attention was concentrated on wiping dirt and blood from the numerous cuts and abrasions Ben had suffered during his fight with Kallendbor.

"I screwed up. I mishandled the whole thing. I let Kallendbor trick me into accepting his stupid challenge. I lost my composure; I let the entire affair get out of hand." He sighed and leaned back against the stall side. "I should have done a better job of arguing my case. Some lawyer, right? Some King!"

"I think you handled matters rather well, High Lord."

Ben looked at him skeptically. "You do?"

"It was obviously intended that you should fail in your attempt to gain a pledge from the Lords of the Greensward unless you were willing to gain that pledge on their terms. Had you agreed to marry a daughter of one of their households, the pledge would have been yours. You would have had a wife and a dozen in-laws for the balance of your reign as King—a reign that would have been considerably shorter than you would have liked." The wizard shrugged. "But you knew what they intended as well as I, didn't you?"

"I knew."

"So you were right to refuse the offer, and I think you showed great composure under the circumstances. I think that if the game had been allowed to continue, you might have beaten him."

Ben laughed. "I appreciate the vote of confidence. I notice, however, that you left nothing to chance."

"What do you mean?"

"I mean that you ignored my order not to use the magic and conjured up that image of the Paladin when it looked as if I was going down for the count!"

The owlish face studied him, a faint outline in the dark. Questor set aside the bloodied cloths. "I did nothing of the sort, High Lord. That *was* the Paladin."

There was a long silence. "Then he has come three times now," Ben whispered finally, his bewilderment evident. "He came when I was caught in the time passage with the Mark, he came when the demons appeared at the coronation, and now he has come to the Greensward. But he seems just exactly what you called him, Questor—a ghost! He looks as if he's only an image made of light! What is he really?"

The other shrugged. "Maybe what he appears—maybe something more."

Ben hunched his knees up close against his body, trying to stay warm. "I think that he's out there. I think that he's trying to come back again." He looked at Questor for confirmation.

Questor shook his head. "I do not know, High Lord. Maybe so."

"What was it that brought him in the past? There must be something you can tell me about him—about why and how he appeared to the old King."

"He appeared when he was summoned," the other replied. "The summons has always come from the wearer of the medallion. The medallion is a part of the magic, High Lord. There is a link between it, the Kings of Landover, and the Paladin. But only the Kings of Landover have ever fully understood what that link was."

Ben pulled the medallion from beneath his tunic and studied it. "Maybe if I rub it, or talk to it, or just grasp it—maybe that will bring the Paladin. What do you think?"

Questor shrugged. Ben tried all three and nothing happened. He tried wishing for the Paladin's appearance, hands clutched about the medallion so tightly he could feel the impression of its carved surface. Nothing happened.

"I suppose I should have known it wouldn't be that easy." He sighed and dropped the medallion back down the front of his tunic, feeling it catch on the chain that lay looped about his neck. He looked up through a hole in the barn roof as the wind rattled the shingles against their fastenings. "Tell me about the dragon and the Lords of the Greensward."

The wizard's stooped form bent closer still. "You heard most of it from Kallendbor yourself. The Lords of the Greensward are at war with Strabo. The dragon is their nemesis. He has preyed upon them for the better part of twenty years—ever since the old King died. He burns their crops and their buildings; he devours their livestock and occasionally their thralls. He hunts their lands at will, and they are powerless to stop it."

"Because the dragon is part of the magic—isn't that it?"

"Yes, High Lord. Strabo is the last of his kind. He was a creature of the world of fairy until his exile thousands of years ago. He cannot be harmed by mortal weapons, only by the magic from which he was created. That was why Kallendbor felt safe in challenging you to rid him of the dragon—he believes you a fraud. A true King of Landover would command the magic of the medallion and could summon the Paladin to do his bidding."

Ben nodded. "It all comes back to the Paladin, doesn't it? Tell me, Questor, why is it that the dragon hunts the Greensward as he does?"

The wizard smiled. "He is a dragon."

"Yes, I know. But he didn't always hunt like this, I gather—at least, not while the old King lived."

"True. He kept to his own land in times previous. Perhaps he feared the old King. Perhaps the Paladin kept him there until the old King was dead. Your guess is as good as mine."

Ben grunted irritably and leaned back against the stall side. His entire body hurt. "Why is it that you can't manage an answer to any of these questions, damn it? You're supposed to be the court wizard and my personal advisor, but you don't seem to know much of anything!"

Questor looked away. "I do the best I can, High Lord."

Ben immediately regretted his words. He touched the other on the shoulder. "I know. I'm sorry I said that."

"I was away from the court when the old King was alive, and my half-brother and I were never close. Had we been close, perhaps I could have learned at least some of the answers to your questions."

"Forget it, Questor. I'm sorry I said anything."

"It has not been easy for me either, you know."

"I know, I know."

"I have had to master the magic practically alone. I have had no tutor, no master to instruct me. I have had to preserve the throne of Landover while shepherding about a flock of Kings who were frightened by the sight of their own shadow and who wanted nothing more challenging than the spectacle of knights at a joust!" His voice was rising. "I have given everything that I have so that the monarchy might endure, even while beset by miseries that would break the back of an ordinary . . ."

Abernathy's growl interrupted rudely. "Please, wizard, enough of your soliloquies! We are already bored to tears by this account of your sufferings and can bear no more!"

Questor's mouth snapped shut with an audible click of his teeth.

Ben smiled in spite of himself. It hurt his face to do so. "I hope that I do not number among those unfortunate Kings you have just described, Questor," he said.

The other's baleful gaze was still turned on Abernathy. "Hardly."

"Good. Tell me one thing more, then. Can we rely on Kallendbor to be as good as his word?"

Questor looked back now. "About the dragon—yes. He swore an oath."

Ben nodded. "Then we must find a way to get rid of the dragon."

There was an endless moment of silence. Ben could sense the others looking at each other in the dark. "Any ideas as to how we go about doing that?" he asked.

Questor shook his head. "It has never been done."

"There is a first time for everything," Ben replied lightly, wondering as he said it just whom it was he was trying to convince. "You said that it would take magic to rid us of the dragon. Who could help us find that magic?"

Questor considered. "Nightshade, of course. She is the most powerful of those come from the world of fairy. But she is as dangerous as the dragon. I think we might have better luck with the River Master. He, at least, has proven loyal to the Kings of Landover in the past."

"Is he a creature of magic?"

"He was, once upon a time. He has been gone from the world of fairy for centuries. Still, he retains something of the knowledge of the old ways and may have help to offer. It was to him that I would have suggested we go next—even if the Lords of the Greensward *had* given their pledge."

Ben nodded. "Then it's settled. Tomorrow we travel to the country of the

River Master." He stretched, hunched down into his blankets, hesitated a moment and said, "This may not count for much, but I want to thank you all for standing by me."

There was a mutter of acknowledgment and the sound of the others rolling into their bed coverings. Everything was silent for a moment except for the sound of the rain falling and the soft rush of the wind.

Then Abernathy spoke. "High Lord, would it be asking too much that we refrain from camping out in barns after tonight? I think there are fleas in this straw."

Ben smiled broadly and drifted off to sleep.

Daybreak brought an end to the rain, and a glimmer of sunshine appeared through the haze of mist and clouds that lingered on. The little company resumed the journey through the valley of Landover, this time turning south for the country of the River Master. They traveled all day, Ben, Questor and Abernathy on horseback, the kobolds afoot. Once again, Bunion went ahead to announce their coming. They passed from the lowland estates of the Lords of the Greensward at midafternoon, leaving behind their broad, open stretches of meadow and farmland, and by dusk were deep into the rolling hill country of the River Master.

The color of life was different here, Ben saw. The cast of things was brighter and truer—as if the failing of the magic had not penetrated so deeply. It was a country of lakes and rivers nestled within hollows and valleys, of orchards and woods scattered on gentle slopes, of grasses and ferns that shimmered in the wind like the waves of some ocean. The mists were thicker in the hill country, trapped in pockets like harnessed clouds, stirring and wending their way from hollow to valley and back again. But the greens of grasses and trees and the blues of lakes and rivers were brighter than in the Greensward, and the splashes of pinks, crimsons, and lavenders did not have that wintry tone that marked so distinctly the plains. Even the Bonnie Blues seemed not so blighted, though darkening spots still marred their beauty.

Ben asked Questor why this was.

"The River Master and those who serve him are closer to the old ways than most. Bits and pieces of the magic are still theirs to command. What magic they still retain they use to keep the earth and waters of their homeland clean." Questor gave a cursory glance about and then shrugged. "The River Master's magic protects against a failing of the land's magic only marginally. Already, signs of wilt and graying are evident. The River Master and his followers fight a holding action at best. The land will fail here in the end as it fails everywhere else."

"All because Landover has no King?" Ben still found the corrolation between the two difficult to accept.

"*Had* no King, High Lord—no King for twenty years."

"The thirty-two failures don't count for much, I gather?"

"Against a failing of the magic of the sort you see now? Nothing. You will be the first to count for anything."

Maybe yes, maybe no, Ben thought grimly, reminded of his lack of success with the Lords of the Greensward. "I really don't understand—doesn't anyone recognize the problem? I mean, the land is dying all about them and it's all because they can't get together long enough to settle on a King!"

"I do not think they perceive matters quite that way, High Lord," Abernathy said quietly, edging forward on his horse.

Ben glanced back. "What do you mean?"

"He means that the connection between the loss of a King and the failing of the land's magic is one that only I have made," Questor interrupted, obviously irritated with the scribe. "He means that no one else sees the problem the same way I do."

Ben frowned. "Well, what if they're right and you're wrong?"

Questor's owlish face tightened into a knot. "Then everything you and I are trying to do is a colossal waste of time! But it happens that they are not right and I am not wrong!" Questor glared back at Abernathy momentarily and then faced forward. "I have had twenty years to consider the problem, High Lord. I have observed and studied; I have employed what magic I command to test my theory. It is with some confidence that I tell you that Landover must have a King again if it is to survive!"

He was so adamant in his defense that Ben remained silent. It was Abernathy who spoke first.

"If you have finished momentarily with your attempt at self-vindication, Questor Thews, perhaps you will allow me to get a word in edgewise to explain what I really meant when I said others do not perceive matters as we." He looked down at Questor over the rims of his glasses, while the wizard stiffened in his saddle but refused to turn. "What I *meant* was that the lack of perception on the part of others was not as regards the problem, but the solution to it. Most see quite clearly that the failing of the magic came about with the death of the old King. But none agree that coronation of a new King will necessarily solve the problem. Some believe restrictions should be placed on the solution sought. Some believe another solution altogether should be sought. Some believe no solution should be sought at all."

"No solution at all—who thinks that?" Ben asked disbelievingly.

"Nightshade thinks that." Questor reined his horse back to them, his irritation with Abernathy momentarily put aside. "She cares only for the Deep Fell, and her own magic keeps the hollows as she wishes them. Should the magic of the land fail, hers would be the most powerful."

"The Lords of the Greensward would accept one of their own as King, but no other," Abernathy added to his explanation. "They accept the solution, but would place restrictions on it."

"And the River Master seeks to find another solution altogether—his solution being one of self-healing," Questor finished.

"*That* was what I meant in the first place," Abernathy huffed.

The wizard shrugged. "Then you should have said so."

Shadows were gathering rapidly across the land as they turned their horses into a small grove of poplar to set camp for the night. A wooded ridgeline crested the skyline west, and the sun had already settled into its branches, filtering daylight into streamers of hazy gold. A lake stretched south of their campsite, a broad stretch of shimmering gray water over which mist floated in thick clouds while trees screened away dozens of tiny inlets and coves. Birds flew in wide, lazy circles against the night.

"The lake is called Irrylyn," Questor told Ben as they dismounted and handed the reins of their horses to Parsnip. "It is said that, on certain nights of the high summer, the sprites and nymphs of the River Master bathe within these waters to keep their youth."

"That should be exciting." Ben yawned and stretched, wishing nothing more exciting at this point than a good night's sleep.

"Some believe that the waters have the power to preserve youth." Questor was caught up in his musings. "Some believe that the waters can turn back old age and make one young again."

"Some believe anything." Abernathy grunted, shaking himself until his hair ruffled back from beneath the dust that matted it. "I have washed in those waters more than once and gained nothing for my efforts beyond a better smell."

"Something you might give thought to now," Questor advised, wrinkling his nose in distaste.

Abernathy growled in response and padded off into the dark. Ben watched him go, then turned to Questor. "That sounds like a good idea for me, as well, Questor. I feel like somebody's doormat. Is there any reason I can't wash off some of this dirt?"

"No reason at all, High Lord." The wizard was already turning away, searching for Parsnip. "I suppose that I had better see to dinner."

Ben started for the lake and then stopped. "Anything dangerous down there that I ought to know about?" he called back, remembering suddenly the bog wump, the cave wight, and whatever else it was he hadn't even seen during his morning run about Sterling Silver.

But Questor was already out of hearing, his stooped form a vague shadow in the mists. Ben hesitated, staring after him, then shrugged and started for the lake once more. If nymphs and sprites could bathe in the waters of the Irrylyn, how dangerous could it be? Besides, Abernathy was already down there.

He picked his way through the shadows to the water's edge. The lake spread away before him, a sheen of silver that mirrored trailers of mist and the colored spheres of Landover's moons. Willows, cottonwood, and cedar canopied him, like drooping giants against the failing light, and birds called sharply through the twilight. Ben stripped off his clothes and boots, searching the dark for Abernathy. The dog was nowhere in sight, and he could not hear him moving.

Naked, he stepped out into the water. Shock registered in his face. The water was warm! It was like a bath—a soft, pleasant heat that soothed and relaxed the muscles of the body. He reached down and touched it with his hand, certain that the difference in air and water temperature must account for the odd sensation of warmth. But, no, the water was truly warm—as if a giant hot springs.

He shook his head. Cautiously, he stepped out until he was knee-deep in the lake, the shadow of his body stretched back against the waters. Something else was odd. It felt as if he were walking in sand. He reached down again and brought up a handful of the lake bottom. It *was* sand! He checked it carefully in the moonlight to make certain. He was inland at a forested lake where there should only have been mud or rock, and instead there was sand!

He walked ahead, beginning to wonder if perhaps there was indeed some sort of magic at work in the Irrylyn. He glanced about once again for some sign of Abernathy, but the dog was missing. Slowly he lowered himself neck-deep into the water, feeling its warmth soak through him, giving himself over to the sensation. He was several dozen yards from shore by now, the slope from the water's edge a gradual one that receded no more than several inches every ten feet or so. He swam into the dark, stretching his body out, breathing at regular intervals. When he came up for air, he saw a second inlet curve back from his own and swam toward it. It was tiny, barely a hundred feet across, and he swam past it toward a third. He switched from the crawl to a soundless breaststroke, head lifted toward his destination. Moonlight flooded the water with streamers of color, and the mist snaked past in shadowy screens of gray. Ben closed his eyes and swam.

The third inlet was smaller still, barely two dozen yards wide. Rushes screened the shoreline, and cedars and willows canopied above the waters, throwing dark shadows toward the lake. Ben dove beneath the water and swam silently into the cove, pulling his way toward the shallows.

He surfaced a dozen yards from the shoreline—and a woman was directly in front of him. She stood not ten feet away, a little more than ankle-deep in the lake's waters, as naked as he. She made no attempt to turn away or to cover herself. She was like a frightened animal caught in the light, frozen in that split second of hesitation before it would be gone.

Ben Holiday stared, seeing momentarily in his mind someone he had thought forever lost. Water ran down into his eyes and he blinked it away.

"Annie?" he whispered in disbelief.

Then the shadows and the mist shifted where they fell across her, and he saw that she was not Annie—that she was someone else.

And perhaps some*thing* else as well.

Her skin was pale green, smooth and flawless and almost silvery as the waters of the Irrylyn shimmered against it. Her hair was green as well, deep forest green, the tresses tumbling to her waist, braided with flowers and ribbons. But her hair grew in narrow lines along the backs of her forearms as well and along the backs of her calves, silken manes that stirred gently with the whisper of the night wind over the lake.

"Who are you?" she asked softly.

He could not bring himself to answer. He was seeing her clearly now, finding her exquisite beyond anything he would have imagined possible. She was an artist's flawless rendering of a fairy queen brought suddenly to life. She was the most beautiful creature he had ever seen.

She came forward a step in the moonlight. Her face was so youthful that it made her seem hardly more than a girl. But her body . . .

"Who are you?" she repeated.

"Ben." He could barely make himself answer, and it never occurred to him to answer any other way.

"I am Willow," she told him. "I belong to you now."

He was stunned anew. She came toward him, her body swaying with the movement, and now it was he who had become the frightened animal poised to flee.

"Ben." Her voice assumed a sweet, lilting cadence as she spoke to him. "I am a sylph, the child of a sprite become human and a wood nymph stayed wild. I was conceived on the midyear's passing in the heat of the eight moons full, and my fates were woven in the vines and flowers of the gardens in which my parents lay. Twice each year, the fates decreed, I was to steal to the Irrylyn in darkness and bathe in her waters. To the man who saw me thus, and to no other, would I belong."

Ben shook his head quickly, his mouth working. "But that's craz . . . that's not right! I don't even know you! You don't know me!"

She slowed before him, close enough now that she might reach out and touch him. He wanted her to do that. The need for that touch burned through him. He fought against it with everything he could muster, feeling trapped in the emotions that rushed through him.

"Ben." She whispered his name and the sound of it seemed to wrap about him. "I belong to you. I feel that it is so. I sense that the fates were right. I am given, as with the sylphs of old. I am given to the one who sees me thus." Her face lifted, the perfect features radiating back the rainbow colors of the moons. "You must take me, Ben."

He could not force his eyes away from her. "Willow." He used her name now, desperate to turn back the emotions that raged through him. "I cannot take . . . what does not belong to me. I am not even from this world, Willow. I barely know . . ."

"Ben," she whispered urgently, cutting short the rest of what he would say. "Nothing matters but that this has happened. I belong to you." She came a step closer. "Touch me, Ben."

His hand came up. Thoughts of Annie flashed with lightning clarity through his mind, and still his hand came up. The warmth of the waters of the Irrylyn and the air about him wrapped him so close that it seemed he could not breathe. The fingers of her hand touched his.

"Come away with me, Ben," she whispered.

Fire burned through him, a white-hot heat that consumed his reason. She was the need he had never known. He could not refuse her. Colors and warmth blinded him to everything but her, and the whole of the world about him dropped away. His hand closed tightly about hers, and he felt them join.

"Come away with me, now." Her body pressed close.

He reached for her, his arms wrapping her close, the softness of her body astonishing to him.

"High Lord!"

Everything blurred. There was a crashing of underbrush and the sound of footsteps. Rushes stirred, and the silence of the evening was shattered. Willow slipped from his arms.

"High Lord!"

Abernathy shoved his way into view at the shore's edge, panting with near exhaustion, his glasses askew on his furry nose. Ben stared at him in stunned silence, then glanced wildly about. He stood in the tiny inlet alone, naked and shivering now. Willow was gone.

"Goodness, do not wander off like that again without one of us!" Abernathy snapped, a mix of irritation and relief in his voice. "I would have thought that your experience at Sterling Silver would have been lesson enough!"

Ben barely heard him. He was scanning the inlet waters and shoreline for Willow. The need for her still burned through him like fire, and he could think of nothing else. But she was nowhere to be found.

Abernathy sat back on his haunches, grumbling to himself. "Well, I suppose that it is not your fault. It is mostly the fault of Questor Thews. You did tell him that you wished to bathe in the lake and he should have known better than to send you off without Parsnip for company. The wizard seems incapable of understanding the risks this land poses for you." He paused. "High Lord? Are you all right?"

"Yes," Ben answered at once. Had Willow been some sort of bizarre hallucination? She had seemed so real . . .

"You appear a bit distressed," Abernathy said.

"No, no, I'm fine . . ." He trailed off. "I just thought that I . . . saw something, I guess."

He turned then and moved to the shoreline, stepping from the waters of the Irrylyn to dry ground. Abernathy had brought a blanket and wrapped it about him. Ben pulled the blanket close.

"Dinner is waiting, High Lord," the dog advised, studying Ben closely over the rims of his glasses. Carefully, he straightened them. "Perhaps some soup will warm you."

Ben gave a perfunctory nod. "Sounds good." He hesitated. "Abernathy, do you know what a sylph is?"

The dog studied him some more. "Yes, High Lord. A sylph is a sort of woods fairy, the female offspring of sprites and nymphs, I'm told. I have never seen one, but they are supposed to be very beautiful." His ears cocked. "Beautiful in human terms, that is. Dogs might differ."

Ben stared off into the dark. "I suppose." He took a deep breath. "Soup, you say? I could use a bowl."

Abernathy turned and started away. "The campsite is this way, High Lord. The soup should be quite good if the wizard has managed to refrain from trying to improve on it by using his sadly limited magic."

Ben cast a quick glance back at the inlet. The waters of the lake glimmered undisturbed in the moonlight. The shoreline stood empty.

He shook his head and hurried after Abernathy.

The soup was good. It steamed down inside Ben Holiday and took away the chill that had left him shaking when he had discovered he was alone in that inlet. Questor was relieved to see him safely back and quarreled with Abernathy all during the meal as to who should assume responsibility for the High Lord's disappearance. Ben didn't listen. He let them argue, spoke when spoken to, and kept his thoughts to himself. Two bowls of soup and several glasses of wine later, he was comfortably drowsy as he stared into the flames of the small fire Parsnip had built. It hadn't even occurred to him to worry about drinking the wine.

He went to sleep shortly after. He rolled into his blankets and turned away from the fire, his gaze directed to the silver waters of the lake, the trailers of mist that hovered and swirled above them, and the night beyond. He listened to the silence that settled quickly over the hill country. He searched the darkness for shadows.

He slept well that night and, while he slept, he dreamed. He did not dream of Annie or Miles. He did not dream of the life he had left when he crossed over into Landover, nor of Landover or the myriad problems he faced as her King.

He dreamed instead of Willow.

RIVER MASTER

Bunion returned at dawn. The morning was chill and damp; mist and shadows settled thick across the forest like a gray woolen blanket pulled close about a still-sleeping child. The remainder of the little company was at breakfast when the kobold appeared from the trees, a phantasm slipped from the dreams of last night. He went directly to Questor, spoke to him in that unintelligible mix of grunts and hisses, nodded to the others, and sat down to finish off what was left of the cold bread, berries, and ale.

Questor advised Ben that the River Master had agreed to receive them. Ben nodded wordlessly. His thoughts were elsewhere. Visions of Willow still lingered in his mind, images so real that they might have been something other than the dreams they were. Waking, he had sought to banish them, feeling them a betrayal somehow of Annie. But the visions had been too strong and he had been strangely anxious to preserve them in spite of his guilt. Why had he dreamed of Willow? he pondered. Why had the dreams been so intense? He finished his meal wrapped in his private reverie and saw nothing of the looks exchanged by Questor and Abernathy.

They departed the campsite shortly thereafter, a ragged little procession of ghosts, winding silently through the half-light. They made their way single file about the Irrylyn, following the shoreline along a pathway barely wide enough for one. It was a journey through fantasia. Steam lifted snakelike from the valley floor in a mix of warm earth and cool air to mingle with the trailers of mist that swirled about the forest. Trees stood dark and wet against the gray, a tangle of huge, black-barked oaks, elms, gnarled hickories, willows, and cedars. Wraiths of the imagination whisked into view and were gone in the blink of an eye, lithe creatures that teased and taunted. Ben found himself numbed by the intransiency of it all—feeling as if he could not come fully awake from last night's sleep, as if he had been drugged. He rode in a fog that shrouded mind and eyes both, straining for a glimpse of what was real through the maze of shadow pictures. But only the mist-dampened trees and the flat, hard surface of the lake were certain.

Then the lake was gone with the rest of the world, and only the trees remained. Morning lengthened, and still the mist and shadows wrapped the land close and would do no more than whisper of hidden secrets. Sounds filtered softly through the deep haze, bits and pieces of other lives and other happenings that Ben could only guess at. He searched the haze at every turn for a glimpse of Willow, a prodding voice within him whispering that she was there somewhere among the sounds and shadows, watching. He searched, but he did not find her.

It was shortly thereafter that the wood sprite appeared to them.

They had turned their horses down a draw formed by a series of fallen trees, Bunion leading the way on foot, when the sprite slipped from the mists at the kobold's shoulder. He was a lean, wiry figure, barely taller than Bunion, skin as brown and grainy as the bark of a sapling, hair grown thick down the back of his neck and along his arms. Earth-colored clothing hung loosely against his body; his sleeves and pant legs were cut short, his feet slipped into a boot that laced about the calves with leather. He barely slowed the procession as he appeared, falling in beside Bunion, moving forward through the haze in an almost birdlike manner, quick and restless.

"Questor!" Ben's voice was a rough hiss, louder than he had intended it to be. "Who is that?"

The wizard, riding just ahead, leaned back in his saddle, a finger to his lips. "Gently, High Lord. Our guide is a wood sprite in service to the River Master. There are others all about us."

Ben's gaze shifted quickly to the mist. He saw no one. "Our guide? Our guide to what?" His voice had dropped to a whisper.

"Our guide to Elderew, the home of the River Master."

"We need a guide?"

Questor shrugged. "It is safer to have one, High Lord. Marsh lies all about Elderew and more than a few have been lost to it. The lake country can be treacherous. The guide is a courtesy extended us by the River Master—a courtesy extended to all guests upon their arrival."

Ben glanced once more into the opaque curtain of the fog. "I hope the same courtesy is extended to guests upon their departure," he muttered to himself.

They moved ahead into the trees. Other forms appeared suddenly from the mist, lean, wiry shapes like their guide, some with the same wood-grained appearance, some sticklike and gnarled, some smooth and sleek with skin that was almost silver. They fell in silently on either side of the column, hands grasping the reins of the horses, guiding the animals ahead. Pools of water and reed-grown marsh materialized all along the trail they followed, vast patches of swamp in which nothing moved but the fog. The trail narrowed further and at times disappeared altogether, leaving them in water that rose to their guides' waists and the horses' haunches. Creatures swam in the water, some with fins, some with reptilian scales, some with faces that were almost human. Creatures darted through the mist, dancing across the mire's surface like weightless skip-flies. They surfaced far out in the fog, and there were only flashes before they were gone again. Ben felt himself waking now, the dreams of last night dissipated finally, no more than faint memories and disconnected feelings. His mind sharpened as he peered through the gloom and studied the beings about him with mingled incredulity and disbelief. He was enveloped in a sudden, biting sense of hopelessness. Sprites, nymphs, kelpies, naiads, pixies, elementals—the names came back to him as he watched these marsh creatures appear and fade again. He recalled his early, exploratory reading of fantasy and horror fiction, an almost forbidden trespass, and relived his wonder at the strange beings he had encountered. Such creatures could only exist in the writer's mind and come to life through his pen, he had believed—wishing secretly at the same time that it could be otherwise. Yet here those creatures were, the inhabitants of the world into which he had come, and he knew less of them than he did of those make-believe writer's creations he had encountered in his youth—and they, in turn, knew nothing at all of him. How, in God's name, could he convince them then to accept him as their King? What could he say that would persuade them to pledge to him?

The hopelessness of the task was appalling. It terrified him so that for a moment he was paralyzed with indecision. The lean, shadowy figures of the River Master's people slipped through the mist all about him, and he saw them as alien beings for whom he was nothing more than a curiosity. It had been different with the Lords of the Greensward. There had been a similarity in appearance, at least, a sense of sameness. But there was nothing of that with the people of the River Master.

He shoved the indecision and the fear from his mind. He swept back into its cubicle the hopelessness he felt. He banished them with a fury that was surprising. Such feelings were merely excuses to quit, and he would never do that. Bridges could be built between beings of any kind. There had been Kings that had served these people before; he could serve them just as well. He would find a way to make them see that. He would do whatever was necessary, but he would never quit. Never.

"High Lord?"

Abernathy was at his elbow, liquid brown eyes questioning. Ben looked down. His hands were gripping the pommel of his saddle so tightly that the knuckles were white. Sweat dampened the back and underarms of his tunic. He knew his face reflected the intensity of his feelings.

He took a deep breath and steadied himself, hands releasing their death-grip. "It was just a chill," he alibied, forced his gaze away, and kicked Wishbone ahead so that Abernathy was safely behind him once more.

A great gathering of hoary cypress loomed darkly through the mist ahead, trailers of moss hanging from their branches, gnarled roots digging into the marshy soil like claws. The little company and their wraithlike guides passed into their midst, swallowed in shadows and the smell of fetid earth. Their path was snakelike through the ancient trees, circumventing black pools that mirrored, like opaque glass, and patches of marsh that steamed. The grove of cypress was massive, and they became lost within it. The minutes slipped away, and daylight took on the guise of fading dusk.

Then the sheltering trees thinned and the ground began to rise. Slowly the company worked its way upward through the forest to where the mist burned away and the day brightened with sun. Marsh gave way to hardened earth, cypress to oak and elm. The raw smell of the lowland lake country filtered out into sweeter smells of pine and cedar. The faces in the mist became distinct now as elusive figures darted all about, but had the substance of real beings. Voices lifted out of the forest ahead. Ben sensed the end of their journey was at hand, and his pulse quickened.

A rush of color filtered through the trees, garlands of flowers strung from limbs and swaybars, and the sound of rushing water filled the air. The trees parted before them, the trail broadened, and a massive open-air amphitheater stood cradled in the light. Ben stared. The amphitheater was formed of living trees wrapped in a three-quarter circle about an arena of grasses and flowers; there were lines of walkways and seats constructed of limbs and sawn logs, fastened and shaped about the framework of the amphitheater's bowl. Branches from the trees canopied overhead to form a natural covering, and traces of sunlight broke through the mist where it thinned at the roof of the forest, falling in long, rainbow streamers to the grasses below in the manner of light in a rain forest when the monsoons have passed.

"High Lord," Abernathy called softly back to him. "Look."

He pointed—not to the amphitheater, but to what lay beyond. Ben felt his breath catch in his throat. What he was seeing was something almost surreal. Trees twice the size of those which framed the amphitheater lifted skyward in the forest beyond, pillars of such monstrous proportions that they dwarfed even the redwoods he had once visited when traveling with Annie through California. Great, angular branches laced together, binding one tree to the next, creating a complex and intricate network of limbs that joined each to the other until all were one.

An entire city lay cradled within and below those branches.

It was a magnificent, sprawling artist's rendering of an imagined fairy homeland. Cottages and shops sat high within the branches of the giant trees, interconnected by lanes and walkways that descended gradually toward the forest floor where the greater part of the city sat astride a series of canals fed by a river that cut through the center of the city. It was the soft rush of the river's waters that they had heard before. The forest's leafy roof screened away the sky, but sunlight broke through in scattered patches. Color from flowers and bushes brightened homes and shops, gardens and hedgerows, waterways and treelanes. The mists shrouded the city like a soft filter, and the gray, wintry cast that characterized so much of the valley was banished.

The fairy-born people of the River Master filled the treelanes and waterways, angular faces and bodies bits and pieces of the land's shadows as they passed through the mist.

"That is Elderew," Questor announced needlessly, for Ben had already surmised that much.

The members of the little company turned into the amphitheater, the slight forms of their guides slipping from them one by one until only the guide who had appeared first to them remained. They passed through the open quarter section to the arena bowl—Bunion in the lead, stride for stride with their guide; Questor and Ben next; Abernathy a few paces behind, bravely hoisting aloft once more the scarlet and white King's standard with the armored figure of the Paladin; Parsnip and the pack animals trailing. A reception committee was waiting, just emerged from one of several tunnels leading into the amphitheater from beneath its seats, gathered now in a knot at the tunnel's entrance. There were men and women both in the group; while Ben could not discern faces from so great a distance, he could easily identify items of forest clothing similar to that worn by their guide and swatches of the same wood-grained skin.

They drew to a halt at the center of the arena, dismounted, and walked forward to where the reception committee waited. The kobolds and Abernathy trailed Ben and Questor now, and the guide had remained behind with the animals. Ben cast a quick glance over at the wizard.

"If you have any last minute advice, Questor, I would appreciate it," he whispered.

"Hmmmmm?" The wizard's thoughts were elsewhere once again.

"About the River Master? About what sort of person he is?"

"What sort of creature, you mean," Abernathy interjected acidly from behind them.

"A sprite, High Lord," Questor answered. "A fairy who become half-human when he crossed into Landover and adopted this valley as his home, a woods and water being, a . . . a, uh . . ." The wizard paused thoughtfully. "He is really quite hard to describe, when you come right down to it."

"Best that he discover for himself," Abernathy declared pointedly.

Questor thought a moment, then nodded in agreement. "Yes, perhaps so."

They were too close to the gathering that awaited them for Ben to discuss the matter further—though in light of what had just been implied, he would have dearly loved to do so—and he turned his attention instead to a quick study of his hosts. He identified the River Master at once. The River Master stood central and foremost among those gathered, a tall, lean figure garbed in pants, tunic and cloak that were forest green, polished boots and leather cross-belts, and a slim silver diadem bound about his forehead. His skin was of a silver cast and grained like that of their guide—almost scaled—but his hair was black and thick about the nape of his neck and forearms. There was an odd, chiseled appearance to his eyes and mouth, and his nose was almost nonexistent. He had the look of something carved of wood.

The remaining members of the gathering stood grouped about him, younger for the most part, men and women of varying shapes and sizes, a scattering of faces as nut-brown and grained as that of their guide, one or two silver like the River Master, one sticklike and almost featureless, one covered with fur that was a russet color, one reptilian in looks and coloring, one a ghostly white with deep black eyes, and one . . .

Ben slowed abruptly, fighting to keep from his face the sudden shock that raced through him. One of those gathered, the one standing at the River Master's left hand, was Willow.

"Questor!" His voice was a low hiss. "The girl on the left—who is she?"

Questor stared over at him. "Who?"

"The girl on the left! The one with the green skin and hair, damn it!"

"Oh, the sylph?" Questor smiled benignly to those ahead, speaking to Ben out of the side of his mouth. "Her name is Willow. She is one of the River Master's children." He paused. "What difference does . . ."

Ben hushed him into immediate silence. They kept walking, Ben's mind working frantically, his eyes flitting from the faces of the others gathered to Willow's. She stared back at him boldly, her own eyes challenging.

"Welcome, High Lord," the River Master greeted as Ben and his companions reached him. He bowed briefly, little more than a nod, and those with him bowed as well. "Welcome to Elderew."

Masking his surprise at seeing Willow, Ben drew his scattered thoughts together with a vengeance. "I appreciate the greeting. I appreciate as well your receiving me in your home on such short notice."

The River Master laughed. It was a big, hearty laugh that filled the amphitheater with its sound, but the grainy, chiseled face was like stone. "The fact that you come at all does you much credit, High Lord. You are the first to do so since the old King died. I would be a poor host indeed if I were to refuse to receive you after so long a wait!"

Ben smiled politely, but the smile gave way to shock when he noticed that the River Master had gills at the side of his neck. "Apparently it has been a long wait for everyone," he managed.

The River Master nodded. "Quite long." He turned. "This is my family, High Lord—my wives, my children, and my grandchildren. Many have never seen a King of Landover and asked to be in attendance."

He introduced them one by one, the gills at the side of his neck fluttering softly as he spoke. Ben listened patiently, nodding to each, nodding to Willow as to the others as she was brought forward, feeling the heat of her eyes burn through him. When the River Master had finished, Ben introduced those in his own company.

"All are welcome," the River Master announced in response, and he gave his hand to each. "There will be a celebration in your honor this evening and a processional. You are to think of Elderew as your home while you are with us." He gave Ben what was meant to pass for a smile. "And now I think that you and I should speak of what has brought you here, High Lord. It is the way of things in the lake country to dispose of business directly and with expedience. While your companions are boarded in the village, you and I shall have our conference—just the two of us. Will you consent to that?"

Ben nodded. "I will." He did not even glance at Questor to see if the wizard approved. Questor could not help him in this. He knew what it was that he had to do, and he knew that he had to do it alone. Besides, the River Master did not seem a bad sort, Abernathy's cryptic comments notwithstanding.

The River Master dispatched his family with instructions to conduct Questor, Abernathy, and the kobolds to their lodgings. Then he turned to Ben. "Would you like to see something of the village while we talk, High Lord?" he asked.

It was more a suggestion than a question, but Ben nodded agreeably nevertheless. The River Master beckoned him down into one of the tunnels that cut beneath the amphitheater and he followed wordlessly. He had a last glimpse of Willow staring after him from the misty sunlight and then the shadows closed about.

When he emerged at the far end of the tunnel, the River Master took him along a canal bank lined with flowerbeds and hedgerows, carefully trimmed and tended, into a park that bordered the perimeter of the amphitheater. There were children playing in the park, small darting forms of varying sizes and shapes that reflected the diversity of their parentage, their voices bright and cheerful in the comparative stillness of the afternoon. Ben smiled wistfully. It had been a long time since he had listened to the sound of children playing; except for their different appearance, they might have been the children of his own world.

But, of course, *this* was his world now.

"I know that you have come to Elderew to ask my pledge to the throne, High Lord," the River Master informed him suddenly, his silver face a tight, expressionless mask. It seemed that his face never altered, reflecting nothing of his thoughts. "I know, as well, that you went first to the Lords of the Greensward with this same request and that the request was refused." Ben glanced quickly at him, but the River Master brushed the look aside with a shrug. "Oh, you needn't be surprised that I know such things, High Lord. I am once and always of the fairy world, and I still have something of the magic I once wielded. I have eyes in most corners of the valley."

He paused, digressing momentarily on the construction of the park and the canal system that ran through Elderew. Ben listened patiently, seeing that he meant to conduct the discussion at his own pace, content to let him do so. They walked from the park into a grove of elm bordering the giant trees that were the framework of the village.

"I respect the initiative and the courage that you have shown in undertaking your journey to the peoples of the valley, High Lord."The River Master returned now to the matter of Ben's visit. "I believe you to be a stronger man than those who laid claim to the throne of Landover before. Your actions at Rhyndweir would suggest that you are, in any case. I think you are also a straightforward and decisive man, so I will spare you the evasive maneuverings of diplomacy. I have considered your request—knowing what it is, as I have said—and I must reject it."

They walked on in silence. Ben was stunned. "May I ask why?" he said finally.

"I can see no advantage to granting it."

"I would argue that you should see many advantages."

The River Master nodded. "Yes, I know. You would argue that there is strength in numbers—that a central government would benefit the whole of the people of the land. You would argue that the people of the land cannot trust one another while there is no King. You would argue that we are threatened from without by neighboring worlds and from within by the Mark and his demons. You would argue that the land is stricken with a blight that is caused by a failing of the magic that made her, and that eventually she will die." He looked over. "Have I correctly stated the arguments that you would make?"

Ben nodded slowly. "How would you answer them?"

"I would tell you a story." The River Master slowed and led Ben to a bench chiseled from a massive rock. They sat. "The people of the lake country came from the fairy world, High Lord—most in a time long since forgotten by everyone but us. We are a fairy people who choose to live in a world of humans. We have become mortals by choice, affected by time's passage where once we were virtually immortal. We are elementals—creatures of wood, earth, and water—sprites, nymphs, kelpies, naiads, pixies, and dozens more. We left the fairy world and claimed the lake country as our own. We made it what it is—a country of beauty, grace, and health. We made it so because that was our purpose for coming into Landover in the first place. We came to give her life—not simply the lake country, but all of the valley."

He paused. "We have that power, High Lord—the power to give life." He bent close, an earnest teacher instructing his pupil. "We have not lost all of the magic, you see. We still possess the power to heal. We can take a land that suffers from sickness and blight and make it whole again. Come with me a moment. See what I mean."

He rose and walked a short distance to a gathering of brush nestled at the perimeter of the elm grove. The leaves were showing signs of wilt and spotting, much as the Bonnie Blues Ben had observed on his journey to Sterling Silver.

"See the sickness in the leaves?" the River Master asked.

He reached down and placed his hand upon the brush, close to where it rooted in the earth. There was concentration in his face. His breathing slowed and his head bent until his chin rested on his chest. Slowly the brush stirred, responding to his touch. The wilt and spotting disappeared, the color returned, and the brush grew straight again in the afternoon light.

The River Master rose. "We have the power to heal," he repeated, the intensity still visible in his eyes. "We would have used it to benefit the whole of the land had we been allowed to do so. But there are many who distrust us. There are many more who care nothing for the work that we do. They prefer us confined to the lake country, and we have honored their wishes. If they choose to think us dangerous because we are different, then so be it. But they will not leave well enough alone, High Lord. They continue to harm the land through their use of it. They cause sickness to spread through their carelessness and disregard. They bring sickness not only to their own homes in the valley, but to ours as well—to the rivers and the forests that belong to us!"

Ben nodded. Perhaps they shared common ground after all. "Your world is really not so different from my own, River Master. There were many who pollute the land and water in my world as well, and they disregard the safety and health of others in doing so."

"Then, High Lord, you will understand the ending that I put to my story." The River Master faced him squarely. "The lake country belongs to us—to the people who live within and care for it. This is our home. If the others in the valley choose to destroy their homes, that is of no concern to us. We have the power to heal our rivers and forests, and we will do so for as long as it is necessary. The loss of the magic that came with the death of the old King caused no greater problem for us than had already existed. The Lords of the Greensward, the trolls, kobolds, gnomes, and all of the others had spread their sickness through Landover long before that. Nothing has changed for us. We have always been a separate people, and I suspect that we always will be."

He shook his head slowly. "I wish you success, High Lord, but I will not pledge to you. Your coming to the throne of Landover changes nothing for the people of the lake country."

Ben glanced down again at the bit of brush the River Master had healed and then folded his arms across his chest solemnly. "I was told by Questor Thews that the River Master and his people worked to cure the sickness that spreads through Landover. But isn't it true that your work to keep the sickness out grows more difficult each day? The loss of the magic spreads the sickness too quickly, River Master. There will come a day when even your skill will not be enough, a day when the blight is so strong that the magic of the land itself will die."

The River Master's face was a stone. "The others may perish because they lack the skills to survive, High Lord. That will not happen with us."

Ben frowned. "That declaration of independence seems rather overoptimistic, don't you think? What of the Mark and his demons? Can you survive them?" There was a trace of irritation in his voice.

"They cannot even see us if we do not wish it. We can disappear into the mist in a moment. They pose no danger to us."

"They don't? What if they occupy Elderew?"

"Then we would build again. We have done so before. The land always offers the means to survive when you possess the magic."

His placid certainty was infuriating. He was a mirror image of the proverbial scholar who lived inside of his books and saw nothing of the world that was not printed there. It appeared that Abernathy's cynicism had some foundation in fact after all. Ben's mind raced, sorting through arguments and discarding them just as quickly. The River Master had obviously decided that he would not pledge to *any* King of Landover, and it did not seem that there was anything that could make him change his mind. Yet Ben knew that he must find a way.

A light clicked on inside his head. "What of the reason that you came to Landover in the first place, River Master? What of your work here?"

The chiseled face regarded him thoughtfully. "My work, High Lord?"

"Your work—the work that brought all of your people out of the fairy world and into Landover. What of that? You left paradise and timeless, immortal life to cross into a world with time and death. You accepted that you would be human. You did that because you wanted to cleanse Landover, to make her earth, trees, mountains, and waters healthy and safe! I don't know why you made that choice, but you did. Now you seem to be telling me that you have given up! You don't seem that sort of man to me. Are you willing to sit back and let the whole valley turn sick and wither away into nothing just to prove a point? Once the sickness spreads far enough and deep enough, how will you ever find the magic to drive it out!"

The River Master stared at him wordlessly, a small frown appearing, a hint of doubt in his eyes.

Ben charged quickly ahead. "If you pledge to me, I will put an end to the pollution of the waterways and the forests. I will stop the spread of the sickness—not just here, in the lake country, but throughout the valley."

"A noble ambition, High Lord." The River Master seemed almost sad. "How will you do that?"

"I will find a way."

"How? You lack even the small magic of the old King, the magic that gave him mastery over the Paladin. You wear the medallion—I see it beneath your tunic—but it is little more than a symbol of your office. High Lord, you are a King in name only. How can you do any of what you promise?"

Ben took a deep breath. The words stung, but he was careful to keep the anger from his voice. "I don't know. But I will find a way."

The River Master was silent a moment, lost in thought. Then he nodded slowly. His words were slow and carefully measured. "Very well, High Lord. Nothing is lost by letting you try. You make a promise I will hold you to. Put an end to the pollution. Put a stop to the spreading of the sickness. Extract a promise from the others who inhabit this valley that they will work with us to preserve the land. When you have done that, then I will give you my pledge."

He extended his hand. "A bargain, High Lord?"

Ben gripped the hand firmly in his own. "A bargain, River Master."

They shook. The sound of the children's laughter rang softly in the distance. Ben sighed inwardly. Another conditional pledge extracted. He was a man building a house of cards.

He gave the River Master his best courtroom smile. "You wouldn't happen to know a way to keep the dragon out of the Greensward, would you?"

ELDEREW

The River Master did not know a way to keep the dragon out of the Greensward. No one did, so far as he knew. Nightshade might, he speculated as he guided Ben back through the grove of elm and into the park with its children. The witch of the Deep Fell had magic more powerful than that of any other creature in the valley—although even Nightshade had never dared offer challenge to Strabo. In any case, Nightshade would never agree to help him, even if she had the means to do so. She had always hated the Kings of Landover because they commanded the services of the Paladin, and the Paladin was more powerful than she.

Times change, Ben thought dismally.

There were the fairies, of course, the River Master added almost as an afterthought. The fairies had always been able to control the dragons. That was why the dragons had fled from or been driven out of their world and come over into the valley. But the fairies would not help Ben either. The fairies helped no one, unless it was their idea first. They stayed within the mists, hidden in their timeless, ageless world, and lived their own lives according to their own rules. Ben could not even go to them to ask their help. No one ever went into the fairy world and came out again.

They walked down together through Elderew, the River Master describing the history of his city and its people, Ben wondering how on God's green earth—or this one, for that matter—he was ever going to make a success out of being King. The afternoon slipped away; while the city was a marvelous and exciting creation, the tour was wasted on Ben. He listened dutifully, commented in all of the appropriate places, asked the proper questions, and waited with a saint's patience for a chance to excuse himself.

The chance never came. Dusk settled, and the River Master deposited him at his lodging for the night—a ground-level cottage with several open-air porches and walkups, secluded gardens and an impressive stand of Bonnie Blues. Overhead, the brightly lighted treelanes of the city spiraled through the mist of the forest roof in arcs of hazy gold. Laughter and light banter echoed through the shadows. For some, the day's work was finished.

Ben trooped into the cottage, the daylight fading quickly to nightfall behind him, the River Master's promise of an evening of celebration hanging over him like a pall. The last thing he felt like doing was celebrating.

The others of the little company were waiting for him as he entered. He gave them a cursory hello and plopped down in a comfortably cushioned wicker rocker.

"I struck out again," he announced wearily.

Questor took a seat across from him. "He refused his pledge, High Lord?"

"More or less. He promised to give it only after I've found a way to put a stop to the pollution of the valley by the others who live here. I have to extract their sworn vow to work with the lake country people to keep the valley clean."

"I warned you he would be difficult, High Lord," Abernathy declared triumphantly. Ben glanced over. He remembered his scribe's admonishment somewhat differently, but there was nothing to be gained by arguing the point.

"I think you have done rather well, High Lord," Questor informed him, ignoring Abernathy.

Ben groaned. "Questor, please . . ."

"I am quite serious about this, I assure you," the wizard added quickly. "I was worried he would refuse you unconditionally. He was loyal to the old King out of a sense of respect for a monarchy that had governed hundreds of years and out of a desire not to provoke trouble by refusing obeisance. But the lake country people have never truly had a sense of belonging; there has never been an acceptance of them by the others."

"The River Master said something along those same lines. Why is it such a problem?"

Questor shook his head. "Mostly, it is a lack of understanding. The people of the lake country are fairies and they command magic the others in the valley do not and never will. The people of the lake country chose self-exile from a world viewed by most as perfect, a world that is timeless and changeless, a world where one can be immortal. The people of the lake country live differently from the others, and their conception of life's priorities is different. All of that breeds mistrust, jealousy, envy—a lot of very destructive emotions."

"There is another side to the story, of course," Abernathy interjected from behind Questor. "The people of the lake country have always had difficulty associating with the others of Landover. They remain aloof for the most part, arguing that their values should be imposed while they as a people remain apart.

They rail against the others for spreading sickness and blight through poor management of the land and waters, yet they stay hidden within their mist and forest."

Ben frowned. "Is the pollution they complain about really that bad?"

Questor shrugged. "Bad enough. The Lords of the Greensward strip the land for their fields and livestock and hunt the forests for food. The trolls mine the mountains north for ores and their smelts poison the streams that feed the valley. Others contribute their share as well."

"It is difficult to accommodate everyone, High Lord," Abernathy added quietly, eyes blinking thoughtfully beneath his shaggy brows.

"Words of wisdom." Ben found himself thinking suddenly of the life he had left behind him in Chicago. "The more things change, the more things stay the same," he muttered.

Questor and Abernathy looked at each other. "High Lord?" Questor asked.

Ben rose, stretched and shook his head. "Forget it. How soon do tonight's festivities commence?"

"Quite soon, High Lord," the wizard replied.

"A bath, High Lord?" Abernathy asked quickly. "A change of clothes?"

"Both. And some ideas, if anyone has any, on how we can go about pleasing everyone long enough to persuade them all to acknowledge the damn throne!"

Bunion and Parsnip hissed and grinned eagerly from across the room. Ben gave them a dark look, started from the room, then stopped. "You know, I wouldn't mind tonight so much if I thought I could find a way to change the River Master's mind—but I don't see it happening." He paused, considering. "Still, how much time do I have to work with?"

"These celebrations usually last all night, High Lord," Questor replied.

Ben sighed wearily. "Terrific," he muttered and left the room.

Questor's prediction proved to be right on target. The celebration began shortly after sunset and lasted until dawn. It was ostensibly held in honor of Landover's visiting High Lord, but Ben was left with the distinct impression that the people of the lake country would have been willing to hold a celebration for almost any reason. Certainly neither pace nor order, orchestration nor duration, was in any way dictated by him.

The festivities began with a processional. Ben was seated in the amphitheater with the members of his little company, the River Master and his family, Willow among them, and several hundred others, as children and young people with torches and colored banners streamed through the open quarter section and circled the arena in a kaleidoscope of color and light, singing songs as they came. Concentric circles formed and turned slowly about one another, and the cheers and shouts of the people gathered lifted in appreciation. Music from flutes, horns, stringed instruments, and pipes rose from a band of players gathered directly below where Ben sat. The music was high and lilting, whisking the processional along, increasing its tempo as the minutes slipped past.

Soon the broad concentric circles dissolved into smaller wheels, and the marchers became dancers who spun and whirled in the grasses, torches and banners fluttering above them as the music quickened. Wine and ale passed freely about the arena and the amphitheater seats above, and all joined in the clapping and singing. The sound rose to echo through the great forest trees of Elderew, filling the night until no other sound could be heard. Mist dissipated and the moons of Landover filled the skies, bright spheres of color that hung suspended like oversized balloons. Streamers of rainbow light filtered down through the trees to mingle with the fire of the torches and cast back the shadows.

Ben quickly gave up looking for an opportunity to talk further with the River Master about pledging to the throne. No one was interested in doing anything except having a good time. The singing and shouting drowned out all efforts at normal conversation, and the wine was consumed with a speed he found astonishing. He accepted a glass warily and as a courtesy and found it quite good. He drank another—because what the hell difference did it make?—then several more; in no time at all, he was three sheets to the wind and having one hell of a good time. Questor and the kobolds drank with him, seemingly as relaxed as he, and only Abernathy abstained, muttering something about wine not being good for animals. Soon they were all singing and clapping, and it didn't really matter what the singing and the clapping was for.

The River Master seemed pleased that Ben was having such a good time. He came over often, his chiseled, expressionless face flushed and dark eyes bright, welcoming Ben once again to Elderew, wishing him well, asking him if there was anything he might need. Ben was tempted to give him the obvious answer, but held his tongue. The River Master clearly meant well, and the merriment was infectious. He had not enjoyed himself this much since long before he had come into this strange land.

The night slipped on, the festivities grew heightened, and the people in the amphitheater seats began to pour down into the arena to mingle with those who had made up the processional. The singing and dancing became more frenzied, the fairies of the lake country flitting through the shadows and light as if they were yet the magical people they had once been. The River Master took the hand of one of his several wives, a slender river sprite, and pulled her after him toward the field. He called to Ben and the others, to the members of his family, and to his people to join him. Most went. Ben rose, hesitated, looked back to where Willow had been seated, found her gone, and sat down again. What was he thinking? What cause had he to celebrate? The wine's effects wore off with astonishing swiftness as he faced the unpleasant truths of his efforts at Kingship, and he lost his taste for celebrating.

He rose again, still unsteady, excused himself hastily to the others, and hurried toward the closest amphitheater exit. Abernathy came after him, but he sent the scribe scurrying with a sharp admonishment. Sprites, nymphs, kelpies, naiads, and pixies milled past him, dancing and singing, caught up in the spirit of the celebration. Ben brushed quickly past them. He had had enough of people for one day, and he wanted to be alone.

Shadows closed about him in the tunnel beneath, and then he was back in the forest. Lights winked from the treelanes overhead, and the sounds of the celebration began to diminish. He pushed ahead into the dark, anxious to be returned to his lodging and to be away from the festivities he had abandoned. His stomach churned with the wine, and suddenly he was sick at the pathside. He straightened, waited for his head and stomach to clear, and went on. When he reached the cottage, he climbed the walkway to an open-air side porch and slumped down in a high-backed wicker chair.

"Aren't you wonderful?" he congratulated himself.

He felt depressed and discouraged. He had believed so strongly in himself in the beginning. He knew he could be King of Landover. He possessed intelligence and ability, he was compassionate, he had experience working with people, and he understood the application of laws in society. Most important of all, he needed this challenge and he had thought himself ready for it. But all of that seemed to count for nothing in the greater scheme of things. His progress toward gaining even the minimal amount of recognition a King required had met with no success whatsoever—just a lot of conditional bargains. The old King's closest allies had rebuffed him; the others had ignored him. He had lost the services of the King's protector, now become something very much akin to a ghost haunting a deserted house, and the Mark and his demons were footsteps creeping up on him with the passing of each day.

He stretched and stared out into the night. Well, what the hell? he thought obstinately. Nothing at stake here but his self-respect, was there? All he had to do was use the medallion and he'd go back to Chicago, a million dollars lighter, but safe and sound. He had failed before at things, and he would undoubtedly fail again. Face it—this might be one of the failures.

He played with the idea in his mind a moment, then found himself thinking of the faces of those few who had come to his coronation, the farmers and their families, the hunters, the ones who still looked for a King they might believe in. Too bad for them, of course, he thought, wondering even as he did so how he could be so damn flip.

"So maybe you're not so wonderful after all," he muttered wearily.

Something moved in the shadow of the trees close beside the porch, and he jerked about.

"Ben?"

It was Willow. She slipped from the trees and came toward him, a ghostly figure in white silk, her green hair shimmering in the light. She was like a bit of moonlit mist crossing a midnight lake, ephemeral but impossibly beautiful. She came up to him, the silk hanging close against her body.

"I followed you, Ben," she told him softly, but with no apology in her voice. "I knew you would tire and come to sleep. But do not sleep yet. Come first with me. Come with me and watch my mother dance."

He felt his throat tighten as she neared him. "Your mother?"

"She is a wood nymph, Ben—so wild that she will not live among the people of Elderew. My father has never been able to bring her to him. But the music will draw her and she will yearn to dance. She will come to the old pines and she will look for me. Come, Ben. I want you there."

She came onto the porch, reached down for his hand and stopped. "Oh, your face! You have been hurt!" He had almost forgotten the beating Kallendbor had administered. Her hand touched his forehead softly. "I did not see your injuries at the Irrylyn. Here."

She swept her fingers swiftly about his face and at once the pain was gone. He could not hide the astonishment in his eyes.

"The small hurts can be healed, Ben," she whispered. "The ones that can be seen."

"Willow . . ." he began.

"I will not ask you to come away with me again—not until you are ready." Her fingers lingered on his cheek, warm and gentle. "I know who you are now. I know you to be of another world and not yet at peace with ours. I will wait."

He shook his head. "Willow . . ."

"Come, Ben!" She grasped his hand firmly and pulled him from the chair. "Come, hurry!" She led him from the porch and into the trees. "My mother will not wait!"

Ben no longer thought to resist. They ran into the forest, she a vision of something he had not believed could exist and he the shadow she drew after her. They darted through the trees, his hand in hers, and soon he was hopelessly lost and did not care. The heat of her touch burned through him, and the need for her began to grow anew within him.

They slowed after a time, deep in a woods become misted and shadowed far beyond that of Elderew. The sounds of the celebration still echoed through the trees, but distant and soft. Colored slivers of moonlight slipped downward from the forest roof and dappled the earth like paint spots. Willow held

Ben's hand tightly in her own, the warmth of her like a fire that drew him. The mane of hair from her forearm brushed against his wrist like corn silk. She crept now through the trees and brush, soundlessly skirting the giant sentinels and their offspring, a bit of fragmented night.

Then the hardwood trees gave way to pine, evergreens that were giant and aged. Willow and Ben pushed through their needled boughs, and a clearing opened before them.

There Willow's mother danced in a prism of colored moonlight.

She was a tiny thing, barely larger than a child, her features delicate and fine. Silver hair hung below her waist, and the skin of her slender body and limbs was pale green, like her daughter's. She was clothed all in white gauze, and a radiance emanated from her that seemed born of some self-generated inner light. Spinning and leaping as if she were driven by a madness peculiar to her alone, she danced through the moonlit clearing to the rhythm of the distant music.

"Mother!" Willow breathed softly, and there was excitement and happiness reflected in her eyes.

The wood nymph's eyes met her own for just an instant, but she did not slow her dance. Willow knelt wordlessly at the clearing's edge, pulling Ben down gently beside her. Together they sat in silence and watched the phantasm before them do magic.

How long she danced and how long they watched, Ben did not know. Time seemed to come to a standstill in that clearing. All that had troubled him on his return from the amphitheater lost significance and was forgotten. There was only Willow and he and the lady who danced. He felt them made one by the grace and beauty of that dance. He felt them bond in a way he did not understand, but desperately needed. He felt the bonding take place, and he did not resist.

Then the dance was finished. There was a sudden stillness, a hush, and it seemed that the music had ceased to play. Willow's mother turned for a fleeting moment to view them and was gone. Ben stared, hearing again the music of the celebration. But the wood nymph had disappeared as if she had never been.

"Oh, Mother!" Willow whispered, and she was crying. "She is so beautiful, Ben. Isn't she beautiful?"

Ben nodded, feeling her small hand grasping his own. "She is very beautiful, Willow."

The sylph rose, drawing him up with her. "Ben," she spoke his name so softly he almost missed it. "I belong to you now. High Lord and the daughter of fairies, we shall be one. You must ask my father to allow me to go with you when you leave. You must tell him that I am needed—for I truly am, Ben—and when you have told him that, he will let me go."

Ben shook his head quickly. "Willow, I cannot ask for . . ."

"You are the High Lord, and your request cannot be refused." She hushed him, a finger resting on his lips. "I am but one of my father's many children, one whose mother will not even live with the man she lay with to give me birth, one whose favor in her father's eyes varies with his moods. But you must ask for me, Ben."

Annie's face flashed in his mind, a counterpoint to the fire that this girl kindled within his body. "I can't do that."

"You do not understand the magic of the fairy people, Ben. I see that in your eyes; I hear it in your voice. But Landover *is* the heart of that magic, and you must accept what that means."

She released his hand and stepped softly away. "I must go now. I must nourish in the soil that my mother has graced. Leave me, Ben. Go back through the forest; the way will open up to you."

"No, wait, Willow . . ."

"Ask for me, Ben. My father must give me up." Her delicate face lifted to the colored streamers of moonlight that bathed the clearing. "Oh, Ben, it is as if my mother were all about me, wrapping me close, drawing me to her. I can feel her still. The essence of her reaches to me from the soil. This night I can be with her. Leave now, Ben. Hurry away."

But he stood rooted before her, stubbornly refusing to do as she asked. Why was she insisting that she belonged to him? Why couldn't she see that what she was seeking was impossible?

She spun in the clearing's center, beautiful, sensuous, delicate. He wanted her so badly in that instant that tears came to his eyes.

"Willow!" he cried out, starting forward.

She came out of her spin and faced him, feet planted firmly in the clearing's earth, arms raised skyward, face lifted. Ben stopped. A sudden radiance began to emanate from the sylph, the same radiance that her mother had given off while dancing. Willow shimmered, turned transparent in the light and began to swell and distort. Ben shielded his eyes, dropping to one knee in shock. Willow was changing before him, turning into something different entirely, arms and legs darkening and turning gnarled, sweeping outward like a canopy, splitting and lengthening . . .

He blinked, and Willow was gone. A tree had taken her place. It was the tree from which she took her name. She had become that tree.

Ben stared. He felt a wave of shock and repulsion wash through him. He fought to deny it, but it would not give way. She had said she would nourish in the soil. She had said she could feel her mother reaching up to her. My God, what manner of being was she?

He waited for the answer to come to him, a solitary figure in the mist and shadows of the forest. He waited, but the answer would not come.

He might have waited there all night if Bunion had not appeared, stepping suddenly from the trees to take his arm and lead him away like a disobedient child. He went with the kobold without argument, too stunned to do anything else. Conflicting emotions raged through him, battering him. Willow was so beautiful and vibrant, and the need for her within him was impossibly strong. Yet at the same time he was repulsed by her, a creature who gave every appearance of being amorphous, who could become a tree as easily as a human.

He did not look back as he left the clearing; he could not bear to. He was too ashamed of what he was feeling. He pushed his way through the ancient pines, trailing after Bunion in silence. The kobold must have followed after him, he realized. Questor or Abernathy must have sent him. They were taking no chances after his disappearance at the Irrylyn.

He wished suddenly that they had not found him that night. He wished that he had disappeared. He wished a thousand other things that might have happened and now never would.

The journey back was a short one. The others were waiting for him at the cottage, anxious looks on their faces. They sat him down and gathered around him.

"You should have told us of the sylph, High Lord," Questor said quietly, after exchanging a few brief words with Bunion. "We could have warned you what to expect."

"I warned him once already that the people of the lake country were not like us," Abernathy advised, and Ben didn't know whether to laugh or cry. Questor hushed the scribe quickly.

"You have to understand something, High Lord," the wizard went on, turning back to Ben. "Willow is the child of a sprite and a wood nymph. Her father is only half human. Her mother is less so, more a part of the forest than a part of man, an elemental who finds life within the soil. Something of that was passed on to Willow at birth, and she requires the same nourishment. She is a changeling; she owes her life to both plant and animal forms. It is natural for her to take the form of each; she could be no other way. But it must seem strange, I know, to you."

Ben shook his head slowly, feeling some of the conflict within dissipate. "No stranger than anything else that's happened, I guess." He felt sick at heart and weary; he needed to sleep.

Questor hesitated. "She must care deeply for you."

Ben nodded, remembering. "She said that she belongs to me."

Questor glanced quickly at Abernathy and away again. The kobolds stared at Ben with bright, questioning eyes. Ben stared back.

"But she doesn't," he said finally. "She belongs to the lake country. She belongs to her family and to her people."

Abernathy muttered something unintelligible and turned away. Questor said nothing at all. Ben studied them wordlessly a moment, then climbed to his feet. "I'm going to bed," he announced.

He started from the room, and their eyes followed after him. Then he stopped momentarily at the doorway to his bedroom. "We're going home," he told them and waited. "Tomorrow, at first light."

No one said anything. He closed the door behind him and stood alone in the dark.

G'HOME GNOME

They left Elderew the next morning shortly after daybreak. Mist hung across the lake country like a shroud, and the dawn air was damp and still. It was the kind of day in which ghosts and goblins came to life. The River Master was there to see them off and looked to be neither. Questor had summoned him, and he appeared without complaint. He could not have slept, for the festivities had barely ended, but he looked fresh and alert. Ben extended his thanks on behalf of the company for the hospitality they had been shown, and the River Master, his grainy, chiseled face still as expressionless as flat stone, bowed briefly in acknowledgment. Ben glanced about several times for Willow, but she was nowhere to be seen. He considered again her request that she be allowed to accompany him back to Sterling Silver. Part of him wanted her with him; part of him would not allow it. Indecision gave way to expediency; time ran out on the debate. He left without speaking of it to her father.

The company rode north for the remainder of the day, passing out of the lake country and its mists into the gray, open expanse of the western end of the Greensward and from there to the forested hills surrounding Sterling Silver. Sunlight barely pierced a clouded sky that stretched above them the whole of the journey back, and there was the smell of rain in the air. It was nightfall when they stepped once more from the lake skimmer and walked the final few yards to the gates of the castle. A smattering of raindrops was just beginning to fall.

It rained all that night. The rain was steady and hard and it blotted out the entire world beyond the immediate walls. That was perfectly all right with Ben. He fished out the bottle of Glenlivet he had been saving for a special occasion, gathered Questor, Abernathy, and the two kobolds at the table in the dining hall, and proceeded to get roaring drunk. He got drunk alone. The other four sipped gingerly from their tumblers as he consumed nearly the whole of the bottle by himself. He talked to them as he drank about life in his world, about Chicago and its people, about his friends and family, about anything and everything but Landover. They responded politely, but he had no memory later of what they said and frankly didn't care. When the scotch was gone and there was no longer anything left to talk about, he rose to his feet and stumbled off to bed.

Questor and Abernathy were both at his bedside when he awoke the next morning. He felt like hell. It was still raining.

"Good morning, High Lord," they greeted together, faces somber. They had the look of pallbearers at a funeral.

"Come back when I'm dead," he ordered, rolled over and went back to sleep.

He came awake a second time at noon. This time there was no one there. The rain had stopped, and the sun was sending a few faint streamers of light earthward through a veil of mist. Ben pushed himself into a sitting position and stared into space. His head throbbed and his mouth tasted of cotton. He was so angry with himself that he could barely keep from screaming.

He washed, dressed and trooped down the castle stairs to the great hall. He took his time, studying the stone walls, the tarnished silver trappings, the worn tapestries and drapes. He felt the warmth of the castle reaching out to him, a comforting mother's touch. It had been a long time since he had felt that touch. His hands brushed the stone in response.

Questor, Abernathy, and the kobolds were all gathered in the great hall, engaged in various make-work tasks. All looked up quickly as he entered. Ben came up to them and stopped.

"I'm sorry about last night," he apologized immediately. "I guess that was just something that I had to get out of my system. I hope you all rested well, because we have a great deal of work to do."

Questor glanced at the others, then back to Ben. "Where are we going now, High Lord?" he asked.

Ben smiled. "We're going to school, Questor."

The lessons began that afternoon. Ben was the student; Questor, Abernathy, Bunion, and Parsnip were his teachers. Ben had thought it all through—much of it in fits and starts while in various stages of inebriation and repentance—but carefully. He had spent most of his time since his arrival in Landover running about pointlessly. Questor might argue that the visits to the Greensward and Elderew had served a good purpose—and perhaps they had. But the bottom line was that he was floundering. He was a stranger in a land he had never dreamed could exist. He was trying to govern countries he had not even seen. He was trying to bargain with rulers and headmen he knew nothing about. However competent, hard-working, and well-intentioned he might be, he could not expect to assimilate as rapidly as he was trying to. There were lessons to be learned, and it was time that he learned them.

He began with Sterling Silver. He took the remainder of the afternoon and toured the castle from cellar to turret, Questor and Abernathy at his side. He had the scribe relate the history of the castle and her Kings from as far back as his records and memory would record. He had the wizard fill in the gaps. He learned everything he could of what had transpired in and about those halls and chambers, towers and parapets, grounds and lakes. He used eyes and nose and touch to ingest her life, and he made himself feel as one with her.

He ate dinner late that night in the great hall and spent the dinner hour and two hours after with Parsnip learning to recognize the consumables and poisons of the valley. Questor stayed with him, interpreting everything Parsnip said.

The next day he used the Landsview. He took Questor with him the first several times out, traversing the valley from one end to the other, studying the geography, the provinces, the towns, the fortresses and castles, and the people who inhabited them all. By midafternoon, he was making the trip alone, feeling more comfortable with the magic, learning to expand the vast range of the Landsview to suit his needs, and replaying in his mind the bits and pieces of information imparted to him by the wizard.

He went out by Landsview again the following day, and each day after that, his attention focused now on the history of the valley, matching events with places and people. Questor was his teacher once again, and the wizard proved infinitely patient. It was difficult for Ben to match dates and times to places and things where he had so little previous background in either. Questor was forced to repeat the lessons over and over. But Ben had a good memory and he was determined. By the end of the first week of lessons, he had a decent working knowledge of Landover.

He engaged in outings closer to Sterling Silver as well, journeys made afoot and not through the magic of the Landsview. Bunion was his guide and mentor on these excursions. The kobold took him from the valley into the forests and hills about the castle to study more closely the life forms that inhabited the region. They tracked down a timber wolf, hunted to his lair a cave wight, and uncovered a pair of bog wumps. They unearthed tunnel rats, snakes, and reptiles of various forms, treed a variety of cats, and spied upon the distant, rock-sheltered eyries of hunting birds. They studied the plant life. Questor went with them on the first outing to interpret; after that, he was left behind. Ben and the kobold found that they could communicate well enough on their own.

Ten days later, Ben used the Landsview to seek out Strabo. He went alone. He intended this outing to be a measure of his progress in learning to control the magic. He had thought at first to seek out Willow, but it would be as if he were spying on her and he did not want that. So he settled on the dragon instead. The dragon terrified him, and he wanted to see how he could handle his fear. He searched most of the day before finding the monster engaged in devouring half a dozen cattle at the north end of the Greensward, gnawing and crunching on carcasses shredded and broken almost beyond recognition. The dragon seemed to sense his presence as he brought himself to within a dozen yards of the feast. The crusted snout raised and jagged, blackened teeth snapped at the air before him. Ben held his ground for a long five count, then pulled quickly away, satisfied.

He wanted to make a foray alone into the forests about Sterling Silver to test what he had learned from Bunion, but Questor put his foot down. They compromised on a daytime hike in which Bunion would trail and not interfere if Ben was not threatened. Ben trooped out at dawn, trooped back again at dusk and never saw Bunion once. He also never saw the cave wight and the tree adder that the kobold dispatched as they were about to make a meal of him. He consoled himself with the knowledge that, while he had seen neither of these, he had seen and avoided several bog wumps, wolves, other wights and reptiles, and a big cat, all of whom would have made a meal of him just as quickly.

Two weeks later, he could recite from memory recent history, geographical landmarks and routes to and from the same, consumables and poisons, the creatures inhabiting the valley, the workings of the social orders that dominated the major races, and the rules that any manual of basic survival in Landover would include. He was still working on the Landsview. He had not yet developed his confidence in its magic to undergo the final test that he had set for himself—a search for the witch Nightshade in the hollows of the Deep Fell. Nightshade never ventured out of the oppressively dark confines of the Deep Fell, and he did not yet trust himself to attempt an intrusion.

He was still wrestling with his uncertainty when a more immediate problem appeared at the castle gates.

"You have visitors, High Lord," Abernathy announced.

Ben was bent over a worktable in one of the lower sitting rooms, perusing ancient maps of the valley. He looked up in surprise, seeing first the scribe and then Questor a few discreet steps behind him.

"Visitors?" he repeated.

"Gnomes, High Lord," Questor advised him.

"G'home Gnomes," Abernathy added, and there was a hint of disdain in his voice.

Ben stared at them. He shoved back the maps. "What in the world are G'home Gnomes?" His lessons with Questor had never gotten this far.

"A rather pathetic species of gnome, I am afraid," Questor replied.

"A rather worthless species, you mean," Abernathy corrected coldly.

"That is not necessarily so."

"It is definitely so."

"I am sorry to say that you reflect only your own prejudices, Abernathy."

"I reflect a well-reasoned opinion, Questor Thews."

"What is this—Laurel and Hardy?" Ben broke in. They stared back at him blankly. "Never mind," he told them, impatiently brushing the reference aside with a wave of one hand. "Just tell me what G'home Gnomes are."

"They are a tribe of gnomes living in the foothills north below the high peaks of Melchor," Questor answered, his owlish face shoving forward past Abernathy. "They are burrow people; they inhabit tunnels and dens they dig out of the earth. Most of the time they stay in the ground . . ."

"Where they ought to stay," Abernathy interjected.

". . . but now and again they forage the surrounding countryside." He gave Abernathy a withering glance. "Do you mind?" His eyes shifted back to Ben. "They are not well liked. They tend to appropriate things that do not belong to them and give back nothing in exchange. Their burrowing can be a nuisance when it encroaches on pastureland or grain fields. They are extremely territorial and, once settled in, will not move. It doesn't matter who owns the land they have settled on—once there, they stay."

"You have not told him the worst!" Abernathy insisted.

"Why not tell him yourself," Questor huffed, stepping back.

"They eat dogs, High Lord!" Abernathy snapped, unable to contain himself any longer. His muzzle drew back to reveal his teeth. "They are cannibals!"

"Unfortunately, true." Questor shoved forward once more, crowding Abernathy aside with his shoulder. "They eat cats as well, however, and I have never heard you complain about that!"

Ben grimaced. "Terrific. What about the name?"

"An abbreviation, High Lord," Questor said. "The gnomes became so vexatious with their burrowing and their thieving that everyone began to express openly their wish that they would simply 'go home' to wherever it was they had come from. After a while, the admonishment 'go home, gnomes' became the nickname by which they were known—G'home Gnomes."

Ben shook his head in disbelief. "Now there's a story right out of the brothers Grimm. The G'home Gnomes. Well, what brings these gnomes to us?"

"They will speak of that only with you, High Lord. Will you see them?"

Abernathy looked very much as if he wanted to bite Questor, but he managed to refrain from doing so, his shaggy muzzle frozen in a half-snarl. Questor rocked back on his heels, cyes fixed on Ben expectantly.

"The royal appointment calendar isn't exactly bulging at the seams," Ben answered, looking first at Abernathy, then at Questor. "I can't see where meeting someone who has taken the trouble to come all this way can hurt anything."

"I trust you will remember later that it was you who said that, High Lord." Abernathy sniffed. "There are two of them waiting. Shall I show both in?"

Ben had to fight to keep from grinning. "Please do."

Abernathy left and was back a few moments later with the G'home Gnomes.

"Fillip and Sot, High Lord," Abernathy announced, teeth showing.

The gnomes came forward and bowed so low their heads touched the castle stone. They were the most miserable-looking creatures Ben had ever seen. They were barely four feet tall, their bodies stout and covered with hair, their faces ferretlike and bearded from neck to nose. They wore clothes that the lowliest bum would have refused, and they looked as if they hadn't bathed since birth. Dust coated their bodies and clothing; dirt and grime were caked in the seams of their skin and under fingernails that looked dangerously diseased. Tiny, pointed ears jutted from either side of skull caps with red feathers stuck in the bands, and toes with curled nails peeked out from the ends of ruined boots.

"Great High Lord," one addressed him.

"Mighty High Lord," the other added.

They took their heads off the floor and faced him, eyes squinting. They looked like moles come to the surface for a glimpse of daylight.

"I am Fillip," one said.

"I am Sot," the other said.

"We have come to offer our pledge of fealty to the High Lord of Landover on behalf of all of the G'home Gnomes," Fillip said.

"We have come to offer felicitations," Sot said.

"We wish you long life and health," Fillip said.

"We wish you many children," Sot said.

"We extend to you our skills and our experience to be used in whatever manner you may choose," Fillip said.

"We extend to you our services," Sot said.

"But first we have a small problem," Fillip said.

"We do," Sot agreed.

They waited, their presentation apparently finished. Ben wondered if they had simply run out of gas. "What sort of problem do you have?" he asked solicitously.

They glanced at each other. Sharp mole faces crinkled and tiny, pointed teeth showed liked daggers.

"Trolls," Fillip said.

"Crag Trolls," Sot said.

Again they waited. Ben cleared his throat. "What about them?" Whereas he had known nothing of the G'home Gnomes, he did know something of the Crag Trolls.

"They have taken our people," Fillip said.

"Not all of our people, but a rather substantial number," Sot corrected.

"They missed us," Fillip said.

"We were away," Sot said.

"They raided our burrows and dens, and they carried our people off with them," Fillip said.

"They seized everyone they found," Sot said.

"They took them to Melchor to work the mines and the furnaces," Fillip said.

"They took them to the fires," Sot grieved.

Ben was beginning to get the picture. The Crag Trolls were a rather primitive race of beings living in the mountains of Melchor. Their primary business was mining ores from the rock and converting them in their furnaces to weapons and armor which they sold to the other inhabitants of the valley. The Crag Trolls were a reclusive and unfriendly bunch, but they seldom provoked trouble with their neighbors and had never used slave labor.

He glanced past the gnomes to Questor and Abernathy. The wizard shrugged and the scribe gave him one of his patented 'I told you so' looks.

"Why did the Crag Trolls seize your people?" Ben asked the gnomes.

Fillip and Sot glanced at each other thoughtfully, then shook their heads.

"We do not know, great High Lord," Fillip said.

"We do not," Sot said.

They were without doubt the worst liars Ben had ever encountered. Nevertheless, he decided to be tactful. "Why do you *think* the Crag Trolls seized your people?" he pressed.

"That would be difficult to say," Fillip said.

"Very difficult," Sot agreed.

"There could be any number of reasons," Fillip said.

"Any number," Sot echoed.

"It is possible, I suppose, that in foraging we might have appropriated property which the trolls felt belonged to them," Fillip speculated.

"It is possible that we might have claimed property we believed abandoned but which, in truth, still belonged to them," Sot added.

"Mistakes of that sort sometimes do happen," Fillip said.

"Sometimes," Sot said.

Ben nodded. He didn't believe for a minute that any foraging from the Crag Trolls had been anything short of deliberate. The only mistake had been in the gnomes' belief that they could get away with it.

"If a mistake of this sort were to happen," Ben observed carefully, "wouldn't the Crag Trolls simply have asked for the missing property back?"

The gnomes looked decidedly uncomfortable. Neither said anything.

Ben frowned. "What sort of property might have been misappropriated, do you think?" he asked them.

Fillip glanced down at his boots, and the toes wriggled uneasily. Sot's ferret features twisted about and looked as if they might like to disappear into his fur.

"The trolls like to keep pets," Fillip said finally.

"The trolls are very fond of pets," Sot added.

"They like the furry tree sloths most of all," Fillip said.

"They give them to their children to play with," Sot said.

"How can one tell wild furry tree sloths from pet furry tree sloths?" Fillip queried.

"How can one know which is which?" Sot queried.

A terrible suspicion crossed Ben's mind. "You can always give back misappropriated pets, can't you?" he asked them.

"Not always," Fillip said, somehow managing to look mortified.

"No, not always," Sot agreed.

Ben caught a glimpse of Abernathy out of the corner of his eye. His scribe's hackles were raised up like the spikes of a cornered porcupine.

He looked back at the gnomes. "You ate those tree sloths, didn't you?" he demanded.

Neither said a word. They looked down at their boots. They looked aside at the walls. They looked everywhere but at Ben. Abernathy gave a low, menacing growl, and Questor hushed him into silence.

"Wait outside, please," Ben told the gnomes.

Fillip and Sot turned about quickly and scurried from the room, small rodent bodies swaying awkwardly with the movement. Fillip glanced back once as if he might say something more, then reconsidered and hurried out. Questor followed them to the door and closed it tightly behind them.

Ben looked at his aides. "Well, what do you think?"

Questor shrugged. "I think it is easier to catch and devour a tame furry tree sloth than a wild one."

"I think someone should eat a few of them and see how they like it!" Abernathy snapped.

"Would such a meal interest you?" Questor asked.

Ben stepped forward impatiently. "I'm not asking what you think about what they did. I'm asking what you think about helping them."

Abernathy was appalled. His ears flattened back and his glasses slipped askew on his nose. "I would sooner bed down with fleas, High Lord! I would sooner share lodgings with cats!"

"What about the fact that the trolls have forced these people into slavery?" Ben pressed.

"It seems clear to me that they brought it on themselves!" his scribe answered stiffly. "In any case, you have far more important concerns than the G'home Gnomes!"

Ben frowned. "Do I?"

"High Lord," Questor interrupted and stepped forward. "The Melchor is dangerous country and the Crag Trolls have never been the most loyal of the King's subjects. They are a tribal people, very primitive, very unreceptive to intervention from anyone not of their own country. The old King kept them in line primarily by staying out of their business. When he had to intervene, he did so with an army to stand behind him."

"And I have no army to stand behind me, do I?" Ben finished. "I don't even have the services of the Paladin."

"High Lord, the G'home Gnomes have been nothing but trouble for as long as anyone can remember!" Abernathy stepped over to join Questor. "They are a nuisance wherever they go! They are cannibals and thieves! Why would you even consider helping them in this dispute?"

Questor nodded in agreement. "Perhaps this kind of request is one best refused, High Lord."

"No, Questor," Ben replied at once. "This is exactly the kind of request that I cannot refuse." He looked at the wizard and the scribe in turn and shook his head. "You don't understand, do you? I came into Landover to be King. I cannot pick and choose when I will be King and over whom. I am King now and always and for everyone who needs me. That is the way it works with monarchies. I know that much from the history of my own world. A King must proclaim and administer the laws of the Kingdom fairly and equally to all of his subjects. There can be no favorites; there can be no exceptions. What I would do for the Lords of the Greensward and the sprites and nymphs of Elderew I must do for the G'home Gnomes. If I back away once, I set a precedent for doing so the next time and the time after that and so on any time it seems convenient."

"But you have no support in this, High Lord," Questor argued.

"Perhaps not. But if I am successful in helping the gnomes, then I might have that support the next time out. The gnomes have given their pledge, which is one pledge more than I had before they made the journey here. They deserve something for that. Maybe the others will pledge as well if they see that the throne can be of use even to the G'home Gnomes. Maybe they will reconsider their position."

"Maybe cows will fly over the castle," Abernathy grumbled.

"Maybe," Ben agreed. "I've seen stranger things since I arrived."

They stared at each other wordlessly for a moment.

"I do not care for this idea at all," Questor said, his owlish face lined with doubt.

"Nor I," Abernathy echoed.

"Then we agree," Ben concluded. "I don't like it either. But we are going anyway. We are going because that's what we have to do. School's out, as the saying goes. It's time to face life in the real world again. Now let's have the gnomes back in here."

Questor and Abernathy bowed in acknowledgment and left the room muttering to themselves.

The G'home Gnomes returned with protestations of good intent spilling forth. The furry tree sloths were a favorite food of their people, Fillip insisted. Yes, the furry tree sloths were quite delicious, Sot agreed. Ben cut them short. Their request would be granted, he told them. He would go with them to the Melchor to see what could be done to gain the release of those taken by the Crag Trolls. They would depart Sterling Silver at dawn. Fillip and Sot stared at him, then fell to their knees before him, groveling in a most disgusting manner. Ben had them removed at once.

He went up to the Landsview alone that evening after dinner. The gnomes had been sequestered in their rooms by Abernathy (who refused to trust them anywhere else in the castle), and the others were occupied with preparations for the journey north. Ben had time to use as he chose. He decided to take a quick peek into the lake country.

The night was misted and dark, no different from dozens of others, seven of Landover's brightly colored moons faintly visible over the line of the horizon, stars a distant sprinkling of street lights through a midnight fog. The Landsview took him instantly to the lake country, and he descended slowly into Elderew. The city was bright with torchlight atop treelanes and along roadways, and her people were still abroad. The sound of laughter and light conversation made him feel uneasy somehow—more an intruder than he already was. He slipped over the amphitheater, down across the city dwellings and shops, past the cottage that had been his lodging, and into the deep woods. He found the old pines where Willow's mother had danced. They were deserted. The tree into which Willow had transformed herself was gone. Willow was nowhere to be found.

He let himself remain in the deep woods for a time, thinking of Annie. He could not explain why, but he needed to think of her. He needed to be with her, too, but he knew that Annie was gone and it was pointless to dwell on it. He felt alone, a traveler come far from home and friends. He was adrift. He felt that he had cut himself off from everything, and that his reasons for doing so were proving to be poor ones. He needed someone to tell him that it would all work out, that he was doing the right thing, that there were better times ahead.

There was no one to do that, however. There was only himself.

Midnight came and went before Ben finally refocussed on Sterling Silver. He took his hands reluctantly from the railing of the Landsview and he was home again.

CRAG TROLLS

Morning followed night, as it always does, but Ben awoke questioning the assumption that it necessarily must. His mood was dark, and his nerves were on edge after a sleep troubled with a vicious and depressing dream of death and personal futility. There had been people dying in his dream; they had died all about him, and he had been powerless to save them. He had known none of them in his waking life, but they had seemed quite real in his sleep. They had seemed his friends. He had not wanted them to die, but he had been unable to prevent it. He had tried in desperation to come awake so that he could escape what was happening, but he could not. There had been in his sleep that frightening sense of timelessness that occurs when the subconscious suggests that waking will never come, that the only reality is in the dream. When his eyes finally slipped open, he saw the dawn filtering down, misted and gray, through the windows of his sleeping chamber. It had been misted and gray in the world of his dream, too—a twilight in which neither day nor night could seize upon the other.

He found himself wondering then if there were some worlds where morning could not follow night—where there was only the one or the other or a constant mix of both. He found himself wondering if, with the failing of the magic, Landover might not become one.

The prospect was too dark to contemplate, and he dismissed it with a flourish of activity. He rose, washed, dressed, finished gathering up his gear for the journey north, greeted Questor, Abernathy, Bunion, Parsnip, Fillip, and Sot at breakfast, ate, saw his possessions to the pack animals on the far side of the lake shore, mounted Wishbone, and gave the command to ride. He had been careful not to permit himself time to think back on the dream. It was nearly forgotten now, a fading memory better gone. Landover's King, with the members of his court and the G'home Gnomes in tow, sallied forth once more.

They journeyed north through the hill country all that day, traversing forested steeps, scrub-covered hollows and glens, and the shores of thicketed lakes. They passed west of the Greensward, east of the Deep Fell. The sun shone above them, veiled by clouds and mist, a fuzzy white ball of light that barely cast out night's shadows. The land they traveled looked wintry and ill. Leaves and brush were dark and spotted with wilt, grasses looked dried and burned as if by frost, and trees were blanketed with fungus that sapped away their juices. The land was growing sicker; its life was seeping away.

Strabo passed over the little company toward evening. The dragon appeared from out of the west, a massive winged shadow darker than the skies he flew. The G'home Gnomes saw him at the same moment and together scrambled from the back of the horse they shared and disappeared into the brush. The remainder of the company watched in silence as the dragon passed east. It took fifteen minutes after he was gone for Ben and his companions to persuade the gnomes to surface from their hiding place and continue the journey.

They camped that night in a glen sheltered by apple trees and clumps of birch. The light disappeared quickly in the dusk, and they ate their evening meal in darkness. No one had much of anything to say. Everyone seemed preoccupied with his own thoughts. They finished eating and went directly to sleep.

The following day was much the same as the first—gray, misted, and unfriendly. They crossed from the borders of the Greensward into the foothills leading upward to the Melchor. The mists of the fairy world which rimmed the valley seemed to have drifted far down across the shoulders of the Melchor, forming a mantle of gray that obscured everything. They rode toward it and then into it. It was past midday when they were swallowed.

Bunion guided them ahead, sure-footed and unswerving, his eyes sharper than those of his companions. They followed a rock-strewn road that quickly became a pathway and then a narrow, rutted trail. Cliff walls and shadows closed about. They were within the Melchor. The light began to fail rapidly with the coming of dusk. They were forced to walk their horses now, the way forward too uncertain to risk a fall. Fillip and Sot clung to each other as the company pressed ahead, mumbling to themselves, their uneasiness apparent. Ben squinted through the mist and darkness, trying to see what lay beyond. He might as well have been peering through paint.

There was a growing sense of desperation in Ben Holiday. He had been struggling to deny it all day, but it was persistent and claimed him in the end. This expedition into the country of the Crag Trolls to secure the release of the captured G'home Gnomes was more important than he had been willing to admit. It was, quite possibly, his last chance. He had failed to gain the pledge of a single ally to the throne. He had failed to accomplish a single positive act since assuming the Kingship. If he failed again here—with these universally disdained and pitifully dependent gnomes—where would he go next? The word of his failure would travel quickly. No one else was likely to seek his help. He would become the play-King that the Lord Kallendbor had labeled him.

Night settled in. The way forward grew more uncertain and the pace slowed to a walk. There was thunder in the distance, a low rumbling punctuated by the sharp crack of lightning. A dull, reddish glow began to stain the darkness. Ben peered at the glow uncertainly. The thunder and lightning took on new tones, no longer the sounds of a storm approaching, but of something else.

Bunion brought the company to a halt. He exchanged a few words with Questor, and the wizard turned to Ben. The reddish glow was the fire of the troll furnaces. The thunder and lightning were the sounds of bellows being pumped and metal being forged.

Ben had Abernathy unfurl the King's banner and hoist it over them. The little company went forward.

Minutes later they crested a rise, the narrow trail broadened as the defile ended, and they found themselves poised at the entrance to Hell. At least, that was how it appeared to Ben. Hell was a valley surrounded by great, towering cliffs that disappeared into a ceiling of mist and darkness. Fires burned everywhere. They burned in monstrous rock kilns, the stone so hot that it glowed, in iron kettles, molten ore bubbling and steaming, in pits dug out of the rock and earth, flames licking at waste and fuel, and in iron stanchions set to give light to the valley perimeter and to aid in the keeping of the watch. The fires burned red, so that everything was bathed in crimson light. A narrow river wound its way through the valley basin, its waters the color of blood. Shadows flickered like chained beings across the cliffs and boulders, thrown against the stone by the flames. Squat houses of stone blocks and tiles lay scattered between the fires, and close beside them were the pens. The pens were formed of iron stakes and wire. The pens held living beings—livestock, but humans as well. The center pen contained a gathering of some fifty-odd gnomes, ragged, frightened-looking creatures, their ferret faces buried in bowls of food and pails of water. There were gnomes outside the pen as well, these engaged in feeding the fires. Backs bent, heads lowered, their furry bodies singed and blackened, they hauled fuel, fed raw ore, stoked the kilns, and hammered molten metal. They were the damned of the earth, sent to their eternal reward.

The trolls were there to see that this reward was properly bestowed. There were hundreds of them, dark, misshapen forms that slouched purposefully about the valley from fire to fire, some engaged in the work allotted, some engaged in directing its course. The trolls were sullen, heavy-limbed beings, their faces closed and virtually featureless, their bodies muscled and disproportionately fashioned. Limbs were long and rangy, heavier than the lean bodies. Torsos were bent at the spine, shoulders too broad for the ligaments and sinew that bound them, heads oblong and sunk down into chests matted with wiry hair. Their skin had the look of burned toast, an uneven cast that failed to reflect the fires' light but seemed only to absorb it. Gnarled, splayed feet gripped rock and earth with the sureness of a mountain goat's hooves.

Ben felt the air go out of his lungs as if it had been sucked away by the fires. Despite the suffocating heat that washed over him, he turned cold. Heads swung about and misshapen bodies lumbered forward. The little company had already been seen. Bright, yellowed eyes fixed on them as the Crag Trolls advanced.

"Dismount," Ben ordered quietly.

He climbed down, Questor and Abernathy beside him. Parsnip came forward to stand with Bunion, and the kobolds hissed in warning at the trolls, their teeth showing white against the fires' crimson light. Fillip and Sot cowered behind Ben, their small bodies pressed down close against his legs.

Two dozen Crag Trolls were in front of them almost immediately. They crowded to within several yards, slouched forms bumping mindlessly, yellow eyes decidedly unfriendly. A geyser of fire erupted from one of the waste pits in the valley behind them, exploding in a booming cough. Not a head turned.

"Show them the flag," Ben ordered Abernathy.

The scribe dropped the flag forward at an angle so that its insignia rolled clear of the folds. The trolls studied it without interest. Ben waited a moment, glanced briefly at Questor and stepped forward.

"I am Ben Holiday, High Lord of Landover!" he shouted. His voice reverberated from the rock walls and died. "Who is your headman?"

The trolls studied him. Not a one moved. There was a headman of this tribe; Ben knew that much from his studies with Questor. "Who speaks for you?" he demanded, keeping his voice steady and commanding.

Other Crag Trolls had joined the first gathering. They parted now, and a single troll slouched forward, a rugged, battered creature with a collar of silver studs. He spoke quickly, a tongue that Ben did not recognize.

"He wants to know what we are doing here, High Lord," Questor interpreted the response. "He sounds irritated."

"Does he understand what I'm saying?"

"I do not know, High Lord. Possibly."

"Speak to him in his own language, Questor. Tell him again who I am. Tell him that because he failed to attend the coronation when summoned I have come to see him instead, and that now he must give me his pledge."

"High Lord, I don't think . . ."

Ben's face was hard. "Tell him, Questor!"

Questor spoke briefly to the troll, and there was a rumble of discontent through the ranks of those gathered behind him. The troll lifted one arm and the rumble ceased. The troll said something more to Questor.

Questor turned to Ben. "He says that he knows nothing of any coronation, that there is no King of Landover and hasn't been since the old King died. He says that he will give his pledge to no one."

"Wonderful." Ben kept his eyes on the headman. Slowly he extracted the medallion from beneath his tunic and held it out where it could be seen. There was a murmur of recognition. The Crag Trolls glanced at one another and shuffled back uneasily. "Tell them I command the magic, Questor," Ben ordered. "And be ready to give them a show of proof if I call for it."

Questor's owlish face tightened sharply as he glanced at Ben, hesitating.

"Do it, Questor," Ben said softly.

Questor spoke again. The trolls mumbled among themselves, still shifting about. The headman looked confused. Ben waited. The heat from the fires washed over him; sweat soaked through his clothes. He could feel the faces of the G'home Gnomes pressed up against his pant legs, peering past them at the trolls. The seconds slipped by, and nothing happened. He knew he had to do something quickly or he would lose whatever small advantage he might have gained.

"Questor, tell the headman again that he must give his pledge to the throne. Tell him that he must give over to me as a show of good faith the G'home Gnomes he has taken so that they might serve me instead. Tell him he must do so immediately, that I have little time to waste on him, that I go next to the witch of the Deep Fell. Tell him not to challenge me."

"High Lord!" Questor breathed in disbelief.

"Tell him!"

"But what if he challenges you and I cannot summon the magic?"

"Then we fry in the fire with the gnomes, damn it!" Ben's face was flushed and angry.

"Caution, High Lord!" Abernathy warned suddenly, his muzzle shoving into view.

"The hell with being cautious!" Ben wheeled on him. "Bluff or no bluff, we have to try something . . . !"

Abernathy cut him short with a hiss of warning. "High Lord, I think he understands what you have both been saying!"

Ben froze. The headman was studying him, his yellow eyes suddenly cunning. He *had* understood everything; Ben knew it instantly. The troll gave a quick command to those behind him and they began to fan out about the little company.

"Use the magic, Questor," Ben whispered.

The wizard's face was gray with uncertainty. "High Lord, I do not know if I can!"

"If you don't, we are in big trouble!" Ben kept his eyes fixed on Questor's. "Use it!"

Questor hesitated, his tall, rainbow-colored form a statue against the fires and the night. Then abruptly he wheeled on the Crag Trolls, his arms lifting. The trolls shrieked. Questor's arms windmilled, words poured forth from his throat and the air exploded with light.

It began to rain flowers.

They showered down from out of nowhere—roses, peonies, violets, lilies, daisies, chrysanthemums, orchids, daffodils and every other kind of flower under the sun. They descended on the little company and the Crag Trolls in buckets, tumbling off them and bouncing to the ground.

It was difficult to decide who was the most surprised. It was certain that everyone had expected something else—including Questor, who made a valiant effort to recover after his initial shock, arms lifting a second time as he tried again to engage the magic. He was far too slow. The Crag Trolls had already recovered. They launched themselves at the members of the little company somewhat in the manner of linebackers in a full blitz. They looked monstrous. Ben shouted in warning to the others. He saw the kobolds leap up, heard them hiss, heard Abernathy's teeth snap, felt the gnomes Fillip and Sot grappling at him for protection, and smelled an instant's mix of charred ash and smoke.

Then the Crag Trolls piled into him. He was hammered back—thrown from his feet with the force of the rush. His head struck the hard earth, and the air before him exploded instantly into blinding light. Then everything went dark.

He came awake a prisoner in Dante's *Inferno.* He was chained to a post in the central holding pen, heavy bracelets and locks fastened to his wrists and ankles. He sat slumped against the post, the faces of dozens of furry gnomes peering at him through a haze of smoke. His head throbbed and his body was bathed in sweat and grime. The stench of the kilns and waste pits filled the air and made him instantly nauseous. The fires burned all about, crimson light falling like a mantle across the valley rock.

Ben blinked and turned his head slowly. Questor and Abernathy were chained to posts close by, awake and whispering together guardedly. The kobolds were trussed hand and foot by chains and bound to iron rings fixed to spikes driven into the stone floor. Neither appeared conscious. Crag Trolls patrolled the perimeter of the compound, their misshapen forms little more than shadows drifting silently through the night.

"Are you awake, High Lord?"

"Are you unhurt, High Lord?"

Fillip and Sot edged forward out of the sea of faces peering at him. Ferret eyes regarded him solicitously, squinting. Ben wanted nothing so badly at that instant as to break free long enough to throttle them both. He felt like the prize exhibit at the zoo. He felt like a freak. Most of all, he felt like a failure. It was their fault that he felt like that. It was because of them that he was here in the first place. Damn it, all of this had happened because of them!

But that wasn't true, and he knew it. He was here because it had been his choice to come, because this was where he had put himself.

"Are you all right, High Lord?" Fillip asked.

"Can you hear us, High Lord?" Sot asked.

Ben shoved his misplaced anger aside. "I can hear you. I'm all right. How long have I been unconscious?"

"Not long, High Lord," Fillip said.

"Not more than a few minutes," Sot said.

"They seized us all," Fillip said.

"They threw us into this pen," Sot said.

"No one escaped," Fillip said.

"No one," Sot echoed.

So tell me something I don't know, Ben thought bitterly. He glanced about the compound. They were caged by wire fences that were six foot high and barbed. The gates were of heavy wood lashed with chains. He tugged experimentally at the chains secured to his ankles and wrists. They were firmly locked and fixed in their rings. Escape was not going to be easy.

Escape? He laughed inwardly. What in the hell was he thinking about? How was he going to escape from this place?

"High Lord!" He turned at the sound of his name. Questor had discovered that he was awake. "Are you hurt, High Lord?"

He shook his head no. "How are you and Abernathy? And the kobolds?"

"Quite well, I think." The owlish face was black with soot. "Bunion and Parsnip got the worst of it, I am afraid. They fought very hard for you. It took more than a dozen trolls to subdue them."

The kobolds stirred in their chains, as if to substantiate the wizard's claim. Ben glanced at them a moment, then turned again to Questor. "What will they do to us?" he asked.

Questor shook his head. "I really do not know. Nothing very pleasant, I would think."

Ben could imagine. "Can you use the magic to free us?" he asked.

Questor shook his head once more. "The magic does not work when my hands are chained. It has no power when iron binds me." He hesitated a moment, his long face twisting. "High Lord, I am sorry that I have failed you so badly. I tried to do as you asked—to invoke the magic to aid us. It simply would not respond. I . . . cannot seem to master it . . . as I would wish." He stopped, his voice breaking.

"It's not your fault," Ben interjected quickly. "I'm the one who got us into this mess—not you."

"But I am the court wizard!" Questor insisted vehemently. "I should have magic enough at my command to deal with a handful of trolls!"

"And I should have brains enough to do the same! But it would appear that this time we both came up a bit short, so let's just forget it, Questor. Forget the whole business. Concentrate on finding a way out of this cattle yard!"

Questor Thews slumped back in dejection. He seemed broken by what had happened, no longer the confident guide that had brought Ben into the land. Even Abernathy made no response. Ben quit looking at them.

Fillip and Sot edged closer to where he was chained.

"I am thirsty," Fillip said.

"I am hungry," Sot said.

"How soon can we leave this place, High Lord?" Fillip asked.

"How soon?" Sot asked.

Ben stared at them in disbelief. How about the twelfth of never? How about next decade? Did they think that they were just going to walk out of here? He almost laughed. Apparently they did.

"Let me give it some thought," he suggested and smiled bravely.

He turned away from them and stared out over the pen yard. He found himself wishing he had brought some sort of weapon with him from the old world. A bazooka, maybe? A small tank, perhaps? Bitterness welled up within him. That was the trouble with hindsight, of course—it gave you perfect vision when it was too late to be of any use. It had never occurred to him when he had decided to come into Landover that he would ever have need of a weapon. It had never occurred to him that he would ever find himself in this sort of predicament.

He wondered suddenly why the Paladin had failed to appear when the trolls had come at him. Ghost or not, the Paladin had always appeared before when he was threatened. He would have welcomed an appearance on this occasion as well. He mulled the question over in his mind for a moment before deciding that the only difference between this time and the others was that this time he had failed to think about the medallion when threatened. But that seemed a tenuous link. After all, he had tried to summon the Paladin by willing his appearance when he was testing the medallion's power, and absolutely nothing had happened.

He sagged back against the holding post. The throbbing was beginning to ease in his head. Hell wasn't as bad as it had been five minutes ago. Before it had been intolerable; now it was almost bearable. He reflected momentarily on his life, dredging up all the bad things that had gone before to hold up in comparison to this. The comparison failed. He thought of Annie, and he wondered what she would say if she were alive to see him like this. Annie would probably have dealt with the situation much better than he; she had always been the more flexible, always the more resilient.

There were tears in his eyes. They had shared so much. She had been his one true friend. God, he wished he could see her just once more!

He brushed furtively at his eyes and straightened himself. He tried thinking of Miles, but all he could think about was Miles telling him "I told you so" over and over. He thought about his decision to come to Landover, to the fairy-tale Kingdom that couldn't exist. He thought about the world he had left to come here, about all of the little amenities and irritations he would never experience again. He began to catalogue the wishes and dreams that he would never see fulfilled.

Then he realized what he was doing. He was giving up on himself. He was writing himself off as dead.

He was immediately ashamed. The iron-hard determination that had carried him through so many fights reasserted itself swiftly. There would be no quitting, he swore. He would win this fight, too.

He smiled bitterly. He just wished he knew how.

Two familiar ferretlike faces shoved into view once more.

"Have you had enough time to think about it yet, High Lord?" Fillip asked.

"Yes, have you decided when we will leave, High Lord?" Sot asked.

Ben sighed. "I'm working on it," he assured them.

The hours slipped away. Midnight passed, and the Crag Trolls began to shuffle off to bed. A few stayed on duty to tend the kilns and watchfires, but the rest disappeared into their stone huts. Questor and Abernathy dropped off to sleep. Most of the G'home Gnomes joined them. Fillip and Sot curled up at his feet. Only the kobolds remained awake with Ben. They lay on their sides, unable to get to a sitting position, their narrow eyes fixed on him watchfully, their white teeth showing through those maddening grins. Ben smiled back at them once or twice. They were tough little creatures. He admired them and he regretted getting them into this mess. He regretted getting them all into this mess.

It was nearing morning when he felt a hand lightly touch his face. He had been dozing, and he came awake with a start. Mist and smoke hung like a pall across the valley floor. Shadows cast by the fires chased one another through the haze, red and black wraiths. There was a chill in the air; the fires burned low.

"Ben?"

He looked around and Willow was there. She was crouched directly behind him, huddled close to the chaining post. Slate- and earth-colored clothing concealed her slim form and a hooded cloak shadowed her face and hair. He blinked in disbelief, thinking her a part of some half-remembered dream.

"Ben?" she repeated, and her sea-green eyes stared out at him from beneath the hood. "Are you all right?"

He nodded mechanically. She was real. "How did you find me?" he whispered.

"I followed you," she answered, moving closer. Her face was inches from his own, the shadows drawn clear of her exquisite features. She was so impossibly beautiful. "I told you that I belonged to you, Ben. Did you not believe me?"

"It was not a question of believing you, Willow," he tried to explain. "You cannot belong to me. No one can."

She shook her head determinedly. "It was decided long ago that I should, Ben. Why is it that you cannot understand that?"

He felt a wave of helplessness wash through him. He remembered her naked in the waters of the Irrylyn; he remembered her changing into that gnarled tree within the pines. She excited and repelled him both, and he could not come to terms with the mix of feelings.

"Why are you here?" he asked in frustration.

"To set you free," she answered at once. She slipped from beneath the cloak a ring of iron keys. "You should have asked my father for me, Ben. He would have given his permission if you had asked. But you did not ask, and because you did not, I was forced to leave anyway. Now I cannot go back again."

"What do you mean, you can't go back?"

She began working the keys into the locks of his chains, trying each in turn. "It is forbidden for any to leave the lake country without my father's permission. The penalty is exile."

"Exile? But you're his daughter!"

"No longer, Ben."

"Then you shouldn't have come, damn it! You shouldn't have left, if you knew that this would happen!"

Her gaze was steady. "I had no choice."

The third key fitted and the chains fell away. Ben stared at the sylph in anger and frustration, and then in despair. She slipped from his side and moved to Questor, Abernathy, and the kobolds. One by one, she set them free. Daylight was beginning to lighten the eastern sky across the mountains. The trolls would be waking soon.

Willow slipped back to him. "We must go quickly, Ben."

"How did you get in here without being seen?" he asked.

"There are none who can see the people of the lake country if they do not wish it, Ben. I slipped into the valley after midnight and stole the keys from the watch. The gates stand open, the chain only draped through its rings. But we must leave at once; the deception will be discovered."

She passed the ring of keys to him, and he took them. His fingers brushed hers. He hesitated, thinking suddenly of what she had risked to come after him. She must have shadowed him since he had left the lake country. She must have been watching over him all that time.

Impulsively he reached for her and hugged her close. "Thank you, Willow," he whispered.

Her arms wrapped about his body and she hugged him back. He felt the warmth of her body burn into him, and he welcomed it.

"High Lord!" Questor was pulling urgently on his arm.

He released Willow and glanced about hurriedly. The G'home Gnomes were stirring in their sleep, rubbing their eyes and stretching their furry limbs. Some were awake already.

"Is it time to leave, High Lord?" Fillip asked, coming drowzily to his feet.

"Yes, is it time, High Lord?" Sot echoed, rising with him.

Ben stared at them, remembering what had brought him here in the first place. Abernathy suddenly leaned close. "High Lord, it will be difficult enough for five of us to slip away unnoticed. We cannot hope to take an entire company of gnomes in the bargain!"

Ben glanced about once more. Mist and smoke were beginning to dissipate. The sky was growing lighter. There were signs of life in several of the stone huts. The entire village would be awake in the next few minutes.

He looked down at the anxious faces of Fillip and Sot. "Everyone goes," he said quietly.

"High Lord . . . !" Abernathy tried to protest.

"Questor!" Ben called softly, ignoring his scribe. Questor stepped close. "We need a diversion."

The wizard went pale. The owlish face twisted into a knot. "High Lord, I have already failed you once . . ."

"Then don't do so again," Ben cut him short. "I need that diversion—as soon as we're through the gates of this cattle pen. Do something that will distract the Crag Trolls. Explode one of their kilns or drop a mountain on them. Anything—but do it!"

He took Willow's arm and started across the compound. Bunion and Parsnip were ahead of him at once, clearing the way, creeping through the fading dark. Furry, ferret-faced forms squirmed and bunched close as he went.

He caught a glimpse of a lean, misshapen figure approaching the compound gates. "Bunion!" he warned with a hiss.

The kobold was through the gate in an instant, shoving free the chains from their rings. He caught the surprised troll before the creature knew what was happening and silenced him.

Ben and Willow rushed from the compound, Questor and Abernathy a step behind. The G'home Gnomes poured through after. Shouts of alarm broke through the stillness almost immediately, deep-throated cries that shattered the sleep of the Crag Trolls. The trolls stumbled from their huts, grunting. The gnomes scattered, stocky forms moving much faster than Ben would have thought possible. He drew up short. There were Crag Trolls at every turn.

"Questor!" he yelled frantically.

Brilliant white light exploded overhead, and Strabo appeared. The dragon flew across the valley breathing fire everywhere. Crag Trolls scrambled frantically for cover, and G'home Gnomes screamed in terror. Ben stared in disbelief. Where had the dragon come from?

Then he caught sight of Questor, arms thrust out of his robes and windmilling madly as the wizard stumbled back. He saw at the same instant that Strabo had only one leg, that the wings were not centered properly on the barrel-shaped body, that there were odd clumps of feathered plumage about the leathered neck, and that the dragon's fire lanced earthward but burned nothing. The dragon was a fake. Questor had given them their diversion.

Willow saw it, too. She seized his arm, and together they broke for the valley pass that had brought the little company in the previous night. The others followed, Questor bringing up the rear. Already the illusory dragon was beginning to fade, bits and pieces of his body disintegrating as he flew back and forth above the astonished trolls. Ben and his companions dashed through their midst. Twice they were intercepted, but Bunion dispatched the attackers with a swiftness that was frightening. They gained the defile in moments, the way before them clear.

Ben risked a final glance back. The dragon had come apart completely, pieces of magic falling into the mist and smoke like a broken puzzle. The trolls remained in a state of complete confusion.

The little company dashed into the shadows of the defile, and the trolls, the fires, the valley, and the madness were left behind.

CRYSTAL

It was nearing midmorning when Ben and his companions finally ended their flight. They were safely out of the Melchor by then, well below the shadowed, misted cliffs and defiles, back within the foothills from which the G'home Gnomes had originally been taken. The gnomes had long since disappeared, the Crag Trolls appeared to have lost interest in the matter, and there no longer seemed to be any reason to continue running.

Make no mistake, Ben thought, lowering himself gingerly to rest his back against an oak trunk—they had been running. It was an ignominious admission. It would have been far more satisfying to couch their flight in terms of making an escape, or some such. But the truth of the matter was that they had been running for their lives.

Willow, Questor, Abernathy, and the kobolds gathered about him, seating themselves in a circle on a patch of wintry saw grass colored a faint pink. Clouds rolled overhead in a thick blanket of gray, and the smell of rain was in the air. They ate a brief meal of leaves and stalks from Bonnie Blues that grew close at hand, and they drank the water of a spring that ran down out of the mountains. They had nothing else to eat or drink. All of their possessions, horses included, had been lost to the trolls.

Ben chewed and sipped disinterestedly and tried to gather his thoughts. He could argue the relative merits of the matter until the cows came home, but things were not going well for the ruler of Landover. His track record was abysmal. With the exception of those seated about him, he had not gained a single ally. The Lords of the Greensward, traditional supporters of the throne, had received him coolly, tried unsuccessfully to bribe him, then practically thrown him through Rhyndweir's gates. The River Master had been more congenial in his reception, but only because he was completely disinterested in anything the throne said or did, believing the salvation of his people lay entirely in his own hands. The Crag Trolls had imprisoned him and would have undoubtedly fried him had he not managed to escape their cattle pens—thanks, he reminded himself, not to anything he had done but to Willow's perseverance and to a fortuitous turn of events that finally enabled Questor to conjure up the magic in more or less the right way for a change.

There were the G'home Gnomes, of course. Fillip and Sot had pledged for them. But what was that worth? What good was the pledge of a burrow people who were despised by everyone for being thieves and scavengers and worse?

"So what exactly do we have here?" he asked aloud, and everyone looked up in surprise. "We have this. The Lords of the Greensward—Kallendbor, Strehan and the rest—will pledge to the throne on the day I rid them of the dragon, something that no one has ever been able to do. The River Master will pledge to the throne on the day that I gain the promise of the Lords of the Greensward and various others to cease pollution of his lands and waters and to work with him to keep the valley clean. Fat chance. The Crag Trolls will pledge to the throne on the day I can walk back into the Melchor without fear of being offered up for roast beef. Good luck there, as well." He paused. "I'd say that about covers the situation, doesn't it?"

No one said anything. Questor and Abernathy exchanged uncertain glances. Willow looked as if she did not understand—which, indeed, she might not, he conceded. The kobolds stared at him with their bright, knowing eyes and grinned their needle-sharp smiles.

He flushed with a mix of sudden embarrassment and anger. "The truth of the matter is I have made absolutely no progress whatsoever. Zero. Nil. Zip. Any arguments?" He hoped someone would try.

Questor obliged him. "High Lord, I think you are being entirely too hard on yourself."

"Am I? What part of what I said was untrue, Questor Thews?"

"What you said was true as far as it went, High Lord. But you overlook an important consideration in your appraisal."

"I do? What consideration is that?"

Questor held his ground. "The difficulty of your position. It is not easy to be King of Landover under the best of circumstances."

The others nodded in agreement. "No," Ben shook his head at once. "I can't accept that. I can't blame this on the circumstances. You take the circumstances as you find them and make the best of them."

"Why do you think that you have not done this, Ben?" Willow wanted to know.

The question confused him. "Because I haven't! I couldn't persuade the Lords of the Greensward or your father or those damned trolls to do any of the things that I wanted them to do! I almost got us killed back there with the trolls! If you hadn't followed us and if Questor hadn't managed to get his magic working, we would probably all be dead!"

"I would not make too much out of any help you gained from my magic." Questor muttered softly, owlish face twisting uncomfortably.

"You did succeed in freeing the gnomes, High Lord," Abernathy reminded him stiffly. His brown eyes blinked. "I personally consider it wasted effort, but such value as their lives might hold is owed now entirely to you. You were the one who insisted that we take them with us."

The others nodded once more. Ben glanced from face to face, frowning. "I appreciate the vote of confidence, but I think it's misplaced. Why don't we just accept what we all know—I'm just not doing the job."

"You are doing the best that you can, High Lord," Questor replied at once. "No one can ask anything more."

"Nor do anything more," Abernathy added.

"But maybe someone else *can* do more," Ben declared pointedly. "Maybe someone else *should.*"

"High Lord!" Abernathy rose stiffly. He pushed his glasses back on his long nose and his ears cocked back. "I have been scribe to the throne for more years than you have lived. Perhaps that is difficult to realize given my present form," he cast a withering glance at Questor, "but I ask you to accept my word nevertheless. I have witnessed Kings of Landover come and go—the old King and those many who followed after him. I have observed them all in their attempts to govern. I have seen them exercise their wisdom and their compassion. Some have been capable; some have not." His right paw pointed dramatically. "But I will tell you now, High Lord, that none—not even the old King—have ever shown more promise than you!"

He finished and sat back on his haunches slowly. Ben was stunned. He would not have expected in his wildest dreams to receive such a ringing endorsement from the cynical scribe.

He felt Willow take his hand. "Ben, you must listen to him. The part of me that is my mother senses something very special about you. It tells me that you are different. I think that you are meant to be King of Landover. I think no one else should even try."

"Willow, you cannot make that judgment . . ." he started to tell her, but a sudden hissing from the kobolds cut him short. They spoke between themselves a moment, and then Bunion said something quickly to Questor.

The wizard looked at Ben. "The kobolds agree with the sylph. There is something different about you, they feel. You show courage and strength. You are the King they wish to serve."

Ben sagged back weakly against the tree trunk, shaking his head reprovingly. "What do I have to do to convince you that you are mistaken about me? There is nothing different about me, nothing special, nothing that would make me a better King than the next guy. Don't you see? You're doing the same thing I did when I took the kingship—you're deceiving yourselves! This may be a fantasy kingdom on paper, but it is real enough in the flesh—and we have to accept the fact that no amount of wishing or make-believe is going to solve its problems!"

No one responded. They stared at him silently. He thought about saying something further to persuade them, but decided against it. There wasn't anything else worth saying.

Finally, Questor rose. He came to his feet as if the weight of the world were suddenly on his shoulders. His owlish face was screwed up so tightly that he appeared to be in pain. Slowly, he straightened.

"High Lord, there is something that you should know." He cleared his throat nervously. "I told you before that my half-brother chose you quite deliberately as buyer of the throne of Landover. I told you that he chose you because he believed that you would fail as King and that the Kingship would revert once again to him—just as it has each time it has been sold since the old King's death. He believed you one of life's more obvious failures, High Lord. He depended on it, in fact."

Ben folded his arms defensively across his chest. "Then I guess he won't be disappointed when he discovers the way things are working out, will he?"

Questor cleared his throat again, shifting his weight uncomfortably. "As it happens, High Lord, he knows exactly how things are working out and he is extremely disappointed."

"Well, frankly, Questor, I don't give a . . ." Ben stopped short. He stared hard at the other man. "What did you say? Did you say he knows how things are working out—*exactly* how they're working out?"

He came to his feet and faced the wizard. "How can that be, Questor? His magic doesn't reach into this world anymore, does it? You said he couldn't take anything with him when he left Landover except the medallion. Everything else had to be left behind. If that's so, then how does he know what's happening back here?"

Questor was eerily calm, his face composed like a death mask. "I tell him what is happening, High Lord," he said quietly.

There was an endless silence. Ben could not believe what he had just heard. "You tell him?" he repeated in astonishment.

"I must, High Lord." Questor's eyes dropped. "It was the bargain I made with him when he departed Landover with the old King's son. I could be court wizard in his absence, but I had to agree to report to him on the progress of the would-be Kings of Landover sent over from your world. I was to let him know of their failures, and should they occur, of their successes. He planned to use this information in his selection process of candidates for future sales of the throne; he would look for weaknesses that the information revealed."

The others had come to their feet as well. Questor ignored them. "I want no more secrets between us," he went on quickly. "There have been too many secrets already, I fear. So I will tell you the last of what I have kept from you. You asked once how many Kings of Landover there have been since the death of the old King. I told you more than thirty. What I did not tell you was that the last eight came from Rosen's, Ltd.—all within a span of less than two years! Five of those lasted less than the ten-day trial period permitted under the terms of your agreement. Consider for a moment what that means, High Lord. It means that five times, at least, the store would have had to refund to the customer the money paid—five times my half-brother would have lost his sale. One million dollars each time, High Lord. Bad publicity, bad business. I think that neither the store nor my brother would have tolerated such losses. That suggests to me the losses were never discovered. I think that most, if not all, of those sales were kept hidden from the store. And I think that the subsequent dissatisfaction of the customers was covered up in the most expeditious way possible."

He paused deliberately. "Questor, what are you saying?" Ben whispered.

"That were you to use the medallion now to return to your own world, High Lord, you would find your money gone and your life expectancy shortened considerably."

Abernathy was furious, his muzzle drawn back to reveal all of his numerous teeth. "I *knew* you were not to be trusted, Questor Thews!" he growled ominously.

Ben brought his hand up quickly. "No, wait a moment. He didn't have to tell me this; he chose to do so freely. Why, Questor?"

The wizard's smile was strangely gentle. "So that you would know how much I believe in you, High Lord Ben Holiday. The others have argued their belief persuasively and eloquently, but you appear unwilling to listen. I am hoping that this admission to you will accomplish what they, apparently, have not and make you believe in yourself. I think you the King that Landover has waited for. I think that my half-brother fears this as well. He has shown more than a little concern over your refusal to give up when so many before you would have done so long ago. He worries that you will find a way to keep the throne. He is frightened of you, High Lord."

Willow seized Ben's arm tightly. "Listen to him, Ben. I believe him."

Questor sighed wearily. "I had what I believed to be good reason for doing as my half-brother asked. I would not have been given the position of court wizard had I refused. I knew that I could do nothing to help the land if the position were not mine. I believed that the help I could give as court wizard would outweigh any damage my reports might do. It was not until just recently that I began to surmise the fate of those who had purchased the Kingship and failed to stay on. By then it was too late to help them . . ."

His voice broke. "My half-brother made a further bargain with me, High Lord—a bargain that, I am ashamed to admit, I could not bring myself to refuse. His books of magic, the secrets of the conjuring acquired by wizards since the dawn of the land, are concealed within the Kingdom. Only he knows where. He could not take them out with him, and he has promised them to me. Each time a new King fails, he gives me a bit more of the magic with which to work. I do nothing to aid his plan, High Lord—but the need for the magic is an irresistible lure. Bits and pieces aid me in my learning. I know that he will never give the books to me; I know that he uses me as his pawn. But I believe that sooner or later he will say one word more than he should or give up one secret too many, and I will be able to find the books without him and use them to put an end to him!"

The owlish face twisted sharply in on itself, lines cutting to the bone. "I let myself be used, High Lord, because I saw no other way. My intentions have always been good ones. I want this land restored to what it was. I would do anything to achieve that. I love this land more than my own life!"

Ben studied him silently, conflicting emotions washing through him. Willow still grasped his arm, her fingers insistent, their pressure telling him that she thought Questor spoke the truth. Abernathy still looked wary. The kobolds stood mute beside him, and he could read nothing in their dark faces.

He looked back again at the wizard. His own voice was rough. "Questor, you suggested to me more than once that I could use the medallion to return safely to my own world."

"It was necessary that I test the depth of your commitment, High Lord!" the other whispered fiercely. "It was necessary that you be given the choice!"

"And if I had elected to use the medallion?"

The silence was endless. "I would like to believe, High Lord . . . that I would have stopped you."

There were sudden tears in the other's eyes. Ben read the mix of shame and hurt reflected there. "I would like to believe so, too, Questor," he said softly.

He thought a moment, then put his hand on the wizard's shoulder. "How do you communicate with Meeks, Questor? How do you speak with him?"

Questor took a moment to compose himself, then dug into the folds of his clothing and pulled something free. Ben stared. It was the crystal that Questor had been wearing when Ben had first crossed into Landover. Ben had all but forgotten it. He had seen it several times since, but had never given it more than a passing thought.

"The crystal is his, High Lord," Questor explained. "He gave it to me when he departed Landover. I warm it with my hands, and his face appears within it. I can speak with him then."

Ben studied the crystal wordlessly for a moment, looking into the depthless facets, peering through the rainbow of colors that shimmered within. The crystal hung from a silver chain fastened to a ring screwed into its apex.

He looked at Questor. "Has Meeks any other source of contact with Landover?"

The wizard shook his head. "I think not."

Ben hefted the crystal experimentally. "Do you have enough faith in me to give the crystal up, Questor?" he asked, his voice almost a whisper.

"The crystal is yours, High Lord," the wizard replied at once.

Ben nodded and smiled faintly. He passed the crystal back to Questor. "Summon up Mr. Meeks for me, would you, please?"

There was a moment's hesitation, and then Questor placed the crystal within his palms and cupped them together. Willow, Abernathy, and the kobolds pressed close. Ben felt his heart race. He had not expected to encounter Meeks so soon again; but now that it was about to happen, he looked forward to it eagerly.

Questor opened his palms carefully and picked the crystal up by its chain. Meeks peered out of the crystal's center, surprise mirrored in his sharp eyes.

Ben bent down so that his eyes were even with those of Meeks. "Good day, Mr. Meeks," he greeted. "How are things in New York?"

The craggy old face went dark with anger, the eyes baleful as they stared back. Ben had never seen such hatred.

"Don't feel like talking?" Ben smiled his best courtroom smile. "Can't say that I blame you. Things aren't working out all that well for you, are they?"

The black-gloved hand came up in warning as Meeks tried to say something.

"No, don't bother answering," Ben cut him short. "Nothing you have to say would interest me. I just want you to know one thing." He took the crystal from Questor and held it up before him. The smile disappeared. "I just want you to know that the wheels are about to come off your wagon!"

Then he carried the crystal to a stand of rocks that jutted through the earth of a nearby hillside and smashed the orb against them until it was reduced to fragments. He ground the fragments into the earth with his boot.

"Good-bye, Mr. Meeks," he said quietly.

He turned. His companions were watching him, standing in a knot where he had left them. He walked slowly back to where they waited. Their eyes remained riveted on him.

"I guess that's the last of Mr. Meeks," he offered. "It appears that we are back to square one."

"High Lord, please allow me to say something," Questor asked. He was agitated, but he composed himself. "High Lord, you cannot give up." He glanced awkwardly at the others. "Perhaps I have lost everyone's trust because of what I have done. Perhaps it would be best if I were to go no further with you. I accept that. But you, at least, must go on. Abernathy, Bunion, Parsnip, and Willow, too, will stay with you. They believe in you, and they are right to do so. You have the wisdom, compassion, strength, and courage of which they spoke. But you have something else, High Lord Ben Holiday. You have something that no other King of Landover has shown for many a year—something a King of Landover must have. You have determination. You refuse to quit when another man would. A King needs that quality most of all."

He paused, his stooped form straightening. "I did not lie when I told you that my half-brother sees that determination in you and is frightened by it." He shook his head admonishingly. "Do not quit now, High Lord. Be the King that you have wished to be!"

He had finished, and he waited for Ben's response. Ben glanced at the others—at Willow, the fire in her eyes a reflection of more than her trust; at Abernathy, sardonic and wary; at Parsnip and Bunion, their monkey faces sharp and cunning with hidden knowledge. Each face was like an actor's mask in some bizarre piece of theater, and the play a thing not yet finished. Who were they really, he wondered—and who was he?

Suddenly he was a lifetime away from everything that had come before his journey into this strange world. Gone were the corporate high rises, the lawyers, the judicial system of the United States of America, the cities, the governments, the codes, and the laws. It was all gone, everything that had ever been. There was only what never was—dragons, witches, fairy creatures of all sorts, castles and knights, damsels and wizards, things of magic and things of enchantment. He was starting life over, and all of the rules were new. He had jumped into the abyss, and he was still falling.

Quite unexpectedly, he started to grin. "Questor, I have no intention of quitting." The grin broadened. "How could I possibly quit in the face of such an eloquent testimonial of faith? How could I possibly quit with friends such as you to stand with me?" He shook his head slowly, as much at his own madness as at theirs. "No, the beat goes on, and so do we."

Willow was smiling. The kobolds hissed their approval. Questor looked relieved. Even Abernathy nodded his agreement.

"One condition, however." The grin disappeared from his face. He stepped forward and put his hand gently on Questor's shoulder. "We started together, and we finish together. What's past is past, Questor. We need you with us."

The wizard stared at him in disbelief. "High Lord, I would do anything you asked of me, but . . . I cannot . . ." He glanced at the others self-consciously.

"A vote," Ben called out at once. "Does Questor go with us? Bunion? Parsnip?" The kobolds nodded. "Willow?" The sylph nodded as well.

He paused and looked at Abernathy. "Abernathy?"

Abernathy faced him silently and made no gesture either way. Ben waited. The scribe might have been chiseled out of stone. "Abernathy?" he repeated softly.

The dog shrugged. "I think he knows less about character than he does about magic, but I also think he meant no real harm. Let him come."

Ben smiled. "Well done, Abernathy," he commended. "We are a company once more." He looked at Questor. "Will you come with us?"

Flushing, a smile tugging at the corners of his mouth, the wizard nodded eagerly. "Yes, High Lord, I will."

Ben glanced at each of them in turn, thinking momentarily that they were all nuts, then turned to study the sky. The sun was a fuzzy white glow through the mist and clouds, its center directly overhead. It was nearing midday.

"I suppose that we had better be going, then," he said.

Abernathy's teeth clicked sharply. "Umm . . . going where, High Lord?" he asked hesitantly.

Ben came up to him and put his hands on the dog's furry shoulders. He glanced conspiratorially at the others. "Where I told the Crag Trolls we were going, Abernathy; where we should have been going all along."

The scribe stared at him. "And where is that, High Lord?"

Ben smiled solemnly. "To the Deep Fell, Abernathy. To Nightshade."

DEEP FELL

They thought Ben Holiday mad. They thought it to varying degrees, perhaps, but the vote was unanimous. The kobolds expressed it with a quick hiss and frightening, humorless grins. Willow's green eyes mirrored it, and she shook back her waist-length hair in disapproval. Questor and Abernathy were aghast, and both began talking at once.

"You have taken leave of your senses, High Lord!" the scribe exploded.

"You cannot risk placing yourself in the hands of the witch!" the wizard admonished.

Ben let them go on a bit, then sat them all down and patiently explained himself. He had not taken leave of his senses, he assured them. On the contrary, he knew exactly what he was doing. He might be taking some risk in going down into the Deep Fell and confronting Nightshade, but there was risk in almost any alternative left to him at this point and no other alternative made as much sense or offered the same opportunities.

Think about it, he urged. The key to every door closed against him lay in use or acquisition of magic. It was magic that had given life to the land and those who lived upon it in the beginning; it was loss of magic that threatened to steal that life away now. The medallion was a thing of magic, enabling him to pass from his world into theirs and—if need be—out again. The Paladin was a thing of magic, and magic was needed to bring him back to them. The castle at Sterling Silver was a thing of magic, and magic was needed to save it. Most of the land's creatures were creatures of magic, and magic was what they understood, respected and feared. The Lords of the Greensward wanted Ben to rid them of the dragon, and it would take magic to do that. The River Master wanted the land's inhabitants to work with him to heal the land, and that would probably take some form of magic as well. The Mark and his demons were a dark magic that threatened to destroy them all, and it would take a very powerful form of white magic, indeed, to prevent that from happening.

He paused. Who was most likely, then, to have access to the magic that he needed in order to begin to put things right again? Who possessed magic that the others did not?

Sure, there was risk. There was always risk. But no one had gone to Nightshade in many years; no one had even thought to try. No King of Landover had sought her allegiance since the death of the old King. Since before that, Abernathy interjected firmly—the old King wanted nothing to do with her either. All the more reason to see her now, Ben insisted. She could be talked to. Perhaps she could be persuaded. Possibly, if all else failed, she could be tricked.

His companions stared at him in horror.

He shrugged. Very well, forget the part about tricking her. She was still their best bet. She was possessor of the land's most powerful magic—Questor had said as much in their lessons. The others fixed accusing eyes on the wizard. A bit of that magic might turn things about for him. He wouldn't need much; enough to solve just one of the problems facing him would be plenty. Even if she refused her own magic, she might agree to arrange a meeting with the fairies; perhaps he could enlist their help.

He saw Willow cringe slightly at mention of the fairies, and for an instant he was no longer quite so sure of himself. But he shrugged the feeling off and went on with his argument. He had reasoned it through, and the solution to his problem was unmistakable. He had need of an ally to help bring the other inhabitants of Landover to terms. He would not find a more powerful ally than Nightshade.

Nor a more dangerous one, Questor pointed out bluntly.

But Ben was not to be dissuaded. The matter was decided and the journey about to commence. They were off to the Deep Fell. Anyone who didn't care to go with him could stay behind—he would understand.

No one stepped back. But there were a lot of uneasy looks.

It was midday by now, and they traveled south through the hill country until nightfall. The weather remained foul, the clouds continuing to mass, the onslaught of rain to draw closer. Mist turned to fog as night descended, and it began to drizzle. The company made camp beneath an outcropping of rocks below a ridgeline draped by a grove of weathered ash. The damp and the dark closed about quickly, and the six travelers hunched down together in their shelter and ate a sparse meal of spring water, Bonnie Blues, and some odd roots collected by the resourceful Parsnip. The air turned chill, and Ben found himself wishing for a shot of his now-departed Glenlivet.

Dinner was completed rather quickly, and they began to give thought to their sleeping accommodations. They were without bedding of any kind; everything had been lost in their flight from the trolls. Questor volunteered his use of the magic, and this time Ben agreed. The kobolds seemed hardy enough, but the rest of them might well catch pneumonia by morning if they didn't have something to help ward off the cold. Besides, Questor had shown improved control over the magic at the Melchor.

Such was not the case this night, however. The magic sparked and poofed, and several dozen flowered hand towels materialized. Questor grumbled about the weather and tried again. This time he produced burlap sacks. Now Abernathy was grumbling as well, and tempers were heating up faster than bodies. On the third try, the wizard conjured up a colorfully striped pavilion tent complete with sitting cushions and dressing boards, and Ben decided that they would settle for that.

They settled themselves in and one by one drifted off to sleep. Abernathy kept watch as he slept, his nose pointed out the tent flap, not entirely convinced that the trolls had given up on them.

Only Ben remained awake. He lay in the dark and listened to the sound of the rain as it drummed against the tent. He was beset with uncertainties that until now he had successfully ignored. He felt time slipping inexorably from him. Sooner than he wished, he knew, it was going to run out altogether. Then the Mark would have him or some other evil that he had no real protection against. Then he would be forced to use the medallion to save himself, even though he had sworn that he would not. What choice would he make then? What would he do when his life was *really* threatened—not by manor lords looking to box his ears or trolls looking to pen him up, but by some monster that could snuff his life out with nothing more than a thought? Such monsters were out there, he knew. Nightshade was out there.

He forced himself to think about the witch of the Deep Fell for a time. He had not let himself do so earlier; it was easier not to. He knew he had to go to her. It did not help matters to think about how dangerous that might be. Nightshade frightened the others badly, and nothing besides the Mark had done that. He might be biting off more than he could chew once again; he might be putting them all in a worse predicament than the one they had experienced in the camp of the Crag Trolls. He chewed his lower lip thoughtfully. He could not afford to do that. There might be no one to rescue them this time. He would have to be more careful; he would have to take steps to protect them.

Especially Willow, he thought. He glanced over to where she lay in the dark, trying to follow the line of her sleeping form. She had not transformed herself into and taken root as a tree this night. Evidently, she did so only periodically. He found that he was less repelled by the idea than he had previously been. Perhaps it was only the strangeness of the change that had bothered him so at first, and now he was used to the idea. Sometimes familiarity bred acceptance, not contempt.

He shook his head admonishingly. What you really mean, Holiday, is that she saved your skin, so now you can accept her. Bully for you.

His breathing evened out and his eyes closed. He wished she hadn't given up so much to follow him. He wished that she had been a little less impulsive. It made him feel responsible for her, and he didn't want that. She wanted it, of course. She saw things the way some child would see them—their fate told in the winding of vines on a bridal bed, their lives joined by a chance meeting at some midnight swim. She expected things from him that he wasn't prepared to give to anyone.

His thoughts wandered, and his obstinacy slowly diffused. Perhaps the problem was not with her at all; perhaps it was with him. Maybe the real problem was that he simply didn't have the things to give her that she was asking for. Perhaps he had lost everything good about himself when Annie had died. He didn't want to think that, but perhaps it was so.

He was surprised to find tears in his eyes. He brushed them silently away, grateful that no one could see.

He let his thoughts slip away then, and he drifted down into himself. His dreams overtook him, and he slept.

He was awake early, the daylight still a faint blush against the eastern horizon where the mist rolled across the hills. The others of the little company were awake as well, stretching muscles cramped from sleeping in the damp and chill, yawning against the too quick passing of the night. The rain had died away to a spattering of drops from the leaves of the trees. Ben stepped from the pavilion tent into the half-light and walked to where a trickle of water spilled down out of the rocks through a gathering of heavy brush. He was bending down to catch a drink in his cupped hands when a pair of ferretlike faces poked out suddenly from the brush.

He jumped backward, water flying up into his face, a startled oath on his lips.

"Great High Lord," a voice greeted quickly.

"Mighty High Lord," a second voice echoed.

Fillip and Sot. Ben recovered his composure, forced himself with considerable effort to discard his impulse to throttle them both, and waited patiently as they worked their way free of their concealment. The G'Home Gnomes were a bedraggled pair, their clothing ripped and their fur matted with the rain. They appeared even dirtier than usual, if that was possible.

They waddled forward, eyes peering up at him in the near dark.

"We experienced some difficulty eluding the Crag Trolls, High Lord," Fillip explained.

"We were hunted until dark, and then we could not determine where you had gone," Sot added.

"We were frightened that you had been taken again," Fillip said.

"We were afraid that you had not escaped," Sot added.

"But we found your trail and followed it," Fillip continued.

"We see poorly, but we have an excellent sense of smell," Sot added.

Ben shook his head helplessly. "Why did you bother coming at all?" he asked, kneeling down so they were all at eye-level. "Why didn't you simply go on home with the rest of your people?"

"Oh, no, High Lord!" Fillip exclaimed.

"Never, High Lord!" Sot declared.

"We gave our promise to serve you, if you should aid us in freeing our people," Fillip said.

"We gave our word," Sot said.

"You kept your part of the bargain, High Lord," Fillip said.

"Now we intend to keep ours," Sot finished.

Ben stared at them in disbelief. Loyalty was the last thing he had ever expected from these two. It was also the last thing he needed. Fillip and Sot were more likely to prove a source of trouble than a well of relief.

He almost told them so, but then he caught the look of determination on their faces and in their half-blind eyes. He reminded himself that the G'home Gnomes were the first to step forward and offer their pledge to Landover's throne—the first, when no one else would. It seemed wrong to dismiss their offer of help out of hand when they were so willing to serve.

He straightened slowly, watching as their eyes followed him up. "We are going to the Deep Fell," he advised them. "I plan to meet with Nightshade."

Fillip and Sot looked at each other expressionlessly and nodded.

"Then we can be of service to you, High Lord," Fillip said.

"Indeed, we can," Sot agreed.

"We have gone into the Deep Fell on many occasions," Fillip said.

"We know the hollows well," Sot said.

"You do?" Ben didn't even try to hide his amazement.

"Yes, High Lord," Fillip and Sot said together.

"The witch pays little attention to creatures such as us," Fillip said.

"The witch does not even see us," Sot said.

"We will guide you safely in, High Lord," Fillip offered.

"Then we will guide you safely out again," Sot added.

Ben extended his hand and shook heartily each grimy paw. "You have yourselves a deal." He grinned. The gnomes beamed. He drew back. "One question. Why did you wait until now to show yourselves? How long have you been crouching back there in the brush?"

"All night, High Lord," Fillip admitted.

"We were afraid of the dog," Sot whispered.

Ben brought them into the camp and announced to the others that the gnomes would be accompanying them to the Deep Fell. Abernathy was thoroughly dismayed and expressed the fact in no uncertain terms. It was one thing to agree to accept the wizard back into their company on the theory that he might prove useful—though he questioned how much use he would, in fact, be—but the gnomes were clearly of no use at all. He growled, and the gnomes shrank back uneasily. The kobolds hissed at them, and even Willow looked doubtful. But Ben was firm in his decision. The G'home Gnomes were coming with them.

They resumed their journey shortly after sunrise. They ate a quick breakfast of stems and leaves from the Bonnie Blues, Questor made the pavilion tent disappear in a flash of light and a puff of smoke, frightening the gnomes half to death in the process, and they were on their way. They traveled south and west on a meandering course that took them down out of the hill country and back into the forestland and lakes bordering the Greensward. Bunion led and the rest followed. It rained on and off, frequently misting like a veil of cold steam. The valley lay socked in by clouds and fog that formed an oddly bluish haze that rolled and mixed against the treetops and the dark, distant walls of the mountains. Flowers bloomed in the rain, and Ben found that odd. The flowers were pastel in color, fragile blooms that lasted only minutes and then withered. Rain flowers, Questor called them—evidencing a sorry lack of originality. They came with the rain and then they were gone. Once, in better times, they had enjoyed a lifespan of a dozen hours or more. But now, like everything else in the valley, they were stricken by the sickness. The magic no longer gave them more than a brief life.

The little company took a short break at mid-morning, settling themselves beside a spring grown thick with reeds, lilies, and cypress. The spring had a greenish-brown cast to it and nothing growing near looked healthy. Bunion set off in search of drinking water. It had begun to rain again, and the others clustered in twos and threes beneath the branches of the trees. Ben waited for a time, then caught Willow's eye and took her aside where they could be alone.

"Willow," he said gently. He knew this was going to be difficult. "I have been thinking about your coming with us into the Deep Fell—and wherever else we end up going. I don't think that you should go any further. I think that you ought to return to your home in Elderew."

She looked at him steadily. "I do not want to return home, Ben. I want to stay with you."

"I know that. But I think that it is too dangerous for you to do so."

"It is no more dangerous for me than it is for you. It may be that you will have need of my help again. I will stay."

"I will write a letter explaining to your father that I wished you with me until now so that you will not be in trouble with him," he went on. "I will come later to explain it to him myself."

"I don't want to go, Ben," she said again.

The green cast of her face was darkened by the shadows of the cypress, and she seemed to Ben almost a part of the tree. "I appreciate your willingness to take the same risks that I take," he said, "but there is no reason for you to do so. I cannot allow it, Willow."

Her face tilted back slightly, and now there was sudden fire in her green eyes. "You have nothing to say about it, Ben. The decision is mine." She paused, and it seemed as if she were staring right through him. "Why not tell me what is really on your mind, High Lord of Landover."

He stared back at her in surprise, then slowly nodded his agreement. "Very well. I'm not sure how to say this. If I could keep you with me and be honest with myself, I think I would do so. But I cannot. I don't love you, Willow. It may be that the fairy people discover love in a single sighting, but it doesn't happen that way with me. I don't believe in what the vines and the portents told you about how this would happen. I don't believe that you and I are meant to be lovers. I think you and I are meant to be friends, but I can't let you risk your life for me because of that!"

He stopped, feeling her hands catch up his own and gently hold them.

"You still do not understand, do you, Ben?" she whispered. "I belong to you because that is what is meant to be. It is truth woven in the fabric of the land's magic, and though you may not see it, nevertheless it will come to pass. I feel love for you because I love in the way of the fairies—at first sighting and by promise. I do not expect that of you. But you will come to love me, Ben. It will happen."

"Maybe so," he acknowledged, gripping her hands tightly in response in spite of himself, finding her so desirable that he could almost admit that she might be right. "But I do not love you now. I find you the most beautiful creature I have ever seen. I find myself wanting you so badly that I have to fight back the need for you." He shook his head. "But, Willow, I cannot believe in the future that you seem to see so clearly. You don't belong to me! You belong to yourself!"

"I belong to nothing if I do not belong to you!" she insisted fiercely. Her face leaned close to his. "Are you frightened of me, Ben? I see fear in your eyes, and I do not understand it."

He took a deep breath. "There was someone else, Willow—someone who truly belonged to me and I to her. Her name was Annie. She was my wife, and I loved her very much. She was not as beautiful to look at as you, but she was pretty and she was . . . special. She died two years ago in an accident and I . . . I haven't been able to forget her or to quit loving her or to love anyone else."

His voice broke. He hadn't realized it would be so difficult talking about Annie after all this time.

"You have not told me why are you afraid, Ben," Willow pressed, her voice gentle, but insistent.

"I don't know why I'm afraid!" He shook his head, confused, "I don't know. I think it's because when Annie died I lost something of myself—something so precious that I'm not sure I'll ever get it back again. Sometimes I think I can't feel anymore. I just seem to pretend . . ."

There were sudden tears in her eyes, and he was shocked. "Please don't cry," he asked her.

Willow smiled bitterly. "I think you are afraid to let yourself love me, because I am so different from what she was," the sylph said softly. "I think you are afraid that if you let yourself love me, you will somehow lose her. I wouldn't want that. I want what you were and are and will be—all that is you. But I cannot have that because you are afraid of me."

He started to deny it, then stopped. She was right when she said that he was frightened of her. He saw her in his mind as she danced in the clearing of aged pines at midnight, changing from sylph to willow tree, rooting in the soil that her mother had danced upon. The transformation repelled him still. She was not human; she was something beyond and apart from that.

How could he ever love a creature so different from Annie . . . ?

Her fingers brushed at the tears that were slipping now from his own eyes. "I am life of the magic and subject to its will, Ben. So must you be; so will you be. Earth mother and heaven father made us both, and the land binds us." She bent forward and kissed him on his cheek. "You will lose your fear of me and one day you will love me. I believe that." Her breath was soft against his face. "I will wait for as long as that takes, Ben, but I will not leave you—not if you beg me, not if you command me. I belong to you. I belong with you. I will stay with you, though the risk is ten times as great as it is now. I will stay, though my own life be given up for yours!"

She rose, a rustle of long hair and clothing in the mid-morning stillness. "Do not ever ask me to leave you again," she told him.

Then she walked quickly away. He stared after her wordlessly and knew that he would not.

The little company arrived at the Deep Fell shortly before midday. The rain had passed and the day brightened, though clouds still screened the whole of the sky. The smell of damp hung thick in the air, and the morning chill had sharpened.

Ben stood with his companions at the edge of the Deep Fell and stared downward. All but the rim of the bowl was screened away by a blanket of mist. The mist hung over everything, swirling sluggishly across a scattering of tree tops and ridges that poked through the haze like jagged bones from a broken corpse. Scrub choked the rim and upper slopes of the hollows, brambles and thickets that were wintry and stunted. Nothing moved in the pit. No sound came out of it. It was an open grave that waited for an occupant.

Ben eyed it uneasily. It was frightening to look upon—the more so from its edge than from the safety of the Landsview. It appeared monstrous to him, a sprawling, misshapen chasm carved from the earth and left to gather rot. He glanced momentarily at a stand of Bonnie Blues that grew close to the rim. They were blackened and withered.

"High Lord, it is not too late to rethink your decision," Questor advised softly, standing at his elbow.

He shook his head wordlessly. The decision had been made.

"Perhaps we should wait until morning," Abernathy muttered, glancing uneasily at the clouded sky.

Ben shook his head a second time. "No. No more delays. I'm going in now." He turned to them, glancing from one face to the next as he spoke. "I want you to listen carefully and I don't want any arguments. Fillip and Sot will go with me as guides. They say that they know the Deep Fell. I will take one other. The rest of you will wait here."

"High Lord, no!" Questor exclaimed in disbelief.

"You would trust yourself to those . . . those cannibals!" Abernathy raged.

"You may have need of our protection!" Questor went on.

"It is madness for you to go alone!" Abernathy finished.

The kobolds hissed and bared their teeth in unmistakable disapproval, the G'home Gnomes chittered and shrank from the conflict, and the scribe and the wizard kept arguing, both at the same time. Only Willow said nothing, but she stared at Ben so hard that he could feel it.

He put up his hands to quiet them. "Enough, already! I told you that I didn't want any arguments, and I don't! I know what I'm doing. I've thought it through pretty carefully. We're not going to have a replay of what happened in the Melchor. If I don't come out when I should, I want someone free to come in after me."

"It may be far too late for you by then, High Lord," Abernathy pointed out bluntly.

"You said you were taking one other, High Lord," Questor interjected quickly. "I assume you meant me. You may have need of my magic."

"I may, indeed, Questor," he agreed. "But not unless I run into trouble with Nightshade and need my chestnuts pulled out of the fire. You're staying here with Abernathy and the kobolds. I'm taking Willow."

The sylph's hard stare turned to one of surprise.

"You would take the girl?" Questor exclaimed. "But what protection can she offer you?"

"None." Ben watched her eyes turn introspective. "I'm not looking for protection. I'm looking for common ground. I don't want the witch to think the King of Landover *needs* protection, and that is what she is likely to think if I descend on her with all of you. Willow is not so threatening. Willow is a fairy creature like the witch. They share a common background, and together Willow and I may be able to find the means to enlist Nightshade to our cause."

"You do not know the witch, High Lord!" Questor insisted vehemently.

"You certainly do not!" Abernathy agreed.

Willow came forward then, and she took his arm gently. "They may be right, Ben. Nightshade is not likely to offer her help simply because of me. She cares nothing more for the lake country people than for the court at Sterling Silver. She cares nothing for anyone. This is very dangerous."

He noticed that she did not offer to remain behind. She had already stripped away boots and forest cloak and stood next to him, barefoot in a pair of short pants and sleeveless tunic. "I know," he answered her. "That is why Questor, Abernathy, and the kobolds will remain here—to come to our rescue if we need it. If we all go in at once, we all risk falling victim to the same treachery. But if the strongest of us remain behind, the chances of rescue are improved." He looked at the others. "Do you understand?"

There was a general grumbling of acknowledgment. "I respectfully submit that this whole idea is both dangerous and foolish, High Lord," Abernathy declared.

"I would prefer to be there to advise you," Questor argued.

Ben nodded patiently. "I respect your feelings, but I've made up my mind. Whatever risk there is, I don't want anyone sharing it with me who doesn't have to. If I could do this myself without endangering anyone, that's what I would do. Unfortunately, I can't."

"No one has ever asked you to, High Lord," Questor replied quietly.

Ben met his eyes. "I know. I could not have had better friends than you have been." He paused. "But this is where it all ends, Questor. You have done for me all that you can. Time and choices are running out. I have to make something happen if I wish to be Landover's King. I have that responsibility—to you, to the land, and to myself."

Questor said nothing. Ben glanced briefly at the others. No one spoke. He nodded and reached for Willow's hand. He fought back against the chill that had suddenly settled through him.

"Lead on," he ordered Fillip and Sot.

Together, they started down into the pit.

NIGHTSHADE

It was like stepping off into a pool of blackened, fouled water. The mist rose to greet them, lapping anxiously at their boots. It climbed to their thighs and curled to their waists. It tugged at their shoulders and finally their necks. A moment later, they were submerged in it completely. Ben had to suppress a sudden urge to hold his breath against its suffocating tide.

His hand gripped Willow's tightly.

The mist was an impenetrable screen, closing about them as if a blanket that would smother them. It clung to their skin with fingers of damp insistence, and its touch was an itch that scratching would not cure. The smell of rotting wood and earth filled the air, permeating the mist, giving it the texture of toxic liquid splashed upon the skin. An unpleasant warmth issued out of it, as if something huge were trapped within the murk and sweating in terror as its lifeblood was sucked steadily away.

Ben sensed the terror to be his own, and he fought back against it. The back and underarms of his tunic were damp, and his breathing was ragged. He had never been so frightened. It was worse than when the Mark had come for him in the time passage. It was worse than his encounter with the dragon. It was a fear of something felt and not seen. His feet picked their way mechanically down the scrub-choked slope; he was barely aware of their movement. He could see the stocky forms of the gnomes a few feet ahead of him as they doggedly worked their way forward. He could see Willow beside him, her green-skinned form ghostlike, the cornsilk hair on her head, calves and forearms trailing out behind her as if stirred by the mist. He could see bits and pieces of the scrub and rock about him, and of trees and ridges somewhere far ahead. He saw them and was blind to them. It was what he could not see and could only feel that commanded the focus of his attention. It was what was hidden that he seemed suddenly to see best.

His free hand searched for the medallion tucked within his tunic, and he fingered it reassuringly through the cloth.

The minutes dragged on as the four companions groped their way through the haze, eyes searching sightlessly. Then the slope leveled out, the mist thinned, and scrub turned to brush and forest. They had reached a plateau several dozen feet above the hollows floor. Ben blinked. He could see again. Trees spread away before him in a tangle of trunks, limbs, and vines, and ridges thrust upward sharply into their mass, cresting against a skyline that was canopied in roiling mist. The hollows rim had disappeared. Everything beyond was gone.

Ben pushed past the gnomes to stand on a small promontory that jutted out from the slope, and he stared into the wilderness. His breath caught sharply in his throat.

"Oh, my God!" he whispered.

The hollows spread away for as far as the eye could see—farther than was conceivably possible. The Deep Fell had mushroomed into something so vast that its walls could no longer contain it. The Deep Fell had grown as big as all of Landover!

"Willow!" he whispered urgently.

She was beside him at once. He pointed out into the forest, into the vast, endless tract of it, terror reflected in his eyes as he struggled to comprehend what he was looking at. She understood at once. Her hands closed about his, squeezing. "It is only illusion, Ben," she said quickly. "What you see is not really there. It is only Nightshade's magic at work. She has mirrored back a thousand times the whole of the hollows to frighten us away."

Ben looked again. He saw nothing different, but he nodded as if he did anyway. "Sure—just a trick with magic to scare us off." He took a deep breath. He was calm again. "Want to know something, Willow? It works pretty well."

He gave her a quick smile. "How is it that you aren't fooled?"

She smiled a pixie grin back. "The fairy in me senses such tricks."

They continued their descent toward the hollows floor. Fillip and Sot seemed unbothered by the illusion. That was probably because their eyesight was so poor that they were unaware of the illusion, Ben decided. Sometimes ignorance *was* bliss.

They reached the hollows floor and paused. The tangle of the wilderness spread away before them, seemingly endless. Gnarled trunks and limbs twisted like spiders' webs against the ceiling of mist, vines clung like snakes, and brush choked on itself in thick tangles. The earth was damp and yielding.

Fillip and Sot sniffed the air a moment, then started forward. Ben and Willow followed. They pushed ahead through the wilderness, finding paths where it seemed there could be none. The hollows wall disappeared behind them and the jungle closed about. It was eerily still. They neither saw nor heard another living thing. No animals called, no birds flew, no insects hummed. The light was weak, sunlight screened into a dim gray haze by the clouds of mist. Shadows lay over everything. There was a sense of having been swallowed whole. There was a feeling of having been snared.

They had not gone far when they encountered the lizards.

They were at the edge of a deep ravine and about to start down when Ben saw movement at the bottom. He brought the others to a hurried halt and peered cautiously into the shadows. Dozens of lizards clustered together in the pit of the ravine, their scaled, greenish black bodies slithering across one another, their wicked-looking tongues flicking at the misted air. They were all sizes, some as large as alligators, some as small as frogs. They blocked all passage forward.

Willow took Ben's hand and smiled. "Another illusion, Ben," she assured him.

"This way, High Lord," advised Fillip.

"Come, High Lord," invited Sot.

They descended into the pit and the lizards disappeared. Ben was sweating again and wishing he didn't feel like such a fool.

Other illusions awaited them, and Ben was fooled each time. There was a monstrous old ash tree clustered thick with giant bats. There was a stream filled with piranhalike fish. Worst of all, there was the clearing in which vaguely human limbs stretched from the broken earth, clawed fingers grasping at anything that sought to pass through. Each time Willow and the gnomes led him resolutely forward, and the imagined dangers evaporated into the mist.

More than an hour slipped by before they reached the swamp. It was past midday. A vast marsh of reeds and quicksand stretched across their path for as far as the eye could see. Steam lifted from the marsh, and the quicksand bubbled as if fed by gasses from the earth below.

Ben glanced quickly at Willow. "Illusion?" he asked, already prepared for the answer she would give.

But this time she shook her head. "No, the swamp is real."

The gnomes were sniffing the air again. Ben glanced out across the swamp. A crow sat on a branch of deadwood halfway across, a large, ugly bird with a streak of white cresting its head. It stared at him with its tiny, dark eyes, and its head cocked reflectively.

Ben glanced away. "What now?" he asked the others.

"There is a trail further on, High Lord," Fillip answered.

"A pathway across the marsh," Sot agreed.

They waddled ahead, following the line of the swamp, ferret faces lifted, testing the air with their noses. Ben and Willow trailed slowly after. A hundred feet further on, the gnomes turned into the swamp and proceeded to cross. The swamp looked no different here than anywhere else, but the ground was firm enough to hold them, and they were safely past in a few minutes' time. Ben glanced back at the crow. It was still watching him.

"Let's not get paranoid," he muttered to himself.

They pressed on into the jungle. They had gone only a short distance further when Fillip and Sot became suddenly excited. Ben pushed quickly forward and found that the gnomes had discovered a nest of forest mice and flushed the family out. Fillip slipped into the brush on his belly, snaked through it soundlessly and emerged with one of the unfortunates firmly in hand. He bit off its head and gave the body to Sot. Ben grimaced, kicked Sot in the backside, and angrily ordered them both to get moving. But the memory of the headless mouse stayed with him.

He forgot about the mouse when they came up against the wall of brambles. The brambles lifted better than a dozen feet into the air, mingling with the trees and vines of the forest, stretching away into the distance. Again, Ben glanced at Willow.

"The brambles are real, too," she announced.

Fillip and Sot tested the air, walked up and down the wall both ways, then turned right. They had gone about fifty feet when Ben saw the crow. It was sitting on the crest of the wall of brambles just above them and staring down. Sharp eyes fixed on Ben. He stared back momentarily and could have sworn the bird winked.

"Here, High Lord," Fillip called.

"A passage, High Lord," Sot announced.

The gnomes pushed through the brambles as if they didn't exist, and Ben and Willow followed. The brambles parted easily. Ben straightened on the other side and glanced back. The crow was gone.

He saw the crow several times after that, sitting in trees or perching on logs, motionless as it watched him with those same secretive eyes. He never saw it fly and he never heard it call. Once he asked Willow if she saw it, too—none too certain that this wasn't just another illusion. She said that she did see it, but that she had no idea what it was doing there.

"It seems to be the only bird in the hollows," he pointed out doubtfully.

She nodded. "Perhaps it belongs to Nightshade."

That was not a very reassuring thought, but there was nothing Ben could do about it, so he put the matter out of his mind. The jungle had begun to thin, the trunks, limbs, and vines giving way to small clearings in which pockets of mist hung like tethered clouds. There was a brightening in the sky ahead, and a hint of the jungle's end. But there was no sign of the walls of the hollow as there should have been, and the Deep Fell was as sprawling and endless as it had first seemed.

"Can you tell where we are or how far we've come?" he asked the others, but they shook their heads wordlessly.

Then abruptly the jungle gave way and the four companions stood on the threshold of a castle fortress that dwarfed anything Ben had ever seen or even imagined could exist. The castle rose up before them like a mountain, its towers lifting into the clouds and mist so that they were screened from view, its walls receding into the distant horizon for miles. Turrets, battlements, parapets, and ramparts were constructed one upon the other in dazzling geometrical designs, the whole so vast in scope that it might have enclosed an entire city within its stone-block shell. It sat upon a great plateau with the jungle grown thick at its base. A rock-strewn trail led from where they stood to the open castle gates and a raised portcullis.

Ben stared at the castle in disbelief. Nothing could be this huge, his instincts told him. Nothing could be of such monstrous size. It had to be an illusion—a trick of magic, like his vision of the hollows and the things they had encountered. . . .

"What is this place, Willow?" he blurted out, cutting short his speculation, and the disbelief and awe he felt were apparent in his voice.

"I do not know, Ben." She stood with him, her own gaze fixed on the monstrosity. She shook her head slowly. "I do not understand it. This is not an illusion, Ben—and yet it is. There is magic at work, but the magic accounts for only part of what we see."

The G'home Gnomes, too, were confused. They shifted about uneasily, their ferretlike faces casting about for a scent they could rely upon. They failed to find one and began mumbling in guarded tones.

Ben forced his gaze away from the castle and looked carefully about for anything that would give him a clue as to its origin and purpose. He saw nothing at first, save for the jungle and the mist.

Then he saw the crow.

It was perched on a tree limb several dozen yards away, wings folded carefully in, eyes fixed on him. It was the same crow—glossy black feathers crested in white. Ben stared at it. He could not explain it, but he was certain that the crow knew what this was all about. It infuriated him that the bird was sitting there so placidly, as if waiting to see what they would do next.

"Come on," he told the others and started up the trail.

They walked cautiously ahead and the castle loomed closer. It didn't shimmer and disappear as Ben had expected it might. Instead, it took on an ominous, grim appearance as the weathered rock grew more detailed and the sound of wind whistling through towers and ramparts grew pronounced. Ben was leading now, with Willow a step behind. The gnomes had fallen back, their paws fastened to Ben's pants, their furry faces apprehensive as they peered out from behind his legs. Dry leaves and twigs rustled across the stone pathway, and the warmth of the jungle had faded to a chill.

The entrance to the castle gaped open before them, a black hole with iron teeth. Shadows wrapped everything beyond in an impenetrable shroud. Ben slowed at the gates and peered guardedly into the gloom. He could just make out what appeared to be a kind of courtyard with a few scattered benches and tables, a cluster of blackened stanchions and a weather-beaten throne covered with dust and spiderwebs. He could see nothing beyond that.

He went forward once more, the others trailing. They passed beneath the shadow of the portcullis and entered the courtyard. It was massive, unkempt, and empty. Their footsteps rang in hollow cadence through the stillness.

Ben was halfway across when he saw the crow. Somehow it had gotten there before them. It sat upon the throne, eyes fixed directly on him. He slowed and stopped.

The crow's eyes blinked and suddenly turned blood-red.

"Nightshade!" Willow whispered quickly in warning.

The crow began to change. It seemed to expand against the gloom, shimmering with an aura of crimson light, its shadow rising up against the throne like a wraith set free. Blackened stanchions flared and caught fire, and light exploded through the darkness. The G'home Gnomes gasped in dismay, bolted back through the gates of the castle, and were gone. Willow stood next to Ben, her hand gripping his as if it were a lifeline that kept her from drowning. Ben watched the crow transform into something darker still, and he was suddenly afraid that he had made an awful mistake.

Then the crimson aura died away and there was only the light from the fires that burned in the iron stanchions. The crow was gone. Nightshade sat upon the crumbling throne.

"Welcome to Deep Fell, great and mighty High Lord," she greeted, her voice barely more than a soft hiss.

She was not what Ben had expected. She didn't really look much like a witch at all—although it never crossed his mind even for an instant that she wasn't. She was tall and sharp-featured, her skin white and flawless, her hair raven black except for a single streak of white that ran down its center. She was neither old nor young, but somewhere in between. There was an ageless look to her features, a sort of marble statue quality that suggested an artist's creation that might survive all human life. Ben didn't know what artist had created the witch, whether god or devil, but some thought had gone into the sculpting. Nightshade was a striking woman.

She rose, black robes falling all about her tall, spare form. She came down off the throne and stopped a dozen feet in front of Ben and Willow. "You show more determination than I had thought possible for a pretender. The magic does not frighten you as it should. Is that because you are stupid or merely reckless?"

Ben's mind raced. "It's because I'm determined," he replied. "I didn't come into the Deep Fell to be frightened off."

"More's the pity for you, perhaps," she whispered, and the color of her eyes seemed to change from crimson to green. "I have never liked the Kings of Landover; I like you no better. It matters nothing to me that you are from another world, and it matters nothing why you have come. If you wish something of me, you are a fool. I have nothing I wish to give."

Ben's hands were sweating. This was not going well at all. "What if I have something I wish to give to you?"

Nightshade laughed, black hair shimmering as her body rocked. "You would give something to me? Landover's High Lord would give something to the witch of the Deep Fell?" The laughter stopped. "You are a fool after all. You have nothing that I want."

"Perhaps you are mistaken. Perhaps I do."

He waited and would say nothing more. Nightshade came nearer, her ghostly face bent down to view him more closely, her sharp features taut against the bones of her face. "I know of you, play-King," she said. "I have watched you travel from the Greensward to the lake country to the Melchor and finally to here. I know you seek the pledge of the valley's people and can command nothing more than the misguided loyalty of this girl, that charlatan Questor Thews, a dog, two kobolds, and those pathetic gnomes. You hold the medallion, but you do not command the magic. The Paladin stays gone from you. The Mark hunts you. You are a single step from being yesterday's memory!"

She loomed over him, a head taller, her dark form hanging like death's specter. "What can you give to me, play-King?"

Ben edged a step in front of Willow. "Protection."

The witch stared at him speechlessly. Ben kept his eyes fixed on hers, trying to back her away from him by sheer force of will, the closeness of her dark form suffocating. But Nightshade did not move.

"I am King of Landover, Nightshade, and I intend to remain King," he said suddenly. "I am not the play-King that you believe me, and I am not a fool. I may not be of this world, and I may not yet know everything about it I should. But I know enough to recognize its problems. Landover needs me. You need me. If you lose me, you risk losing yourself."

Nightshade stared at him as if he were mad, then glanced at Willow as if to ascertain whether or not the sylph thought him mad as well. Her eyes glittered as they sought his again. "What risk is there to me?"

Ben had her close attention now. He took a deep breath. "The magic goes out of the land, Nightshade. The magic fails. It fails because there is no King as a King was meant to be. Everything fragments, and the poison settles deeper. I see it happening, and I know its cause. You need me. The Mark claims the land, and sooner or later he will have it. The demon will not tolerate you. He will drive you out. He will not abide strength greater than his own."

"The Mark will not challenge me!" she sneered and there was fury in her eyes.

"Not yet, he won't," Ben pressed quickly. "Not in the Deep Fell. But what happens when the rest of the land has withered into an empty husk and only the Deep Fell remains? You'll be all alone. The Mark will have everything. He'll have strength enough to challenge you then!"

He was guessing, but something in the witch's eyes told him he was guessing right. Nightshade straightened, her black form rising up against the gloom. "And you believe that you can protect me?"

"I do. If the valley's people pledge to me, the Mark will not be so quick to challenge. He cannot stand against all of us. I don't think he will even try. And if you pledge first, the others must do the same. You are the most powerful, Nightshade; your magic is the strongest. If you give your allegiance to me, the others will follow. I ask nothing else from you. I promise in return to guarantee that the hollows will belong to you alone—always. No one shall bother you here. Not ever."

She almost smiled. "You offer nothing that I do not already have. I don't need you to stand against the Mark. I can do that whenever I choose. I can call the others to me and they will come because they are afraid!"

Oh, brother, Ben thought. "They won't come, Nightshade. They will hide or run from you or they will fight you. They will not allow you to lead them as they might allow me."

"The lake country will never accept you, Nightshade," Willow whispered in agreement.

Nightshade's brow furrowed. "The River Master's daughter would say as much," she sneered. "But you mistake whom you deal with, sylph. My magic would sicken ten times over what your father's would cure—and more quickly than this!"

Her hand shot out, seized Willow's wrist and turned the sylph's arm black and withered. Willow shrieked, and Ben yanked the stricken arm free. Instantly, the arm was restored, the sickness gone. Willow was flushed and there were angry tears in her eyes. Ben faced the witch.

"Seize me as you did her!" he challenged, and his hand closed about the medallion.

Nightshade saw the movement and drew back. Her eyes veiled. "Do not threaten me, play-King!" she warned darkly.

Ben held his ground. He was as angry now as she. "Nor you me or those who are my friends, witch," he replied.

Nightshade seemed to retreat within her robes. Her sharp face lowered into her raven hair, and one hand lifted slowly to point at Ben. "I grant you your determination, play-King. I grant you a measure of courage. But I do not grant you my pledge. If you would have that, you must first prove to me that you deserve it. If you are weaker than the Mark, then I ally myself to my disadvantage. I might as easily ally myself with the demon and bind him in a pledge of magic that he could not break. No, I will not risk myself for you until I know what strength you possess."

Ben knew he was in trouble. Nightshade had made a decision about him that she was not likely to alter. His mind worked frantically. The darkness of the castle, the vastness of its chambers, seemed to weigh down upon him. Nightshade was his last chance; he could not afford to lose her. He felt his hopes begin to fade, and he fought to hold on to them.

"We need each other, Nightshade," he argued, searching for a way out. "How can I convince you that I possess the strength necessary to be King?"

The witch seemed to think the matter through for a moment, her pale face lost again within her hair. Then slowly she looked up. There was an unpleasant smile on her thin lips. "Perhaps we do need each other—and perhaps there is something that can help us both. What if I were to tell you that there is a magic that could rid the Greensward of the dragon?"

Ben frowned. "Strabo?"

"Strabo." The smile stayed fixed. "There is such a magic—a magic that can make you master of the dragon, a magic that can give you command over everything that he does. Use it, and he will do as you say. You can send him from the Greensward, and then the Lords must give you their pledge."

"So you know of that as well," Ben mused, trying to give himself time to think. He studied the pale face carefully. "Why would you agree to give such a magic to me, Nightshade? You've already made it clear how you feel about me."

The witch smiled with the intensity of a wolf eyeing dinner. "I said nothing about *giving* the magic to you, play-King. I said, what if I were to *tell* you of such a magic. The magic is not in my possession. You must retrieve it from where it is hidden and bring it to me. Then we will share the magic, you and I. Bring it to me, and I will believe in your strength and accept you as King. Do so, and you will hold the promise of your own future."

"Ben . . ." Willow began, a note of caution in her voice.

Ben dismissed her with a shake of his head. He had already committed himself. "Where is this magic to be found?" he asked Nightshade.

"It will be found in the mists," she answered softly. "It will be found in the fairy world."

Willow's hand clamped on Ben's. "No, Ben!" she exclaimed.

"The magic is called Io Dust," Nightshade continued, ignoring the girl. "It grows from a midnight-blue bush with silver leaves. It nurtures in pods the size of my fist." She clenched her hand before Ben's face. "Bring two pods—one for me, one for yourself. The dust from a single pod will be enough to give you mastery over the dragon!"

"Ben, you cannot go into the fairy world!" Willow was frantic. She wheeled on the witch. "Why not go yourself, Nightshade? Why send Ben Holiday when you will not go yourself?"

Nightshade's head lifted in disdain. "I am admonished by one whose people left the fairy world for this valley when the choice to remain was theirs? You are quick to forget, sylph. I cannot go back into the fairy world. I was cast out from it and am forbidden to return. It is certain death for me if I go back." She smiled coldly at Ben. "But perhaps this one will have better fortune than I. He, at least, is not forbidden entry."

Willow yanked Ben about to face her. "You cannot go, Ben. It is death if you do. No one can go into the fairy world and survive who is not born to and kept by it. Listen to me! My people left that world because of what it was—a world in which reality was a projection of emotion and thought, abstraction and imagery. There was no reality apart from what we were, and no substantive truth apart from ourselves! Ben, you cannot survive in such an environment. It requires disciplines and familiarities that you lack. It will destroy you!"

He shook his head. "Maybe not. Maybe I'm more capable than you think."

Tears glistened in her eyes. "No, Ben. It will destroy you," she repeated tonelessly.

There was an intensity in her face and voice that was frightening. Ben stared into her eyes and hardened himself against the plea that was mirrored there. Slowly he pulled her close against him. "I have to go, Willow," he whispered so that only she could hear. "I have no other choice!"

"She tricks you, Ben!" Willow whispered back, her face hard against his. "This is a trap! I hear the deception in her voice!" She was shaking. "I see now what this castle is! This castle is a projection of the magic against the wall of the mists! Journey far enough through it and you stand within the fairy world! Ben, she arranged this deception! She knew you were coming to her and she knew why! She has known all along!"

He nodded and pushed her gently away. "That doesn't change anything, Willow. I still have to go. But I'll be careful, I promise. I'll be very careful." She shook her head wordlessly, and the tears ran down her cheeks. He hesitated, then leaned forward and kissed her gently on the mouth. "I'll be back."

She seemed to find herself again in that instant. "If you go, so do I."

"He goes alone," Nightshade interjected coldly, her face impassive. "I want no aid being given by a creature born of the fairy world. I want no interference from anyone. I want to see for myself whether the play-King possesses the strength he claims. If he brings the pods of Io Dust to me, I will have my proof."

"I have to go," Willow insisted, shaking her head slowly. "I belong to him."

"No," Ben told her gently. He struggled to find the right words. "You belong to Landover, Willow—and I don't yet. Maybe I never will. But I have to belong to the land before I can ever even think of belonging to her people. I haven't earned that right yet, Willow—and I have to!" His smile was tight. "Wait for me here. I will come back for you."

"Ben . . ."

"I will come back," he insisted.

He stepped away, turning again to find Nightshade. He felt empty and directionless, as if some tiny bit of life was turned loose in a sea of debris and blowing winds. He was about to be alone for the first time since he had come into Landover, and he was frightened almost beyond reason.

"Where do I go?" he asked Nightshade, fighting to keep his voice calm.

"Follow the corridor—there." She pointed behind her, and torchlight glimmered along a shadowed corridor in which mist swirled like a living thing. "You will find a door at its end. The fairy world lies beyond."

Ben nodded and walked past her without a word. His mind reeled with whispered warnings that he was forced to ignore. He slowed at the corridor entrance and glanced back. Willow stood where he had left her, her slender form a pale green shadow, her strange, beautiful face streaked with tears. He was filled with sudden wonder. How could this girl care so much for him? He was just a stranger to her. He was just someone she had happened across. She had blinded herself to the truth with fables and dreams. She imagined love where there was none. He could not understand.

Nightshade stared after him, her cold face expressionless.

He turned slowly away and walked into the mists.

FAIRY

Everything disappeared at once. The mists closed about like a shroud, and Ben Holiday was alone. The corridor tunneled ahead, coiling snakelike through pairs of torches that gave off dim halos of light in a haze of shadows and gloom. Ben followed it blindly. He could barely see the passage walls against which the halos cast their feeble glow, blocks of stone charred by flame and stained by damp. He could hear only faintly the sound of his boots as they thudded against the flooring. He could see or hear nothing else.

He walked for a long time, and the fear which had already taken seed within him spread like a cancer. He began to think about dying.

But the corridor ended finally at an iron-bound, wooden door with a great curved handle. Ben did not hesitate. He gripped the handle and twisted. The door opened easily, and he stepped quickly through.

He was standing in an elevator facing forward. A panel of lighted buttons to the right of the closed doors told him he was going up.

He was so astonished that for an instant he could only stare at the doors and the buttons. Then he wheeled about, searching for the door through which he had passed. It was gone. There was only the rear wall of the elevator, simulated oak with dark plastic trim. He felt along the edges with his fingers, testing for a hidden latch. There was none.

The elevator stopped on the fifth floor, and a janitor got on.

"Morning," he greeted pleasantly and punched button eight.

Ben nodded wordlessly. What in the hell was going on? He stared at the control panel, finding it oddly familiar. He glanced hurriedly about the interior and realized that he was on the elevator that serviced the building where his law offices were situated.

He was back in Chicago!

His mind spun. Something had gone wrong. Something *must* have gone wrong. Otherwise, what was he doing here? He braced himself against the wall railing. There was only one explanation. He had gone back through the mists completely; he had passed right through the fairy world into his own.

The elevator stopped at eight, and the janitor got off. Ben stared after him as the doors slipped closed. He had never seen the man before in his life, and he thought he knew all of the help that serviced the building—by sight, if not by name. They cleaned the offices on Sundays; that was the only time they were permitted to ride the elevators. He was always there, too, catching up on his paperwork. But he didn't know this man. Why didn't he?

He shook his head. Maybe it was someone new, he decided—someone the building supervisor had just hired. But new help wouldn't work the offices on Sunday alone, not when they had access to . . . He caught himself. He smiled, suddenly giddy. Sunday! It must be Sunday if the janitors were using the elevators! He almost laughed. He hadn't thought to ask the day of the week since he had crossed into Landover!

The elevator began to rise. He saw the panel buttons blink in front of him and watched them climb toward fifteen. The elevator was taking him to his office. But he hadn't punched the button, had he? He glanced down in confusion and jumped. He was no longer wearing the clothes he had worn when Nightshade had sent him into the mists. He was wearing the running suit and Nikes he had worn when he had gone into the Blue Ridge.

What was happening?

The elevator stopped at fifteen, the doors slid open and he stepped out into the hallway. A jog left and he was at the glass doors that fronted the lobby to the offices of Holiday and Bennett, Ltd. The doors were open. He pushed through and stepped inside.

Miles Bennett turned from the reception desk, a sheaf of papers in his hands. He saw Ben, and the papers slipped from his fingers and tumbled to the floor. "Doc!" he whispered.

Ben stared. It was Miles who stood before him, but not the Miles he had left behind. This Miles was a shell of that other man. He was no longer simply heavy; he was bloated. His face was florid in the manner of a man who drinks too much. His dark hair had gone gray and thin. Worry lines marked his face like an etching.

The shock faded from his partner's eyes and was replaced with undisguised rancor. "Well, well—Doc Holiday." Miles spoke his name with distaste. "Goddamn if it isn't old Doc."

"Hello, Miles," he greeted and stuck out his hand.

Miles ignored it. "I can't believe it. I can't believe its really you. I thought I'd never see you again—thought no one ever would. Goddamn. I thought you long since gone to hell and shoveling brimstone, Doc."

Ben smiled, confused. "Hey, Miles, it hasn't been that long."

"No? You don't call ten years a long time? Ten goddamn years?" Miles smiled as he saw the stunned look on Ben's face. "Yeah, that's right, Doc—ten years. Not a living soul has heard a word from you in ten years. No one—me, least of all, your goddamn partner, in case you'd forgot!" He stumbled over the words, swallowing. "You poor, dumb jerk! You don't even know what's happened to you while you've been off in your fairy world, do you? Well, let me clue you in, Doc. You're broke! You've lost everything!"

Ben felt a chill settle through him. "What?"

"Yeah, everything, Doc." Miles leaned back against the desk top. "That's what happens when you're presumed legally dead—they take everything away and give it to your heirs or to the state! You remember your law, Doc? You remember how it works? You remember anything, goddamn it?"

Ben shook his head disbelievingly. "I've been gone ten years?"

"You always were a quick study, Doc." Miles was sneering openly at him now. "The great Doc Holiday, courtroom legend. How many cases was it you won, Doc? How many shoot-outs did you survive? Doesn't much matter anymore, does it? Everything you worked for is gone. It's all gone." The veins on his cheeks were red and broken. "You don't even have a place with this firm anymore. You're just a collection of old stories I tell the young bucks!"

Ben wheeled about and looked at the lettering over the glass entry doors. It read, Bennett and Associates, Ltd. "Miles, it seemed like only a few weeks . . ." he stammered helplessly.

"Weeks? Oh, damn you to hell, Doc!" Miles was crying. "All those dragons of the law you thought you'd slay, all those witches and warlocks of injustice that you thought you'd take on and straighten out—why the hell didn't you stay here and do it? Why'd you leave here for your goddamn fairy land? You weren't a quitter before, Doc. You were too stubborn to quit. Maybe that's why you were such a good lawyer. You were, you know. You were the best I'd ever seen. You could have done anything. I'd have given my right arm just to help you do it, too. I admired you that much. But, no, you couldn't survive in the same world with the rest of us. You had to have your own goddamn world! You had to jump ship and leave me with the rats! That's what happened, you know. The rats came out of their holes and took over—the rats, sniffing around the old cheese. I couldn't handle it alone! I tried, but the clients wanted you, the business couldn't function without you, and the whole goddamn mess went down the tubes!"

He sobbed. "Look at you, damn you! You don't look like you've aged a day! And look at me—a boozed-up, burned-out wreck . . ." He shoved forward, neck muscles straining against the collar of his shirt. "You know what I am, Doc? I'm dead weight, that's what I am. I'm something that takes up space—something the younger bucks are trying to find a way to shove quietly out the door!" He sobbed again. "And one day, they're gonna do it, Doc! They're gonna shove me right out of my own damn office . . ."

He broke down completely. Ben felt sick inside as he watched his old friend's composure disintegrate completely. He wanted to step forward, to go to him, but he was unable to move. "Miles . . ." he tried.

"Get out, Doc," the other cut him short, his voice breaking. He motioned roughly with his arm. "You don't belong here. They took everything you had long ago. You're a dead man, Doc. Get the hell out!"

He left the reception room in a rush and stumbled down the hall into his office. Ben stood rooted in place for an instant, then followed. When he reached Miles' office, the door was closed. He grasped the handle and stepped inside.

Mist swirled past his face . . .

The mist disappeared. He stood in an orchard of apple trees ripe with fruit. Green grasses waved gently in the summer breeze, and the smell of honeysuckle was in the air. A pasture fenced with board rail painted white was visible in the distance, and horses grazed in its enclosure. A stables sat close by, and a sprawling ranch house of brick and stained fir overlooked it all from a tree-shaded knoll.

He wheeled about in shock, already knowing that Miles, the office, and the elevator would all be gone. They were. There was nothing left. Had he imagined them? Had he imagined everything? The terrible confrontation with Miles was still replaying itself hatefully in his mind, the emotions it had triggered razor sharp as they cut against his memory. Had he imagined the whole thing?

He glanced quickly down at his clothing. The running suit and Nikes had been replaced by slacks, a short-sleeved shirt and loafers.

What in the hell was happening?

He fought to control the fear that raced through him and brought what was left of his common sense to bear. Had he jumped through time, he wondered? He didn't think so. But he might have imagined that he had. It could have all been just an illusion. It hadn't seemed an illusion, but it could have been. The mists could have blinded him. His passage through the fairy world could have deceived him somehow. He could have gone nowhere at all. But if he had gone nowhere and if everything he had seen was an illusion, then what was he seeing now . . . ?

"Ben?"

He turned, and there was Annie. She looked exactly as he remembered her, a small, winsome girl with huge brown eyes, button nose, and shoulder-length auburn hair. She was dressed in white, a summer frock with ribbons at the waist and shoulders. Her skin was pale and freckled, and the air about her seemed to shimmer in the flush of the sun's midday light.

"Annie?" he whispered in disbelief. "Oh, my God. Annie, is it really you?"

She smiled then, that unaffected little-girl smile she always gave him when she found something amusing in his expression, and he knew that it truly was her. "Annie," he repeated and there were tears in his eyes.

He started toward her, the tears almost blinding him, but her hands came up quickly in warning. "No, Ben. Don't touch me. You mustn't try to touch me." She stepped back a pace, and he stopped, confused. "Ben, I'm not alive anymore," she whispered, tears in her own eyes. She tried to smile through them. "I'm a ghost, Ben. I'm only an image of what you remember. If you try to take hold of me, I will disappear."

He stood before her, confused all over again. "What . . . what are you doing here if you're a ghost?"

She laughed gaily and it was as if he had never lost her. "Ben Holiday! Your memory is as selective as ever. Don't you remember this place? Look about you. Don't you know where we are?"

He glanced about, seeing again the pastureland, the stables, the horses, the ranch house on the knoll—and suddenly he did remember. "Your parents' home!" he exclaimed. "This is your parents' country home, for Christ's sake! I'd forgotten about it! I haven't been out here for . . . oh, I don't remember how long!"

Her laughter crinkled the corners of her eyes. "It was your special hideaway when the rigors of city life became too much. Remember? My parents used to kid you about being a city boy who didn't know a horse's front end from its hind. You used to say there wasn't much difference. But you loved it here, Ben. You loved the freedom it gave you." She glanced about wistfully. "That's why I still come here, you know. It reminds me of you. Isn't that odd? We spent so little time here, but still it's the place that reminds me most of you. I think it was the sense of freedom it seemed to give you that made me feel so good about it—that more so than my own love of the country."

She wheeled about, pointing back toward the ranch. "Remember the dormer passageways that connected the sleeping rooms through their closets? We used to laugh about those, Ben. We used to talk about gremlins living there—as in the movie. We used to threaten to board them up if anything strange ever happened while we were staying over. You said we'd own that house someday, after my parents were gone, and then we'd board them up for sure!"

Ben nodded, smiling. "Annie, I did always love it here—always."

She folded her arms across her breast, her smile fading. "But you didn't keep the house, Ben. You don't even come back to visit."

He winced at the pain in her eyes. "Your parents were gone, Annie. It . . . hurt too much to come back after losing you, too."

"You should have kept the home, Ben. You would have been happy here.

We could have still been with each other here." She shook her head slowly. "At least you should have come to visit. But you never came even once. You still don't come. I wait for you to come, but you never do. I miss you so much, Ben. I need to have you by me . . . even though I can't touch you or hold you as I once did. Just having you near helps me . . ." She trailed off. "I can't make you see me in the city, Ben. You don't see anything there. I don't like the city. If I must be a ghost, I would much prefer to haunt the country where everything is fresh and green. But it is no good living here either when you never come."

"I'm sorry, Annie," he apologized quickly, anxiously. "I never thought that it would be *possible* for me to see you again. I would have come had I known that you were here."

She smiled. "I don't think you would have, Ben. I don't think I mean anything to you anymore. Even your coming now was an accident. I know what you are about in your life. Ghosts have better sight than the living. I know that you have chosen to leave me and travel to another world—a world where I will become only a memory. I know of the girl you have met. She is very pretty—and she loves you."

"Annie!" He almost reached for her in spite of the warning. He had to force his hands to remain at his sides. "Annie, I don't love this girl. I love you. I have always loved you. I left because I couldn't stand what was happening to me with you gone! I thought I had to try something or I would lose everything that was left of me!"

"But you never came looking for me, Ben," she insisted, her voice soft and filled with hurt. "You gave up on me. Now I've lost you forever. You've gone into this other world, and I can never have you back. I can't come to you there. I can't have you close to me like this and I need that, Ben. Even a ghost needs the closeness of the one she loves."

Ben felt his grip on his emotions start to slip. "I can still come back, Annie. I have the means to do so. I don't have to stay in Landover."

"Ben," she whispered, her brown eyes sad and empty. "You no longer belong in this world. You chose to leave it. You can't come back. I know that you have spoken with Miles Bennett. What he told you was true. Ten years have passed, Ben. You've nothing to come back to. Everything you once had is gone—your possessions, your position with the firm, your standing with the bar, everything. You made a choice ten years ago, and you have to accept the fact that it's too late to change it now. You can never come back."

Ben's struggled in vain to respond. This was madness! How could it be happening? Then he caught himself sharply. Maybe it wasn't happening. Maybe it was all part of the illusion he had suspected before, a trick of the mists and the fairy world, none of it real. The enormity of that possibility stunned him. Annie seemed real, damn it! How could she not be?

"Daddy?"

He turned. A small child stood a dozen feet away in the shadow of a giant apple tree, a little girl no more than two, her tiny face a mirror of Annie's. "This is your daughter, Ben," he heard Annie whisper. "Her name is Beth."

"Daddy?" the little girl called to him, and her small arms reached up.

But Annie intercepted her, pulled her back, and held her close. Ben dropped slowly to one knee, his tall form stooped over, his arms folded against his chest to stop himself from shaking. "Beth?" he repeated dully.

"Daddy," the little girl said again, smiling.

"She lives with me, Ben," Annie told him, swallowing against her own pain. "We visit the country, and I try to teach her what life would have been like for her if . . ."

She couldn't finish. She bent her head into Beth's shoulder, hiding her face. "Don't cry, Mommy," the little girl said softly. "It's all right."

But it wasn't all right. Nothing was all right, and Ben knew that it never would be again. He felt himself breaking apart inside, needing to be with them, wanting to hold them both, unable to do anything but stand there helplessly.

"Why did you leave us, Ben?" Annie was asking again, her eyes searching his. "Why did you cross over into that other world when we needed you so badly in ours? You should never have quit on us, Ben. Now we've lost you—and you've lost us. We've lost each other forever!"

He was on his feet then, a cry breaking from his throat, stumbling blindly toward where they knelt, arms outstretched. He saw Beth's small arms trying to reach back.

Mist swirled past his face . . .

He stumbled, pitched forward, and fell sprawling to the ground. There was a moment of dizziness as he fought to regain the breath that had been knocked from his body. A rush of cool air swept over him, and the sunlight was gone. He blinked against the dusk that closed about, and his hands clutched at an earth turned barren and hard.

Annie and Beth—where were his wife and child?

Slowly he pushed himself back to his feet. He stood at the rim of a valley that was shrouded in mist and twilight. The valley had the look of a dying creature whose death had been a long and painful ordeal. Forests were stripped of their leaves and vines, the limbs and trunks of the trees gnarled and rotting. Plains had turned wintry, the grasses stunted, the flowers sapped of their color. Mountains crested against the misted skyline, but their slopes were stark and barren. A scattering of dwellings and castles hunched down against the earth, ill-kept and worn. Steam rose from lakes and rivers turned foul, their waters sluggish with filth.

Ben caught his breath in horror. He recognized the valley. It was Landover.

He looked down at his clothing. It was the clothing that he had been wearing when he had gone down into the Deep Fell.

"No!" he whispered.

Annie and Beth were forgotten. He searched frantically for some sign of life upon the ravaged land. He sought out movement about the dwellings and castles, but found none. He sought out Sterling Silver and found only an empty island in a lake of black water. He sought out the Deep Fell, Rhyndweir, the lake country, the Melchor, and all of the landmarks he had come to know. Each time, he found nothing but devastation. Everything had disappeared.

"Oh, my God!" he breathed.

He stumbled forward, breaking quickly into a run as he dashed down the slope of the hillside, still searching for something of the valley he had left behind him when he had ventured into the fairy world. Grasses rustled dry and stiff against his legs as he ran, and the brittle branches of dying scrub snapped off their stems like gunshots. He passed a stand of Bonnie Blues turned black, their leaves withered and curled. He scanned the trees of the nearest fruit grove and found them bare. No birds flew against the twilight. No small animals scattered at his approach. No insects hummed or darted past.

He grew quickly winded and slowed to a staggering halt. The valley lay blackened and empty before him. Landover was a graveyard.

"This can't be . . ." he started to protest softly.

Then a shadow materialized within the mist before him. "So Landover's King has finally found his way back to us," a caustic voice greeted.

The speaker stepped into view. It was Questor Thews, the gray robes and gaily colored silk scarves shredded and soiled, the white hair and beard ragged and unkempt. One leg was gone, and he hobbled forward on a crutch. Welts and scars marked his face and arms. His fingers were black with disease, and his eyes were bright with fever.

"Questor!" Ben whispered, horrified.

"Yes, High Lord, Questor Thews, once court wizard and advisor to the Kings of Landover, now a homeless beggar wandering in a land where only the forgotten still live. Are you pleased to see me so?"

His voice was so bitter that Ben shrank from it. "Pleased? Why would I be pleased?" he managed finally. "What happened, Questor?"

"What happened, High Lord? Do you truly not know? Look about you, then. That which you see is what happened! The land died for lack of the magic which a King could have given it! The land died. When the land died, her people died as well. There is nothing left, High Lord—everything is gone!"

Ben shook his head in confusion. "But how could that happen . . . ?"

"It could happen because Landover's King abandoned her!" the other cut him short, fury and pain in his voice. "It could happen because you were not here to prevent it! You were off in the fairy world in pursuit of your own ends, and we were left to manage as best we could! Oh, we tried to find you and bring you back; but once within the fairy world, you were lost to us. I warned you, High Lord. I told you that no one could go safely into the fairy world. But you did not listen to me. No, you listened only to your own foolish reasoning and you wandered into that world of mists and dreams and were lost to us. You were gone an entire year, High Lord. An entire year! No one could find you. The medallion was lost. All hope of finding a King was lost. It was the finish for us!"

He stumbled closer, hunching brokenly against the crutch. "The magic faded quickly, High Lord; the poison spread. Soon the creatures of the land, human and otherwise, began to sicken and die. It happened so fast that no one could defend against it—not the River Master with all his healing magic, not Nightshade with all her power. Now all are dead or scattered. Only a few remain—a few like me! We live only because we cannot manage to die!" His voice shook. "I thought that you would come back to us in time, High Lord. I kept hoping that you would. I was a fool. I believed in you, when I should have known you were not worth believing in!"

Ben shook his head sharply. "Questor, don't . . ."

A mottled hand brushed his protest aside. "It remains only for the Mark and his demons to come now, High Lord. There is no one left to stand against them, you see—no one. All are dead. All are destroyed. Even the strongest could not survive the passing of the magic." He shook his head in anguish. "Why did you not come back to us sooner, High Lord? Why did you stay gone so long when you knew you were needed? I loved this land and her people so! I thought it was the same with you. Oh, if I had strength enough left in me, I would take this crutch and . . ."

His body trembled, and he lifted the crutch threateningly. Ben stepped back in horror, but Questor could lift the crutch only inches, and the effort brought him to ground, a collapsed rag doll. Tears streamed down his ravaged face.

"I hate you so much for what you have done!" he cried. Slowly his face lifted. "Do you know how much I hate you? Do you have any idea? Let me show you!" There was madness in his eyes. "Do you know what became of your beloved sylph after you abandoned her? Do you know what became of Willow?" His face was a mask of fury. "Do you remember her need to nourish within the land's once fertile soil? Look down into the valley, close by that lake! Look down where the shadows lie deepest! Do you see that twisted, blackened trunk with its roots rotted away into . . . ?"

Ben could listen no more. He turned and ran. He ran without thinking, consumed with anger and horror that he could not control, desperate to escape the words of this hateful old man who blamed him for all that had happened. He ran, heedless of direction, pushing mindlessly forward through shadows and mist. Screams echoed after him, whether from within his own mind or outside, he could not tell. His world was collapsing about him like a house of cards brought down by an errant wind. He had lost everything—his old world, his new, his old friends, his new, his past, and his future. Familiar faces pushed in about him—Miles, Annie, Questor—their accusing voices whispering of his failures, hurt and anger in their eyes. Words pummeled him, insidious warnings of the losses he had caused.

He ran faster, his own cries strident against the beating of his heart.

Then suddenly he quit moving altogether. He was still running, but the ground had been taken out from under him and he was suspended in air. There was sudden pain. He jerked about violently, searching for the cause . . .

Taloned feet had fastened on his shoulders, digging deep into clothing and flesh. A massive, twisted form hovered above him, scaled body smelling fetid and rank, the disease of the land sunk deep within it. Ben stared upward wildly, and Strabo's maw gaped open as the dragon reached down for him.

He screamed.

Mist swirled past his face . . .

It was happening again. Time and place were shifting. He closed his eyes instantly and kept them closed. The act was accomplished almost before the directive was issued. Something was terribly wrong. His instincts told him so. His instincts told him that the swift changes of time and place that he had been experiencing were impossible. They seemed to be happening, but in reality they were not. They were illusions or dreams or something very close. Whatever they were, they were taking over his life and tearing him apart. He had to stop them now before he was destroyed.

He hid quietly in the darkness of his mind, eyes tightly shut, his voice stilled. He forced himself to concentrate on the sound of his heart beating within his body, on the feeling of the blood coursing through his veins, on the silence that shrouded him. Be at rest, he whispered. Be at peace. Do not give way to what seems to be happening.

Slowly he regained control of himself. But still he kept his eyes closed. He was afraid that if he opened them some new horror would await. He must understand what had been happening to him first.

Meticulously, he reasoned it through. He had gone nowhere, he decided. He was still within the fairy world, still within the mists. Nor had ten years or even one year lapsed. They couldn't have. The shifts in time and place were illusions brought about by the fairy world or its inhabitants or his reaction to either or both. What he needed to do now was to discover what was causing this. He just needed to understand why.

He built the foundation for his understanding one block at a time. Nothing he had seen was real—that was his beginning premise. If nothing was real, then everything must be false, and if everything was false, there had to be a reason for it taking the form that it had. Why was he seeing these particular visions? He retreated deep into his mind, down into its blackest, most silent regions, where there was nothing beyond the sound of his own thinking. Questor, Miles, and Annie—why had he seen them depicted as he had? He let himself relax in the inky darkness. Willow had warned him of the dangers of the fairy world. What was it that the sylph had said? She had said that in the fairy world reality was a projection of emotion and thought. She had said that there was no reality, no substantive truth apart from what you were. If that were so, what he had seen was what he had projected from within himself. What he had seen was a manifestation of his emotions . . .

He took a long, slow breath and let it out again. His understanding was beginning to take shape. His visions were the creation of his emotions—but which emotions? He replayed in his mind what he had seen of Miles, Annie and Beth, and Questor Thews. All had been angered or disappointed by what he had caused them to suffer. All had blamed him for their misfortunes. Illusions, but that was the way he had seen them. He had seen them as victims of his own poor judgment and inaction. Why had he seen them so? His mind raced through the possibilities, and suddenly he had his answer. He was afraid that what he had envisioned might really happen! He was afraid that it might all be true! Fear! Fear was the emotion that had shaped his thinking!

It made perfect sense. Fear was the strongest emotion of all. Fear was the least controllable emotion. That was why he had jumped through time and space to witness the horrors that had seemed to befall his friends and loved ones—the fear was breathing life into his worst imaginings. He had been frightened that he would fail in what he had undertaken from the moment he had made his decision to cross into Landover. The natural result of such a failing would be the scenarios he had just experienced. He would be cut off from his old life entirely with no chance to return, he would be stripped of all that he had believed he would gain in his new life, and he would fail his friends and family alike. He would be a man who had lost everything.

A sense of relief rushed through him. Now he understood. Now he knew what to do. If he could control his emotions, he could prevent the nightmares. If he could shut off the fear, conscious or subconscious, he could bring himself back into the present. It was a tall order, but it was his only chance.

He took several long moments to collect his thoughts and to focus them on the task at hand. He told himself to remember the kind of lawyer he had once been, to remember the courtroom skills that had made him so. He told himself to remember that everything he had experienced before was a lie, an imagining of his own making. He pictured instead the world he had seen when traveling through the time passage that had brought him to Landover—the forest with its shroud of mist.

Then slowly he opened his eyes. The forest was back again, deep, solitary, primeval. Mist swirled gently through its trees. Faint visions danced upon the mists, but they did not trouble him. The nightmares were gone, the lies banished. His reasoning had not failed him. He breathed deeply, letting himself drift through the cool, peaceful darkness, in and out of the substanceless visions. Cautiously, he began to search for the magic he had come here to find, for the Io Dust. He thought he caught glimpses of silver and midnight-blue, but nothing whole. He continued to drift, and suddenly he was fragmenting like ice shattered on stone. He was breaking apart, splitting into separate pieces that would not rejoin. Frantically, he forced the feeling down within himself to feel the solidity of the earth beneath his feet.

The sense of dissipation faded. The mist closed about.

He was no longer alone. Voices whispered.

—You are welcome, High Lord of Landover—

—You have found yourself and in doing so you have found us—

He struggled to speak, but found he could not. Faces crowded close, lean and sharp, their features somehow muddied in the twilight. They were the faces he had seen when he had crossed into Landover through the time passage. They were the faces of the fairies.

—Nothing is lost that we do not first see as lost, High Lord. Believe it saved, and it may be. Visions born of fear give birth to our failing. Visions born of hope give birth to our success—

—What is possible lives within us, and it only remains for us to discover it. Can you give life to the dreams that live within you, High Lord? Look into the mists and see—

Ben stared deep into the mists, then watched them swirl and part before him. A land of incredible beauty appeared, sunlight spreading out across it like a golden mantle. Life flourished in the land, and it was filled with boundless energy. There was excitement and promise beyond anything he would have believed possible. He felt himself cry out at the sight and feel of it.

Then slowly the vision faded and was gone. The voices whispered.

—Another time and place for such visions, High Lord. Another life. Bondings such as this must wait their birthings—

—You are a child among elders, High Lord, but you are a child who shows promise. You have seen the truth behind the lies that would deceive you and know it to be your own. You have earned the right to discover more—

Then show me, he wanted to shout! But he could not, and the voices whispered on.

—You have unmasked the fear that would have destroyed you, High Lord. You have shown great presence. But fear has many disguises and assumes many forms. You must learn to recognize them. You must remember what they truly are when next they come for you—

Ben's throat worked soundlessly. He didn't understand. What was the fairy's meaning?

—You must go back now, High Lord. Landover needs your help. Her King must be there to serve her—

—But you may take with you that which you came to find—

Ben saw a bush materialize within the mist before him—a bush of midnight-blue with silver leaves. He felt something pressed into the palm of each hand. He looked down and found that he was holding a pair of oblong pods.

The voices whispered.

—Io Dust, High Lord. Inhale it, and you belong to the giver until released. A single breath is all it takes. But beware. The witch Nightshade seeks the dust for uses of her own and plans to share nothing of it with you. Once you have secured it for her, you will have no further value—

—Be quicker than she, High Lord. Be swift—

Ben nodded mutely, determination etched into the lines of his face.

—Go now. One day only has been lost to you—but that day must remain lost. To bring you back more quickly would cause you harm that could not be repaired. Understand, therefore, that things must necessarily be as you find them—

—Come back to us, High Lord, when the magic is found again—

—Come back to us when the need is there—

—Come . . . —

— . . . back—

Voices, faces, and slender forms faded into the mist and were gone. The mist drew back in a tight swirl and disappeared.

Ben Holiday blinked in disbelief. He stood once more in the twilight of the Deep Fell, a pod of Io Dust gripped tightly in each hand. He glanced about cautiously and found that he was alone. Fragments of his imagined encounters with Miles, Annie, and Questor Thews darted momentarily through his memory, cutting like tiny knives. He winced at the pain they caused and quickly brushed them away. They had never been real. They had been lies. His meeting with the fairies had been the only truth.

He lifted the pods of Io Dust and stared thoughtfully at them. He could not help himself. He began to smile like the Cheshire Cat. He had done the impossible. He had gone into the fairy world and, despite everything, he had come out again.

He felt as if he had been reborn.

IO DUST

The Cheshire Cat smile and the good feelings that went with it lasted about thirty seconds—the time it took Ben Holiday to remember the fairies' warning about Nightshade.

He glanced hurriedly about, eyes sweeping the misted gloom of the Deep Fell. There was no sign of the witch, but she was out there somewhere, waiting for him, planning to dispose of him the instant she got her hands on the Io Dust. That must have been her intention from the beginning—to send him into the fairy world to do what she could not and then to do away with him on his return. He frowned. Had she known that he *would* return? Probably not. It would make no difference to her if he didn't. It cost her nothing to let him try. But the fairies had spoken as if she expected that he would come back. That bothered him. How could the witch have known that he would succeed in doing something that no one else could?

His hands closed reassuringly about the pods and he took a deep breath to steady himself. There wasn't time just now to worry about what the witch did or didn't know. He had to find Willow and escape the Deep Fell as quickly as he could. He was frightened for the sylph; Nightshade was unlikely to treat her any better than she had treated Ben. Anything might have happened to the girl in his absence, and whatever happened would most certainly be his fault. A whole day lost, the fairies had said. That was far too much time for the girl to have been left alone. Willow was no match for Nightshade. Worse, the others from the little company might have come down into the Deep Fell looking for their missing King and run afoul of the witch as well.

Gritting his teeth angrily against the unpleasant possibilities, he cast about a second time in a effort to get his bearings. Mist and forest rose about him like a wall, and one direction looked the same as another. Clouds hung low across the forest roof, concealing sun and sky. There was nothing to tell him where he was or where he should go.

"Damn!" he whispered softly.

Throwing caution to the winds, he began walking. A lot had happened to Ben Holiday since he had come into Landover from his own world, and most of it had been bad. Each time he had tried to take a step forward, he had been forced to take two steps back. It seemed as if nothing could go right. But all that was about to change. For once, he was going to succeed. He had gone into the fairy world and come out again with the Io Dust when every shred of logic said he couldn't. He had the means to rid the Greensward of the dragon Strabo and gain the pledge of his most important ally. It would be a giant leap forward toward accomplishing everything he had set out to accomplish—never mind the single steps he had been experimenting with so far. He didn't care if there were a dozen Nightshades lurking about in the forest mist; he was not about to let this opportunity slip through his fingers.

A pair of furry faces pushed through the brush directly in front of him, and he jumped back with a startled cry.

"Great High Lord!"

"Mighty High Lord!"

It was Fillip and Sot. Ben exhaled sharply and waited for his heart to drop back out of his throat. So much for his brave determination!

The G'home Gnomes stepped out of the bushes guardedly, their ferret faces hawking the forest scents, noses twitching expectantly.

"High Lord, is it really you? We never thought to see you again!" Fillip said.

"Never! We thought you lost in the mist!" Sot said.

"Where have you two been?" Ben asked, remembering that they had fled the castle at the witch's transformation from the crow.

"Hiding!" Fillip whispered.

"Watching!" Sot whispered.

"The witch looked for us long and hard," Fillip said.

"But she couldn't find us," Sot said.

"Not when we went underground," Fillip said.

"Not in our burrows," Sot said.

Ben sighed. "Bully for you." He glanced about. "Where is she now?"

"Back where you left her in that clearing, High Lord," Fillip said.

"Still waiting for your return," Sot said.

Ben nodded. "And Willow?"

Fillip glanced quickly at Sot. Sot looked at the ground.

Ben knelt before them, a hollow feeling opening in the pit of his stomach. "What happened to Willow?"

Furry faces wrinkled uncomfortably and grimy paws twisted together.

"High Lord, we don't know," Fillip said finally.

"We don't," Sot agreed.

"When you failed to return, the others came looking for you," Fillip said.

"They came down from the valley's rim," Sot said.

"We didn't even know they were in the valley," Fillip said.

"If we had, we would have warned them," Sot said.

"But we were hiding," Fillip said.

"We were frightened," Sot said.

Ben brushed the explanations aside with an impatient wave of his hand. "Will you just tell me what happened!"

"She took them all prisoner, High Lord," Fillip said.

"She took them all," Sot echoed.

"Now they have disappeared," Fillip finished.

"Not a trace of them," Sot agreed.

Ben sat back slowly on his heels; the color drained from his face. "Oh, my God!" he said quietly, his worst fears realized. Willow, Questor, Abernathy, and the kobolds—Nightshade had them all. And it was his fault. He took a long moment to consider the dilemma, then came back to his feet. There could be no thought of escape now—not without his friends. Io Dust or no Io Dust, he wasn't about to leave them behind.

"Can you take me to Nightshade?" he asked the gnomes.

Fillip and Sot regarded him with undisguised horror.

"No, High Lord!" Fillip whispered.

"No, indeed!" Sot agreed.

"She will make you a prisoner as well!" Fillip said.

"She will make you disappear with the others!" Sot said.

Entirely possible, Ben thought to himself. Then he gave the G'home Gnomes an encouraging smile. "Maybe not," he told them. He pulled one of the pods of Io Dust from beneath his tunic and held it up thoughtfully. "Maybe not."

He took five minutes or so to prepare for his encounter with Nightshade. Then he explained the plan he had devised to the gnomes, who listened dutifully and regarded him with perlexed stares. They seemed uncertain what it was he was talking about, but there was no point in trying to explain it further.

"Just try to remember what it is that you're to do and when you're to do it," he cautioned finally and gave up on the matter.

They set out through the forest, the gnomes in the lead, Ben trailing. The afternoon light was fading, passing slowly toward dusk. Ben glanced about uneasily, pausing briefly at the sight of shadows that flickered through the mists behind him. The fairy world was back there somewhere and with it the ghosts of his imagination. He could feel their eyes on him yet, the living and the dead, the past and the present, the old world and the new. What he had seen had been lies, his own fears brought to life. But the lies lingered, whispers of truths that might yet be. He had failed no one in the ways the fairy mists had shown. But he might, if he were not as swift as the fairies had warned that he must be. He might fail them all.

The minutes slipped by. Ben felt them pass with agonizing swiftness. He wanted to urge the gnomes to hurry faster, to quicken their studied pace through the forest maze. But he kept his peace; Fillip and Sot were taking no chances with Nightshade and neither should he.

Then a clearing opened ahead through a screen of pine and heavy brush, barely visible in the gloom. Fillip and Sot dropped into a crouch and glanced hurriedly back at Ben. He crouched with them, then inched ahead cautiously for about another yard or so and stopped.

Nightshade sat statuelike on the webbed, dust-covered throne where she had first appeared to him, eyes fixed on the ground before her. Weather-beaten tables and benches were scattered about before her, ringed by a line of blackened stanchions in which tiny fingers of flame licked at the shadows. The courtyard, the portcullis, and the entire castle were gone. There was only the forest and these few ruined bits of furniture sheltering the witch.

Blood-red eyes blinked, but did not lift.

Ben crept slowly back again, taking the G'home Gnomes with him. When they were safely out of earshot, he dispatched them to carry out their assignment. Soundlessly, they disappeared into the trees. Ben watched them go, lifted his eyes skyward in a silent prayer, and settled back to wait.

He let fifteen minutes pass, judging the time as best he could, then stood up and started forward boldly. He passed through the screen of pine and brush and stepped into the clearing where Nightshade waited.

The witch looked up slowly, head and eyes lifting to watch his approach. Her stark, sharp-featured face reflected a mix of pleasure and surprise—and something else. Excitement. Ben came toward her cautiously, knowing he must be careful. He was still a dozen paces off when she stood up and signaled for him to stop.

"Do you have it?" she asked softly.

He nodded, saying nothing.

Her thin hand ran back through her raven hair, smoothing out the white streak like a trail of foam stirred in dark waters. "I knew you to be better than the play-King I called you," she whispered, her smile suddenly dazzling. She was tall and majestic standing there before him, robes spread against the forest, marble skin flawless. "I knew you to be . . . special. I have always had the sight." She paused. "The Io Dust—show it to me."

He glanced about, as if searching. "Where is Willow?"

The red eyes narrowed almost immeasurably. "Waiting, safely kept. Now show me!"

He started forward, but her hand came up like a shield and her voice was a hiss. "From there!"

Both hands were in his pockets. Slowly he extracted the left, producing an oblong pod for her inspection.

Her face came alive with excitement. "Io Dust!" She was shaking as she beckoned him closer. "Bring it to me. Carefully!"

He did as he was told, but stopped just out of reach, glancing about once again. "I think you ought to tell me where Willow is first," he hedged.

"First the Dust," she insisted, reaching.

He let her take the pod, saying, "Oh, that's all right, I see her now, back there in the trees." He started past her, looking anxiously. "Willow! Over here!"

His call and the fervent prayers that accompanied it were both answered on cue. There was a rustling within the brush and a glimpse of someone coming into view. Nightshade turned in startled surprise, red eyes narrowing, following Ben's gaze. Words of disclaimer were already forming on her lips.

Ben's right hand came out of his pocket and he flung a handful of the concealed Io Dust directly into Nightshade's face. The witch gasped in surprise—inhaling the dust as she did so. Surprise and fury twisted her thin features with a look of sudden horror. Ben threw a second fistful of the dust into her face—and again she inhaled it, tripping over her robes as he pushed her roughly back. The pod flew from her hands and she sprawled back upon the earth in a tangle.

Ben was on her like a cat. "Don't touch me!" he cried in warning. "Don't even think about hurting me! You belong to me; you will do anything and everything I tell you and nothing else!" He saw her lips draw back in a snarl of rage, and felt the sweat soak the back and underarms of his tunic. "Tell me that you understand," he whispered quickly.

"I understand," she repeated and her hatred for him burned in her eyes.

"Good." He took a deep breath and slowly climbed back to his feet. "Stand up," he ordered.

Nightshade stood, straightening herself slowly, her body stiff and unyielding, as if constricted from within by some iron will that she fought to resist and could not. "I will destroy you for this!" she snarled. "I will see you suffer in ways that you could not imagine!"

"Not today, you won't," he muttered, more to himself than to her. He glanced hurriedly about. "Fillip! Sot!"

The G'home Gnomes crept cautiously from the bushes where they had been hiding, waiting for Ben's signal to pretend that they were Willow answering his call. They emerged with looks of apprehension etched into their furry faces, their ferret eyes peering almost blindly toward the witch.

"Great High Lord," Fillip whispered.

"Mighty High Lord," Sot whispered.

Neither sounded quite so certain he was either, inching forward like rats prepared to bolt at the slightest move. Nightshade swung her gaze on them like a hammer and they cringed from its blow.

"She can't hurt you," Ben assured them—working at the same time at assuring himself. He walked over to pick up the discarded pod and brought it back. He held it up for Nightshade to inspect. "Empty," he said, pointing to a tiny hole he had carved in its bottom. "I took out all the dust and put it in my pocket to use on you. Just about what you had planned for me, wasn't it? Answer me."

She nodded. "It was." The words were laced with venom.

"I want you to stand here and do only what I tell you. We'll start with some questions. I'll ask them and you'll answer them. But tell me the truth, Nightshade—no lies. Understand?" She nodded wordlessly. Ben reached into his tunic front and extracted the second pod of Io Dust. He held it out to her. "Will the dust contained in this pod be enough to gain control of the dragon?"

She smiled. "I don't know."

He hadn't expected that. A suspicion of doubt tugged at his mind. "Have I given you enough dust that you must do as I say?"

"Yes."

"For how long?"

She smiled again. "I don't know."

He kept his expression neutral. There would be little margin for error, it appeared. "If you feel your need to obey me fading, you must tell me. Do you agree?"

The hatred in her eyes burned deeper. "I agree."

He didn't trust her, Io Dust or no Io Dust. He wanted to get this over with and get out of the Deep Fell. Fillip and Sot looked as if they were at least a dozen steps ahead of him already. They were crouched down in the shadow of one of the ruined tables, snouts buried in their chests like confused ostriches.

His eyes returned to Nightshade. "What have you done with Willow and the others who came with me?"

"I took them prisoner," she said.

"Questor Thews, Abernathy the scribe, the two kobolds? All of them?"

"Yes. They came looking for you, and I took them."

"What have you done with them?"

"I kept them for a time and then I sent them away."

She looked almost pleased with the way this was going, and Ben hesitated in spite of himself. "What do you mean, you sent them away?" he pressed.

"I had no use for them, so I sent them away."

Something was wrong. Nightshade had not planned to release him. She would never have released his friends. He stared at her, watching her eyes change suddenly from crimson to green. "Where did you send them?" he asked quickly.

Her eyes glittered. "To Abaddon. To the Mark."

He went cold all over. The lies he had imagined had become truths. He had failed his friends after all. "Bring them back!" he ordered sharply. "Bring them back now!"

"I cannot." She sneered openly. "They are beyond my reach!"

He seized the front of her dark robes, enraged. "You sent them there—you can bring them back again!"

She was smiling in delight. "I cannot, play-King! Once sent to Abaddon, they are beyond my power! They are trapped!"

He released her and stepped back, fighting to regain control of himself. He should have foreseen this! He should have done something to prevent it from happening! He stared about the shadowed clearing futilely, anger and disgust coursing through him as he considered and discarded possibility after possibility in rapid succession.

He wheeled back on her. "You will go into Abaddon and bring them back!" he ordered triumphantly.

Her smile was a thing of near ecstasy. "I cannot do that either, play-King! I have no power in Abaddon! I would be as helpless as they!"

"Then I'll go myself!" he said. "Where is the entrance, witch!"

She laughed, her face taut. "There *is* no entrance, fool! Abaddon is forbidden! Only a few . . . !"

Her triumph was so complete that she failed to catch herself in time. Her mouth snapped shut, but she was already too late. Ben seized the front of her robes.

"A few? What few? Who besides the demons can go there? You?" Her head twisted back and forth wordlessly. "Then who, damn it? Tell me!"

She shuddered and stiffened as if jerked by a hook embedded deep within. Her reply came out almost a scream. "Strabo!"

"The dragon!" he breathed, seeing now. He released her and walked away. "The dragon!" He wheeled and came back again. "Why can the dragon enter and not you?"

Nightshade was beside herself with rage. "His magic . . . encompasses a greater range than mine, reaches farther . . . !"

And is more powerful, Ben finished what she could not bring herself to say. He felt himself go limp, sweat soaking through him, weariness sapping at his strength. It made sense. He had first encountered Strabo at the fringes of the mists, still within the fairy world. If the dragon could pass into the fairy world, it stood to reason that he could pass into Abaddon.

And he could take Ben with him.

He almost smiled. The sudden coming together of circumstance and need was frightening. He had thought to use the Io Dust simply to send the dragon out of Landover. That would have been difficult and dangerous enough. Now he must use the Io Dust to force Strabo to carry him down into Abaddon where his friends were trapped and then carry them all out again. The enormity of the task was staggering. He must do this without direction or guidance. He must do this alone. But there was never any question of his not doing it. Willow, Questor, Abernathy, Bunion, and Parsnip had risked themselves for him time and time again. It was an imperative beyond that of Kingship that required he do the same for them.

His eyes found those of the witch. He could see an undisguised satisfaction mirrored there. "You have sworn to destroy me, Nightshade, but it is I who ought to destroy you," he whispered in fury.

Fillip and Sot had slipped from behind the table and were tugging tentatively at his legs.

"Can we go now, High Lord?" Fillip asked.

"Can we leave this place, High Lord?" Sot echoed.

"She frightens me," Fillip said.

"She wants to hurt us," Sot said.

Ben glanced down at them, saw the fear in their eyes, and watched their noses twitch expectantly. They looked like dirty children about to be punished, and he felt sorry for them. They had been through a lot.

"Just a moment more," he promised. He looked back at Nightshade. "How long has it been since you sent my friends into Abaddon?"

The witch narrowed her green eyes. "I disposed of them this morning—quite early."

"Did you harm them in any way?"

Her face pinched sharply. "No."

"They are well, then?"

She laughed. "Perhaps—if the demons haven't tired of them."

He wanted to throttle her, but he managed to keep control of himself. "Once I am within Abaddon, how can I find them?"

Nightshade's body seemed to fold itself deeper into the dark robes. "The dragon can find them for you—if he still obeys!"

Ben nodded wordlessly. There was that problem on top of everything else. How long would the Io Dust render the dragon helpless against him? How long before the effects of its magic wore off? There was only one way to find out, of course.

He shrugged the thought aside. "Where will I find the dragon?" he asked the witch.

Nightshade smiled darkly. "Everywhere, play-King."

"I'm sure." He rethought the question. "Where is he certain to go that I can wait for him to come?"

"The Fire Springs!" Her voice was a thin hiss. "He makes his home in the flame-waters!"

Ben remembered the Springs from his studies at Sterling Silver. Lava pools or oil pits or some such, they lay east beyond the Greensward, deep within the wastelands.

"High Lord!" Fillip called urgently, interrupting his thoughts.

"High Lord!" Sot tugged at his leg.

Ben nodded in response one time more. The day was coming to a close, the sun's light giving way to darkness, the shadows of dusk lengthening through the trees. He did not want to be caught in the Deep Fell after dark.

He stepped forward and stood directly before Nightshade. "I am King of Landover, Nightshade. You may not think so and others may not think so, but, until I decide otherwise, that's the way it is. A King has certain responsibilities. Among them is a responsibility to protect his subjects. You took it upon yourself to interfere with that responsibility and to place people who were not only subjects, but friends, in extreme danger—so extreme that I may never see any of them again!"

He paused, watching the hate glitter in her eyes as they turned from green back to red again. "You have passed judgment on yourself, Nightshade. What you have done to my friends, I now do to you. I command you to transform yourself into that crow and to fly back into the mists of the fairy world. Do not deviate from your course. Fly until you are once again within the old world and keep flying until . . . whatever happens, happens."

The witch shook with rage and frustration, and a sudden glimmer of fear crept into her eyes. "The fairy magic will consume me!" she whispered.

Ben was unmoved. "Do what I have told you, Nightshade. Do it now!"

Nightshade went rigid, then shimmered with crimson light. Flames exploded skyward in the iron stanchions. The witch and the light disappeared and in their place was the crow. Shrieking, it spread its wings against the dusk and flew away into the forest.

Ben stared after her, half expecting that she would return again. She did not. Nightshade was gone. She would fly as he had commanded until she entered the mists and the fairy world that was forbidden to her. He didn't know what would happen to her when she arrived, but he doubted that it would be pleasant. Too bad. He had given her at least as much chance to survive as she had given his friends. Fair was fair.

He shook his head. He had a bad feeling about it nevertheless.

"Let's find our way out of here," he muttered to Fillip and Sot, and the three of them hurried from the clearing.

STRABO

Ben slept that night in a poplar grove a few miles south of the rim of the Deep Fell. When he awoke at sunrise, he began his journey east to the Fire Springs.

He took Fillip and Sot with him, despite their obvious reluctance to go. He had no choice. He was afraid that without them he might become lost or side-tracked. He knew the country reasonably well from his studies at the castle, but there was always the possibility of encountering something those studies had missed or becoming stymied through ignorance, and he couldn't risk letting either happen. Time was something that he didn't have to waste, and the G'home Gnomes would have to bear with him a little while longer.

As it was, the journey took the better part of three days. It would have taken longer if Fillip and Sot hadn't appropriated a pair of plow horses whose day had clearly come and gone. They were so swaybacked and rough-gaited that it jarred his bones just to watch them amble about the campsite. Riding them was worse, but the pace of travel improved and they covered more distance, so he kept his peace. He never asked the gnomes where they got the horses. Moral principle took a backseat to expediency on this occasion.

They came down out of the forested hill country below the Deep Fell, skirted the broad plains of the Greensward, and passed east into the wasteland that stretched to the far rim of the valley. Their journey seemed endless. It dragged with the weight of a millstone tied about their necks. Ben was consumed by fear for his missing friends; too much could happen, all of it bad, before he would be able to reach them. Fillip and Sot were consumed by fear for their own skins; they believed themselves sacrificial lambs being led to the dragon's dinner table. The three talked to one another as little as possible, uncomfortable with the journey, its purpose, and each other.

Ben thought frequently of Nightshade as they traveled, and his thoughts were not pleasant ones. It was bad enough that he had left Willow alone and unprotected when he had gone into the mists, bad enough that Questor and the others had come down into the hollows looking for him when he had failed to return that first day, and worse than bad that all of them had been whisked off to Abaddon and the demons on a whim, while Nightshade idled about waiting for his return. But it was unforgivable that he hadn't made better use of the witch when he had held her captive under the power of the Io Dust. There were any number of things he should have done and hadn't. He should have had her use her magic to bring the dragon to him—to lure it there, if nothing else. Had she been unable to do that, he should have had her use the magic to send *him* to the dragon. That would have saved three days of traipsing all over the valley on a plow horse! He should have had her supply him with some of her magic. A little extra protection wouldn't have hurt. And he never should have let her off so easy—not after what she had done. He should have made certain she would cause him no further problems. Or at least he should have made her pledge to him in case she did escape.

But as the journey wore on, such thoughts fragmented, faded and died away. Should have, could have—what the hell difference did it make now? He had done the best he could; he simply hadn't thought of everything. A pledge made under duress was probably worthless. Unknown magic was probably more dangerous than no magic. Things were better as they were; he would find a way to make do with what he had.

They reached the Fire Springs late on the third day out. The gnomes had taken him deep into the wasteland east of the Greensward, a country of mixed horrors—barren plains of desert sand and dust, hills of saw grass, scrub, and gnarled short trees, sucking swamp that oozed red mud and quicksand, and petrified forests where the trees were tangled, broken bones that jutted from the earth. The land had a wintry cast beyond anything that Ben had seen in the other parts of the valley, a washed and colorless mix from dying vegetation and broken earth. Even the Bonnie Blues did not grow here. The three had worked their way through hills and ridges grown thick with stunted briar and tangled brush to a forest of deadwood, cresting a deep ravine. They walked their horses, unable to ride them through the heavy undergrowth. Mist floated in thick clouds over everything, a blanket that smelled of the land's death.

"There, High Lord!" Fillip cried suddenly, bringing Ben to a halt with a hasty tug on one sleeve.

"The Fire Springs, High Lord!" Sot announced, pointing into the distance.

Ben peered through the mist and trees. He couldn't see a thing. He peered harder. Now he caught a glimpse of something flickering against the gloom—a sort of light that reflected on the mist.

"Let's get a bit closer," he urged. "I can't see anything from here."

He started forward again and then stopped. Fillip and Sot were not moving. They glanced at each other, then at him, then at each other again. Their furry faces lowered and their noses twitched.

"This is close enough, High Lord," Fillip advised.

"As close as we're going, High Lord," Sot agreed.

"We have no protection against the dragon."

"No protection at all."

"He would eat us without thinking twice about it."

"He would burn us to the bone!"

Fillip hesitated. "The dragon is too dangerous, High Lord. Leave him and come away."

Sot nodded solemnly. "Let the dragon be, High Lord. Let him be."

Ben studied them a moment, then shook his head. "I can't let him be, fellows. I need him." He smiled ruefully and walked back. He placed a hand on the shoulder of each. "Will you wait here for me? Until I come back?"

Fillip looked up at him, eyes squinting. "We will wait for you, High Lord. Until you come back."

Sot rubbed his paws together absently. "*If* you come back," he muttered.

Ben left them with the plow horses and forged ahead into the tangled undergrowth. He picked his way cautiously, trying to be as quiet as possible. He could see geysers of steam rising from beyond the ridgeline to mingle with the mist. The flickering light shone more clearly, a shimmer of brightness dancing against the sky. He could smell something as well—something unpleasantly reminiscent of spoiled meat.

Sweat and dust streaked his face and arms, but he was cold inside. He had been anxious for this until now.

One hand stole to the pockets of his tunic. What remained of the Io Dust from the emptied pod was in his right pocket. The full pod was in his left. He really hadn't devised a plan yet for using the dust. He didn't have any idea at all what sort of plan would work. His sole objective was to get as close to the dragon as possible and hope that an opportunity presented itself.

A King of Landover ought to have a better plan than that, he thought gloomily, but he couldn't seem to come up with one.

He crested the ridgeline and peered over. A broad, misshapen ravine sprawled away before him, pitted with craters of all sizes and shapes, their bowls filled with an unidentifiable bluish liquid on which yellowish flames danced and burned, casting flickers of light against the shroud of mist. Tangled thickets and mounds of earth and rock clogged the floor of the ravine between craters, a formidable array of obstacles to anyone who sought to enter.

Ben looked the ravine over carefully. The dragon was nowhere to be seen. "It figures," he muttered.

He debated for a time what to do next. He could either wait where he was until Strabo returned or make his way down into the ravine and wait there. He opted for the second choice. He wanted to be as close as possible to the dragon when he finally faced it.

He slipped over the crest of the ridge and started down. A voice somewhere deep inside kept whispering that he was crazy. He fully agreed. He could not believe he was doing this. He was terrified of the dragon; he would have preferred to turn tail and run out of there as quickly as his shaking legs could manage it. He was not particularly brave; he was just desperate. He hadn't realized until this moment exactly how desperate he was.

But I won't let them down, he promised himself, thinking of Willow and the others. Whatever happens, I won't.

He reached the bottom of the ravine and glanced about. Steam geysered sharply from a crater close at hand, a whooshing sound that startled him. Flames lifted with the explosion and flickered hungrily against the mist. He could barely see where he was going this close to the springs, but he made his way forward resolutely. He supposed that someplace in the middle of the Fire Springs might be the best place to wait—although not *too* far out in the middle. His breathing was quick and ragged. He wished he had command of the Paladin. He wished Questor and the kobolds were with him. He wished *anyone* was with him. He wished he were somewhere else.

Steam and heat seared his nose and mouth, and he wrinkled his face in distaste. The smell was terrible. There were bones on the floor of the ravine, some of them quite new. He forced himself to ignore them. Brush and scrub blocked his way, but he pushed steadily through. He skirted a pile of broken rock, a boulder cluster, and the skeleton of a rather large animal. He thought he had come far enough. There was a massive earth mound just ahead with a curl of rock at one end. It appeared a good hiding place. He would wait there for the dragon to return.

He wondered suddenly how long that might be. The Fire Springs might be Strabo's home, but that didn't mean he came there all that often. Maybe he came only once a year, for pete's sake! His impatience with himself flared. He should have asked the witch, damn it! He should have . . .

He came to an abrupt and startled halt. He was less than a dozen feet from his chosen hiding place, the curl of rock against the massive earthen mound—and the mound had just moved.

He stared. No, he must have imagined it.

The mound moved again.

"Oh, my God," he whispered.

A tiny cloud of dust rose from just above what he had believed to be the tip of the rock curls and a huge, lidded eye slipped open.

Ben Holiday, lawyer extraordinaire, intrepid adventurer, and would-be King of Landover had just made a very big mistake.

The dragon stirred lazily, shaking off the layer of earth and dust that covered it, and uncurled from its sleep. It kept its eyes on Ben, watching him the way a snake watches its cornered prey. Ben was frozen where he stood. He should have used the Io Dust. He should have turned and run. He should have done something—anything!—but he could not move an inch. It was all over but the shouting. He found himself wondering in a rush of black humor if he would be fried or sautéed.

Strabo blinked. The crusted head swung slowly about and the long snout split wide. Blackened teeth slipped free, and a long, split tongue flicked at the misted air.

"I know you from somewhere, don't I?" the dragon asked.

Ben was floored. He had expected a good many things from the dragon, but talking wasn't one of them. The fact that the dragon talked changed everything. It took the edge off the fear he felt for the beast. It revised in an instant's time his whole perspective on what was happening to him. If the dragon could be talked to, maybe the dragon could be reasoned with! He forgot about being fried or sautéed. He forgot about defending himself. He searched instead for something to say in reply.

Strabo's head snapped up. "The mists at the edge of the fairy world—that's where I saw you. Several weeks ago wasn't it? I was asleep and you wandered past me. Stared at me so hard you woke me. Rude of you to do that, I might add." He paused. "That was you, wasn't it?"

Ben nodded mechanically, an image flashing in his mind of the dragon blowing him away head-over-heels like a feather caught in the wind. He brushed the image aside. He was still unable to believe that he was actually hearing the beast talk. The dragon had an odd voice, a sort of machinelike hiss that reverberated as if released from an echo chamber.

"Who are you?" the dragon asked, head lowering again. "What were you doing in the mists?" He showed his teeth as his lips curled back from his gums. "Are you one of the fairies?"

Ben shook his head. "No, I'm not." He gathered his wits quickly now. "I'm Ben Holiday, from Chicago. From another world, really. I'm Landover's new King."

"Are you?" The dragon seemed unimpressed.

"Yes." Ben hesitated, his courage slowly returning. "You know, I didn't think dragons talked."

Strabo shifted his bulk slightly, undulating his long, serpentine body so that his backside rested against a series of smaller pools, the flames dancing close against his scaled hide. "Oh, one of those," he sniffed.

Ben frowned. "One of which?"

"One of those humans who think dragons are illiterate, mindless beasts who spend their time wreaking havoc on poor, hard-working, simple folk until some champion appears to do them in. You're one of those, aren't you?"

"I suppose I am."

"You read too many fairy tales, Holiday. Who do you think spreads those stories about dragons? Not the dragons, you can be sure. No, humans spread those stories, and humans are not about to characterize themselves as the bad folk and the dragon as the one mistreated, are they? You must consider the source, as they say. It is much easier to cast the dragon as the villain—burning fields, devouring livestock and peasants, seizing beautiful princesses, and challenging knights in armor. It all makes great reading, even if it isn't the truth."

Ben stared. What kind of dragon was this?

"There were dragons before there were humans, you know. There were dragons before most of the fairy creatures came into being." Strabo bent down. His breath was terrible. "The trouble didn't start with the dragons; it started with the others. No one wanted the dragons around. The dragons took up too much space. Everyone was frightened of the dragons and what they were capable of doing—never mind that it was only a few giving the rest a bad name! And our magic was so much stronger than theirs that they could not control us as they wished."

The crusted head shook slowly. "But there are always ways of getting what you want if you work hard enough at it, and they worked very hard at getting rid of us. We were exiled, hunted, and destroyed, one after the other, until now there is only me. And they would destroy me as well, if they could."

He didn't specify who "they" were, but Ben guessed he meant everyone in general. "Are you saying you aren't responsible for any of the things for which you are blamed?" he asked, looking a bit doubtful.

"Oh, don't be stupid, Holiday—of course I'm responsible! I'm responsible for practically all of them!" The voice hissed softly. "I kill the humans and their tame animals when I wish. I burn out their crops and homes if I choose. I steal their mates because it pleases me. I hate them."

The tongue flicked. "But it wasn't always so, you see. It wasn't so until it became easier for me to be the thing they thought me than to try to survive as the creature I once was . . ." He trailed off, as if remembering. "I've been alive for almost a thousand years, you know, and all alone for the past two hundred of those. There are no more dragons. They're all legends. I'm all there is—like the Paladin. You know of him, Holiday? We're both the last of our kind."

Ben watched the dragon nuzzle at a Fire Spring, drinking the burning waters, inhaling the flames slowly. "Why are you telling me all of this?" he asked, genuinely puzzled.

The dragon looked up. "Because you're here." The snout dipped. "Why are you here, by the way?"

Ben hesitated, remembering suddenly what had brought him. "Well . . ."

"Oh, yes." The dragon cut him short. "You're Landover's newest King. Congratulations."

"Thanks. I haven't been at it very long."

"No, I assume not—otherwise you wouldn't be here."

"I wouldn't?"

"Hardly." The dragon bent closer. "When the old King was alive, he kept me exiled here in this wasteland. I was forbidden the rest of the valley. The Paladin was used to keep me here because the Paladin was as strong as I. I flew the skies at night, sometimes, but could not let myself be seen by the humans nor interfere in their lives . . ." The dragon's voice had grown hard. "I promised myself that one day I would be free again. This valley was as much mine as anyone's. And when the old King died and the Paladin disappeared, I *was* free, Holiday—and no King of Landover shall ever put me back again."

Ben was aware of a none-too-subtle shift in the atmosphere between them, but he pretended not to notice. "I'm not here for that," he said.

"But you *are* here to ask for my pledge to the throne, aren't you?"

"I'd thought about it," Ben admitted.

Strabo's snout split wide with a low, hissing laugh. "Such courage, Holiday! Wasted, though. I have never given my pledge to Landover's Kings—never, in the thousand years of my life. Why should I? I am not as those others who live here! I am not confined to Landover as they! I can travel anywhere I choose!"

Ben swallowed. "You can?"

The dragon shifted, tail curling back behind Ben. "Well . . . not anywhere, I suppose. But almost anywhere. I cannot travel deep into the fairy world nor into worlds where they do not believe in dragons. Do they believe in dragons in your world?"

Ben shook his head. "I don't think so."

"That explains why I have never been there. I travel only to lands where dragons are real—or, at least, where dragons once were real. I frequent half a dozen worlds close at hand. Most I have hunted. I had to hunt them when the old King forbid me the valley." His look turned sly, eyes lidding. "But hunting beyond the valley is more work than I care to do. It is easier to hunt here. It is more *satisfying*!"

The atmosphere had now gone decidedly chilly. The dragon could be talked to, but it looked doubtful that he could be reasoned with. Ben felt doors closing all about him. "Well, I don't suppose that there's much point in my suggesting that you do anything else then, is there?"

Strabo lifted slightly on his hind legs, dust rising from his massive body. "I have enjoyed our conversation, Holiday, but it appears to be at an end. Unfortunately, that means the end of you."

"Oh, wait a minute, let's not be so hasty." Ben couldn't get the words out fast enough, his mind racing. "Our conversation doesn't have to be over, does it? I think we should talk a bit more!"

"I can understand why you would might want to," the dragon hissed softly. "But I grow bored."

"Bored! Okay, let's change the subject!"

"That wouldn't help."

"No? Well, how about if I just leave, then—just walk away, say good-bye, so long?" Ben was desperate now.

The dragon loomed above him, a huge, scaled shadow. "That just postpones the inevitable. Eventually you would come back again. You would have to, because you are Landover's King. Face it, Holiday—I am the enemy. Either you have to destroy me or I have to destroy you. I much prefer the latter."

Ben glanced about wildly. "For God's sake, why does one of us have to destroy the other?"

"Why? Because that's the way it is between dragons and Kings. That's the way it's always been."

Ben's frustration had reached the breaking point. "Well if that's the way it's always been, then why the long dissertation on the disservice being done to dragons by story-telling humans? Why did you waste time telling me all that if you planned to fry me right after?"

The dragon actually laughed. "What a quaint way of putting it!" He paused. "Yes, why bother telling you anything under the circumstances? Good point." He thought about it for a moment, then shrugged. "I suppose because it was something to do. There's not a lot to do out here, you know."

Ben felt the last of his hope drain away. This was the end. He had dodged one silver bullet in the mists of the fairy world and a second in his confrontation with Nightshade. But this third one was going to do him in. He watched the dragon lift higher above him and begin to inhale slowly. One blast of fire and that would be it. His mind worked frantically. He had to do something! Damn it, he couldn't just stand there and let himself be incinerated!

"Wait!" he called out sharply. "Don't do it!" His hand reached into his tunic front and yanked free the medallion. "I still have this! I'll use its magic if I have to."

Strabo exhaled slowly, steam, smoke and flame singeing the misted air. He stared at the medallion and his tongue licked out. "You don't command the magic, Holiday."

Ben took a deep breath. "You're wrong. I do. I'll bring the Paladin if you don't let me go."

There was a long moment of silence. The dragon studied him thoughtfully and said nothing. Ben sent up a silent prayer. This was his last hope. The Paladin had come to him before when he was in trouble. Maybe . . .

His hand tightened about the face of the medallion, feeling the engraved surface press against his palm. A sudden, unexpected revelation came to him. What was he thinking? He could escape right now, if he chose! He had forgotten momentarily that the medallion gave him the means to do so! The medallion would take him back to his old world in an instant—all he had to do was take it off!

But that would mean leaving his friends trapped in Abaddon. That would mean leaving Landover forever. That would mean giving up.

That would also mean staying alive. He weighed the prospect, undecided.

"I think you're lying, Holiday," the dragon said suddenly and began to breathe in again.

Good-bye, world, Ben thought and prepared to make a futile dash for safety.

But suddenly there was a sharp glimmer of light through the mist and steam that rose above the flames of the springs, and the Paladin *did* appear! Ben could not believe it. The knight materialized out of nothingness, a solitary, battered form atop his aging mount, lance hoisted in the crook of one arm before him. Strabo turned at once, clearly startled. Flames burst from his maw in an explosive roar, enveloped the knight and horse, and died into smoke. Ben flinched, feeling the backlash of the tremendous heat. He turned away, shielding his eyes, then quickly looked back again.

The Paladin was unharmed.

Strabo rose slowly on his massive hind legs, wings lifting like a shield, lidded eyes casting about to find Ben again. "Twenty years—it's been twenty years!" he whispered in a low hiss. "I thought him gone forever! How did you bring him back, Holiday? How?"

Ben started to stammer something in reply, as surprised as Strabo by the Paladin's reappearance, then quickly caught himself. This was the opportunity he had been waiting for.

"The medallion!" he exclaimed at once. "The medallion brought him! The words of magic are inscribed here—on the medallion's back! Look for yourself!"

He held the disk out obligingly, dangling it from its silver chain so that the misted light reflected brightly from its surface. Strabo bent down, serpentine neck angling from his massive body, crusted head drawing close. The huge maw split open, the long tongue licking. Ben caught his breath. The dragon's shadow fell over him, blocking away the light.

"Look—you can see the writing!" Ben urged and thought, *just a little closer . . .*

One hooked foreleg reached for the medallion.

Ben's free hand jerked clear of his tunic pocket, and he flung a fistful of the Io Dust directly into Strabo's nostrils. The dragon inhaled in surprise, then sneezed. The sneeze nearly blew Ben off his feet, but somehow he held his ground. He snatched back the medallion, reached into his other pocket and produced the pod. Strabo's head was already swinging about to find him, jaws widening. Ben hurled the pod into the open maw. The dragon was quick, catching the pod in midair, biting down on it in fury, grinding it into pulp.

Too late Strabo realized his mistake. Io Dust flew everywhere, expoding from the dragon's mouth in jets of white smoke. Strabo gave a dreadful roar and flames burst forth. Ben threw himself aside, rolled twice, scrambled to his feet again and raced for the clump of boulders he had passed coming in. He gained it half a dozen yards ahead of the fire and dove frantically behind it. Strabo had gone completely beserk. He was thrashing above the floor of the Fire Springs in a frenzy, his massive body smashing earth and rock alike. A crater of flames geysered skyward with a booming cough. The dragon roared and breathed fire everywhere. Flames and smoke filled the afternoon air, obscuring everything. The Paladin disappeared. The springs disappeared. Ben huddled in his shelter and prayed he had been quick enough that the dragon had lost sight of him.

After a time, the thrashing and the flames ceased, and it grew quiet again. Ben waited patiently in his shelter, listening to the muffled sounds of the dragon as he moved slowly about. The booming explosions of the Fire Springs faded back into a soft hissing.

"Holiday?"

The dragon's voice was harsh with anger. Ben stayed where he was.

"Holiday? That was Io Dust, Holiday! That was an entire pod of Io Dust! Where did you get it? You said you weren't one of the fairies! You lied!"

Ben waited. He hadn't heard anything he liked yet. He listened as Strabo moved somewhere off to his left—listened to the heavy sound of his body dragging.

"Do you know how dangerous such magic is, Holiday? Do you know the harm you could have caused me? Why did you trick me like that?"

The moving stopped. Ben heard the dragon shift himself, then heard the sound of drinking. Maybe he had made a mistake, he thought suddenly. Maybe an entire pod of Io Dust was too much for anyone. Maybe the dragon was hurt.

There was a lengthy sigh. "Holiday, why have you done this to me? What is it that you want of me? Tell me and be done with it!"

The dragon sounded more hurt than angry. Ben decided to risk it. "I want your word that you will do nothing to harm me!" he called out.

The dragon's reply was a soft hiss. "You have it."

"I want you to tell me that you will do whatever I tell you to do and nothing else. You have to anyway, you know."

"I know, Holiday! I agree! Tell me what it is that you want!"

Ben slipped cautiously from behind the shelter of the boulders. Streamers of mist and smoke still hung over the pit of the Fire Springs, casting everything in an eerie half-light. Strabo crouched several dozen yards away between a series of burning craters, looking like an angry, trapped animal. His ugly, crusted head swung slowly about, lidded eyes catching sight of Ben. Ben tensed, prepared to dive back behind the boulders. But the dragon only looked at him and waited.

"Come over here," Ben ordered.

The dragon came—meekly. There was undisguised hatred in his eyes. Ben watched the monster approach. The barrel-shaped body hunched along above thick, armored legs. Wings flapped with the movement, and the long tail snaked about restlessly. Ben felt like Fay Wray with King Kong.

"Set me free!" Strabo demanded. "Set me free, and I'll let you live!"

Ben shook his head. "I can't do that."

"You mean you won't!" the dragon whispered, his voice like sandpaper rubbed across slate. "But you can't keep me like this forever, and when I do get free of you . . ."

"Let's just skip the threats, shall we?"

". . . there won't be enough left of you to fill a gnome's thimble goblet, not enough to feed the smallest cave wight—and I'll cause you such pain that you won't believe . . ."

"Are you ready to listen to me?"

The dragon's head lifted disdainfully. "I won't pledge to you, Holiday! It would mean nothing given this way!"

Ben nodded. "I understand that. I don't want your pledge."

There was a long moment of silence as the dragon studied him. The hatred in the beast's eyes had given way to curiosity. It appeared that the worst was over. The dragon was his—for the moment, at least. Ben felt a welcome easing of tension within himself, a dissipation of the fear and sharp anticipation. He had dodged silver bullet number three. He still held the medallion clasped tightly in one hand, and he slipped it back into his tunic now. He glanced about momentarily for the Paladin, but the knight had disappeared again.

"Like a ghost . . ." he murmured.

He turned back to the dragon. Strabo was still studying him. The wicked tongue licked nervously at the misted air. "Very well, Holiday. I give up. What *do* you want from me?"

Ben smiled. "Why don't you make yourself comfortable, and I'll tell you."

ABADDON

It was nearing dusk when Ben tightened the last of the straps on the makeshift leather riding harness he had fashioned, ordered Strabo to kneel down and climbed aboard. He settled himself carefully in the seat that rested at the juncture of several clusters of bony spikes that ribbed the dragon's spine, tested the cinch straps for slippage and fitted his boots into the iron stirrups.

At least he had the riding harness. He was lucky to have that. It was an unwieldy apparatus, constructed from traces, straps, buckles, and rings that had belonged to various field animals fallen victim to the dragon and brought to the Fire Springs for leisurely consumption. He had picked it out from among the bones and fastened it all together. It was bound about the dragon's neck just above and behind the forelegs, the saddle on which he sat settled forward of the haunches. Reins ran to the neck just behind the crested head. Ben didn't think for a moment that he would be able to guide the dragon as he would a horse; the reins were just one more precaution to keep him from falling off.

"If you fall, you're in trouble, Holiday," the dragon had warned him earlier.

"Then you'd better make sure that I don't," Ben had replied. "You are *ordered* to make sure that I don't."

He wasn't convinced, however, that Strabo could do that, Io Dust or no Io Dust. They were descending into the netherworld of Abaddon, and both lives would be at risk. Strabo would have difficulty keeping them safe under the best of circumstances—and the proposed rescue of his missing friends from the realm of the demons did not promise the best of anything.

He paused momentarily, seated atop the dragon, and gazed out across the wasteland. They had moved to the rim of the Fire Springs, clear of the burning craters and the thick undergrowth. The day was dying into evening; as the sun slipped down behind the distant mountains, mist and gloom settled over the valley. Landover was a murky gathering of shadows and vague shapes. Ben could almost watch the failing of the daylight from one moment to the next. It was as if the valley were disappearing before his eyes. He had the uneasy sensation that it was, the unpleasant feeling that he would never see it again.

He straightened himself in the stirrups, hardening his resolve against such thoughts. He forced a grim smile. Ben Holiday was about to sally forth, a knight atop his steed, off to the rescue. He almost laughed. Don Quixote, off to tilt with windmills—what a picture he could send home again if he had his camera! Damn, but he had never thought—never believed—that he would be doing anything like this with his life! All those years of living behind concrete and steel walls; all those stuffy courtrooms and musty law libraries; all those sterile pleadings and legal briefs; all those lawbooks and statutes and codes—how far removed from that he was now!

And he knew, with a certainty that surprised him, that he could never go back again to any of it.

"What are you doing up there, Holiday—admiring the view?" Strabo's hiss of displeasure interrupted his thoughts. "Let's be on our way!"

"All right," Ben agreed softly. "Take me up."

The dragon's wings spread wide, and he lifted from the ground with a lurch. Ben held tightly to the reins and harness straps, watching the land drop away quickly beneath him. He had a momentary glimpse of bramble, thicket, and deadwood forests fading into trailers of mist and dusk's lengthening shadows, and then there was only gloom. Fillip and Sot were down there somewhere, hidden from view. He had gone back to them long enough to let them know that he was riding Strabo down into Abaddon to rescue the others. He had dispatched them back again to Sterling Silver to await his return. They had been only too quick to go, their horror-stricken faces clearly reflecting their unspoken conviction that they had seen the last of him.

Maybe they had, he mused. Maybe he should have told them to go on home and forget about him. They probably wouldn't have done that, though. They still took their pledge to him quite seriously.

He reflected momentarily on all the help they had given him—a pair of larcenous, grimy little cannibals. Who would have thought it? Silently, he wished them well.

Strabo flew into the coming night, passing from the eastern wasteland to the fringes of the Greensward and then west. The daylight failed completely, darkness descended, and Landover's moons began to shine. They were all visible on this night—white, peach, washed-out mauve, burnt rose, sea green, beryl, turquoise, and jade—their colors unobstructed by the mists that shrouded the valley below. They were like giant balloons, Ben thought and wondered where the party was.

The minutes slipped rapidly past. Strabo's massive body undulated rhythmically beneath Ben as the leathered wings beat against the night winds and carried them westward. Ben gripped the reins and harness and hung on for dear life. Air currents buffeted and chilled him. Landover was a vast bowl of steaming soup over which he hung suspended. He was exhilarated by the sensation of flying like this, but he was frightened, too. He hadn't liked horseback riding and he didn't like dragon riding any better. The dragon kept a steady pace and that helped, but Ben still distrusted the situation. He knew the Io Dust could wear off at any time and that would be the end of him.

"This is a foolish venture!" Strabo called back to him moments later, as if reading his thoughts. The crusted, misshapen head swung about, eyes glinting. "All this for a handful of humans!"

"My friends!" Ben shouted in reply, the wind whipping the words back into his face.

"Your friends mean nothing to me!"

"Fair enough—you mean nothing to them! Except Questor Thews, I suppose—he thinks you special!"

"The wizard? Pah!"

"Just do what I told you to do!" Ben ordered.

"I hate you, Holiday!"

"Sorry—I don't care!"

"You will! Sooner or later, I'll get free of you and when I do you'll be sorry you ever decided to use me this way!"

The head swung back again, the cold, mechanical voice dying into the rush of the wind. Ben said nothing. He gripped the reins and the harness straps tighter.

They flew deep into the Greensward toward the center of the valley. Ben did not know where they were going. He knew the dragon was taking him to Abaddon, but he had no idea where Abaddon was. Abaddon was the netherworld of Landover, but its gates were time passages of the sort that had brought him from his own world. They were not, however, the *same* time passages. They were not to be found within the mists that ringed the valley. They were hidden somewhere within the valley, Strabo had told him—somewhere only the demons and the dragon could reach . . .

Strabo slowed suddenly and began a long sweep back that became a widening circle. Ben looked down. The valley was a shroud of mist and gloom. Strabo's wings spread wider, and the dragon began to bank sharply on the night winds.

"Hold tight to me, Holiday!" the dragon cried back to him.

Strabo dipped suddenly and started down. Wings flattened back and the long neck stretched forward. They began to pick up speed as the dragon's dive steepened. The wind rushed past Ben Holiday's ears in a vicious roar that drowned out everything. The ground began to come into focus, a shapeless blur sharpening with the passing of each second they dropped. Ben was cold all the way through. They were going too fast! They were going to dive right into the middle of the Greensward!

Then abruptly the dragon fire exploded from Strabo's throat, a huge, brilliant arc of crimson flame. The air seemed to melt before it, cellophane that wrinkled and expanded at its edges, leaving a jagged hole. Ben squinted against the rush of the wind and saw the blackness of the hole open out of the night. Dragon fire died away, but the hole remained. They were passing through it, flying into the empty dark. Landover disappeared; the misted Greensward was gone. There was a sucking noise as the hole closed behind them and then sudden stillness.

Strabo leveled off within the black. Ben lifted slightly from where he had crouched down against the dragon's spine and stared about, awestruck. The world had undergone a radical change. Moon and stars were gone. There was a sky of inky black, canopied over a sprawling mass of jagged peaks and deep gorges. Flashes of lightning danced at the juncture of earth and sky, filling the fringes of the horizon with a bizarre light show. Volcanos growled in the distance, their reddish fires glimmering from out of mountainous cones of rock; streams of lava flowed in long red trailers like blood. The earth shook and grumbled with the eruptions, and geysers of flame and molten rock exploded skyward against the blackness.

"Abaddon!" Strabo advised, his voice a slow hiss.

He dropped downward with sickening speed, and Ben felt the pit of his stomach lurch. Mountain peaks rushed past, and the fire from the volcanos burst skyward all about. Ben was terrified. Abaddon was the realization of his worst nightmare. He had never seen anything so inhospitable. Nothing could survive in such a world.

A shadow rocketed past, winged and elusive. Strabo hissed in warning. Another shadow slipped past, then another. There were sharp hisses and flashes of teeth. Dragon fire burst suddenly from Strabo's maw, and one of the shadows screamed and dropped earthward. Ben flattened himself within the nest of spikes that protected the dragon's spine. The fire burst forth again and again. Another of the shadows exploded into ash and fell. Strabo was weaving evasively as more of the shadows appeared. He stretched out his massive body and increased his speed. The black things fell behind and were gone.

A series of rugged peaks whipped past, and then the dragon slowed once more. "Gnats!" he growled contemptuously. "No match for me!"

Ben was drenched with sweat and could barely catch his breath. "How much farther?"

The dragon's laugh was harsh. "A bit, Holiday. What seems to be the matter? Is this more than you bargained for?"

"I'll be fine. You do what you were told to do and get to my friends!"

"Temper, Holiday."

The dragon flew on through the fire-streaked blackness. The "gnats" came at them twice more, and twice more Strabo burned a handful of them before flying past. The world of Abaddon stretched on below, unchanging in its look, a world of rock and fire. White light danced frantically on the horizons all about, and lava flared within the craters of the mountain peaks, but in the valleys and gorges below all remained impenetrably black. If there was something living down there, it could not be seen from the air.

Ben began to experience a growing sense of futility. His friends had been trapped in this world for almost five days!

Strabo banked left between two monstrous volcanic peaks and started down. Wind rushed past, and trailers of fire laced the mountain rock on both sides. Ben peered down into the lava. Things were swimming in the fire! Things were playing there!

A monstrous black shadow heaved up from out of the shadows on one peak, tentacled arms reaching. Strabo hissed and the dragon fire burned at the arms. The arms shuddered and drew back. The shadow disappeared.

Then they were through the mountains and within a valley ringed by jagged peaks. Strabo dove sharply and leveled off less than fifty feet above its floor. Pools of fiery lava bubbled at the fringes of the valley, throwing rocks and flame skyward in small bursts. Cracks and crevices split the barren floor, dropping away into blackness. Creatures scurried everywhere, small and misshapen in the crimson half-light, things barely human. Cries rose up at the sight of the dragon, shrieks that disappeared as quickly as they sounded in the distant roar of the volcanos. Ben heard the dragon screech in reply.

The "gnats" reappeared, dozens strong. Other things winged into view, larger and more fearsome-looking. Strabo leveled out and flew faster. Ben was hunched down so close to the dragon's spine that he could feel the pulsing of his hide. Straps and cinches strained with the effort of the dragon's flight. Ben could feel things beginning to loosen.

Then a monstrous pit of fire appeared before them, its throat thousands of feet deep. A tiny slab of rock hung suspended by chains across that throat—a disk of stone that measured no more than a dozen feet across. The slab of rock danced and bobbled unsteadily on its webbing of iron, and the fire licked up at it hungrily from far below.

Ben caught his breath sharply. There were a handful of tiny figures crouched on that slab of rock, fighting to keep their balance.

His friends!

Strabo dove for them, gnats and other flying demons in pursuit. Other demons still, hundreds strong, were gathered about the fire pit, throwing rocks at the figures crouched upon the slab and shaking the chains that secured it. All were yelling gleefully. It was a game they were playing, Ben realized in horror. The demons had trapped or placed his friends on that slab and were waiting now to see them fall into the fire!

The pit drew closer. The demons turned, seeing the dragon now, crying out. Hands reached for the pins that fastened the chains to the pit wall. The demons were trying to drop the slab and his friends into the fire before he could reach them!

Ben was frantic. Chains fell away quickly, one after another, and the slab of rock buckled and shook. Strabo breathed fire at the demons and burned dozens to ash, but the rest continued to work at the chains. Ben screamed in fury as he saw clearly now the faces of Questor Thews, Abernathy, the kobolds—and Willow! Strabo rocketed clear of the rim of the pit, past the demons working to release the chains that bound the rock slab. Too late, Ben thought. They were going to be too late!

There was an instant then in which time froze. There was no time and all the time in the world. Ben seemed to see everything that happened with a frightening detachment that held him suspended in the instant of its happening. The chains at one section fell away completely and the slab of rock buckled and sagged. His friends dropped to their hands and knees and began to slide toward the pit.

Strabo dove sharply, dragging Ben with him toward the fire. He reached the slab of rock as the people on it slipped away. Clawed feet snatched two out of midair. With a quick snap of his jaws, he caught another, and his great head twisted back to deposit a kobold in front of Ben. The second kobold flung himself at the harness and grasped the straps.

The final figure dropped into the pit. It was Questor Thews.

Ben saw him fall, watching in horror as the gray robes with their rainbow-colored sashes flared and billowed like a failing parachute. Strabo arced downward, then rose quickly again into the night. He was too far away to reach the wizard. He could not save him.

"Questor!" Ben screamed.

Then something truly magical happened, something so bizarre that even with all that had happened in the few moments past, it left Ben stunned. Questor's plunge into the fire seemed to slow and then to stop altogether. The wizard's arms spread wide against the crimson light of the flames and slowly the sticklike figure began to rise from the pit.

Ben caught his breath, his mind racing. There was only one possible answer. Questor Thews had finally conjured up the right spell! He had made the magic work!

Strabo arced downward quickly, bursts of fire incinerating the "gnats" and other flying demons that sought to intercede. He reached Questor Thews just as the wizard levitated above the rim of the pit, flew under him, and caught him on his back so that he was settled just behind Ben.

Ben turned hurriedly and stared. Questor sat there like a statue, his face ashen, his eyes bright with astonishment. "It . . . it was all in a proper twist of the fingers, High Lord," the wizard managed before fainting.

Ben reached back and secured him, one hand firmly fixed to the gray robes as Strabo began to climb. Shrieks rose from the demons, a cacophony of epithets that faded quickly as the dragon outdistanced them. The ground dropped away below, transformed into a rumpled black shroud rent by jagged holes and cracks of flame. The lightning at the edges of the world danced wildly, streaking across the horizon's sweep, and all of Abaddon seemed to shake and rumble.

Then Strabo breathed dragon fire into the air before them, and once again the sky melted and gave way. Edges frayed and crinkled about a jagged hole, and the dragon and his passengers passed through.

Ben had to squint against a sudden change of light. When he opened his eyes wide again, stars and colored moons brightened a misted night sky.

They were back in Landover once more.

It took Ben several moments to regain his bearings. They were in Landover, but not over the Greensward. They were north, almost to the wall of the valley. Strabo circled for a time, winging over thick forestland and barren ridge line, then eased down gently into a deserted meadow.

Ben scrambled down from the dragon's back. Bunion and Parsnip greeted him with hisses and gleaming teeth, so agitated they could barely contain themselves. Abernathy dropped rudely to the ground, picked himself up, brushed himself off, and denounced the day he had ever let himself become mixed up with any of them. Questor, conscious again, lowered himself gingerly along the harness straps and stumbled over to Ben, barely aware of what he was doing, his eyes fixed on the dragon.

"I had never believed I would see the day that *anyone* would rule this . . . this marvelous creature!" he whispered, awestruck. "Strabo—last of the old dragons, the greatest of the fairy creatures, brought to the service of a King of Landover! It was the Io Dust, of course, but still . . ."

He stumbled into Ben and suddenly remembered himself. "High Lord, you are safe! We thought you lost for certain! How you found your way clear of the fairy world, I will never know! How you accomplished what you did . . ." His enthusiasm left him momentarily speechless, and he reached for Ben's hand and pumped it vigorously. Ben grinned in spite of himself. "We came looking for you after you failed to return that first day, and the witch took us," the wizard went on hastily. "She sent us to Abaddon and dropped us on that slab of rock for the demons to play with. Almost five days, High Lord!

That's how long we have been trapped there! Days of being teased and taunted by those loathsome, foul . . ."

The kobolds hissed and chittered wildly, pointing.

Questor nodded at once, his enthusiasm fading. "Yes, you are correct to intercede—I had indeed forgotten." He took Ben's arm. "I ramble, High Lord, when there are more pressing concerns. The sylph is very ill." He hesitated, then pulled Ben after him. "I am sorry, High Lord, but she may be dying."

Ben's smile was gone instantly. They hurried forward of where Strabo crouched, watching them with lidded eyes. Abernathy was already kneeling in the grass next to Willow's inert form. Ben knelt with him, and Questor and the kobolds gathered close.

"Her time for joining with the earth came when she was trapped in Abaddon," Questor whispered. "She could not deny the changeling need, but the rock would not accept her."

Ben shuddered. Willow had tried to transform, unable to resist the need, and the attempt had been only partially completed. Her skin had gone wrinkled and barklike, her fingers and toes had turned to gnarled roots, her hair had become slender branches, and her body had twisted and split. She was so hideous to look upon that Ben could barely manage to do so.

"She still breathes, High Lord," Abernathy said softly.

Ben fought down his revulsion. "We have to save her," he replied, trying desperately to think of what to do. He stared in horror as Willow's body convulsed suddenly, and more roots split from the skin beneath one wrist. The sylph's eyes fluttered blindly and closed again. She was in agony. Anger coursed through Ben like a fire. "Questor, use your magic!"

"No, High Lord." Questor shook his head slowly. "No magic that I possess can help. Only one thing can save her. She must complete the transformation."

Ben wheeled on the wizard. "Damn it, how is she supposed to do that? She's barely alive!"

No one said anything. He turned back to the girl. He should never have left her alone with Nightshade. He should never have permitted her to come with him in the first place. It was his fault that this had happened. It would be his fault if she died . . .

He swore softly and thrust the thought aside. His mind raced.

Then suddenly he remembered. "The old pines!" he exclaimed. "The grove in Elderew where her mother danced and she transformed herself that last night! It was special to her! Perhaps she could complete the transformation there!" He was already on his feet, directing the others. "Here, help me carry her! Strabo—bend down!"

They bore the sylph to the dragon and bound her to his back. Then they climbed up beside her, fastening themselves where they could to the makeshift harness. Ben rode in front of the unconscious girl, Questor and Abernathy behind, the kobolds to either side at the stirrups.

Strabo grunted irritably in response to a command from Ben and then lifted into the night sky. They flew south, the dragon leveling out and straining to increase his speed, the wind threatening to tear them all loose from the creaking harness. The minutes slipped past, and the hill country north gave way to the plains of the Greensward. Ben's hand reached back to touch the body of the sylph and found the barklike skin cold and hard. They were losing her. There wasn't enough time. The Greensward passed away and the forests and rivers of the lake country appeared, dim patches of color through the haze of mist. The dragon dropped lower, skimming the treetops and the ridgelines. Ben was shaking with impatience and frustration. His hand still clasped Willow's arm, and it seemed as if he could actually feel the life passing from her.

Then Strabo banked sharply left and dove downward into the forest. Trees rushed up to greet them, then there was a small clearing through the wall of branches; as quick as that, they were on the ground once more. Ben scrambled down wordlessly, the others with him, all working frantically to free Willow. The forest loomed about them like a wall, trailers of mist swirling through the rows of dark trunks. Bunion hissed at them and led the way, his instincts sure. They moved into the trees, slipping and groping their way through the near black, carrying the rigid form of the girl.

They reached the pine grove in seconds. The pines stood empty and silent in the mist, sentinels against the dark. Ben directed the procession to the grove's center, the earthen stage on which Willow's mother had danced the last night before he had departed Elderew.

Gently, they laid Willow down. Ben felt the girl's wrist above the mass of roots and tendrils that had broken the skin. The wrist was cold and lifeless.

"She is not breathing, High Lord!" Questor whispered in a low hiss.

Ben was frantic. He lifted the stricken sylph in his arms and held her close against him. He was crying. "Damn it, you can't die, Willow, you can't do this to me!" He cradled her, feeling the roughness of her skin chafe his face. "Willow, answer me!"

And suddenly he was holding Annie, her body broken and bloodstained from the accident that had taken her life, another piece of wreckage to be swept from the scene. The sensation was so sharp that he gasped. He could feel bone and blood and torn flesh; he could feel the small, frail life of his unborn child. "Oh, God, no!" he cried softly.

He jerked his head up, and the image faded. He was holding Willow again. He bent close, kissing the sylph's cheek and mouth, his tears running down her face. He had lost Annie and the child she carried. He could not stand it if he were to lose Willow, too. "Don't die," he begged her. "I don't want you to die. Willow, please!"

Her frail body stirred, responding almost miraculously, and her eyes opened to his. He looked into those eyes, past the ravaged face and body, past the devastation wrought by the half-completed transformation. He reached for the flicker of life that still burned within.

"Come back to me, Willow!" he begged her. "You must live!"

The eyes closed again. But the body of the sylph stirred more strongly now, and convulsions became spasms of effort to regain muscle control. Willow's throat swallowed. "Ben. Help me up. Hold me."

He brought her quickly to her feet, and the others stepped back from them. He held her there, feeling the lifeblood work itself through her, feeling the transformation begin again. Her roots snaked deep into the forest soil, her branches lengthened and split, and her trunk stretched and hardened.

Then everything went still. Ben looked up. The change was complete. Willow had become the tree that was her namesake. It was going to be all right.

His eyes squeezed tightly shut. "Thank you," he whispered.

He lowered his head, wrapped his arms about the slender trunk, and cried.

The demon appeared toward dawn, materializing out of the gloom, a black and misshapen thing wrapped in armor. It happened very suddenly. The wind whispered, the mist swirled, and the demon was there.

Ben was awake almost instantly. He had been dozing, sleeping in fits and starts, cramped from leaning against Willow, from holding her. Strabo was presumably still back in the clearing where Ben had left him.

The demon approached, and Ben rose to meet it. The kobolds interposed themselves instantly, moving to block the demon's way. Abernathy jerked awake and kicked Questor roughly. The wizard awoke as well and scrambled to his feet. The demon's helmeted head swung slowly about, and its crimson eyes surveyed the company and the pine grove with studied caution.

Then it spoke. Ben could not understand anything of what was said, and the speech was over almost before it began. Questor hesitated, then looked back at him. "The Mark issues you a challenge, High Lord. He demands that you meet him in combat three dawns from now at the Heart."

Ben nodded wordlessly. What had been promised from the beginning was finally here. Time had run out. He was only half awake, still near exhaustion from his ordeal of the past several days, but he grasped the significance of the challenge instantly.

The Mark had had enough of him. The demon was angry.

But perhaps—just perhaps—the demon was worried, too. Questor had once told him that the demon always challenged at midwinter—and it was nowhere near midwinter yet. The demon was rushing things.

He thought about it a moment, tried to reason it through, then shook his head numbly. It didn't matter. He had made the decision to stay long ago, and nothing would change that decision now. It surprised him that his resolve was so strong. It gave him a good feeling.

He nodded to the messenger. "I'll be there."

The demon was gone in a swirl of mist. Ben stared after it a moment, then gazed off into the trees where the first light of dawn was still a faint silver tinge against the far horizons. "Go back to sleep," he told the others gently.

He settled down again by Willow, rested his cheek against her roughened trunk and closed his eyes.

Dawn had broken when he came awake once more. He was stretched full length upon the earth in the shadow of the aged pines. His head rested in Willow's lap and her arms cradled him. She had transformed back again.

"Ben," she greeted softly.

He looked at her slender arms, her body and then her face. She was just as she had been when he had seen her that first night bathing in the waters of the Irrylyn. The color, the beauty, and the vibrancy had been restored. She was the vision he had wanted and been afraid to seek. Yet it was no longer the vision that mattered to him; it was the life inside. The repulsion, the fear, and the sense of alienation he had once felt were gone. They had been replaced by hope.

He smiled. "I need you," he whispered and meant it.

"I know, Ben," she said to him. "I have always known."

She bent her face to his and kissed him, and he reached up to draw her close.

IRON MARK

The first thing Ben did that morning was to release Strabo from the spell of the Io Dust that bound the dragon to him. He gave Strabo his freedom on the condition that the dragon not hunt the Greensward or any other settled part of the valley or any of its citizens so long as Ben was King.

"The duration of your rule in Landover amounts to a splash of water in the ocean of my lifetime, Holiday," the dragon advised him coldly, eyes lidded against his thoughts. They stood together in the clearing where Strabo had waited the night.

Ben shrugged. "Then the condition should be easy to accept."

"Conditions from a human are never easy to accept—especially when the human is as deceitful as you."

"Flattery will gain you nothing more than I have already offered. Do you agree or not?"

The crusted snout split wide, teeth gleaming. "You risk the possibility that my word means nothing—that extracting it while the magic binds me renders it worthless!"

Ben sighed. "Yes or no?"

Strabo hissed, the sound rising up from deep within. "Yes!" He spread his leathered wings and arced his long neck skyward. "Anything to be free of you!" Then he hesitated and bent close. "Understand—this is not finished yet between you and me, Holiday. We will meet again another day and settle the debt owed me!"

He rose with a rush of beating wings until he was atop the trees, banked eastward, and disappeared into the rising sun. Ben watched him go and then turned away.

Questor Thews could not understand. First he was astonished, then angry, and finally just mystified. Whatever could the High Lord have been thinking?

Why would he release Strabo like that? The dragon was a powerful ally, a weapon that none would dare to challenge, a lever which could be used to exact the pledges the High Lord so desperately needed!

"But that's precisely what's wrong with keeping him." Ben tried to explain it to the wizard. "I'd end up using him like a club; I'd have my pledges not because the people of Landover felt they should give them but because they were terrified of the dragon. That's no good—I don't want loyalty from fear! I want loyalty from respect! Besides, Strabo is a two-edged sword. Sooner or later the effects of the Io Dust are going to wear off anyway, and then what? He'd turn on me in a minute. No, Questor—better that I let him go now and take my chances."

"Aptly put, High Lord," the wizard snapped. "You will indeed take your chances. What happens to you when you face the Mark? Strabo could have protected you! You should at least have kept him until then!"

But Ben shook his head. "No, Questor," he answered softly. "This isn't the dragon's fight; it's mine. It always has been, I think."

He left the matter there, refusing to discuss it further with any of them. He had thought it through carefully. He had made up his mind. He had learned a few things he had not known earlier and deduced a few more. He saw clearly what a King of Landover must be if he were to have any value at all. He had come full circle in many respects from the time he had first entered the valley. He wanted his friends to understand, but he did not think he could explain it to them. Understanding would have to come another way.

Happily, there was no further opportunity to dwell on the subject right then. The River Master appeared, alerted by his people that something strange was going on in the grove of the old pines. Strabo had flown in toward midnight and flown out again that dawn. He brought with him a handful of humans, including the man named Holiday who claimed Landover's throne, the wizard Questor Thews, and the River Master's missing daughter. Ben greeted the River Master with apologies for the intrusion and a brief explanation of what had befallen them all during the past several weeks. He told the River Master that Willow had followed him at his invitation, that it was his oversight in not advising the sprite earlier, and that he wished the sylph to remain with him for a few days more. He asked that they meet again three dawns hence at the Heart.

He said nothing of the challenge issued by the Mark.

"What purpose will be served, High Lord, in meeting with you at the Heart?" the River Master asked pointedly. His people were all about them, faint shapes in the mist of the early dawn, eyes that glimmered in the haze of the trees.

"I will ask again your pledge to the throne of Landover," Ben answered. "I think that this time you will want to give it."

Skepticism and a hint of alarm reflected in the sprite's chiseled features, and the gills on his neck ceased their steady flutter. "I have given you my conditions for such a pledge," the River Master said softly. There was a warning note in his voice.

Ben kept his gaze steady. "I know."

The River Master nodded. "Very well. I will be there."

He embraced Willow briefly, gave his permission for her to stay on with Ben and was gone. His people disappeared with him, melting back into the forest gloom. Ben and the members of his little company were left alone.

Willow moved close, her hand closing about his. "He does not intend to give you his pledge, Ben," she whispered, lowering her voice so that the others could not hear.

Ben smiled ruefully. "I know. But I'm hoping that he won't have any choice."

It was time to be going. He dispatched Bunion to Rhyndweir castle with a message for Kallendbor and the other Lords of the Greensward. He had done as they had asked and rid them of Strabo. Now it was their turn. They were to meet him at the Heart three dawns hence and give him their pledge of loyalty.

Bunion disappeared into the forest wordlessly, and Ben and the remaining members of the little company turned homeward toward Sterling Silver.

It took them longer returning from Elderew and the lake country this time than it had before, because this time they traveled afoot. Ben didn't mind. It gave him time to think, and he had a great deal to think about. Willow walked with him as they traveled, staying close, saying little. Questor and Abernathy questioned him repeatedly about his plans for dealing with the Mark, but he put them off. The truth of the matter was he didn't have any plans yet, but he didn't want them to know that. It was better if they thought that he was simply being closemouthed.

He spent much of his time surveying the country they traveled through and imagining how it had been before the failing of the magic. His memory of the vision shown him by the fairies recalled itself often, a gleaming, wondrous painting where the mists, the gloom and the wilting of the land's life were absent. How long ago had this valley been like that, he wondered? How long before it could be made that way again? The vision of the fairies had been more than a memory; it had been a promise. He pondered the sluggish swirl of the deep mists that screened the sunshine and shrouded the mountains, the thinning groves of Bonnie Blues dotted with wilt and spotting, the lakes and rivers turned gray and clouded, and the meadows and grasslands grown sparse and wintry. He pondered the valley's people and their lives in a world turned suddenly harsh and unproductive. He thought again of the faces of those few that had appeared for his coronation—of the many who had lined the roads leading into Rhyndweir. That could all be changed if the failing of the magic could be halted.

A King to serve the land and lead her people would accomplish that end, Questor Thews believed. Twenty years of no King upon Landover's throne had caused the problem in the first place.

But the concept was a difficult one for Ben to grasp. Why would such a simple thing as the loss or gain of a King have so great an effect upon the life of this valley? A King was just a man. A King was just a figurehead. How could one man make such a difference?

It could, he decided finally, where the land took its life from the magic that had created it, and the magic was sustained by the rule of a King. Such a thing might not be possible in a world governed solely by natural laws, but it could be so here. The land took its life from the magic. Questor had told him so. Perhaps the land took its life from the King as well.

The implications of that possibility were staggering, and Ben could not begin to comprehend all of the ramifications that they suggested. Instead, he reduced their number to those relevant to his most immediate problem—staying alive. The magic failed without him; the land failed without the magic. There was a bond among the three. If he could understand it, he could save himself. He knew it instinctively. The fairies had not created Landover one day to see it fall apart the next simply because of the loss of a King. They had to have foreseen and provided a way to bring that King back again—a new King, a different King, but a King to rule and keep the magic strong.

But what provision had they made?

The first day of the journey back seemed endless. When night finally descended and the others of the little company slept, Ben lay awake, still thinking. He was awake a long time.

The second day passed more quickly, and by midday they had reached once more the island castle of Sterling Silver. Bunion was waiting at the gates, already returned from his journey to the Greensward. He spoke rapidly, punctuating his sentences with sharp gestures. Ben couldn't begin to follow him.

Questor interceded. "Your message was delivered, High Lord." His voice was bitter. "The Lords of the Greensward reply that they will come to the Heart as commanded—but they will postpone until then any decision as to whether or not they will pledge to the throne."

Ben grunted. "Hardly surprising." He ignored the look exchanged by the wizard and Abernathy and moved ahead through the entry. "Thanks for the effort, Bunion."

He walked quickly down the connecting passageway to the inner court and crossed, the others trailing. He had just stepped inside the front hall when a pair of bedraggled apparitions darted frantically from the shadows of an alcove and threw themselves at his feet.

"Great High Lord!"

"Mighty High Lord!"

Ben groaned in recognition. The G'home Gnomes Fillip and Sot fell to their knees before him, groveling and whimpering so pitifully that it was embarrassing. Their fur was matted and spiked, their paws were caked with mud, and they had the look of something dredged from the sewers.

"Oh, High Lord, we thought you devoured by the dragon!" Fillip wailed.

"We thought you lost in the depths of the netherworld!" Sot cried.

"Ah, you have great magic, High Lord!" Fillip praised him.

"Yes, you have returned from the dead!" Sot declared.

Ben wanted to kick them into next week. "Will you kindly let go of me!" he ordered. They had fastened themselves to his pant legs and were kissing his feet. He tried to shake free, but the gnomes would not release their death grip. "Let go, already!" he snapped.

They fell back, still hugging the stone flooring, their lidded eyes peering up at him expectantly.

"Great High Lord," Fillip whispered.

"Mighty High . . ." Sot began.

Ben cut him short. "Parsnip, Bunion—get these two mud bunnies into a bath and don't let them up for air until you can tell what they are again." The kobolds dragged the G'home Gnomes from the foyer, still groveling. Ben sighed, suddenly weary. "Questor, I want you and Abernathy to take one last look through the castle histories. See if there is anything—anything at all—that refers to the way that Landover, her Kings and the magic are joined." He shook his head sadly. "I know we've been this route before; I know we haven't found anything, but . . . well, maybe we missed something . . ." He trailed off.

Questor nodded bravely. "Yes, High Lord, it is possible that we missed something. It doesn't hurt to look again."

He disappeared down the hallway with Abernathy in tow. Abernathy looked doubtful.

Ben stood alone in the foyer with Willow for a few moments after the others had gone, then took the sylph gently by the hand and climbed the tower stairs to the Landsview. He felt a need to explore the valley one last time—he bit his tongue at the thought—and he wanted the girl to go with him. They hadn't spoken much since her recovery from the transformation, but they had stayed close to each other. It helped him having her there. It gave him an assurance that he didn't entirely understand. It gave him strength.

He tried to tell her. "I want you to know something, Willow," he said as they stood together on the platform of the Landsview. "I don't know how all this is going to turn out, but I do know that, whichever way it goes, I'm the better by a long sight for having had you for a friend."

She did not reply. Her hand closed tightly over his. Together they grasped the railing, and the castle walls fell away into the clouded gray skies.

They were gone all afternoon.

Ben slept soundly that night and did not wake until midday. Questor met him on his way downstairs. The wizard looked exhausted.

"Don't tell me." Ben smiled sympathetically. "Let me guess."

"Guessing is not required, High Lord," Questor replied. "We worked all night, Abernathy and I, and we found nothing. I am sorry."

Ben put his arm around the sticklike frame. "Nothing to be sorry for—you tried. Go get some sleep. I'll see you for dinner."

He ate some fruit and cheese and drank some wine in the kitchen while Parsnip watched silently, then went alone to the chapel of the Paladin. He stayed there for some time, kneeling in the shadows, wondering what had become of the champion and why he would not return, trying to draw some small measure of understanding and strength from the armored shell that rested on the pedestal before him. Dreams and wishes paraded before his eyes, vague images in the musted air, and he let himself feel the sweetness of the life he had enjoyed. Old world and new, the good things recalled themselves and gave him peace.

He walked back through Sterling Silver in the late afternoon hours. He took his time, trailing silently through her halls and passageways, brushing her stone with his hands, feeling the warmth of her body. The magic that gave her life still burned somewhere deep within, but it was weakening. The Tarnish had grown worse; the discoloration had moved deeper within the castle walls. She was failing rapidly. He remembered the promise he had made to himself—that one day he would find a way to help her. He wondered now if he ever would.

He gathered his friends in the dining hall for dinner that evening—Willow, Questor, Abernathy, Bunion, Parsnip, Fillip, and Sot. There was little to eat. The castle larder was nearly empty and the magic could no longer produce the needed food. Everyone pretended the meal was fine. Conversation was subdued. No one complained; no one argued. They all worked very hard at avoiding any mention of what lay ahead.

When the meal was almost ended, Ben stood up. He had difficulty speaking. "I hope that you will excuse me, but I should try to get at least a few hours' sleep before I, uh . . ." He stopped. "I thought I'd leave around midnight. I don't expect any of you to go with me. In fact, it might be better if you didn't. I appreciate the way you've all stood by me up to this point. I couldn't ask for better friends. I wish there was something I . . ."

"High Lord," Questor interrupted gently. He came to his feet, thin arms folding into his gray robes. "Please don't say anything more. We all decided earlier that we would come with you tomorrow. Good friends could do no less. Now why don't you go on to bed?"

They stared silently at him—the wizard, the scribe, the sylph, the kobolds, and the gnomes. He nodded slowly and smiled. "Thank you. Thank you all again."

He walked from the room and stood alone for a moment in the hall beyond. Then he climbed the stairs to his bedroom.

Willow came to wake him at midnight.

They stood together in the darkness of the bedroom after Ben had risen and held each other. Ben's eyes closed wearily and he let the warmth of the girl seep through him.

"I'm afraid of what's going to happen, Willow," he whispered to her. "Not of what might happen to me . . ." He cut himself short. "No, that's a lie—I'm scared to death of what might happen to me. But I'm more afraid of what might happen to Landover if the Mark kills me. If I fail to survive this confrontation, Landover may be lost. And I'm afraid I *will* fail, because I still don't know how to prevent him from winning!"

She hugged him tightly, and her voice was fierce. "Ben! You have to believe in yourself! You have accomplished so much more than anyone ever imagined that you would. The answers you need are there. You have found them before when you needed them; I think you can do so again."

He shook his head. "I don't have enough time left to find them, Willow. The Mark hasn't left me enough time."

"You will find the answers in the time that you have."

"Willow, listen to me." Ben moved his face away from hers. "Only one thing can prevent the Mark from killing me—only one. The Paladin. If the Paladin appears to defend me, I have a chance. It's possible that he might. He's saved me several times now since I came into the valley."

He bent close again. "But, Willow, he's a ghost! He lacks substance and strength! He's a shadow, and shadows don't frighten anyone for very long! I don't need a ghost—I need the real thing! And, damn it, I don't even know if the real thing still exists!"

Her green eyes were calm in the aftermath of his fury. "If he has come to you before, Ben, he will do so again." She paused. "Do you remember when I told you that you were the one promised me by the fates woven in the marriage bed of my parents? You did not believe me, but you have seen since that it was so. I told you something more, Ben. I told you I sensed you were different; I told you I believed you were meant to be King of Landover. I still believe that. And I believe that the Paladin will come to you again. I believe that he will protect you."

He looked at her for a very long time without speaking. Then he kissed her lightly on the mouth. "Guess there's only one way to find out."

He gave her a brave smile and took her hands in his. Together, they started for the door.

Dawn stalked the Heart on cat's feet; the first faint tinges of silver were beginning to lighten the eastern skies above the tree line. Ben and the members of his little company had arrived several hours earlier and were gathered now on the dais. Others had been arriving all night. The River Master was there, standing close against the screen of the forest, surrounded by dozens of his people, all faint shadows in the mist and night. The Lords of the Greensward were there as well, dressed in battle harness, bristling with arms. War horses stamped and knights stood close like iron statues. Fairy people and humans, they faced one another across the rows of white velvet kneeling pads and armrests, eyes watchful in the gloom and half-light.

Ben sat quietly on the throne at the center of the dais, Willow at one hand, Questor and Abernathy at the other. The kobolds crouched directly in front of him. Fillip and Sot were nowhere to be seen. The G'home Gnomes had vanished once more.

Tunneled down about twenty feet, Ben surmised with faint amusement.

"Abernathy." Ben turned abruptly to find his scribe.

The dog jumped at the sound of his voice, then collected himself and bowed stiffly. "Yes, High Lord?"

"Go to Kallendbor and the Lords of the Greensward, then to the River Master. Ask that they join me before the dais."

"Yes, High Lord."

He went immediately. Abernathy hadn't quarreled once with Questor since they had left the castle. Both were on their best behavior—both walking on eggshells. It made Ben more nervous than he would have been if they had simply acted normal.

"High Lord." Questor bent close, his voice a whisper. "It nears dawn. You wear no armor and you have no weapons. Let me suggest that you allow me to equip you with some of each—now."

Ben looked up at the scarecrow figure with his gray robes and colored scarves, his wispish hair and beard, and his lined, anxious face and he smiled gently. "No, Questor. No weapons and no armor. They wouldn't do me any good against a creature like the Mark. I can't defeat him that way. I have to find another."

Questor Thews cleared his throat. "Do you happen to have such a way in mind, High Lord?"

Ben felt the cold that had settled deep within him burn sharply. "I might," he lied.

Questor stepped back. The shadows that cloaked the clearing were beginning to fade with the coming of daylight. Figures appeared from out of the gloom to either side—the Lords of the Greensward and the River Master and members of his family. Ben stood up and walked to the edge of the dais, stepping past the watchful kobolds. The iron forms of the Lords and the slim shadows of the fairies converged before him.

He took a deep breath. There was no point in mincing words. "The Mark comes to challenge me at dawn," he told them quietly. "Will you stand with me against him?"

There was complete silence. Ben looked from one face to the next, then nodded. "Very well. Let me put it another way. Kallendbor, the Lords of the Greensward gave me their word that they would pledge to the throne if I rid them of the dragon Strabo. I have done so. He is banished from the Greensward and all of the settled parts of the valley. I ask you now for your pledge. If your word means anything, you will give it to me."

He waited. Kallendbor looked uncertain. "What guarantee have we that you have done as you say—that the dragon is gone for good?" demanded Strehan harshly.

He isn't gone for good, Ben was tempted to say. He's gone for as long as I'm King and not a moment more, so you ought to think seriously about helping me stay alive!

But he didn't say that. Instead, he ignored Strehan and kept his eyes on Kallendbor. "Once your pledge is given, I will command that the people of Greensward cease all violation of the waters that feed into and sustain the lake country. Your people will work with the people of the River Master to clean those waters and to keep them clean."

He turned. "You, River Master, will then fulfill your promise and give to me your pledge as well. And you will begin again to teach to the people of the Greensward the secrets of your healing magic. You will help them to understand."

He paused again, eyes fixed now on the chiseled face of the sprite. There was uncertainty in the River Master's face as well. No one said anything.

The wind brushed suddenly against his face, sharp and quick. From somewhere distant, there was a low rumble like thunder. Ben forced himself to remain outwardly calm. The dawn had begun to break against the skyline.

"No one," he said softly, "will be forced to stand with me against the Mark."

He felt Questor's hand clamp roughly on his arm, but he ignored it. The clearing had gone still but for the quickening of the wind and the growing sound of the thunder. Shadows faded into streaks of silver and rose. The people of the lake country slipped deeper into the forest gloom; the knights and their war horses began to grow restless.

"High Lord." Kallendbor came forward a step. His dark eyes were intense. "It matters nothing what promises passed between us. If the Mark has challenged you, you are a dead man. You would be so even if we chose to take your part in this. None of us—Lords or fairy people—can withstand the Mark. His is the strength that only the greatest magic can overcome. We lack such magic, all of us. Humans have never had it and the people of the lake country have long since lost it. Only the Paladin had such magic—and the Paladin is gone."

The River Master came forward as well. Those with him were glancing about apprehensively. The wind had risen to a low whistle and the thunder was beginning to reverberate through the forest earth. The clearing behind them was suddenly deserted, the rows of pads and rests like grave markers neatly placed.

"Fairy magic banished the demons centuries ago, High Lord. Fairy magic had kept them from this land. The talisman of that fairy magic is the Paladin, and none here can withstand the Iron Mark without the Paladin to aid us. I am sorry, High Lord, but this battle must be yours."

He turned and walked from the dais, his family hastening to follow.

"Strength to you, play-King," Kallendbor muttered, and then he wheeled away as well. The other Lords trailed wordless after, armor clanking.

Ben stood alone at the forefront of the dais and stared after them for a moment. Then he shook his head hopelessly. He guessed he hadn't really expected them to help, anyway.

Thunder shook the dais to its foundation, rolling through the earth beneath in a long, sustained rumble of dissatisfaction. The dawn's faint silver light disappeared in a sudden press of shadows.

"High Lord—get back!" Questor was at his side, his gray robes whipping wildly in the wind. Willow appeared as well, and Abernathy and the kobolds. They surrounded him protectively, hands taking hold firmly. Bunion and Parsnip hissed ferociously.

The darkness thickened. "Stand away—all of you!" Ben shouted. "Stand down off the dais! Now!"

"No, High Lord!" Questor cried in response, his head shaking emphatically.

There was resistance from all, and he shrugged free of them. The wind began to howl furiously. "I said stand away, damn it! Get back away from me and do it now!"

Abernathy went. The kobolds bared their long teeth against the wind and darkness, and they hesitated still. Ben grasped Willow and shoved her into their hands, pushing all three aside. They went, a stricken Willow looking back frantically.

Questor Thews stood his ground. "I can help, High Lord! I have control over the magic now, and I . . . !"

Ben grasped his shoulders and swung him about, fighting the thrust of the wind as it broke free from the netherworld and stung with its force. "No, Questor! No one stands with me this time! Get off the dais at once!"

He propelled the wizard a good half-dozen feet with a single shove and motioned him to continue on. Questor looked back briefly, saw the determination in Ben's eyes, and went.

Ben stood alone. The Lords of the Greensward and their knights and the River Master and his fairies huddled in the shadows of the forest, shielding their faces against the darkness and wind. Questor and the others crouched down against the side of the dais. Flags snapped and rippled as the wind tore at them. Silver stanchions shuddered and bent. Thunder rolled in one continuous, frightening shudder.

Ben was shaking. Great special effects, he thought absurdly.

Shadows and mist swirled and joined at the far edge of the clearing, separating humans and fairies crouched within the trees. The thunder boomed sharply, as if exploding.

Then the demons appeared, a horde of dark, misshapen forms breaking from invisibility into being, spilling over from the black. Serpentine mounts snarled and pawed at the earth, and weapons and armor clanked and rattled like bones. The mass expanded and spread like a stain against the frail dawn light, pushing forward toward the dais, clogging the rows of kneeling pads and rests.

The thunder and the wind died away, and the sound of breathing and snarling filled the sudden stillness. The demons occupied almost the whole of the Heart. Ben Holiday and his small band of friends were an island in a sea of black forms.

A corridor opened at the army's center, and a massive, black, winged creature surged through the gap, half snake, half wolf, bearing on his back an armored nightmare. Ben took a deep breath and straightened resolutely.

The Iron Mark had come for him.

MEDALLION

It was the most terrifying moment of Ben Holiday's life.

The Iron Mark advanced the wolf-serpent through the ranks of the demons, slowly closing the distance that separated them. The black armor was scarred and battered, but it gleamed wickedly in the half-light. Weapons jutted from their sheaths and bindings—swords, battle axes, daggers, and a half-dozen more. Serrated spines ran the length of the Mark's limbs and back, bristling like a porcupine's quills. The helmet with the death's head had the visor closed down; but through iron slits, eyes glimmered a bright crimson.

Ben had never noticed before. The Mark was at least eight feet tall. The Mark was huge.

The wolf-serpent lifted its crusted head, its massive jaws parted and its teeth bared. It hissed, the sound like steam released under enormous pressure, and a snake's tongue licked at the morning air.

All about, the breathing of the demons was a harsh and eager reply.

Ben was suddenly paralyzed. He had been frightened before by the things he had encountered and the dangers he had faced during his brief time in Landover—but never like this. He had thought he would be equal to this confrontation, and he was not. The Mark was going to kill him, and he didn't know how to stop it from happening. He was captive to his fear, frozen in the manner of an animal who has been brought to bay at last by its most persistent enemy. He would have run in that instant if he could have made himself do so, but he could not. He could only stand there, watching the demon advance on him, waiting for his inevitable destruction.

It was with great effort that he managed to reach within his tunic and clasp tightly the medallion.

The carved surface pressed its outline of island castle, rising sun and mounted knight into the palm of his hand. The medallion was the only hope he had, and he clung to it with the desperation of a drowning man clinging to a lifeline.

Help me, he prayed!

There was a sharp hiss of anticipation from the demons. The Mark slowed his wolf-serpent and the helmet with the death's head lifted watchfully.

It isn't too late—I can still escape, Ben screamed out in the silence of his mind. I can still use the medallion to save myself!

Something tugged at his memory then—something indefinable. Fear has many disguises, the fairies had warned. You must learn to recognize them. The words were just a nudge, but it was enough to ease the iron grip of his fear and let him reason again. The floodgates opened. Bits and pieces of conversations and events surrounding the medallion recalled themselves in a frantic rush. They spun and swirled like debris in a stream's sudden eddy, and he grasped for them desperately.

Willow's calm voice whispered to him in the midst of his confusion: The answers you need are there.

But, damn it, he couldn't find them!

Then the fingers of his memory closed about a single, small admonishment that he had nearly forgotten in the chaos of the days and weeks now past, and he snatched it clear of the others. It had come from Meeks, of all people. It had been contained in the letter that had accompanied the medallion when it was first given to him.

No one can take the medallion from you, the letter had said.

He repeated the words, sensing something important hidden in them, not yet understanding what it was. The medallion was the key. He had always known that. He had sworn his oath of office upon it. It was the symbol of his rule. It was recognized by all as the mark of his Kingship. It was the key to passage in and out of Landover. It was the link between Landover's Kings and the Paladin.

The Mark dug iron spurs sharply into the scaled body of the wolf-serpent, and the beast heaved forward once more, hissing with rage. The demon army came with it.

He cannot take the medallion from me, Ben decided suddenly. The Mark must have the medallion, but he cannot take it from me. Somehow, I know it is so. He waits for me to use it so that I will be gone from Landover forever. That is what he expects me to do. That is what he really wants.

Meeks had wanted that as well. All of his enemies seemed to want that.

And that was reason enough not to allow it.

His hand lifted the medallion clear of his tunic, and he let it fall gently against his chest, free of his clothing where all could see it. He would not remove it. He would not use it to escape. He would not leave Landover when he had worked so hard to stay. This was where he belonged, alive or dead. This was his home.

This was his commitment.

He thought suddenly, once again, of the Paladin.

The Iron Mark closed on him, and a lance with spikes jutting from its tip lowered toward his chest. Ben waited. He no longer felt the fear. He no longer felt anything but a renewed stubbornness and determination.

It was enough.

Light flashed at the far edge of the clearing, brilliant and white against the shadows and gloom. The Mark wheeled about and there was a low hiss of recognition from among the ranks of the demons.

The Paladin appeared out of the light.

Ben shuddered. Something deep within drew him almost physically to the apparition—pulled him in the manner of an invisible magnet. It was as if the ghost were reaching for him.

The Paladin rode forward to the forest's edge and stopped. Behind him, the light died away. But the Paladin did not fade with the light as he had each time before. This time he remained.

Ben was twisting inside of himself, separating away from his being in a way he had not thought possible. He wanted to scream. What was happening? His mind spun. The demons seemed to have gone mad, crying out, shrieking, milling about as if they had lost all direction. The Mark spurred forward through their midst, his carrier grinding them underfoot as if they were blades of grass. Ben heard Questor cry out to him; he heard Willow cry out as well—and he heard the sound of his own voice calling back.

He recognized something grand and terrible then through his haze of confusion and physical distress. The Paladin was no longer a ghost. He was real!

He felt the medallion burn against his chest, a flare of silver light. He felt it turn to ice, then to fire and then to something that was neither. Then he watched it streak across the Heart to where the Paladin waited.

He watched himself be carried with it.

There was just enough time left for a single, stunning revelation. There was one question he had never asked—one that none of them had asked. Who was the Paladin? Now he knew.

He was.

All he had ever needed to do to discover that was to give himself over to this land of magic when it truly meant something. All he had ever needed to do to bring the Paladin back was to forgo the option of escape and to commit finally and irrevocably to a decision to remain.

He was astride the Paladin's charger. Silver armor closed about him, encasing him in an iron shell. Clasps and fasteners snapped shut, clamps and screws tightened, and the world became a rush of memories. He was submerged within those memories, a swimmer fighting to come up for air. He lost himself in their flow. He changed and was born anew. He was from a thousand other times and places, and he had lived a thousand other lives. The memories were now his. He was a warrior whose skill in battle and combat experience had never been equalled. He was a champion who had never lost.

Ben Holiday ceased to be. Ben Holiday became the Paladin.

He was aware momentarily of the present King of Landover standing statuelike on the dais at the center of the Heart. Time and motion seemed to slow to a standstill. Then he spurred his horse forward, and he forgot everything but the monstrous black challenger that rose to meet him.

They met in a frightening clash of armor and weapons. The spike-studded lance of the Mark and his own of white oak splintered and broke apart. Their mounts screamed and shuddered with the force of the impact, then raced past each other and wheeled recklessly about. Fingers of metal plating and chain mail gripped the hafts of battle axes and the curving blades lifted into the dawn air.

They came at each other again. The Mark was a black monstrosity that dwarfed the worn and battered figure of the silver knight. It was an obvious mismatch. They thundered toward each other and collided in a resounding crash. Axe blades bit deep, lodging in metal joints, slicing through armor. Both riders lost their balance and careened wildly astride their chargers. They wheeled and broke apart, axes hammering. The Paladin was yanked violently backward and pulled from his horse. He fell, clinging to the harness straps of the wolf-serpent.

It seemed the end of him. The wolf-serpent twisted violently, reaching back with its jaws to finish him. He was just out of reach. The Iron Mark wielded his battle axe with both hands. The axe hammered down, blow after blow, as the Mark sought to shatter his enemy's helmet.

The Paladin dangled from the harness straps, twisting to avoid the terrible blows. He could not release his grip. If he were to fall backward, the weight of his armor would not let him rise again and he would be trampled to death. He groped blindly for his assailant, finding at last the weapons harness the demon wore strapped about his waist.

His fingers closed on the handle of a four-edged dirk.

He wrenched the weapon free and buried it in the Mark's knee where the jointed metal armor gaped open. The Mark shuddered, and the battle axe dropped from his nerveless fingers. The Paladin grappled with the demon, trying to yank him off balance, seeking to pull him clear of the harness seat. The wolf-serpent wheeled wildly, hissing with rage as he felt his rider slipping. The Mark clung desperately to the reins and harness straps, kicking out at the Paladin. Kneeling pads and armrests shattered like deadwood as the combatants careened through the center of the Heart, and howls rose from the demons caught within.

Then abruptly the Paladin jerked the four-edged dirk from the Mark's armored knee and jammed it downward into the wolf-serpent's shoulder where it joined the scaled body. The monster reared and bolted, throwing both knight and demon to the ground in a crash of armor.

The Paladin landed on hands and knees, fighting to keep his balance. Dizziness washed through him. The Mark sprawled a dozen feet away, but he lurched unsteadily to his feet despite the massive weight of his armor. Both hands reached down to a giant broadsword sheathed at his waist.

The Paladin heaved himself upright then and freed his own broadsword just as the Mark reached him. Sword blades hammered into each other in a frightening clash of metal, the sound ringing out against the sudden stillness. The Paladin was thrust back by the heavier form of the Mark, yet kept his feet. Again they lunged and again the swords hammered down. Back and forth across the Heart the combatants staggered as the broadswords rose and fell in the half-light.

The Paladin experienced a sudden, unfamiliar sensation. He was losing this battle.

Then the Mark feinted and reversed the swing of his broadsword so that it cut downward in a sweeping motion toward the Paladin's feet. It was a glancing blow that careened off the tarnished armor, yet it caught the knight by surprise and knocked him sideways. He went down heavily and his weapon spun out of reach. The Mark was atop him at once. The demon's giant broadsword arced downward, and the blade caught and lodged in the Paladin's shoulder plates, wedged between the joints. Had the Mark released the sword, it would have been the end of the Paladin. But the demon clung fast to the weapon, struggling to free it, refusing to let go. It gave the Paladin one last chance. Desperately he groped his way up the demon's armored body, grappling for the weapons harness once more.

His fingers closed about the haft of the iron-headed mace.

The Paladin reared up, one hand clinging to the Mark's armored body, the other bringing up the mace. The ridged crown crashed into the helmeted death's head and the Mark shuddered. The Paladin swung the weapon upward a second time, the whole of his strength behind the blow. The metal visor split wide, and the face within was a nightmare of blood and twisted features. Silver light flared from the body of the Paladin. Once more the mace rose and fell, and the death's head disintegrated.

The Iron Mark tumbled to the earth, a shapeless mass of black metal. The Paladin rose slowly and stepped away.

A stillness shrouded the Heart, a mantle of hushed silence that was its own terrifying sound. Then the wind rose with a howl, the thunder reverberated through the forest earth, the air swirled black with shadows and gloom, and the gateway to Abaddon opened suddenly about the demons. Howling and crying, they disappeared back into the netherworld.

The clearing stood empty once more. Gloom and shadows dissipated. The dawn's new light fell across the Paladin as he climbed back astride his charger. The light gleamed on armor that was no longer tarnished or worn, but like new. The light flared, reflecting momentarily from the knight to the medallion worn by Landover's King as he stood alone at the forefront of the dais.

Then the light faded and the Paladin was gone.

Ben Holiday breathed the morning air and felt the warmth of the sunlight on his body. He felt momentarily weightless in the light clothing of Landover's King, free once more from the Paladin's armor. Time and motion thawed and quickened until all was as it had been.

He was himself again. The dream, the nightmare, whichever part of both he had survived, was over.

Shadowy figures stirred within the forest trees and emerged into the Heart, humans and fairies, Lords and knights of the Greensward, and the River Master with his people of the lake country, picking their way carefully through the debris. Ben's friends appeared from their shelter at the base of the dais, stunned looks on their faces. Willow was smiling.

"High Lord . . ." Questor began helplessly and trailed off. Then slowly he knelt before the dais. "High Lord," he whispered.

Willow, Abernathy, and the kobolds knelt with him. Fillip and Sot reappeared, as if by magic, and they, too, knelt. All across the clearing the men of the Greensward and the men of fairy dropped to one knee—the River Master, Kallendbor, Strehan, the Lords of the Greensward, all that had come.

"High Lord," they acknowledged.

"High Lord," he whispered back.

KING

It was all pretty simple after that. Even a neophyte monarch like Ben didn't have much difficulty figuring out what to do with all those astonished subjects. He got them back on their feet and marched them directly to Sterling Silver for a victory feast. Things might have been tough up until this morning and they might be tough again by tomorrow; but for the remainder of this day, at least, it looked like smooth sailing.

He ferried his friends, the River Master and his immediate family, and the Lords of the Greensward and their retainers across in the lake skimmer and left soldiers and assorted entourages to camp along the shoreline. It took several trips to bring everyone invited across, and he made a mental note to construct a bridge before the next get-together.

"There *was* a bridge in the old days, High Lord," Questor whispered surreptitiously, as if reading his thoughts, "but when the old King died, the people ceased coming to the castle, the army drifted away, and traffic eventually stopped altogether. The bridge fell into a terrible state of disrepair, boards cracked and rotted, bindings frayed, nails rusted—just a large clog in the lake that reflected the sorry state of the entire kingdom. I tried to salvage it with magic, High Lord, but things just didn't work out quite the way I had planned . . ." He stopped rambling and trailed off.

Ben's eyebrows lifted. "Things?"

Questor leaned closer. They were midway across the lake on their final trip. "I am afraid I sank the bridge, High Lord."

He peered reluctantly over the skimmer's bow. Ben peered with him. It was hard to keep from grinning, but he did.

He gathered his guests in the great hall and seated them about a series of tressel tables pulled together. He worried belatedly that Sterling Silver could not find the means to feed them all, but his fears were groundless. The castle reproduced provisions from her larder with newfound strength and determination—as if she could sense the victory that had been won—and there was food and drink enough for everyone, inside and out.

It was a marvelous feast—a celebration in which all shared. Food and drink were consumed with relish, toasts were exchanged and adventures recounted. There was a fellowship that transcended lingering skepticism; there was a strange sense of renewal. One by one those gathered rose to their feet, at Questor's urging, and pledged once more their loyalty and unconditional support to Landover's newest King.

"Long life, High Lord Ben Holiday," the River Master prayed. "May all your future successes match today's."

"May you keep the magic close and use it well," Kallendbor advised, the warning in his voice unmistakable.

"Strength and judgment, High Lord," wished Strehan, his brow clouded with a continuing mix of awe and doubt.

"Great High Lord!" Fillip cried.

"Mighty High Lord!" Sot echoed.

Ah, well—it was a mixed bag, but a welcome one. One after another, they gave him their pledges and good wishes, and Ben acknowledged each courteously. There was cause for optimism, no matter how difficult tomorrow might turn out to be. The Paladin was returned—brought back from a place in which no one would have thought to look, freed from the prison of Ben's own heart. The magic was returned to the valley, and Landover would begin its transformation back to the pastoral land it had once been. The changes would be slow, but they would come. The mist and gloom would clear and there would be sunlight again. The Tarnish would fade; Sterling Silver would be Castle Dracula no more. The blight that had stricken the Bonnie Blues would weaken and die. Forests, grasslands, and hills would heal. Lakes and rivers would come clean. Wildlife would flourish anew. Everything would be reborn.

And one day, a day far in the future, perhaps past the time that he would live, the golden vision of life in the valley that he had been shown by the fairies would come to pass.

It can happen, he told himself firmly. I need only believe. I need only remain true. I need only continue to work for it.

He rose when they had finished. "I am your servant, first and always—yours and the land's," he told them, his voice quiet. The noise died away and they turned to listen. "I am that to you and I ask that you be the same to each other. We have much to accomplish together. These things we shall do immediately. We shall cease polluting the waterways and ravaging the forestlands of our neighbors. We shall work with each other and teach each other what we can to protect and restore all the land. We shall devise commerce agreements that facilitate free trade between all our peoples. We shall institute public works programs for our roads and waterways. We shall revise our laws and establish courts to enforce them. We shall exchange ambassadors—here and with all of the peoples of the valley—and we shall convene regularly at Sterling Silver to air our grievances in a peaceful and constructive fashion."

He paused. "We shall find a way to be friends."

They toasted him, more for the thought than the feasibility of what he was proposing, he knew—but it was a start. There were other ideas to be implemented as well: a workable taxing system, a uniform currency exchange, a census, and various reclamation projects. He had ideas he hadn't even begun to think through thoroughly enough to propose yet. But the time would come. He would find a way to put them all to work.

He passed down the table, pausing by Kallendbor and the River Master. He bent close. "I rely on you, most of all, to stand by your promises. Each must help the other as you have sworn you would. We are all allies, now."

There were solemn nods and murmured assurances. But a veil of doubt remained in their eyes. Neither was certain that Ben Holiday was the man to hold their enemies in check. Neither was convinced that he was the King they needed. His victory over the Mark was impressive; but it was only a single victory. They would wait and see.

Ben accepted that. At least he had their pledge. He would find a way to win their trust.

He thought back momentarily to the battle fought between the Paladin and the Mark. He had told no one what he had learned of the link between the knight-errant and himself. He wasn't sure yet if he ever would. He wondered if he could bring the Paladin back again if the knight were needed. He thought that he could. But it chilled him to think about the transformation he had undergone within that suit of iron—the feelings and emotions he had shared with his champion, the memories of battles and deaths over so many years. He shook his head. There would have to be a very compelling reason for him to call the Paladin back again . . .

Another toast was proposed by one of the Lords—his good health. He acknowledged it and drank. Count on it, he promised silently.

He switched subjects. He must begin work immediately on restoration of the Heart. So much had been damaged during the battle with the Mark; the ground had been torn, the white velvet kneeling pads and armrests had been destroyed, and the staffs of the flags and the tall stanchions had been shattered. The Heart must be put right again. It meant something special to them all, but to no one more than him.

"Ben." Willow left her seat and moved next to him. She lifted her wine glass. "Happiness, High Lord," she wished him, her voice soft against the background of noise.

He smiled. "I think I've found that happiness, Willow. You and the others have helped me find it."

"Is this true?" She looked at him carefully. "And does the pain of what you lost in your old life no longer haunt you, then?"

She spoke of Annie. A momentary image of his dead wife passed within his mind and then faded. His old life was over; he would not be going back to it. He felt he could accept that now. He could never forget Annie, but he could let her go.

"It no longer haunts me," he answered.

Her green eyes held his own. "Perhaps you will permit me to remain with you long enough to make certain, Ben Holiday?"

He nodded slowly. "I wouldn't want it any other way."

She bent close and kissed his forehead, his cheek and his mouth. The party continued unnoticed around them.

It was after midnight when the festivities ended and the guests began to retire to the rooms that had been prepared for them. Ben had finished saying good night to all who remained and was giving thought to the comforts of his own bed when Questor approached, looking a bit embarrassed.

"High Lord," he began and stopped. "High Lord, I regret troubling you with so small a problem at this hour, but it needs attending to, and I believe you best suited to deal with it." He cleared his throat. "It seems that one of the Lords brought a canine pet with him into Sterling Silver—quite a close member of the family, I am given to understand—and now it has disappeared."

Ben lifted his eyebrows. "A dog?"

Questor nodded. "I have said nothing to Abernathy . . ."

"I see." Ben glanced about. Fillip and Sot were nowhere in sight. "And you think . . . ?"

"Merely a possibility, High Lord."

Ben sighed. Tomorrow's troubles were already upon him. But then, of course, so was tomorrow. He grinned in spite of himself. "What do you say, Questor—let's go find out if the gnomes are planning a midnight snack."

High Lord Ben Holiday, King of Landover, began the new day rather earlier than expected.

THE BLACK UNICORN

For Amanda
She sees unicorns that are hidden from me . . .

"How do you know she is a unicorn?" Molly demanded. "And why were you afraid to let her touch you? I saw you. You were afraid of her."

"I doubt that I will feel like talking for very long," the cat replied without rancor. "I would not waste time in foolishness if I were you. As to your first question, no cat out of its first fur can ever be deceived by appearances. Unlike human beings, who enjoy them. As for your second question—" Here he faltered, and suddenly became very interested in washing; nor would he speak until he had licked himself fluffy and then licked himself smooth again. Even then he would not look at Molly, but examined his claws.

"If she had touched me," he said very softly, "I would have been hers and not my own, not ever again."

—Peter S. Beagle, *The Last Unicorn*

CONTENTS

PROLOGUE

The black unicorn stepped from the morning mists, almost as if born of them, and stared out over the kingdom of Landover.

Daybreak hovered at the crest of the eastern horizon, an intruder that peeked from its place of concealment to catch a glimpse of night's swift departure. The silence seemed to deepen further with the appearance of the unicorn—as if that one small event in that one tiny corner was sensed somehow throughout the whole of the valley. Everywhere sleep gave way to waking, dreams to being, and that moment of transition was as close as time ever came to being frozen.

The unicorn stood near the summit of the valley's northern rim, high in the mountains of the Melchor, close to the edge of the world of fairy. Landover spread away before it, forested slopes and bare rock crags dropping toward foothills and grasslands, rivers and lakes, forests and scrub. Color glimmered in hazy patches through the fading dark where streaks of sunlight danced off morning dew. Castles, towns, and cottages were vague, irregular shapes against the symmetry, creatures that hunkered down in rest and breathed smoke from dying embers.

There were tears in the eyes of green fire that swept the valley end to end and glittered with newfound life. It had been so long!

A stream trickled down and collected in a basin of rocks a dozen yards from where the unicorn stood. A tiny gathering of forest creatures crouched at the edge of that pool and stared in awe at the wonder that had materialized before them—a rabbit, a badger, several squirrels and voles, an opossum and young, a solitary toad. A cave wight melted back into the shadows. A bog wump flattened back into its hole. Birds sat motionless upon the branches of the trees. All were stilled. The only sound was the ripple of the stream over mountain rock.

The black unicorn nodded its head in recognition of the homage being paid. Ebony body gleamed in the half light, mane and fetlocks shimmering like silk thrown in the wind. Goat's feet shifted and lion's tail swished, restless movements against the backdrop of the still-life world. The ridged horn knifed the darkness, shining faintly with magic. There had never before been a thing of such grace and beauty in all of creation as the unicorn and never would be again.

Dawn broke sharply over the valley of Landover, and the new day was begun. The black unicorn felt the sun's heat on its face and lifted its head in greeting. But invisible chains still bound it, and the cold of their lingering presence dispelled almost instantly the momentary warmth.

The unicorn shivered. It was immortal and could never be killed by mortal things. But its life could be stolen away all the same. Time was the ally of the enemy who had imprisoned it. And time had begun to move forward again.

The black unicorn slipped like quicksilver through shadows and light in search of its freedom.

DREAMS . . .

"I had a dream last night," Ben Holiday announced to his friends at breakfast that morning.

He might as well have been giving a weather report. The wizard Questor Thews did not appear to hear him, his lean, owlish face furrowed in thought, his gaze directed some twenty feet above the breakfast table at an invisible point in space. The kobolds Bunion and Parsnip barely looked up from eating. The scribe Abernathy managed a look of polite curiosity, but for a shaggy-faced dog whose normal look *was* one of polite curiosity, that was not particularly difficult.

Only the sylph Willow, just come into the dining hall of castle Sterling Silver and seated next to him, showed any real interest—a sudden change of expression that was oddly disquieting.

"I dreamed about home," he continued, determined to pursue the matter. "I dreamed about the old world."

"Excuse me?" Questor was looking at him now, apparently returned from whatever planet he had been visiting. "Excuse me, but did I hear you say something about . . . ?"

"Exactly *what* did you dream about the old world, High Lord?" Abernathy interrupted impatiently, polite curiosity become faint disapproval. He looked at Ben meaningfully over the rims of his eyeglasses. He always looked at him like that when Ben mentioned anything about the old world.

Ben forged ahead. "I dreamed about Miles Bennett. You remember my telling you about Miles, don't you—my old law partner? Well, I dreamed about him. I dreamed that he was in trouble. It wasn't a complete dream; there wasn't a true beginning or end. It was as if I came in halfway through the story. Miles was in his office, working, sorting through these papers. There were phone calls coming in, messages being delivered, people in the shadows where I couldn't see them clearly. But I could see that Miles was practically frantic. He looked terrible. He kept asking for me. He kept wondering where I was, why I wasn't there. I called out to him, but he didn't hear me. Then there was a distortion of some sort, a darkness, a twisting of what I was seeing. Miles kept calling, asking for me. Then something came between us, and I woke up."

He glanced briefly at the faces about him. They all were listening now. "But that doesn't really tell you everything," he added quickly. "There was a sense of . . . some impending disaster lurking behind the whole series of images. There was an intensity that was frightening. It was so . . . real."

"Some dreams are like that, High Lord," Abernathy observed, shrugging. He pushed the eyeglasses back on his nose and folded his forelegs primly across his vested chest. He was a fastidious dog. "Dreams are frequently manifestations of our subconscious fears, I've read."

"Not this dream," Ben insisted. "This was more than your average, garden-variety dream. This was like a premonition."

Abernathy sniffed. "And I suppose the next thing you are going to tell me is that on the strength of this emotionally distressing, but rationally unfounded, dream you feel compelled to return to your old world?" The scribe was making no effort to conceal his distress now, his worst fears about to be realized.

Ben hesitated. It had been more than a year since he had passed into the mists of the fairy world somewhere deep in the forests of the Blue Ridge Mountains twenty miles southwest of Waynesboro, Virginia, and entered the kingdom of Landover. He had paid a million dollars for the privilege, answering an advertisement in a department store catalogue, acting more out of desperation than out of reason. He had come into Landover as King, but his acceptance as such by the land's inhabitants had not come easily. Attacks on his claim to the throne had come from every quarter. Creatures whose very existence he had once believed impossible had nearly destroyed him. Magic, the power that governed everything in this strangely compelling world, was the two-edged sword he had been forced to master in order to survive. Reality had been redefined for him since he had made his decision to enter the mists, and the life he had known as a trial lawyer in Chicago, Illinois, seemed far removed from his present existence. Still, that old life was not completely forgotten, and he thought now and then of going back.

His eyes met those of his scribe. He didn't know what answer to give. "I admit that I am worried about Miles," he said finally.

The dining hall was very quiet. The kobolds had stopped eating, their monkey faces frozen in those frightening half grins that showed all their considerable teeth. Abernathy was rigid in his seat. Willow had gone pale, and it appeared that she was about to speak.

But it was Questor Thews who spoke first. "A moment, High Lord," he advised thoughtfully, one bony finger placed to his lips.

He rose from the table, dismissed from the room the serving boys who stood surreptitiously on either side, and closed the doors tightly behind them. The six friends were alone in the cavernous dining hall. That apparently wasn't enough for Questor. The great arched entry at the far end of the room opened through a foyer to the remainder of the castle. Questor walked silently to its mouth and peered about.

Ben watched curiously, wondering why Questor was being so cautious. Admittedly, it wasn't like the old days when there were only the six of them living at Sterling Silver. Now there were retainers of all ages and ranks, soldiers and guardsmen, emissaries and envoys, messengers and assorted others that comprised his court, all stumbling over one another and into his private life when it was least convenient. But it wasn't as if the subject of his going back to the old world hadn't been discussed openly before—and by practically everyone. It wasn't as if the people of Landover didn't know by this time that he wasn't a native Landoverian.

He smiled ruefully. Ah, well—there was no harm in being cautious.

He stretched, loosening muscles still tightened from sleep. He was a man of ordinary appearance, his height and build medium, his weight evenly distributed. His movements were quick and precise; he had been a boxer in his youth and still retained much of his old skill. His face was brown from sun and wind, with high cheekbones and forehead, a hawk nose, and a hairline that receded slightly at the corners. Age lines were beginning to show at the corners of his eyes, but the eyes themselves were brilliant blue and icy.

His gaze shifted ceilingward. Morning sunlight streamed through high glass windows and danced off polished wood and stone. The warmth of the castle seeped through him, and he could feel her stir restlessly. She was always listening. He knew that she had heard him speak of the dream and was responding with a measure of discontent. She was the mother who worried for her brash, incautious child. She was the mother who sought always to keep that child safe beside her. She didn't like it when he talked of leaving.

He glanced covertly at his friends: Questor Thews, the wizard whose magic frequently misfired, a ragtag scarecrow of patchwork robes and tangled gestures; Abernathy, the court scribe become a soft-coated Wheaten Terrier through Questor's magic and left that way when the magic couldn't be found to change him back again, a dog in gentleman's clothing; Willow, the beautiful sylph who was half woman, half tree, a creature of the fairy world with magic of her own; and Bunion and Parsnip, the kobolds who looked like big-eared monkeys in knickers, a messenger and a cook. He had found them all so strange in the beginning. A year later, he found them comfortable and reassuring and felt protected in their presence.

He shook his head. He lived in a world of dragons and witches, of gnomes, trolls, and other strange creatures, of living castles and fairy magic. He lived in a fantasy kingdom in which he was King. He was what he had once only dreamed of being. The old world was long past, the old life gone. Odd, then, that he still thought of that world and life so frequently, of Miles Bennett and Chicago, of the law practice, of the responsibilities and obligations he had left behind. Threads from the tapestry of last night's dream entwined within his memory and tugged relentlessly at him. He could not forget easily, it seemed, what had comprised so many years of his life . . .

Questor Thews cleared his throat.

"I had a dream last night as well, High Lord," the wizard declared, returned from his reconnaissance. Ben's eyes snapped up. The tall, robed figure hunched down over his high-backed chair, green eyes clear and distant. The bony fingers of one hand scratched the bearded chin, and the voice was a wary hiss. "My dream was of the missing books of magic!"

Ben understood the other's caution now. Few within Landover knew of the books of magic. The books had belonged to Questor's half-brother, the former court wizard of Landover, a fellow Ben had known in the old world as Meeks. It was Meeks, in league with a disgruntled heir to the throne, who had sold Ben the kingship of Landover for one million dollars—certain that Ben would fall victim to one of any number of traps set to destroy him, certain that when Ben was finally dispatched the kingship would become his to sell again. Meeks had thought to make Questor his ally, the promise of knowledge from the hidden books of magic the carrot used to entice his half-brother to his cause. But Questor and Ben had become allies instead, eluding all the traps that Meeks had set and severing the old wizard's ties with Landover for good.

Ben's eyes fixed Questor's. Yes, Meeks was gone—but the books of magic still remained concealed somewhere within the valley . . .

"Did you hear what I said, High Lord?" Questor's eyes sparkled with excitement. "The missing books—magic gleaned by wizards of Landover since the dawn of her creation! I think I know where they are! I saw where they were in my dream!" The eyes danced. The voice dropped to a whisper. "They are hidden in the catacombs of the ruined fortress of Mirwouk, high in the Melchor! In my dream, I followed after a torch that no hand carried, followed it through the dark, through tunnels and stairways to a door marked with scroll and runes. The door opened; there were blocks of stone flooring and one marked with a special sign. It gave at my touch and the books were there! I remember it all . . . as if it really happened!"

Now it was Ben's turn to look dubious. He started to say something in reply and stopped, not knowing what to say. He felt Willow stir uneasily beside him.

"I did not know whether to speak of my dream or not, to be honest with you," the wizard confided, his words coming in a rush. "I thought maybe I should wait until I was able to discover if the dream was false or true before I said anything. But then you spoke of your dream, and I . . ." He hesitated. "Mine was like yours, High Lord. It was not so much a dream as a premonition. It was strangely intense, compelling in its vividness. It was not frightening like yours; it was . . . exhilarating!"

Abernathy, at least, was not impressed. "All this could be the result of something you ate, wizard," he suggested rather unkindly.

Questor seemed not to hear him. "Do you realize what it would mean if I were to have the books of magic in my possession?" he asked eagerly, hawk face intense. "Do you have any idea of the magic I would command?"

"It seems to me you command quite enough already!" Abernathy snapped. "I would remind you that it was your command—or lack thereof—over magic that reduced me to my present state some years back! There is no telling what damage you might cause if your powers were enhanced further!"

"Damage? What of the good I might accomplish?" Questor wheeled on the other, bending close. "What if I were to find a way to change you back again!"

Abernathy went still. It was one thing to be skeptical—another to be foolishly so. He wanted nothing more in all the world than to be human again.

"Questor, are you sure about this?" Ben asked finally.

"As sure as you, High Lord," the wizard replied. He hesitated. "Odd, though, that on a single night there should be two dreams . . ."

"Three," Willow said suddenly.

They stared at her—Questor, his sentence unfinished; Ben, still trying to grasp the significance of Questor's revelation; Abernathy and the kobolds speechless. Had she said . . . ?

"Three," she repeated. "I, too, had a dream—and it was strange and disturbing and perhaps more vivid than either of yours."

Ben saw the disquieting expression again, more pronounced, more intense. He had been preoccupied before and had not paid close attention. Willow was not given to exaggeration. Something had shaken her. He saw a worry in her eyes that bordered on fear.

"What was it that you dreamed?" he asked.

She did not speak immediately. She seemed to be remembering. "I was on a journey through lands that were both familiar and at the same time foreign. I was in Landover and yet I was somewhere else. I was seeking something. My people were there, dim shadows that whispered urgently to me. There was a need for haste, but I did not understand why. I simply went on, searching."

She paused. "Then daylight passed away into darkness, and moonlight flooded a woods that rose all about me like a wall. I was alone now. I was so frightened I could not call for help even though I felt I must. There was a mist that stirred. Shadows crowded so close that they threatened to smother me."

Her hand crept over Ben's and tightened. "I needed you, Ben. I needed you so badly I could not stand the thought of not having you there. A voice seemed to whisper within me that if I did not complete my journey quickly, I would lose you. Forever."

Something in the way Willow spoke that single word chilled Ben Holiday to the bone.

"Then suddenly a creature appeared before me, a wraith come from the mists of the predawn night." The sylph's green eyes glittered. "It was a unicorn, Ben, so dark that it seemed to absorb the white moon's light as a sponge would absorb water. It was a unicorn, but something more. It was not white as the unicorns of old, but ink black. It barred my passage, its horn lowered, hooves pawing at the earth. Its slender body seemed to twist and change shape, and I saw it was more demon than unicorn, more devil than fairy. It was blind in the manner of the great marsh bulls, and it had their fury. It came for me, and I ran. I knew, somehow, that I must not let it touch me—that if it were to touch me I was lost. I was quick, but the black unicorn followed close behind. It wanted me. It meant to have me."

Her breath came quickly, her slender body tense with the emotions that raged within. The room was deathly still. "And then I saw that I held in my hands a bridle of spun gold—real gold threads drawn and woven by the fairies of the old life. I didn't know how I had come to possess that bridle; I only knew that I mustn't lose it. I knew that it was the only thing in the world that could harness the black unicorn."

The hand tightened further. "I ran looking for Ben. The bridle must be taken to him, I sensed, and if I did not reach him with it quickly, the black unicorn would catch me and I would be . . ."

She trailed off, her eyes fastened on Ben's. For an instant, he forgot everything she had just told him, lost in those eyes, in the touch of her hand. For an instant, she was the impossibly beautiful woman he had come upon bathing naked in the waters of the Irrylyn almost a year ago, siren and fairy child both. The vision never left him. He recaptured it each time he saw her, the memory become life all over again.

There was an awkward silence. Abernathy cleared his throat. "It seems to have been quite a night for dreams," he remarked archly. "Everyone in the room but me appears to have had one. Bunion, how about you? Did you dream about friends in trouble or books of magic or black unicorns? Parsnip?"

The kobolds hissed softly and shook their heads in unison. But there was a wary look to their sharp eyes that suggested they did not wish to treat the matter of these dreams as lightly as Abernathy did.

"There was one thing more," Willow said, still looking only at Ben. "I came awake while I ran from the thing that hunted me—black unicorn or devil. I came awake, but I felt certain the dream had not ended—that there was still something more to come."

Ben nodded slowly, his reverie broken. "Sometimes we dream the same dream more than once . . ."

"No, Ben," she whispered, her voice insistent. Her hand released his. "This dream was like yours—more premonition than dream. I was being warned, my High Lord. A fairy creature is closer to the truth of dreams than others. I was being shown something that I am meant to know—and I have not yet been shown all."

"There are stories of sightings of a black unicorn in the histories of Landover," Questor Thews advised suddenly. "I remember reading of them once or twice. They happened long ago, and the reports were vague and unconfirmed. The unicorn was said to be a demon spawn—a thing of such evil that even to gaze once upon it was to become lost . . ."

The food and drink of their breakfast sat cooling on plates and in cups on the table before them, forgotten. The dining hall was still and empty, yet Ben could sense eyes and ears everywhere. It was an unpleasant feeling. He glanced briefly at Questor's somber face and then back at Willow's once more. Had he been told of her dream—and perhaps even of Questor's as well—and not experienced his own, he might have been inclined to dismiss them. He did not put much stock in dreams. But the memory of Miles Bennett in that darkened office, nearly frantic with worry because Ben was not there when he was needed, hung over him like a cloud. It was as real as his own life. He recognized a similar urgency in the narrative of the dreams of his friends, and their insistence simply reinforced a nagging conviction that dreams as vivid and compelling as theirs should not be dismissed as the byproducts of last night's dinner or a collection of overactive subconsciousnesses.

"Why are we having these dreams?" he wondered aloud.

"This is a land built on dreams, High Lord," Questor Thews replied. "This is a land where the dreams of fairy world and mortal world come together and are channeled one to the other. Reality in one is fantasy in the other—except here, where they meet." He rose, spectral in his patchwork robes. "There have been instances of such dreams before, frequently in scatterings of up to half a dozen. Kings and wizards and men of power have had such dreams throughout the history of Landover."

"Dreams that are revelations—or even warnings?"

"Dreams that are meant to be acted on, High Lord."

Ben pursed his lips. "Do you intend to act on yours, Questor? Do you intend to go in search of the missing books of magic—just as your dream has advised?"

Questor hesitated, his brow furrowed in thought.

"And should Willow seek out the golden bridle of her dream? Should I return to Chicago and check out Miles Bennett?"

"High Lord, please—a moment!" Abernathy was on his feet, a decidedly harried look about him. "It might be wise to think this matter through a bit more carefully. It could be a very grave mistake for the lot of you to go running off in search of . . . of what may very well turn out to be a collection of gastrically induced falsehoods!"

He faced Ben squarely. "High Lord, you must remember that the wizard Meeks is still your greatest enemy. He cannot reach you as long as you stay in Landover, but I am certain he lives for the day you are foolish enough to venture back into the very world in which you left him trapped! What if he discovers that you have returned? What if the danger that threatens your friend is Meeks himself?"

"There is that chance," Ben agreed.

"Yes, there most certainly is!" Abernathy pushed his glasses firmly back on his nose, his point made.

He glanced now at Questor. "And you should be wise enough to appreciate the dangers inherent in any attempt to harness the power of the missing books of magic—power that was the tool of wizards such as Meeks! There were rumors long before you and I came into being that the books of magic were cast in demon iron and conjured for evil use. How can you be certain that such power will not consume you as quickly as fire would a piece of dried parchment? Such magic is dangerous, Questor Thews!

"As for you—" He turned quickly to Willow, cutting short Questor's attempts at protest. "—yours is the dream that frightens me most. The legend of a black unicorn is a legend of evil—even your dream tells you that much! Questor Thews failed to advise in his recitation of the histories of Landover that all those who claimed to have seen this creature came to a sudden and unpleasant demise. If there is a black unicorn, it is likely a demon strayed from Abaddon—and best left alone!"

He finished with a snap of his jaws, rigid with the strength of his conviction. His friends stared at him. "We are only surmising," Ben said, attempting to sooth his agitated scribe. "We are only considering possible alternatives . . ."

He felt Willow's hand close again about his own. "No, Ben. Abernathy's instincts are correct. We are past considering alternatives."

Ben fell silent. She was right, he knew. Not one of the three had said so, but the decision had been made all the same. They were going on their separate journeys in pursuit of their separate quests. They were resolved to test the truth of their dreams.

"At least one of you is being honest!" Abernathy huffed. "Honest about going if not about the danger of doing so!"

"There are always dangers . . ." Questor began.

"Yes, yes, wizard!" Abernathy cut him short and focused his attention on Ben. "Have you forgotten the projects presently under way, High Lord?" he asked. "What of the work that requires your presence to see it to completion? The judiciary council meets in a week to consider the format you have implemented for hearing grievances. The irrigation and road work at the eastern borders of the Greensward is set to begin, once you have surveyed the stakings. The tax levy requires an immediate accounting. And the Lords of the Greensward are to visit officially three days from now! You cannot just leave all that!"

Ben glanced away, nodding absently. He was thinking all at once of something else. Just when was it he had decided that he would leave? He couldn't remember making the decision. It was almost as if somehow the decision had been made for him. He shook his head. That wasn't possible.

His eyes shifted back to Abernathy. "Don't worry. I won't be gone long," he promised.

"But you cannot know that!" his scribe insisted.

Ben paused, then smiled an entirely unexpected smile. "Abernathy, some things must take precedence over others. Landover's business will keep for the few days it will take me to cross over to the old world and back again." He rose and walked to stand close to his friend. "I can't let this pass. I can't pretend the dream didn't happen and that I'm not worried for Miles. Sooner or later, I would have to go back in any case. I have left too many matters unfinished for too long."

"Such matters will keep better than those of this kingdom, should you fail to return, High Lord," his scribe muttered worriedly.

Ben's smile broadened. "I promise I will be careful. I value the well-being of Landover and her people as much as you."

"Besides, I can manage affairs of state quite nicely in your absence, High Lord," Questor added.

Abernathy groaned. "Why is it that I feel no reassurance whatsoever at such a prospect?"

Ben cut off Questor's response with a cautionary gesture. "Please, no arguing. We need each other's support." He turned to Willow. "Are you determined in this as well?"

Willow brushed back her waist-length hair and gave him a studied, almost somber look. "You already know the answer to that question."

He nodded. "I suppose I do. Where will you start?"

"The lake country. There are some there who may be able to help me."

"Would you consider waiting for me until I return from my own journey so that I might go with you?"

The sea green eyes were steady. "Would you wait instead for me, Ben?"

He squeezed her hand gently in reply. "No, I guess not. But you are under my care, nevertheless, and I don't wish you to go alone. In fact, I don't wish either Questor or you to go alone. Some sort of protection may prove necessary. Bunion will go with one of you, and Parsnip with the other. No, don't argue with me," he continued quickly, seeing words of protest forming on the lips of the sylph and the wizard both. "Your journeys could prove dangerous."

"And yours as well, High Lord," Questor pointed out.

Ben nodded. "Yes, I realize that. But our circumstances are different. I can take no one with me from this world into the other—at least not without raising more than a few eyebrows—and it is in the other world that such danger as might threaten me awaits. I will have to be my own protector on this outing."

Besides, the medallion he wore about his neck was protection enough, he thought. He let his fingers stray down the front of his tunic to the medallion's hard outline. Ironically, Meeks had given him the medallion when he had sold him the kingship—the key to the magic that was now his. Only the bearer could be recognized as King. Only the bearer could pass through the fairy mists from Landover to the worlds beyond and back again. And only the bearer could summon and command the services of the invincible armored champion known as the Paladin.

He traced the image of the knight-errant riding out from the gates of Sterling Silver against the sunrise. The secret of the Paladin was his alone. Even Meeks had never understood the full extent of the medallion's power or its connection with the Paladin.

He smiled tightly. Meeks had thought himself so clever. He had used the medallion to pass over into Ben's world and then let himself be trapped there. What the old wizard wouldn't give to get that medallion back now!

The smile faded. But that would never happen, of course. No one but the bearer could remove the medallion once it was in place—and Ben never took it off. Meeks was no longer any threat to him.

Yet somewhere at the back of his mind, almost buried in the wall of determination that buttressed everything to which he committed himself, a tiny fragment of doubt tugged in warning.

"Well, it appears that there is nothing I can say on the matter that will change your minds," Abernathy declared to the room at large, drawing Ben's attention back again. The dog peered at him over the rims of his glasses, pushed the spectacles farther up on his nose, and assumed the posture of a rejected prophet. "So be it. When will you depart, High Lord?"

There was an awkward silence. Ben cleared his throat. "The quicker I go, the quicker I can return."

Willow rose and stood before him. Her arms went about his waist, drawing him close. They held each other for a moment as the others watched. Ben could feel something stir in the sylph's slender body—a kind of shiver that whispered of unspoken fears.

"I imagine it would be best if we all got about our business," Questor Thews said quietly.

No one replied. The silence was enough. Dawn was already stretching into midmorning and there was a shared need to make use of the day ahead.

"Come back safe to me, Ben Holiday," Willow spoke into his shoulder.

Abernathy heard the admonishment and glanced away. "Come back safe to us all," he said.

Ben did not waste any time in setting out.

He retired directly to his bedroom after departing the dining hall and packed the duffel he had brought with him from the old world with the few possessions he felt he would need. He changed back into the navy blue sweat suit and Nikes he had worn over. The clothes and shoes felt odd after Landover's apparel, but comfortable and reassuringly familiar. He was going back at last, he thought as he changed. He was finally going to do it.

He went from the bedchamber down a set of back stairs and through a number of private halls to a small courtyard just off the front gates where the others waited. The morning sun shone from a cloudless blue sky against the white stone of the castle, flashing in blinding streaks where it caught the silver trim. Warmth eased from the earth of the island on which Sterling Silver sat and gave the day a lazy feel. Ben breathed the freshness of the day and felt the castle stir in response beneath his feet.

He locked hand to wrist firmly with the kobolds Bunion and Parsnip, returned Abernathy's stiff, formal bow, embraced Questor, and kissed Willow with a passion usually reserved for deepest night. There was not much talking. All the talking had already been done. Abernathy again warned against Meeks, and this time Questor cautioned him as well.

"Be careful, High Lord," the wizard advised, one hand gripping Ben's shoulder as if to hold him back. "Though shut in a foreign world, my half-brother is not entirely shorn of his magic. He is still a dangerous enemy. Watch out for him."

Ben promised he would. He walked with them through the gates, past the sentries stationed on day watch and down to the shore's edge. His horse waited on the far bank, a bay gelding he had named Jurisdiction. It was his private joke that wherever he traveled on horseback, he always had Jurisdiction. No one other than himself understood what he was talking about.

A squad of mounted soldiers waited there as well. Abernathy had insisted that within the kingdom, at least, Landover's King would not travel without adequate protection.

"Ben." Willow came to him one final time, her hands pressing something into his. "Take this with you."

He glanced down covertly. She had given him a smooth, milky-colored stone intricately marked with runes.

Willow closed his hands back about it quickly. "Keep the stone hidden. It is a talisman often carried by my people. If danger threatens, the stone will heat and turn crimson. That way you will be warned."

She paused, and one hand reached up to stroke his cheek softly. "Remember that I love you. I will always love you."

He smiled reassuringly, but the words bothered him as they always did. He didn't want her to love him—not so completely, not so unconditionally. He was frightened of what that meant. Annie had loved him like that—his wife, Annie, now dead, a part of his old life, his old world, killed in that car accident that sometimes seemed as if it had happened a thousand years ago, but more often seemed to have happened yesterday. He wasn't willing to risk embracing that kind of love and losing it a second time. He couldn't. The prospect terrified him.

A sudden twinge of sadness passed through him. It was strange, but until he met Willow he had never dreamed he might experience again those feelings he had shared with Annie . . .

He gave Willow a brief kiss and shoved the stone deep into his pocket. The touch of her hand lingered on his face as he turned away.

Questor took him across in the lake skimmer and waited until he was mounted. "Keep safe, High Lord," the wizard bade him.

Ben waved back to them all, took a final look at the spires of Sterling Silver, wheeled Jurisdiction about, and galloped away, with the squad of soldiers in tow.

Morning slipped into midday and midday into afternoon as Ben rode westward toward the rim of the valley and the mists that marked the boundaries of the fairy world. Late-year colors carpeted the countryside through which he passed in bright swatches. Meadows were thick with grasses of muted greens, blues, and pinks, and with white clover dotted crimson. Forest vegetation still retained much of its new growth. Bonnie Blues, the trees that were a staple of life within the valley with their offering of drink and food, grew in clusters everywhere—half-grown pin oaks colored a brilliant blue against the various shades of forest green. Two of Landover's eight moons hung low against the northern horizon, visible even in daylight—one peach, the other a pale mauve. Harvesting was under way in the fields of the small farms scattered about the countryside. Winter's week-long stay was still a month distant.

Ben drank in the smell, taste, sight, and feel of the valley as if sampling a fine wine. Gone was the mistiness and wintry gray blight that had marked the land when he had first come over and the magic had been dying. The magic was well now, and the land was whole. The valley and her people were at peace.

Ben was not. He set a steady pace as he traveled, but not a quick one. The need for haste he had felt earlier had given way to a strange anxiety at the thought of actually leaving. This would be his first trip out of Landover since his arrival, and although the idea of leaving had not bothered him before, it was beginning to bother him now. A nagging concern lurked about the edges and corners of his determination—that once he left Landover he would not be able to come back again.

It was ridiculous, of course, and he tried valiantly to beat it down, seeking to convince himself that he was experiencing the same misgivings any traveler encountered at the beginning of a trip away from home. He tried arguing that he was a victim of his friends' repeated warnings and humming "Brigadoon" to lighten the mood.

Nothing helped, however, and he finally gave it up. Some things you simply had to put up with until they lost their grip on you.

It was midafternoon when his party reached the lower slopes of the valley's western rim. He left the soldiers there with the horses and instructions to set up camp and wait for his return. He might be gone as long as a week, he told them. If he wasn't back by then, they were to return to Sterling Silver and advise Questor. The captain of the squad gave him a funny look, but accepted the orders without argument. He was used to his King going off on strange errands without his guard—although usually he had one of the kobolds or the wizard in tow.

Ben waited for the captain's salute, then slung the duffel bag over one shoulder and began the hike up the valley slope.

It was nearing sunset when he reached the summit and crossed toward the misted forest line that marked the boundaries of the fairy world. Daytime's warmth was slipping rapidly toward evening's cool, and his elongated shadow trailed after him like a grotesque silhouette. There was a deep, pervasive stillness in the air, and he felt a sense of something hidden.

Ben's hand strayed to the medallion that hung about his neck, and his fingers closed about it firmly. Questor had told him what to expect. The fairy world was everywhere and nowhere at the same time, and all of its many doorways to the worlds beyond were settled within. The way back was whatever way he chose to go and it could be found at whatever point he chose to enter. All he need do was fix in his mind his destination and the medallion would see him to the proper passageway.

That was the theory, at least. Questor had never had the opportunity to test it.

The mist swirled and stirred within the great forest trees, its trailers twisting like snakes. The mist had the look of something alive. There's a cheerful thought, Ben chided himself. He stopped before the mist, regarded it warily, took a deep breath to steady himself, and started in.

The mist closed about him instantly and the way back became as uncertain as the way forward. He pushed on. A moment later, a tunnel opened before him—the same vast, empty, black hole that had brought him across from the old world a year earlier. It burrowed through mist and trees and disappeared into nothingness. There were sounds in the tunnel, distant and uncertain, and shadows dancing at its rim.

Ben's pace slowed. He was remembering what it had been like when he had passed through this tunnel the last time. The demon known as the Mark and his black, winged carrier had come at Ben from out of nowhere; by the time he had decided they were real, they had very nearly finished him. Then he had practically stumbled over that sleeping dragon . . .

Slender shapes darted at the fringes of the darkness within the trees and mist. *Fairies.*

Ben quit remembering and forced himself to walk more quickly. The fairies had helped him once, and he should have felt comfortable among them. But he did not. He felt alien and alone.

Faces materialized and vanished again in the mists, sharp-eyed and angular with hair the consistency of willow moss. Voices whispered, but the words were indistinct. Ben was sweating. He hated being in the tunnel; he wanted out of there. Ahead, the darkness pressed on.

Ben's fingers still clutched the medallion in a death grip, and he thought suddenly of the Paladin.

Then the darkness before him brightened to dusky gray, and the tunnel's length shortened to less than fifty yards. Indefinable shapes swayed unevenly in the half-light, an interlacing of spider webs and bent poles. Voices and movement in the walls of the tunnel gave way to a sharp hissing. A sudden wind rose and howled sharply.

Ben peered ahead into the gloom. The wind whipped at him from the edges of the tunnel's end and carried the hissing sound into his face with a wet, stinging rush.

And there was something else . . .

He stepped from the tunnel's shelter into a blinding rainstorm and found himself face to face with Meeks.

. . . AND MEMORIES

Ben Holiday froze. Lightning streaked from skies leaden and packed with low-hanging clouds that shed their rain in torrents. Thunder boomed, reverberating across the emptiness, shaking the earth beneath with the force of its passing. Massive oak trees rose all about like the staked walls of some huge fortress, their trunks and leaf-bare limbs glistening blackly. Shorter pine and fir bristled in clumps through the gaps left by their taller sisters, and the rugged slopes of the Blue Ridge Mountains lifted darkly against the nearly invisible horizon.

The spectral figure of Meeks stood pinned against this backdrop. He stood without moving, tall and bent and old, white hair grizzled, craggy face as hard as iron. He looked almost nothing of the man Ben remembered. That man had been human; this man had the look of an enraged animal. Gone were the pressed woolen slacks, corduroy jacket, and loafers—the trappings of civilization that had complemented an urbane, if gruff, sales representative of a highly respected department store. Those reassuringly familiar business clothes had been replaced by robes of gunmetal blue that billowed like sailcloth and seemed to absorb the light. A high collar jutted from the shoulders to frame a ghastly, pitted face twisted by fury that bordered on madness. The empty sleeve of his right arm still hung limp. The black leather glove that covered his left hand was yet a claw. But each was more noticeable somehow, as if each were a scar left bare for viewing.

Ben's throat constricted sharply. There was a tension in the old man that was unmistakable—the tension of an attacker poised to strike.

My God, he has been waiting for me, Ben thought in shock. He knew I was coming!

Then Meeks started for him. Ben took one step back, his right hand tightening frantically about the medallion. Meeks was almost on top of him. The wind shifted, and the sounds of the storm echoed through the mountains with renewed sharpness. The rain swept back against his face, forcing him to blink.

When he looked again, Meeks was gone.

Ben stared. Meeks had disappeared as completely as if he had been a ghost. Rain and darkness cloaked the whole of the surrounding forestland in a shroud of gray wetness. Ben glanced about hurriedly, disbelief twisting his face. There was no sign of Meeks.

It took only a moment for Ben to regain his scattered thoughts. He caught sight of the dim outline of a pathway directly before him and started for it. He moved quickly ahead through the trees, following the pathway's curve as it wound down the mountainside and away from the time passage that had brought him back to his old world from Landover. And he was indeed back—of that much he was certain. He was back in the Blue Ridge Mountains of Virginia, deep in the George Washington National Forest. This was the same pathway that had brought him into Landover more than a year ago. If he followed it far enough, it would take him down out of the mountains to Skyline Drive, a turn-around with the black number 13 stenciled on a green sign, a weather shelter, and—most important of all—a courtesy telephone.

He was soaked through in moments, but he kept moving steadily ahead, the duffel clutched tightly under one arm. His mind worked rapidly. That wasn't Meeks he had seen, hadn't even looked like the old Meeks, had been barely recognizable, for Pete's sake! Besides, Meeks wouldn't have just disappeared like that if it had really been him, would he?

Doubt tugged sharply at his mind. Had he simply imagined it all, then? Had it all been some sort of mirage?

Belatedly, he thought of the rune stone that Willow had given him. Slowing, he fished through the pocket of his jacket until he found the stone and brought it out into the light. It was still milky in color and gave off no heat. That meant no magic threatened him. But what did that tell him about the phantom vision of Meeks?

He pushed ahead, slipping on the damp, water-soaked earth, pine boughs slapping at his face and hands. He was aware suddenly of how cold it was in these mountains, the chill settling through him with an icy touch. He had forgotten that late autumn could be unpleasant, even in western Virginia. Illinois could be frigid. It might even be snowing in Chicago . . .

He felt something catch in his throat. Shadows moved through the mist and rain, darting and sliding from view. Each time, he saw Meeks. Each time, he felt the wizard's gloved hand reaching for him.

Just keep moving, he told himself. Just get yourself to that phone.

It seemed to take much longer, but he reached the courtesy phone some thirty minutes later, climbing down from among the trees and crossing the parkway to the weather shelter that housed it. He was soaked to the skin and freezing, but he felt none of it. The entirety of his concentration was focused on the Plexiglas-enclosed black and silver metal box.

Please let it be working, he prayed.

It was. Rain beat down on the shelter roof in a steady thrum, and mist and gloom closed tightly about. He thought he heard footsteps. He rummaged through his duffel for the coins and credit card he still carried in his wallet, rang information for the name of a limo service out of Waynesboro, and called for a car to come up and get him. It was all done in a matter of minutes.

He sat down then to wait on the wooden bench fastened to the side of the shelter. He was surprised to discover that his hands were shaking.

By the time the limo reached him and he was safely inside, he had regained his composure enough to reason through what had happened to him.

He no longer thought that he had imagined the appearance of Meeks. What he had seen had been real enough. But it hadn't been Meeks he had seen; it had been an image of Meeks. The image had been triggered by his crossing back through the time passage. He had been meant to see the image. It had been placed there at the tunnel's end so that he would see it.

The question was, why?

He hunched down in the backseat of the limo as it sped down the parkway toward Waynesboro and considered the possibilities. He had to assume that Meeks was responsible. No other explanation made any sense. So what was Meeks trying to accomplish? Was he trying to warn Ben off—to chase him back through the time passage? That didn't make any sense. Well, no, the warning part did. Meeks was arrogant enough to want to let Ben know that he was aware of his coming back. But there had to be more to it than that. The image must have been placed there to accomplish something else as well.

He had his answer almost immediately. The image had not only warned Ben of Meeks; it had warned Meeks of Ben! The image was a device to alert the wizard that Ben had come back from Landover!

It made perfect sense. It was only reasonable to expect that Meeks would employ some contrivance—magic or otherwise—to warn him when Landover's failed Kings crossed back into their old world with the medallion. Once alerted, Meeks could then come after them . . .

Or, in this case, after him.

It was late afternoon when the driver deposited him at the front steps of a Holiday Inn in downtown Waynesboro, the rain still falling, the daylight completely gone. Ben told the fellow he was on vacation and had hiked the parkway north from Staunton until the bad weather forced him to abandon the plan and call for help. The driver looked at him as if he were nuts. The weather had been like this for better than a week, he snapped. Ben shrugged, paid him in cash, and hurried inside.

On his way to the front desk, he paused long enough to check the date on a newspaper someone had left lying on a table in the lobby. It read Friday, December 9. It was ten days more than a year since he had first walked through the time passage from the Blue Ridge Mountains of Virginia into Landover. Time in the two worlds did indeed pass synchronously.

He booked a room for the night, sent out his clothes to be cleaned and dried, took a steaming-hot shower to warm himself, and ordered dinner sent in. While he waited for the meal and his clothes, he called the airport for reservations to Chicago. There was nothing until morning. He would have to fly to Washington, then transfer to Chicago. He booked the reservation, billed it to his credit card, and hung up.

It was while he was eating dinner that it occurred to him that using a credit card to pay for his air fare wasn't exactly the smartest thing he could have done. He was sitting on the edge of his bed in front of the TV, the tray balanced on his lap, a Holiday Inn towel wrapped about him, and the room temperature at about eighty. His clothes were still out. Tom Brokaw was giving the news, and it suddenly struck Ben that in a world of sophisticated communications a computerized credit-card trace was a relatively simple matter. If Meeks had gone to the trouble of placing that image at the opening of the time passage to warn of Ben's return, then he would almost certainly take the matter a step further. He would know that Ben would attempt a visit to Chicago. He would know that Ben would probably elect to fly. A credit-card trace would tell him the airline flight, date of travel, and destination.

He could be waiting when Ben stepped off the plane.

That possibility ruined what was left of the meal. Ben put the tray aside, clicked off the TV, and began to consider more carefully what he was up against. Abernathy had been right. This was turning out to be more dangerous than he had imagined. But he really didn't have any choice. He had to go back to Chicago and see Miles long enough to discover whether there was any truth to his dream. Meeks would probably be waiting for him somewhere along the line. The trick was to avoid bumping into him.

He permitted himself a brief smile. No problem.

He had his clothes back by nine o'clock and was asleep by ten. He awoke early, had breakfast, shouldered the duffel, and caught a cab to the airport. He flew to Washington on the previous night's reservation, then canceled the balance of the ticket, walked over to another airline, booked a seat to Chicago on standby under an assumed name, paid for this ticket with cash, and was airborne before noon.

Let's see Meeks pick up on that one, he thought to himself.

Eyes closed, he leaned back in his seat and reflected on the strange set of circumstances that had taken him away from his home in Chicago to Never-Never Land. The memories made him shake his head reprovingly. Maybe, like Peter Pan, he had just never grown up. He had been a lawyer then, a damn good one, one from whom great things were expected by those who were the movers and shakers in the business. He was in practice with his friend and longtime associate Miles Bennett, a shared partnership in which the two complemented each other like old shoes and work jeans—Ben the outspoken, audacious trial lawyer, Miles the steady, conservative office practitioner. Miles often deplored Ben's judgment in taking cases, but Ben always seemed to land on his feet despite the heights from which he insisted on jumping. He had won more courtroom battles than the average bear—battles in which his corporate opponents had thought to bury him under an avalanche of money-backed rhetoric and paperwork, legal dodges, delays, and gamesmanship of all sorts. He had so surprised Miles after his victory in the Dodge City Express case that his partner had begun referring to him as Doc Holiday, courtroom gunfighter.

He smiled. Those had been good, satisfying times.

But the good times faded when Annie died. The satisfaction disappeared like quicksilver. His wife had died in a car accident, three months pregnant, and he seemed to lose everything after that. He turned reclusive, shunning everyone but Miles. He had always been something of a loner and he sometimes thought that the death of his wife and baby had just reinforced what was always there. He began to drift, the days running together, their events merging indecipherably. He sensed that he was slowly slipping away from himself.

It was difficult to know what might have happened had he not come across the bizarre offering in the Rosen's Department Store Christmas Wishbook for the purchase of the throne of the kingdom of Landover. He had thought it ridiculous at first—a fantasy kingdom with wizards and witches, dragons and damsels, knights and knaves for sale for one million dollars. Who would be foolish enough to believe that? But the desperate dissatisfaction he was experiencing in his life had led him to take the chance that something in this impossible fantasy might be real. Any risk was worth taking if it could bring him back to himself. He had shelved his doubts, packed his bags, and flown to Rosen's New York office to see what was what.

He was required to undergo an interview in order to complete the sale. The interviewer had been Meeks.

The familiar image of Meeks flashed instantly to mind—the tall old man with the whispered voice and dead eyes, a veteran of wars Ben could only imagine. The interview was the only time they had ever met face to face. Meeks had found him an acceptable candidate to be Landover's King—not to succeed as Ben had believed, but to fail. Meeks had convinced him to make the purchase. Meeks had charmed him like a snake its prey.

Meeks had also underestimated him.

He let his eyes slip open again and he whispered, "That's right, Ben Holiday—he did underestimate you. Now be sure that you don't underestimate him."

The plane touched down at Chicago O'Hare shortly after three, and Ben caught a cab into the city. The driver talked all the way in, mostly about sports: the Cubs' losing season, the Bulls' playoff hopes with Jordan, the Blackhawks' injury problems, the Bears at 13 and 1. The Chicago Bears? Ben listened, replying intermittently, a small voice at the back of his mind telling him there was something wrong with this conversation. He was nearly downtown before he figured out what it was. It was the language. He understood it, even though he had neither heard it nor spoken it for more than a year. In Landover, he heard, spoke, wrote, and thought Landoverian. The magic made it possible for him to do so. Yet here he was, back in his old world, back in good old Chicago, listening to this cab driver speak the English language—or a reasonable facsimile thereof—as if it were the most natural thing in the world.

Well, maybe that's exactly what it was, he thought and smiled.

He had the cab driver deposit him at the Drake, unwilling to return to his old penthouse apartment or to contact any friends or acquaintances just yet. He was being careful now. He was thinking about Meeks. He checked in under an assumed name, paid cash in advance for one night, and let the bellhop guide him to his room. He was increasingly grateful for the fact that he had decided to carry several thousand dollars in cash as a precaution when he had crossed into Landover a year ago. The decision had been almost an afterthought, but it was turning out to be a sound one. The cash was saving him from using the credit card.

Leaving the room with the cash and the billfold in one pocket of his running suit, he took the elevator down, left the hotel, and walked several blocks to Water Tower Place. He shopped, bought a sport coat and slacks, dress shirts, tie, socks and underwear, and a pair of dress loafers, paid cash, and headed back again. There was no point in being conspicuous, and a running suit and Nikes in the middle of the downtown Chicago business district was far too conspicuous. He simply didn't look the type. Sometimes appearances were everything—particularly in the short view. That was exactly why he hadn't brought any of his friends with him. A talking dog, a pair of grinning monkeys, a girl who became a tree, and a wizard whose magic frequently got the better of him would hardly escape notice on Michigan Avenue!

He regretted the superficial characterization of his friends almost immediately. He was being needlessly flip. Odd as they might be, they were genuine friends. They had stood by him when it counted, when it was dangerous to do so, and when their own lives were threatened. That was a whole lot more than you could say for most friends.

He bowed his head against a sudden gust of wind, frowning.

Besides, wasn't he as odd as they?

Wasn't he the Paladin?

He shoved the thought angrily to the darkest corners of his mind and hurried to catch the crossing light.

He bought several newspapers and magazines in the hotel lobby and retired to his room. He ordered room service and killed time waiting for his dinner by skimming the reading material to update himself on what had been happening in the world during his absence. He stopped long enough to catch an hour of world and local news, and by then his meal had arrived. He continued reading through the dinner hour. It was closing in on seven o'clock by this time, and he decided to call Ed Samuelson.

There were two reasons for Ben's return to Chicago. The first was to visit with Miles and discover whether the dream about his friend had been accurate. The second was to set his affairs in order permanently. He had already decided that the first would have to wait until morning, but there was no reason to put off the second. That meant a call to Ed.

Ed Samuelson was his accountant, a senior partner in the accountancy firm of Haines, Samuelson & Roper, Inc. Ben had entrusted management of his estate—an estate that was considerable in size—to Ed before he had left for Landover. Ed Samuelson was exactly the sort of person one would hope for in an accountant—discreet, dependable, and conscientious. There had been times when he thought Ben clearly mad in his financial judgment, but he respected the fact that it was Ben's money to do with as he chose. One of those times had been when Ben decided to purchase the throne of Landover. Ed had liquidated the assets necessary to collect the one million dollar purchase price and had been given power of attorney to manage the balance of Ben's assets while Ben was away. He had done all this without having the faintest idea what Ben was about.

Ben had not told him then and he had no intention of telling him now. But he knew Ed would accept that.

Calling Ed Samuelson was something of a risk. He had to assume that Meeks knew Ed was his accountant and would be contacted eventually. Anticipating that contact, Meeks might have tapped the accountant's phone. That was a somewhat paranoid assumption perhaps, but Meeks was no one to fool with. Ben only hoped that, if Meeks had decided on a phone tap, he had opted for one at Ed Samuelson's office and not one at his home.

He called Ed, found him just finished with his evening meal, and spent the next ten minutes convincing him that it really was Ben Holiday who was calling. Once he got that job done, he warned Ed that no one—and that meant absolutely no one—was to know about this call. Ed was to pretend that he had never received it. Ed asked the same question he always asked when Ben made one of his bizarre requests: Was Ben in some sort of trouble? No, Ben assured him, he was not. It simply wasn't convenient for anyone to know he was in town at the moment. He did plan on seeing Miles, he assured Ed. He did not think he would have time to see much of anyone else.

Ed seemed satisfied. He listened patiently while Ben explained what he wanted done. Ben promised he would stop by the office tomorrow about noon to sign the necessary papers if Ed could arrange to be there. Ed sighed stoically and said that would be fine. Ben said good night and placed the phone receiver back on its cradle.

Twenty minutes in the shower helped wash away the tension and the growing weariness. He came back out of the bathroom and crawled into his bed, a few of the magazines and newspapers stacked next to him. He started to read, gave it up, and let his thoughts drift and his eyes close.

Moments later, he was asleep.

He dreamed that night of the Paladin.

He was alone at first, standing on a pine-sheltered bluff looking down over Landover's misted valley. Blues and greens mixed as sky and earth joined, and it was as if he could reach out and touch them. He breathed, and the air was fresh and chill. The clarity of the moment was stunning.

Then shadows deepened and closed down about him like night. Cries and whispers filtered through the pines. He could feel the shape of the medallion pressing against his palm as he clutched at it in anticipation. He had need of it once more, he sensed, and was glad. The being he kept trapped inside could be let loose again!

There was a darting movement to one side and a monstrous black shape surged forward. It was a unicorn, eyes and breath of fire. But it changed almost instantly. It became a devil. Then it changed again.

It was Meeks.

The wizard beckoned, a tall, stooped, menacing form, face scaled over like a lizard's. He came for Ben, growing in size with each step, changing now into something unrecognizable. There was the smell of fear in Ben's nostrils, the smell of death.

But he was the Paladin, the knight-errant whose strayed soul had found a home within his body, the King's champion who had never lost a battle, and nothing could stand against him. He brought that other self to life with a frightening rush of elation. Armor closed about him, and the smell of fear and death gave way to the acrid smells of iron, leather, and oil. He was no longer Ben Holiday, but a creature of some other time and place whose memories were all of battle, of combat and victory, of fighting and dying. Wars raged in his mind, and there were glimpses of struggling behemoths encased in iron, surging back and forth against a haze of red. Metal clanged, and voices huffed and grunted in fury. Bodies fell in death, torn and broken.

He felt himself exhilarated!

Oh, God, he felt himself reborn!

The darkness broke against him, shadows reaching and clawing, and he went to meet them in a rage. The white charger he rode carried him forward like a steam engine driven by fires he could not begin to control. The pines slipped past him in a blur, and the ground disappeared. Meeks became a wraith he could not touch. He raced forward, flying out from the edge of the bluff into nothingness.

The sense of exhilaration vanished. Somewhere in the night, there was a frightening scream. He realized as he fell that the scream was his own.

The dreams left him after that, but he slept poorly for the remainder of the night anyway. He rose shortly after dawn, showered, called room service for breakfast, ate, dressed in the clothes he had bought yesterday, and caught a cab out front of the hotel shortly after nine. He took his duffel bag with him. He did not think he would be returning.

The cab took him south on Michigan Avenue. It was Saturday, but the streets were already beginning to clog with Christmas shoppers anxious to beat the weekend rush. Ben sat back in the relative seclusion of the cab and ignored them. The joys of the approaching holiday were the furthest thing from his mind.

Traces of last night's dream still whispered darkly to him. He had been badly frightened by that dream and by the truths that it contained.

The Paladin was a reality he had not fully come to grips with. He had become the armored knight only once—and then as much by chance as by intention. It had been necessary to become the Paladin in order to survive, and he had therefore done what was necessary. But the transformation had been a frightening thing, a shedding of his own skin, a crawling into someone else's—someone or something. The thoughts of that other being were hard and brutal, a warrior's thoughts, a gladiator's. There was blood and death in those thoughts, an entire history of survival that Ben could only begin to comprehend. It frankly terrified him. He could not control what this other thing was, he sensed—not entirely. He could only *become* what it was and accept what that meant.

He was not sure he could ever do that again. He had not tried and did not wish to try.

And yet a part of him did—just as in the dream. And a part of him whispered that someday he must.

He had the cab take him to the offices of Holiday & Bennett, Ltd. The offices were closed on Saturdays, but he knew Miles Bennett would be there anyway. Miles was always there on Saturdays, working until noon, catching up on all the dictating and research that he hadn't gotten to during the week, taking advantage of the absence of those bothersome interruptions that seemed to dog him during regular business hours.

Ben paid the cab driver to drop him at the end of the block across the street from his destination, then stepped quickly into the doorway of another building. Pedestrians passed him by, oblivious to what he was about, caught up in their own concerns. Traffic moved ahead at a rapid crawl. There were cars parked on the street, but no one seemed to be keeping watch in them.

"Doesn't hurt to be careful," he insisted softly.

He stepped back out of the doorway, crossed the street with the light, moved up the block, and pushed through the storm glass doors to the lobby of his building. He saw nothing out of place, nothing odd.

He hurried to an open elevator, stepped inside, punched the button to floor fifteen, and watched the doors slide closed. The elevator started up. Just a few moments more, he thought. And if Miles wasn't there for some reason, he would simply track him down at his home.

But he hoped he wouldn't have to do that. He sensed that he might not have the time. Maybe it was the dream, maybe it was simply the circumstances of his being here—but something definitely felt wrong.

The elevator slowed and stopped. The doors slid open, and he stepped into the hallway beyond.

His breath caught sharply in his throat. Once again, he was face to face with Meeks.

Questor Thews brushed at the screen of cobwebs that hung across the narrow stone entry of the ruins of the castle tower and pushed inside. He sneezed as dust clogged his nostrils and muttered in distaste at the damp and dark. He should have had the sense to bring a torch . . .

A spark of fire flared next to him, and flames leaped from a brand. Bunion passed the handle of the light to Questor.

"I was just about to use the magic to do that for myself!" the wizard snapped irritably, but the kobold just grinned.

They stood within the failing walls of Mirwouk, the ancient fortress Questor had seen in his dream of the missing books of magic. They were far north of Sterling Silver, high within the Melchor, the wind whipping about the worn stone to howl down empty corridors, the chill settling through stale air like winter's coming. It had taken the wizard and the kobold the better part of three days to get here, and their travel had been quick. The castle had welcomed them with yawning gates and vacant windows. Its rooms and halls stood abandoned.

Questor pushed ahead, searching for something that looked familiar. The late afternoon was settling down about them, and he had no wish to be wandering about this dismal tomb after dark. He was a wizard and could sense things hidden from other folk, and this place had an evil smell about it.

He groped about for a time, then thought he recognized the passageway he had entered. He followed its twists and turns, eyes peering through the gloom. More cobwebs and dust hindered his progress, and there were spiders the size of rats and rats the size of dogs. They scurried and crawled, and he had to watch for them at every step. It was decidedly annoying work. He was tempted to use his magic to turn the lot of them into dust bunnies and let the wind sweep them away.

The passageway took a downward turn, and the shape of its walls altered noticeably. Questor slowed, peering at the stonework. Abruptly, he straightened.

"I recognize this!" he exclaimed in an agitated whisper. "This is the tunnel I saw in my dreams!"

Bunion took the torch from his hand without comment and led the way down. Questor was too excited to argue the matter and followed quickly after. The passage broadened and cleared, free of webbing, dust, rodents, and insects. There was a new smell to the stone, a kind of sickly-fragrant musk. Bunion kept up a brisk pace, and sometimes all that Questor could see before him was the halo of the torch.

All was just as it had been in the dream!

The tunnel went on, angling deeper into the mountain rock, a coil of hollowed corridors and curving stairs. Bunion stayed in front, eyes sharp. Questor was practically breathing down his neck.

Then the tunnel ended at a stone door marked with scroll and runes. Questor was shaking with excitement by now. He felt along the markings and his hands seemed to know exactly where to go. He touched something and the door swung open with a faint grating sound.

The room beyond was massive, its floor constructed of granite blocks polished smooth. Questor led the way now, following the vision inside his head, the memory of his dream. He walked to the center of the chamber, Bunion at his side, the sound of their footfalls a hollow echo.

They stopped before a piece of granite flooring on which the sign of a unicorn had been carved.

Questor Thews stared. A unicorn? One hand tugged uneasily at his chin. Something was wrong here. He did not recall anything about a unicorn in his dream. There had been a sign cut into the stone, but had the sign been that of a unicorn? It seemed a rather large coincidence . . .

For just an instant, he considered turning about, walking directly back the way he had come, and abandoning the entire project. A small voice inside whispered that he should. There was danger hidden here; he could sense it, feel it, and it frightened him.

But the lure of the missing books was too strong. He reached down, and his fingers traced the ridges of the creature's horn—again, almost of their own volition. The block stirred and slid aside, fitting into a neatly constructed chute.

Questor Thews peered downward into the hole that was left.

There was something there.

Nightfall draped the lake country in shadows and mist, and the light of colored moons and silver stars was no more than a faint glimmer as it reflected off the still surface of the Irrylyn. Willow stood alone at the shoreline of a tiny inlet ringed in cottonwood and cedar, the waters of the lake lapping at her toes. She was naked, her clothes laid carefully upon the grass behind her. A breeze blew softly against her pale green skin, wove its careless way through the waist-length emerald hair, curled and ribboned, and ruffled the fetlocks that ran the length of her calves and forearms. She shivered with the touch. She was a creature of impossible beauty, half human, half fairy, and she might have been a descendant of the sirens of myth who had lured men to their doom on the rocks of ancient seas.

Night birds called sharply from across the lake, their cries echoing in the stillness. Willow's whistle called back to them.

Her head lifted and she sniffed the air as an animal might. Parsnip was waiting patiently for her in the campsite fifty yards back, the light of his cooking fire screened by the trees. She had come alone to the Irrylyn to bathe and to remember.

She stepped cautiously into the water, the lukewarm liquid sending a delicious tingle through her body. It was here that she had met Ben Holiday, that they had seen each other for the first time, naked as they bathed, stripped of all pretentions. It was here that she had known that he was the one who was meant for her.

Her smile brightened as she thought back on how it had been—the wonder of the moment. She had told him what was to be, and while he had doubted it—still doubted it, in truth—she had never faltered in her certainty. The fates of her birth, told in the fairy way by the manner of entwining of the bedded flowers of her seeding, could never lie.

Oh, but she loved the outlander Ben Holiday!

Her child's face beamed and then clouded. She missed Ben. She worried for him. Something in the dream they had shared troubled her in a way she could not explain. There was a riddle behind these dreams that whispered of danger.

She had said nothing of it to Ben because she had read in his voice when he told her of his dream that he had already decided he would go. She knew then that she could not turn him from his purpose and should not try. He understood the risks and accepted them. The urgency of her concern paled beside the strength of his determination.

Perhaps it was for that reason that in telling him of her dream she had not told him all. Something in her dream was different than in his—or Questor Thews'. It was a subtle thing and difficult to explain, but it was there nevertheless.

She crouched in the shallows, emerald hair fanning out across her shoulders like a shawl. Her finger traced patterns on the still surface, and the memory of the dream returned. The wrong feeling was in the texture of the dream, she thought. It was in the way it played against her mind. The visions had been vivid, the events clear. But the telling was somehow false—as if it were all something that could happen in a dream, but not in waking. It was as if the memory was a mask that hid a face beneath.

She ceased her tracing motion and rose. What face was it, she wondered, that lay concealed beneath that mask?

The frown that clouded her face deepened, and she wished suddenly she had not been so accepting of Ben's decision. She wished she had argued his going after all or that she had insisted that he take her along.

"No, he will be well," she whispered insistently.

Her eyes lifted skyward and she let the moonglow warm her. Tomorrow she would seek the advice of her mother, whose life was so close to that of the fairy creatures in the mists. Her mother would know of the black unicorn and the bridle of spun gold and would guide her; soon she would be back again with Ben.

She stepped further out into the darkened lake, let the waters close about her, and drifted at peace.

SHADOWS . . .

The second appearance of Meeks did not elicit in Ben Holiday the panic that the first had. He did not freeze; he did not experience the same sense of confusion. He was surprised, but not stunned. After all, he had a better idea of what to expect this time around. This was just another apparition of the outcast wizard—tall, stooped, cloaked in the robes of gunmetal blue, white hair grizzled, face craggy and sallow, black leather glove lifted like a claw, but an apparition nevertheless.

Wasn't it?

Meeks started for him, and suddenly he wasn't so sure. The pale blue eyes were alive with hatred, and the hard features seemed to twist into something not quite human. Meeks closed on him, gliding down the empty, fluorescent-lit corridor soundlessly, growing huge in the silence. Ben stood his ground with difficulty, one hand searching out the reassuring bulk of the medallion beneath his shirt. But what protection did the medallion offer him here? His mind raced. The rune stone, he thought suddenly! The stone would tell him if he was threatened! His free hand rummaged frantically in his pants pocket, fumbling for the stone as the robed figure loomed closer. Despite his resolve, Ben took a quick step backward. He could not find the stone!

Meeks was directly in front of him, dark and menacing. Ben flinched as the wizard blocked the light . . .

And then he looked up and found himself alone in the deserted corridor, staring into empty space, listening to the silence.

Meeks was gone—another substanceless apparition.

He had found the rune stone, nestled in the corner of his pants pocket, and he pulled it into the light. It was blood red and burned at the touch.

"Damn!" he muttered, angry and frightened both at once.

He took a moment to gather his wits, scanning the hallway swiftly to be certain that he had missed nothing. Then he straightened, finding himself in a sort of defensive half-crouch, and stepped away from the elevator doors. Nothing moved about him. It appeared he really was alone.

But what was the reason for this second vision? Was this another warning? Was it a warning *from* Meeks or *to* Meeks?

What was going on?

He hesitated only a moment before turning sharply left toward the glass doors that fronted the offices of Holiday & Bennett, Ltd. Whatever was going on, he felt it wise to keep moving. Meeks had to know that eventually he would come to Miles. That didn't mean that Meeks was there—or even anywhere close. The apparition might be just another signal to warn him of Ben's coming. If Ben were quick enough, he would be there and gone before Meeks could do anything about it.

The lights in the office lobby were off. He pulled at the handle on the entry doors and found them locked. That was normal. Miles never unlocked the front doors or turned on the lights when he worked alone. Ben had come prepared for that. He pulled out his office key and inserted it into the lock. The lock turned easily, and the door opened. Ben stepped inside, pocketed the key, and let the door close behind him.

A radio was playing softly in the silence—Willie Nelson, the kind of stuff Miles liked. Ben looked down the inner hallway and saw a light shining out of Miles' office. He grinned. The old boy was at home.

Maybe. A new wave of doubt and mistrust washed over him, and the grin faded. Better safe than sorry, he cautioned himself, worrying that old chestnut as if it were a spell to cast out evil spirits. He shook his head. He wished there was some way to be sure about Meeks . . .

He eased his way silently down the hall until he stood before the lighted doorway. Miles Bennett sat alone at his desk, hunched over his law books, a yellow pad crammed with notes open beside him. He had come to work wearing a coat and tie, but the knot in the tie had been pulled loose, and the coat had been shed in favor of rolled-up sleeves and an open collar. He glanced up as he sensed Ben's presence, and his eyes widened.

"Holy Saint Pete!" He started up, then eased back down again. "Doc—is that really you?"

Ben smiled. "It's me all right. How are you doing, buddy?"

"How am I doing? How am *I* doing?" Miles was incredulous. "What the hell kind of question is that? You go trouping off to Shangri-La or whatever, you're gone better than a year, no one hears a word from you, then one day back you come—right out of nowhere—and you want to know how *I* am? Pretty damn cheeky, Doc!"

Ben nodded helplessly and groped for something to say. Miles let him struggle with it a moment, then laughed and pushed himself to his feet, a big, rumpled teddy bear in business clothes.

"Well, come on in, Doc! Don't stand out there in the hallway like the prodigal son returned—even if that's what you are! Come on in, have a seat, tell me all about it! Damn, I can't believe it's really you!"

He hastened around the desk, his big hand extended, took Ben's, and pumped it firmly. "I'd just about given up on you, you know that? Just about given up. I thought something had happened to you for certain when I didn't hear anything. You know how your mind works overtime in this business anyway. I began imagining all sorts of things. I even considered calling the police or someone, but I couldn't bring myself to tell anyone my partner was off chasing little people and dragons!"

He was laughing again, laughing so hard his eyes were tearing, and Ben joined in. "They probably get calls like that all the time."

"Sure, that's what makes Chicago the great little town it is!" Miles wiped his eyes. He wore a rumpled blue shirt and dress pants. He looked a little like a giant Smurf. "Hey, Doc—it's good to see you."

"You, too, Miles." He glanced around. "Doesn't appear that anything has changed since I left."

"Naw, we keep the place a living shrine to your memory." Miles glanced around with him, then shrugged. "Wouldn't know where to start anyway, the place is such a monumental piece of art deco." He smiled, waited a moment for Ben to say something, and, when Ben didn't, cleared his throat nervously. "So, here you are, huh? Care to tell me what happened out there in fairyland, Doc? If it's not too painful to relate, that is. We don't have to discuss it if you'd rather . . ."

"We can discuss it."

"No, we don't have to. Forget I asked. Forget the whole business." Miles was insistent now, embarrassed. "It's just such a surprise to have you come waltzing in like this . . . Hey, look, I've got something for you! Been saving this for when we got together again. Look, got it right here in the drawer." He hastened back around behind the desk and rummaged quickly through the bottom drawer. "Yeah, here we go!"

He pulled out a bottle of Glenlivet, still sealed, and plopped it on the desk. Two glasses followed.

Ben shook his head and smiled with pleasure. His favorite scotch. "It's been a long time, Miles," he admitted.

Miles broke the seal, uncorked the bottle, and poured two fingers into each glass. He pushed one across the desk to Ben, then lifted his own glass in salute. "To crime and other forms of amusement," he said.

Ben touched glasses with him, and both drank. The Glenlivet was smooth and warm going down. The two old friends took seats across the desk. Willie Nelson continued to sing through the momentary silence.

"So you gonna tell me or what?" Miles asked finally, changing his mind once more.

"I don't know."

"Why not? You don't have to be coy with me, you know. You don't have to feel embarrassed if this thing didn't turn out the way you expected."

Memories flooded Ben's thoughts. No, it surely hadn't turned out the way he had expected. But that wasn't the problem. The problem was in deciding how much he should tell Miles. Landover wasn't something that could be easily explained. It was sort of like the way it was when you were a kid and your parents wanted to know about Susie at the freshman sock hop.

It was like telling them that Santa Claus really *did* exist.

"Would it be enough if I told you that I found what I was looking for?" he asked Miles after a moment's thought.

Miles was silent for a moment. "Yeah, if that's the best you can do," he replied finally. He hesitated. "*Is* that the best you can do, Doc?"

Ben nodded. "It is just now."

"I see. Well, what about later? Can you do better later? I'd hate to think that this was the end of it and I'd never learn anything more. Because I don't think I could stand that. You left here in search of dragons and damsels in distress, and I told you you were crazy. You believed all that hype about a kingdom where magic was real and fairy tale creatures lived, and I told you it was impossible. See, Doc, I need to know which of us was right. I need to know if dreams like yours are still possible. I *have* to know."

Disappointment reflected in the roundish face. Ben felt sorry for his old friend. Miles had been in on this business from the beginning. He was the only one who knew that Ben had spent a million dollars to purchase a fantasy kingdom that sane men knew couldn't possibly exist. He was the only one who knew that Ben had gone off in search of that kingdom. He knew how the story started, but he didn't know how it ended. And it was eating at him.

But there was more to consider here than Miles' discomforting curiosity. There was his safety. Sometimes knowledge was a dangerous thing. Ben still didn't know how great a threat Meeks posed—to either of them. He still didn't know how much truth there was to his dream. Miles appeared to be well, but . . .

"Miles, I promise I'll tell you everything one day," he answered, trying to sound reassuring. "I can't tell you exactly when, but I promise you'll know. It's a difficult thing to talk about—sort of the way it used to be about Annie. I could never talk about her without . . . worrying about what I said. You remember, don't you?"

Miles nodded. "I remember, Doc." He smiled. "Have you made peace with her ghost finally?"

"I have. Finally. But it took a lot of time, and I went through a lot of changes." He paused, remembering when he had stood alone in the mists of the fairy world and come face to face with the fears he had harbored deep within himself that somehow he had failed his dead wife. "I guess talking about where I've been and what I've found there will take a little time and help as well. I still have to work a few things through . . ."

He trailed off, the glass of scotch twirling through his fingers on the desk before him.

"It's all right, Doc," Miles said quickly, shrugging. "It's enough just having you back again and knowing you're all right. The rest will come later. I know that."

Ben stared at the scotch for a moment, then lifted his eyes to Miles. "I'm only here for a short time, buddy. I can't stay."

Miles looked uncertain, then forced a quick grin. "Hey, what are you telling me? You've come back for something, haven't you? So what was it? You missed the Bulls' nosedive last winter, the Cubs' el foldo this spring, the marathon, the elections, all the rest of the vintage Chicago season. You want to catch a Bears game? The monsters of the midway are thirteen and one, you know. And they still serve Bud and nachos at the food stands. What do you say?"

Ben laughed in spite of himself. "I say it sounds pretty good. But that's not what brought me back. I came back because I was worried about you."

Miles stared at him. "What?"

"I was worried about you. Don't make that sound like such an astounding event, damn it. I just wanted to be sure you were all right."

Miles took a long pull on the scotch, then eased back carefully in the padded desk chair. "Why wouldn't I be all right?"

Ben shrugged. "I don't know." He started to continue, then caught himself. "Oh, what the hell—you already think I'm nuts, so what's a few more pecans in the fruitcake. I had this dream. I dreamed you were in real trouble and you needed me. I didn't know what the trouble was, only that it was my fault that you were in it. So I came back to find out if the dream was true."

Miles studied him a moment the way a psychiatrist might study a prize patient, then drained off the rest of his scotch and tipped forward in the chair once more. "You are nuts, Doc—you know that?"

"I know."

"Fact is, your conscience must be working overtime."

"You think so?"

"I do. You're just feeling guilty because you bailed out on me in the middle of the pre-Christmas season court rush, and I was left with all those damn cases! Well, I've got news for you! I took care of those cases, and office routine never skipped a beat!" He paused, then grinned. "Well, maybe half a beat. Proud of me, Doc?"

"Yeah, sure, Miles." Ben frowned. "So there aren't any problems at the office—nothing wrong with you, nothing that needs me back here?"

Miles rose, picked up the Glenlivet, and poured them each another finger. He was smiling broadly. "Doc, I hate to tell you this, but things couldn't be better."

And right then and there, Ben Holiday began to smell a rat.

Fifteen minutes later he was back on the streets. He had visited with Miles just long enough to avoid giving the impression that anything was seriously wrong. He had stayed even when everything inside him was screaming that he ought to run for his life.

Taxis were at a premium Saturday mornings, so he caught a bus south to Ed Samuelson's office for his noon meeting. He sat alone two seats from the back, clutched the duffel to him like a child's security blanket, and tried to shake the feeling that there were eyes everywhere watching him. He sat hunched down in his suit and dress coat and waited for the chill to steal from his body.

Think like a lawyer, he admonished himself! Reason it through!

The dream had been a lie. Miles Bennett was not in trouble and had no need of his assistance. Maybe the dream had only been his sense of guilt at leaving his old friend behind working overtime. Maybe it was only coincidence that Questor and Willow had experienced similar dreams on the same night. He didn't think so. Something had triggered those dreams—something or someone.

Meeks.

But what was his enemy up to?

He left the bus at Madison and walked several doors down to Ed Samuelson's building. The eyes followed after him.

He met with his accountant and signed various powers-of-attorney and trust instruments enabling management of his affairs to continue in his absence for as long as several years. He didn't anticipate being gone that long, but you never knew. He shook Ed's hand, exchanged good-byes, and was back out the door at 12:35 P.M.

This time he waited until he found a taxi. He had the driver take him directly to the airport and caught a 1:30 P.M. flight on Delta to Washington. He was in the nation's capital by 5:00 P.M. and an hour later caught the last flight out that night on Allegheny to Waynesboro. He kept his eyes open for Meeks the whole time. A man in a trench coat kept looking at him on the flight from

Chicago. An old woman selling flowers stopped him in the main terminal at National. A sailor with a duffel bumped him as he turned away too quickly from the Allegheny ticket counter. But there was no sign of Meeks.

He checked the rune stone twice on the flight from Washington to Waynesboro. He checked it almost as an afterthought the first time and reluctantly once after. Both times it glowed blood red and burned at the touch.

He did not go any further that night. He was desperate to continue on—the need for haste was so strong he could barely control it—but reason overcame his sense of urgency. Or maybe it was fear. He did not relish venturing into the Blue Ridge in the dark. It was too easy to become lost or hurt. And it was likely that Meeks would be waiting for him at the entrance to the time passage.

He slept poorly, rose at daybreak, dressed in the warm-up suit and Nikes, ate something—he couldn't remember later what it was—and called the limo service to pick him up. He stood in the lobby with his duffel in hand and kept an uneasy watch through the plate glass windows. After a moment, he stepped outside. The day was cold and gray and unfriendly; the fact that it was dry offered what little comfort there was to be found. The air smelled bad and tasted worse, and his eyes burned. Everything had an alien look and feel. He checked the rune stone half-a-dozen times. It still glowed bright red.

The limo arrived a short time later and sped him on his way. By midmorning he was hiking back up into the forested mountains of the George Washington National Park, leaving Chicago, Washington, Waynesboro, Miles Bennett, Ed Samuelson, and everything and everyone else in this world in which he now felt himself a stranger and a fugitive far behind.

He found the mists and oaks that marked the entrance to the time passage without incident. There was no sign of Meeks—not in the flesh, not as an apparition. The forest was still and empty; the way forward was clear.

Ben Holiday fairly ran to gain the tunnel's entrance.

He stopped running on the other side.

Sunshine streamed down out of lightly clouded skies and warmed the earth with its touch. Brightly colored meadows and fruit orchards spread down valley slopes like a quilt of patchwork swatches. Flowers dotted the landscape. Birds flew in dashes of rainbow silk. The smells were clean and fresh.

Ben breathed deeply, chasing the spots that danced before his eyes, waiting for the strength that had been sapped by his flight to return. Oh, yes, he had run. He had flown! It frightened him that he had allowed himself to panic like that. He breathed, deep and slow, refusing to look back again at the dark and misted forests that rose like a wall behind him. He was safe now. He was home.

The words were a litany that soothed him. He let his eyes lift skyward and pass down again across the length and breadth of Landover, comforted by the unexpected sense of familiarity he experienced. How strange that he should feel this way, he marveled. His passing back was like the passing from winter's slow death to spring's life. Once he would never have believed he could feel this way. Now it seemed the most logical thing in the world.

It was closing on midday. He walked down from the valley's rim to the campsite where he had left his escort. They were waiting for him and accepted his return without surprise. The captain greeted him with a salute, brought Jurisdiction around, got his men mounted, and they were on their way. From a world of jet liners and limousines to a world of walking boots and horses—Ben found himself smiling at how natural the transition seemed.

But the smile was a brief one. His thoughts returned to the dreams that Questor, Willow, and he had shared and the nagging certainty that something was very wrong with those dreams. His had been an outright lie. Had those of Questor and Willow been lies as well? His was tied in some way to Meeks—he was almost certain of it. Were those of Questor and Willow tied to Meeks as well? There were too many questions and no answers in sight. He had to get back to Sterling Silver quickly and find his friends.

He reached the castle before nightfall, pressing for a quicker pace the entire way. He scrambled down from his horse, gave the escort a hurried word of thanks, called for the lake skimmer, and crossed quickly to his island home. Silver spires and glistening white walls beamed down at him, and the warmth of his home-mother reached out to wrap him close. But the chill within him persisted.

Abernathy met him just inside the anteway, resplendent in red silk tunic, breeches and stockings, white polished boots and gloves, silver-rimmed glasses, and appointment book. There was irritation in his voice. "You have returned none too soon, High Lord. I have spent the entire day smoothing over the ruffled feelings of certain members of the judiciary council who came here expressly to see you. A number of problems have arisen with next week's meeting. The irrigation fields south of Waymark have sprung a leak. Tomorrow the Lords of the Greensward arrive, and we haven't even looked at the list of concerns they sent us. Half-a-dozen other representatives have been sitting about . . ."

"Nice to see you again, too, Abernathy," Ben cut him off in midsentence. "Are either Questor or Willow back yet?"

"Uh, no, High Lord." Abernathy seemed at a momentary loss for words. He trailed along silently as Ben moved past him toward the dining hall. "Did you have a successful trip?" he asked finally.

"Not very. You're certain neither has returned?"

"Yes, High Lord, I am certain. You are the first one back."

"Any messages from either?"

"No messages, High Lord." Abernathy crowded forward. "Is something wrong?"

Ben did not slow. "No, everything is fine."

Abernathy looked uncertain. "Yes, well, that is good to know." He hesitated a moment, then cleared his throat. "About the judiciary council's representatives, High Lord . . . ?"

Ben shook his head firmly. "Not today. I'll see them tomorrow." He turned toward the dining hall and left Abernathy at the door. "Let me know the minute Questor or Willow returns—no matter what I'm doing."

Abernathy pushed his glasses further up his long nose and disappeared back down the passageway without comment.

Ben ate a quick meal and climbed the stairs to the tower that held the Landsview. The Landsview was a part of the magic of Sterling Silver, a device that gave him a quick glimpse into the happenings of Landover by appearing to allow him to fly the valley end to end. It was a circular platform with a silver guard rail that looked out from the tower through an opening in the wall that ran ceiling to floor. A lectern fastened on the guard rail at its midpoint. An aged parchment map of the kingdom was pinned to the lectern.

Ben stepped up onto the platform, fastened both hands firmly to the guard rail, fixed his eyes upon the map, and willed himself northward. The castle disappeared about him an instant later, and he was sailing through space with only the silver railing and the lectern for support. He sped far north to the mountains of Melchor, swept across their heights and down again. He sped south to the lake country and Elderew, the home city of the people of the River Master. He crisscrossed the forests and hills from one end of the lake country to the other. He found neither Questor Thews nor Willow.

An hour later, he gave it up. His body was drenched with sweat from the effort, and his hands were cramped from gripping the railing. He left the tower of the Landsview disappointed and weary.

He tried to soak the weariness and disappointment away in the waters of a steaming bath, but could not come entirely clean. Images of Meeks haunted him. The wizard had lured him back with that dream of Miles; Ben was certain of it and was also certain that the wizard had some plan in mind to gain revenge on him for Meeks' exile. What Ben was not certain about was what part the dreams of his friends played in all this—and what danger they might be in right now because of it.

Night descended, and Ben retired to his study. He had already decided to send out search parties for both his missing friends by morning. Everything else would have to wait until he solved the mystery of the dreams. He was becoming increasingly convinced that something was terribly wrong and that he was running out of time to set it right again.

Evening deepened. He was immersed in catching up on the paperwork that had piled up during his absence when the door to his study flew open, a sudden gust of wind scattered the stacks of documents he had arranged carefully on the work table before him, and the gaunt figure of Questor Thews stalked out of the darkness into the light.

"I have found them, High Lord!" Questor exclaimed with an elaborate flourish of one arm, a canvass-wrapped bundle clutched to his chest with the other. He crossed to where Ben was working and deposited the bundle on the table with a loud thump. "There!"

Ben stared. A rather bedraggled Bunion trudged through the door behind him, clothes torn and muddied. Abernathy appeared as well, nightshirt twisted and nightcap askew. He shoved his glasses in place and blinked.

"It was all just exactly as the dream promised," Questor explained hurriedly, hands working at the canvass wrapping. "Well, not quite as promised. There was the matter of the demon imp hidden in the stonework. A nasty surprise, I can tell you. But Bunion was its equal. Took it by the throat and choked the life out of it. But the rest was just as it was in the dream. We found the passages in Mirwouk and followed them to the door. The door opened, and the room beyond was covered with stonework. One stone had the special markings. It gave at the touch, I reached down and . . ."

"Questor, you found the missing books?" Ben asked incredulously, cutting him short.

The wizard stopped, stared back at him in turn, and frowned. "Of course I found the books, High Lord. What do you think I have been telling you?" He looked put upon. "Anyway, to continue, I was about to reach down for them—I could see them in the shadows—when Bunion pulled me back. He saw the movement of the imp. There was a terrific struggle between them . . . Ah, here we are!"

The last fold of canvass fell back. A pair of massive, aged books nestled amid the wrappings. Each book was bound in a leather covering that was scrolled in runes and drawings, the gilt that had once inscribed each marking worn to bits and tracings. Each book had its corners and bindings layered in tarnished brass, and huge locks held the covers sealed.

Ben reached down to touch the cover of the top book, but Questor quickly seized his hand. "A moment, High Lord, please." The wizard pointed to the book's lock. "Do you see what has happened to the catch?"

Ben peered closer. The catch was gone, the metal about it seared as if by fire. He checked the catch on the second book. It was still securely in place. Yes, there was no doubt about it. Something had been done to the first book to break the lock that sealed it. He looked back at Questor.

"I have no idea, High Lord," the wizard answered the unasked question. "I brought the books to you exactly as I found them. I have not tampered with them; I have not attempted to open them. I know from the markings on the covers that they are the missing books of magic. Beyond that, I know no more than you." He cleared his throat officiously. "I . . . thought it proper that you be present when I opened them."

"You thought it proper, did you?" Abernathy growled, hairy face shoving into view. He looked ridiculous in his nightcap. "What you mean is you thought it *safer*! You wanted the power of the medallion close at hand in case this magic proved to be too much for you!"

Questor stiffened. "I have significant magic of my own, Abernathy, and I assure you that . . ."

"Never mind, Questor," Ben cut him short. "You did the right thing. Can you open the books?"

Questor was rigid with indignation by now. "Of course I can open the books! Here!"

He stepped forward, hands hovering over the first of the aged tomes. Ben moved back, his own hands closing on the medallion. There was no point in taking any chances with this sort of . . .

Questor touched the fastenings, and green fire spit sharply from the metal. Everyone jumped back quickly.

"It would appear that you have underestimated the danger of the situation once again!" Abernathy snapped.

Questor flushed, and his face tightened. His hands came up sharply, sparked, then came alive with a fire of their own—a brilliant crimson fire. He brought his fire down slowly to the metal fastenings, then held it there as it slowly devoured the green fire. Then he brushed his hands together briskly, and both fires were gone.

He gave Abernathy a scornful look. "A rather insignificant measure of danger, wouldn't you say?"

He reached again for the fastenings and pulled the metal clasp free. Slowly he opened the book to the first page. Aging yellow parchment stared back at him. There was nothing there.

Ben, Abernathy, and Bunion pressed forward about him, peering down through the shadows and half-light. The page was still empty. Questor thumbed to the second page. It was empty as well. He thumbed to the third. Empty.

The fourth page was empty, too, but its center was seared slightly as if held too close to a flame.

"I believe it was you who used the word *insignificant,* wizard?" Abernathy goaded.

Questor did not reply. There was a stunned look on his face. Slowly he began to leaf through the book, turning one blank page after another, finding each sheet of yellowed parchment empty, but increasingly seared. Finally pages began to appear that were burned through entirely.

He thumbed impulsively to the very center of the book and stopped.

"High Lord," he said softly.

Ben peered downward at the ruin that lay open before him. A fire had burned the center of the book to ashes, but it was as if the fire had somehow been ignited from within.

High Lord and wizard stared at each other. "Keep going," Ben urged.

Questor paged through the remainder of the book quickly and found nothing. Each sheet of parchment was just like the others—empty save for where the mysterious fire had burned or seared it.

"I do not understand what this means, High Lord," Questor Thews admitted finally.

Abernathy started to comment, then changed his mind. "Perhaps the answers lie in the other book," he suggested wearily.

Ben nodded for Questor to proceed. The wizard closed the first book and set it aside, gloved his hands in the red fire, brought them carefully down, and drew free the green fire that protected the lock on the second book. It took somewhat longer this time to complete the task, for the lock was still intact. Then, the fires extinguished, he released the lock and cautiously opened the book.

The outline of a unicorn stared back at him. The unicorn was drawn on parchment that was neither yellowed nor seared, but pristine white. The unicorn was standing still, its silhouette perfectly formed by dark lines. Questor turned to the second page. There was a second unicorn, this one in motion, but drawn the same way. The third page revealed another unicorn, the fourth still another, and so on. Questor leafed quickly through the entire book and back again. Each page of the book appeared new. Each page held a unicorn, each drawn in a different pose.

There were no writings or markings of any kind other than the drawings of the unicorns.

"I *still* do not understand what this means." Questor sighed, frustration etched into his lean face.

"It means these are not the books of magic you believed them to be," Abernathy offered bluntly.

But Questor shook his head. "No, these are the books. The dream said so, the markings on the bindings say so, and they appear as the old stories described them. These are the missing books, all right."

They were silent for a moment. Ben stared thoughtfully at the books, then glanced about until his eyes found the shadowy figure of Bunion peering from behind Questor. The kobold grinned ominously.

Ben looked back again at the books. "What we have here," he said finally, "is one book with unicorns drawn on every page and another book with no unicorns drawn anywhere, but a burned-out center. That has to mean *something,* for Pete's sake! Questor, what about Willow's dream of a black unicorn? Couldn't the unicorns here have something to do with that?"

Questor considered the possibility for a moment. "I do not see any possible connection, High Lord. The black unicorn is essentially a myth. The unicorns drawn here are not inked in black, but sketched deliberately in white. See how the lines define the features?" He turned a few pages of the second book to illustrate his point. "A black unicorn would be shaded or marked in some way to indicate its color . . ."

He trailed off, brows knitting tightly in thought. His bony fingers traced the seared lock on the first book delicately. "Why has this lock been broken and the other left intact?" he asked softly, speaking to no one in particular.

"There have not been any unicorns in the valley since its inception, according to the histories of the Kings of Landover," Abernathy interjected suddenly. "But there were unicorns once—a whole raft of them. There was a legend about it, as a matter of fact. Now let me think . . . Yes, I remember. Just wait here a moment, please."

He hurried from the room, nails clicking on the stone, nightshirt trailing. He was back a few moments later, a book of the royal histories of Landover cradled in his arms. The book was very old and its covers worn.

"Yes, this is the one," the scribe announced. He placed it next to the books of magic, thumbed through it quickly, and stopped. "Yes, right here." He paused, reading. "It happened hundreds of years ago—very close to the time of the valley's creation. The fairies dispatched a large gathering of unicorns into our valley from out of the mists. They sent them here for a very particular reason. It seems that they were concerned about a growing disbelief in the magic in many of the outlying worlds—worlds such as your own, High Lord—" The scribe extended him a disapproving look. "—and they wished to give some sign to those worlds that the magic did indeed still exist." He paused, frowning as he squinted at the aged writing. "I think I have that right. It is difficult to read this clearly because the language is very old."

"Perhaps it is your *eyes* that are old," Questor suggested, none too kindly, and reached for the book.

Abernathy snatched it away irritably. "My eyes are twice what yours are, wizard!" he snapped. He cleared his throat and went on. "It appears, High Lord, that the fairies sent the unicorns as proof to the disbelieving worlds that the magic was still real. One unicorn was to travel to each of these worlds out of Landover through the time passages." He paused again, read some more, then closed the book with a bang. "But, of course, that never happened."

Ben frowned. "Why not?"

"Because all the unicorns disappeared, High Lord. They were never seen again by anyone."

"Disappeared?"

"I remember that story," Questor declared. "Frankly, it always struck me as a rather strange story."

Ben frowned some more. "So the fairies send a raft of white unicorns into Landover and they all disappear. And that's the last of the unicorns except for a black unicorn that may or may not be real and appears only occasionally from God knows where. Except now we also have the missing books of magic that contain nothing about magic at all—just a lot of drawings of unicorns and some half-burned empty pages."

"One lock broken and one still sealed," Questor added.

"Nothing about Meeks," Ben mused.

"Nothing about changing dogs back into men," Abernathy huffed.

They stared at one another in silence. The books lay open on the table before them—two of magic that didn't seem very magical at all and one of history that told them nothing historically useful. Ben's uneasiness grew. The further they followed the threads of these dreams, the more confused matters got. His dream had been a lie; Questor's had been the truth. The source of their dreams had been different . . .

Apparently.

But maybe not. He was not sure of anything just now. It was growing late. The trip back had been a long one, he was tired, and the fatigue dulled his thinking. There wasn't enough time, and he didn't have enough energy to reason it all through tonight. Tomorrow would be soon enough. When morning came, they would search out Willow; once they found her, they would pursue this matter of the dreams until they understood exactly what was going on.

"Lock up the books, Questor. We're going to bed," he declared.

There was muttered agreement from all quarters. Bunion went off to the kitchen to clean up and eat. Abernathy went with him, carrying the aged history. Questor scooped up the books of magic and carted them out wordlessly.

Ben watched them go, left alone in the shadows and half-light. He almost wished he had asked them to stay while he forced himself to work on this puzzle a bit longer.

But that was foolish. It would all keep.

Reluctantly, he trudged off to sleep.

. . . AND NIGHTMARES

Later, Ben Holiday would remember how ill-conceived his advice to himself had been that night. He would remember the words clearly. It will all keep. Tomorrow will be soon enough. He would remember those words as he ate them. He would reflect bitterly on the undiscerning reassurance he had allowed himself to take from them.

That was the beauty of hindsight, of course. It was always twenty-twenty.

The trouble began almost immediately. He retired directly to his bed chamber from the study, slipped on a nightshirt, and crawled beneath the covers. He was exhausted, but sleep would not come. He was keyed up from the day's events, and the mystery of the dreams played about like a cornered rat in his mind. He chased the rat, but he couldn't catch it. It was a shadow that eluded him effortlessly. He could see its outline, but could not grasp its form.

Its eyes glowed crimson in the darkness.

He blinked and shoved himself up on his elbows. The rune stone that Willow had given him shone fire red on the nightstand where he had placed it. He blinked, aware suddenly that he must have been nearly asleep when the light had brought him back. The color of the stone meant danger threatened—just as it must have threatened during the whole of the trip back.

But where was the danger to be found, damn it?

He rose and walked about the room like a creature stalking prey. There was nothing there. His clothes still lay draped over the chair where he had thrown them; his duffel still occupied its spot on the floor by the dressing room. He stood in the center of the room for a moment and let the warmth of the castle's life reach out to him. Sterling Silver responded with a deep, inner glow that wrapped him from head to foot. She was undisturbed.

He frowned. Perhaps the stone was mistaken.

It was distracting, in any case, so he covered it with a towel and climbed back into his bed. He waited a moment, closed his eyes, opened them again, closed them a second time. The darkness cloaked him and did not tease. The rat was gone. Questions and answers mixed and faded in the night. He began to drift.

He might have dreamed for a time, then. There were images of unicorns, some black, some white, and the slender, timeless faces of the fairies. There were images of his friends, both past and present, and of the dreams he had envisioned for his kingdom and his life. They ran through his subconscious, and their fluid motion lulled him as the rolling of an endless sea.

Then a curious fire flared to sudden life within his mind, disrupting the flow. Hands reached from out of nothingness, and fingers clasped the chain about his neck—his hands, his fingers. What were they doing?

And suddenly there was an image of Meeks!

The image appeared from out of a black mist, the wizard a tall, skeletal form cloaked in gunmetal blue with a face as rough and hard as raw iron. He loomed over Ben as if he were death come for its latest victim, one sleeve empty, the other a black claw that reached down, down . . .

Ben jerked awake with a start, kicking back the bedclothes, sweeping blindly at the dark with one hand. He blinked and squinted. A candle's flame lit one corner of the room, a solitary pinprick of white-gold against a haze of crimson fire given off by Willow's rune stone as it blazed in frantic warning on the nightstand, the towel that had covered it gone. Ben could feel the presence of the danger it signaled. His breath came in sharp gasps, and it was as if a giant hand pressed down upon his chest. He fought to push it off, but his muscles would not obey. His body seemed locked in place.

Something moved in the dark—something huge.

Ben tried to shout, but the sound was no more than a whisper.

A figure materialized, scarlet light covering it like blood. The figure stood there and, in a voice that sounded of nails on slate, whispered, "We meet again, Mr. Holiday."

It was Meeks.

Ben could not speak. He could only stare. It was as if the image that had haunted him during his visit to the old world had somehow managed to follow him back into this one. Except that this was no image. He knew it instantly. This was real!

Meeks smiled thinly. He was quite human in appearance now, the predatory look vanished. "What—no clever words of greeting, no brave admonishments, not even a threat? How unlike you, Mr. Holiday. What seems to be the matter? Cat got your tongue?"

The muscles of Ben's throat and face tightened as he struggled to regain control of himself. He was paralyzed. Meeks' flat, terrifying eyes bound him with cords he could not break.

"Yes, yes, the will is there, isn't it, Mr. Holiday—but the way is so dark! I know that feeling well! Remember how it was when you left me last? Remember? You taunted me in the vision crystal—my sole link with this world—and then you shattered it! You broke my eyes, Mr. Holiday, and you left me blind!" His voice had become a hiss of fury. "Oh, yes, I know what it is like to be paralyzed and alone!"

He moved forward a step further and stopped, his gaunt, craggy face bent against the crimson light of the rune. He seemed impossibly huge. "You are a fool, play-King—do you know that? You thought to play games with me and you did not even bother to understand that it was I who made all the rules. I am the games master, little man, and you are but a novice! I made you King of this land; I gave you all that it had to offer. You took that from me as if you were entitled to it! You took it as if it belonged to you!"

He was shaking with anger, the fingers of his gloved hand knotted in front of his robes in a clawed fist. Ben had never been so terrified in his life. He wanted to shrink down into himself, to crawl beneath the covers once more. He wanted to do anything—*anything*—that would let him escape this terrible old man.

Then Meeks straightened, and abruptly the anger in his face was replaced by cold indifference. He looked away. "Well, it hardly matters now. The game is over. You have lost, Mr. Holiday."

Sweat ran down Ben's rigid back. How could this have possibly happened? Meeks had been trapped in the old world; he had been denied any possible entrance into Landover as long as Ben held the medallion!

"Would you like to know how I got here, Mr. Holiday?" Meeks seemed to have read his mind. The wizard swung slowly back on him. "It was simple, really. I let you bring me." He saw the look in Ben's eyes and laughed. "Yes, Mr. Holiday—that's right. *You* were responsible for bringing me back again. What do you think of that?"

He came forward until he was standing next to the bed. His craggy face bent close. Ben could smell the stench of him. "The dreams were mine, Mr. Holiday. I sent them to you—to you, my half-brother, and the sylph. I sent them. Not all of my powers were lost in the destruction of the crystal! I could still reach you, Mr. Holiday! In your sleep! I could bridge the two worlds through your subconscious! My foolish half-brother forgot to think of that in cautioning you against me. Dreams were the only tools I needed to take control of you again. How vivid the imagination can be! Did you find the dream I sent you compelling, Mr. Holiday? Yes, of course you did. Your dream was sent to bring you to me, and bring you to me it did! I knew you would come if you thought your friend Mr. Bennett needed you. I knew you *must* come. It was simple after that, Mr. Holiday. The image at the end of the time passage was magic that alerted me to your return and let me trace your movements. It settled down within you, and you were never free of me after!"

Ben's heart sank. He should have known that Meeks would use the magic to keep track of him in some way. He should have known the wizard would leave nothing to chance. He had been a fool.

Meeks was smiling like the Cheshire Cat. "The second image was an even more interesting ploy. It diverted you from what I was really about. Oh, yes, I was there with you, Mr. Holiday! I was *behind* you! While you were preoccupied with my image, *I* slipped down into your clothing, a thing no bigger than a tiny insect. I concealed myself upon you and I let you carry me back into Landover. The medallion allows only your passage, Mr. Holiday—yet if I am a part of you, it also allows mine!"

He was hidden within my clothing, Ben thought in despair, with me all the way back, and I never realized it. That was why the rune stone glowed in warning. The threat was always there, but I couldn't see it!

"Ironic, isn't it, Mr. Holiday—you bringing me back as you did?" The skin on Meeks' cheeks and forehead was pulled back with the intensity of his smile, and his face was like a skull. "I had to come back, you know. I had to come back immediately because of your damnable, insistent meddling! Have you any idea of the trouble you have caused me? No—no, of course not. You have no idea. You do not even know what I am talking about. You understand nothing! And, in your ignorance, you have very nearly destroyed what it has taken years to create! You have disrupted everything—you and your campaign to become King of Landover!"

He had worked himself into a rage again, and it was only with great effort that he brought himself back under control. Even so, the words spit from him like bile. "No matter, Mr. Holiday, no matter. This all means nothing to you, so there is no point in belaboring it. I have the books now, and there is no further damage that you can do. I have what I need. Your dream has given me mastery of you, my half-brother's dream has given me mastery of the books, and the sylph's dream will give me . . ."

He stopped sharply, almost as if he had erred. There was a curious uneasiness in the pale, hard eyes. He blinked and it was gone. One hand brushed the empty air in dismissal. "Everything. The dreams will give me everything," he finished.

The medallion, Ben was thinking frantically. If I could only manage to put my hands on the medallion . . .

Meeks laughed sharply. "There is undoubtedly much that you wish to say to me, isn't there, Mr. Holiday? And surely much that you wish to do!" The craggy face shoved close before his own once more. The hard eyes bored into him. "Well, I will give you your chance, play-King. I will give *you* the opportunity that you were so quick to deny *me* when you smashed the crystal and exiled me from my home!"

One bony finger crooked before Ben's frozen eyes. "But first I have something to show you. I have it right here, looped safely about my neck." His hand dipped downward into the robes. "Look closely, Mr. Holiday. Do you see it?"

He withdrew his hand slowly. There was a chain gripped tightly in the fingers. Ben's medallion hung fastened at its end.

Meeks smiled in triumph as he saw the look of desperation that flooded Ben's eyes. "Yes, Mr. Holiday! Yes, play-King! Yes, you poor fool! It *is* your precious medallion! The key to Landover—and it belongs to me now!" He dangled it slowly before Ben, letting it twirl to catch the mixed light of blazing rune stone and candle's flame. His eyes narrowed. "Do you wish to know what happened to separate you from the medallion? You gave it to me in a dream I sent you, Mr. Holiday. You took the medallion off and passed it to me. You gave the medallion to me willingly. I could not take it by force, but you *gave* it to me!"

Meeks was like a giant that threatened to crush Ben—tall, dark, looming out of the shadows. His breath hissed. "I think there is nothing I can tell you that you do not already know, is there, Mr. Holiday?"

He made a quick gesture with his hand, and the invisible chains that held Ben paralyzed dropped away. He could move again and speak. Yet he did neither. He simply waited.

"Reach down within your nightshirt, Mr. Holiday," the wizard whispered.

Ben did as he was told. His fingers closed on a medallion fastened to the end of a chain. Slowly he withdrew it. The medallion was the same shape and size as the one he had once worn—the one Meeks now possessed. But the engraving on the face was changed. Gone was the Paladin, Sterling Silver, and the rising sun. Gone was the polished silver sheen. The medallion was tarnished black as soot and embossed with the robed figure of Meeks.

Ben stared at the medallion in horror, touched it disbelievingly, then let it drop from his fingers as if it had burned him.

Meeks nodded in satisfaction. "I own you, Mr. Holiday. You are mine to do with as I choose. I could simply destroy you, of course—but I won't. That would be too easy an end for you after all the trouble you have caused me!" He paused, the smile returning—hard, ironic. "Instead, Mr. Holiday, I think I will set you free."

He moved back a few steps, waiting. Ben hesitated, then rose from the bed, his mind working frantically to find a way out of this nightmare. There were no weapons close at hand. Meeks stood between him and the bedroom door.

He took a step forward.

"Oh, one thing more." Meeks' voice stopped him as surely as if he had run into a wall of stone. The hard, old face was a mass of gullies and ridges worn by time. "You are free—but you will have to leave the castle. Now. You see, Mr. Holiday, you do not belong here anymore. You are no longer King. You are, in fact, no longer even yourself."

One hand lifted. There was a brief sweep of light and Ben's nightshirt was gone. He was dressed in laborer's clothing—rough woolen pants and tunic, a woolen cloak, and worn boots. There was dirt on him and the smell of animals.

Meeks studied him dispassionately. "One of the common folk, Mr. Holiday—that is who you will be from this day forward. Work hard and you may find a way to advance yourself. There is opportunity in this land even for such as you. You will not be King again, of course. But you may find some other suitable occupation. I hope so. I would hate to think of you as destitute. I would be most distressed if you were to suffer inconvenience. Life is a long time, you know."

His gaze shifted suddenly to Willow's rune stone. "By the way, you will not be needing that any more, will you?" His hand lifted, and the rune stone flew from the nightstand into his gloved palm. His fingers closed, and the stone shattered into dust, its red glow winking out abruptly.

He looked back again at Ben, his smile cold and hard. "Now where were we? Oh, yes—we were discussing the matter of your future. I can assure you that I will monitor it with great interest. The medallion with which I have supplied you will tell me all I need to know. Be careful you do not try to remove *that* medallion. A certain magic protects against such foolishness—a magic that would shorten your life rather considerably if it were challenged. And I do not want you to die, Mr. Holiday—not for a long, long time."

Ben stared at the other man in disbelief. What sort of game was this? He measured quickly the distance to the bedroom door. He could move and talk again; he was free of whatever it was that had paralyzed him. He had to try to escape.

Then he saw Meeks watching him, studying him as a cat might a cornered mouse, and fear gave way to anger and shame. "This won't work, Meeks," he said quietly, forcing the edge from his voice. "No one will accept this."

"No?" Meeks kept the smile steady. "And why is that, Mr. Holiday?"

Ben took a deep breath and a couple of steps forward for good measure. "Because these old clothes you've slapped on me won't fool anyone! And medallion or no medallion, I'm still me and you're still you!"

Meeks arched his eyebrows quizzically. "Are you certain of that, Mr. Holiday? Are you quite sure?"

There was a tug of doubt at the back of Ben's mind, but he kept it from his eyes. He glanced sideways at the floor-length mirror to catch a glimpse of himself and was relieved to find that physically, at least, he was still the same person he had always been.

But Meeks seemed so certain. Had the wizard changed him in some way that he couldn't see?

"This won't work," he repeated, edging closer to the door as he spoke, trying to figure out what it was that Meeks knew that he didn't—because there most certainly was *something* . . .

Meeks' laughter was sharp and acrid. "Why don't we see what works and what doesn't, Mr. Holiday!"

The gloved hand swept up, the fingers extended, and green fire burst from the tips. Ben sprang forward with a lunge, tumbling past the dark form of the wizard, rolling wildly to dodge the fire, and scrambling back to his feet. He reached the closed door in a rush and had his fingers on the handle when the magic caught up with him. He tried to scream, but couldn't. Shadows wrapped him, smothered him, and the sleep that wouldn't come earlier couldn't now be kept away.

Ben Holiday shuddered helplessly and dropped slowly into blackness.

STRANGER

Ben came awake again in shadows and half-light, eyes squinting through a swirl of images that rocked like the flotsam and jetsam an ocean's waters tossed against a beachhead. He lay on a pallet of some sort, the touch of its leather padding cool and smooth against his face. His first thought was that he was still alive. His second was to wonder why.

He blinked, waiting for the images to stop moving and take definite shape. The memory of what had happened to him recalled itself with painful intensity. He could feel again the anger, frustration, and despair. Meeks had returned to Landover. Meeks had caught him unprepared, smashed the rune stone given him by Willow, stripped him of his clothing, turned the dark magic on him until consciousness was gone, and . . .

Oh, my God!

His fingers groped down the front of his tunic, reached inside, and withdrew the medallion that hung from its chain about his neck. Frantically, he held it up to the twilight, the warnings already whispering urgently in his mind, the certainty of what he would find already taking shape in his thoughts. The carved metal face of the medallion seemed to shimmer. For an instant, he thought he saw the familiar figure of the Paladin riding out of Sterling Silver against the rising sun. Then the Paladin, the castle, and the sun were gone, and there was only the cloaked form of Meeks, black against a surface tarnished with disuse.

Ben swallowed against the dryness he felt in his throat, his worst fears realized. Meeks had stolen the medallion of the Kings of Landover.

A sense of desperation flooded through him, and he tried to push himself to his feet. He was successful for a moment, a small rush of adrenaline giving him renewed strength. He stood, the swirl of images steadying enough that he could recognize something of his surroundings. He was still within Sterling

Silver. He recognized the room as a sitting chamber situated at the front of the castle, a room reserved for waiting guests. He recognized the bench on which he had been lying, with its rust-colored leather and carved wooden feet. He knew where he was, but he didn't know why—just as he didn't know why he was still alive . . .

Then his strength gave out again, his legs buckled, and he crumpled back onto the bench. Wood scraped and leather creaked, the sounds alerting someone who waited without. The door opened inward. Gimlet eyes glittered from out of a monkey face to which large ears were appended.

It was Bunion!

Bunion stepped into view and peered down at him.

Ben had never been so happy to see anyone in his entire life. He would have hugged the little kobold if he could have found the strength to do so. As it was, he simply lay there, grinning foolishly and trying to make his mouth work. Bunion helped him back onto the bench and waited for him to get the words out.

"Find Questor," he managed finally. He swallowed again against the dryness, the inside of his mouth like chalk. "Bring him. Don't let anyone know what you're doing. And be careful. Meeks is here in the castle!"

Bunion stared at him a moment longer, an almost puzzled look on his gnarled face, then turned and slipped from the room wordlessly. Ben lay back again, exhausted. Good old Bunion. He didn't know what the kobold was doing there—or even what *he* was doing there, for that matter—but it was exactly the piece of good fortune he needed. If he could find Questor quickly enough, he could rally the guard and put an end to any threat Meeks might pose. Meeks was a powerful wizard, but he was no match for so many. Ben would regain the stolen medallion, and Meeks would regret the day he ever even *thought* about sneaking back into Landover!

He closed his eyes momentarily, marshaling what inner resources he could, then pushed himself upright once more. His eyes swept the room. It was empty. Candlelight from a wall bracket and a table dish chased the shadows. Light from without crept through the crack beneath the closed door. He stood, bracing the backs of his legs against the bench for support. He was still dressed in the peasant garb with which Meeks had clothed him. His hands were black with grime. Cute trick, Ben thought—but it won't work. I'm still me.

He took a dozen deep breaths, his vision steadying, his strength rebuilding. He could feel the warmth of the castle reaching out from the flooring through his battered work boots. He could feel the vibrancy of her life. There was an urgency to her touch that was disturbing. She seemed to sense the danger he was in.

Don't worry; it's going to be all right, he reassured her silently.

Footsteps approached and the door opened. Questor Thews stood there with Bunion. He hesitated, then entered the room wordlessly. The kobold followed, closing the door behind them.

"Questor, thank God you're here!" Ben blurted out. He started forward, hands reaching out in greeting. "We have to act quickly. Meeks is back—here, now, somewhere in the castle. I don't know how he managed it, but he stole the medallion. We have to alert the guard and find him before . . ."

He came to an abrupt stop half-a-dozen feet from his friend, his words trailing off into silence. The wizard's hands were still at his sides—not extended to receive his own. The owlish face was hard, and the bushy eyebrows furrowed.

Questor Thews was looking at Ben as if he had never seen his King before in his life.

Ben stiffened. "Questor, what's the matter?"

The wizard continued to stare at him. "Who are you?"

"Who am I? What do you mean, who am I? It's me, Ben!"

"Ben? You call yourself Ben?"

"Of course, I call myself Ben! What else would I call myself? That's my name, isn't it?"

"Apparently *you* believe so."

"Questor, what are you talking about? I believe so because it *is* so!"

Questor Thews frowned. The lines about his brows furrowed even more deeply. "*You* are Ben Holiday? *You* are Landover's High Lord?"

Ben stared back at him speechlessly. The disbelief in the other's voice was unmistakable. "You don't recognize me, do you?" he ventured.

The wizard shook his head. "I do not."

Ben felt a sharp sinking sensation in the pit of his stomach. "Look, it's just the clothes and the dirt, for Pete's sake! Look at me! Meeks did this—changed the clothes, messed me up a bit. But it's still me!"

"And you are Ben Holiday?"

"Yes, damn it!"

Questor studied him a moment, then took a deep breath. "You may believe yourself to be Ben Holiday. You may even believe yourself to be High King of Landover. But you are not. I know because I have just come from the King—and he was not you! You are an intruder in this castle. You are a spy and possibly even worse. You have entered uninvited, you have listened in on conversations that were private, you have attacked the High Lord in his bedchamber, and now you are claiming to be someone you clearly are not. If the choice were mine, I would have you imprisoned at once! It is only because the High Lord has ordered your release that you are free now. I suggest you go quickly. Seek help for your affliction, whatever it is, and stay far, far away from here!"

Ben was stunned. He could not think of what to do. He heard himself telling Meeks, "Medallion or no medallion, I'm still me and you're still you!" He heard Meeks reply, "Are you certain of that?"

What had been done to him?

He turned quickly to Bunion, searching for some hint of recognition in the kobold's sharp eyes. There was none. He rushed past them both to a mirror that hung upon the wall next to the doorway. He peered through the half-light at his image reflected in the glass. It was his face! He was exactly the same as he had always been! Why couldn't Questor and Bunion see that?

"Listen to me!" He wheeled on them, frantic. "Meeks has come back from the old world, stolen the medallion, and somehow disguised from everyone but myself who I am! I look the same to me, but not to you!"

Questor folded his arms across his chest. "You look different to everyone but yourself?"

It sounded so ridiculous that for a moment Ben just stared at him. "Yes," he replied finally. "And he has made *himself* appear as me! Somehow he has stolen my identity. I didn't attack him in his bedchamber! He attacked me in mine!" He came forward a step, eyes darting from one face to the other. "He sent the dreams, don't you see? He arranged all of this! I don't know why, but he did! This is part of his revenge for what we did to him!"

There was irritation in Questor's eyes, indifference in Bunion's. Ben felt his grip on the situation slipping. "You can't let him do this, damn it! You can't let him get away with this!" His mind raced. "Look, if I'm not who I say I am, how do I know all that I do? How do I know about the dreams—mine of Miles Bennett, yours of the missing books of magic, Willow's of the black unicorn! For God's sake, what about Willow? Someone has to warn her! Listen, damn it! How do I know about the books you brought in last night—the ones with the unicorns? I know about those. I know about the medallion, about . . . Ask me something! Go on, ask me anything! Test me!"

Questor shook his head solemnly. "I do not have time for these games, whoever-you-are. You know what you know because you are a spy and learned these things by spying. You listened to our conversations and you adapted them to your own purposes. You forget that you already confessed all this to the High Lord when he caught you sneaking about his bedchamber. You admitted everything when pressed. You are fortunate you were not dispatched by the guard when you attempted to flee. You are fortunate you . . ."

"I did not flee anything!" Ben shouted in fury. He tried to reach out to Questor, but Bunion interceded at once and kept him away. "Listen to me! I am Ben Holiday! I am High Lord of Landover! I . . ."

The doors opened and guards appeared, alarmed by the frenzy in his voice. Questor beckoned, and they seized hold of his arms.

"Don't do this!" he screamed. "Give me a chance . . ."

"You have been given that chance!" Questor Thews interjected coldly. "Take advantage of it and leave!"

Ben was dragged from the room struggling, still screaming his identity, still protesting what had been done to him, while his mind spun with anger and frustration. He caught a glimpse of a tall, dark-robed figure standing in the distance, watching. Meeks! He screamed louder, trying to break free. One of the guards cuffed him and he saw stars. His head drooped and his voice trailed away. He had to do something! But what? What?

The robed figure disappeared. Questor and Bunion were left behind. Ben was dragged through the entry to the castle gates and beyond the walls. The bridge he had rebuilt after he had assumed the throne was bright with torch-light. He was dragged across it. When he reached the far side, he was thrown to the ground.

"Good night, your Majesty," one of the guards mocked.

"Come visit again soon," said another.

They walked away laughing. "Next time we'll have his ears," one said.

Ben lay upon the ground momentarily, head spinning. Slowly he pushed himself upright and looked back across the bridge at the castle lights. He stared at the towers and battlements as they glistened silver in the light of Landover's eight moons and listened to the fading sound of voices and the heavy thud of the gates being closed.

Then all was silent.

He still could not believe that this was happening to him.

"Mother!" Willow whispered, and there was excitement and longing in her voice.

Moonlight draped the great forests of the lake country in a mix of rainbow colors, its cool brightness a beacon against the shadows. Parsnip was encamped somewhere far back within those shadows, patiently awaiting her return. Elderew lay distant, the city of the River Master wrapped in silence, her inhabitants asleep. Elderew was Willow's home and the River Master was her father, but it was neither her home nor her father that she had come to see this night.

It was the wood nymph who danced before her like a vision out of fairy.

Willow knelt at the edge of a clearing surrounded by aging pines and watched the magic unfold. Her mother spun and leaped through the night's stillness, light and ephemeral, born of air and blown on the wind. She was a tiny thing, little more than a wisp of life. White gauze clothed her, transparent and weightless, and the pale green skin of her child's body glimmered beneath the covering. Waist-length silver hair rippled and shimmered with each movement she made, a trailer of white fire against the night's dark. Music that she alone could hear swept her on.

Willow watched in rapture. Her mother was a wild thing, so wild that she could not live among humans, even the once-fairy people of the lake country. She had bonded briefly to Willow's father, but that had been long ago. They had bonded once only, her father nearly driven mad with need for the wood nymph he could not have, and then her mother had disappeared back into the forests again. She had never come back. Willow had been born of that brief union, her father's constant reminder of the fairy being he forever wanted and could never have. His impossible longing aroused in him both love and hate. His feelings for Willow had always been ambivalent.

Willow understood. She was a sylph, an elemental. She was the child of both her parents, her constant water sprite father and her mercurial wood nymph mother. Her father's domesticity gave her stability, but she was imbued with her mother's wildness as well. She was a creature of contradictions. Amorphous, she was both flesh and plant. She was human in the greater part of the moon's cycle and plant briefly in the cycle's apex—a single night each twenty-day. Ben had been shocked to see her transformation that first night. She had changed from human to tree in this very clearing, feeding on the energy implanted by her mother in the earth where she danced. Ben had been shocked, but she was what she was, and he had come to accept that. One day he would even love her for it, she believed. It was not so with her father. His love was conditional and always would be. He was still a captive of the insatiable need her mother aroused in him. Willow only seemed to emphasize the weight of the chains that bound him.

So Willow had not come to her father in her effort to understand the dream of the black unicorn. She had come instead to her mother.

Her mother spun closer, whirling and twisting with grace and strength that defied understanding. Although wild and captive in her own way to desires she could not resist, her mother loved her nevertheless—without condition, without measure. She came when Willow needed her, the bond that linked them so strong that they could often sense each other's thoughts. They spoke now in the silence of their minds, trading images of love and want. The bonding grew stronger, an entwining that expanded thoughts into words . . .

"Mother," Willow whispered a second time.

She felt herself dream. Her mother danced, and she saw in the balletic, frenzied movements the vision that had brought her. The black unicorn appeared once more, a creature of exquisite, terrible beauty. It stood before her in the dark wood of which she had first dreamed, slender shape shimmering in moonlight and shadows, in the manner of a wraith. Willow shook to see it so. One moment it was a creature of fairy, the next a demon of Abaddon. Its spiraled horn flared and its hooves pawed the forest earth. Head lowered, it feinted with a quick rush, then backed cautiously away. It seemed trapped with indecision.

What bothers it so? Willow wondered in surprise.

She looked down suddenly and the answer lay cradled in her hands. She was holding again the bridle of spun gold. It was the bridle that kept the unicorn at bay; she knew it instinctively. She caressed it and felt the weave and draw of the threads run smooth against the touch of her fingers. A strange rush of emotions coursed through her. Such power the bridle offered! It could make the unicorn hers, she sensed. There were no unicorns left in all the world, none but in fairy, where she might never go again, none but this one only, and it might be hers if she wished it. All she need do was to stretch out her hand . . .

But, no, she cautioned abruptly, if she were to touch this creature for even the briefest instant, she would be lost to herself. She knew that; she had always known that. She must take the bridle to Ben because it belonged to him . . .

And then the unicorn's head lifted, all beauty and grace. The dark face was perfectly symmetrical, the long mane blown like silk on a whisper of wind. There was fear in its eyes, fear of something other than the sylph and her bridle of spun gold, fear of something beyond her comprehension. Willow was paralyzed with the horror of it. The eyes of the black unicorn threatened to engulf her. The dream closed about. She blinked rapidly to break the spell and caught for just an instant something more than fear in the creature's eyes. She saw an unmistakable plea for help.

Her hands lifted, almost of their own volition, and she held the bridle before her like a talisman.

The black unicorn snorted, an indelicate, frightened sound, and the shadows of the wood seemed to shimmer in response. Abruptly, the dream faded into vapor and the unicorn was gone. Willow's mother danced alone again in the pine-sheltered clearing. The wood nymph spun one final time, a bit of moonlight against the dark, slowed in her pirouette, and flitted soundlessly down to where her daughter knelt.

Willow sank back upon her heels in exhaustion, the strength drained from her by the effort she had given over to the dream. "Oh, Mother," she murmured and clasped the slender, pale green hands. "What have I been shown?" Then she smiled gently and there were tears in her eyes and on her cheeks. "But there is no purpose in asking you, is there? You know no more of this than I. You dance only what you feel, not what you know."

Her mother's delicate features changed in a barely perceptible manner—

a lowering of her eyes, a slight twisting of her mouth. She understood, but could not help. Her dance was a conduit to knowledge, but not its source. The magic worked that way with elementals.

"Mother." Willow clasped the pale hands more tightly, drawing strength from their touch. "I must know the reason for these dreams of the unicorn and the bridle of gold. I must know why I am being shown something that both lures and frightens me as this does. Which vision am I to believe?"

The small hands tightened back on her own, and her mother answered in a brief, birdlike sound that echoed of the forest night.

Willow's slender form bent close, and something like a chill made her shiver. "There is one in the lake country who can help me understand?" she asked softly. "There is one who might know?" Her face grew intense. "Mother, I must go to him! Tonight!"

Again her mother responded, quick, eerie. She rose and spun swiftly across the clearing and back again. Her hands beckoned frantically. *Tomorrow,* they said. *Tonight is taken. It is your time.*

Willow's face lifted. "Yes, Mother," she whispered obediently.

She understood. She might wish it otherwise—and indeed had done so more than once before—but she could not deny the fact of it. The twenty-day cycle was at its end; the change was upon her. The need was already so strong that she could barely control herself. She shivered again. She must hurry.

She thought suddenly of Ben and wished he were there with her.

She stood up and walked to the clearing's center. Her arms lifted skyward as if to draw in the colored moonlight. A radiance enveloped her, and she could feel the essence of her mother emanating from the earth upon which she had danced. She began to feed.

"Stay close to me, Mother," she pleaded as her body shimmered. Her feet arched and split into roots that snaked downward into the dark earth, her hands and arms lengthened into branches, and the transformation began.

Moments later it was finished. Willow had disappeared. She had become the tree whose namesake she bore and would stay that way until dawn.

Her mother sank down next to her, a child's ghost slipped from the shadows. She sat motionless for a time. Then her pale, slender arms wrapped about the roughened trunk that harnessed her daughter's life and held it tight.

Dawn was approaching. Landover's moons were fading away, one after the other, and night's shadows were giving ground before a broadening golden hue that edged its way slowly out of the eastern horizon.

Questor Thews stalked the halls of Sterling Silver, a skeletal, ragtag figure in his gray robes with the colored sashes, looking for all the world as if he had lost his best friend. He rounded a corner near the front entry hall and bumped up against Abernathy.

"Taking an early constitutional?" the scribe inquired archly.

Questor grunted and the furrows lining his forehead deepened. "I find I cannot sleep, and I do not for the life of me know why that is. There is reason enough to be tired, heaven knows."

Abernathy's shaggy face revealed nothing of what he thought of that. He shrugged and turned to walk next to the wizard. "I understand someone was caught breaking into the High Lord's bedchamber this evening—someone who claimed to be the King."

Questor grunted a second time. "A madman. He was lucky to be released. But the High Lord ordered it. 'Put him across to the mainland,' he said. I would not have been so generous about the matter had the decision been mine, I assure you."

They walked a bit further. "Odd that the High Lord simply released him," Abernathy remarked finally. His nose twitched. "He usually finds better uses for his enemies."

"Hmmmmmm." Questor didn't seem to hear. He was shaking his head at something. "It bothers me that the man knew so much about the dreams. He knew of the books of magic, of the High Lord's visit back, of the unicorn . . ." He trailed off momentarily. "He seemed to know everything. He seemed so sure of himself."

Neither spoke for a time. Questor led the way up a stairwell to a walk overlooking the outer parapets at the front of the castle. Below, the bridge which connected the island to the mainland stretched out across the lake, misted and empty. Questor peered through the fading gloom to the far shore, scanning the water's edge. His owlish face tightened like a drawn knot.

"The stranger appears to be gone," he said finally.

Abernathy glanced at him curiously. "Did you expect anything else?" he asked.

He waited in vain for an answer to his question. Questor continued to stare out across the lake and said nothing.

EDGEWOOD DIRK

The new day did not find Ben Holiday standing about the gates of Sterling Silver with his nose pressed up against the timbers as might have been expected. It found him hiking his way south into the lake country. He walked quickly and purposefully. By the time the sun had crested the rim of the valley east above the mists and tree line, he was already half-a-dozen miles into his journey and determined to complete at least a dozen more before the day was finished.

The decision to leave had not been an easy one. It had taken him a long time to make it. He had sat out there in the dark and the chill, staring back at the lights of the castle and wondering what had hit him, so stunned he didn't even move for the first half hour; he just sat there. His emotions ran the gamut from shock to fear to anger and back again. It was like a bad dream from which you are certain you will escape—even after the time for escape is long past. He recounted the events of the night over and over again in his mind, trying to construct some rational explanation for their being, to discover some purpose to their order. He failed. It all came down to the same thing—Meeks was in and he was out.

It was with a sense of desperation that he finally acknowledged that what had happened to him was for real. He had given up a life and a world that were familiar and safe to come into Landover; he had risked losing everything he had on the chance that he would find something better. Obstacles had confronted him at every turn, but he had overcome them. He had gained in reality what most found only in dreams. Now, just when he had begun to feel comfortable with what he had, just when it seemed the worst was past, everything he had struggled so hard to find had been snatched away from him, and he was faced with the distinct possibility that he would end up losing it all.

It wasn't possible. It wasn't fair.

But it was a fact, and he hadn't been a successful trial lawyer for all those years in the old world by avoiding the reality of facts. So he choked down his desperation, got over being too stunned to move, swept away the anger and the fear, and forced himself to deal with his situation. His repeated replays of what had happened to him failed to yield the information he might have wished. Meeks had tricked him into returning to the old world, and he had carried the wizard back with him into Landover. Meeks had done that by sending him a false dream about Miles. But Meeks had also sent the dreams of the missing books of magic and the black unicorn to Questor Thews and Willow. Why had he done that? There had to be a reason. The dreams were all tied together in some way; Ben was certain of it. He was certain as well that something had forced Meeks to choose this particular time to return to Landover. His diatribe in the bedchamber had made that clear. In some way Ben had messed up his plans—and it was more than simply the thwarting of the wizard's sale of the throne of Landover to others or the exiling of the wizard from his home world. It was something else—something of far greater importance to Meeks. The wizard's anger at Ben was fueled by events and circumstances that Ben hadn't yet uncovered. They had compelled Meeks to return—almost out of desperation.

But Ben had no idea why.

He did know that, despite what should have been adequate provocation, Meeks hadn't killed him when he could have. That was puzzling. Clearly Meeks hated him enough to want him to suffer awhile as an outcast, but wasn't it a bit risky letting him wander around loose? Sooner or later someone was going to see through the deception and recognize the truth of things. Meeks could not assume his identity and Ben remain a stranger to everyone indefinitely. There had to be some way to counter the magic of that vile amulet Meeks had stuck him with, and he would surely search it out eventually. On the other hand, maybe what he accomplished in the long run didn't matter. Perhaps time was something he didn't have. Maybe the game would be over for him before he understood all the rules.

The possibility terrified him. It meant he had to act quickly if he didn't want to risk losing the chance of acting at all. But what should he do? He had stared back across the lake at the dark shape of the castle and reasoned it through. He was wasting his time here where he was a stranger to everyone—even to his closest friends. If neither Questor nor Bunion recognized him, there was little chance anyone else at Sterling Silver would. Meeks was King of Landover for the moment; he would have to concede that much. It grated on him like sand rubbed on raw flesh, but there was nothing to be done about it. Meeks was Ben—and Ben himself was some fellow who had slipped uninvited into the castle and tried to cause trouble. If he attempted to break in a second time, he would undoubtedly wind up in worse shape than he was in now.

Maybe Meeks was hoping for that. Maybe he was expecting it. Ben did not want to chance it.

Besides, there were better alternatives to choose from. Admittedly he did not know exactly what Meeks was about, but he knew enough to know how to cause the wizard problems if he could act fast enough. Meeks had sent three dreams, and two of them had already served their purposes. Meeks had regained entry into Landover through Ben, and he had used Questor to bring him the missing books of magic. Make no mistake, Ben admonished himself—Meeks had those books by now as surely as the sun would rise in the east. That left only the third dream to be satisfied—the dream sent to Willow of the black unicorn. Meeks was looking for something from that third dream as well; he had let a hint of it slip in his anger. He was looking for the golden bridle that would harness the black unicorn and he fully expected Willow to bring it to him. And why shouldn't she, after all? The dream had warned her that the unicorn was a threat to her, that the bridle was the only thing that would protect her, and that she must bring the bridle to Ben. That was exactly what she would think she was doing, of course, once she found the bridle—except that it would be Meeks disguised as Ben who would be waiting to greet her. But if Ben could reach the sylph first, he could prevent that from happening. He could warn Willow, and perhaps the two of them could discover the importance of the bridle and the unicorn to the wizard and throw a monkey wrench into his plans.

So off Ben went, heading south, the difficult decision made. It meant forgoing his responsibilities as King of Landover and conceding those responsibilities to Meeks. It meant abandoning the problems of the judiciary council, the irrigation fields south of Waymark, the always-impatient Lords of the Greensward, the tax levy, and all the others who still waited for an audience with Landover's High Lord. Meeks could act in his place with impunity in the days ahead—or fail to act, as the case might be. It meant abandoning Sterling Silver and leaving his friends, Questor, Abernathy, and the kobolds. He felt like a traitor and a coward going this way. A part of him demanded that he stay and fight. But Willow came first. He had to find her and warn her. Once that was accomplished, he could turn his attention to exposing Meeks and setting things right.

Unfortunately, finding Willow would not be easy. He was traveling down into the lake country because that was where Willow had said she would go to begin her search for the unicorn and the golden bridle. But Willow had been gone almost a week, and that search might have taken her anywhere by now. Ben would appear a stranger to everyone, so he could not trade on his position as Landover's King to demand help. He might be ignored totally or not even be allowed into the lake country. If that happened, he was in trouble.

On the other hand, it was difficult to imagine being in worse trouble than he was in already.

He walked all that day, feeling better about himself as he went, for no better reason than the fact that he was doing something positive and not simply sitting around. He wound his way southward out of the lightly forested hill country around his island home into the more densely grown woods that comprised the domain of the River Master. The hills smoothed to grasslands, then thickened to woods damp with moisture and heavy with shadow. Lakes began to dot the countryside, some no larger than marshy ponds, some so vast they stretched away into mist. Trees canopied and closed about, and the smell of damp permeated the failing light. A stillness settled down about the land as dusk neared, then began to fill slowly with night sounds.

Ben found a clearing by a stream feeding down out of the distant hills and made his camp. It was a short project. He had no blankets or food, so he had to content himself with the leaves and branches from a stand of Bonnie Blues and the spring water. The fare was filling, but hardly satisfying. He kept thinking that something was moving in the shadows, watching him. Had the lake country people discovered him? But no one showed. He was quite alone.

Being so alone eroded his confidence. He was all but helpless when you got right down to it. He had lost his castle, his knights, his identity, his authority, his title, and his friends. Worst of all, he had lost the medallion. Without the medallion, he did not have the protection of the Paladin. He was left with only himself to rely upon, and that was precious little against the dangers posed by Landover's denizens and their mercurial forms of magic. He had been lucky to survive his arrival in Landover when he had enjoyed the benefit of the medallion's protection. What was he to do now without it?

He stared off into the dark, finding the answers as elusive as the night's shadows. What distressed him most was the fact that he had lost the medallion to Meeks. He could not figure out for the life of him how that could have happened. No one was supposed to be able to take the medallion from him. That meant he must have given it over willingly. But how had Meeks compelled him to do something so stupid?

He finished his meager dinner and was still brooding over the turn of events that had brought him to this sorry state when he saw the cat.

The cat was sitting at the edge of the clearing, perhaps a dozen feet or so away, watching him. Ben had no idea how long the cat had been there. He hadn't seen it until now, but it was keeping perfectly still, so it might have been occupying that same spot for some time. The cat's eyes gleamed emerald in the moonlight. Its coat was silver-gray except for black paws, face, and tail. It was a slender, delicate thing—seemingly out of place in the forest wild. It had the look of a strayed house pet.

"Hello, cat," Ben ventured with a wry smile.

"Hello, yourself," the cat replied.

Ben stared, certain that he must not have heard correctly. Had the cat spoken? He straightened. "Did you say something?" he asked cautiously.

The cat's gleaming eyes blinked once and fixed on him, but the cat said nothing. Ben waited a few moments, then leaned back again on his elbows. It wasn't as if it were surprising to imagine that the cat *might* have said something, he told himself. After all, the dragon Strabo spoke; and if a dragon could speak, why not a cat?

"Too bad you can't talk," he muttered, thinking it would be nice to share his misery with someone.

The night brought a chill with it, and he shivered briefly in the rough work clothes. He wished he had a blanket or a fire to help ward off the damp; or better, that he were back in his own bed at the castle.

He glanced over again at the cat. The cat hadn't moved. It simply sat there, staring back at him. Ben frowned. The cat's steady gaze was a bit unnerving. What was a cat doing out here in the woods alone like this anyway? Didn't it have a home? The emerald eyes gleamed brightly. They were sharp and insistent. Ben shifted his own gaze to the shadowed woods. He wondered again how he was going to find Willow. He would need help from the River Master and he hadn't the foggiest idea as to how he would convince that being of his true identity. His fingers brushed the tarnished medallion that hung about his neck, tracing the outline of Meeks. The medallion certainly wouldn't be of any help.

"Maybe the River Master's magic will help him recognize me," he thought aloud.

"I wouldn't count on it, if I were you," someone replied.

He started and looked quickly in the direction of the speaker. There was no one there but the cat.

Ben's eyes narrowed. "I heard you that time!" he snapped, irritated enough that he didn't care how foolish he sounded. "You *can* speak, can't you?"

The cat blinked and answered. "I can when it pleases me."

Ben fought to regain his composure. "I see. Well, you might at least have the courtesy to announce the fact instead of playing games with people."

"Courtesy has nothing to do with the matter, High Lord Ben Holiday. Playing games is a way of life with cats. We tease, we taunt, and we do exactly as we please, not as others would have us do. Playing games is an integral part of our personae. Those who wish to have any sort of relationship with us must expect as much. They must understand that participation in our games is necessary if they wish communication on any level."

Ben stared at the cat. "How do you know who I am?" he asked finally.

"Who else would you be but who you are?" the cat replied.

Ben had to stop and think that one through a minute. "Well, no one," he said finally. "But how is it that *you* can recognize me when no one else can? Don't I look like someone else to you?"

The cat lifted one dainty paw and washed it lovingly. "Who you look like counts for little with me," the cat said. "Appearances are deceiving, and who you look like might not be who you really are. I never rely on appearances. Cats can appear as they choose. Cats are masters of deception and masters of an art cannot be deceived by anyone. I see you for who you really are, not who you appear to be. I have no idea if how you appear just now is how you really are."

"Well, it isn't."

"Whatever you say. I do know that however you might appear, you are in any case Ben Holiday, High Lord of Landover."

Ben was silent a moment, trying to decide just what it was he was dealing with here, wondering where on earth this creature had come from.

"So you know who I am in spite of the magic that disguises me?" he concluded. "The magic doesn't fool you?"

The cat studied him a moment, then cocked its head, reflecting. "The magic wouldn't fool you either, if you didn't let it."

Ben frowned. "What do you mean by that?"

"Much and little. Deception is mostly a game we play with ourselves."

The conversation was turning a bit oblique. Ben sat back wearily. "Who are you, Mr. Cat?" he asked.

The cat stood up and came forward a few feet, then sat back down again, prim and sleek. "I am a great many things, my dear High Lord. I am what you see and what you don't. I am real and imagined. I am something from the life you have known and something from dreams of life you have not yet enjoyed. I am quite an anomaly, really."

"Very insightful," Ben grunted. "Could you be a bit more precise, perhaps?"

The cat blinked. "Certainly. Watch this."

The cat shimmered suddenly in the dark, glowing as if radioactive, and the sleek body seemed to alter shape. Ben squinted until his eyes closed, then looked again. The cat had grown. It was four times the size it had been, and it was no longer just a cat. It had assumed a slightly human face beneath cat's ears, whiskers, nose and fur, and its paws had become fingers. It swished its tail expectantly as it stared at him.

Ben started half-a-dozen questions and gave up. "You must be a fairy creature," he said finally.

The cat grinned—an almost-human grin. "Exactly so! Very well reasoned, High Lord!"

"Thank you so much. Would you mind awfully telling me what sort of fairy creature you are?"

"What sort? Well, um . . . hmmmmm. I am a prism cat."

"And what is that?"

The grin disappeared. "Oh, I don't think I can explain it—not even if I wanted to, which I really don't. It wouldn't help you to know anyway, High Lord. You wouldn't understand, being human. I will tell you this. I am a very old and very rare sort of cat. I am but one of just a few still remaining. We were always a select breed and did not propagate the species in the manner of common animals. It is that way with fairy creatures—you have been told this, haven't you? No? Well, it is that way. Prism cats are rare. We must spread ourselves quite thin to accomplish our purposes."

"And what purpose is it that you are trying to accomplish here?" Ben asked, still trying to make some sense out of all the verbiage.

The cat flicked its tail idly. "That depends."

"Depends on what?"

"Oh you. On your . . . intrinsic self-worth."

Ben stared at the cat wordlessly. Things were becoming a bit too muddled for him to stay with this conversation. He had been assaulted in his own home and bounced out like a stranger. He had lost his identity. He had lost his friends. He was cold and he was hungry. He felt as if any intrinsic self-worth he might possess rated just about zero.

The cat stirred slightly. "I am deciding whether or not I shall be your companion for a time," the creature announced.

Ben grinned faintly. "My companion?"

"Yes. You certainly need one. You don't see yourself to be who you really are. Neither does anyone else, apparently, save for me. This intrigues me. I may decide to stay with you long enough to see how it all turns out for you."

Ben was incredulous. "Well, I'll say one thing for you. You're a different sort—whether cat, human, fairy, or whatever. But maybe you'd better think twice about sticking with me. You might be letting yourself in for more than you can handle."

"Oh, I rather doubt that," the cat replied. "I seldom encounter anything that difficult these days."

"Is that so?" Ben's patience slipped a notch. This cat was insufferable! He hunched closer to the prim creature. "Well, try this on for size, Mr. Cat. What if I were to tell you that there is a wizard named Meeks who has stolen my identity, my throne, and my life and consigned me to exile in my own land? What if I were to tell you that I intend to get all of that back from him, but that to do so I need to find a sylph who in turn searches for a black unicorn? And what if I were to tell you that there is every chance that I—and anyone brash enough to offer to help me in this endeavor—will be disposed of most unpleasantly if found out?"

The cat said nothing. It simply sat there as if considering. Ben leaned back, both satisfied and disgusted with himself. Sure, he could congratulate himself for having laid all of his cards on the table and setting the cat straight. But he had also just destroyed the one chance he might have had of finding someone to help him. You can't have it both ways, he admonished himself.

But the cat seemed unperturbed. "Cats are not easily discouraged once they have decided on something, you know. Cats are quite independent in their behavioral patterns and cannot be cajoled or frightened. I fail to see why you bother trying such tactics with me, High Lord."

Ben sighed. "I apologize. I just thought you ought to know how matters stand."

The cat stood up and arched its back. "I know exactly how matters stand. You are the one who is deceived. But deception needs only to be recognized to be banished. You have that in common with the black unicorn, I think."

Once more, Ben was surprised. He frowned. "You know of the black unicorn? There really is such a creature?"

The cat looked disgusted. "You search for it, don't you?"

"For the sylph more than the unicorn," Ben answered hastily. "She had a dream of the creature and of a bridle of spun gold that would hold it; she left to search for both." He hesitated, then plunged ahead. "The dream of the unicorn was sent by the wizard. He sent other dreams as well—to me and to Questor Thews, another wizard, his half-brother. I think that in some way the dreams are all tied together. I am afraid that Willow—the sylph—is in danger. If I can reach her before the wizard Meeks . . ."

"Certainly, certainly," the cat interrupted rather rudely. There was a bored look on its face. It sat down again. "It appears I had better come with you. Wizards and black unicorns are nothing to be fooling about with."

"I agree," Ben said. "But you don't appear to be any better equipped than I to do what needs to be done. Besides, this isn't your problem. It's mine. I don't think I would feel comfortable risking your life as well as my own."

The cat sneezed. "Such a noble expression of concern!" Ben could have sworn he caught a hint of sarcasm, but the cat's face revealed nothing. The cat circled briefly and sat down again. "What cat is not better equipped than *any* human to do *anything* that needs to be done? Besides, why do you persist in thinking of me as simply a cat?"

Ben shrugged. "Are you something more?"

The cat looked at him for a long time, then began to wash. It licked and worried its fur until it had groomed itself to its satisfaction. All the while, Ben sat watching. When the cat was at last content, it faced him once more. "You are not listening to me, my dear High Lord. It is no wonder that you have lost yourself or that you have become someone other than who you wish to be. It is no wonder that no one but I can recognize you. I begin to question if you are worth my time."

Ben's ears burned at the rebuke, but he said nothing. The cat blinked. "It is cold here in the woods; there is a chill in the air. I prefer the comfort of a hearth and fire. Would you like a fire, High Lord?"

Ben nodded. "I'd love one—but I don't have the tools."

The cat stood and stretched. "Exactly. But I do, you see. Watch."

The cat began to glow again, just as it had before, and its shape within the glow grew indistinct. Then suddenly there was a crystalline glimmer, and the flesh and blood creature of a moment earlier disappeared completely and was replaced by something that looked as if it were a large glass figurine. The figurine still retained the appearance of a cat with human features, but it moved as if liquid. Emerald eyes blazed out of a clear body in which moonlight reflected and refracted off mirrored surfaces that shifted like tiny plates of glass. Then the light seemed to coalesce in the emerald eyes and thrust outward like a laser. It struck a gathering of deadwood a dozen feet away and ignited it instantly into a blazing fire.

Ben shielded his eyes, then watched as the fire diminished until it was manageable—the size of a campfire. The emerald eyes dimmed. The cat shimmered and returned to its former shape. It sat back slowly on its haunches and regarded Ben solemnly. "You will recall now, perhaps, what I told you I was?" it said.

"A prism cat," Ben responded at once, remembering.

"Quite right. I can capture light from any source—even so distant a source as the land's eight moons. I can then transform such light into energy. Basic physics, actually. At any rate, I have abilities somewhat more advanced than your own. You have seen but a small demonstration of those abilities."

Ben nodded slowly, feeling a bit uneasy now. "I'll take your word for it."

The cat moved a bit closer to the fire and sat down again. The night sounds had died into stillness. There was a sudden tension in the air. "I have been places others only dream about and I have seen the things that are hidden there. I know many secrets." The cat's voice became a whisper. "Come closer to the fire, High Lord Ben Holiday. Feel the warmth." Ben did as he was told, the cat watching. The emerald eyes seemed to flare anew. "I know of wizards and missing books of magic. I know of black unicorns and white, some lost, some found. I even know something of the deceptions that make some beings seem other than what they are." Ben started to interrupt, but the cat hissed in warning. "No, High Lord—just listen! I am not disposed to converse so freely on most occasions, so it would behoove you to let me finish! Cats seldom have anything to say, but we always know much! So it is in this instance. I know much that is hidden from you. Some of what I know might be useful, some not. It is all a matter of sorting out. But sorting out takes time, and time requires commitment. I give commitment to things but rarely. You, however, as I said, intrigue me. I am thinking about making an exception. What do you think?"

Ben wasn't sure what he thought. How could this cat know about black unicorns and white? How could he know about missing books of magic? How much of this was just talk in general and how much specific to him? He wanted to ask, but he knew as surely as it was night that the cat was not about to answer him. He felt his questions all jumble together in his throat.

"Will you come with me, then?" he asked finally.

The cat blinked. "I am thinking about it."

Ben nodded slowly. "Do you have a name?"

The cat blinked once more. "I have many names, just as I am many things. The name I favor just now is Edgewood Dirk. But you may call me Dirk."

"I am pleased to make your acquaintance, Dirk," Ben said.

"We shall see," Edgewood Dirk answered vaguely. He turned and moved a step or two closer to the fire. "The night wearies me; I prefer the day. I think I shall sleep now." He circled a patch of grass several times and then settled down, curling up into a ball of fur. The glow enveloped him momentarily, and he was fully cat once more. "Good night, High Lord."

"Good night," Ben replied mechanically. He was still taut with the emotions that Dirk had aroused in him. He mulled over what the cat had said, trying to decide how much the creature really knew and how much he was generalizing. The fire crackled and snapped against the darkness, and he moved closer to it for warmth. Whatever the case, Edgewood Dirk might have his uses, he reasoned and stretched his hands toward the flames. If only this strange creature were not so mercurial . . .

And suddenly an unexpected possibility occurred to him.

"Dirk, did you come looking for me?" he asked.

"Ah!" the cat replied softly.

"Did you? Did you deliberately seek me out?"

He waited, but Edgewood Dirk said nothing more. The stillness of a few moments earlier began to fill again with night sounds. The tension within him dissipated. Flames licked against the deadwood and chased the forest shadows. Ben stared over at the sleeping cat and experienced an odd sense of serenity. He no longer felt quite so alone.

He breathed deeply the night air and sighed. No longer alone? Who did he think he was kidding?

He was still trying to decide when he finally fell asleep.

HEALER SPRITE

Ben Holiday awoke at dawn and could not figure out where he was. His disorientation was so complete that for several moments he could remember nothing of the events of the past thirty-six hours. He lay on grasses damp with morning dew in a clearing in a forest and wondered why he wasn't in his own bed at Sterling Silver. He glanced down his body and wondered why he was wearing such shabby clothing. He stared off into the misted trees and wondered what in the hell was going on.

Then he caught sight of Edgewood Dirk perched on a fallen log, sassy and sleek, preening with studied care as he licked himself, all the while studiously ignoring his human company. Ben's situation came back to him then in a rush of unpleasant memories, and he found himself wishing rather ruefully that he had remained ignorant.

He rose, brushed himself off, drank a bit of spring water, and ate a stalk from the Bonnie Blues. The fruit taste was sweet and welcome, but his hunger for more substantial fare was to go unassuaged for yet another meal. He glanced once or twice in Dirk's direction, but the cat went on about the business of washing himself without noticing. Some things obviously took precedence over others.

When Dirk was finally finished, he rose from his sitting position, stretched, and said, "I have decided to come with you."

Ben refrained from saying what he was tempted to say and simply nodded.

"For a while, at least," Dirk added pointedly.

Ben nodded a second time. "Do you know where it is that I intend to go?" he asked.

Dirk gave him one of those patented "must you be such an idiot?" looks and replied, "Why? Don't you?"

They departed the campsite and walked in silence through the early morning hours. The skies were gray and oppressive. A heavily clouded sun lifted sluggishly from out of the tree line, its mist-diffused light sufficiently bright to permit small patches of dull silver to chase the shadows and dot the pathway ahead like stepping stones across a pond. Ben led, Dirk picking his way carefully a yard or two behind. There were no forest sounds to keep them company; the woods seemed empty of life.

They reached the Irrylyn at midmorning and followed its shoreline south along a narrow footpath that wound through forest trees and deadwood. Like the woods surrounding, the lake seemed lifeless. Clouds hung low across its waters, and there was no wind. Ben's thoughts drifted. He found himself reliving his first meeting with Willow. He had come to the lake country seeking the support of the River Master in his effort to claim Landover's throne. Willow and Ben had chanced upon each other bathing naked at night in the warm, spring-fed waters of this lake. He had never seen anyone as beautiful as the sylph. She had given back to him feelings he had thought dead and gone.

He shook his head. The memory left him oddly sad, as if it were an unpleasant reminder of something forever lost. He stared out across the gray, flat surface of the Irrylyn and tried to recapture the moment. But all he found were ghosts at play in the mists.

They broke away from the lake at its southern end and moved back into the forest. It was beginning to spit rain. The small patches of gray sunlight disappeared and shadows closed about. The character of the woods underwent a sudden and distinct change. The trees turned gnarled and damp, monstrous sentinels for a surreal world of imaginary wraiths that slipped like smoke through a mist that shrouded everything. Sounds returned, but they were more haunting than comforting, bits and pieces of life that sprinkled the gloom with hints of what lay hidden. Ben slowed, blinking his eyes, wiping the water from his face. He had made the trip down into the lake country on several occasions since that first meeting with Willow, but each time it had been in the company of the sylph or Questor Thews, and one of the fairy people had always met them. He could find his way as far as the Irrylyn by himself, but he could not find his way much farther than that. If he expected to find the River Master and his people, he was going to have to have some help—and he might not get it. The lake country people lived in Elderew, their home city, hidden somewhere in these forests. No one could find Elderew without help. The River Master could either bring you in or he could leave you out—the choice was his.

He walked a bit farther, saw the path before him disappear completely, and stopped. There was no indication of where to go next. There was no sign of a guide. The forest about him was a sullen wall of damp and gloom.

"Is there a problem of some sort?"

Edgewood Dirk appeared next to him and sat down gingerly, flinching as the rain struck him. Ben had forgotten the cat momentarily. "I'm not sure which way to go," he admitted reluctantly.

"Oh?" Dirk looked at him, and Ben could have sworn the cat shrugged. "Well, I suggest we trust to our instincts."

The cat stood up and padded silently ahead, moving slightly left into the mist. Ben stared after the beast momentarily, then followed. Who knew? Maybe the cat's instincts were worth trusting, he thought. They certainly couldn't be any worse than his own.

They picked their way slowly ahead, slipping through the massive trees, ducking low-hanging branches with mossy trailers, stepping over rotting logs, and skirting marshy patches of black ooze. The rain quickened, and Ben felt his clothing grow damp and heavy. The forest and the mist thickened and wrapped about him like a cloak; everything disappeared outside a ten-foot sweep. Ben heard things moving all about him, but saw nothing. Dirk kept padding steadily on, seemingly oblivious.

Then abruptly a shadow detached itself from the gloom and brought them to a halt. It was a wood sprite, lean and wiry, small as a child, his skin browned and grainy, his hair thick and dark, grown like a mane down the back of his neck and arms. Dressed in nondescript, earth-colored clothing, he seemed as much a part of the forest as the trees and, had he wished, might have disappeared as quickly as he had come. He said nothing as he glanced first at Ben, then at Dirk. He hesitated as he caught sight of the cat, seemed to consider something, then beckoned them forward.

Ben sighed. Halfway home, he thought.

They walked ahead silently, following a narrow trail that wound snakelike through vast, empty stretches of swamp. Fog rolled over the still surface of the water, clouds of impenetrable gray. A thin sheet of rain continued to fall. Shapes darted and glided wraithlike through the gloom, some with faces that were almost human, some with the look of forest creatures. Eyes blinked and peered out at him, then were gone—sprites, nymphs, kelpies, naiads, pixies, elementals of all forms. The fairy worlds of dozens of childhood stories came suddenly to life, an impossible mix of fantasy and truth. As always, it left Ben filled with wonder—and slightly afraid.

The path he followed was unfamiliar to him. It was like that whenever he came to Elderew; the River Master always brought him in a different way. Sometimes he passed through water that rose to his waist; sometimes he passed along marshy earth that sucked eagerly at his boots. Whichever way he came, the swamp was always close about, and he knew that to stray from any of the paths would bring a quick end to him. It always bothered him that not only could he not find his way in, but he could not find his way out again either. That meant he was trapped here if the River Master did not choose to release him. That would not have been a consideration in the past. After all, he had been Landover's King and he had possessed the power of the medallion. But all that was changed now. He had lost both his identity and the medallion. He was just a stranger. The River Master could do as he chose with a stranger.

He was still thinking about his dilemma when they entered a great stand of cyprus, brushed aside curtains of damp moss trailers, wove past massive gnarled roots, and emerged at last from the marsh. Ben's boots found firmer ground, and he began a short climb up a gentle slope. The mist and gloom thinned, cyprus gave way to oak and elm, fetid smells dissipated, and the sweeter scent of open woodlands filled the morning air. Colors reappeared as garlands of rain-soaked flowers strung along hedges and roped from sway bars lined the path. Ben felt a tinge of relief. The way forward was familiar again. He quickened his pace, anxious that the journey be done.

Then the slope crested, the trees parted at the path's end, and there he was. Elderew stretched away before him, the city of the lake country fairies. The great, open-air amphitheater where the people held their festivals stood in the foreground, gray and empty in the rainfall. Massive trees framed its walls, the lower branches connected by sawn logs to form seats, the whole ringing an arena of grasses and wild flowers. Branches interlaced overhead to create a leafy roof, the rain water dripping from its eaves in a steady trickle. Beyond, trees twice the size of California's giant redwoods rose over the amphitheater against the clouded horizon and cradled in their branches the city proper—a broad cluster of cottages and shops interconnected by an intricate network of tree lanes and stairways that stretched from forest earth to treetop and down again.

Ben stopped, stared, and blinked away the rain that ran down his forehead into his eyes. He realized suddenly that he was gaping like the country boy come to the city for the first time. It reminded him of how much a stranger he really was in this land—even after having lived in it for over a year, even though he was its King. It underlined in bold strokes the precariousness of his situation. He had lost even the small recognition he had enjoyed. He was an outsider stripped of friends and means, almost completely reliant on the charity of others.

The River Master appeared from a small stand of trees to one side, flanked by half-a-dozen guards. Tall and lean, his strange scaled skin gleaming with a silver cast where it shone beneath his forest green clothing, the lord of the lake country fairies stalked forward determinedly. His hard, chiseled face did not evidence much in the way of charity. His demeanor, normally calm and unhurried, seemed brusque. He said something to the guide in a dialect Ben did not recognize, but there was no mistaking the tone. The guide stepped back quickly, his small frame rigid, his eyes turned away.

The River Master faced Ben. The silver diadem about his forehead flashed dully with rain water as he tilted his head up. Coarse, black hair rippled along the back of his neck and forearms. There were to be no preliminaries. "Who are you?" he demanded. "What are you doing here?"

Ben had anticipated some resistance, but nothing like this. He had expected that the River Master wouldn't recognize him, and, sure enough, he hadn't. But that didn't explain why the ruler of the once-fairy people was being so deliberately unfriendly. The River Master was surrounded by guards, and they were armed. He had left the members of his family behind where always before he had gathered them about him to receive visitors. He had not waited for Ben to reach the amphitheater, the traditional greeting place for visitors. And his voice reflected undisguised anger and suspicion. Something was dreadfully wrong.

Ben took a deep breath. "River Master, it's me, Ben Holiday," he announced and waited. There wasn't even a hint of recognition in the other's dark eyes. He forged ahead. "I know I don't look like myself, but that's because something has been done to me. A magic has been used to change my appearance. The wizard who served the old King's son, the one who abandoned Landover—he calls himself Meeks in my world—has returned and stolen both my identity and the throne. It's a long story. What's important is that I need your help. I have to find Willow."

The River Master stared, obviously surprised. "*You* are Ben Holiday?"

Ben nodded quickly. "I am—even though I don't appear to be. I'll try to explain. I traveled back to . . ."

"No!" The River Master cut him short with an irritated chop of one hand. "There is only one explanation I wish to hear from you—whoever you are. I wish to know why you brought the cat."

Now it was Ben's turn to stare. Rain water tricked steadily down his face, and he blinked it from his eyes. "The cat?"

"Yes, the cat! The prism cat, the fairy creature who sits next to you—why did you bring it here?" The River Master was a water sprite and there were gills directly below his chin at either side of his throat. He was so agitated now that the gills fluttered uncontrollably.

Surprised, Ben glanced at Dirk, who sat a dozen paces away and washed his paws with what appeared to be total disinterest in the conversation taking place. "I don't understand," he replied finally, looking back again at the River Master. "What's the problem with . . . ?"

"Am I not making myself clear to you?" the River Master interrupted once more, rigid with anger now.

"Well, no, not . . ."

"The cat, I asked you—what is the cat doing here?"

Ben gave up trying to be diplomatic. "Now look. I didn't bring the cat; the cat chose to come. We have a nice working arrangement—I don't tell him where to go or what to do, and he doesn't tell me. So why don't you quit being difficult and tell me what's going on. The only thing I know about prism cats is that they can start campfires and change shape. Obviously you know something more."

The River Master's face tightened. "I do. And I would think that the High Lord of Landover would make it *his* business to know as well!" He came forward a step. "You still claim that you *are* the High Lord, don't you?"

"I most certainly do."

"Even though you look nothing like Ben Holiday at all, you wear a workman's clothing, and you travel without retainers or standard?"

"I explained all that . . ."

"Yes, yes, yes!" The River Master shook his head. "You certainly have the High Lord's boldness, if nothing else."

He seemed to consider the matter for a moment, saying nothing. The guards about him and the chastened guide were like statues. Ben waited impatiently. A handful of faces appeared from behind the trunks of surrounding trees, materializing through the rain and gloom. The River Master's people were growing curious.

Finally, the River Master cleared his throat. "Very well. I don't accept that you are Landover's High Lord, but whoever you are, allow me to explain a few things about the creature with whom you travel. First, prism cats are fairy creatures—true fairy creatures, not exiles and emigrants like the people of the lake country. Prism cats are almost never seen beyond the mists. Second, they do not normally keep company with humans. Third, they are uniformly unpredictable; no one pretends to understand fully what they are about. And fourth, wherever they journey, they bring trouble. You are fortunate that you were allowed into Elderew at all in the company of a prism cat. Had I known that you traveled with one, I would almost certainly have kept you out."

Ben sighed wearily, then nodded. Apparently superstitions about cats weren't confined to just his world. "Okay, I promise to keep all that in mind in the future," he replied, fighting to keep the irritation from his voice. "But the fact remains you did *not* keep me or the cat out, so here we are and whether you believe that I am High Lord of Landover or not doesn't really matter a rat's whiskers. I still need your help if I . . ."

A sudden gust of rain blew into his face, and he choked on what he was about to say next. He paused, shivering within the cold and damp of his clothing. "Do you suppose that we could continue this discussion somewhere dry?" he asked quietly.

The other man studied him silently, his expression unchanged.

"River Master, your daughter may be in great danger," Ben whispered. "Please!"

The River Master continued to study him a moment longer, then beckoned him to follow. A wave of one hand dismissed the guide. The faces of the watching villagers disappeared just as quickly. They walked a short distance through the trees to a gazebolike shelter formed of sculpted spruce, the guards trailing watchfully. A pair of benches sat within the shelter facing each other over a broad, hollowed stump converted to a planter of flowers. The River Master seated himself on one bench, and Ben took the other. The rain continued to fall all about them, a soft, steady patter on the forest trees and earth, but it was dry within the shelter.

Dirk appeared, jumped up beside Ben, settled down with all four paws tucked away, and closed his eyes sleepily.

The River Master glanced at the cat with renewed irritation, then squared around to Ben once more. "Say what you would," he advised.

Ben told him the whole story. He felt he had nothing to lose in doing so. He told him about the dreams, the journeys embarked upon by Questor, Willow, and himself, the discovery of the missing books of magic, the unexpected appearance of Meeks, the theft of both his identity and the medallion, and his exile from Sterling Silver. The River Master listened without comment. He sat there as if he had been carved from stone, unmoving, his eyes fastened on Ben's. Ben finished, and the lord of the lake country people remained a statue.

"I don't know what else I can say to you," Ben said finally.

The River Master responded with a barely perceptible nod, but still said nothing.

"Listen to me," Ben pleaded. "I have to find Willow and warn her that this dream of the black unicorn was sent by Meeks and I don't think I can do that without your help." He paused, suddenly reminded of a truth that he still had difficulty acknowledging—even to himself. "Willow means a great deal to me, River Master. I care for her; you must know that. Now tell me—has she been here?"

The River Master pulled his forest cloak closer about him. The look in his eyes was distant. "I think perhaps you are who you claim to be," he said softly. "I think perhaps you are the High Lord. Perhaps."

He rose, glanced from his shelter at the guards who ringed them, motioned all but one of them away, and came over to stand next to Ben. He bent down, his strange, wooden face right next to Ben's. "High Lord or fraud, tell me the truth now—how is it that you come to travel with this cat?"

Ben forced himself to stay calm. "It was a matter of chance. The cat found me at the edge of the lake country last night and suggested his company might be useful. I'm still waiting to find out if that's true."

He looked down at Dirk momentarily, half expecting the cat to confirm what he had said. But Dirk sat there with his eyes closed and said nothing. It occurred to Ben suddenly that the cat hadn't said a word since they had arrived in Elderew. He wondered why.

"Give me your hand," the River Master said suddenly. He reached down with his own and clasped Ben's tightly. "There is one way in which I may be able to test the truth of your claim. Do you remember when you first came to Elderew and we walked alone through the village and talked of the magic of the lake country people?" Ben nodded. "Do you remember what I showed you of the magic?"

The pressure of his grip was like an iron bar. Ben winced, but did not try to pull away. "You touched a bush stricken with wilt and healed it," he replied, his eyes locked on those of the other man. "You were attempting to show me why the lake country people could manage on their own. Later, you refused to give your pledge to the throne." He paused deliberately. "But you have given it since, River Master—and you have given it to me."

The River Master studied him a moment, then pulled him effortlessly to his feet. "I have said that you could be Ben Holiday," he whispered, his hard face bent close. "I believe it possible." He placed both of Ben's hands in his own. "I do not know how your appearance was altered, but if magic changed you to what you are, then magic can be used to change you back again. I possess the power to heal much that is sickened and distressed. I will use that power to help you if I can." The scaled hands tightened harder about Ben's. "Stand where you are and do not move."

Ben took a quick breath. The River Master's grip warmed his own, and the chiseled features lowered into shadow. Ben waited. The other's breathing slowed and a sudden flush spread through Ben's body. He shivered at the feeling, but remained stationary.

Finally the River Master stepped back. There was a hint of confusion in the dark eyes. "I am sorry, but I cannot help you," he said finally. "Magic has indeed been used to alter your appearance. But the magic is not of another's making—it is of your own."

Ben stared. "What?"

"You have made yourself who and what you are," the other said. "You must be the one to change yourself back again."

"But that doesn't make any sense!" Ben exploded. "I haven't done a thing to change what I look like—it was Meeks! I watched him do it! He stole the medallion of the Kings of Landover and gave me . . . this!"

He yanked the tarnished image of Meeks from his tunic and thrust it out angrily, almost as if to snap it from its chain. The River Master studied it a moment, touched it experimentally, then shook his head. "The image graven here is clouded in the same manner as your appearance. The magic at work is again of your own making."

Ben's jaw tightened, and he snatched the medallion back again. The River Master was talking in riddles. Whatever magic was at work was most assuredly not of Ben's making. The River Master was either mistaken or misled—or he was deliberately trying to confuse Ben because he still didn't trust him.

The River Master seemed to read his mind. He shrugged. "Believe me or don't—the choice is yours. What I tell you is what I see." He paused. "If this new medallion you wear was given to you by your enemy, perhaps you should discard it. Is there a reason you keep it?"

Ben sighed. "Meeks told me that the medallion would let him know what I was about. He warned that a certain magic protects against trying to remove it—a magic that could kill me."

"But is that so?" the other asked. "Perhaps the wizard lied."

Ben hesitated before replying. He had considered that possibility before. After all, why should he believe anything Meeks told him? The problem was that there was no way to test the truth of the matter without risking his life.

He lifted the tarnished medallion before him experimentally. "I have given it some thought . . ." he began.

Then out of the corner of his eye, he saw Edgewood Dirk stir. The cat's head lifted, and the green eyes snapped open. It was almost as if the cat had roused himself from his near-comatose state for the express purpose of seeing what Ben would do. The strange eyes were fixed and staring. Ben hesitated, then slowly lowered the medallion back inside his tunic. "I think maybe I need to give it some more thought," he finished.

Dirk's eyes slipped closed again. The black face lowered. Rain beat down steadily in the momentary stillness, and a long peal of thunder rolled across the lake country from somewhere east. Ben experienced a strange mix of frustration and anger. What sort of game was the cat playing now?

The River Master moved back to the other bench and remained standing. "It appears I cannot help you after all," he advised. "I think that you had better go—you and the cat."

Ben saw his chance for any help slipping away. He rose quickly. "At least tell me where to find Willow," he begged. "She said she was coming here to the lake country to learn the meaning of her dream. Surely she would come to you for help."

The River Master studied him silently for a moment, considering in his own mind things hidden from Ben, then shook his head slowly. "No, High Lord or pretender—whichever you are—she would not."

He came partway around the stump once more, then stopped. Wind blew sharply at his cloak, and he pulled it close to ward away the chill of the rain. "I am her father, but not the parent from whom she would seek help when it was needed. I was never that. I have many children by many wives. Some I am closer to than others. Willow has never been close to me. She is too much like her mother—a wild thing who seeks only to sever ties, not to bind them. Neither seeks companionship from me; neither ever did. The mother came to me only once, then was gone again, back into the forest . . ."

He trailed off, distracted. "I never even knew her name," he continued after a moment. "A wood nymph, no more than a tiny bit of silk and light, she dazzled me so that names were of no consequence for that one night. I lost her without ever really having had her. I lost Willow, I think, because of what that did to me. I begrudged the mother her freedom, and Willow was forced to live with my anger and resentment. That caused her to slip gradually from me, and there was no help for it. I loved her mother so much that I could neither forgive nor forget what she had done to me. When I gave Willow permission to live at Sterling Silver, I severed the only tie that still bound us. She became forever her own woman and my daughter no longer. Now she sees me as a man who has more children than he can ever truly be father to. She chooses not to be one of those."

He turned away, lost perhaps in memories. His confession was a strange one, Ben thought—told simply and directly, but without a trace of emotion. There had been no inflection in the River Master's voice, no expression in his face. Willow meant much to him, and yet he could demonstrate nothing of it—he could only relate the fact of its being. It made Ben wonder suddenly about his own feelings for the sylph and question what they were.

The River Master stared out into the rain for a time, motionless, silent, and then he shrugged. "I could heal so much, but not that," he said quietly. "I did not know how." Suddenly he looked back again at Ben—and it was as if he were seeing him for the first time. "Why is it that I tell this to *you*?" he whispered in surprise.

Ben had no idea. He kept silent as the River Master stared at him as if mystified by his even being there. Then the lord of the lake country people seemed simply to dismiss the matter. His voice was flat and cold. "You waste your time with me. Willow will go to her mother. She will go to the old pines and dance."

"Then I will search for her there," Ben said. He rose to his feet. The River Master watched him, silent. Ben hesitated. "You need not send a guide with me. I know the way."

The River Master nodded, still silent. Ben started away, walked a dozen paces from the shelter, stopped, and turned. The single remaining guard had faded back into the trees. The two men were alone. "Would you like to come with me?" Ben asked impulsively.

But the River Master was staring out into the rain again, lost in its dull silver glitter, lost in its patter. The gills on his neck slowed to a barely perceptible flutter. The hard, chiseled face seemed emptied of life.

"He doesn't hear you," Edgewood Dirk said suddenly. Ben glanced down in surprise and found the cat at his feet. "He has gone inside of himself to discover where he's been. It happens like that sometimes after revealing something so carefully guarded for so long."

Ben frowned. "Carefully guarded? Do you mean what he said about Willow? About her mother?" The frown deepened as he knelt next to the cat. "Dirk, why *did* he tell me all that? He's not even sure who I am."

Dirk looked over at him. "There are many forms of magic in this world, High Lord. Some come in large packages, some in small. Some work with fire and strength of body and heart . . . and some work with revelation."

"Yes, but why . . . ?"

"Listen to me, High Lord! Listen!" Dirk's voice was a hiss. "So few humans listen to anything a cat has to say. Most only talk to us. They talk to us because we are such good listeners, you see. They find comfort in our presence. We do not question and we do not judge. We simply listen. They talk, and we listen. They tell us everything! They tell us their innermost thoughts and dreams, things they would tell no other. Sometimes, High Lord, they do all this without even understanding why!"

He was still again, and suddenly it occurred to Ben that Dirk wasn't speaking in general terms, but in very specific ones. He wasn't talking about just everyone, but about someone definite. His eyes lifted to find the solitary figure of the River Master.

And then he thought suddenly about himself.

"Dirk, what . . . ?"

"Shhhhhh!" The cat hushed him into silence. "Let the stillness be, High Lord. Do not disturb it. If you are able, listen to its voice—but let it be."

The cat moved slowly off into the trees, picking his way gingerly over the damp, water-soaked forest earth. Rain fell in steady sheets out of skies clouded over from horizon to horizon, a gray ceiling canopied above the trees. Silence filled the gaps left by the sound of the rain, cloaking the city of Elderew, the houses and tree lanes, the walkways and parks, and the vast, empty amphitheater that loomed behind the still-motionless figure of the River Master. Ben listened as Dirk had said he should and he could almost hear the silence speak.

But what was it saying to him? What was it that he was supposed to learn? He shook his head hopelessly. He didn't know.

Dirk had disappeared into the haze ahead of him, a pale gray shadow. Abandoning his efforts to listen further, Ben hurried after.

DANCE

That there was something inordinately peculiar about Edgewood Dirk was no longer a matter for debate with Ben Holiday. You might have argued that *all* cats were somewhat peculiar and that it should come as no surprise therefore that a cat out of the fairy world would turn out to be even *more* peculiar than your average feline, but Ben would have disagreed. The sort of peculiar exhibited by Dirk went far beyond anything encountered in—oh, say—*Alice in Wonderland* or *Dick Whittington*. Dirk lent a whole new meaning to the word, and the most aggravating part of all was the fact that, try as Ben might, he could not decipher what it was that the beast was about!

In short, who was this cat, and what was he doing here with Ben?

He would have loved to find immediate answers to his questions, but time did not permit it. The cat was leading the way once more—presumptuous beast that it was—and he was forced once again to hurry after. Rain pelted his face in a quickening downpour, and the wind gusted in chill swipes. Nightfall was approaching and the weather was growing worse. Ben was drenched, cold, hungry, and discouraged, despite his resolve to continue, and he found himself wishing fondly for a warm bed and dry clothes. But he was unlikely to find either just now. The River Master was barely tolerating his presence as it was, and he must use the time that remained to him to try to find Willow.

He passed through the city of Elderew, head bent against the weather, another of dusk's faceless shadows, then plunged into the forest beyond. The lights of cottages and homes disappeared behind him, and the darkness closed about in a wet, rain-sodden curtain. Trailers of mist floated past like kite tails broken free from their winged flyers, touching and rubbing, forming into gradually thickening sheets. Ben ignored it all and pushed on. He had gone to the old pines often enough to know the way blindfolded.

He arrived at the clearing moments later—several steps behind Edgewood Dirk. He glanced about expectantly, but there was nothing to be found. The clearing sat empty, ringed by the old pines, ancient sentinels of the forest, as damp and cold as the rest of the land. He cast about briefly for tracks or other signs of Willow's passing, but there was nothing to indicate whether the sylph had been there or not.

Edgewood Dirk paced the clearing once, sniffing at the earth, then retreated to the shelter of a pine's spreading boughs and sat down daintily. "She was here two nights ago, High Lord," he announced. "She was seated close to where you stand while her mother danced, then let the change take her. She left at dawn."

Ben stared at the cat. "How do you know all this?"

"A good nose," Dirk advised disdainfully. "You should cultivate one. It can tell you all sorts of things you would miss otherwise. My nose tells me what your eyes cannot tell you."

Ben moved over and hunched down in front of the cat, ignoring the water that dripped off the pine's branches and ran down his face in steady streams. "Does your nose tell you where she has gone now?" he asked quietly.

"No," the cat answered.

"No?"

"You are repeating me without need," Dirk sniffed.

"But if your nose told you all the rest, why can't it tell you that?" Ben demanded. "Is your nose always this selective?"

"Sarcasm does not become you, High Lord," Dirk admonished, head cocking slightly. "Besides, I deserve better than that. I am, after all, your sole companion and supporter in this venture."

"Which needs some explaining, I might point out," Ben snapped. "You persist in taunting me with what you know, then tell me only what you wish, I realize that you have a perfectly good excuse for this behavior, being a cat, but I hope I can impress on you how aggravating it is to me!" His temper was getting the better of him, and his voice was rising. "I simply asked how you could determine that Willow was here, that her mother danced, that she transformed, and yet not be able to tell me where . . ."

"I don't know."

". . . she might have gone after leaving . . . What? You don't know? You don't know what?"

"I don't know why I don't know."

Ben stared once more.

"I should be able to read her passing from the clearing, but I can't," Dirk finished calmly. "It is almost as if it was deliberately hidden."

Ben took a moment to consider this new piece of information, then shook his head. "But why would she hide where she was going?"

Dirk did not answer. Instead, he hissed softly in warning and rose to his feet once more. Ben stood up with him and turned. The River Master's dark figure reappeared from out of the mist, striding the length of the clearing to where Ben waited. He was alone.

"Has Willow been here?" he asked abruptly.

Ben hesitated, then nodded. "Been and gone. The cat says her mother danced for her two nights ago."

There was anger reflected in the eyes of the water sprite, but he smoothed it away quickly. "She would appear to her daughter, of course," he murmured. "They share that bond. The dance would reveal truth in the fairy way, would show what was sought . . ." He trailed off, as if thinking of something else, then straightened. "Have you determined where she has gone, High Lord?"

Again Ben hesitated, this time as much in surprise as out of caution. The River Master had called him High Lord. Had he now decided to accept Ben's claim? Ben met his steady gaze. "Her trail has been concealed from us," he said. "Hidden deliberately, the cat thinks."

The River Master glanced briefly at Dirk, frowning. "Perhaps." His chiseled face swung back on Ben. "But my daughter lacks the guile and her mother the means. The concealment, if there be one, comes from another source. There are some who would help her and not tell me. There are some." The anger in his eyes flared anew, then was gone. "Still, it hardly matters. I have the means to find her anyway. And anything else I wish."

Abruptly he turned, muttering. "Time slips away. The rain and the dark will hamper my efforts as it is. I must act quickly if I am to be effective." There was an urgency in his voice—and a determination. "I will not have these games played behind my back. I will know the meaning of the dream of the black unicorn and the golden bridle and I will know it whether Willow and her mother wish me to or not!"

He disappeared back into the forest in a rush, not bothering to see if Ben was following. He needn't have worried. Ben was right on his heels.

Edgewood Dirk stayed beneath the pine boughs and watched them go. After a moment, he began to clean himself.

The River Master had undergone such a complete transformation that Ben could scarcely believe it. One moment he was disinterested in the matter of his daughter and the black unicorn, the next he could not find out about them quickly enough. He strode back through the forest to the edge of the city, calling his guard to him as he went. Retainers appeared from everywhere, hanging at his side momentarily for their instructions, then disappearing back into the night. Like shadows, they came and disappeared again, a smattering of sprites, kelpies, naiads, and others—voiceless, momentary appendages to the dark figure of their lord. The River Master spoke rapidly and precisely, then turned away from each, his pace never slowing. He skirted almost furtively the boundaries of Elderew proper and turned back into the forest. Ben trailed after, all but forgotten.

The moments slipped by as they passed deeper into the forest trees, east and north of the city now. Nightfall had closed down so tightly that nothing beyond a dozen feet was visible. The rain washed over both of them in sheets, a steady downpour that showed little sign of abating. Thunder rolled out of the skies in long peals, and lightning split the clouds from somewhere distant. The worst of the storm had not reached them yet. It was still coming.

The River Master seemed oblivious. His concentration was absolute. Ben began to wonder what was going on and to grow uneasy.

Then they emerged from the trees onto a broad hillside clearing that stretched downward to a vast lake into which a pair of rivers fed at opposite ends. The rivers, swollen with rain water, cascaded down through rocky gorges that fell away from heights anchored by massive clusters of the giant redwood-like trees. The lake roiled with the pumping action, and the flare of new lightning danced and glimmered with a mix of torchlight from stanchions that ran the length and breadth of the hills in widening arcs and lit the whole of the slope. Ben slowed and stared out into the black. The lake country people seemed to be everywhere—or were there simply a few amid the vast number of torches? Wind whipped the rain into his eyes, and he could not tell.

The River Master turned, saw he was still there, and beckoned him forward to a shelf of rock that jutted out from the hillside and overlooked the rivers, the lake, and the weaving lines of torchlight. The fury of the storm broke over them as they stood on the unsheltered platform, pressed close against each other, their words almost lost in the howl of the wind.

"Watch now, High Lord!" the River Master shouted, his strange, chiseled face inches from Ben's. "I cannot command Willow's mother to dance for me as she danced for her daughter, but I can command her kindred! I will know what secrets are kept from me!"

Ben nodded mutely. There was a frenzy in the other's eyes that he had never seen before—a frenzy that hinted of passion.

The River Master signaled, and a sticklike being approached from out of the night, a creature so thin that it appeared to have been fashioned of deadwood. Rough woolen clothing hung about its body, whipped by the wind, and green cornsilk hair ran from the crown of its head to the nape of its neck and along its spine and the backs of its arms and legs. Its features were formed of what looked to be a series of slits cut into the wood of its face. It carried a set of music pipes in one hand.

"Play!" the River Master commanded, one hand sweeping the valley slope. "Call them!"

The stick creature hunched down against the sodden earth, settled itself with its legs crossed before it, and brought the pipes to its lips. The music began softly, a sweet, lilting cadence that rocked in the troughs of momentary stillness left by lulls in the wind's deep howl. It meshed and blended with the sounds of the storm, weaving its way through the fabric like thread hand-sewn. It had the texture of silk, smooth and quiet, and it wrapped itself about the listeners like a blanket. Downward along the slope it carried, and there was the sense of something changing in the air.

"Hear it!" the River Master said in Ben's ear, exultant.

The player of the pipes lifted the pitch gradually, and the song rose higher into the fury of the storm. Slowly it transcended the dark and the wet and the chill, and the whole of their surroundings began to alter. The howl of the storm diminished as if blanketed away, the chill gave way to warmth, and the night brightened as if dawn had come already. Ben felt himself lifted as on a cushion of air. He blinked, disbelieving. Everything about him was changing—shape, substance, time, everything. There was a magic in the music that was greater than any he had ever encountered, a power that could alter even nature's great force.

Torchlight brightened as if the fires had been given new life, and the slope was lit with their glow. But there was a new glow as well, a glow that hung on the night air like incandescence. It radiated out across the slope and downward to the waters of the lake. The waters had gone still, the churning smoothed away as a mother's hand would smooth a sleeping child's ruffled hair. The glow danced at the water's edge, a living thing.

"There, High Lord—look!" the River Master urged.

Ben stared. Bits and pieces of the glow had begun to take shape. Dancing, whirling, lifting against the torchlight, they had begun to assume the forms of fairy creatures. Slight, airy things, they gathered strength from the glow and from the music of the pipes and took life. Ben knew them instantly. They were wood nymphs, the same as Willow's mother—childlike creatures as insubstantial as smoke. Limbs flashed and glistened nut-brown, hair tumbled waist-length, tiny faces lifted skyward. Dozens of them appeared as if from nowhere and danced and flitted at the shores of the mirrored lake in a kaleidoscope of movement.

The music heightened. The glow radiated the warmth of a summer's day, and colors began to appear in its brightness—rainbow shades that mixed and spread like an artist's brush strokes on canvass. Shape and form began to alter, and Ben felt himself transported to another time and place. He was young again, and the world was all new. The lifting sensation he had experienced earlier intensified, and he was floating free of the earth, free of gravity's pull. The River Master and the player of the pipes floated with him, birdlike in the sweep of sound and color. Still the wood nymphs danced below him, whirling with a new exhilaration into the glow, into the air. They spun outward from the shore's edge, skipping weightless across the waters of the still lake, their tiny forms barely touching the mirrored surface. Slowly they came together at the lake's center, forming intricate patterns as they linked briefly and broke away again, linked and broke away.

Above them, an image began to take shape in the air.

"Now it comes!" the River Master breathed from somewhere so distant that Ben could barely hear him.

The image came clear, and it was Willow. She stood alone at the edge of a lake—this lake—and held in her hand the bridle of spun gold that was the vision of her dream. She was clothed in white silk, and her beauty was a radiance that outshone even that created by the music of the player and the dance of the wood nymphs. Flushed with life, her face lifted against the colors that spun about her, and her long green tresses fanned out in the whisper of the wind. She held the bridle out from her as if it were a gift and she waited.

Beware! a voice warned suddenly, a voice so tiny as to be almost lost in the whirl of the vision.

Ben wrenched his eyes momentarily from Willow. From what seemed an impossible distance below, Edgewood Dirk stared up at him.

"What's wrong?" Ben managed to ask.

But the question was irretrievably lost in what happened next. The music had reached a fever pitch, so intense that it locked away everything. The world was gone. There was only the lake, the whirl of the wood nymphs, and the vision of Willow. Colors flooded Ben's vision with impossibly bright hues, and there were tears in his eyes. He had never known such happiness. He felt as if he were breaking apart inside and had been transformed.

Then something new appeared at the edge of the lake, beyond the nymphs and the vision of Willow—something at once both impossibly lovely and terrifying. Ben heard the muffled cry of the River Master. It was a cry of fulfillment. The whirl of sound and color shimmered and bent like fabric stretched, and the intrusion from without stepped gingerly into its weave.

It was the black unicorn.

Ben felt his breath catch in his throat. There was a burning in his eyes and a sudden, impossible sense of need. He had never seen anything as beautiful as the unicorn. Even Willow in the vision of the wood nymphs was but a pale shadow next to the fairy creature. Its delicate body seemed to sway with the music and the dance as it emerged from the dark into the sweep of color, and its horn glowed white with the magic of its being.

Then Dirk's warning came again, no more than a memory this time. *Beware!*

"What is happening?" Ben whispered.

The River Master turned back to him now, head swinging about in slow motion. The hard face was alive with feelings that danced across its chiseled surface in waves of light and color. He spoke, yet the words seemed to come not from his mouth, but from his mind. "I will have him, High Lord! I will have his magic for my own, and it will become a part of my land and my people! He must belong to me! He must!"

And Ben saw suddenly, through the blanket of pleasant feelings and through the music and the dance, the truth of what the River Master was about. The River Master had not summoned the piper and the wood nymphs for the purpose of discovering anything of Willow or her mother. His ambition was much greater than that. He had summoned piper and nymphs to bring him the black unicorn. He had used music and dance to create the illusion of his daughter and her bridle of spun gold to draw the unicorn to the lakeside where it might be taken. The River Master had believed Ben's story all right—but he had decided that the black unicorn would better serve his own purposes than the purposes of a dethroned and powerless King. He had taken Willow's dream and made it his own. This whole business was an elaborate charade—the piper and the wood nymphs and the instruments used to create it.

And, oh, God, it had worked! The black unicorn had come!

He watched the unicorn now in fascination, unable to turn away, knowing he must do something to prevent what was about to happen, but frozen by the beauty and intensity of the vision. The unicorn shone like a bit of flawless night against the sweep of colors that had drawn it in. It nodded its slender head to the call of the music and cried once to the vision of the girl with her golden bridle. It was a fairy-tale rendering brought to life, and the loveliness of it was compelling. Goat's feet pranced and lion's tail swished, and the unicorn stepped further into the trap.

I have to stop it! Ben felt himself trying to scream.

And then the fabric through which the black unicorn had passed so easily seemed to shred at its center point high above the vision and the wood nymphs, and a nightmare born of other minds and needs thrust its way into view. It was a loathsome thing, a creature of scales and spikes, of teeth and claws, winged and coated in a black ooze that steamed at the warmth of the air. A cross between a serpent and a wolf, it forced its way in from the night and the storm and plummeted toward the lake, shrieking.

Ben went cold. He had seen this being before. It was a demon out of the netherworld of Abaddon—a twin to the monster once ridden in battle by the Iron Mark.

It came for them in a fury, then veered sharply as it caught sight of the black unicorn. The unicorn saw the demon as well and screamed a terrifying, high-pitched cry. The ridged horn glowed white-hot with magic, and the unicorn leaped sideways as the demon swept by it, talons raking the empty air. Then the unicorn was gone, fled back into the night, having disappeared as suddenly as it had come.

The River Master cried out in anguish and fury. The demon swung back around, and fire lanced from its open maw. The flames engulfed the piper and turned the sticklike figure to ash. Sound and color dissipated into mist, and the night returned. Darkness flooded inward as the vision of Willow and the golden bridle collapsed. Ben stood once more on the shelf of rock beside the River Master, and the fury of the storm washed over them anew.

But the wood nymphs whirled on, still caught up in the frenzy of their dance. It was as if they could not stop. All about the lake's shores they spun, tiny bits of glowing light in the black and the wet. Torches fizzled and went dark, blown out by the rain and the wind, and only the light of the wood nymphs was left against the night. It drew the demon like a hunter to its prey. The monster swung back and down, sweeping the lake end to end, fire bursting from its throat and turning the helpless dancers to ash. The screams as they died were tiny shrieks that lacked real substance, and they disappeared as if candles snuffed. The River Master howled in despair, but could not save them. One by one they died, burned away by the demon as it passed back and forth across the night like death's shadow.

Ben was beside himself. He could not bear the destruction. But he could not turn away. He acted finally because the horror was too much to stand further. He acted without thinking, yanking the tarnished medallion from beneath his tunic as he would have in the old days, thrusting it out against the night, shouting in fury at the winged demon.

He had forgotten momentarily what medallion it was he wore.

The demon turned and glided toward him. Ben was suddenly conscious of Dirk at his feet, sitting motionless next to him. He was conscious now, too, of the fact that by drawing attention to himself he had just signed his own death warrant.

Then lightning flashed, and the demon saw clearly the medallion, Ben Holiday, and Edgewood Dirk. The beast hissed with the fury of steam released through a fissure in the earth, and swung abruptly away. It flew back into the night and was gone.

Ben was shaking. He didn't know what had happened. He only knew that for some unexplainable reason he was still alive. Below, the last of the wood nymphs had ceased finally to dance and disappeared back into forest, the loss of light from their passing leaving dark the whole of the lake and hills. Wind and rain lashed the emptiness that remained.

Ben stilled his hands. Slowly he placed the medallion back within his tunic. It burned against his skin.

The River Master had sunk to one knee. His eyes were fixed on Ben. "That thing knew you!" he cried in anger.

"No, it couldn't have . . ." Ben began.

"The medallion!" the other cut him short. "It knew the medallion! There is a tie between you that you cannot explain away!" He rose to his feet, his breath a sharp hiss. "You have made me lose everything! You have cost me the unicorn! You have caused the destruction of my piper and my wood nymphs. You and that cat! I warned you about that cat! Trouble follows a prism cat everywhere! Look what you have done! Look what you have caused!"

Ben recoiled. "I haven't . . ."

But the River Master cut him short once more. "I want you gone! I am no longer sure who you are and I no longer care! I want you gone from my country now—and the cat as well! If I find you here come morning, I will put you into the swamp in a place from which you will never escape! Now go!"

The fury in his voice defied argument. The River Master had been cheated of something he had wanted very badly and he had made up his mind that Ben was at fault. It made no difference that his wants had been selfish ones or that he had been deprived of something to which he had not been entitled in the first place. It was of no importance that he had misused Ben. All he could see was the loss.

Ben felt an odd emptiness within him. He had expected better of the River Master.

He turned without a word and walked away into the night.

EARTH MOTHER

The rain and the chill turned Ben Holiday into a sodden, disheveled mess as he trudged back through the forest trees from the empty hillside and the angry River Master, and his appearance became an accurate reflection of his mood. The mix of emotions he had experienced from the music of the pipes, the dance of the wood nymphs, the vision of Willow and what followed was still tearing at him with all the savagery and persistence of a wolf pack. He could still feel twinges of the ecstasy and freedom of self that the music and dance had brought, but the predominant feelings were of dismay and horror.

The images played out in the dark solitude of his mind: the River Master, anxious to seize the black unicorn so that its magic might be his alone; that winged demon, burning the frail wood nymphs to ash as they whirled helplessly at the water's edge; Ben himself, instinctively holding forth the blackened image of Meeks as if it were a talisman that would somehow be recognized . . .

And perhaps it was.

Damn, what had happened there? What was it that had happened? The winged creature had come for him to destroy him, then turned aside as if it had flown into a wall! Had it been the medallion, Ben, Edgewood Dirk, or perhaps something else entirely?

The River Master clearly thought it was the medallion. He was convinced that Ben was bound to the demon—and to Meeks—in some foul way that protected all three. Ben shivered. He had to admit to the possibility. The image of Meeks might have been enough to turn back the demon . . .

He stopped. That was assuming that the demon had been sent by Meeks, of course. But wasn't it the only possibility that made sense? Hadn't Meeks invited the demons out of Abaddon in the first place when the old King died? Ben started walking again. Yes, it had to be Meeks. He must have sent the demon because he knew the River Master was close to capturing the black unicorn, and he wanted the unicorn for himself—for whatever reason. But that meant he must have had some way of knowing that the River Master was about to capture the unicorn, and that in turn meant that Ben's medallion might have provided such a way. Meeks had warned that the medallion would let him know what Ben was about. The medallion might have done exactly that. Ben might indeed have been responsible for the destruction of the wood nymphs.

The screams of the dying fairy creatures still echoed in the dark corners of his mind, a savage reminder. Until they died, he had not even thought of them as real—just bits and pieces of light with human images cast upon the glow; slender, lyrical figurines that would shatter like glass if dropped . . .

The whole mixed and teased in his mind until at last he shoved all the pieces aside violently. His questions bred more questions, and there seemed to be answers for none of them. The rain beat down in a wet staccato, drumming, puddling in mud and grasses, and running across the pathway he followed in small rivers. He could feel the cold and the dark pressing in about him and he wished faintly for a moment's warmth and a spark of light. He walked; yet he was not really aware of where it was he was going. Away, he decided. Away from the River Master and the lake country, away from the one good chance he had of finding Willow before Meeks.

His boots slapped at the mud and damp. But where was he to go?

He cast about suddenly for Edgewood Dirk. Where was that confounded cat? It was always there when he didn't need it; where was it now that he did? Dirk always seemed to know which way to go. The cat seemed to know everything.

Dirk had even known what the River Master was trying to do with the music of the piper and the dance of the wood nymphs, Ben thought as he reflected on the events that had just taken place.

Beware, the cat had warned.

Convenient, that.

His thoughts twisted, and he found himself thinking again of the medallion. Had it really brought the demon? Had it really been responsible for the destruction of the wood nymphs and the piper? He couldn't live with that. Perhaps he ought simply to get rid of the thing. After all, what if it actually did work to the benefit of the wizard if Ben kept it on? Maybe that was exactly what Meeks wanted. The warning against trying to remove it might be a ruse. If he took it off, maybe he would be free of the wizard.

He stopped once more and reached down into his tunic. He placed his fingers about the chain from which the medallion hung and slowly lifted it free. Staring at it in the dark, seeing its muted, tarnished image glimmer in the brief flashes of lightning that streaked the forest skies, he had an incredibly strong urge to fling the unsettling piece of metal from him. If he did so, he might set himself free, redeem himself in part at least for the destruction of the wood nymphs. He might begin anew . . .

"Ah, my dear High Lord, there you are—wandering about in the dark like some blind 'possum. I thought I had lost you completely."

Edgewood Dirk stepped delicately from the trees, his immaculate coat glistening with rain water, his whiskers drooping slightly with the damp. He walked over to a fallen log and sat down on the dampened bark with studied care.

"Where have *you* been?" Ben snapped irritably. He hesitated, then let the medallion drop back into his tunic.

"Looking for you, of course," Dirk replied calmly. "It seems that you need a great deal of looking after."

"Is that so?" Ben was steamed. He was weary, frightened, disgusted, and a dozen other unpleasant things, but most of all he was sick and tired of being treated like a lost puppy by this damn cat. "Well, if ever there was someone suited to the task of looking after people, it's you, isn't it? Edgewood Dirk, caretaker of lost souls. Who else possesses such marvelous insight into human character? Who else discerns the truth of things with such remarkable consistency? Tell me again, Dirk—how is it that you know so much? Come on, tell me! How did you know what the River Master was doing back there before I did? How did you know he was summoning the unicorn? Why did you let me just stand there and be part of it? Those wood nymphs probably died because of me! Why did you let that happen?"

The cat stared at him pointedly for a moment, then began to wash. Ben waited. Dirk seemed oblivious to his presence.

"Well?" Ben said finally.

The cat looked up. "You do have a lot of questions, don't you, High Lord?" The pink tongue licked out. "Why is it that you keep looking to me for the answers?"

"Because you seem to have them, damn it!"

"What seems to be and what actually is are quite different, High Lord—a lesson you have yet to learn. I have instinct and I have common sense; sometimes I can discern things more easily than humans. I am not, however, a vast reservoir of answers to questions. There is a difference." He sneezed. "Besides, you mistake the nature of our relationship yet again. I am a cat and I don't have to tell you anything. I am your companion in this adventure, not your mentor. I am here at my own sufferance and I can leave when I choose. I need answer to no one—least of all you. If you desire answers to your questions, I suggest you find them yourself. The answers are all there if you would make the necessary effort to look for them."

"You could have warned me!"

"You could have warned yourself. You simply didn't bother. Be grateful that I chose to intervene at all."

"But the wood nymphs . . ."

"Why is it," the cat cut him short, "that you continually insist on asking for things to which you are not entitled? I am not your *deus ex machina*!"

Ben choked back whatever he was about to say next and stared. *Deus ex machina!* "You speak Latin?" he asked in disbelief.

"And I read Greek," Dirk answered.

Ben nodded, wishing as he did that he might solve even a small part of the mystery of the cat. "Did you know ahead of time that the wood nymphs were going to be destroyed?" he asked finally.

The cat took its time answering. "I knew that the demon would not destroy you."

"Because ?"

"Because you are the High Lord."

"A High Lord no one recognizes, however."

"A High Lord who won't recognize himself."

Ben hesitated. He wanted to say, "I do, but my appearance has been changed and my medallion has been stolen, and so on and so forth." But he didn't because this was a road they had traveled down already. He simply said, "If the demon couldn't recognize me, then how did you know he wouldn't destroy me?"

Dirk almost seemed to shrug. "The medallion."

Ben nodded. "Then I think I should get rid of the medallion. I think the medallion caused what happened back there—the appearance of the demon, the destruction of the wood nymphs, all of it. I think I should chuck it as far away as I can, Dirk."

Dirk rose and stretched. "I think you should see what the mud puppy wants first," he said.

His gaze shifted and Ben's followed. Rain and gloom almost hid the small, dark shape that crouched a dozen feet away on a scattering of pine needles. It was an odd-looking creature, vaguely reminiscent of a beaver with long ears. It stared back at him with eyes that glowed bright yellow in the dark.

"What is it?" he asked Dirk.

"A wight that scavenges and cleans up after other creatures—a sort of four-legged housekeeper."

"What does it want?"

Dirk managed to look put upon. "Why ask me? Why not ask the mud puppy?"

Ben sighed. Why not, indeed? "Can I do something for you?" he asked the motionless shape.

The mud puppy dropped back down on all fours and started away, turned back momentarily, started away, and turned back again.

"Don't tell me," Ben advised Dirk. "It wants us to follow."

"Very well, I won't tell you," Dirk promised.

They followed the mud puppy through the forest, angling north once more away from the city of Elderew and the people of the lake country. The rain lessened to a slow drizzle, and the clouds began to break, allowing some light to seep through to the forestland. The chill continued to hang in the air, but Ben was so numb with cold already that he no longer noticed. He plodded after the mud puppy in silence, wondering vaguely how the creature got its name, wondering where they were going and why, what he should do about the medallion, and most of all what he should do about Dirk. The cat trailed after him, picking its way with cautious steps and graceful leaps, avoiding the mud and the puddles, and working very hard at keeping itself clean.

Just like your typical cat, Ben thought.

Except that Edgewood Dirk was anything but a typical cat, of course, and it didn't matter how long or how hard he protested otherwise. The real question was, what was Ben going to do about him? Traveling with Dirk was like traveling with that older person who always made you feel like a child and kept telling you not to be one. Dirk was obviously there for a reason, but Ben was beginning to wonder if it was a reason that would serve any useful purpose.

The hardwood trees of the high forest began to give way to swamp as they approached the far north boundary of Elderew. The land began to slope away, and mist to appear in long, winding trailers. The gloom thickened and the chill dampness turned to a clinging warmth. Ben was not comforted.

The mud puppy continued on without slowing.

"Do these creatures do this sort of thing often?" Ben whispered at last to Dirk. "Ask you to follow them, I mean?"

"Never," Dirk responded and sneezed.

Ben scowled back at the cat. I hope you catch pneumonia, he thought darkly.

They passed down into the murk, into stands of cypress and willow and thickets of swamp growth that defied description or identification. Mud sucked at his boots and water oozed into the impressions they left. The rain abated completely, and there was a sullen stillness. Ben wondered what it felt like to be dry. His clothing felt as if it were weighted with lead. The mist was quite heavy now, and his vision was reduced to a distance of no more than a few feet. Maybe we've been brought here to die, he decided. Maybe this is it.

But it wasn't "it" or anything else of immediate concern; it was simply a trek through the swamp that ended at a vast mudhole. The mud puppy brought Ben and Dirk to the mudhole, waited until they were at its edge, and then disappeared into the dark. The mudhole stretched away into the mist and dark for better than fifty feet, a vast, placid sinkhole that belched air bubbles from time to time and evidenced no interest in much else. Ben stared out at the mudhole, glanced down at Dirk, and wondered what was supposed to happen next.

He found out a moment later. The mudhole seemed to heave upward at its centermost point, and a woman rose from the depths to stand upon its surface.

"Good morning, High Lord," she greeted.

She was naked, it appeared, although it was hard to be certain because she was plastered from head to foot with mud, and it clung to her as if it were a covering. There was a glimmer of light from her eyes as they fastened on him; but, except for the eyes, there was only the shape of her beneath the mud. She rested on the surface of the sinkhole as if weightless, relaxed and quite at home.

"Good morning," he replied uncertainly.

"I see that you have a prism cat traveling with you," she said, her voice oddly flat and resonant. "Quite a stroke of good fortune. A prism cat can be a very valuable companion."

Ben was not sure he agreed with that assessment, but held his tongue. Dirk said nothing.

"I am known as the Earth Mother, High Lord," the woman continued. "The name was given to me some centuries ago by the people of the lake country. Like them, I am a fairy creature bound to this world. Unlike them, the choice to come was mine, and it was made at the time of the beginning of the land when there was need for me. I am the soul and spirit of the earth. I am Landover's gardener, you might say. I keep watch over her soil and the things that grow upon it. The province of protection and care of the land is not mine alone, because those who live upon its surface must share responsibility for its care—but I am an integral part of the process. I give possibility from beneath and others see that possibility to fruition." She paused. "Do you understand, High Lord?"

Ben nodded. "I think I do."

"Well, some understanding is necessary. The earth and I are inseparable; it is part of my composition, and I am one with it. Because we are joined, most of what happens within Landover is known to me. I know of you especially, because your magic is also a part of me. There is a bond between Landover's High Lord and the land that is inseparable. You understand that as well, don't you?"

Ben nodded again. "I have learned as much. Is that how you know me now, even with my appearance altered?"

"I know you as the prism cat knows you, High Lord; I never rely on appearances." There was the vaguest hint of laughter, not unkind. "I watched you arrive in Landover and I have followed you since. You possess courage and determination; you lack only knowledge. But knowledge will come in time. This is a land not easily understood."

"It is a bit confusing just now," Ben agreed. Already he liked the Earth Mother a whole lot better than he liked Edgewood Dirk.

"Confusing, yes. But less so than you believe." She shifted slightly within the swirl of mist, her opaque form featureless and immutable. Her eyes glistened wetly. "I had the mud puppy bring you to me so that I could give you some information about Willow."

"You've seen her?" Ben demanded.

"I have. Her mother brought her to me. Her mother and I are close in the manner of true fairy creatures and the earth. We share the magic. Her mother is ill-used by the River Master, who thinks only to possess her and not to accept her for what she is. The River Master seeks to dominate in the manner of humans, High Lord—a great failing that I hope he will come to recognize in time. Possession of the land and her gifts is not meant to be. The land is a trust to be shared by all of finite lives and never to be taken for private use. But that has never been the way of things—not in Landover, not in all the worlds beyond. The higher orders seek to dominate the lower; all seek to dominate the land. An Earth Mother's heart is often broken in that way."

She paused. "The River Master tries, and he is better than some. Still, he, too, seeks domination in other, less obvious ways. He would use his magic to turn the land pure without understanding that his vision is not necessarily true. Healing is needed, High Lord, but not all healing is advisable. Sometimes the process of dying and regeneration is intrinsic to development. A recycling of life is a part of being. No one can predict the whole of the cycle, and a tampering with any period can be harmful. The River Master fails to see this—just as he fails to see why Willow's mother cannot belong to him. He only sees what needs are immediately before him."

"Such as his need for the black unicorn?" Ben interjected impulsively.

The Earth Mother studied him closely. "Yes, High Lord—the black unicorn. *There* is a need that none can resist—not even you, perhaps." She was silent a moment. "I digress. I brought you here to tell you of Willow. I have felt you with her, and the feeling is good. There is a special bond between you that promises something I have long waited for. I wish to do what I may to preserve that bond."

One dark arm lifted. "Listen, then, High Lord. Willow's mother brought her to me two days ago at dawn. Willow would not go to her father for help, and her mother could not give her what she needed. She hoped that I could. Willow has dreamed twice now of the black unicorn—once when she was with you, once after. The dreams are a mix of truth and lies, and she cannot separate the one from the other. I could not help her with that; dreams are not a province of the earth. Dreams live in the air and in the mind. She asked then if I knew whether the black unicorn was a thing of good or evil. I told her that it would be both until the truth of it was clearly understood. She asked if I could show her that truth. I told her that truth was not mine to give. She asked me then if I knew of a bridle of spun gold. I told her that I did. She has gone to find it."

"Where?" Ben asked at once.

The Earth Mother was silent again for a moment, as if debating something with herself. "High Lord, you must promise me something," she said finally. "I know you are troubled. I know you are afraid. Perhaps you will even become desperate. The road you travel now is a difficult one. But you must promise me that whatever befalls you and however overwhelming your feelings because of it, your first concern will always be for Willow. You must promise that you will do whatever it lies within your power to do to keep her safe."

Ben hesitated a moment before replying, puzzled. "I don't understand. Why do you ask this?"

The Earth Mother's arms folded into her body. "Because I must, High Lord. Because of who I am. That has to be answer enough for you."

Ben frowned. "What if I cannot keep this promise? What if I choose *not* to keep it?"

"Once the promise is given, it must be kept. You will keep it because you have no choice." The Earth Mother's eyes blinked once. "You give it to me, remember, and a promise given to me by you cannot be broken. The magic binds us in that way."

Ben weighed the matter carefully for several long moments, undecided. It wasn't so much the idea of committing himself to Willow that bothered him; it was the fact of the promise itself. It was a foreclosure of all other options without knowing yet what those options might be, a blind vow that lacked future sight.

But then again, that was how life often worked. You didn't always get the choices offered to you up front. "I promise," he said, and the lawyer part of him winced.

"Willow has gone north," the Earth Mother said. "Probably to the Deep Fell."

Ben stiffened. "The Deep Fell? Probably?"

"The bridle was a fairy magic woven long, long ago by the land's wizards. It has passed through many hands over the years and been all but forgotten. In the recent past, it has been the possession of the witch Nightshade. The witch stole it and hid it with her other treasures. She hordes the things she finds beautiful and brings them out to view when she wishes. But Nightshade has had the bridle stolen from her several times by the dragon Strabo, who also covets such treasures. The theft of the bridle has become something of a contest between the two. It was last in the possession of the witch."

A lot of unpleasant memories surged to the fore at the mention of Nightshade and the Deep Fell. There were a good many places that Ben did not care to visit again soon in the Kingdom of Landover, and the home of the witch was right at the top of the list.

But, then, Nightshade was gone, wasn't she, into the fairy world . . . ?

"Willow left when I told her of the golden bridle, High Lord," the Earth Mother interrupted his thoughts. "That was two days ago. You must hurry if you are to catch her."

Ben nodded absently, already aware of a lightening of the sky beyond the swamp's unchanging murk. Dawn was almost upon them.

"I wish you well, High Lord," the Earth Mother called. She had begun to sink back into the swamp, her shape changing rapidly as she descended. "Find Willow and help her. Remember your promise."

Ben started to call back to her, a dozen unanswered questions on his lips, but she was gone almost at once. She simply sank back into the mudhole and disappeared. Ben was left staring at the empty, placid surface.

"Well, at least I know which way Willow's gone," he said to himself. "Now all I have to do is find my way out of this swamp."

As if by magic, the mud puppy reappeared, slipping from beneath a gathering of fronds. It regarded him solemnly, started away, turned back again, and waited.

Ben sighed. Too bad all of his wishes weren't granted so readily. He glanced down at Dirk. Dirk stared back at him.

"Want to walk north for a while?" he asked the cat.

The cat, predictably, said nothing.

HUNT

They were four days gone from Elderew, east and slightly south of Rhyndweir in the heart of the Greensward, when they came upon the hunter.

"Black it was, like the coal brought down out of the north mines, like some shadow that hasn't ever seen the daylight. Sweet mother! It came right past me, so close that it seemed I might reach out and touch it. It was all grace and beauty, leaping as if the earth couldn't hold it to her, speeding past us all like a bit of wind that you can feel and sometimes see, but never touch. Oh, I didn't want to touch it, mind. I didn't want to touch something that . . . pure. It was like watching fire—clean, but it burns you if you come too close. I didn't want to come too close."

The hunter's voice was quick and husky with emotions that lay all too close to the surface of the man. He sat with Ben and Dirk in the early evening hours about a small campfire built in the shelter of an oak grove and a ridgeline. Sunset scattered red and purple across the western horizon, and blue-gray dusk hovered east. The close of the day was still and warm, the rain clouds of four nights past a memory. Birds sang their evening songs in the trees, and the smell of flowers was in the air.

Ben watched the hunter closely. The hunter was a big, rawboned man with sun-browned, weathered skin and calloused hands. He wore woodsman's garb with high leather boots softened by hand for comfort and stealth, and he carried a crossbow and bolts, long bow and arrows, a bolo, and a skinning knife. His face was long and high-boned, a mask of angles and flat planes with the skin stretched tightly across and the features strained by the tension. He had the look of a dangerous man; in other times, he might have been.

But not this night. This night he was something less.

"I'm getting ahead of myself," the man muttered suddenly, an admonishment as much as a declaration. He wiped at his forehead with one big hand

and hunkered down closer to the flames of the campfire as if to draw their warmth. "I almost wasn't there at all, you know. I was almost gone to the Melchor hunting bighorn. Had my gear all packed and ready when Dain found me. He caught up with me at the crossroads out, running like his woman had found out the worst, calling after me like some fool. I slowed and waited, and that made *me* the real fool. 'There's a hunt being organized,' he said. 'The King himself has called it. His people are out everywhere, drawing the best and the quickest to net something you won't believe. A black unicorn! Yea, it's so,' he says. 'A black unicorn that's to be hunted down if it takes all month, and we have to chase the beast from valley's end to valley's end. You got to come,' he says. 'They're giving each man twenty pieces a day and food and, if you're the one who snares him, another five thousand!' "

The hunter laughed sullenly. "Five thousand pieces. Seemed like the best chance I'd ever get at the time—more money than I'd see in ten years' work any other way. I looked at Dain and wondered if he'd lost his mind, then saw the way his eyes were lit and knew if was all real, that there was a hunt, that there was a bounty of five thousand, that some fool—King or otherwise—believed there was a black unicorn out there to be caught."

Ben glanced momentarily at Dirk. The cat sat a few feet from him, eyes fixed intently on the speaker, paws curled up underneath so that they didn't show. He hadn't moved or spoken since the hunter had come across their tiny camp and asked if he might share their meal. Dirk was to all outward appearances a normal cat. Ben couldn't help wondering what he might be thinking.

"So we went, Dain and me—us and another two thousand of the same mind. We went to Rhyndweir where the hunt was to begin. The whole plain between the split in the rivers was packed tight with hunters camped and waiting. There was beaters and drivers, there was the Lord Kallendbor and all the other high-and-mighty landsmen with all their knights in armor and foot soldiers. There was horses and mules, wagons loaded down with provisions, carriers and retainers, a whole sea of moving parts and sounds that would have frightened any other prey from ten miles distant! Mother's blood, it was a mess! But I stayed on anyway, still thinking about the money, but thinking about something else now, too—thinking about that black unicorn. There wasn't any such creature, I knew—but what if there was? What if it was out there? I might not catch it, but, Lord, just to see it!

"That same evening we were all called before the castle gates. The King wasn't there; his wizard was—the one they call Questor Thews. He was a sight! Patchwork robe and sashes made him look like a scarecrow! And there was this dog with him that dressed like you and me and walked on his hind legs. Some said he could talk, but I never heard it. They stood up there with the Lord Kallendbor and whispered to him things no one else could hear. The wizard had a face like chalk—looked scared to death. Not Kallendbor, though—not him. He never looks afraid of anything, that one! Sure as death itself and ready to pronounce judgment. He called out to us in that big, booming voice you could hear for a mile on those plains. He called out and told us that this unicorn was a real live beast and it could be tracked and caught like any other beast. There were enough of us and we would have it or know the reason why! He gave us our places and the line of sweep and sent us off to sleep. The hunt was to begin at dawn."

The hunter paused, remembering. His eyes looked past Ben in the growing darkness to some point distant in time and place from where they sat now. "It was exciting, you know. All those men gathered together like that—a hunt greater than any I had ever heard tell. There were to be Trolls north along the Melchor and a number of the fairy tribes south above the lake country. They didn't seem to think the unicorn would be south of there—don't know why. But the plan was to start on the eastern border and drive west, closing the ends north and south like a huge net. Beaters and horsemen would work from the east; hunters and snares would set up west in moving pockets. It was a good plan."

He smiled faintly. "It started right on schedule. The line east began to move west, clearing out everything in its path. Hunters like myself set up in the hill country where we could see everything that moved in the grasslands and beyond. Some rode chaser all along the front and ends, flushing whatever was hidden there. It was something, all those men, all that equipment. Looked like the whole valley was gathered in that one huge hunt. Looked like the whole world. The line came west all that day from the wastelands to Rhyndweir and beyond—beaters and chasers, horsemen and foot soldiers, wagonloads of provisions going back and forth from castles and towns. Don't know how they got it organized so fast and still made it work—but they did. Never saw a thing, though. Camped that night in a line that stretched from the Melchor down to Sterling Silver. Campfires burned north to south like a big, winding snake. You could see it from the hills where Dain and I were set up with the other hunters. We stayed out of the main camps. We're more at home up there anyway—can see as well at night as in day and had to keep watch so that nothing sneaked past in the dark.

"The second day went the same. We got to the western foothills at the edge of the grasslands, but saw nothing. Camped again and waited. Watched all that night."

Ben was thinking of the time he had wasted since leaving Elderew just to get this far north. Four days. The weather had slowed his travel in the lake country, and he had been forced to skirt east of Sterling Silver to avoid an encounter with the guard—his guard—because they might recognize him as the stranger that the King had ordered out of the country. He had been forced to travel afoot the entire way, because he had no money for horses and was not yet reduced to stealing. He must have missed the hunt by less than twenty-four hours. He was beginning to wonder what that had cost him.

The hunter cleared his throat and continued. "There was some unpleasantness by now among the men," he advised solemnly. "Some felt this was a waste of time. Twenty pieces a day or not, no one wants to be part of something foolish. The Lords were having their say, too, griping that we weren't doing our share, that we weren't watching as close as we should, that something might have sneaked through. We knew that wasn't the case, but that wasn't something they wanted to hear. So we said we'd try harder, keep looking. But we wondered among ourselves if there was anything out there to look for.

"The third day we closed the line west to the mountains, and that's when we found it." The hunter's eyes had suddenly come alive, bright in the firelight with excitement. "It was late afternoon, the sun screened away by the mountains and the mist, and the patches of forest we searched in that hill country were thick with shadows. It was the time of day when everything seems a little unclear, when you see movement where there is none. We were working a heavy pine grove surrounded by hardwood and thick with scrub and brush. There were six of us, I think, and you could hear dozens more all about, and the lines of beaters shouting and calling from just east where the line was closing. It was hot in the hills—odd for the time of day. But we were all worn down to the bone and weary of chasing ghosts. There was a feeling that this hunt had come down to nothing. Sweat and insects made the work unpleasant now; aches and pains slowed us. We had shoved away thoughts of the unicorn beyond completing the hunt and getting home again. The whole business was a joke."

He paused. "Then suddenly there was movement in the pine—just a shadow of something, nothing more than that. I remember thinking that my eyes were playing tricks on me yet another time. I was going to say something to Dain; he was working just off to my left. But I held my tongue—too tired, maybe, to want to say anything. I just sort of stopped what I was doing there in the brush and the heat and I watched the place of the movement to see if there was going to be any more."

He took a deep breath, and his jaw tightened down. "There was this darkening of the little sunlight that remained then—as if clouds had screened it away for a moment. I remember how it felt. The air was all hot and still; the wind had died down into nothing. I was looking, and the brush came apart and there it was—the unicorn, all black and fluid like water. It seemed so tiny. It stood there staring at me—I don't know how long. I could see the goat's feet, the lion's tail, the mane that ran down its neck and back, the fetlocks, that ridged horn. It was just as the old stories described it—but more beautiful than they could ever make it. Sweet mother, it was glorious! The others saw it, too, a few of them anyway. Dain caught a glimpse; another two said they saw it close up. But not as close as me, Lord! No, I was right next to it, it seemed! I was right there!

"Then it bolted. No, not bolted—it didn't flee like that. It bounded up and seemed to fly right past me; all that motion and grace, like the shadow of some bird in flight cast down on the earth by the sun passing. It came by me in the blink of an eye—*whisk!*—and it was gone. I stood there looking after it, wondering if I'd really seen it, knowing I had, thinking how marvelous it was to view, thinking it truly was real . . ."

He choked on the words as they tumbled out one after the other, released from his throat in a rush of strange emotion. His hands were raised before him, knotting with the intensity of the telling of his story. Ben quit breathing momentarily, awed by what he was seeing, not wanting to break the spell.

The hunter's eyes lowered then, and the hands followed. "I heard later that it flew right into the teeth of the chase. I heard it went past the whole mess of them like wind through a forest of rooted trees. Dozens saw it. There was a chance to hold it, maybe—but I kind of wonder. It came right over the nets. There was a chase, but . . . but you know what?" The eyes lifted again. "The unicorn came right up against the Lords of the Greensward and the King's men—right up against them, sweet mother! And the wizard—the very one that organized all this—conjured up some nonsense and it rained flowers and butterflies all over everything. The chase broke up in the confusion, and the unicorn was gone before you could spit!" He smiled suddenly. "Flowers and butterflies—can you imagine that?"

Ben smiled with him. He could.

The hunter drew up his knees then and hugged them. The smile disappeared. "That was it, then. That was all she wrote. The hunt was done. Everyone sort of broke up and went away after that. There was some talk of continuing, of taking the whole line back east again, but it never came to anything. No one wanted any part of that. It was like the heart had gone out of the chase. It was like everyone was glad the unicorn got away. Or maybe it was just that no one thought it could ever be caught anyway."

The hard eyes lifted. "Strange times we live in. The King sacked the wizard and the dog, I hear. Threw them out the minute he heard what had happened. Just dismissed them out of hand for what the wizard had done—or what he thought he'd done. I don't think the wizard could have done much one way or the other anyway. Not with that creature, not with it. No one could have. It was too much a ghost for anything mortal, too much a dream . . ."

There were sudden tears in the hunter's eyes. "I think I touched it, you know, when it went past me. I think I touched it. Sweet mother, I can still feel the silk of its skin brushing me, like fire, like . . . a woman's touch, maybe. I had a woman touch me once that way, long ago. The unicorn felt like that. Now I can't forget it. I try to think of other things, try to be reasonable about the fact of it having happened at all, but the sense of it stays with me." He tightened his face against what he was feeling. "I been looking for it on my own since I left, thinking maybe one man could have better luck than a whole hunting party. I don't want to catch it exactly; I don't think I could. I just want to see it again. I just want to maybe touch it one more time—just once, just for a moment . . ."

He trailed off again. The campfire sparked suddenly in the stillness, a sharp crackling. No one moved. Darkness had settled down across the valley, and the last daylight had dropped from view. Stars and moons had appeared, their light faint and distant, their colors muted. Ben glanced down at Edgewood Dirk. The cat had his eyes closed.

"I just want to touch it once more," the hunter repeated softly. "Just for a moment."

He stared vacantly at Ben. The ghost of who and what he had been was swallowed in the silence that followed.

That same night Willow dreamed again of the black unicorn. She slept huddled close to the faithful Parsnip in a gathering of pine at the edge of the Deep Fell, concealed within a covering of boughs and shadows. Her journey north from Elderew was five days gone. She was now only hours ahead of Ben Holiday. The hunt for the black unicorn had delayed her for almost a day as it swept the hill country west of the Greensward and turned her east. She had no idea what the hunt was about. She had no idea that Ben was searching for her.

The dream came at midnight, stealing into her sleep like a mother to her slumbering child's room, a presence that was warm and comforting. There was no fear this time, only sadness. Willow moved through forest trees and grassland spaces, and the black unicorn watched, as if a ghost come from some nether region to trail the living. It appeared and faded like sunshine from behind a cloud, now in the shade of a massive old maple, now in the lea of a copse of fir. It was never all visible, but only in part. It was black and featureless save for its eyes—and its eyes were a mirror of all the sadness that ever was and would ever be.

The eyes made Willow cry, and her tears stained her cheeks as she slept. The eyes were troubled, filled with pain she could only imagine, haunted beyond anything she had believed possible. The black unicorn of this dream was no demon spawn; it was a delicate, wondrous creature that somehow had been terribly misused . . .

She came awake with a start, the image of the unicorn clearly etched in her mind, its eyes fixed and staring. Parsnip slept next to her, undisturbed. Dawn was still hours away, and she shivered with the night's chill. Her slim body trembled at the whisper of the dream's words in her memory, and she felt the magic of their presence in her fairy way.

This dream was real, she realized suddenly. This dream was the truth.

She straightened back against the pine's roughened trunk, swallowed the dryness in her throat, and forced herself to consider what the dream had shown her. Something required it—the eyes of the unicorn, perhaps. They sought something from her. It was no longer enough to think simply of retrieving the golden bridle and carrying it to Ben. That was the command of her first dream, the dream that had brought her on this quest—but the truth of that dream was now in doubt. The unicorn of that dream was entirely different than the unicorn of this. One was demon, the other victim. One was pursuer, the other . . . hunted? She thought perhaps so. There was a need for help in the unicorn's eyes. It was almost as if it was begging her for that help.

And she knew she must give it.

She shuddered violently. What was she thinking? If she even came close to the unicorn, she could be lost. She should forget this madness! She should go to Ben . . .

She let the unfinished thought trail off, huddled down against the night and the stillness, and wrestled with her indecision. She wished her mother were there to comfort her or that she could seek again the counsel of the Earth Mother.

She wished most of all for Ben.

But none of them was there. Except for Parsnip, she was alone.

The moments slipped by. Suddenly she rose, a soundless shadow, left Parsnip asleep in the gathering of pines, and disappeared silently into the Deep Fell. She went not on reason, but on instinct, without doubt or fear, but with certainty that all would be well and she would be kept safe.

By dawn, she had returned. She did not have the golden bridle in her possession, but she knew now where it was. Her fairy senses had told her what even the Earth Mother could not. The bridle had been stolen yet again.

She woke Parsnip, gathered together her few things, cast a brief glance back at the dark bowl of the hollows, and started walking east.

THIEVES

When Ben Holiday and Edgewood Dirk awoke the following morning, the hunter was gone. Neither had heard him leave. He had departed without a word, disappearing so completely that it was almost as if he had never been. Even his face was just a vague memory for Ben. It was only his story of the hunt for the black unicorn that lingered on, still vivid, still haunting.

Breakfast was a solemn affair. "I hope he finds what he's looking for," Ben muttered at one point.

"He can't," Dirk replied softly. "It doesn't exist."

Ben was beginning to wonder about that. The black unicorn seemed as elusive as smoke and about as substantive. The unicorn was seen, but never for more than a few moments and never as more than a fleeting shadow. It was a legend that had assumed a scant few of the trappings of reality, but which remained for all intents and purposes little more than a vision. It was altogether possible that a vision was all the unicorn was—some strayed bit of magic that took form but never body. In Landover, you never knew.

He thought about asking Dirk, but then decided against it. Dirk wouldn't give him a straight answer if he knew one, and he was tired of playing word games with the cat.

He decided to change the subject.

"Dirk, I've been giving some thought to what the Earth Mother told us about the golden bridle," he said when breakfast was finished. "She told Willow that it was last in the possession of Nightshade, but she didn't say anything about what had become of the witch since I sent her into the fairy mists." He paused. "You knew I had done that, didn't you? That I had sent Nightshade into the mists?"

Dirk, seated on an old log, shifted his front paws experimentally. "I knew."

"She sent my friends into Abaddon, and I decided to give her a taste of her own medicine," he went on by way of explanation. "I was given Io Dust by the fairies, a powder that, if breathed, made you subject to the commands of the one who fed you the Dust. I used it later on the dragon Strabo, too, as a matter of fact. At any rate, I used it on Nightshade first and caused her to change herself into a crow and fly off into the mists." Again he paused. "But I never knew what happened to her after that."

"This rather boring recapitulation is leading somewhere, I trust?" Dirk sniffed.

Ben flushed. "I was wondering whether or not Nightshade had found her way out of the mists and back into the Deep Fell. It might help if we knew that before we waltzed blindly on in."

Dirk took a long moment to clean his face, causing Ben's flush to heighten further with impatience. At last the cat looked up again. "I have not been down into the Deep Fell myself in quite some time, High Lord. But I understand that Nightshade might well be back."

Ben took a moment to let the news sink in. The last thing he needed just now was an encounter with Nightshade. He no longer had the medallion to protect him—if indeed it could protect him anyway from a creature as evil as the witch. If she recognized him, he was dead. Even if she didn't, she was hardly likely to welcome him with open arms. And she was hardly likely to welcome Willow either—especially once she learned what the sylph was after. She wasn't about to hand over the golden bridle, however convincing the arguments Willow might offer. She would probably turn Willow into a toad—and turn *him* into a toad. He thought wistfully of the Io Dust and wished he had just a single handful. That would even the odds considerably.

His eyes fixed intently on Dirk. "What do you think about a quick trip back into the fairy world?" he asked abruptly. "I did it once; I could do it again. The fairies would recognize me, magic or no magic. Maybe they could help me change back again. At the very least, they could give me another pod of the Io Dust to use on Nightshade. After all, I promised the Earth Mother I would do my best to look after Willow, and I can't look after her if I can't look after myself."

Dirk studied him a moment, blinked and yawned. "Your problem is not one anyone else can help you with—least of all the fairies."

"Why not?" Ben snapped, irritated with the cat's insufferable smugness.

"Because, in the first place, the magic that has changed you is your own—as you have been told at least half-a-dozen times now. And in the second place, the fairies won't necessarily help you just because you ask. The fairies involve themselves in people's lives when and where they choose and not otherwise." The prim muzzle wrinkled distastefully. "You knew that before you asked the question, High Lord."

Ben fumed silently. The cat was right, of course—he had known. The fairies hadn't interceded in Landover's problems when he had first come into the valley and the tarnish and the Iron Mark had threatened, and they were unlikely to do so now. He was King, and the problems facing him were his.

So how was he going to solve them?

"C'mon," he ordered suddenly, springing to his feet. "I have an idea that might work." He pulled on his boots, straightened his clothing, and waited for Dirk to ask what the idea was. The cat didn't. Finally, he said, "Don't you want to know the details?"

The cat stretched and jumped down from its perch to stand next to him. "No."

Ben ground his teeth and silently swore that, all right then, it would be a cold day somewhere damn hot before *he* would say another word about it!

They walked north through the early morning, skirting the grasslands of the Greensward, veering slightly east toward the foothills that lay below the Melchor. Ben led, but as usual Dirk seemed to know where they were going anyway and often traveled a parallel course, picking his way through the high grasses, seemingly oblivious to what Ben was about. Dirk continued to be a mystery without a solution, but Ben forced himself to concentrate on the task at hand rather than dwell on Dirk, because dwelling on Dirk just made him nuts. It was easier to accept the cat the way one accepted changes in the weather.

The grasslands were still marked from the passing of the hunt. Booted feet had flattened portions of the tall grass and broken down the scrub. Debris from the provision wagons littered the plains, and the ashes of huge campfires scarred the multicolored meadows. The Greensward had the look of a giant picnic ground at the close of July fourth. Ben wrinkled his nose in distaste. Meeks was already using the land selfishly again.

There were other signs of misuse as well. Signs of the wilt that had marked the valley in his early days in Landover had returned to the plants and trees—signs that could only have been brought about by a lessening of the power of the King's magic. When there was no King in Landover, the land lost strength; he had learned that on his first visit. Meeks was not the true King, despite any outward appearance, and Landover was beginning to show the effects. The signs were tiny yet, but they would grow worse. Eventually, the tarnish would return to Sterling Silver and the whole valley would begin to sicken. Ben pressed ahead at a quicker pace, as if somehow speed might help.

A caravan of traders traveling north into the Melchor to obtain metal implements and weapons from the Trolls crossed their path around midday, and they shared lunch. The gossip was all connected with the hunt for the black unicorn and the strange events of the past few days. The King had gone into seclusion, refusing to see anyone, even the Lords of the Greensward. Public works projects had been put on hold, judicial and grievance councils had been dismissed, envoys had been sent home from Sterling Silver, and everything in general had come to a dead halt. No one knew what was happening. There were rumors of demons flying the night skies, monstrous things that carried off livestock and stray children in the manner that the dragons once had. There were even rumors that the King himself was responsible, that he had made some devil's bargain to give the demons of Abaddon their way in Landover if they in turn would bring him the unicorn.

Everything seemed to revolve around the unicorn. The King had let it be known in no uncertain terms that he meant to have the creature, and the one who brought it to him would be hugely rewarded.

"If you can catch smoke, you're a rich man," one trader joked, and the others all laughed.

Ben didn't laugh. He took his leave hastily and continued north at an even quicker pace. Things were getting out of hand, and a good part of that was clearly his fault.

By midafternoon, he was in the country of the G'home Gnomes.

The G'home Gnomes were a burrow people he had encountered during his early days as Landover's King. They were small, furry, grimy creatures that looked something like overgrown moles. They were scavengers and thieves and they couldn't be trusted any farther than your pet dog could be with the evening roast. As a matter of fact, they couldn't be trusted *with* your pet dog, because they considered dogs, cats, and other small domesticated animals quite a delicacy. Abernathy considered the G'home Gnomes cannibals. Questor Thews considered them trouble. Everyone considered them a nuisance. The appellation "G'home Gnome" came from the almost universally expressed demand of those who had the misfortune to come in contact with them: "Go home, gnome!" Two of these gnomes, Fillip and Sot, had made a pilgrimage to Sterling Silver to seek Ben's aid in freeing some of their people from Crag Trolls after the Trolls had carted the unfortunates away for stealing and eating a number of their pet tree sloths. Ben had almost lost his life in that venture, but the G'home Gnomes had proven to be among the most loyal of his subjects—if not the most reformed.

And Fillip and Sot had once confided to him that they knew the Deep Fell as they knew the backs of their hands.

"That's exactly the kind of help we need," Ben told Dirk, despite his vow not to tell the cat anything. "Nightshade will never be persuaded to give up the bridle willingly. Willow has to know that, too—but that won't stop her from trying. She'll probably be direct rather than circumspect; she's too honest for her own good. Whatever the case, if she's gone into the Deep Fell, she's likely in trouble. She'll need help. Fillip and Sot can let us know. They can sneak down without being seen. If Willow or Nightshade is there, they can tell us. If the bridle is there, perhaps they can steal it for us. Don't you see? They can go where we can't."

"Speak for yourself," Dirk replied.

"Do you have a better plan?" Ben snapped back immediately.

Dirk was oblivious to his anger. "I have no plan," he answered. "This is your problem, not mine."

"Thank you very much. I gather you wouldn't consider undertaking this reconnaissance and theft yourself then?"

"Hardly. I am your companion, not your lackey."

"You are a pain, Dirk."

"I am a cat, High Lord."

Ben terminated the discussion with a scowl and stalked off toward the burrow community. The G'home Gnomes lived in towns in the same manner as prairie dogs, and sentinels warned of his approach long before he could see anything. By the time he reached the town, there wasn't a G'home Gnome anywhere—just a lot of empty-looking holes. Ben walked to the center of the town, seated himself on a stump and waited. He had been here a number of times since becoming King, and he knew how the game was played.

A few minutes later, Dirk joined him. The cat curled up beside him without a word and closed its eyes against the late afternoon sun.

Shortly after that, a furry face poked up from one of the burrows. Eyes squinted weakly against the daylight, and a wrinkled nose sniffed the air tentatively.

"Good day, sir," the gnome addressed Ben and tipped his battered leather cap with its single red feather.

"Good day," Ben replied.

"Out for a walk, are you, sir?"

"Out for a healthy dose of fresh air and sunshine. Good for what ails you."

"Yes, oh yes indeed, good for what ails you. Must be careful of colds that settle in the throat and chest during the passing of fall."

"Certainly must. Colds can be tricky." They were dancing on eggshells, and Ben let the music play itself out. The G'home Gnomes were like this with strangers—scared to death. One always tested you. If you posed no threat, the rest came out. If any menace was sensed, you never saw more than the one. "I hope your family is well?" Ben went on, trying to sound casual. "And your community?"

"Oh, quite well, thank you, sir. All quite well."

"That's good to hear."

"Yes, good to hear." The gnome glanced about furtively, looking to see if Ben was alone, looking to see if he was hiding anything. "You must have walked quite a distance north from the Greensward, sir. Are you a craftsman?"

"Not exactly."

"A trader, then?"

Ben hesitated a moment and then nodded. "On occasion, I am."

"Oh?" The gnome's squint seemed to deepen. "But you do not appear to have any wares with you this trip, sir."

"Ah! Well, sometimes appearances are deceiving. Some trading wares can be quite small, you know." He patted his tunic. "Pocket-sized."

The gnome's front teeth flashed nervously out of its grimy face. "Yes, of course—that is so. Could it be that you are interested in trading here, sir?"

"Could be." Ben set the hook and waited.

The gnome did not disappoint him. "With someone in particular?"

Ben shrugged. "I have done some business in the past with two members of your community—Fillip and Sot. Do you know them?"

The gnome blinked. "Yes, Fillip and Sot live here."

Ben smiled his most disarming smile. "Are they about?"

The gnome smiled back. "Perhaps. Yes, perhaps. Would you wait a moment, please? Just a moment?"

He ducked back into his burrow and was gone. Ben waited. The minutes slipped past and no one appeared. Ben kept his place on the stump and tried to look as if he were enjoying himself. He could feel eyes watching him from everywhere. Doubts began to creep into his mind. What if Fillip and Sot took a look at him and decided he was no one they had ever seen? After all, he wasn't the Ben Holiday they knew any longer. He was a stranger—and not a particularly well-dressed one either. He glanced down at his clothing, reminded of his sorry state. He made a rather shabby-looking trader, he thought ruefully. Fillip and Sot might decide he wasn't worth their bother. They might decide to stay right where they were. And if he couldn't get close enough to talk to them, he wasn't about to have any success obtaining their help.

The afternoon shadows lengthened. Ben's patience simmered like hot water over an open fire. He glanced irritably at Edgewood Dirk. No help was there. Eyes closed, paws tucked under, breathing slowed to nothing, the cat might have been sleeping or it might have been stuffed.

The burrow holes continued to yawn back at him in empty disinterest. The sun continued to slip into the western hills. No one appeared.

Ben had just about decided to throw in the towel when a furry, dirt-lined face poked up suddenly from a burrow opening not a dozen yards away, closely followed by a second directly beside it. Two snouts sniffed the late afternoon air warily. Two pairs of weakened eyes peered cautiously about.

Ben heaved a sigh of relief. They were Fillip and Sot.

The squinting eyes fixed on him.

"Good day, sir," said Fillip.

"Good day, sir," said Sot.

"Good day, indeed." Ben beamed, sitting up straight again on the stump.

"You wish to trade, sir?" asked Fillip.

"You wish to trade with us?" asked Sot.

"Yes. Yes, I most certainly do." Ben paused. "Would you gentlemen mind coming over here? That way I can be certain you understand what it is that I have to trade."

The G'home Gnomes glanced at each other, then emerged into the fading sunlight. Stout, hairy bodies were clothed in what looked like Salvation Army rejects. Bearded, ferretlike faces with tiny, squinted eyes and wrinkled noses tested the air like weather vanes directed by the wind. Dirt and grime covered them from head to foot.

Fillip and Sot without a doubt.

Ben waited until they had stopped just a few feet in front of him, beckoned them closer still, then said, "I want you to listen to me very closely, do you understand? Just listen. I'm Ben Holiday. I'm High Lord of Landover. A magic has been used to change my appearance, but that's only temporary. I'll change myself back sooner or later. When I do, I'll remember who helped me and who didn't. And I need your help right now."

He glanced from one furry face to the other. The gnomes were staring at him voicelessly, eyes squinting, noses testing. They looked for a moment at each other, then back again at Ben.

"You are not the High Lord," said Fillip.

"No, you are not," agreed Sot.

"Yes, I am," Ben insisted.

"The High Lord would not be here alone," said Fillip.

"The High Lord would come with his friends, the wizard, the talking dog, the kobolds, and the girl Willow—the pretty sylph," said Sot.

"The High Lord would come with his guards and retainers," said Fillip.

"The High Lord would come with his standards of office," said Sot.

"You are not the High Lord," repeated Fillip.

"No, you are not," repeated Sot.

Ben took a deep breath. "I lost all those things to a bad wizard—the wizard who brought me into Landover in the first place, the wizard we saw in the crystal after we freed ourselves from the Crag Trolls—remember? You were the ones who came to Sterling Silver to ask my help in the first place. I went with you to help you free your people from the Trolls—the same gnomes who had eaten the furry tree sloths that were the Trolls' favorite pets. Now if I'm not the High Lord, how do I know all this?"

Fillip and Sot looked at each other again. They looked a bit uncertain this time.

"We don't know," admitted Fillip.

"No, we have no idea," agreed Sot.

"But you are not the High Lord," repeated Fillip.

"No, you are not," agreed Sot.

Ben took another deep breath. "I smashed the crystal against some rocks after we discovered its purpose. Questor Thews admitted his part in its use. You were there, Abernathy and Willow were there, the kobolds Bunion and Parsnip were there. Then we went down into the Deep Fell. You took Willow and me in. Remember? We used Io Dust to turn Nightshade back into a crow and fly her into the fairy mists. Then we went after the dragon Strabo. Remember? How could I know this if I'm not the High Lord?"

The gnomes were shifting their feet as if fire ants had crawled into their ruined boots.

"We don't know," Fillip said again.

"No, we don't," Sot agreed.

"Nevertheless, you are not the High Lord," repeated Fillip.

"No, you are not," repeated Sot.

Ben's patience slipped several notches despite his resolve. "How do you *know* that I'm not the High Lord?" he asked tightly.

Fillip and Sot fidgeted nervously. Their small hands wrung together, and their eyes shifted here and there and back again.

"You don't smell like him," said Fillip finally.

"No, you smell like us," said Sot.

Ben stared, then flushed, then lost whatever control he had managed to exercise up to this point. "Now you listen to me! I *am* the High Lord, I *am* Ben Holiday, I *am* exactly who I said I was, and you had better accept that *right now* or you are going to be in the biggest trouble of your entire lives, bigger even than when you stole and ate that pet dog at the celebration banquet after the defeat of the Iron Mark! I'll see you hung out to dry, damn it! Look at me!" He wrenched the medallion from his tunic, covering the face and the image of Meeks with his palm, and thrust it forward like a weapon. "Would you like to see what I can do to you with this?"

Fillip and Sot collapsed prone upon the earth, tiny bodies shaking from head to foot. They went down so fast it looked as if their feet had been yanked from beneath them.

"Great High Lord!" cried Fillip.

"Mighty High Lord!" wailed Sot.

"Our lives are yours!" sobbed Fillip.

"Yours!" sniffled Sot.

"Forgive us, High Lord!" pleaded Fillip.

"Forgive us!" echoed Sot.

Now that's much better, Ben thought, more than slightly astonished at the rapid turnabout. A little intimidation seemed to go a whole lot further than a reasonable explanation with the G'home Gnomes. He was a bit ashamed of himself for having had to resort to such tactics, but he was more desperate than anything.

"Get up," he told them. They climbed to their feet and stood looking at him fearfully. "It's all right," he assured them gently. "I understand why this is confusing, so let's just put it all behind us. All right?" Two ferretlike faces nodded as one. "Fine. Now we have a problem. Willow—the pretty sylph—may be in a lot of trouble, and we have to help her the same way she helped us when the Crag Trolls had us in their pens. Remember?" He was using that word "remember" a lot, but dealing with gnomes was like dealing with small children. "She's gone down into the Deep Fell in search of something, and we have to find her to be certain that she's all right."

"I do not like the Deep Fell, High Lord," complained Fillip hesitantly.

"Nor I," agreed Sot.

"I know you don't," Ben acknowledged. "I don't like it either. But you two have told me before that you can go down there without beeing seen. I can't do that. All I want you to do is to go down there long enough to look around and see if Willow is there—and to look for something that I need that's hidden down there. Fair enough? Just look around. No one has to know you're even there."

"Nightshade came back to the Deep Fell, High Lord," announced Fillip softly, confirming Ben's worst fears.

"We have seen her, High Lord," agreed Sot.

"She hates everything now," said Fillip.

"But you most," added Sot.

There was a period of silence. Ben tried to imagine for a moment the extent of Nightshade's hatred for him and could not. It was probably just as well.

He bent close to the gnomes. "You've been back to the Deep Fell, then?" Fillip and Sot nodded miserably. "And you weren't seen, were you?" Again, the nods. "Then you can do this favor for me, can't you? You can do it for me and for Willow. It will be a favor that I won't forget, I can promise you that."

There was another long moment of silence as Fillip and Sot looked at him, then at each other. They bent their heads close and whispered. Their nervousness had been transformed into agitation.

Finally they looked back at him again, eyes glinting.

"If we do this, High Lord, can we have the cat?" asked Fillip.

"Yes, can we have the cat?" echoed Sot.

Ben stared. He had forgotten Dirk momentarily. He glanced down at the cat, and then back at the gnomes. "Don't even think about it," he advised. "That cat is not what it seems."

Fillip and Sot nodded reluctantly, but their eyes remained locked on Dirk.

"I'm warning you," Ben said pointedly.

Again the gnomes nodded, but Ben had the distinct feeling that he was addressing a brick wall.

He shook his head helplessly. "Okay. We'll sleep here tonight and leave at daylight." He took an extra moment to draw their attention. "Try to remember what I just said about the cat. All right?"

A third time the gnomes nodded. But their eyes never left Dirk.

Ben ate another Spartan meal of Bonnie Blues, drank spring water, and watched the sun sink into the horizon and night settle over the valley. He thought of the old world and the old life and wondered for the first time in a long time whether he might have been better off staying where he was instead of coming here. Then he pushed his maudlin thoughts aside, wrapped himself in his travel cloak, and settled down against the base of the stump for an uncomfortable night's rest.

Dirk hadn't moved from the stump top. Dirk looked dead.

Sometime during the night there was a shriek so dreadful and so prolonged that it brought Ben right up off the ground. It sounded as if it were almost on top of him; but when he finally got his bearings and peered bleary-eyed about the campsite, all he found was Dirk crouched down atop the stump with his hackles up and a sort of steam rising from his back.

In the distance, something—or someone—whimpered.

"Those gnomes are persistent to the point of stupidity," Dirk commented softly before settling back down again, eyes glistening in the night like emerald fire.

The whimpering faded and Ben lay back down as well. So much for his well-intentioned advice to Fillip and Sot. Some lessons had to be learned the hard way.

That same night found an altogether different scene unfolding some miles south of Rhyndweir at an abandoned stock pen and line shack perched on a ridgeline that overlooked the eastern expanse of the Greensward. A sagging roof and shutterless windows marked the line shack as a derelict, and the stock pen was missing rails in half-a-dozen spots. Shadows draped the whole in a web of black lace. A white-bearded scarecrow and an Ozian shaggy dog, both decidedly unkempt, bracketed a brightly burning campfire built a dozen yards or so from the line shack and hurtled accusations at each other with a vehemence that seemed to refute utterly the fact that they had ever been best friends. A wiry, monkey-faced creature with elephant ears and big teeth watched the dispute in bemused silence.

"Do not attempt to ask my understanding of what you have done!" the shaggy dog was saying to the scarecrow. "I hold you directly responsible for our predicament and am not inclined to be in the least forgiving!"

"Your lack of compassion is matched only by your lack of character!" the scarecrow replied. "Another man—or dog—would be more charitable, I am sure!"

"Ha! Another man—or dog—would have bidden farewell to you long ago! Another man—or dog—would have found decent company in which to share his exile!"

"I see! Well, it is not too late for you to find other company—decent or not—if such is your inclination!"

"Rest assured, it is under consideration right now!"

The two glowered at each other through the red haze of the campfire, their thoughts as black as the ashes of the crumbling wood. The monkey-faced watcher remained a mute spectator. Night hung about all three like a mourner's shroud, and the ridgeline was spectral and still.

Abernathy shoved his glasses further back on his nose and picked up the argument once more, his tone of voice a shade softer. "What I find difficult to understand is why you let the unicorn get away, wizard. You had the creature before you, you knew the words that would snare it, and what did you do? You called down a thunderburst of butterflies and flowers. What kind of nonsense was that?"

Questor Thews tightened his jaw defiantly. "The kind of nonsense that you, of all people, should understand."

"I am inclined to think that you simply panicked. I am compelled to believe that you simply failed to master the magic when you needed to. And what do you mean, 'the kind of nonsense that *I* should understand'?"

"I mean, the kind of nonsense that gives all creatures the chance to be what they should be, despite what others think best for them!"

The scribe frowned. "One moment. Are you telling me that you *intentionally* let the unicorn escape? That the butterflies and the flowers were not accidental?"

The wizard pulled on his chin whiskers irritably. "Congratulations on your astute, if belated, grasp of the obvious! That is exactly what I am telling you!"

There was a long silence between them as they studied each other. They had been traveling together since daybreak, inwardly seething at the turn of events that had brought them to this end, outwardly distanced from each other by their anger. This was the first time that the subject of the unicorn's escape had been discussed openly.

The moment of testing passed. Questor looked away first, sighed, and pulled his patchwork robes closer about him to ward off the deepening night chill. His face was worn and lined from worry. His clothing was dusty and torn. Abernathy looked no better. They had been stripped of everything. Their dismissal had come immediately after the High Lord had learned of their failure to capture the black unicorn. The High Lord had given them no chance to explain their actions nor had he offered any explanation for his. They had been met on their return to Sterling Silver by a messenger, who had delivered a curt handwritten directive. They were relieved of their positions. They could go henceforth where they chose—but they were never to return to the court.

Bunion, apparently given his choice in the matter, went with them. He had offered no reason.

"It was not my intention when we began the hunt to allow the unicorn to escape," Questor continued softly. "It was my intention that it be captured and delivered to the High Lord just as he had ordered. I believed it a dangerous undertaking because the black unicorn has long been reported a thing of ill fortune. But, then again, the High Lord has shown an extraordinary capacity for turning ill fortune to his advantage." He paused. "I admit I was bothered by his insistence on the unicorn's immediate capture and by his refusal to explain that insistence to us. Yet I still intended that the unicorn be taken." He took a deep breath. "But when I saw the beast before me in that wood, standing there—when I saw what it was . . . I could not allow it to be taken. I don't know why, I just couldn't. No, that is not true—I do know why. It wasn't right. I could feel inside me that it wasn't right. Didn't you sense it, too, Abernathy? The unicorn was not meant to belong to the High Lord. It was not meant to belong to anyone." He glanced up again uncertainly. "So I used the magic to see that it wouldn't. I let it escape."

Abernathy snapped at something that flew past him, then shoved his dust-encrusted glasses back on his nose and sneezed. "Well, you should have said so sooner, wizard, instead of letting me think that your magic had simply bested you once again. This, at least, I can understand."

"Can you?" Questor shook his head doubtfully. "I wish I could. I have acted against the wishes of the High Lord when I am sworn to his service, and the only reason I can give is that serving him in this instance felt wrong. He was right to dismiss me from the court."

"And me also, I suppose?"

"No, he should not have dismissed you. You had no part in what happened."

"The fact of the matter is, he was wrong to dismiss either of us!"

Questor shrugged helplessly. "He is the High Lord. Who are we to question his judgment?"

"Humph!" Abernathy snorted derisively. "The hunt was an ill-advised exercise of judgment, if ever there was one. He knew the history of the black unicorn. We told him the beast would not be trapped in a hunt, and he completely ignored us. He has never done that before, wizard. I tell you, he is obsessed with this beast. He thinks of nothing else. He has spoken of Willow only once—and that a tirade over her failure to return to him with the golden bridle. He ignores his duties, he keeps to his rooms, and he confides in no one. Not a single mention has been made of the books of magic since you returned them to him. I had hoped that the High Lord might give at least some *brief* consideration into looking for a way to use them to return me to my former self. Once, the High Lord would have done so without even having to think about it . . ."

The scribe trailed off self-consciously, glowering at the flames of the little fire. "Well, no matter. The point is, he is not himself these days, Questor Thews. He is not himself."

The wizard's owlish face twisted thoughtfully. "No." He glanced momentarily at Bunion and was surprised to find the kobold nodding in agreement. "No, he most certainly is not."

"Hasn't been since . . ."

"Since we discovered that impostor in his bed chamber?"

"Since then, yes. Since that night."

They were silent again for a moment. Then their eyes met, and they were startled by what they found mirrored there. "Is it possible that . . ." Abernathy began uncertainly.

"That the impostor *was* the High Lord?" Questor finished. He frowned his deepest frown. "I would not have thought so before, but now . . ."

"There is no way we can be certain, of course," Abernathy interrupted quickly.

"No, no way," Questor agreed.

The fire crackled and spit, the smoke blew across them with a shift in the wind, and sparks danced into the ashes. From somewhere far away, a night bird sounded a long, mournful cry that brought shivers down Questor's spine. He exchanged quick glances with Abernathy and Bunion.

"I hate sleeping out-of-doors," Abernathy muttered. "I don't like fleas and ticks and crawly things trying to assume occupancy of my fur."

"I have a plan," Questor said suddenly.

Abernathy gave him a long, hard look, the kind he always gave when confronted with a pronouncement he would just as soon live without. "I am almost afraid to ask what it is, wizard," he responded finally.

"We will go to the dragon. We will go to Strabo."

Bunion's teeth gleamed in a frightening grin. "That is a plan?" demanded Abernathy, horrified.

Questor leaned forward eagerly. "But it makes perfect sense that we should go to Strabo. Who knows more about unicorns than dragons? Once they were the greatest of enemies—the oldest adversaries in the world of fairy. Now the black unicorn is the last of his kind, and Strabo the last of his. They share a common cause, a natural affinity! Surely we can learn something of the unicorn from the dragon—enough perhaps to unravel its mystery and to discover its purpose in coming to Landover!"

Abernathy stared in disbelief. "But the dragon doesn't like us, Questor Thews! Have you forgotten that? He will roast us for a midday snack!" He paused. "Besides, what good will it do to learn anything more about the unicorn? The beast has caused us trouble enough as it is."

"But if we understand its purpose, we might discover a reason for the High Lord's obsession," Questor replied quickly. "We might even find a way to reinstate ourselves at court. It is not inconceivable. And the dragon will not cause us harm. He will be happy to visit with us once he has learned our purpose in coming. Do not forget, Abernathy, that dragons and wizards share a common background as well. The nature and duration of our professional relationship has always dictated a certain degree of mutual respect."

Abernathy's lip curled. "What a lot of nonsense!"

Questor barely seemed to hear him. There was a faraway look in his eye. "There were games played between wizards and dragons in the old days that would challenge the faint of heart, I can tell you. Games of magic and games of skill." He cocked his head slightly. "A game or two might be necessary here if Strabo chooses to be obdurate. Theft of knowledge is a skill I have mastered well, and it would be fun to test myself once more . . ."

"You are mad!" Abernathy was appalled.

But Questor's enthusiasm was not to be dampened. He came to his feet, excitement in his eyes as he paced the circle of the fire. "Well, no matter. What is necessary must be done. I have made my decision. I shall go to the dragon." He paused. "Bunion will go with me, won't you, Bunion?" The kobold nodded, grinning ear to ear. The wizard's hands fluttered. "There, it is settled. I am going. Bunion is going. And you must come with us, Abernathy." He stopped, hands lowering, tall form stooping slightly as if from the weight of his sudden frown. "We must go, you know. After all, what else is there for us to do?"

He stared questioningly at the scribe. Abernathy stared back, sharing the look. There was a long silence while doubt and uncertainty waged a silent war with self-esteem in the old friends' eyes. There were shadows of times they had believed past come back to haunt their present, and they felt those shadows closing inexorably about. They could not permit that. Anything was better than waiting for such suffocating darkness.

The ridgeline was still again, a dark spine against a sky of stars and moons that seemed cold and distant. The line shack and the stock pen were the bones of an aging earth.

"Very well," Abernathy agreed, sighing his most grievous sigh. "We will all be fools together."

No one spoke up to dispute him.

MASK

Sunrise found Fillip and Sot present and accounted for as promised. They were standing a good twenty yards away when Ben came awake, a pair of motionless, squat shadows in the fading dark, their travel packs strapped to their backs, their caps with solitary red feathers set firmly in place. They appeared bushes at first glance; but after Ben rose to stretch muscles cramped from the chill and the hard earth, they came forward a few tentative steps and gave anxious greetings. They seemed more nervous than usual and kept peering past him as if they expected an onslaught of Crag Trolls at any moment.

It took Ben a moment to realize that they were not on guard against Trolls, but against Edgewood Dirk.

Dirk, for his part, ignored them. He was sitting on the tree stump washing when Ben thought to look for him, his silky coat smooth and glistening as if damp from morning dew. He did not glance up or respond to Ben's good morning. He went on about the business of cleaning himself until he was satisfied that the job was properly completed, then settled down to the contents of a bowl of spring water that Ben had provided. Ben hadn't thought about it before, but Dirk never seemed to eat much. What he survived on was something of a mystery, but it was a mystery that Ben chose to leave unsolved. He had enough puzzles to deal with without adding another.

They departed shortly after waking, Ben and Dirk leading—depending on how you defined the word "leading," for once again Dirk seemed to know where Ben was going almost before he did. The gnomes trailed. Fillip and Sot clearly wanted no part of Edgewood Dirk. They stayed well back of the cat and watched him the way you would a snake. Fillip was limping noticeably and Sot appeared to have burned a good portion of the fur off his wrists and the backs of his hands. Neither had anything to say about their injuries, and Ben let them be.

They traveled through the morning at a steady pace, the sun shining brightly from out of a cloudless sky, the smell of wild flowers and fruit trees scenting the air. Signs of the wilt prevailed. They remained small but noticeable, and Ben thought again of Meeks in his guise, of the demons come back out of Abaddon at his bidding, of the lessening of magic in the land, and the stealing of its life. There was a renewed urgency tugging him along, a sense that time was slipping from him too quickly. He was no closer than he had ever been to discovering what had been done to him. He still had no idea why the black unicorn had come back into Landover or what its importance was to Meeks. He knew only that there was a tie connecting all that had happened and he had to unknot it if he were ever to straighten this mess out.

Thinking of that led him to think once again about Edgewood Dirk. It continued to grate on him that the cat chose to remain such an enigma when he could obviously explain himself. Ben was reasonably sure by now that Dirk had not simply stumbled across him that first night in the lake country, but had deliberately sought him out. He was also reasonably sure that Dirk was staying with him for a reason and not simply out of curiosity. But Dirk was not about to explain himself to Ben until he felt like it; and given the cat's peculiar nature, that explanation was likely to be offered along about the twelfth of never. Still, it seemed abhorrent to Ben simply to accept the beast's presence without making any further effort whatsoever to learn something of what had brought it to him in the first place.

As morning lengthened toward noon and the shadow of the Deep Fell began to grow visible, he decided to take another crack at the cat. He had been busy during the trek, mulling over the possibility of a common link between the various unicorns he had encountered since his dream. There were, after all, quite a number of them. There was the black unicorn. There were the sketched unicorns contained in the missing books of magic—correction, one of the missing books of magic; the other was a burned-out shell. And there were the fairy unicorns that had disappeared centuries ago on their journey through Landover to the mortal worlds. It was the legend of the fairy unicorns that concerned him just now. He already believed that there must be a link between the black unicorn and the drawings contained in the books of magic. Otherwise, why had Meeks sent dreams of both? Why did he want them both so badly? The real question was whether they also had some connection with the missing fairy unicorns. He realized that it would be something of a coincidence if there actually were a connection among the three, but he was beginning to wonder if it wouldn't be an even bigger coincidence if there weren't. Magic tied all three in a single bond, and he would have bet his life that it was some sort of control over the magic that Meeks was after.

So. Enough debate. Maybe solving one of the little puzzles would aid in solving the big one. And maybe—just maybe—Edgewood Dirk would be less reticent to help . . .

"Dirk, you've been a lot of places and seen a lot of things." He opened the conversation as casually as he could manage, not giving himself a chance to dwell further on it. "What do you think about this legend of the missing fairy unicorns?"

The cat didn't even look at him. "I don't think about it at all."

"No? Well what if you did think about it? You said you knew something of the missing white unicorns when we first met, didn't you?"

"I did."

"About the unicorns the fairy people sent into the other worlds? The ones who somehow disappeared?"

"The very same." Dirk sounded bored.

"So what do you think happened to them? How did they disappear?"

"How?" The cat sniffed. "They were stolen, of course."

Ben was so astonished at getting a straight answer for a change that he failed to follow up on it for a moment. "But . . . stolen by whom?" he managed finally.

"By someone who wanted them, High Lord—who else? By someone who had the ability and means to capture them and hold them fast."

"And who would that have been?"

Dirk sounded irritated. "Now who do you think that would have been?"

Ben hesitated, considering. "A wizard?"

"Not *a* wizard—*wizards*! There were many in those days, not simply one or two as there are now. They had their own guild, their own association—loosely formed, but effective when it chose to be. The magic was stronger then in Landover, and the wizards hired out to anyone who needed their skills most and could best afford it. They were powerful men for a time—until they chose to challenge the King himself."

"What happened?"

"The King summoned the Paladin, and the Paladin destroyed them. After that, there was only one real wizard permitted—and he served the King."

Ben frowned. "But if the unicorns were stolen by the wizards, what happened to them after the wizards were . . . disposed of? Why weren't they set free?"

"No one knew where they were."

"But shouldn't someone have looked for them? Shouldn't they have been found?"

"Yes and yes."

"Then why weren't they?"

Dirk slowed, stopped, and blinked sleepily. "The question no one asked then is the one you fail to ask now, High Lord. Why were the unicorns stolen in the first place?"

Ben stopped as well, thought momentarily, and shrugged. "They were beautiful creatures. The wizards wanted them for themselves, I suppose."

"Yes, yes, yes! Is that the best you can do?"

"Well, uh . . ." He paused again, feeling very much a fool. "Why can't you just explain it to me, damn it?" he demanded, exasperated.

Dirk eyed him steadily. "Because I don't choose to," he said softly. "Because you have to learn how to see things clearly again."

Ben stared at him momentarily, glanced back at the G'home Gnomes who were watching from a safe distance back, and folded his arms across his chest wearily. He had no idea what Dirk was talking about, but it didn't do any good to argue with the cat.

"All right," he said finally. "Let me try again. The wizards discovered that the fairies were sending unicorns through Landover into the mortal worlds. They stole the unicorns for themselves instead. They stole them because . . ." He stopped, remembering suddenly the missing books and the drawings. "They stole the unicorns because they wanted their magic! That's what the drawings in that book mean! They have something to do with the missing unicorns!"

Edgewood Dirk cocked his head. "Do you really think so, High Lord?"

He was so genuinely curious that Ben was left not knowing what to think. He had expected the cat to agree with him, but the cat looked as surprised as he!

"Yes, I really think so," he declared at last, wondering nevertheless. "I think the missing unicorns and the missing books are tied together and the black unicorn has something to do with both."

"That does stand to reason," Dirk agreed.

"But how were the unicorns stolen? And how could the wizards steal their magic? Weren't the unicorns as powerful as the wizards?"

"I am told so," Dirk agreed once more.

"Then what happened to them? Where are they hidden?"

"Perhaps they wear masks."

"Masks?" Ben was confused.

"Like your own. Perhaps they wear masks, and we cannot see them."

"Like my own?"

"Would you mind not repeating everything I say?"

"But what are you talking about, for Pete's sake?"

Dirk gave him a "Why bother asking me?" look and sniffed the late morning air as if the answers he sought might be found there. The black tail twitched. "I find I am quite thirsty, High Lord. Would you care to join me for a drink?"

Without waiting for a response, he stood and trotted off into the trees to one side. Ben stared after him a moment, then followed. They walked a short distance to a pool fed from a small rapids and bent to drink. Ben drank rapidly, more thirsty than he had expected. Dirk took his time, dainty to the point of annoyance—lapping gently, pausing frequently, carefully keeping the water from his paws. Ben was conscious of Fillip and Sot in the background watching, but paid them no mind. His attention was given over entirely to the cat and to what Dirk was going to say next—because he most certainly was going to say something or Ben was as mistaken as he had ever been in his life!

Ben was not mistaken. A moment later, Dirk sat back on his haunches and glanced over. "Look at yourself in the water, High Lord," he ordered. Ben did and saw a dilapidated version of himself, but himself nevertheless. "Now look at yourself out of the water," Dirk continued. Ben did and saw ragged clothes and cracked boots, dirt and grime, an unshaved, unkempt, unwashed body. He could see nothing of his face. "Now look at yourself in the water again—look closely."

Ben did, and this time he saw the image of himself shimmer and change into the image of someone he did not recognize, a stranger whose clothes were the same ones he wore.

He looked up sharply. "I don't look like me anymore—not even to myself!" There was a hint of fear in his voice that he could not disguise, even though he tried.

"And that, my dear High Lord, is because you are beginning to *lose* yourself," Edgewood Dirk said softly. "The mask you wear is becoming you!" The black face dipped closer. "Find yourself, Ben Holiday, before that happens. Take off your mask, and perhaps then you can find a way to unmask the unicorns as well."

Ben looked back hurriedly at the pool of water and to his relief found his old face back again in the reflection of the waters. But the definition of his features seemed weak. It was almost as if he were fading away.

He looked up again for Dirk, but the cat was already trotting away, scattering the fearful gnomes before him. "Best hurry, High Lord," he called back. "The Deep Fell is no place to be looking for oneself after nightfall."

Ben climbed slowly to his feet, not only more confused than ever but also frightened now as well. "Why do I ask that damn cat anything?" he muttered in frustration.

But he already knew the answer to that question, of course. He shook his head at matters in general and hastened after.

By midafternoon, they had reached the Deep Fell.

It was unchanged and unchanging—a dark, impenetrable smudge on an otherwise brightly sunlit expanse of forestland, hunched down against the earth in the manner of a creature in hiding, tensed to flee or strike. Shadows and mist played hide and seek in its sprawling depths, crawling with slow, irregular movements over trees and swamp and murk. Nothing else could be seen. What life forms there were lay in wait, pawns in a hard and vicious game of survival that rewarded only the quick and the strong. Sounds were muted and colors shaded gray. Only death was at home within the Deep Fell, and only death was immutable. Ben and his companions could sense that truth. Standing at the hollows rim, they stared downward into its darkness and thought their separate thoughts.

"Well, we might as well get at it," Ben muttered finally. He was remembering the last time he had come into the Deep Fell and the terrifying illusions that Nightshade had created to keep him out—the illusions of endless swamp, lizards, and worse. He was thinking of his encounter with the witch—an encounter that had almost cost him his life. He was not looking forward to a repeat performance.

"Well," he said again, the word trailing off into silence.

No one was paying any attention to him. Dirk sat next to him, eyes lidded and sleepy-looking as he basked in a small patch of sunlight and watched the movement of the mists in the Deep Fell. Fillip and Sot stood a good dozen yards left, well away from the cat and the hollows. They were whispering in small, anxious voices.

He shook his head. "Fillip. Sot."

The G'home Gnomes cringed away, pretending not to hear him.

"Get over here!" he snapped irritably, his patience with gnomes and cats in general exhausted.

The gnomes came sheepishly, tentatively, edging forward with uneasy looks at Dirk, who as usual paid them no heed. When they were as close as they were going to get without being dragged, Ben knelt down to face them, his eyes finding theirs.

"Are you certain that Nightshade is down there?" he asked quietly.

"Yes, High Lord."

"She is, High Lord."

Ben nodded. "Then I want you to be careful," he told them quietly. This was no time for impatience or anger, and he suppressed both. "I want you to be very careful, all right? I don't want you to do anything that will place you in any real danger. Just go down there and look around. I need to know if Willow is there—or even if she's been there earlier. That's first. Find out any way you can."

He paused, and the wide brown eyes of the gnomes shifted uneasily. He waited a moment, captured them again with his own. "There is a bridle made out of spun gold," he continued. "Nightshade has it hidden down there somewhere. I need that bridle. I want you to see if you can find it. If you can, I want you to steal it."

The brown eyes widened suddenly to the size of saucers. "No, it's all right, don't be afraid," Ben soothed quickly. "You don't have to steal it if the witch is anywhere about—only if she's not or if you can take it without her knowing. Just do what you can. I'll protect you."

That was probably the worst lie he had told in his entire life; he didn't really have any way to protect them. But he had to do something to reassure them or they would simply bolt at the first opportunity. They might do that anyway, but he was hoping the majesty of his office would hold them in thrall just long enough to get this job done.

"High Lord, the witch will hurt us!" Fillip declared.

"Hurt us badly!" Sot agreed.

"No, she won't," Ben insisted. "If you're careful, she won't even know you're down there. You've been down there before, haven't you?" Two heads nodded as one. "She didn't see you then, did she?" Two heads nodded again. "Then there's no reason she will see you this time either, is there? Just do as I told you and be careful."

Fillip and Sot looked at each other long and hard. There was enough doubt in their eyes to float a battleship. Finally, they looked back again at Ben.

"Just go down once," said Fillip.

"Just once," echoed Sot.

"All right, all right, just once," Ben agreed, casting an anxious glance at the fading afternoon sun. "But hurry, will you?"

The gnomes disappeared reluctantly into the hollows gloom. Ben watched them until they were out of sight, then sat back to wait.

As he waited, he found himself thinking about Edgewood Dirk's repeated references to masks. He wore a mask. The missing unicorns wore masks. That's what the cat had said, but what did the cat mean? He propped himself up against the base of a tree trunk some dozen yards from where Dirk basked in the sunlight and tried to reason it through. It was, after all, about time he reasoned *something* through. Lawyers were supposed to be able to do that; it was indigenous to their profession. King or no in Landover, he was still a lawyer with a lawyer's habits and a lawyer's way of thinking. So think, he exhorted himself! Think!

He thought. Nothing came. Masks were worn by actors and bandits. You wore them to disguise yourself. You put them on and then you took them off when you were done with the disguise. But what did that have to do with him? Or the unicorns? None of us are trying to disguise ourselves, he thought. Meeks is trying to disguise me. Who's trying to disguise the unicorns?

The wizards who took them, that's who.

The answer came instantly to him. He shifted upright. The wizards stole the unicorns and then hid them by disguising them. He nodded. It made sense. So how did they disguise them? With masks? What, turned them into cows or trees or something? No. He frowned. Start over again. The wizards took the unicorns—how did they do that—so they could steal their magic. The wizards wanted the magic for their own. But what would they do with it? What use would they find for it? Where was the magic now?

His eyes widened. There were no longer any other true wizards besides Meeks. The source of his power was in the missing but now found books of magic, the books that were supposedly a compilation of the magics acquired by wizards down through the years—the books with the drawing of the unicorns! Sure, the unicorns in the books—or the one book, at least—were drawings of the missing unicorns!

But why make drawings?

Or are they the unicorns themselves?

"Yes!" he whispered in surprise.

It was so impossible that he hadn't seen it before—but impossible only in his own world, not in Landover where magic was the norm! The missing unicorns, the unicorns no one had seen for centuries, their magic intact, were trapped in the wizards' books! And the reason that there was nothing else in the books but the drawings of the unicorns was that the magic of the books was entirely that of the unicorns—magic that the wizards had stolen!

And harnessed to their own use?

He didn't know. He started to say something to Dirk, then checked himself. There was no point in asking the cat if he was right; the cat would simply find a way to confuse him all over again. Figure it out for yourself, he admonished! The unicorns had been transformed by wizard magic into the drawings in the missing books—that would explain the disappearance of the unicorns for all these years, the reason that Meeks had sent the dream of the books to Questor, and the need Meeks had for the books. It would even explain Dirk's reference to masks.

Or was he just reaching now?

He paused. There were a few other matters still lacking explanation, he realized. What about the black unicorn? Was it simply a white unicorn that had escaped from the books—the first book, perhaps, the one with the burned-out core? Why was it black now if it had been white before? Ash or soot? Ridiculous! Why had it appeared and then disappeared again at other times over the years if it were a prisoner in the wizards' books? Why was Meeks so desperate to get it back now?

His hands twisted in knots. If one unicorn could break free, why couldn't the rest?

His confusion began to compound. Meeks had hinted that Ben had done something to wreck his plans, but hadn't said what. If that was so, it had to have something to do with the unicorns, black and white. But Ben hadn't the foggiest idea what that something was.

He sat puzzling matters through without success as afternoon stretched toward nightfall and the sun disappeared westward. Shadows lengthened almost imperceptibly across the forest. Slowly, the darkness and mist of the Deep Fell crept out of their daytime confinement to link hands with those shadows and close about Ben and Dirk. The day's warmth faded into evening chill.

Ben ceased his musings and concentrated on the slope of the hollows. Where were Fillip and Sot? Shouldn't they have been back by now? He climbed to his feet and stalked to the edge of the pit. There was nothing to be seen. He walked its rim for several hundred yards in both directions, through patches of scrub and brush, peering into the gloom. No luck. A growing uneasiness settled through him. He hadn't really believed the little gnomes were in any danger or he wouldn't have sent them down alone. Maybe he had been mistaken. Maybe that was the way he had wanted to see it and not the way it was.

He stalked back to his starting point and stood staring at the smudge of the Deep Fell helplessly. The dangers of the hollows had never bothered the gnomes before. Had something changed that? Damn it, he should have gone with them!

He glanced over at Dirk. Dirk appeared to be sleeping.

Ben waited some more because he didn't have much choice. The minutes dragged interminably. It was growing darker. It was becoming difficult to distinguish things clearly as the twilight deepened.

Then suddenly there was movement at the hollows rim. Ben straightened, came forward a step, and stopped. A mass of brush parted, and Fillip and Sot pushed their way into view.

"Thank heavens you're all . . ." Ben started and trailed off.

The G'home Gnomes were rigid with fear. Paralyzed. Their furry faces were twisted into masks of foreboding, their eyes bright and fixed. They looked neither right nor left nor even at Ben. They stared straight ahead and saw nothing. They stood with their backs to the mass of brush and held hands in the manner of small children.

Ben rushed forward, frightened now. Something was dreadfully wrong. "Fillip! Sot!" He knelt down before them, trying to break whatever spell it was that held them fast. "Look at me. What happened?"

"*I* happened, play-King!" an unpleasantly familiar voice whispered.

Ben looked up, past the frozen gnomes, at the tall, black shape that had materialized behind them as if by magic and found himself face to face with Nightshade.

WITCH AND DRAGON, DRAGON AND WITCH

Ben stared voicelessly into the cold green eyes of the witch and, if there had been some place to run, he would have been halfway there already. But there was no running away from Nightshade. She held him fast simply by the force of her presence. She was a wall that he could neither scale nor get around. She was his prison.

Her voice was a whisper. "I never believed it possible that you would be so foolish as to come back here."

Foolish, indeed, he agreed silently. He forced himself to reach out to the terrified gnomes and draw them to him, away from the witch. They fell into him like rag dolls, shaking with relief, burying their furry faces in his tunic.

"Please help us, High Lord!" was the best Fillip could manage, his own voice a whisper.

"Yes, please!" echoed Sot.

"It's all right," Ben lied.

Nightshade laughed softly. She was just as Ben remembered her—tall and sharp-featured, her skin as pale and smooth as marble, her hair jet black, save for a single streak of white down its center, her lean, angular frame cloaked all in black. She was beautiful in her way, ageless in appearance, a creature who had somehow come to terms with her mortality. Yet her face failed to reflect the emotions that would have made her complete. Her eyes were depthless and empty. They looked ready to swallow him.

Well, I asked for this, he thought.

Nightshade's laughter died away then, and there was the barest hint of uncertainty in her eyes. She came forward a step, peering at him. "What is this?" she asked softly. "You are not the same . . ." She trailed off, confused. "But you must be; the gnomes have named you High Lord . . . Here, let me see your face in the light."

She reached out. Ben was powerless to resist. Fingers as cold as icicles fastened on his chin and tilted his head to the moonlight. She held him there a moment, muttering. "You *are* different—yet the same, too. What has been done to you, play-King? Or is this some new game you seek to play with me? Are you not Holiday?" Ben could feel Fillip and Sot shivering against his body, tiny hands digging into him. "Ah, there is *magic* at work here," Nightshade whispered harshly, fingers releasing his face with a twist. "Whose magic is it? Tell me, now—quickly!"

Ben fought back an urge to scream, fought to keep his voice steady. "Meeks. He's come back. He's made himself King and changed me into . . . this."

"Meeks?" The green eyes narrowed. "That pathetic charlatan? How has he found magic enough to accomplish this?" Her mouth twisted with disdain. "He lacks the means to tie his own shoes! How could he manage to do this to you?"

Ben said nothing. He didn't have an answer to give her.

There was a long moment of silence as the witch studied him. Finally, she said, "Where is the medallion? Let me see it!"

When he didn't immediately respond, she made a quick motion with her fingers. Despite his resolve, he found himself withdrawing the tarnished emblem from his tunic for her inspection. She stared at it a moment, then stared again at his face, then slowly smiled the smile of a predator eyeing dinner.

"So," she whispered.

That was all she said. It was enough. Ben knew instantly that she had figured out what had been done to him. He knew that she understood the nature of the magic that had changed him. Her realization of it was infuriating to him. It was worse than being held like this. He wanted to scream. He *had* to know what she had learned, and there was no way in the world that she was going to tell him.

"You are pathetic, play-King," she went on, her voice still soft but insinuating now as well. "You have always been lucky, but never smart. Your luck has run out. I am almost tempted to leave you as you are. Almost. But I cannot forget what you did to me. I want to be the one to make you suffer for that! Are you surprised to see me again? I think perhaps you are. You thought me gone forever, I imagine—gone into the world of fairy to perish. How foolish of you."

She knelt down before him so that her eyes were level with his. There was such hate that he flinched from it. "I flew into the mists, play-King—just as you commanded that I must, just as I was bidden. The Io Dust held me bound to your command, and I could not refuse. How I despised you then! But I could do nothing. So I flew into the mists—but I flew slowly, play-King, slowly! I fought to break the spell of the Io Dust as I flew; I fought with all the power that I could summon!"

The smile returned again, slow and hard. "And I *did* break the spell finally. I shattered it and turned back again. Too late, though, play-King, much too late—for I was already within the fairy mists and there was damage done to me! I hurt as never before; I was scarred by the pain of it! I escaped with my life and little else. It took me months to regain even the smallest part of my magic. I lay within the swamp, a creature in hiding, as helpless as the smallest reptile! I was broken! But I would not give in to the pain and the fear; I thought only of you. I thought only of what I would do to you once I had you in my hands again. And I knew that one day I would find a way to bring you back to me . . ."

She paused. "But I never dreamed it would happen so soon, my foolish High Lord. What great good fortune! It was the change that brought you to me, wasn't it? Something about the change—but what? Tell me, play-King. I will have it from you anyway."

Ben knew this was so. There was no sense in trying to keep anything from the witch. He could see in the empty green eyes what was in store for him. Talking was the only thing that was keeping him alive, and as long as he was alive he had a chance. Chances at this point were not to be tossed aside lightly.

"I came looking for Willow," he answered, pushing the gnomes behind him now. He wanted them out of the way—just in case. He had to keep his eyes open for the right opportunity. The gnomes, however, continued to cling to him like Velcro.

"The River Master's daughter? The sylph?" Nightshade's look was questioning. "Why would she come here?"

"You haven't seen her?" Ben asked, surprised.

Nightshade smiled unpleasantly. "No, play-King. I have seen no one but you—you and your foolish burrow people. What would the sylph want with me?"

He hesitated, then took a deep breath. "The golden bridle."

There, it was out. Better to tell her and see if he could learn anything than to play it cute. Fencing with Nightshade was too dangerous.

Nightshade looked genuinely surprised. "The bridle? But why?"

"Because Meeks wants it. Because he sent Willow a dream about the bridle and a black unicorn." Quickly he told the witch the story of Willow's dream and of the sylph's decision to try to learn what she could of the bridle. "She was told that the bridle was here in the Deep Fell." He paused. "She should have arrived here ahead of me."

"A pity she didn't," Nightshade replied. "I like her little better than I like you. Destroying her would have given me almost as much satisfaction as destroying you." She paused, thinking. "The black unicorn, is it? Back again? How interesting. And the bridle can hold it fast, the dream says? Yes, that could be possible. After all, it was created by wizard magic. And it was a wizard I stole it from years back . . ."

Nightshade laughed. She studied him, a cunning look creeping into her eyes. "These pathetic burrow people who belong to you—were they sent to steal the bridle from me?"

Fillip and Sot were trying to crawl inside Ben's skin, but Ben was barely aware of them. He was thinking of something else altogether. If Meeks had once possessed the bridle, then that meant the wizard probably once used it—might even have used it to hold captive the black unicorn. Had the unicorn somehow escaped then? Was the dream Meeks had sent to Willow designed to regain possession of the bridle so that the unicorn could be recaptured? If so, what did the unicorns in the missing books of magic have to do with . . .

"Do not bother answering, play-King," Nightshade interrupted his thoughts. "The answer is in your eyes. These foolish rodents crept into the Deep Fell for just that reason, didn't they? Crept into my home like the thieves they are? Crept down on their little cat's paws?"

The mention of cat's paws reminded him suddenly of Edgewood Dirk. Where was the prism cat? He glanced around before he could think better of it, but Dirk was nowhere to be seen.

"Looking for someone?" Nightshade demanded at once. Her eyes swept the darkened forest behind Ben like knives. "I see no one," she muttered after a moment. "Whoever it is you look for must have abandoned you."

Nevertheless, she took a moment to make certain that she was right before turning back to him. "Your thieves are as pathetic as you, play-King," she resumed her attack. "They think themselves invisible, but they remain unseen only when I do not *wish* to see them. They were so obvious in their efforts on this misadventure that I could not fail to see them. The minute they were mine, they called for you. 'Great High Lord; mighty High Lord!' How foolish! They gave you up without my even having to ask!"

Fillip and Sot were shaking so hard Ben was in danger of being toppled. He put a hand on each to try to offer some sort of reassurance. He felt genuinely sorry for the little fellows. After all, they were in this mess because of him.

"Since you have me, why not let the gnomes go?" he asked the witch suddenly. "They're foolish creatures, as you say. I tricked them into helping me. They really didn't have a choice. They don't even know why they're here."

"Worse luck for them." Nightshade dismissed the plea out of hand. "No one goes free who stands with you, play-King." Her face lifted, black hair sweeping back. Her eyes scanned the darkness once more. "I no longer like it here. Come."

She rose, a black shadow that gained in size as she spread her arms. Her robes billowed out like sailcloth. There was a sudden wind through the trees, cold and sharp, and mist from the Deep Fell lifted to wrap them all. Moons and stars vanished into its murk, and there was a sudden sense of lifting free, of floating. The G'home Gnomes clutched Ben tighter than ever, and he in turn held them for lack of something better to hold. There was a *whoosh*ing sound and then silence.

Ben blinked against the cold and the mist, and slowly the light returned. Nightshade stood before him, smiling coldly. The smells of swamp and mist hung thick on the air. Torchlight revealed a row of stanchions and the bones of tables and benches scattered across an empty court.

They were somewhere within the Deep Fell, down in Nightshade's home.

"Do you know what is to happen to you now, play-King?" she asked softly.

He had a pretty good idea. His imagination was working overtime on the possibilities despite his efforts to restrain it. His chances appeared to have run out. He wondered fleetingly why it was that Willow hadn't gotten here before him. Wasn't this where the Earth Mother had told her to go? If she wasn't here, where was she?

He wondered what had become of Edgewood Dirk.

Nightshade's sudden hiss jarred him free of his thoughts. "Shall I hang you to dry like a piece of old meat? Or shall I play games with you awhile first? We must take our time with this, mustn't we?"

She started to say something more, then paused as a new thought struck her. "But, no—I have a much better idea! I have a much grander and more fitting demise in mind for you!"

She bent into him. "Do you know that I no longer have the golden bridle, play-King? No? I thought not. It was stolen from me. It was stolen while I was too weak to prevent it, still recovering from the hurt that *you* caused me! Do you know who has the bridle now? Strabo, play-King! The dragon has the fairy bridle, the bridle that rightfully belongs to me. How ironic! You come to the Deep Fell in search of something that isn't even here! You come to your doom pointlessly!"

Her face was only inches from his own, skin drawn tight against the bones, the streak in her black hair a silver slash. "Ah, but you give me a chance to do something I could not otherwise do! Strabo dotes on things made of gold, though he has no use for them except as baubles! He has no true appreciation of their worth—especially the bridle with its magic! He would never give it back to me, and I cannot take it from him while he keeps it hidden within the Fire Springs. But he would trade it, play-King. He most certainly would trade it for something he values more."

Her smile was ferocious. "And what does he value more in all the world than a chance to gain his revenge against you?"

Ben couldn't imagine. Strabo had been a victim of the Io Dust as well, and he had left Ben with the promise that one day he would repay him. Ben felt the bottom drop out of his stomach. This was like being *pushed* from the frying pan into the fire. He tried to keep the witch from seeing what he was feeling and failed.

Nightshade's smile broadened in satisfaction. "Yes, play-King—I will be most content to leave the means of your destruction to the dragon!"

She brought her hands up in a sharp swirl of motion, mists rising as if bidden, chill wind returning in a rush. "Let us see what fun Strabo will have with you!" she cried, and her voice was a hiss.

The G'home Gnomes whimpered and fastened once again on his pant legs. Ben felt himself floating and watched the hollows begin to disappear . . .

The eastern wastelands lay empty and desolate in the fading afternoon light as Questor Thews, Abernathy, and Bunion worked their way steadily ahead through tangled brush and deadwood, over ridgelines and down ravines, across brief stretches of desert, and around swamp and bog. They had walked all day, pushing aside fatigue and uneasiness in equal measure, determined to reach the home of the dragon by nightfall.

It was going to be close.

Nothing lived in the wastelands of Landover—nothing but the dragon. He had adopted the wastelands as his home when driven from the mists of fairy centuries ago. The wastelands suited the dragon fine. He liked it there. His disposition found proper solace in the devastation wrought by nature's whims, and he kept the whole of the vast expanse his own. Shunned by the other inhabitants of the valley, he was an entirely solitary being. He was the only creature in the valley—with the exception of Ben Holiday—who could cross back and forth between Landover and the mortal worlds. He could even venture a short distance into the fairy mists. He was unique—the last of his kind and quite proud to be so.

He was not particularly fond of company—a fact not lost on Questor, Abernathy, and Bunion as they hurried now to reach the beast before it got any darker.

It was dusk nevertheless by the time they finally arrived at their destination. They climbed to the crest of a ridgeline that was silhouetted against the coming night by a brightness that flickered and danced as if alive and found themselves staring down into the Fire Springs. The Springs were the dragon's lair. They were settled within a deep, misshapen ravine, a cluster of craters that burned steadily with blue and yellow fire amid tangled thickets and mounds of rock and earth. Fed by a liquid pooled within the craters, their flames filled the air with smoke, ash, and the raw stench of burning fuel. A constant haze hung across the ravine and the hills surrounding, and geysers lifted periodically against the darkness with booming coughs.

They saw the dragon right off. It slouched down within the center of the ravine, head resting on a crater's edge, long tongue licking placidly at a scattering of flames.

Strabo didn't move. He lay sprawled across a mound of earth, his monstrous body a mass of scales, spikes, and plates that seemed almost a part of the landscape. When he breathed, small jets of steam exhaled into the night. His tail was wrapped around a rock formation that rose behind him, and his wings lay back against his body. His claws and teeth were blackened and bent, grown from leathered skin and gums at odd angles and twists. Dust and grime covered him like a blanket.

One red eye swiveled in its socket. "What do you want?" the dragon asked irritably.

It had always amazed Ben Holiday that a dragon could talk, but Ben was an outlander and didn't understand the nature of these things. It seemed perfectly normal to Questor and Bunion that the dragon should talk, and even more so to Abernathy, being a soft-coated Wheaten Terrier who himself talked.

"We wish to speak with you a moment," Questor advised. Abernathy managed an affirming nod, but found himself wondering at the same time why anyone in his right mind would wish to speak with something as awful as Strabo.

"I care nothing for what you wish," the dragon said with a huff of steam from both nostrils. "I care only for what I wish. Go away."

"This will only take a moment," Questor persisted.

"I don't have a moment. Go away before I eat you."

Questor flushed. "I would remind you to whom you are speaking! There is some courtesy owed me, given our long association! Now, please be civil!"

As if to emphasize his demand, he took a meaningful step forward, a scarecrow figure in tattered sashes that looked like nothing so much as a bundle of loosely joined sticks silhouetted against the light. Bunion showed all his teeth in a frightening grin. Abernathy pushed his glasses further up on his nose and tried to calculate how quickly he could reach the safety of the darkened brush at the base of the ravine behind him.

Strabo blinked and lifted his head from the crater fire. "Questor Thews, is that you?"

Questor puffed out. "It most certainly is."

Strabo sighed. "How boring. If you were someone of consequence, you might at least prove a brief source of amusement. But you are not worth the effort it would take me to rise and devour you. Go away."

Questor stiffened. Ignoring Abernathy's paw on his shoulder, he came forward another step. "My friends and I have journeyed a long way to speak with you—and speak with you we will! If you choose to ignore the long and honorable association between wizards and dragons, that is your loss! But you do us both a great disservice!"

"You seem rather ill-tempered tonight," the dragon replied. His voice reverberated in a long hiss, and the serpentine body shifted lazily against the rocks and craters, tail splashing liquid fire from a pool. "I might point out that wizards have done nothing for dragons in centuries, so I see little reason to dwell on any association that might once have existed. Such nonsense! I might also point out that while there is no question about my status as a dragon, there is certainly some question about yours as a wizard."

"I will not be drawn into an argument!" Questor snapped, rather too irritably. "Nor will I depart until you have heard me out!"

Strabo spit at the sulfurous air. "I ought simply to eat you, Questor Thews—you and the dog and that other thing, whatever it is. A kobold, isn't it? I ought to breathe a bit of fire on you, cook you up nicely, and eat you. But I am in a charitable mood tonight. Leave me and I will forgive your unwelcome intrusion into my home."

"Perhaps we should reconsider . . ." Abernathy began, but Questor shushed him at once.

"Did the dog say something?" the dragon asked softly.

"No—and no one is leaving!" Questor announced, planting his feet firmly.

Strabo blinked. "No?"

His crusted head swung abruptly about and flame jetted from his maw. The fire exploded directly beneath Questor Thews and sent him flying skyward with a yelp. Bunion and Abernathy sprang aside, scrambling to get clear of flying rocks, earth, and bits of flame. Questor came down again in a tangled heap of robes and sashes, his bones jarred with the impact.

Strabo chuckled, crooked tongue licking the air. "Very entertaining, wizard. Very amusing."

Questor climbed to his feet, dusted himself off, spit out a mouthful of dirt, and faced the dragon once more. "That was entirely uncalled for!" he declared, struggling to regain his lost dignity. "I can play such games, too!"

His hands clapped sharply, pointed and spread. He tried to do something with his feet as well, but he lost his footing on the loose rock, slipped, and sat down with a grunt. Light exploded above the craters and a shower of dry leaves tumbled down over Strabo, bursting instantly into flames from the heat.

The dragon was in stitches. "Am I to be smothered in leaves?" he roared, shaking with mirth. "Please, wizard—spare me!"

Questor went rigid, owlish face flushed with anger.

"Maybe we should come back another time," Abernathy ventured in a low growl from his position behind a protective mound of earth.

But Questor Thews was having none of it. Again, he brushed himself off and got back to his feet. "Laugh at me, will you, dragon?" he snapped. "Laugh at a master practitioner of the magic arts? Very well then—laugh this off!"

Both hands lifted and wove rapidly through the air. Strabo was preparing to send forth another jet of flame when a cloudburst broke immediately overhead and torrents of rain cascaded over him. "Now, stop that!" he howled, but in seconds he was drenched snout to tail. His flame fizzled into steam, and he ducked his head into one of the pools of fire to escape the downpour. When he came up again for air, Questor made a second gesture and the rain ceased.

"There, you see?" the wizard said to Abernathy, nodding in satisfaction. "He won't be quite so quick to laugh next time!" Then he turned back once more to the dragon. "Rather amusing yourself!" he called over.

Strabo flapped his leathered wings, shook himself off, and glared. "It appears that you will continue to make a nuisance of yourself, Questor Thews, until I either put an end to you or listen to whatever it is that you feel compelled to say. I repeat, I am in a charitable mood tonight. So say what it is you feel you must and be done with it."

"Thank you very much!" Questor replied. "May we come down?"

The dragon plopped his head back on the edge of the crater and stretched out again. "Do what you please."

Questor beckoned to his companions. Slowly, they made their way down the side of the ravine and through the maze of craters and rocks until they were twenty yards or so from where the dragon reposed. Strabo ignored them, eyes lidded, snout inhaling the fumes and fires of the crater on which he rested.

"You know I hate water, Questor Thews," he muttered.

"We have come here to learn something about unicorns," Questor announced, ignoring him.

Strabo belched. "Read a book."

"As a matter of fact, I did. Several. But they lack the information about unicorns that you possess. Everyone knows that unicorns and dragons are the oldest of fairy creatures and the oldest of enemies. Each of you knows more of the other than anyone else, fairy or human. I need to know something of unicorns that no one else would."

"Whatever for?" Strabo sounded bored again. "Besides, why should I help you? You serve that detestable human who tricked me into inhaling Io Dust and then made me pledge never to hunt the valley or its people so long as he remained King! He is still King, isn't he? Bah! Of course he is—I would have heard otherwise! Ben Holiday, Landover's High Lord! I would make a quick meal of him, if he were ever to set foot in the springs again!"

"Well, it is highly unlikely that he will. Besides, we are here about unicorns, not about the High Lord." Questor thought it prudent not to dwell on the subject of Ben Holiday. Strabo had taken great pleasure in ravaging the crops and livestock of the valley before the High Lord had put a stop to it. It was a pleasure the dragon would dearly love to enjoy again—and well might one day the way Holiday was behaving lately. But there was no reason to give the dragon any encouragement.

He cleared his throat officiously. "I assume that you have heard about the black unicorn?"

The dragon's eyes snapped open and his head lifted. "The black unicorn? Of course. Is it back again, wizard?"

Questor nodded sagely. "For some time now. I am surprised that you didn't know. There was quite an effort put forth to capture it."

"Capture it? A unicorn?" Strabo laughed, a series of rough coughs and hisses. His massive body shook with mirth. "The humans would capture a unicorn? How pitiful! No one captures a unicorn, wizard—even you must know that! Unicorns are untouchable!"

"Some think not."

The dragon's lip curled. "Some are fools!"

"Then the unicorn is safe? There is nothing that can ensnare it, nothing that can cause it to be held?"

"Nothing!"

"Not maidens of certain virtue nor silver moonlight captured in a fairy net?"

"Old wives' tales!"

"Not magic of any sort?"

"Magic? Well . . ." Strabo seemed to hesitate.

Questor took a chance. "Not bridles of spun gold?"

The dragon stared at the wizard voicelessly. There was, Questor Thews realized in surprise, a look of disbelief on the creature's face.

He cleared his throat. "I said, 'Not bridles of spun gold?' "

And it was at that moment that Nightshade, the stranger who believed himself Ben Holiday, and two sorry-looking G'home Gnomes appeared abruptly out of a swirl of mist not a dozen feet away.

FIRE AND SPUN GOLD

There was an endlessly long moment in which everyone stared at everyone else. It was impossible to tell who was most surprised. Eyes shifted, fixed, and shifted again. Tall forms crouched and robes billowed. The dragon's hiss of warning mingled with that of the witch. Abernathy growled in spite of himself. Night had closed down upon the little still life in a black mantle that threatened to engulf them all. In the silence, there was only the crackle and spit of the flames as they danced across the cratered pools of blue liquid.

"You are not welcome here, Nightshade," Strabo whispered finally, his rough voice a rasp of iron. He rose up from the edge of the crater on which he had been resting in a guarded crouch, claws digging into the stone until it cracked and broke. "You are *never* welcome."

Nightshade laughed mirthlessly, her pale face streaked with shadow. "I might be welcome this time, dragon," she replied. "I have brought you something."

Questor Thews realized suddenly that the two G'home Gnomes standing next to the witch and the stranger who thought himself Ben Holiday were none other than Fillip and Sot! "Abernathy . . . !" he exclaimed softly, but the dog was already saying, "I know, wizard! But what are they doing here?"

Questor had no idea at all. Questor had no idea about any of what was happening.

Strabo's massive head lifted and the long tongue licked out. "Why would you bother to bring me anything, witch?"

Nightshade straightened gracefully, her arms folding in about her once more, "Ask me first what it is that I bring," she whispered.

"There is nothing you could bring me that I would wish. There is no point in asking."

"Ah, even if what I bring is that which you most desire in all the world? Even if it is that dear to you?"

Ben Holiday was frantically trying to decide how he was going to get out of this mess. There were no friends to be found in this bunch. Questor, Abernathy, and Bunion believed him an impostor and a fool. Fillip and Sot, if they still believed anything about him at all, were interested by this time only in escaping with their hides intact. Nightshade had kept him alive this long strictly for the purpose of striking a bargain with Strabo, who would be only too happy to do away with him for her. He cast about desperately, looking for a way out that apparently didn't exist.

Strabo's tail thrashed within a pool of fire and sent a shower of liquid flames skyward against the dark. Ben flinched. "I tire of games this night," the dragon snapped. "Get to the point!"

Nightshade's eyes glimmered crimson. "What if I were to offer you Landover's High Lord, the one they call Holiday? What if I were to offer you that, dragon?"

Strabo's snout curled and the crusted face tightened. "I would accept that gift gladly!" the dragon hissed.

Ben took a tentative step backward and found he could not. The G'home Gnomes were still fastened to him like leg irons. They were shaking and mumbling incoherently and preventing him quite effectively from making any quick moves. When he tried surreptitiously to pry them free, they just clung to him all the tighter.

"The High Lord is at Sterling Silver!" Questor Thews declared suddenly, anger showing in his owlish face. "You have no power over him there, Nightshade! Besides, he would rid the valley of you in a moment if you were to show yourself!"

"Really?" Nightshade drew the word out lovingly, teasingly. Then she came forward a step, one long finger impaling Questor on its shadow. "When I have finished my business here, wizard—when your precious High Lord is no more—then will I deal with you!"

Ben fixed a pleading gaze on his friends. *Get out of here!* he tried to tell them.

Nightshade swung back again to Strabo. One clawed hand fastened on Ben's arm and dragged him forward. "Here is the one the foolish wizard believes so safe from me, Strabo! Ben Holiday, High Lord of Landover! Look closely now! Magic has been used! Look beneath the exterior of what you first see!"

Strabo snorted derisively, belched a quick burst of flame, and laughed. "This one? This is Holiday? Nightshade, you are mad!" He leaned closer, the ooze dripping from his snout. "This one doesn't even begin to look like . . . No, wait—you are right, there is magic at work here. What has been done . . ." The massive head dipped and raised, and the eyes blinked. "Can this be so?"

"Look closely!" Nightshade repeated once again, thrusting Ben before her so hard his head snapped back.

Everyone was looking at Ben now, but only Strabo saw the truth. "Yes!" he hissed, and the massive tail thrashed once more in satisfaction. "Yes, it is Holiday!" The jaws parted and the blackened teeth snapped. "But why is it that only you and I . . . ?"

"Because only we are older than the magic that does this!" Nightshade anticipated and answered the question before the dragon could complete it. "Do you understand how it has been done?"

Ben, prize exhibit that he was, wanted nothing more than to hear the answer to that question. He had accepted the fact that he was not going to get out of this in one piece, but he hated to think he was going to die without ever knowing how he had been undone.

"But . . . but that's *not* the High Lord!" Questor Thews declared angrily, sounding suddenly as if he were trying to convince himself as much as anyone else. "That *cannot* be the High Lord! If this is . . . is . . . then, the High Lord is . . ."

He trailed off, a strange look of understanding crossing his face, a look of disbelief shredded by horror, a look that screamed soundlessly a single name—Meeks! Bunion was hissing and pulling at his arm, and Abernathy was muttering frantically about how all this could explain someone-or-other's odd behavior.

All three were pointedly ignored by the dragon and the witch.

"Why would you give him to me?" Strabo was demanding of Nightshade, wary now of what was being offered.

"I said nothing of 'giving' you anything, dragon," Nightshade replied softly. "I wish to trade him."

"Trade him, witch? You hate him more than I! He sent you into the fairy world and almost destroyed you. He marked you with the magic! Why would you trade him? What could I possess that you would want more than Holiday?"

Nightshade smiled coldly. "Oh, yes, I hate him. And I wish him destroyed. But the pleasure shall be yours, Strabo. You need only give me one thing. Give me back the bridle of spun gold."

"The bridle?" Strabo's response came with a hiss of disbelief. He coughed. "What bridle?"

"The bridle!" Nightshade snapped. "The bridle that you stole from me while I was helpless to prevent it. The bridle that is rightfully mine!"

"Bah! Nothing you possess is rightfully yours—least of all the bridle! You yourself stole it from that old wizard!"

"Be that as it may, dragon, the bridle is what I wish!"

"Ah, well, of course, if that is what you wish . . ." The dragon seemed to be hedging. "But surely, Nightshade, there are other treasures that I possess that would serve you better than such a simple toy! Suggest something else, something of greater worth!"

The witch's eyes narrowed. "Now who is it that plays games? I have decided on the bridle and it is the bridle that I shall have!"

Ben had been momentarily forgotten. Nightshade had released him and he had slipped back behind her again, the gnomes still clinging to his legs. As he listened to the bartering, he caught Questor Thews studying him with renewed interest. Abernathy peered over the magician's shoulder through smoke-streaked glasses, and Bunion peered from behind a fold of robe. All were clearly trying to decide how he could be someone other than what he appeared. Ben gritted his teeth and motioned them frantically away with a shake of his head. For crying out loud, they were all going to end up fried!

"It is simply that I fail to see why the bridle is of such interest to you," Strabo was saying, neck curving upward into the dark so that he loomed over the witch.

"And I fail to see what difference it makes!" Nightshade snapped, straightening up a bit further herself. Firelight danced across her marble face. "I fail to see why you make such an issue of returning what is mine to begin with!"

Strabo sniffed. "I need explain nothing to you!"

"Indeed, you need not! Just give me the bridle!"

"I think not. You wish it too badly."

"And you wish Holiday not enough!"

"Oh, but I do! Why not accept a chest of gold or a fairy scepter that changes moonbeams into silver coins? Why not take a gemstone marked with runes that belonged to the Trolls when the power of magic was theirs as well—a gemstone that can give truth to the holder?"

"I don't want truth! I don't want gold or scepters or anything else you hold, you fat lizard!" Nightshade was genuinely mad now, her voice rising to a near scream. "I want the bridle! Give it to me or Holiday will never be yours!"

She edged forward threateningly, leaving Holiday and the G'home Gnomes half-a-dozen paces behind her. It was the closest to freedom that Ben had been since his capture at the Deep Fell. As the voices of the witch and dragon grew more strident, he began to think that maybe—just maybe—there might be a way out of this yet.

He pried Fillip forcibly from his right leg, held him dangling from the crook of his arm, and began to work Sot free from his left.

"One last time, dragon," Nightshade was saying. "Will you trade me the bridle for Holiday or not?"

Strabo gave a long sigh of disappointment. "I am afraid, dear witch, that I cannot."

Nightshade stared at him wordlessly for a moment, then her lips peeled back from her teeth in a snarl. "You don't have the bridle anymore, do you? That is why you won't trade it to me! You don't have it!"

Strabo sniffed. "Alas, quite true."

"You bloated mass of scales!" The witch was shaking with fury. "What have you done with it?"

"What I have done with it is my concern!" Strabo snapped in reply, looking more than a bit put upon. He sighed again. "Well, if you must know, I gave it away."

"You gave it away?" The witch was aghast.

Strabo breathed a long, delicate stream of fire into the night air and followed it with a trail of ashy vapor. The lidded eyes blinked and seemed momentarily distant. "I gave it to a fairy girl who sang to me of beauty and light and things a dragon longs to hear. No maiden has sung to me in many centuries, you know, and I would have given much more than the bridle for a chance to become lost again in such sweet music."

"You gave the bridle away for a song?" Nightshade spoke the words as if trying to convince herself that they had meaning.

"A memory means more than any tangible treasure." The dragon sighed once more. "Dragons have always had a weakness for beautiful women, maidens of certain virtue, girls of grace and sweet smiles. There is a bond that joins us. A bond stronger than that of dragons and wizards, I might add," he addressed Questor Thews in a quick aside. "She sang to me, this girl, and asked me in return for the bridle of spun gold. I gave it to her gladly." He actually seemed to smile. "She was quite beautiful, this sylph."

Ben started. A sylph? *Willow!*

The dragon's head dipped solemnly toward Ben. "I helped give her back her life once," he intoned. "Remember? You commanded it, Holiday. I flew her out of Abaddon to her home in the lake country where she could be healed. I didn't mind that so much—the saving of her life. I hated you, of course—you forced me to submit to you. But I rather enjoyed saving the sylph. It reminded me of the old days when saving maidens was routine work for a dragon."

He paused. "Or was it devouring them? I can never remember which."

"You are a fool!" Nightshade spat.

Strabo cocked his head as if thinking it over. Then his snout split wide to reveal all of his considerable teeth. "Do you really think so? A fool? Me? A bigger fool than you, witch? So big a fool as to venture unprotected into the lair of my worst enemy?"

The silence was palpable. Nightshade was a statue. "I am never unprotected, dragon. Beware."

"Beware? How quaint." Strabo suddenly coiled like a spring. "I have endured patiently your venomous assault on my character; I have allowed you to speak what you wished. Now it is my turn. You are a skinny, pathetic excuse for witchhood who believes herself far more powerful than she is. You come into my home as if you belong here, order me about, call me names, demand things you have no right to demand, and think you can go right out again. You mistake yourself, Nightshade. I might, had I the chance to do it over again, keep the bridle of spun gold so that I could trade it to you for Holiday. I might. But I regret nothing that I have ever done, and this least of all. The bridle is gone, and I do not wish it back again."

He bent forward slowly. The rough voice changed to a slow hiss. "But look—Holiday is still here, witch! And since you brought him expressly for me, I rather think I ought to keep him! Don't you?"

Nightshade's fingers were like claws as they lifted before her lean face. "You will take nothing more from me, dragon—not now, not ever!"

"Ah, but you have only yourself to blame. You have made the prospect of destroying Holiday so tempting that I cannot resist your lure! I must have him! He is mine to destroy, bridle or no! I think you had best give him to me—now!"

Flames burst from the maw of the dragon and engulfed Nightshade. At the same moment, Ben ripped Sot free at last of his left leg and flung himself sideways to escape the backlash of heat and fire. Questor Thews was moving as well, all arms and legs as he galloped toward Ben. Bunion sprinted past him, ears flattened back. Abernathy went down on all fours and scurried for the safety of the bushes.

Ben surged back to his feet, still carrying the wailing gnomes. Strabo's fire exploded skyward into the black, filling the air with a shower of sparks and rock. Nightshade stood unharmed in their center, black robes flying like drying bedclothes caught in the wind, pale face lifted, arms gesturing. Fire burst from her fingers and hammered into a surprised Strabo. The dragon flew backward, tumbling into a cratered pool.

"High Lord!" Questor Thews cried out in warning.

Nightshade whirled just in time to be caught by the full force of a magical gesture from the magician that swept the witch up in a blinding flurry of snowflakes. Nightshade swatted at them angrily, screamed, and threw fire back at him. Shards of flame hissed past Ben as he flung himself down again, smothering the gnomes. The fur on Abernathy's hind end caught fire, and the scribe disappeared up the slope of the Fire Springs with a yelp.

Then Strabo surfaced once more from the crater into which he had fallen, roaring in fury. Uncoiling his serpentine body with a lunge, he sprayed the whole of the Springs with fire. Nightshade swung back on him, shrieking with equal fury, spraying fire of her own. Ben was on his feet and running for his life. The fire swept over him, a wall of heat and red pain. But Questor was there now, hands gesturing desperately, and a shield of some impenetrable plastic substance appeared out of nowhere to slow the fire down. Ben kept his arms locked about the struggling, whimpering G'home Gnomes and scrambled desperately to escape the pursuing flames. Bunion's tough arms closed about his waist and helped haul all three toward the lip of the cratered valley. Questor followed, calling out in encouragement.

Moments later, they reached the rim of the Fire Springs and stumbled from the heat and smoke into the cooling scrub. Coughing and gasping, they collapsed in a tangled knot. Abernathy joined them from out of the dark.

Behind them, the witch and the dragon continued their private battle uninterrupted, their shrieks and roars filling the night. They hadn't even realized yet that the object of their struggle had escaped.

Ben glanced hurriedly at his companions. White eyes blinked back at him through the dark. No sense in resting now, they all seemed to agree. It wouldn't take long for the witch and the dragon to realize what had happened.

Stumbling to their feet once again, they disappeared swiftly into the night.

SEARCH

It was sometime after midnight when Ben and his companions finally broke off their flight. The skies had gone black with thunderheads that rolled eastward out of the grasslands. Moons and stars disappeared as if blown from the heavens by the sudden winds, thunder rumbled in long booming peals, and lightning laced the skies. The rains came swiftly, hard and chill, sweeping broomlike across the wastelands. There was barely time to find shelter in a thick copse of fir before the whole of the land surrounding had turned invisible in a wash of impenetrable mist and damp.

The company sat beneath the massive boughs of the centermost fir and peered out through the curtain of needles at the downpour. Wind rushed in stinging swipes through the trees and scrub, and water cascaded down. Everything faded away amid the steady sounds, and the stand of trees became an island in the gloom.

Ben sat back against the fir's massive trunk after a while and stared at the others, eyes shifting from one face to the next. "I am Ben Holiday, you know," he said finally. "I really am."

They looked questioningly at one another and back again at him.

"Save us, mighty High Lord," said Fillip after a moment, the words a toneless whimper.

"Yes, save us," begged Sot.

They looked like drowned rats, fur grimy and matted down by the rain, clothing ragged and torn. Their fingers reached tentatively for his legs.

"Stop that," he admonished wearily. "There is nothing to save you from. You're all right now."

"The dragon . . ." began Fillip.

"The witch . . ." began Sot.

"Far back and not about to go hunting for us in this. By the time they finish trying to set fire to each other and think to wonder what happened to us, the rain will have washed away any trace of where we went." He tried to sound more confident than he felt. "Don't worry. We'll be fine."

Bunion showed all his teeth and hissed. He looked at Ben as he might an errant bog wump. Abernathy didn't seem to want to look at Ben at all.

Questor Thews cleared his throat. Ben glanced expectantly at him, and the wizard seemed suddenly uncertain of what to say. "This is rather difficult," he said finally. He squinted at Ben. "You say you are indeed the High Lord? The witch and the dragon were correct in believing you so?"

Ben nodded slowly.

"And the story you told us at Sterling Silver—that was all true? You were changed somehow by magic? You have lost the protection of the medallion?"

Ben nodded a second time.

"And Meeks *has* returned and taken your place—and made himself appear as you?"

Ben nodded a third time.

Questor's lean features squinched down so hard against each other he appeared to be in danger of causing permanent damage. "But how?" he demanded finally. "How did all this happen?"

Ben sighed. "That is the sixty-four thousand dollar question, I'm afraid."

Briefly he recounted again his confrontation with Meeks in his bedchamber and his transformation into the stranger he appeared to them to be. He took them to the moment of his decision to travel south in search of Willow. "I've been hunting for her ever since," he concluded.

"See—I told you!" Abernathy snapped.

Questor stiffened and he peered down his long nose at the scribe. "Told me *what?*" he demanded, owlish face tightening even further.

"That the High Lord wasn't acting like the High Lord!" Abernathy fairly barked. "That something was definitely wrong! That nothing was what it should be! In fact, wizard, I told you a good deal more than that, if you would bother taking time enough to remember any of it!" He shoved his rain-streaked glasses back on his nose. "I told you that these dreams would bring nothing but trouble. I told you to forget about chasing after them!" He wheeled suddenly on Ben, a prophet whose visions had come to pass. "I warned you as well, didn't I? I told you to stay in Landover where you belonged! I told you Meeks was too dangerous! But you wouldn't listen, would you? Neither of you would listen! Now look where we are!"

He sneezed, shook himself furiously, and showered everyone with water. "Sorry," he muttered, sounding not the least so.

Questor sniffed. "I trust you feel better now?"

Ben decided to head off any further squabbling. "Abernathy is right. We should have listened to him. But we didn't, and what's done is done. We have to put all that behind us. At least we're back together again."

"A lot of good that's going to do us!" Abernathy snapped, still miffed.

"Well, it might do us some good." Ben tried his best to sound positive. "The six of us together might be able to accomplish something more than I could alone."

"The *six* of us?" Abernathy eyed the G'home Gnomes with disdain. "You count two more than I, High Lord. In any case, I am still not convinced that you really are the High Lord. Questor Thews is much too quick to believe. We have already been fooled once; it is possible that we are being fooled again. How do we know that this isn't just another charade? How do we know that this isn't another of Meeks' tricks?"

Ben thought about it a moment. "You don't, I guess. You have to take my word for it. You have to trust me—and trust your instincts." He sighed. "Do you think Meeks could fool both Strabo and Nightshade that badly? Do you think I would be hanging about claiming to be High Lord if I really weren't?" He paused. "Do you think I would still be wearing this?"

He reached down inside his tunic front and produced the tarnished medallion. The image of Meeks gleamed wetly, caught in a flash of distant lightning.

"Why *are* you still wearing it?" Questor asked quietly.

Ben shook his head. "I'm afraid to get rid of it. If Meeks is right and throwing off the medallion will finish me, then who would be left to warn Willow? She doesn't know any of what's happened. She doesn't know that the dreams were sent by Meeks or the danger she's in. I care too much for her, Questor. I can't abandon her. I can't take the chance that she'll fall into the same trap I did and have no one to help her out."

They were all silent for a moment, studying him.

"No, High Lord—you can't," Questor agreed finally. The wizard looked over at Abernathy. "The real Ben Holiday wouldn't even think of such a thing, would he?" he asked pointedly. "Not the real Ben Holiday."

Abernathy considered the possibility silently for a moment, then sighed. "No, I suppose he wouldn't." He glanced at Bunion, who nodded his monkey face approvingly. "Very well. The others accept you as High Lord; I shall do so as well."

"I appreciate that," Ben assured his scribe.

"But I still think that you are no better off with four of us . . ." He glanced once more at the G'home Gnomes. ". . . or six of us—or however many of us can be counted on—than you were by yourself! What is it that six of us are supposed to do that you could not do alone?"

The others looked at him expectantly. He stared past them into the haze of rain and darkness, drew his legs up to his chest to ward off the growing chill, and tried to come up with something. "Find Willow," he said finally. "Protect her."

They stared at him voicelessly.

"Look. The third dream is the key to everything that's happened, and the bridle is the key to the dream. Willow has the bridle now—we know that. Strabo gave it to her. She has it, but what will she do with it?"

"What, Mighty High Lord?" asked Fillip eagerly.

"Yes, what?" echoed Sot.

"She will take it to you, High Lord," Questor answered quickly. Then he paused. "Or at least to the one she believes to be you."

"That's right, Questor," Ben whispered. "That's what the dream told her she must do and that's what she'll do. She'll take the bridle to me. But I won't be me. I'll be Meeks. Or *he'll* be Meeks—the one she'll run to. And then what happens to her?"

"We have to reach her first," Questor insisted quietly.

"As soon as it stops raining," Abernathy added.

Ben nodded. "Six of us will have a better chance than one."

"Bunion will have a better chance than ten times six," Abernathy interjected, sneezing again. "I think I am catching cold," he muttered.

"For once, Abernathy is right!" Questor exclaimed, ignoring the reproving look the dog gave him. "A kobold can track faster and farther than any human. If there is any sign of the girl, Bunion will find it." He looked over at the kobold, who showed all of his teeth in response. "Indeed, Bunion will find her for us—you may depend upon it." He shrugged. "As soon as it stops raining, of course."

Ben shook his head. "We can't wait that long. We don't have . . ."

"But we have to," the wizard interrupted gently.

"But we can't . . ."

"We must." Questor took his arm and held it. "There can be no tracking done in a storm such as this one, High Lord. There would be no signs to follow." His owlish face bent close and there was sudden warmth in his eyes. "High Lord, you have come a long way since Sterling Silver. You have clearly suffered much. Your physical appearance, however distorted it might be, does not lie. Look at yourself. You are worn to the bone. You are exhausted. I have seen beggars who looked healthier than you. Abernathy?"

"You look a wreck," the dog agreed.

"Well, bad enough, at any rate." The wizard tempered the other's assessment with a smile. "You need to rest. Sleep now. There will be time enough later to begin the hunt."

Ben shook his head vigorously. "Questor, I'm not tired. I can't . . ."

"I think you must," the wizard said softly. A bony hand passed briefly before Ben's face, and his eyes grew suddenly heavy. He could barely keep them open. He felt a pervasive weariness slip within his body and weigh him down. "Rest, High Lord," Questor whispered.

Ben fought the command, struggled to rise, and found he could not. For once, the wizard's magic was working right on the first try. Ben was slipping back against the rough trunk of the fir, downward into a bed of needles. His companions drew close. Abernathy's furry, bespeckled face peered at him through a gathering of shadows. Bunion's teeth gleamed like daggers. Fillip and Sot were vague images that wavered and voices that murmured and seemed to draw steadily farther away. He found comfort in their presence, strength, and reassurance—his friends, all there with him except Parsnip—and Willow!

"Willow," he whispered.

He spoke her name once and was asleep.

He dreamed of Willow while he slept, and the dream was a revelation that shocked him, even in his slumber. He searched for the sylph through the forests, hills, and plains of Landover, a solitary quest that drew him on as a magnet would iron. The country through which he traveled was familiar and yet foreign, too, a mix of sunshine and shadows that shimmered with the inconsistency of an image reflected on water. There were things that moved all about him, but they lacked face and form. He hunted alone, his search a seemingly endless one that took him from one end of the valley and back again, swift and certain in its pace but fruitless nevertheless.

He was driven by an urgency that surprised him. There was a need to find the sylph that defied explanation. He was frightened for her without understanding the reason for his fear. He was desperate to be with her, yet his desperation lacked cause. It was as if he were captive to his emotions and they determined his course where reason could not. He could sense Willow's presence as he searched, a closeness that teased him. It was as if she waited behind each tree and beyond each hill, and he need only journey a bit further to find her. Weariness did not slow him as he traveled; strength of purpose carried him on.

After a time, he began to hear voices. They whispered to him from all about, some in warning, some in admonishment. He heard the River Master, distrustful yet of who Ben was, strangely anxious that the daughter he could not quite love and who could not quite love him be found. He heard the Earth Mother, asking him to repeat again the promise he had made to her to find and protect Willow, insistent that he honor it. He heard that solitary, defeated hunter speak once more in hollow tones of the black unicorn, of the touch that had stolen away his soul. He heard Meeks, his voice a dark and vengeful hiss that promised ruin if the girl and the golden bridle should escape him.

Still he went on.

And then he heard Edgewood Dirk.

It was the voice of the prism cat that slowed him, aware suddenly of how frantic his search for Willow had become. He stopped, his breath ragged in his ears, his chest pounding. He stood within a forest glade that was cool and solitary, a mix of shadows and light, of boughs canopied overhead and moss grown thick underfoot. Dirk sat upon a knoll within that glade, prim and sleek and inscrutable.

"Why do you run so, High Lord Ben Holiday?" Dirk asked quietly.

"I must find Willow," he replied.

"Why must you find her?" Dirk pressed.

"Because danger threatens her," he answered.

"And is that all?"

He paused. "Because she needs me."

"And is that all?"

"Because there is no one else."

"And is that all?"

"Because . . ."

But the words he searched for would not come, as elusive as the sylph herself. There were words to be spoken, he sensed. What were those words?

"You work so hard to orchestrate your life," Dirk declared almost sadly. "You work so hard to fit all the pieces together, a vast puzzle you must master. But you fail to understand the reason for your need to do so. Life is not simply form, High Lord; life is feeling, too."

"I feel," he said.

"You govern," Dirk corrected. "You govern your kingdom, your subjects, your work, and your life. You organize—here as you once organized there. You command. You command as King as you commanded as lawyer. Court-of-law stagecraft or royal-court politics—you are no different now than you were then. You act and you react with quickness and skill. But you do not feel."

"I try."

"The heart of the magic lies in feeling, High Lord. Life is born of feeling, and the magic is born of life. How can you understand either life or magic if you do not feel? You search for Willow, but how can you recognize her when you fail to understand what she is? You search with your eyes for something they cannot see. You search with your senses and your body for what they cannot find. You must search instead with your heart. Try now. Try, and tell me what you see."

He did, but there was a darkness all about him that would not let him see. He drew deep inside himself and found passages through which he could not travel. Obstructions blocked his way, shapeless things that lacked clear definition. He tried furiously to push past them, groping, reaching . . .

Then Willow was before him, a misty vision suddenly remembered. She was lithe and quicksilver as she passed, her face stunning in its beauty, her body a whisper of his need. Forest green hair tumbled down about her slender shoulders and fell to her waist. White silk draped and clung like a second skin. Her eyes met his, and he found his breath drawn from him with a sharpness that hurt. She smiled, warm and tender, and her whisper was soundless in his mind. There was no danger that threatened her, no sense of urgency about her. She was at peace with herself. She was at rest.

"Why do you run so, High Lord Ben Holiday?" Dirk repeated from somewhere within the shadows.

"I must find Willow," he answered again.

"Why must you find her?"

"Because . . ."

Again, he could not find the words. The shadows began to tighten. Willow began to fade back into them.

"Because . . ."

She faded further, a memory disappearing. He struggled frantically to find the words he needed to say, but they eluded him still. The sense of urgency returned, quick and hard. The danger to the sylph became real once more, as if somehow resurrected by his indecision. He tried to reach out to her with his hands, but she was too far away, and he was too rooted in place.

"Because . . ."

The shadows were all about, cloaking him now in their blackness, smothering him in their endless dark. He was drawing back out of himself. Dirk was gone. Willow was little more than a patch of light and color against the black, fading, fading . . .

"Because . . ."

Willow!

He came awake with a start, jerking upright from his place of rest, his underarms and back damp with sweat. Night shrouded the eastern wastelands in silence. Clouds masked the skies, though the rain had ceased to fall. Ben's companions slept undisturbed all about him—all except Bunion. Bunion was already gone, his search for Willow begun.

Ben took a deep breath to steady himself. His dream of Willow was still sharp and certain in his mind. He exhaled.

"Because . . . I love her," he finished.

Those were the words he had searched for. And he knew with frightening certainty that the words were true.

He was awake for a time after that, alone with his thoughts in the dark silence of the night. After a while, though, he tired and dropped back off to sleep. When he awoke again, it was nearing dawn, the eastern sky behind the valley rim brightening with faint streaks of gray and gold. Bunion had not returned. The others still slept.

He rolled over on his back, glanced about the storm-dampened campsite, and then blinked in surprise. Edgewood Dirk rested comfortably on a thick bough of the fir just a few feet above his head, paws tucked under his sleek body, eyes squinched closed against the light.

The eyes slipped open as Ben stared. "Good morning, High Lord," the cat offered.

Ben pushed himself up on his elbows. "Good morning, nothing. Where have you been?"

"Oh, here and there."

"More there than here, it seems!" Ben snapped, a great deal of pent-up anger coming quickly to the fore. "I could have used a little help back there in the Deep Fell when you so conveniently disappeared! I was lucky the witch didn't do away with me on the spot! And then I was dragged off to Strabo's den and offered to him as a snack! But all that made precious little difference to you, did it? Thanks for nothing!"

"You are quite welcome," Dirk replied calmly. "I would remind you once again, however, that I signed on as a companion, not as a protector. Besides, it appears you have suffered no harm in my absence."

"But I might have, damn it!" Ben couldn't help himself. He was sick of the cat appearing and disappearing like some wraith. "I might have been fried in dragon oil for all the good you'd have done me!"

"Might have, could have, may have, should have—the haves and the have nots reduced to pointless possibilities." Dirk yawned. "You would do better to forget flogging dead horses and try rounding up a few live ones."

Ben glared. "Meaning?"

"Meaning you have something more important on your mind than chastising me for imagined wrongs."

Ben paused, remembering suddenly his dream, the search he had undertaken, the golden bridle, the black unicorn, Meeks, and all the rest of the puzzle he still didn't understand. Ah, and Willow! Thoughts of the sylph pushed all others aside. I love her, he told himself, trying the words on for size. He found them unexpectedly comfortable.

"There are those who theorize that our dreams are simply manifestations of our subconscious thoughts and desires," Dirk mused, as if delivering an offhand dissertation. "Dreams do not often portray accurately the events upon which those thoughts and desires are formed, but they do demonstrate quite vividly the emotions behind them. We find ourselves involved in bizarre situations and disjointed events, and our tendency is often to dismiss the dream out-of-hand—a self-conscious response. But hidden within the thrashings of our subconscious is a kernel of truth about ourselves that needs to be understood—truth that sometimes we have refused to recognize while awake and now demands recognition while we sleep."

He paused for dramatic effect. "Love is sometimes such a truth."

Ben pushed himself upright, stared at this cat turned philosopher a moment, and then shook his head. "Is all this in reference to Willow?" he asked.

Dirk blinked. "Of course, sometimes dreams lie and the truth can be found only in waking."

"Like with my dream of Miles?" Ben found the cat's conversation needlessly convoluted. "Why don't you just say what you mean for once?"

Dirk blinked again. "Because I am a cat."

"Oh. Sure." The standard answer again.

"Because some things you simply have to figure out for yourself."

"Right."

"Something you have not proven very adept at doing, I'm afraid."

"Certainly not."

"Despite my continuing efforts."

"Hmmmmm." Ben experienced an almost uncontrollable urge to throttle the beast. To suppress the feeling, he glanced about instead at his still sleeping companions. "Why isn't anyone but me awake yet?" he demanded.

Dirk glanced about with him. "Perhaps they are simply very tired," the cat suggested amiably.

Ben gave him a hard look. "What did you do—employ a bit of magic? Fairy magic? As Questor did with me? You did, didn't you?"

"A bit."

"But why? I mean, why bother?"

Dirk rose, stretched, and jumped down next to Ben, pointedly ignoring him. He began to wash himself and continued to do so until he had cleaned himself thoroughly, fur carefully ruffled and smoothed back in place again.

Then he faced Ben, emerald eyes gleaming in the faint dawn light. "The problem is, you do not listen. I tell you everything you need to know, but you do not seem to hear any of it. It really is distressing." He sighed deeply. "I let your companions sleep to demonstrate to you one final lesson about dreams. So much of your understanding of what has happened depends on your understanding of how dreams work. Watch, now, what occurs when your friends awake. And try to pay attention this time, will you? My patience wears exceedingly thin."

Ben grimaced. Edgewood Dirk settled back on his haunches. Together they waited for something to happen. After a moment, Questor Thews stirred, then Abernathy, and finally the gnomes. One by one, they blinked the sleep from their eyes and sat up.

Then they saw Ben, and more especially, Dirk.

"Ah, good morning, High Lord. Good morning, Dirk," Questor greeted brightly. "Slept well the both of you, I hope?"

Abernathy muttered something about all cats being night creatures and not needing sleep anyway, even prism cats, and how it was a waste of time to worry about any of them.

Fillip and Sot eyed Dirk as they would a long-awaited dinner and showed not the slightest trace of fear.

Ben stared in bewilderment, the conversation continuing on about him as if the cat's presence were perfectly normal. No one seemed surprised that the cat was there. Questor and Abernathy were behaving as if his appearance was entirely expected. The gnomes were behaving the way they had at their first encounter with Dirk; neither seemed to remember what their eagerness to make Dirk a meal had cost them.

Ben listened a moment as the others talked and bustled about, then glanced in confusion at the cat. "What . . . ?"

"Their dreams, High Lord," Dirk whispered, interrupting. "I let them discover me in their dreams. I was real to them there, so I am real to them here. Don't you see? Truth is sometimes simply what we perceive it to be—in waking or in dreams."

Ben didn't see. He had paid close attention, he had listened as instructed, and he still didn't see. What was the point of all this and what did it have to do with him?

But there was no more time to consider the matter. A shout from Abernathy—or rather a sort of bark—captured the attention of all. The boughs at the edge of the grove of fir parted and who should appear but Parsnip! Bunion had him in tow, both of them soaked through by the storm, both grimacing ear to ear those wicked, toothy grins. Ben froze. Parsnip was supposed to be guarding Willow! Shaking off his paralysis, he hastened forward with Questor and Abernathy to greet the wiry little creatures, stopped short at the hard, suspicious look directed at him by Parsnip—who, after all, had no idea yet who he was—and finally backed off a step at Questor's urging. Questor and Bunion conversed briefly back and forth in the rough, guttural language of the kobolds with occasional interjections by Parsnip, and then Questor turned hurriedly to Ben.

"Parsnip has kept watch over Willow since she left Sterling Silver, High Lord—just as you commanded—until yesterday. She dismissed him without reason. When he wouldn't leave her, she used the fairy magic and slipped away. Even a kobold can't stay with a sylph when she doesn't wish it. She has the golden bridle, and . . . and she searches for the black unicorn." He shook his owlish features at the look on Ben's face and tugged worriedly at his white beard. "I know. I don't understand this last either, High Lord, and neither does Parsnip. Apparently she has decided *not* to take the bridle to you as her dream instructed!"

Ben fought off the sudden lurch in his stomach. What did this mean, he wondered? "Where is she now?" he asked instead.

Questor shook his head. "Her trail leads north into the Melchor." He hesitated. "Bunion says she appears to be traveling toward Mirwouk!"

Mirwouk? Where the missing books of magic had been hidden? Why would she go there? Ben felt his frustration increase.

"There is more, High Lord," Abernathy interjected solemnly, ignoring the warning tug on his tunic sleeve from Questor. "Strabo and Nightshade are at hunt—presumably for you, Willow, and the bridle. And a demon—a huge, flying thing, a thing that answers to no one, it seems—is rumored to scour the whole of the valley. Bunion saw it last night."

"Meeks' pet," Ben whispered, remembering suddenly the monster that had appeared at the dance of the River Master's nymphs and destroyed them. His face tightened. Edgewood Dirk and the matter of dreams were forgotten. He thought now only of Willow. "We have to reach her before they do," he announced, his voice sounding hollow in his ears as he fought down the fear that raced through him. "We have to. We're all she has."

Everyone reacted. Abernathy barked sharply at the G'home Gnomes and turned the kobolds about once more. Questor put a reassuring hand on Ben's arm. "We will find her, High Lord. You can depend upon it."

Quickly they departed into the wastelands, the stranger who was High Lord, the wizard and the scribe, the kobolds and the gnomes.

Edgewood Dirk sat quietly and watched them go.

MIRWOUK AND FLYNT

Willow felt the glare of the midday heat on her face through breaks in the forest trees and was suddenly thirsty. She made her way gingerly around an outcropping of rock that jutted from the ever-steepening slope, climbed to a shelf of tall grass and brush that disappeared ahead into a grove of deeply shaded fir, and paused to look back. Landover spread away below, an irregular checkerboard of fields and forests, hills and plains, rivers and lakes, swatches of blues and greens with brush strokes of pastel interspersed like webbing. Sunlight poured down over the valley from a cloudless blue sky and deepened the colors until they blinded with their brilliance.

Willow sighed. It seemed impossible that anything could be wrong on a day such as this.

She was deep within the Melchor now, past the threshold of hardwood forests, past the higher plateau of pine-wooded foothills, a fair distance up into the main peaks. The sun was sharp and hot this day where the shade failed to screen away its light, and the climb was thirsty work. Willow carried no water with her; she relied on her instincts to find what she needed. Her instincts had failed her these past few hours since leaving the foothills, but now she sensed water to be close again.

Nevertheless, she stayed where she was a moment longer and looked out across the valley in silent contemplation. Far, far distant to the south she could just catch a glimpse of the misted island that was Sterling Silver, and she thought of Ben. She wished he were here with her or that she understood why it was that she wasn't there with him. She looked out across the valley and felt as if she were all alone in the world.

What was she doing here?

She felt burdened by the weight of the woolen-bundled harness she wore draped across her right shoulder, and she shrugged it off and let it drop into her hands. A burst of sunlight flashed sharply from a stray bit of trapping that slipped from beneath the covering folds. The bridle of spun gold clinked softly. She covered it over and shifted it to her other shoulder. The bridle was heavy, the woven threads and fastenings more cumbersome than she would have believed. She adjusted it carefully and straightened. She had been fortunate that the dragon had agreed to give it to her. All the fairy songs, music, tears, and laughter had been potent magic indeed. Strabo had been charmed. She was still surprised that the ploy had been successful. She was still mystified that she had known somehow that it would be. Dreams, visions, and hunches—such were the vicissitudes that had driven her these past few days, a stray leaf blown by the wind.

Last night it had been a dream again. She frowned at its memory, her smooth, lovely face lined with worry. Last night, the dream had been of Ben.

A breath of wind swept back her waist-length hair and cooled her skin. She remembered her need to drink, but stayed yet another moment to think of her High Lord. The dream had been strange again, a mix of real and surreal, a jumble of fears and hopes. She had come upon the black unicorn once more, the creature hidden in woods and shadows, no demon this time but a hunted thing, frightened and alone. She had feared it, but wept at its terror. What frightened it was uncertain, but the look it spared her was unmistakable. Come to me, it had whispered. Put aside your plan to carry back the bridle of spun gold to Sterling Silver and your High Lord. Forgo your race from the demon you fear me to be and seek instead the truth of what I am. Willow, come to me.

A single look had said all that, so clear, so certain—a dream, and yet real. So she had come, trusting to her fairy instincts as she had always trusted, believing that they alone of all her senses could not be deceived. She had abandoned the call of the first dream that would have taken her to Ben and gone instead in search of . . .

Of what? Truth?

"Why are the dreams so different?" she questioned softly. "Why am I made so confused?"

Sunlight sparkled off distant waters and forest leaves rippled in the passing wind, but no answers came. She breathed the air deeply and turned away. The shadows of the forest drew her to them, and she let herself be swallowed. Mirwouk was near, she realized in surprise—not more than several miles distant, just beyond the peak she climbed. The fact registered briefly and was forgotten. The broad swath of midday sunlight faded into a scattering of narrow bands, and the shade was cool on her heated skin. She worked her way back into the forest trees, massive fir and pine, seeking the water she knew was hidden there. She found it quickly, a small stream trickling down out of the rocks into a pool and meandering from there to a series of shallows and runs. She laid the bridle carefully on the ground next to her and bent to drink. The water was sweet and welcome to her dry throat. She knelt a long time in the stillness.

The seconds slipped away into minutes. When she lifted her head again, the black unicorn stood across from her.

Her breath caught in her throat and she froze. The unicorn was no more than a dozen paces off, half within shadow, half within pale, filtered sunlight. It was a vision of grace and wonder, slender body as ephemeral as a reflection of love remembered, presence as glorious as a rainbow's sweep. It did not move, but simply regarded her. Ebony body with goat's feet and lion's tail, eyes of green fire, immortal life—all the songs of all the bards through all the ages of the world could not begin to express what the unicorn truly was.

Willow felt a rush of emotion tear through her, stripping bare her soul. She felt her heart begin to break with the ecstasy of it. She had never seen a unicorn and never thought it would be like this. There were tears in her eyes, and she swallowed uncontrollably against what she was feeling.

"Oh, you beautiful thing," she whispered.

Her voice was so soft that she believed only she could hear her words. But the unicorn nodded in response, and the ridged horn shone brightly with magic. The green eyes fixed upon her with new intensity and flared from some inner well of being. Willow felt something seize hold within her. Her hand groped blindly the earth next to her and came to rest at last upon the bridle.

Oh, I must have you, she thought. I must make you mine!

But the eyes held her and she could not move to act upon her need. The eyes held her, and they whispered of something remembered from the dream.

Come to me, they said. Seek me.

She felt herself flush with the heat of that memory and then go cool. She saw the memory reflected in her eyes, in her mind, and in her heart. She looked across the tiny stream of water as it rushed and gurgled over the rocks in the forest stillness, and the stream was a river she could not bridge. She listened to the singing of birds in the trees, a mingling of songs that cheered and heartened, and the sound became the voice of all her secrets revealed.

She felt magic rage within her in waves of insistence she had never known could exist. She no longer belonged to herself; she belonged now to the unicorn. She would have done anything for it. Anything.

Then, in the next instant, it was gone, disappearing so suddenly and so completely that it might never have been. Indeed, she wondered—had it? Willow stared at the space the black unicorn had occupied, an emptiness of mingled light and shadow, and she fought against the sharpness of her pain.

Had she seen the unicorn? Truly seen it? Had it been real?

The questions left her dazed. She could not move. Then, slowly, purposefully, she rose to her feet, shouldered again the golden bridle, and moved with quiet determination in search of her answers.

She searched all that day. Yet she did not search so much as follow, for there was a sense of being led that she could not explain. She climbed through the tangle of rocks and trees and scrub that carpeted the uneven heights of the Melchor and sought a thing that might not even be. She thought she saw the black unicorn several times more, brief flashes only—an ebony flank, an emerald eye, a ridged horn shining with magic. It did not occur to her that her efforts might be misdirected. She chased quite deliriously and without regret. She knew that the unicorn was there, just beyond her reach. She could feel it waiting for her; she could sense it watching. She did not know its purpose, but she was certain of its need.

Nightfall found her less than a mile west of Mirwouk, exhausted, still alone. She had traversed the forest all about the aging, crumbling fortress. She had retraced her own steps several times. She was no nearer the black unicorn than she had been when she had first spied it, but she was as determined as ever that she would catch up to it. At dawn, she would try again.

She lay down within a sheltering of birch, hugged the bridle of spun gold within its woolen covering close against her breast, and let the cool night air wash over her. Slowly the heat of the day faded, and her exhaustion slipped away. She slept undisturbed and dreamed once more.

Her dream this night was of dozens of white unicorns chained and fettered and begging to be set free. The dream was like a fever that would not break.

From shadows close at hand, eyes of green fire kept watch through the night.

Ben Holiday and his companions spent that night within the Melchor as well, although they were still some distance from Mirwouk and Willow. They were camped just above the foothills leading into the mountains and lucky to be that far. It had taken them the better part of the day just to get out of the wastelands, and they had trekked on through the late afternoon and evening to reach the base of the mountains. Ben had insisted. The kobolds had found Willow's tracks near sundown, and Ben thought they might catch up to her yet that day. It was only after complete darkness had set in and Questor had pleaded with Ben to be reasonable that the search was temporarily abandoned.

It resumed at daybreak, and the little company found itself less than a mile below Mirwouk by midmorning. It was then that matters began to grow confusing.

The confusion was manifold. In the first place, Willow's trail was leading toward Mirwouk. Since she wasn't carrying the golden bridle to Ben—or Meeks disguised as Ben—it was somewhat uncertain what it was that she was doing with it. Possibly she was searching for the black unicorn, although that didn't make much sense, since in her dream the black unicorn had been a demon creature that threatened her, and she still didn't know that the dream had been sent by Meeks. Whatever she was doing, she was definitely going toward Mirwouk, and Mirwouk was where Questor's dream had taken him in search of the missing books of wizard magic and where, in fact, the missing books had been found.

In the second place, the kobolds had discovered that twice already Willow's tracks had retraced themselves. Sylphs were fairy creatures and not in the habit of getting lost, so that meant either she was searching for something or following something. But there was no indication at all of what that might be.

In the third place, Edgewood Dirk was still among the missing. No one had seen the cat since they had departed their shelter of two nights earlier, following Bunion's return with Parsnip and the news of Willow's tracks. Ben hadn't paid much attention to Dirk's absence until now, too caught up in his search for Willow really to notice. But confronting these other puzzles had led him almost without thinking to look around for Dirk, perhaps in the vain hope of getting a straight answer from the beast for once; but Dirk was nowhere to be found.

Ben took it all in stride. There wasn't much any of them could do to clear up the confusion just now, so he simply ordered them to press on.

They crossed Willow's tracks a third time within a stone's throw of Mirwouk, and this time the kobolds hesitated. The new trail was fresher than the old. Should they follow it?

Ben nodded and they did.

By midday, they had circled Mirwouk almost completely and crossed Willow's tracks yet a fourth time. Now she was moving *away* from the aged fortress. Bunion studied the tracks for several minutes, his face almost pressed up against the earth in his effort to read the markings. He announced finally that he couldn't tell which tracks were more recent. All seemed quite fresh.

The members of the little company stood staring at each other for a moment, undecided. Sweat lay in a thin sheen across the faces of Ben and Questor, and the G'home Gnomes were whining that they were thirsty. Abernathy was panting. Dust covered all of them like a mist. Eyes squinted against the glaring light of the sun, and faces grimaced and tightened with discomfort. They were all weary and cross and they were all sick and tired of running around in circles.

Though anxious to continue, Ben was nevertheless reluctantly considering the idea of a lunch break and a brief rest when a crashing sound brought him sharply about. The crashing sound was of stone breaking and falling. It was coming from the direction of Mirwouk.

He looked at the others questioningly, but no one seemed anxious to venture an opinion.

"Couldn't hurt to check it out at least," Ben declared and resolutely started off to investigate, the others trailing with various degrees of enthusiasm.

They picked their way upward through the tangle of scrub and trees, watching the crumbling walls and towers of Mirwouk appear through breaks in the branches and rise up before them. Parapets loomed against the skyline, ragged and broken, and shutterless windows gaped emptily. Bats darted past in shadowy bursts and cried out sharply. Ahead, the crashing sounds continued—almost as if something was trapped and trying to break free. The minutes slipped away. The little company approached the sagging gates of the fortress and drew to a halt, listening.

The crashing sounds had stopped.

"I don't like this one bit," Abernathy announced darkly.

"High Lord, perhaps we ought to . . ." Questor Thews began, then stopped as he saw a look of disapproval cross Ben's face.

"Perhaps we ought to have a look," Ben finished.

So they did, Ben leading, the kobolds a step behind, the others trailing. They passed through the gates, crossed the broad outer courtyard beyond, and slipped into the passageway that ran from the secondary wall to the inner courtyard and the main buildings. The passageway was long and dark and it smelled of rot. Ben wrinkled his nose in distaste and hurried ahead. There was still only silence.

Ben reached the end of the tunnel a dozen steps ahead of everyone and was thinking to himself that he might have been smarter to send Bunion ahead to look things over when he caught sight of the stone giant. It was huge and ugly, a featureless, rough-hewn monstrosity that looked like the beginning stages of some novice sculptor's efforts at a tribute to Hercules. It appeared to be just a grotesque statue at first, standing there in the middle of the inner courtyard amid a pile of stone rubble. But then the statue moved, turning with a ponderous effort that sounded of rock grating on rock, and it became immediately apparent that this particular statue was very much alive.

Ben stared in bewilderment, not quite certain yet what to do. A sudden tumult rose from the tunnel behind him, and the others of the company emerged in a rush and practically ran over him in their haste to get clear. The G'home Gnomes were no longer whining; they were howling like injured cats. Abernathy and Questor were both yelling at once, and the kobolds were hissing and showing all their teeth in an unmistakable display of hostility. It took Ben a moment to realize that they weren't responding to anything they saw at *this* end of the tunnel but to something they had seen at the *other.*

Ben peered hurriedly past the frenzied group, neck craning. A second stone giant had entered the passageway and was lumbering toward them.

Questor grasped his elbow as if he might strangle it. "High Lord, that is a Flynt! It will smash us to dust if we let it get close enough . . . ! Ecchhh!" He saw the second one now, as it, too, lumbered forward. "Two of them! Run, High Lord—this way!"

The kobolds were already moving, leading the pack of them across the courtyard to an entryway that disappeared into the fortress proper. The first Flynt had joined the second and both were in pursuit, shambling giants that moved like bulldozers.

The company burst through the entryway and galloped up a flight of stairs.

"What's a Flynt?" Ben demanded of Questor as they fled. "I don't remember your telling me anything about Flynts!"

"I probably didn't tell you anything, High Lord," Questor acknowledged, breathing hard now. His robes tangled in his feet and he almost went down. "Drat!" He straightened, moving quickly on. "Flynts are aberrations—a creation of old magic, stone monsters brought to life. Very dangerous! They were sentinels of this fortress once, but I thought they were all destroyed centuries ago. Wizards created them. They don't think, they don't eat, they don't sleep, they barely see or smell—but they hear everything. Their intended purpose was to keep intruders out of Mirwouk, but of course that was a long time ago, so who knows what they think their purpose might be now. They seem rather intent on just smashing things. Ugh!" He slowed momentarily and somehow managed to look genuinely thoughtful. "Odd that I didn't come across them when I was here last."

Ben rolled his eyes and pulled the wizard ahead.

They reached the top of the stairwell and emerged on a parapet roof about the size of a tennis court. Rubble littered the playing surface. There were no referees in sight and only one other way out—a second stairwell at the far end. The company broke for it as one.

When they reached it, they found it blocked with enough timber and stone to build a set of bleachers.

"Wonderful!" Ben groaned.

"I told you I didn't like this!" Abernathy declared with a bark that surprised everyone.

The Flynts emerged from the far stairwell, looked slowly about, and began to lumber toward them. Bunion and Parsnip moved protectively in front of the others.

Now it was Ben's turn to grab Questor. "The kobolds can't stop those things, damn it! Dredge up some magic!"

Questor moved hurriedly forward, robes flying, tall figure swaying as if he might topple over. He muttered something unintelligible, lifted his arms skyward, and brought them down in a grand sweep. Funnel clouds sprang up from out of nowhere, picked up the loose rubble, and hurtled it at the approaching stone monsters. Unfortunately, the funnel clouds also hurtled some of it back at Questor. The rubble bounced harmlessly off the Flynts. It did not bounce harmlessly off Questor; the wizard went down in a heap, unconscious and bleeding.

Ben and the kobolds rushed to pull the wizard back from further harm. The Flynts still lumbered forward, stone blocks and rubble cracking like deadwood beneath their massive feet.

Ben knelt anxiously. "Questor! Get up! We need you!" He slapped the fallen wizard's face desperately, rubbed his wrists, and shook him. Questor didn't move. His owlish face was pale beneath the blood.

Ben leaped back to his feet. Individually, perhaps, the members of the little company were swift and agile enough to evade these stone monsters. Perhaps. But that was before Questor's injury. No one would get away trying to carry out the wizard, and they were certainly not about to leave him. Ben seized the medallion frantically and let go just as quickly. Useless. He was Meeks' creation now, his medallion a worthless imitation. There could be no help from the magic; there could be no summons to the Paladin.

But he had to do something!

"Abernathy!"

The dog's cold nose shoved into his ear, and he jerked away. "High Lord?"

"These things can't see, taste, or smell—but they can hear, right? Hear anything? Anything even close to Mirwouk, maybe?"

"I am given to understand that the Flynts can hear a pin drop at fifty paces, though I often . . ."

"Never mind the editorials!" Ben pulled the dog about to face him, furry features held close, glasses glinting with sunlight. "Can you hit high C?"

Abernathy blinked. "High Lord?"

"High C, damn it—can you howl loud enough to hit high C?" The Flynts were no more than a dozen paces off. "Well, can you?"

"I don't see . . ."

"Yes or no!"

He was shaking his scribe. Abernathy's muzzle drew back, and he barked right in Ben's face. "Yes!"

"Then do it!" Ben screamed.

The whole roof seemed to be shaking. The G'home Gnomes had fastened themselves to Ben once more, crying, "Great High Lord, Mighty High Lord" in chorus and wailing like lost souls. The kobolds were crouched in front of him, ready to spring. The Flynts looked like tanks bearing down.

Then Abernathy began to howl.

He hit high C on the first try, a frightening wail that drowned out the G'home Gnomes and expanded the grimaces on the faces of the kobolds into a whole new dimension. The wail lifted and spread, cutting through everything with the tenacity of gastrically induced stress. The Flynts stopped in their tracks and their massive hands came up against the sides of their heads with a crash as they tried in vain to shut out the sound. It came at them relentlessly—Ben would never have believed Abernathy capable of such sustained agony—and all the while, they battered at themselves.

Finally, the pounding proved to be too much, and the Flynts simply shattered and fell apart. Heads, arms, torsos, and legs collapsed into piles of useless rock. The dust rose and settled again, and nothing moved.

Abernathy stopped howling, and there was a moment of strained silence. The scribe straightened and glared at Ben with undisguised fury. "I have *never* been so humiliated, High Lord!" he snarled. "Howling like a dog, indeed! I have debased myself in a way I would not have thought possible!"

Ben cleared his throat. "You saved our lives," he pointed out simply. "That's what you did."

Abernathy started to say something more, stopped, and simply continued to glare voicelessly. Finally he took a deep breath of air, exhaled, straightened some more, sniffed distastefully, and said, "When we get those books of magic back, the first thing you will do with them is find a way to turn *me* back into a human being!"

Ben hastily masked the smile that would have been his undoing. "Agreed. The first thing."

Hurriedly they picked up Questor Thews and carried him back down the stairway and out of Mirwouk. They encountered no further Flynts. Perhaps the two they had escaped had been the last, Ben thought as they hastened back into the trees.

"Still, it *is* odd that Questor didn't see them the first time," he repeated the wizard's observation to no one in particular.

"Odd? Not so odd if you consider the possibility that Meeks put them there *after* he had the books, expressly to prevent anyone from coming back into the fortress!" Abernathy huffed. He would not look at Ben. "Really, High Lord—I would have thought you could figure that one out by yourself!"

Ben endured the admonishment silently. He could have figured it out by himself, but he hadn't, so what was there to say? What he couldn't figure out now was why Meeks would *bother* placing guards at Mirwouk. After all, the missing books of magic were already in his possession!

He dropped that question into the hopper with all the other unanswered questions and concentrated on helping the others lay Questor on a patch of shaded grass. Parsnip wiped away the dust and blood from the wizard's face and brought him out of his stupor. Questor recovered after a brief period of treatment, Parsnip patched up his injuries, and the little company was back on its feet once more.

"This time we follow Willow's tracks—however many of them there are—until we find her!" Ben declared resolutely.

"*If* we find her," Abernathy muttered.

But no one heard him and off they went again.

DISCOVERY

The heat of the midday sun settled down across the forests of the Melchor in a suffocating blanket and turned its cooling shadows tepid and dank. Morning breezes died away and the air grew thick and still. Insects hummed their toneless songs, leaves hung limp from their branches, and the warm-blooded life of the woodland lay patient and quiet. There was a slowing of time and purpose.

Willow paused at the base of a giant white oak, the weight of the spun gold bridle tugging relentlessly downward on her shoulders where it lay draped across them. A bright sheen of sweat coated the pale green skin of her face and hands, and her lips parted slightly as she worked harder to catch her breath. She had been walking since sunrise, following the black unicorn as it came and went in wisps of dream and shadow, trailing after as if she were a stray bit of dust drawn on in the wake of its passing. She had traveled the whole of the Melchor about Mirwouk half-a-dozen times over, crossing and recrossing her trail time after time, a senseless journey of whim and chance. She was west of Mirwouk now, scarcely a mile from the aged fortress, but she was barely aware of it, and it would have made no difference to her had she taken the time to think about it. She had long since ceased to care about anything but the subject of her search; all else had become irrelevant.

She must find the unicorn. She must know its truth.

She let her eyes glaze slightly with the memory of last night's dream and wondered anew at its meaning.

Then she drew herself upright and continued on, a frail and tiny bit of life amid the giant trees of the mountain forest, a child strayed. She worked her way slowly through a grove of fir and pine clustered so thickly that the boughs interlocked, barely glanced at a stand of Bonnie Blues beyond, and pressed upward along a gentle slope that led to a meadow plateau. She picked her way with careful steps, remembering wearily that she had passed this way before—once, twice, more? She wasn't certain. It didn't matter. She listened to the sound of her heart pounding through her neck and in her ears. It was very loud. It was almost the only sound in the forest. It became the measure of each step she took.

How much farther? she wondered as the heat pressed down. When am I to stop?

She crested the meadowline, paused in the shadow of a long-limbed crimson maple, and closed her eyes against the uncertainty. When she opened them again, the black unicorn stood facing her.

"Oh!" she breathed softly.

The unicorn stood at the center of the meadow, framed in a splash of unclouded sunlight. It was ink black, so perfectly opaque that it might have been sculpted from midnight's shadows. It faced her, head lifted, mane and tail limp in the breezeless air, a statue carved out of ageless ebony. The green eyes regarded her steadily and within their depths called to her. She breathed the sullen heat into her lungs and felt the scorch of the sun's brightness. She listened. The eyes of the unicorn spoke soundlessly, images caught and reflected from dreams remembered and visions lost. She listened, and she knew.

The chase was over. The black unicorn would run from her no longer. It was to this time and place that she had been brought. It only remained for her to discover why.

She came forward tentatively, still half expecting with every step she took that the unicorn would disappear, that it would bolt and run. It did not. It simply stood there—motionless, dreamlike. She slipped the bridle from her shoulders and held it loosely in her hands before her, letting the unicorn see it clearly. Sunlight danced off the traces and fastenings, brilliant flashes that pierced the forest shadows. The unicorn waited. Willow passed from the shade of the crimson maple into the meadow's sunshine, and the sweltering heat enveloped her. Her sea green eyes blinked away a sudden film of moisture, and she shook back her long hair. The unicorn did not move.

She was only a dozen feet from the creature when abruptly she slowed and then stopped. She could not go on. Waves of fear, suspicion, and doubt washed through her, a mingling of whispers that cried out in sudden warning. What was she doing? What was she thinking? The black unicorn was a creature of such ill fortune that no one who had come close to it had been seen again! It was the demon of her dreams! It was the nightmare that had pursued her in her sleep, hunting her as death would!

She felt the weight of the fairy creature's eyes settle on her. She felt its presence as she would a sickness. She struggled to break and run and could not. Desperately, she fought against the emotions that threatened to consume her and banished them. She took deep, long breaths of the sullen midday air and forced herself to look into the creature's emerald eyes. She kept her gaze fixed. There was no hint of sickness or death in those eyes—no hint of demon evil. There was gentleness and warmth—and need.

She came forward another few steps.

Then something new slowed her. There was a flash of intuition that swept her mind momentarily, quick and certain. Ben was near, come in search of . . . of what?

"Ben?" she whispered, waiting.

But there was no one. She was alone with the unicorn. She did not look away from the creature, but she sensed nevertheless that they were alone. She wet her lips and came forward again.

And again she stopped. Her breast heaved. "I cannot touch you," she murmured to the flawless, impossibly wondrous fairy thing. "I cannot. It will be the end of me if I do."

She knew it was so. She knew it instinctively, the way she had always known. No one could touch a unicorn; no one had that right. It belonged to a realm of beauty that no mortal creature should ever attempt to transcend. It had wandered into Landover, a bit of some rainbow broken off from its dark storm's end arc, and it should never be held by hands such as hers. Memories of legends and songs whispered in snatches of warning. She felt tears start down her cheeks and her breath catch in her throat.

Beautiful thing, I cannot . . .

But she did. Almost before she realized what was happening, she was covering those last few paces in quick, mechanical steps, moving without thinking about what she was doing, reaching out to the midnight creature, and placing the bridle of spun gold gently, carefully about its waiting head. She brushed its silken face with her fingers as she worked, and the touch was electric. She felt the whisper of its mane against the backs of her hands, and the sensation was rife with wonder. Fresh images sprang unbidden into her thoughts, jumbled and not yet understandable, but irresistible nevertheless. She touched the unicorn freely now, reveling in the sensations it caused within her. She could not seem to help herself. She could not stop. She was crying anew, her emotions all uncovered, brought close to the surface of her being. Tears ran down her cheeks as she began to sob uncontrollably.

"I love you," she cried desperately, her hands falling away at last when the bridle was in place. "Oh, I love you so much, you beautiful, wondrous thing!"

The black unicorn's horn shone white with magic as it held her gaze, and there were tears now in its eyes as well. For a single moment, they were joined.

Then the moment was gone, and the world beyond intruded with a rush. A huge, dark shadow passed overhead and settled earthward at the clearing's far edge. In the same instant, a familiar scattering of voices called her name frantically from the clearing's other end. Her dreams took life, their images suddenly, terrifyingly all about. Whispers of the warnings that had brought her to this moment turned abruptly to screams of dismay in her mind.

She felt the black unicorn shudder violently next to her and watched the white magic of its horn flare. But it did not bolt into the woods. Whatever happened next, it would run no further.

So be it. Neither would she.

Woodenly, she turned to discover their fate.

Ben Holiday burst from the trees into the meadow and stopped so abruptly that the others of the little company who followed after stumbled into him in their eagerness to keep up and knocked him forward another few steps. They were all yelling at once, calling out to Willow in warning where she stood at the meadow's center, the black unicorn at her side. The shadow of the winged demon had passed overhead a moment earlier, a monstrous cloud against the sun. It was only the worst of luck that could have brought them all together at this same place and time, but the worst of luck seemed to be the only luck Ben could count on. He had tracked Willow to this meadow after escaping the Flynts, believing the worst to be behind him. Now the demon had found them. He saw again in his mind the River Master's doomed nymphs as the demon burned them to ash and he thought of his promise to the Earth Mother to protect Willow. But he was helpless to do that. How was he going to protect Willow without the medallion?

The demon flew overhead a second time, but it did not attack the sylph or the unicorn or even Ben's little group. Instead, it settled slowly earthward at the clearing's far edge, leathered wings folding in against its body, breath steaming with a hiss. Ben squinted against the sunlight. There was a rider atop the demon. The rider was Meeks.

And Meeks, of course, appeared to everyone watching to be Ben.

Ben heard muttered whispers of surprise and confusion from those crowded up behind him. He watched himself climb slowly down from the demon; and even he had to admit that Meeks looked exactly like him. His companions quit yelling, momentary indecision settling in. Ben could feel their eyes bore into his back and could sense the clouds of doubt gathering. He had told them who he was and they had believed him, more or less, until now. But actually *seeing* Ben Holiday standing there in that clearing across from them was something else altogether . . .

Then the black unicorn trumpeted, a high, eerie call, and everyone turned. The fairy beast stamped and its nostrils flared, the bridle of spun gold dancing against the sunlight with each toss of its delicate head. Magic flashed in its ridged horn. The unicorn was a thing of impossible beauty and it drew the eyes of all gathered like moths to the light. It shuddered, but held its ground against the weight of their stares. It seemed to be searching for something.

Slowly Willow turned from the unicorn and began to look about as well. Her gaze was curiously empty.

Ben wasn't sure what was happening, but he decided almost instantly not to wait to find out. "Willow!" he called to the sylph, and her eyes fixed on him. "Willow, it's me, Ben!" He came forward a few steps, saw the lack of recognition in her eyes, and stopped. "Listen to me. Listen carefully. I know I don't look like myself. But it *is* me. Meeks is responsible for everything that's happened. He's come back into Landover and stolen the throne. He's changed me into this. Worse, he's made himself look like me. That's not me over there—that's Meeks!"

She turned now to look over at Meeks, saw Ben's face and body, and gave a quick gasp. But she saw the demon as well. She took a step forward, stopped, and stepped slowly back again.

"Willow, it's all right," Meeks called out to her in Ben's voice. "Bring the unicorn to me. Pass me the reins of the bridle."

"No!" Ben yelled frantically. "No, Willow!" He came forward another few steps, stopping quickly as Willow started to back away. "Willow, don't do it. Meeks sent the dreams—all of them. He has the medallion. He has the missing books of magic. Now he wants the unicorn! I don't know why, but you can't let him have it! Please!"

"Willow, be careful of what you see," Meeks warned in a quiet, soothing voice. "The stranger is dangerous, and the magic he wields confuses. Come over to me before he reaches you."

Ben was beside himself. "Look at whom I'm with, for God's sake! Questor, Abernathy, Bunion, Parsnip, Fillip, and Sot!" He turned and beckoned to those behind him. But no one came forward. No one seemed quite sure that they should. Ben felt a hint of desperation creep into his voice as he faced Willow anew. "Why would they be with me if I'm not who I say I am? They know the truth of things!" He wheeled about once more, anger in his voice. "Damn it, Questor, say something to her!"

The wizard hesitated, seemed to consider the advisability of doing what Ben asked, then straightened. "Yes, he speaks the truth. He is the High Lord, Willow," he said finally.

There were muttered hissings and murmurings of agreement from the others, including a few pleas of "Save us, great High Lord, Mighty High Lord" from the G'home Gnomes, who were hiding now behind Questor's robes.

Ben turned back. "Willow, come over here quickly! Please! Get away!"

But now Meeks had come forward several paces and he was smiling Ben's most reassuring smile. "Willow, I love you," he told her. "I love you and I want to protect you. Come here to me. What you see from the stranger is all illusion. He has no support from our friends; they are just false images. You can see the truth of things if you look. Do you see me? Am I anyone different from the one I always was? What you are hearing are lies! Remember the dream! You must pick up the reins of the bridle and bring the black unicorn to me to be safe from the dangers that threaten! These illusions pretending friendship are the dangers of your dream! Come to me now and be safe!"

Willow was looking first one way and then the other, confusion evident in her face. Behind her, the black unicorn stamped and snorted delicately, a bit of shadow caught in the sunlight, bound in place by ties no one else could see. Ben was frantic. He had to do something!

"Show me the rune stone!" Willow called out suddenly, head jerking from Ben to Meeks and back again. "Let me see the stone I gave you!"

Ben went cold. The rune stone, the milky-colored talisman that warned of danger when it threatened. "I don't have it!" he called back helplessly. "I lost it when . . ."

"I have it right here!" Meeks announced in triumph, cutting him short. The wizard reached beneath his robes and brought forth the rune stone—or something that appeared to be the rune stone—glowing bright red. He held it up for inspection.

"Ben?" Willow asked softly, some of the hope coming back into her face. "Is it you?" Ben felt his stomach lurch as the girl started away from him.

"One moment!" Questor Thews called suddenly, and everyone turned. "You must have dropped this, High Lord," he advised officiously, coming forward a step or two more, the G'home Gnomes shaken free momentarily from his robes. He held out the rune stone Willow had given Ben—at least, his magic made it *seem* like the stone—and let everyone have a good look. The stone glowed crimson.

Ben had never been more grateful to the wizard in his life. "Thank you, Questor," he breathed quietly.

Willow had stopped again. Slowly, she backed away from them all, the indecision returned. There was fear now in her face as well. "I do not know which of you is Ben," she told them quietly. "Perhaps neither of you."

Her words lingered in the sudden stillness that followed. A frightening tension settled down across the sunlit meadow with its chessboard of frozen figures, each ready to move in a different direction, each poised to strike. Willow pressed back toward the black unicorn, eyes shifting from one set of playing pieces to another, waiting. Behind her, the unicorn had gone still.

I have to do something, Ben told himself once more and wondered frantically what it ought to be.

Then out of the woods strolled Edgewood Dirk. The cat might have been out for an afternoon walk, sauntering with an unconcerned air from the trees, picking its way delicately through the scrub grass and flowers, head and tail held high as it stepped, eyes looking neither right nor left. It paid no attention to any of them. It seemed almost to have stumbled onto things by accident. Dirk walked directly to the center of the clearing, stopped, glanced casually around at those assembled, and sat down.

"Good day," he greeted them.

Meeks let out a shriek that brought them all out of their boots and flung back his cloak. The Ben Holiday disguise shimmered like a reflection in the waters of a pond disturbed by a thrown stone and began to disintegrate. Willow screamed. The wizard's clawed hands lifted and extended, and green fire lanced wickedly toward Edgewood Dirk. But the cat had already begun to change, the small furry body growing, shimmering, and smoothing until it was as crystalline as a diamond. The wizard fire struck it and broke apart, scattering like refracted light into the sunlit air, showering the trees and grass and scorching the earth.

Ben was racing desperately toward Willow by this time, yelling like a madman. But the sylph was already beyond his reach. Eyes frantic, she had pressed herself back against the black unicorn and seized the golden bridle that bound the fairy creature. The unicorn was stamping and rearing, crying out its own high-pitched, eerie call, and darting back and forth in small dashes. Willow clung to the beast as a frightened child would to its mother, grappling with it, being dragged along as it went—away from Ben.

"Willow!" he howled.

Meeks was still after Edgewood Dirk. The shards of flame from his first attack had barely been scattered when the wizard struck once more. Fire gathered and arced from his hands in a massive ball, rolling and tumbling through the air to explode into the cat. Dirk arched and shuddered, and the flaming ball seemed to absorb itself into the crystalline form. Then the fire exploded out again, hurtling itself back toward the wizard in a shower of flaming darts. Meeks threw up his cloak like a shield, and the darts deflected everywhere. Some burned into the hide of the demon crouching behind the wizard and it roared and surged skyward with a rasp of fury.

Smoke and fire burned everywhere, and Ben stumbled on blindly through the haze. Behind him, his companions called out. Overhead, the winged demon blocked the sun, its shadow darkening the meadow like an eclipse. The black unicorn sprang forward with a scream, and Willow flung herself atop it. She might have done so out of instinct or out of need, but the result was the same—she was carried away. The unicorn darted past Ben so quickly he barely saw it. He reached for it, but he was far too slow. He had a brief glimpse of Willow's lithe form clinging to its back, and then both disappeared into the trees.

Then the winged demon attacked. It dropped like a stone toward the meadow, diving from the empty skies, flames bursting from its maw. Ben dropped flat and covered his head. From the corner of one eye, he watched as Dirk shimmered, hunched down against the force of the fire, absorbed it, and thrust it back. Flames hammered into the demon and sent the monster catapulting back. Steam and smoke clogged the meadow air.

Meeks struck again, and Edgewood Dirk repelled the assault. The demon struck, and the cat flung the fire back once more. Ben rose, dropped, rose again, and staggered blindly through the carnage. Shouts and cries reached out to him, and visions floated through the haze before his watering eyes. His hands groped and struggled to hold something, anything—and finally fastened on the medallion.

White heat burned into his palms. For just an instant, he thought he saw the Paladin appear, a faint image somewhere in the distance, a silver, armor-clad figure astride the great white charger.

Then the vision was gone again, a vision that had been impossible in any case. No medallion, no Paladin—Ben knew that. His throat constricted and he choked as the fires of wizard and demon continued to hammer down on Edgewood Dirk and be flung back again. Flowers and grasses burned to black ash. Trees shook and their leaves wilted. The whole world seemed to be in flames.

And finally the meadow itself seemed to explode upward in one vast, heaving cough, steam and fire ripping through everything. Ben felt himself hurtled skyward like a bit of deadwood, flying in a graceless scattering of arms and legs, spinning like a pinwheel.

This is it, he thought just before he tumbled earthward. This is how it all ends.

Then he struck with jarring force and everything went dark.

CAT'S PAW

Ben Holiday came awake again in a deeply shaded forest glade that smelled of moss and wild flowers. Birds sang in the trees, their songs bright and cheerful. A small stream wound through the center of the clearing from the woodlands and disappeared back into them again. There was a stillness that whispered of peace and solitude.

Ben was lying on a patch of grass staring up into a network of branches set against the cloudless sky. A glimpse of the sun peeked through the leaves. He pushed himself carefully upright, aware that his clothes were singed and his hands and arms covered with soot. He took a moment to check himself, feeling about for permanent injuries. There were none—only bumps and bruises. But he looked as if he had rolled through half-a-dozen campfires.

"Feeling better, High Lord?"

He turned at the sound of the familiar voice and found Edgewood Dirk sitting comfortably atop a large, mossy rock, paws tucked carefully away. The cat blinked sleepily and yawned.

"What happened to me?" Ben asked, realizing that this clearly wasn't where he had started out; this wasn't the meadow where he had lost consciousness. "How did I get here?"

Dirk stood up, stretched, and sat down again. "I brought you. It was quite a trick, actually, but I have gotten rather good at using energy to transport inert objects. It did not seem advisable to leave you lying about in that burned-out meadow."

"What about the others? What about Willow and . . ."

"The sylph is with the black unicorn, I imagine. I wouldn't know exactly where. Your companions were scattered in every which direction. That last explosion sent them all flying. Such magic is best left unused. Too bad Meeks cannot understand that."

Ben blinked away a final rush of dizziness and studied the cat. "He knew who you were, didn't he?"

"He knew *what* I was."

"Oh. How is that, Dirk?"

The cat seemed to consider the question. "Wizards and prism cats have crossed paths a few times before, High Lord."

"And not as friends, I gather?"

"Not usually."

"He seemed frightened of you."

"He is frightened of many things."

"He's not alone in that respect. What happened to him?"

"He lost interest in the fight and flew off on his pet demon. He has gone for the books of magic, I would guess. He believes he requires their power. Then he will be back. He will hunt you all down this time out, I think. You had better prepare yourself."

Ben went cold. Slowly he straightened himself, feeling the kinks in his body loosen. "I have to find the others," he began, trying to think his way through the wall of fear and desperation that quickly settled in. "Damn! How am I supposed to do that?" He started up, slowed as a dizziness swept through him, and dropped back to one knee. "How am I supposed to help them at all, for that matter? I would have been finished back there if not for you. This whole business has gotten completely out of hand. I'm no better off than I was the day Meeks had me thrown out of the castle. I still don't know why it is that no one can recognize me. I still don't have any idea how Meeks got hold of the medallion. I still don't know what he wants with the black unicorn. I don't know one thing more than I ever did about what is going on!"

Dirk yawned anew. "Don't you?"

Ben didn't hear him. "I'll tell you one thing. I can't handle this by myself. I never could. There isn't any point in kidding myself; I have to have help. I'm going to do what I should have done in the first place. I'm going into the mists, medallion or no medallion, and find the fairies. I'll do what I did before. I'll find them and ask them for a magic that will let me stand up to Meeks. They helped me with Nightshade; they'll help me with Meeks. They have to."

"Ah, but that's not true, is it?" Dirk asked softly. "The fairies help only when they choose. You know that, my dear High Lord. You have always known that. You cannot demand their aid; you can only wish for it. The choice of giving or withholding it is always theirs."

"It doesn't matter." Ben shook his head stubbornly. "I'm going into the mists. When I find them, I'll . . ."

"*If* you find them," Dirk interrupted.

Ben paused, then flushed. "It would be nice to have some encouragement from you for a change! What makes you think I *won't* find them?"

Dirk regarded him for a moment, then sniffed the air. All about, the birds continued to sing indifferently. "Because they don't want you to find them, High Lord," the cat said finally. He sighed. "You see, *they* have already found *you*."

There was a long moment of silence as Ben and the cat stared at each other, eyes locked. Ben cleared his throat. "What?"

Dirk's eyes lidded to half-mast. "High Lord, who do you think sent me?"

Ben sat back down slowly, crossed his legs before him, and dropped his hands into his lap. "The fairies sent you?" The cat said nothing. "But why? I mean, why you, Dirk?"

"You mean, why a cat? Why not a dog? Or a lion or a tiger? Or another Paladin, for that matter? Is that what you mean?" Dirk's fur ruffled on the nape of his neck and down the arch of his back. "Well, a cat is all that you need or deserve, my dear High Lord! More, in point of fact! I was sent to arouse your consciousness—to make you think! I was not sent to provide salvation! If you want salvation, you will have to find it within yourself! That is the way it has always been and that is the way it will always be!"

He stood up, jumped down from the rock, and strode deliberately up to an astonished Ben. "I am tired of pussyfooting around with you. I have told you everything you need to know to counteract the magic that has been used against you. I have done everything but shove your nose in the truth of matters, and that I cannot do! That is forbidden! Fairy kind never reveal truth to mortal creatures. But I have kept you safe on your journey when you needed keeping safe, though you haven't needed it nearly so often as you believed. I have watched over you and guided you when I could. Most important of all, I have kept you thinking and that in turn has kept you alive!" He paused. "Well, all that is finished now. Your time for thinking is just about up!"

Ben shook his head quickly. "Dirk, I can't just . . ."

"Let me finish!" the cat snapped. "When in the world will humans learn to start listening to cats?" The green eyes narrowed. "The fairies sent me to help you, High Lord, but they left it to me to choose the means. They did not advise me on what I was to do or say. They did not tell me why it was that they believed I could help. Such is not the way of the fairies—nor is it the way of cats! We do as we choose in any case and live our lives as we must. We play games because that is who we are. Cat games or fairy games, it is all very much the same. Ours, High Lord, is a much different world from your own!"

One paw lifted. "Hear me well, then. No one is entitled to be given answers to the problems that beset them. No one is given life on a silver platter—cat or King! If you wish to know the truth of things, you must find it out for yourself. If you wish to understand what puzzles you, reason it through for yourself. You believe yourself mired in insolvable dilemmas. You believe yourself incapable of breaking free. Your identity is gone, your kingdom stolen. Your enemies beset you, your friends are lost. It is a chain of complications in which the links are joined, Ben Holiday. Cut free a single link, and the chains fall apart! But you are the one who carries the cutters—not me, not anyone else. That is what I have been trying to tell you from day one! Do you understand?"

Ben nodded hastily. "I understand."

The paw lowered again. "I hope so. Now I will say this one more time. The magic you struggle against is magic of deception—a mirror that alters in its reflection truths and makes them half-truths and lies. If you can see past the mirror, you can set yourself free. If you can set yourself free, you can help your friends. But you had better get busy!"

He stretched, turned, walked several paces away, and turned back again. The forest glade was quiet now; even the birds in the trees had gone still. Sunlight continued to shine out of the skies from overhead, casting the dappled shadows of the leaves and branches across the clearing beneath, leaving Ben and Dirk spotted and striped.

"The dark wizard is frightened of you, Ben Holiday," Dirk advised softly. "He knows you to be close to the answers you need to break free, and he will try to destroy you before that can happen. I have given you the means to find the answers that will defeat him. Use those means. You are an intelligent man. You have been a man who has spent his life ordering other men's lives. Man of law, man of power—order now your own!"

He moved soundlessly to the glade's edge, never looking back. "I have enjoyed our time together, High Lord," he called back. "I have enjoyed our travels. But they are over for now. I have other places to be and other appointments to keep. I will think of you. And one day, perhaps, I will see you again."

"Wait, Dirk!" Ben called after, coming suddenly to his feet, fighting against the continuing dizziness.

"I never wait, High Lord," the cat replied, now almost lost in shadow. "Besides, there is nothing more I can do for you. I have done everything I can. Good luck to you."

"Dirk!"

"Remember what I told you. And try listening to cats once in a while, would you?"

"Dirk, damn it!"

"Good-bye."

And with that Edgewood Dirk disappeared into the forest and was gone.

Ben Holiday stared after the cat for a long time following its departure, half expecting that it would return. It didn't, of course, just as he had known all along somewhere deep inside that it wouldn't. When he finally accepted the fact, he quit looking for it and began to panic. He was all alone for the first time since being cast out of Sterling Silver—all alone and in the worst predicament of his life. He was without his identity or his medallion, and he had no idea at all how to regain either. Edgewood Dirk, his protector, had deserted him. Willow had disappeared with the black unicorn, still believing him the stranger he appeared to be. His friends were scattered to heaven-knew-where. Meeks had gone for the books of magic and would return shortly to put an end to him.

And here he sat, waiting for it to happen.

He was stunned. He could not seem to think clearly. He tried to reason, to think what he should do next, but everything seemed to jumble up, the problems and needs fighting for equal time in his thoughts. He rose, his motions mechanical, his eyes dead, and walked to the edge of the little stream. He glanced once more after Dirk, saw only empty forest, and turned back again, a feeling of bleak resignation settling through him. He knelt down beside the stream and splashed water on his soot-blackened face, rubbing it into his eyes. The water was like ice, and it sent a shock through his system. He splashed some more on, throwing it up over his head and shoulders, letting the cold galvanize him.

Then he sat back, the water dripping off his face, his eyes looking down into the stream.

Reason it through, he admonished himself. You have all the answers. Dirk said you had all the answers. So what in the hell are they?

He resisted an almost overwhelming urge to leap up and charge off into the trees. He forced himself to stay put. Action would have been more immediately gratifying—the sense of doing something, *anything,* better than just sitting around. But running about heedlessly wasn't what the situation called for; thinking was. He had to know what he was doing, had to understand once and for all what had happened.

Links in a chain, Dirk had said. All his problems were links in a chain, all locked together. Cut one, and the chain would fall apart. Okay. He would do that. He would cut that link. But which link should he cut?

He looked down into the waters of the stream, staring at the rippling reflection of his image. A distorted version of Ben Holiday's face glimmered back at him. But it was he, not someone else, not the stranger everyone else saw. What was it that made others see him differently? A mask, Dirk had said—and he was disappearing into it. He stared at himself for a long moment, then looked up again, focusing on a random gathering of wild flowers several yards beyond, seeing them and seeing nothing.

Magic of deception, Dirk had said.

Whose magic? Whose deception?

His own, the River Master had said. The River Master had offered to help, had tried in fact, but in the end couldn't. The magic at work was magic of Ben's own making, the River Master had said—and only he could act to break its hold.

But what magic had he used?

He tried to think it through, but couldn't. Nothing would come. He rocked back on his heels beside the little stream, hunched down in the shadows of the mountain glade and let his mind wander freely for a moment. It all went back to that night in his bedchamber in Sterling Silver when Meeks had appeared before him from out of nowhere. That was when everything had gone wrong and he had lost the medallion. Something grated at the memory, and he grasped futilely at it. He had lost the medallion, he had lost his identity, he had lost his magic, he had lost his kingdom. A chain of links that needed breaking, he thought. He recalled his shock at finding the medallion gone. He remembered his fear.

A sudden thought struck him, and a memory stirred. The fairies had said something to him once about fear. It had been the only time they had spoken to him, long ago now, back when he had gone into the mists in search of the Io Dust, back when he had first come into Landover and been forced to fight to gain recognition for his right to the throne—just as he was fighting now. What was it they had said? *Fear has many disguises. You must learn to recognize them when next they come for you.*

He frowned. Disguises? Masks? Not much difference between the two, he mused. He had wondered what the words had meant. He found himself wondering again now. At the time, he thought they had referred to his impending encounter with the Iron Mark. But what if they had referred to what was happening to him now—to the fear he was experiencing over the loss of the medallion?

Could the fairies have foreseen that loss so long ago? Or was the warning simply generic, simply . . .

About the magic of this land?

Self-consciously, he reached within his tunic and brought forth the medallion he now wore, the medallion Meeks had given him, its face graven with the dark wizard's harsh visage. It all began here—the questions, the mysteries, a jumble of events that had swept him away from everything sane into this mire of fear and doubt. How could it have happened, he wondered for at least the hundredth time? How could he have lost the medallion without knowing it? How had Meeks gotten the medallion from him when only he could remove it? It didn't make sense! Even if he *had* removed it, why couldn't he *remember* removing it?

Unless he hadn't!

There was a sudden, hollow feeling in the pit of his stomach. Oh, God!

Unless he was still wearing it!

Something had nudged his thinking a step farther than it had gone before. He could almost see the cutters working on his chains. Self-deception, Dirk had said. Magic of his own making, the River Master had said. Damn! He felt his breath begin to come in short, ragged gasps of excitement; he could hear his chest pounding. It made sense. It was the only answer that had ever made sense. Meeks couldn't take the medallion from him unless he removed it himself, but he couldn't remember removing it, and the reason he couldn't remember removing it was because he never had removed it!

Meeks had simply made him think so.

But how?

He tried to think it through a step at a time. His hands were shaking with excitement, the medallion spinning in their grip. He still wore the medallion of the High Lords of Landover; he simply hadn't realized it. Was that possible? His mind raced ahead, exploring the possibilities, whispering to him in a quick, urgent voice. He still wore the medallion! Meeks had simply disguised it somehow, made him think it wasn't the real medallion, just a substitute. That would explain why Meeks hadn't simply finished him off in his bedchamber. Meeks was afraid that the Paladin might still appear—that the disguise was too new, too thin perhaps. That's why the wizard had let him go after giving him the strange warning about not taking off the substitute medallion. He had expected Ben to question that warning sooner or later. He had hoped Ben would take off the medallion and throw it away, thinking he was breaking free. Then Meeks would have had the medallion for good!

His mind spun. The language, he thought suddenly! How could he still communicate in the language of Landover if he wasn't wearing the medallion? Questor had told him long ago that the medallion was the reason he could understand the land's language, could write it, and could speak it! Why hadn't he thought of that before? And Questor—Questor had always wondered how Meeks got the medallion back from failed candidates for the kingship who refused to return it voluntarily. He would have done it something like this! He would have tricked them into taking it off, thinking they had already lost it!

My God! Could all this be possible?

He took a deep breath to steady himself. Could it be anything else? He tacked on a negative answer immediately. It was the only answer that made any sense. The winged demon hadn't broken off the attack on the River Master's nymphs at Elderew because of Dirk; it had flown off because it had seen the medallion held in Ben's hands and been frightened of its power. The demon had recognized the truth when Ben couldn't. Magic had disguised the truth from Ben—magic Meeks had employed that night in his bedchamber—an old magic, Ben thought suddenly. That was what Nightshade had said to Strabo. That was why only the witch and the dragon could recognize it!

But how did the magic work? What was needed to break its spell? Was it this same magic that had changed his identity?

The questions tumbled over one another in their efforts to be answered. Deception—that was the key word, the word Dirk had used repeatedly. Meeks must have used his magic to deceive Ben into believing the medallion he wore was another than his own. And Ben had believed the deception to be the truth. He had let the deception become his own. Damn! He had built his own prison! Meeks must have caused him to dream that he had given up the medallion, and he had convinced himself of its truth!

In which case, shouldn't he be able simply to . . .

He couldn't finish the thought. He was afraid to finish it, afraid he might be wrong. He took another deep breath. It didn't matter that he finish it. It mattered only that he test it. He would *have* to test it to know for sure.

He stared down again into the stream, watching his face shimmer and change with the movement of the water. His mask, he thought—not to him, but to everyone else. He steadied himself, then held the medallion out before him, hands grasping the chain, the visage of Meeks dangling and spinning slowly, reflecting the sunlight in small glimmerings of dull silver. He slowed his breathing deliberately, his heartbeat, and time itself. He focused his gaze on the tarnished image, watching the spinning motion slow, watching until the medallion was almost perfectly still. He shoved the image he was seeing from his mind and substituted in its place a picture from his memory of the Paladin riding out from the gates of Sterling Silver against the sunrise. He looked past the tarnish and the wear and envisioned polished silver. He gave himself over to his vision.

Remember, what you're seeing is all a lie, he told himself. Just a lie.

But nothing happened. The medallion before him continued to reflect the image of Meeks. He fought down a renewed surge of panic and forced himself to remain calm. Something more was needed. Something.

His mind sifted, considering and discarding possibilities. He kept his eyes focused on the medallion. The mountain forest was still about him, the silence complete save for brief snatches of bird songs and the rustle of the wind through the leaves. He was right about this; he knew he was right. Break the first link, and the others would follow. The chain would fall apart. He would become himself again, the power of the Paladin would return, and his magic would be freed. He need only find a key . . .

He caught himself in midthought. Slowly his fingers eased along the length of chain to the medallion itself. Lightly they caressed the tarnished surface, then gathered the talisman into his palms. Its feel was abhorrent to him—but then Meeks would want it that way. His hands closed. He held the medallion, gripped it tightly, felt its surface, its graven image, and envisioned not Meeks, but the Paladin riding out of Sterling Silver, riding out at sunrise, riding to him . . .

Something began to happen. The medallion grew warm to the touch, and there was a barely perceptible change in its feel. He gripped it harder, the image he knew to be hidden there locked firmly in the forefront of his thoughts. He closed his eyes. The image was a beacon of whiteness that became his only light. The medallion burned, but he kept his grip on it. He could sense a shifting in its surface as if something were falling away, a skin being shed. *Yes!* The burning continued, then flared sharply, spread through the whole of his body, lifted away, and dissipated into air.

Coolness returned. Slowly he opened his eyes, then his fingers. He looked down at the medallion that nestled in his palm. It was bright and untarnished. He could see himself mirrored in its surface. The image of the Paladin glimmered back at him.

He permitted himself a huge, almost foolish smile. He had been right after all. The medallion had been his all along.

The chain that had bound him was broken!

REVELATION

Willow stirred, consciousness returning as she made the slow, languid slide out of slumber. The sun was warm upon her skin, and tall grasses tickled her face. She blinked, squinted against the sudden brightness, and let her eyes close again. She had dreamed—or had she? She had flown on a cloud, riding wind currents that whipped and buffeted her and bore her over all the world as if she were a bird on wing. She blinked again, feeling the press of the earth against her back. She had been so free.

Then the drifting sensation slipped from her, and a sudden return of memory jarred her completely awake. She sat upright with a start. There had been no dream. There had been only the reality of her flight from Meeks, the winged demon, the others . . .

A shudder passed through her body. She forced her eyes open again, squinting against the sunlight. She sat within a wide clearing in a grove of hardwood trees and scattered pines almost within the shadow of Mirwouk. The walls of the ancient fortress loomed behind her, jagged heights rough against the afternoon sky. Flowers dotted the hillside that spread away below her, their smells filling the still, humid air. The whole of the mountains about her were strangely silent.

Her eyes shifted. A dozen feet away, the black unicorn stood looking at her, the bridle of spun gold still fastened about its slender head.

"I rode you," she whispered almost soundlessly.

The memory was a jumble of images and feelings that washed over her like ice water and shocked her with their intensity. She had barely known what she was doing when she had pulled herself atop the unicorn's back, terrified by what was happening about her, frantic to escape its horror. Nothing was what it appeared—not Ben, not the stranger who claimed to be Ben, not that cat, nothing. There was fire and destruction all about—such hatred! She had only thought to flee, and something in the touch of the unicorn's body against her own as it had surged past had drawn her after. Hands on the golden bridle, fingers locking in the mane, on the sleek body, and about the slender neck, her own face pressed close . . . The images stirred and vanished, feelings more than pictures, a whisper of need and want.

Her breath came in a small gasp. She had mounted the black unicorn without thinking, and her flight—for that indeed was what it had been—had been magical. There had been no sense of place or time; there had been only an acute sense of being. The unicorn had done more than carry her away from that meadow. The unicorn had carried her away from herself, down inside herself to see all about who and what she was and might be, until the thought of it had left her dazed and filled with wonder. The unicorn had shown her a texture and meaning to life that she would never have believed possible. Just its touch had been enough; nothing more was needed. There were tears in her eyes as she remembered how it had felt. The images were strangely clouded now, but the emotions she had experienced remained sharp and clear. How glorious it had been!

She brushed at the tears and let her gaze meet that of the watching unicorn. It still waited on her. It did not run as it might have, perhaps as it should. It simply waited.

But what was it waiting for? What did it want from her?

Confusion swept through her. The truth of the matter was that she didn't know. She looked into the emerald eyes of the black unicorn and wished the fairy creature could tell her. She needed to know. Here it was, this wondrous being, waiting almost resignedly while she pondered, waiting on her once more—and she didn't have any idea at all what she should do. She felt helpless and afraid. She felt herself a fool.

But she knew she could not afford such feelings, and she blocked them roughly from her mind. Meeks might still hunt them—probably did. That cat, whatever it was, would not delay the wizard long. He would come after her, after the unicorn, after them both. Meeks wanted the black unicorn; the stranger had been right about that. That meant that the stranger might have been right about the dreams as well.

And that, in turn, meant that the stranger might really be Ben.

A twinge of desperate longing raced through her, but she brushed it quickly aside. There was no time to consider the possibility now. The black unicorn was in immediate danger, and she had to do something to help it. It was clearly waiting on her, depending on her, and expecting something from her. She had to find out what.

There was only one way. She knew it instinctively. She would have to touch the unicorn, expose herself to its magic. She would have to open herself to its vision.

She breathed deeply, slowly, trying to steady herself. The sudden fear she experienced made her queasy. She was proposing the unthinkable. No one touched a unicorn and was ever herself again. No one. Oh, yes, she had touched the fairy creature already—a brushing against its body as she slipped the golden bridle in place and a clinging as she rode it to safety from that meadow. But both times she had been barely aware of what she was doing; it had all been something from a brief, wondrous dream that might never have been. What she would do now was entirely different, willful and deliberate, and she would be risking everything she was. The legends were uniform. Unicorns belonged to no one but themselves. Touch one and you were lost.

Yet she was going to do it anyway. The decision had already been made. The black unicorn was more than a legend out of tales a thousand years old, more than the dream that had drawn her on, more even than the reality of its physical being. It was an inescapable want that was an integral and undeniable part of her, a mystery that she must solve. The emerald eyes of the creature reflected her most secret urgings. She could keep nothing of herself hidden. Her own body betrayed her, its need for the unicorn an irresistible force. There was desire in her that surpassed anything she had ever known. The dangers that the black unicorn might pose, imagined or real, paled beside such desire. She had to solve its puzzle, whatever the cost. She had to know its truth.

She went hot and cold and she felt feather light as she rose and started forward. She was trembling, the horror and the anticipation mixing within her in equal measures, driving her reason from her, and leaving only her need.

Oh, Ben, she thought desperately! Why aren't you here?

The black unicorn waited patiently, an ebony statue in the dappled shadows, eyes locked on Willow's. There was a curious sense of its both not and always being mirrored in the sylph—as if it were her most carefully guarded wish, projected into being from her mind.

"I have to know," she whispered to the unicorn as she stood at last before it.

Slowly, her hands came up.

The meadow, once grassy and bright with wild flowers, lay in ruins, a charred, smoking stretch of barren earth amid the forest trees. Questor Thews stood at its edge and peered futilely through the haze. He was covered with dust and ash, his tall, stooped figure more ragtag in appearance than ever, gray robes and colored silks singed and torn, harlequin leather boots scuffed and smudged. That last exchange of magic between Meeks, the demon, and Edgewood Dirk had sent him flying. The wind had been knocked from him, and he'd found himself resting rather precariously in the branches of an aged crimson maple, an object of great delight for the squirrels and birds nesting there. Abernathy, the kobolds, and the gnomes were nowhere to be seen. Ben Holiday, Willow, and the black unicorn had disappeared. Questor had climbed down from that maple and gone searching for them all. He hadn't found a one.

Now his wanderings had brought him back to where he had last seen any of them. And none of them appeared to be here either.

He sighed deeply, his owlish face lined with worry. He wished he knew more of what was going on. He accepted now that the stranger who claimed to be Ben Holiday was in fact who he said he was; the man who appeared to be Ben Holiday was in fact Meeks. The dreams Willow, Ben, and he had experienced had been, in fact, the creations of his half-brother, all part of some bigger plan to gain control over Landover and the magic. But acceptance of all this gained him nothing. He still didn't know what the black unicorn had to do with anything nor did he understand yet what plan Meeks was trying to implement. Worst of all, he didn't have any idea at all how to find any of this out.

He rubbed his bearded chin and sighed again. There had to be a way, of course. He just had to figure it out.

"Hmmmmm," he mused thoughtfully. But his thinking produced nothing.

He shrugged. Well, there was nothing more to be accomplished by standing about.

He started to turn away and found himself face to face with Meeks. His half brother had reverted to his normal form, a tall, craggy figure with grizzled white hair and hard, dead eyes. Dark blue robes cloaked his body like a shroud. He stood less than a dozen yards away, just a step or two back in the trees from the clearing's edge. The black-gloved hand of his one good arm cradled the missing books of magic close against his chest.

Questor Thews felt his stomach lurch.

"I have waited a long time for this moment," Meeks whispered. "I have been very patient."

Dozens of random thoughts rushed through Questor's mind and were gone, leaving only one. "I am not frightened of you," he said quietly.

His half-brother's face was unreadable. "You should be, Questor. You think yourself a wizard now, but you are an apprentice still. You will never be more than that. I have power you never even dreamed could exist! I have the means to do anything!"

"Except catch the black unicorn, it appears," Questor answered bravely.

The dead eyes flickered briefly with rage. "You understand nothing—not you, not Holiday, not anyone. You play a game you cannot win and you play it poorly. You are a distraction to be removed." The pale, creased face was a death mask. "I have endured exile and a disruption of my plans— all brought about by you and this play-King—and neither of you understands yet what it is that you have done. You are pathetic!"

The dark robes seemed to twitch where the right sleeve hung empty. "Your time in this world and life is just about over, half-brother. You stand alone. That prism cat no longer threatens me. Holiday is helpless and abandoned. The sylph and the black unicorn have nowhere left to run. Your other friends are already mine—all but the dog, and the dog is of no consequence."

Questor felt his heart sink. The others were prisoners—all but Abernathy?

Meeks smiled now, a cold, empty smile. "You were the last possible threat to me, Questor. And now I have you."

Questor stiffened, anger pushing back his fear. "You do not have me yet! Nor will you ever have me!"

The other's laugh was soundless. "Won't I?"

His head inclined slightly, and dozens of shadows slipped from behind the trees all about him. The shadows materialized with the light into small, crooked children with pointed ears, wizened faces, and scaled bodies. Pig snouts sniffed the forest air and serpent tongues slipped between rows of sharpened teeth.

"Demon imps!" Questor exclaimed softly.

"Rather a few too many for you to do much about, wouldn't you say?" His half-brother's words hissed at him with undisguised pleasure. "I don't care to waste my time with you, Questor. I prefer to leave you to them."

The demon imps had completely surrounded Questor, eyes bright and anxious, tongues licking their snouts. Meeks was right. There were too many. Nevertheless, he held his ground. There was no point in trying to run. His only chance was to catch them off guard . . .

They had closed to within half-a-dozen yards, a tight circle of ugly little faces and sharp teeth, when Questor whirled about, hands pinwheeling, and sent them all flying with a burst of magic. Smoke and steam geysered from out of nowhere, flinging them away, and Questor was loping desperately back into the concealing shadows of the forest, leaping over the squirming, momentarily blinded demon imps as if they were mud puddles. Squeals of rage chased after him. The demon imps were up and skittering in pursuit almost instantly. He whirled to face them. Again he sent an explosion of magic into their midst, and again they were scattered. But there were so many! They came at him from everywhere, chittering and squealing, grasping at his robes. He tried to defend himself, but it was too late. They were all over him, pulling at him, pinning his arms to his body. He swayed with the weight of them and toppled over.

Clawed hands fastened to his clothing, then to his throat. He began to choke, unable to breathe. He struggled valiantly, but there were dozens holding him down. Flashes of light danced before his eyes.

He had just a momentary glimpse through the tangle of demon imps of a smiling Meeks standing over him before he blacked out.

Willow's hands were inches from the black unicorn's delicate ebony head when she heard a faint rustling of leaves and brush, the sound of someone approaching through the trees. She drew back quickly from the unicorn, startled, wary.

A moment later, a shaggy head pushed out from the foliage and peered about intently through eyeglasses knocked partially askew by a veil of interlocking pine boughs.

It was Abernathy.

"Willow, is that you?" the scribe asked in disbelief.

He shoved past the remaining branches and stepped into the clearing. His dress clothes were in shreds, the greater part of his tunic torn from his body. His boots were gone completely. His fur was singed and his face looked as if it had been shoved into an ash pit. He was panting heavily, and his tongue licked out at his black nose.

"I have had better days, I want you to know," he declared. "I may have had worse, but I cannot remember when. First, I traipse all over creation in search of you and this . . . this animal for heaven knows what reason, because I surely do not, then we find, not just you and it, but Meeks and his demon as well, then the cat appears and there is a pointless exchange of magic that seems to do little more than fire up a whole section of the forest, and finally we are all scattered to the four winds and no one can find anyone!"

He gulped a chestful of air, gave out a long sigh and glanced about. "Have you seen any of the others?"

Willow shook her head, distracted. "No, none of them." Her thoughts were of the unicorn, of the need that consumed her, of her desire to reach out and touch . . .

"What are you doing here?" Abernathy asked suddenly, the sound of his voice startling her. The scribe saw her consternation. "Is something wrong, Willow? What are you doing with the unicorn? You know how dangerous that creature is. Come away, now. Come over and let me look at you. The High Lord would want . . ."

"Have you seen him?" she demanded sharply, the mention of Ben a lifeline for which she quickly grasped. "Is he close?"

Abernathy shoved his glasses further up his nose. "No, Willow—I haven't seen him. He was lost with the rest of us." He paused. "Are you all right?"

The lifeline disappeared. She nodded without speaking. She felt the heat of the afternoon sun, the swelter of the day, and the closeness of the air. She was in a prison that threatened to bury her. The sounds of birds and insects faded into silence, the presence of Abernathy lost meaning, and her desire for the black unicorn consumed her anew. She turned from the scribe and began to reach again for the beast.

"Wait!" Abernathy fairly shouted. "What are you doing, girl? Do not touch that creature! Don't you realize what will happen to you?"

"Stay away from me, Abernathy," she replied softly, but hesitated nevertheless.

"Are you as mad as the rest of them?" the dog snapped angrily. "Has everyone gone crazy? Doesn't anyone but me understand what is happening? The dreams are a lie, Willow! Meeks brought us to this place, tricked us into serving his interests, and made fools of us all! That unicorn is probably something that belongs to him! You cannot know what its purpose might be! Do not touch it!"

She glanced quickly back at the dog. "I have to. I need to."

Abernathy started forward, saw the look of warning in the sylph's green eyes, and quickly stopped. "Willow, do not do this! You know the stories, the legends!" His voice dropped to a whisper. "You will be lost, girl!"

She stared silently at him for a long moment, then smiled. "But that is exactly the point, Abernathy. I am already lost."

Her hands came up swiftly and fastened about the neck of the black unicorn.

It was as if a cold fire swept through her. The fire burned from her hands into her arms and down her body. She stiffened against its feel and shuddered heavily. She threw back her head and gasped for breath. She heard Abernathy call out frantically from behind her and then lost track of him. He was there, but no longer visible to her. She could see nothing now but the face of the unicorn before her, a disembodied shape against a backdrop of space. The fire consumed her, mingled with her desire, and turned it into unrestrained passion. She was losing control of herself, beginning to come apart. A moment longer, and she would cease to be herself entirely.

She tried to remove her hands from the fairy creature's neck and found she could not. She was joined to the unicorn. She was one with it.

Then the ridged horn began to glow white with magic, and a jumble of images ripped through her mind. There was a place of empty coldness. There were chains and fire, tapestries of white on which unicorns bounded and leaped, dark-robed wizards, and spells being cast in endless succession. There was Meeks, Ben, and the Paladin.

And finally there was a cry of such terror and longing that it shattered the images as if they had been formed of glass.

Set me free!

The pain of that cry was too much for her to bear. She screamed, and her scream jerked her sharply backward, tearing her free at last of the unicorn. She stumbled and almost fell—would have fallen, had not Abernathy's arms come quickly about her to hold her upright.

"I saw!" she gasped and could speak no more.

But the sound of her scream still echoed through the trees.

COMBAT

The scream reached Ben Holiday as he knelt alone in the forest beside the tiny stream, restored to himself at last, the medallion of Landover's High Lords a brilliant silver wonder cradled gingerly, unbelievingly within the cup of his hands. The scream rose out of the trees, a thin, high wail of anguish and fear, and lingered like the whistle of the wind through canyon drops in the still mountain air.

Ben's head jerked up, his neck craning. There was no mistaking that cry. It was Willow's.

He leaped to his feet, hands closing possessively over the medallion, eyes searching the forest shadows as if whatever threatened the sylph might be waiting there for him as well. A mix of fear and horror raced through him. What had been done to Willow? He started forward, stopped, whirled about desperately, and realized that he could not trace the direction of the scream. It seemed to come from everywhere at once. Damn! Meeks would hear that scream as surely as he—Meeks and that winged demon. Perhaps Meeks already *had* . . .

He was holding the medallion so tightly that it was cutting into his palms. *Willow!* A vision of the sylph blossomed in his mind, a frail and beautiful creature whose life was his special charge. He recalled again the words of the Earth Mother investing him with responsibility for seeing that she stayed safe and his promise to keep her so. His emotions tore at him and left him ragged and frantic. Truths to which he had not yet given heed flayed his soul.

The truths all reduced to one.

He loved Willow.

He experienced a warm rush of surprise and frantic relief. All this time he had denied his feelings, unable to come to terms with them. He had wanted no one close to him again, not after Annie, his dead wife. Love brought responsibility and the possibility of hurt and loss. He had wanted none of it. But the feelings had remained—as such feelings do—because they had never been his to deny in the first place. The reality of their existence had been forced upon him that first night out in the eastern wastes after fleeing Strabo and Nightshade—revealed in a dream in his dialogue with Edgewood Dirk on the reason for the urgency of his hunt for Willow.

Why do you run so? Why must you hurry so? Why must you find Willow? Dirk had asked.

Because I love her, he had answered.

And so he did—but had not allowed himself until this moment to think on it, to reason on it, and to consider what it meant.

Seconds was all it took to do so now. The thoughts, the reasonings, and the considerations all passed through his mind in a smattering of time that was barely measurable. It was as if everything that had taken so long to reach resolution was compressed down into a single instant.

But that instant was enough.

Ben never hesitated. There was a time when he would have, a time that now seemed a thousand years gone. He released the medallion with its silver-engraved image and let it fall against his chest, the sunlight sending shards of brightness into the dappled forest.

He called the Paladin to him.

Light flared and brightened at the edge of the little glade, chasing the shadows and gloom. Ben's head lifted in recognition, and there was excitement in his eyes. He had thought never to do this again, wished it in fact, prayed it might never be necessary. Now he was anxious for it. A part of him was already beginning to break away.

The Paladin appeared out of the light. His white charger stamped and snorted. His silver armor glittered, its harness and traces creaking. His weapons hung ready. The ghost of another age and life was returned.

Ben felt the medallion begin to burn against his chest, ice and fire first, then something else altogether. He felt himself separating, drawing out of his own body.

Willow! he heard himself scream her name once in the silence of his mind.

It was his last thought. A flare of silver light burst from the medallion and streaked across the glade to where the Paladin waited. He felt himself carried with it to merge with the body of the King's knight-errant. Armor clamped all about, fastening and tightening, closing down. An iron shell encased him, and the memory of who and what he had been was gone. The Paladin's memory became his, a rush of images and thoughts that spanned a thousand other times and places, a thousand other lives—all of a warrior whose battle skills had never been surpassed, a champion who had never been defeated.

Ben Holiday disappeared. He had become the Paladin.

He was aware momentarily of the ragged figure that stood statuelike at the edge of the little stream, bearded and unkempt, a worn and battered shell. He knew it to be Landover's King and dismissed the matter.

Wheeling his white charger about, he surged through the brush and scrub into the forest trees and was gone.

Willow's scream brought Meeks almost instantly. He appeared from the shadow of Mirwouk's crumbling walls astride his winged demon, dark robes flying against the sunlit afternoon skies. The demon plummeted to the hillside with a hiss, settling heavily within a gathering of pines at its far edge. Its leathered wings folded in against its wolf-serpent body, and its nostrils flared with small bursts of fire. Steam rose off its back.

Meeks slid slowly down the scaled neck, hard eyes fixed on the black unicorn as it stamped and snorted frantically some fifty feet away. He cradled in the grasp of his good arm the missing books of magic.

Abernathy pulled a still-shaken Willow protectively behind him. "Stay back from us, wizard!" he ordered bravely.

Meeks ignored him. His eyes were on the unicorn. He came forward a few steps, glanced briefly at Willow and Abernathy, looked again at the unicorn, and then stopped. He seemed to be waiting for something. The unicorn danced and shuddered as if already caught, but still it did not flee.

"Willow, what is happening here?" Abernathy growled urgently.

The sylph could barely stand. She shook her head woozily, her words nearly inaudible. "I saw," she repeated. "The images, the whole . . . of it. But there are . . . so many, I cannot . . ."

She was making no sense at all, still in shock, it appeared. Abernathy helped her over to a patch of flowered grass and sat her gently down. Then he turned back to Meeks.

"She cannot hurt you, wizard!" he called out, drawing the hard eyes instantly. "Why not let her go? The unicorn is yours if you wish it, although I cannot imagine why you would. Heaven knows, it has been a thing of misfortune for all who have encountered it!"

Meeks kept looking at him, but said nothing.

"The others will be here in moments, wizard!" Abernathy declared. "You had best hurry away!"

Meeks smiled coldly. "Come over to me a moment, scribe," he invited softly. "Perhaps we can discuss it."

Abernathy hesitated, glanced briefly back at Willow, took a deep breath, and started across the clearing. He was so frightened that he could barely make himself move. The last thing in the world he wanted to do was walk over there to the wizard and his pet demon, and yet here he was doing just exactly that. He straightened himself bravely, determined to see this thing through. He really hadn't any choice in the matter. He had to do something to help the girl, and this appeared to be the only option open to him. The day was warm and still; it was a wonderful day for just about anything other than this. Abernathy moved as slowly as he could and prayed that the others would arrive before he was turned into the wizard's latest burnt offering.

When he was a dozen paces from Meeks, he stopped. The wizard's craggy face was a mask of cunning and false warmth. "Closer, please," Meeks whispered.

Abernathy knew then that he was doomed. There wasn't going to be any escape for him. He might be able to delay matters for a few moments, but that would be all. Still, even a few moments might help Willow.

He came forward half-a-dozen paces and stopped again. "What shall we discuss?" he demanded.

The cold smile was gone. "Why not the possibility that your friends will be here to help you in the next few moments?"

He gestured briefly with the books, and a ring of twisted little figures appeared from out of the trees surrounding the clearing. The figures were everywhere, encircling them. Ugly, piggish faces with sharp teeth and serpents' tongues snorted and squealed anxiously in the silence. Abernathy felt the hair on the back of his spine arch. A dozen of the little monsters pushed Questor Thews, Bunion, Parsnip, and the G'home Gnomes from out of the trees. All were gagged and securely bound in chains.

Meeks turned. The smile was back. "It appears that your friends will not be much help to you after all. But it was good of you to wait until they could join us."

Abernathy saw his last, faint hope of being rescued disappear.

"Run, Willow!" he shouted.

Then, growling savagely, he launched himself at Meeks. He did it with the somewhat vague notion of catching the wizard off-guard and knocking free those precious books of magic. He almost got away with it. Meeks was so busy orchestrating the arrival of his small army of minions that it never occurred to him the dog might decide to fight back. Abernathy was on top of him almost before he realized what was happening. But the magic Meeks commanded was as quick as thought, and he called it to his use instantly. Green fire surged up from the books of magic, and a screen of flame hammered into Abernathy. The soft-coated Wheaten Terrier tumbled backward head-over-heels and lay still, smoke rising lazily from his singed fur. The screen of fire protecting Meeks and the books of magic flared and died.

The wizard stared back across the clearing to where Willow sat slumped upon the ground and the black unicorn waited.

"At last," he whispered, his voice a slow hiss.

He beckoned curtly to the waiting demon imps and the ring began to tighten.

Silence descended across the little clearing—almost as if nature had put a finger to her lips and said "hush" to the world. There was a moment of time in which everything slowed. Meeks waited impatiently as the circle of demon imps crept forward. His winged demon snorted, nostrils steaming. Willow sat with her head bent, still stunned, her long hair cascading down about her like a veil. The black unicorn moved close, a step at a time only, a shadow out of darkness woefully lost in daylight. Its muzzle drooped and brushed the sylph's arm gently. The white magic of its horn had gone dark.

Then a sudden rush of wind broke over the mountain heights and whistled through the trees. The unicorn's head jerked up, its ears perked forward, and its horn flared brighter than the sun. It heard the sounds that no one else could—sounds for which it had listened for centuries.

Trees, brush, and scrub exploded from the wall of the forest at its northern edge as if torn free by some massive fist. Wind howled through the opening left, and light burst free in a brilliant white flash. Meeks and his winged demon shrank back instinctively, and the demon imps threw themselves down upon the earth squealing.

A rumble of thunder turned to a pounding of hooves, and the Paladin rode out from his twilight existence into battle.

Meeks gave a howl of rage and disbelief. His demon imps were already scattering to the four winds, terror sweeping them away as if they were dried leaves at the end of a broom. The demon imps wanted no part of the Paladin. Meeks turned, the books of magic clutched tightly to his dark robes by the leather-gloved hand. He shrieked something unintelligible to the monster behind him, and the creature surged forward, hissing.

The Paladin swerved slightly, white charger barely slowing as it turned to meet the demon.

Fire burst from the demon's maw, engulfing the approaching horse and rider. But the Paladin broke through the wall of flames and came on, a battle lance lowered into place. The demon breathed its fire once more, and again the flames washed over the knight-errant. Willow's head lifted, and she saw the silver knight and horse disappear in the fire. Sudden realization rushed through her. If the Paladin was here, so was Ben!

Flames pyramided off the clearing's grasses and scorched the sheltering trees. Everything wilted momentarily in a white-hot heat. But then the Paladin was clear of the flames once more, his charger and armor covered with ash and smoking. He was almost on top of the demon now, battle lance set. Too late the demon realized the danger as it spread its wings and tried to lift itself skyward. The Paladin's lance ripped through scales and armored plates and pierced its massive chest. The wolf-serpent screamed and surged back, the battle lance breaking off within it. It tried to rise, a weak, fluttering effort it could not manage. Then its heart gave out, and it fell earthward. It crashed into the scorched grasses, shuddered, and lay still.

The Paladin broke off the attack while the demon was in its death throes, swerving to stay clear of the struggling monster. Then he wheeled back again, drew forth the great broadsword, and spurred his white charger toward Meeks to finish the fight.

But this time Meeks was ready for him.

The hard, craggy old face tightened down in concentration, the wizard's thin lips drawing back until his teeth showed. Whatever magic he yet commanded, he was calling on it now.

Wicked green light flared at a point midway between the approaching knight-errant and the waiting wizard. Meeks cried out and stiffened. His head shot back and the green light exploded in shards.

From out of the fire appeared a line of armored skeletons atop fleshless steeds, half goat, half snake. Willow counted. Three, four, five—there were six altogether. The skeletons held broadswords and maces in their gloveless, bony hands. Helmetless death's-heads smiled in frozen grimace. Riders and carriers both were as black as night.

They turned as one and came at the Paladin in a rush. The Paladin rode to meet them.

Willow watched the battle unfold from close beside the black unicorn. Her senses had returned to her now; her thoughts were clear. She saw the Paladin and the black riders come together in a clash of iron, saw the dust swirl up from the impact, and saw one of the black riders go down in a pile of shattered bones. The fighters wheeled and struck at each other, and the sounds were terrifying. She shrank from the conflict, her thoughts focused not on the Paladin, but on Ben. Where was he? Why wasn't he here? Why wasn't Landover's High Lord close to his champion?

Another black rider went down, the bones of its skeleton body snapping apart, crunching like deadwood beneath the hooves of the Paladin's horse. The Paladin broke away, whirled and struck down a third rider, the great broadsword flashing silver light as it swung through its deadly arc. The remaining riders converged, weapons hammering at him, clanging and sparking off his armor, thrusting him back.

Willow pushed to her knees. The Paladin was in danger of being forced down.

Then small bursts of green fire flared over the bones of the three black riders that had fallen, and six new skeletons rose out of the smoky haze to join their fellows. Willow felt her stomach tighten with cold. They had doubled their strength. There were too many now for the Paladin.

She lurched to her feet, determination giving her strength. Questor, the kobolds, and the gnomes were still bound and helpless. Abernathy was still unconscious. Meeks had disabled them all. There was no one left to help the Paladin but her.

No other left to help Ben.

She knew what she must do. The black unicorn stood quietly next to her, emerald green eyes fixed on her own. There was intelligence there that was unmistakable. She could read in those eyes what she must do, and it mirrored what she already knew in her heart.

She took a deep breath, stretched out her arms, and embraced the unicorn once more.

The magic rushed through her instantly, quick and anxious. The unicorn's delicate body shuddered with release, and the images began. They surged into the watershed of the sylph's mind, jumbling together. Willow jerked back from their intensity, wanted to scream, and fought back against the urge. Her need was less this time, her desire more manageable. She struggled to master it. The images slowed then, straightened into an orderly succession, and came on anew. The mix of pain and anguish that had accompanied them lessened, and their brightness dimmed into something bearable.

She began to recognize what she was seeing. Her fingers caressed the silky, delicate neck of the unicorn as the magic joined them.

A voice cried out.

Fairy-kind! Set me free!

The voice belonged to the unicorn and to nothing. Something of the unicorn was real; something else was not. The images appeared and faded in Willow's mind, and she watched them pass. The black unicorn sought freedom. It had come in search of that freedom. It believed it would find it through . . . *why?* . . . through Ben! The High Lord could set it free because the High Lord commanded the magic of the Paladin, and only the Paladin was strong enough to counteract the magic that bound it, the magic that Meeks wielded—but then there was no High Lord to be found and the unicorn had been left alone in this land, searching, and Willow had come instead, searching too, bearing the golden bridle the wizards had made to snare it when it first broke free long ago. The unicorn was frightened of Willow and the bridle, uncertain of her purpose, and it fled from her until it realized that she was good, that she could help, and that she could take it to the High Lord and set it free. Willow would know the High Lord even in his disguise, when the High Lord himself did not know . . .

The images came quicker now, and Willow fought again to slow them so their meaning would not be lost. Her breath came quickly, as if she had run a great distance, and there was a bright sheen of sweat on her face.

The voice cried out in her mind again.

The High Lord's power was lost to him and therefore lost to me! I could not be set free!

The voice was almost frantic. The images whispered urgently. The dreams that had brought Willow in search of it were a mix of truth and lies, dreams from both wizard and fairies . . . *Fairies! Her dreams were sent by the fairies?* . . . All must come together so that truths could be revealed and the power needed could be summoned—so that Paladin and wizard could meet and the stronger prevail, the stronger that was also the good, and then the books of magic could be, finally and forever, could be and must be . . .

Something intruded, other images, other thoughts imprisoned within the black unicorn for countless centuries. Willow stiffened and her arms locked about the sleek neck. She felt the scream rising within her once more, uncontrollable this time, madness! She saw something new in the images. The black unicorn was not a single life, but many! *Oh, Ben!* she cried soundlessly. There were lives in the images that struggled and could not break free, that yearned for things she could not understand in worlds she could not imagine. She shook with the emotions that ripped through her. Souls imprisoned, lives held fast, magics torn away and used wrongly—*Ben!*

Then there was a sudden image of the missing books of magic, locked within a dark, secret place, a place filled with the smell of something evil. There was an image of fire burning outward from one of those books, burning with the intensity of life being born anew, and from out of that fire and that book leaped the black unicorn, free once more, racing from the dark into the light, searching . . .

The voice cried out one final time.

Destroy the books!

The cry was one of desperation. The cry was almost a shriek. It blocked away the images; it consumed everything with its urgency. The pain it released was intolerable.

Willow's scream finally broke free, rising up against the sounds of battle. The sylph tore away from the black unicorn and stumbled back, almost blacking out with the intensity of what she had experienced. She dropped to her knees, head bent against a wave of nausea and cold. She thought she must die and knew in the same instant she would not. She could sense the black unicorn shuddering uncontrollably beside her.

The words of that final cry were a whisper on her lips.

Destroy the books!

She rose to a half-crouch and screamed them out across the battleground of the little clearing.

The words were like tiny wafers of paper caught in a windstorm. The Paladin did not hear them, consumed by the fury of the battle he fought. Meeks did not hear them, the whole of his concentration given over to directing the magic he had called upon to save himself. Questor Thews, Bunion, Parsnip, Fillip, and Sot, abandoned by their demon imp captors, were lying bound and gagged at the clearing's far edge.

Only Abernathy heard.

The dog was semiconscious, and the words seemed to come to him from somewhere out of the darkness of his own thoughts. He blinked hazily, heard the words echo, heard then the sounds of the frightening conflict taking place about him, and forced his eyes all the way open.

The Paladin and the black riders whirled and struck out at each other at the clearing's center, a kaleidoscope of movement and sound. Willow and the black unicorn were small, trapped figures at the clearing's far end. He could see nothing of his other friends.

He panted, his tongue licking out at his nose, and he felt dull, aching pain working its way through his battered body. He remembered what had been done to him and where he was.

Slowly, he twisted himself about so that he could see better. Meeks stood almost next to him. Caught up in the battle between the Paladin and the black riders, the wizard had come forward the half-dozen paces that had separated him from the dog.

The words whispered once more in Abernathy's mind. *Destroy the books!*

The dog tried to get to his feet and found his body would not respond. He sank back. Other thoughts intruded. Destroy the books? Destroy his one chance of ever becoming human again? How could he even consider such a thing?

Another black rider went down, and there was the sound of breaking bones. The Paladin was hemmed in on all sides, armor blackened by ash and rent by sword and axe. He was losing the battle.

Abernathy knew what it would mean for all of them if he did and quit thinking about his own problems. He tried to rise again and found now that he could—but not all the way. His muzzle drew back in a grimace of frustration.

Then Meeks shifted his feet one further time, and suddenly his leg was inches from Abernathy's head. The wizard wore soft shoes; the leg was exposed. Abernathy's grimace turned to a snarl. He had just been given one last chance.

He launched himself headfirst at Meeks, his jaws closed over the wizard's ankle, and he bit down hard. Meeks gave out a shriek of mingled pain and astonishment, his hands flew out, and the books of magic flew up.

Everything happened at once after that. There was a streak of black light that shot across the clearing, past the Paladin and the skeleton riders, past the clouds of dust and bursts of green fire. The black unicorn sped quicker than thought. Meeks jerked his leg frantically, trying to free himself from Abernathy's jaws, groping at the same time for the airborne books. Abernathy would not let go. Willow cried out, and Abernathy bit down harder. Then the black unicorn had reached them. It leaped into the air, its horn flaring white with the magic, speared the tumbling books, shattered their bindings like glass, and scattered their pages everywhere.

Down fluttered the loose pages, those with the drawings of the unicorns mingling with those whose centers were charred from that inner fire. Meeks screamed and yanked free at last of Abernathy's jaws. Green fire burst from his outstretched hands and hammered into the unicorn as it soared, knocking it askew. The unicorn twisted in midair, and white fire arced from its ridged horn into the wizard. Back flew Meeks. Green fire exploded into the unicorn, and white fire hammered into Meeks. The fires raced back and forth between unicorn and wizard, the level of intensity rising with each new burst.

The Paladin whirled swiftly at the clearing's center, broadsword arcing in a circle that cut apart the remaining black riders and scattered their bones. It was a perfunctory task now; the black riders were already disintegrating. The magic that had sustained them had gone out of their hollow forms. They crumbled instantly and were gone.

Then the Paladin was racing toward the unicorn and the wizard. But the Paladin could not reach them in time. The fire had engulfed Meeks, the magic too strong even for him. He shrieked one final time and exploded into smoke. The black unicorn was engulfed in the same moment, the fire all about. Stricken, it arched skyward, leaped into the air and was gone.

The Paladin, too, disappeared. It rode into a sudden burst of white light, the light washing away ash and dust and healing silver armor until it shone like new—all in an instant's time—and knight-errant and light simply faded away.

Abernathy and Willow stared at each other voicelessly across the charred, empty forest clearing.

Then it happened.

They all saw it—Willow and Abernathy as they crouched upon the scorched hillside, still stunned from the fury of the battle just completed; Questor, the kobolds, and the G'home Gnomes as they struggled futilely to sit upright, still secured by the bonds that the demon imps had used to restrain them; and even Ben Holiday as he stumbled breathlessly from the forest trees after having run all the way from the place of his transformation, not knowing what had brought him, knowing only that he must come. They saw it, and they held their collective breath in wonder.

It began as a wind that disturbed the mountain stillness, just a whisper at first, then a rush of sound like the roar of an ocean. The wind sprang up from the earth upon which the pages of the broken books of magic now lay, stirring dust and ash, whipping at the few tiny shards of green flame that still flickered in the meadow grasses. It lifted skyward in the shape of a funnel, catching up those scattered pages in a snowstorm of white. The pages that were burned became suddenly healed, their ragged edges closing, their yellowed surfaces turning pristine white once more. The pages that were filled with the drawings of the unicorns mixed and joined with them until none was distinguishable from the others. A wall of pages rose up across the skyline, crackling and snapping madly as the wind whipped them through the air.

Then the pages began to change. The drawings began to shimmer and flex, and abruptly the unicorns came alive. No longer frozen in still life, they began to race about the funnel's edge. There were hundreds of them, all white, all in motion, a blur of power and speed. The pages and bindings of the books of magic were gone now; there were only the unicorns. They flew through the air and cried out in ecstasy against the roar of the wind.

Free they seemed to be saying! *Free!*

Then the funnel broke apart and the unicorns scattered, flooding the skies above the mountain clearing in a rush of graceful, delicate bodies—like fireworks exploding in an impossibly beautiful shower. The unicorns spread out across the skyline—buoyed by the magic of their transformation—then soared into the distance. Their cries lingered after them momentarily, then faded into silence.

The mountains had gone still again.

LEGEND

"There never was any black unicorn," Willow said.

"There was, but it was only a deception," Ben said.

Questor Thews and Abernathy, Bunion and Parsnip, and Fillip and Sot looked at each other in confusion.

They sat within the shade of a great, old oak at the edge of the meadow clearing, the lingering smell of scorched earth a pungent reminder of all that had befallen. The last of the shards of green flame had flickered out, but trailers of smoke and particles of dust and ash still floated weightless through the sun-streaked afternoon air. Abernathy had been dusted off, the others had been freed of their bonds, and the six of them were gathered about Ben and Willow, who were trying to explain what had happened. It wasn't easy because neither of them knew everything yet, so they were piecing the story together as they went.

"It might be easier if we start at the beginning," Ben offered.

He hunched forward, legs crossing before him. He was ragged and dirty, but at least they all recognized him now. Removing his own deception of who and what he was had removed theirs as well.

"A long time ago, the fairies sent the white unicorns into Landover on a journey to certain of the mortal worlds. We know that much from the histories. The unicorns were the most recognizable magic the fairies possessed, and they sent them to those worlds where belief in the magic was in danger of failing altogether. After all, there has to be *some* belief in the magic—however small—for any world to survive.

"But the unicorns disappeared. They disappeared because the wizards of Landover waylaid and imprisoned them. They wanted the unicorns' magic for their own use. Remember, Questor, when you told me that the wizards were once a powerful guild that hired out—back before the King sent the Paladin to dispose of them? Well, I'm betting a major part of that magic came from the imprisoned unicorns—magic that the wizards siphoned off. I don't know what magic they possessed to trap the unicorns in the first place—a deception of some sort, I'd guess. That seems to be their favorite trick. At any rate, they caught them up, changed them into drawings, and trapped them in those books."

"But not whole," Willow said.

"No, not whole," Ben agreed. "This is where it gets interesting. The wizards separated the body from the spirit of each unicorn in making the transformation. They imprisoned the body in one book and the spirit in the other! That weakened the unicorns and made them easier to hold. The body without the spirit is never as strong. The wizards' magic was potent enough to imprison each separately; the trick was to prevent them from joining again."

"Which was the danger Meeks faced when the black unicorn escaped," Willow added.

"Right. Because the black unicorn was the collective *spirit* of the imprisoned white unicorns!" Ben furrowed his brow. "You see, so long as the wizards could maintain the strength of the magic that bound the books, the unicorns could not break free and the wizards could drain the unicorns' magic as well and put it to their own use. Even after Landover's King sent the Paladin to crush the wizards' guild years ago, the books survived. They were probably kept hidden for a time. Even later, the wizards still remaining, those now in service to the King, were careful not to let anyone know the real source of their power. And the books were passed down from wizard to wizard until at last they came to Meeks."

He touched his index finger to his lips. "But—in the meantime—there was a problem with the unicorns. Every so often, they escaped. Something would happen, the wizards would relax their vigilance, and the unicorns would break free. It didn't happen often, of course, because the wizards kept close watch over the books. But now and again, it did. Each time, it was the *spirit* part of the imprisoned unicorns that managed to escape—the magic of the spirit always being stronger than that of the body. The spirit would burn its way free of the pages of the book of magic that bound it and escape. But it lacked a true physical presence. It was only a shadow formed of need and will, a silhouette given momentary substance and life—and not much more." He glanced quickly at Willow for confirmation, and she nodded. "And because it was black in color, being only a shadow, it was generally assumed to be something evil rather than something good. After all, whoever heard of a black unicorn? The wizards, I am certain, spread the story that the black unicorn was an aberration—a dangerous thing, perhaps even a demon. They probably set a few examples to reinforce the belief. That kept everyone away from it while the wizards worked at getting it back again."

"The bridle of spun gold was used for that purpose," Willow interjected, picking up the story. "The wizards employed their magic to create the bridle after the first escape. The bridle was a magic that could draw and hold the black unicorn, giving the wizards time to imprison it anew. It was always caught quickly; it was never free for long. It was sent back again into the books of magic, the burned pages were restored, and all was as it had been. The wizards took no chances. The books were their greatest magic, and they could not risk damage to or loss of them."

She turned to Ben. "That was why the black unicorn was so frightened of me at first. Even in its need, it was terrified. I felt its fear each time I came close and again, later, when I touched it. It believed me to be a tool of the wizards that had imprisoned it. It couldn't know the truth. It was not until the very end that it seemed to understand that I was not in service to Meeks."

"Which brings us to the present," Ben announced, straightening. "Meeks had gained possession of the books of magic in his turn and had used them as had all the wizards before him. But then the old King died and everything started to fall into ruin. The black unicorn hadn't escaped for a very long time—perhaps centuries—and there hadn't been any need for the golden bridle in all those years. I don't think even the wizards before Meeks had paid a whole lot of attention to it for a while because it was apparently before Meeks' time that it was stolen for the first time by Nightshade. Later it was stolen by Strabo and then went back and forth between the two after that. Meeks knew where it was, I suppose, but the books of magic were safely under his control, and the witch and the dragon didn't know the real purpose of the bridle in any case. The trouble started when Meeks went over to my world to recruit a new King for Landover and hid the books of magic in his absence. I suppose he thought he wouldn't be gone long enough for anything to happen to them, but things didn't work out that way. When I didn't come crawling back to give up the medallion and the Iron Mark didn't finish me off, Meeks suddenly found himself trapped over there with the books of magic still hidden over here. The magic that imprisoned the unicorns weakened once more in his absence, and the spirit part—the black unicorn—burned free of the pages of its book and escaped."

"So that was why my half-brother sent the dreams!" Questor exclaimed, new understanding beginning to reflect on his owlish face. "He had to get back across into Landover, recover the missing books, and find the golden bridle—and quickly! If he didn't, the black unicorn might find a way to free all the white unicorns—its physical selves—and the magic would be lost!"

"And that is exactly what it tried to do," Willow confirmed. "Not only this time, but every time it managed to break free. It tried to find the one magic it believed stronger than the magic of the wizards—the Paladin! Always before, it was caught so quickly that it never had any real chance. It knew the Paladin was the King's champion, but it would never even manage to reach the King. This time it was certain it could—except that there was no King to be found. Meeks was quick to act, once he discovered the unicorn had escaped. A dream was used to lure Ben out of Landover before the unicorn could reach him. Then Meeks crossed back with him and altered his appearance so that no one—including the black unicorn—could recognize him."

"I think it might have recognized me if it hadn't been imprisoned for so long," Ben interjected. "The older fairy creatures such as Nightshade and Strabo could recognize me. But the unicorn had forgotten much of its magic while it was bound."

"It might have lost much as well through the wizards' use of it," Willow added.

"Meeks told me that night in my bedchamber, when he used his magic to change me, that I messed up his plans in some way," Ben went on, returning to the matter of his lost identity. "Of course, I didn't have any idea what it was that I had done. I didn't know what he was talking about. The truth was that everything I had done was inadvertent. I didn't know that the books contained stolen magic and that, if he weren't within Landover, the magic might be lost. I was just trying to stay alive."

"A moment, High Lord." Abernathy was shaking his head in confusion. "Meeks sent three dreams—yours to provide him a way back into Landover, Questor Thews' to give him possession of the missing books of magic, and Willow's to regain for him the stolen bridle. The dreams worked as they were intended except for Willow's. She found the bridle, but she failed to bring it back to you as the dream had told her she must. Why so?"

"The fairies," Willow said.

"The fairies," Ben echoed.

"I said that first morning that my dream seemed incomplete, that I felt I was to be shown more," Willow explained. "There were other dreams after that; in each, the unicorn appeared to be less a demon, more a victim. The fairies sent those dreams to guide me in my search and to teach me that my fears were false ones. Gradually, I came to realize that the first dream was somehow a lie, that the black unicorn was not my enemy, that it needed help, and that I must provide that help. After the dragon gave the bridle of spun gold to me, I was persuaded further—by dreams and visions—that I must go in search of the unicorn myself if I were ever to discover the truth of matters."

"The fairies sent Edgewood Dirk to me." Ben sighed. "They wouldn't intervene to help me directly, of course—they never do that for anyone. Answers to our difficulties must always come from within; they expect us to solve our own problems. But Dirk was the catalyst that helped me to do that. Dirk helped me to discover the truth about the medallion. Meeks had instigated the deception that led me to believe I had lost it. Dirk helped me see that *I* was the one fostering that deception, and that if *I* could recognize the truth of things, others could as well—which is exactly what happened."

"Which is why the Paladin was able to reach us in time, apparently," Questor said.

"And why the books of magic were finally destroyed and the unicorns freed," Willow added.

"And why Meeks was defeated," Abernathy finished.

"That's about it," Ben agreed.

"Great High Lord!" exclaimed Fillip fervently.

"Mighty High Lord!" echoed Sot.

Ben groaned. "Please! Enough already!"

He looked imploringly at the others, but they all just grinned.

It was time to leave. No one much cared for the idea of spending another night in the Melchor. It was agreed they would be better off setting up camp in the foothills below.

So they trudged wearily down out of the mountains through the fading daylight, the sun sinking behind the western rim of the valley in a haze of scarlet and gray. As they walked, Willow dropped back next to Ben, and her arm locked gently about his.

"What do you think will become of the unicorns?" she asked after a moment.

Ben shrugged. "They'll probably go back into the mists, and no one will ever see them again."

"You do not think they will go on to the worlds to which they were sent?"

"Out of Landover?" Ben shook his head. "No, not after all they've been through. Not now. They'll go back home where it's safe."

"It isn't safe in your world, is it?"

"Hardly."

"It isn't very safe in Landover, either."

"No."

"Do you think it is any safer in the mists?"

Ben thought about that a moment. "I don't know. Maybe not."

Willow nodded. "Your world has need of unicorns, doesn't it? The magic is forgotten?"

"Pretty much."

"Then maybe it doesn't matter that it isn't safe there. Maybe the need outweighs the danger. Maybe at least one unicorn will decide to go anyway."

"Maybe, but I doubt it."

Willow's head lifted slightly. "You say it, but you do not mean it."

He smiled and did not reply.

They reached the foothills, passed through a broad meadow of red-spotted wildflowers to a stretch of fir, and the kobolds began scouting ahead for a campsite. The air had gone cool, and the approaching twilight gave the land a muted, silvery sheen. Crickets had begun to chirp, and geese flew low across a distant lake. Ben was thinking about home, about Sterling Silver, and the warmth of the life that waited there for him.

"I love you," Willow said suddenly. She didn't look at him, facing straight ahead as she spoke the words.

Ben nodded. He was quiet a moment. "I've been meaning to say something to you about that. You tell me you love me all the time, and I can never say it back to you. I've been thinking lately about why that is, and I guess it's because I'm afraid. It's like taking a chance you don't have to take. It's easier to pass it by."

He paused. "But I don't feel that way right now, right here. I feel altogether different. When you say you love me, I find I want to say it back to you. So I guess I will. I love you, too, Willow. I think I always did."

They walked on, not speaking. He was aware of the increased pressure of her arm about his. The day was still and restful, and everything was at peace.

"The Earth Mother made me promise to look after you, you know," Ben said finally. "That's part of what started me thinking about us. She made me promise to keep you safe. She was most insistent."

He could feel Willow's smile more than see it. "That is because the Earth Mother knows," she said.

He waited for her to say something more, then glanced down. "Knows what?"

"That one day I shall bear your child, High Lord."

Ben took a deep breath and let it out slowly.

"Oh."

EPILOGUE

It was two days before Christmas.

Southside Chicago was chill and dreary, the snowfall of the previous night turned gray and mushy on walks and streets, the squarish highrise projects and tenements vague shadows in a haze of smoke and mist. Steam rose out of sewer grates in sudden clouds as sleet pelted down. Not much of anything was moving. Cars crawled by like prehistoric beetles, headlights shining their luminous yellow eyes. Pedestrians ducked their heads against the cold, their chins buried in scarves and collars, their hands jammed into coat pockets. Late afternoon watched an early evening's approach in gloomy silence.

The corner of Division and Elm was almost deserted. Two boys with leather jackets, a commuting businessman, and a carefully dressed woman headed home from shopping, stepped from a bus, and started walking in different directions. A shop owner paused to check the locks on the front door of his plumbing business as he prepared to close up for the day. A factory worker on the seven-to-three shift ducked out of Barney's Pub after two beers and an hour of unwinding to begin the trudge two blocks home to his ailing mother. An old man carrying a load of groceries shuffled along a sidewalk path left in the snow by a trail of icy footprints. A small child engulfed by her snowsuit played with a sled by the steps of her apartment home.

They ignored each other with casual indifference, lost in their own private thoughts.

The white unicorn flew past them like a bit of strayed light. It sped by as if its sole purpose in being was to circle the whole of the world in a single day. It never seemed to touch the ground, its graceful, delicate body gathering and extending in a single fluid motion as it passed. All the beauty in the world—all that was or could ever be—was captured by its movement. It was there and gone in an instant. The watchers caught their breath, blinked once, and the unicorn had disappeared.

There followed a moment of uncertainty. The old man's mouth dropped open. The child put down her sled and stared. The two boys ducked their heads and muttered urgently. The businessman looked at the shop owner and the shop owner looked back. The carefully dressed woman remembered all those magical stories of fairies she still enjoyed reading. The factory worker thought suddenly of Christmas as a child.

Then the moment passed, and they all moved on. Some walked more quickly, some more slowly. They glanced over at the misted, empty street. What was it they had seen? Had it really been a unicorn? No, it couldn't have been. There were no such things as unicorns—not really. And not in cities. Unicorns lived in forests. But they had seen something. Hadn't they seen something? Hadn't they? They walked on, silent, and there was a warmth within each of them at the memory of what they had experienced. There was a feeling of having been a part of something magical.

They took that feeling home with them. Some of them kept it for a time. Some of them passed it on.

WIZARD AT LARGE

For Alex
Who is something of a wizard at large himself . . .

At that word the young man let his glass slip through his fingers, and looked upon Keawe like a ghost.

'The price,' says he; 'the price! You do not know the price?'

'It is for that I am asking you,' returned Keawe. 'But why are you so much concerned? Is there something wrong about the price?'

'It has dropped a great deal in value since your time, Mr. Keawe,' said the young man, stammering.

'Well, well, I shall have the less to pay for it,' says Keawe. 'How much did it cost you?'

The young man was white as a sheet. 'Two cents,' said he.

'What?' cried Keawe, 'two cents? Why, then, you can only sell it for one. And he who buys it—' The words died upon Keawe's tongue; he who bought it could never sell it again, the bottle and the bottle imp must abide with him until he died, and when he died must carry him to the red end of hell.

—Robert Louis Stevenson, *The Bottle Imp*

CONTENTS

SNEEZE

Ben Holiday sighed wearily and wished he were somewhere else besides where he was. He wished he were anywhere else.

He was in the garden room at Sterling Silver. The garden room was probably Ben Holiday's favorite of all the many rooms at the castle. It was bright and airy. Flower boxes crisscrossed the tiled floor in dazzling swatches of color. Sunshine streamed through floor length windows that ran the length of its southern wall, tiny motes of pollen dancing on the broad bands of light. The windows stood open and fragrant smells wafted in. The room looked out on the gardens proper, a maze of flower beds and bushes that spread their way downward to the lake on which the island castle rested, mixing and mingling their colors like paints run together on a rain-soaked canvas. The flowers bloomed year-round, reseeding themselves with commendable regularity. A horticulturist from Ben's old world would have killed to study such treasures—species that grew only in the Kingdom of Landover and nowhere else.

Just at the moment, Ben would have killed to escape them.

". . . Great High Lord . . ."

". . . Mighty High Lord . . ."

The familiar calls of supplication grated on him like rough stones and reminded him anew of the cause of his disgruntlement. His eyes rolled skyward momentarily. *Please!* His gaze shifted furiously from flower box to flower bed and back again, as if somewhere among all those tiny petals the escape he so desperately sought might be found. It wasn't, of course, and he sagged back further in his cushioned chair and contemplated the unfairness of it all. It wasn't that he was trying to shirk his duty. It wasn't as if he didn't care about these things. But this was his *refuge,* for Pete's sake! This was supposed to be his place for time away!

". . . and took all of our hard-earned berry stores."

"And all of our ale kegs as well."

"When all we did was to borrow a few laying hens, High Lord."

"We would have replaced those that were lost, High Lord."

"We intended to be fair."

"We did."

"You must see that our possessions are returned . . ."

"Yes, you must . . ."

They went on, barely pausing for breath.

Ben studied Fillip and Sot the way his gardener studied weeds in the flower beds. The G'home Gnomes rambled on unself-consciously and endlessly, and he thought about the vagaries of life that permitted misfortunes such as this to be visited on him. The G'home Gnomes were a pitiful bunch—small, ferret-like burrow people who begged, borrowed, and mostly stole everything with which they came in contact. They migrated periodically and, once settled, could not be dislodged. They were regarded in general as a blight upon the earth. On the other hand, they had proven unswervingly loyal to Ben. When he had purchased the Kingdom of Landover from Rosen's Department Store Christmas Wishbook and come into the valley—almost two years ago now—Fillip and Sot, on behalf of all of the G'home Gnomes, had been the first to pledge their loyalty. They had aided him in his efforts to establish his kingship. They had helped him again when Meeks, the former Court Wizard, had slipped back into Landover and stolen his identity and his throne. They had been his friends when there were precious few friends to be had.

He sighed deeply. Well, he owed them something, certainly—but not this much. They were taking advantage of his friendship in a way that was totally unconscionable. They had traded on it to bring this latest complaint before him, deliberately circumventing the regular channels of a court administration he had worked hard to implement. They had brandished it like a fiery torch until he was hounded to this, his last sanctuary. It wouldn't be so bad if they didn't do this every single time there was a complaint of any sort—which was every five minutes, it sometimes seemed—but, of course, they did. They didn't trust anyone else to be fair and impartial. They wanted their "Great High Lord" and their "Mighty High Lord" to hear them out.

And hear them out, and hear them out . . .

". . . a fair disposition would be a return of all things stolen and a replacement of all things damaged," said Fillip.

"A fair disposition would be for you to order to our service several dozen trolls for a reasonable period of time," said Sot.

"Perhaps a week or two," said Fillip.

"Perhaps a month," said Sot.

It would also help matters if they didn't bring most of their problems on themselves, Ben thought darkly. It was difficult to be either objective or sympathetic when he knew before the first word was out of their mouths that they were *at least* as guilty of causing the dilemma as whomever their latest complaint was to be lodged against.

Fillip and Sot rambled on. Their grimy faces twitched as they talked, their eyes squinting against the light, their fur wrinkled and worn. Their fingers curled and straightened as they gestured, and bits of dirt crumbled and broke away from beneath the nails where it was caked from digging. Their shabby clothes hung on them, leather and sackcloth, colorless save for a single incongruous red feather stuck in the headband of their caps. They were bits of wreckage that had somehow washed up on the shores of his life.

"Perhaps a tribute would help serve as recompense," Fillip was saying.

"Perhaps a token gift of silver or gold," Sot echoed.

Ben shook his head hopelessly. This was quite enough. He was about to cut them off when he was saved from the need to do so by the sudden, unexpected appearance of Questor Thews. His Court Wizard burst through the garden room doors as if catapulted by some giant sling, arms waving, white beard and long hair whipping about, gray robes with their colorful patches trailing after in what appeared to be a desperate effort to keep up with their wearer.

"I have done it, I have done it!" he proclaimed without any preliminaries. He was flushed with excitement, his owlish face made positively glowing by whatever it was that he had done. He seemed oblivious to the presence of the G'home Gnomes, who mercifully stopped their presentation in midsentence and simply stared at him open-mouthed.

"What is it that you have done?" Ben inquired mildly. He had learned to temper his enthusiasm where Questor was concerned, because it was often sadly misplaced. Questor accomplished on the average about one half of what he thought he had accomplished.

"The magic, High Lord! I have found the magic! Finally, I have found the means to . . ." He stopped, hands gesturing emphatically. "No, wait a moment! The others must hear this, too. All of our friends must be present. I have taken the liberty of sending for them. It should only be a few, brief . . . This is such a glorious . . . Ah, ah, here they are now!"

Willow appeared in the open door, stunning as always, more beautiful than all the flowers about her, her slender form a whisper of white silk and trailing lace as she slipped into the sunlit room. Her pale green face glanced toward Ben, and she smiled that special, secret smile that she reserved only for him. A fairy creature, she seemed as ephemeral as the warmth of the midday air. The kobolds, Bunion and Parsnip, trailed after, gnarled bodies skittering along, wizened monkey faces grinning doubtfully, all teeth and sharp angles. Fairy creatures, too, they had the look of something conjured from a nightmare. Abernathy came last, resplendent in his scarlet and gold Court

Scribe uniform, no fairy creature, but a soft-coated Wheaten Terrier who seemed to think he was human. He held his dog's body erect and dignified, his soulful eyes darting at once to the hateful, carnivorous G'home Gnomes.

"I see no reason to be present in the same room as these loathsome creatures . . ." he began indignantly and was cut short by the sight of Questor Thews advancing on him with arms stretched wide.

"Old friend!" the wizard gushed. "Abernathy, the best of news for you! Come, come!"

He seized hold of Abernathy and propelled him into the center of the room. Abernathy stared at the wizard in disbelief, finally shaking himself free of the other entirely.

"Have you lost your mind?" he demanded, brushing at his garments to straighten them. His muzzle twitched. "And what is this old friend business? What are you up to now, Questor Thews?"

"Something you cannot begin to imagine!" The wizard was beaming with excitement as he rubbed his hands together and beckoned them all closer. They crowded in, and Questor's voice lowered conspiratorially. "Abernathy, if you were to wish for that which you most desire in all the world, what would it be?"

The dog stared at him. Then he glanced momentarily at the G'home Gnomes, then back again. "How many wishes do I get?"

The wizard lifted his bony hands and brought them to rest gently on the other's shoulders. "Abernathy." He breathed the scribe's name. "I have found the magic that will change you from a dog back into a man!"

There was stunned silence. Everyone knew the story of how Questor had used the magic to change Abernathy from a man into a dog to protect him from the old King's spiteful son some years earlier, when that reprobate was in one of his more hateful moods, and then had been unable to change him back again. Abernathy had lived since then as an imperfect dog who retained human hands and speech, always with the hope that one day a way would be found to restore his human self. A chagrined Questor had searched in vain for that way, frequently claiming he would find it when he found certain books of magic hidden by Meeks on his departure from Landover. But the books had been destroyed while being recovered, and not much had been heard on the subject since.

Abernathy cleared his throat. "Is this simply an over-generous dose of your usual nonsense, wizard?" he asked cautiously. "Or can you really change me back?"

"I can!" Questor declared, nodding vehemently. He paused. "I think."

Abernathy drew back. "You think?"

"Wait a minute!" Ben was out of his chair and between them with as much speed as he could manage, nearly tripping headfirst over a box of gardenias in his effort to prevent bloodshed. He took a deep breath. "Questor." He waited until the other's eyes found his. "I thought that kind of magic was beyond you. I thought that when you lost the books of magic, you lost any way of even studying the arts mastered by your predecessors, let alone trying to . . ."

"Trial and error, High Lord!" the other interrupted quickly. "Trial and error! I simply expanded on what I already knew, taking matters a step further each time, learning a bit more as I went until I had learned it all. It has taken me until now to master the magic, but master it I have!"

"You think," Ben amended.

"Well . . ."

"This is a waste of time—as usual!" Abernathy snapped, turned, and would have stalked away except that he was hemmed in by the G'home Gnomes, who had crowded close to hear better. Abernathy wheeled back. "The fact of the matter is, you never get *anything* right!"

"Rubbish!" Questor cried out suddenly, quieting them all. He straightened. "For ten long months I have worked on this magic—ever since the old books of magic were destroyed with Meeks, ever since then!" His sharp eyes locked on Abernathy. "I know how much this means to you. I have dedicated myself to mastering the magic that would make it possible. I have used the magic on small creatures with complete success. I have proven so far as it is possible to do so that it can be done. It only remains to try it with you."

No one said anything for a moment. The only sound in the room was the buzz of a solitary bumblebee as it meandered from flower box to flower box. Abernathy frowned at Questor Thews in determined silence. There was disbelief reflected in his eyes, but it couldn't quite mask the hope.

"I think we should give Questor the opportunity to finish his explanation," Willow spoke up finally. She stood a pace or two back from the others, watching.

"I agree," Ben added his approval. "Tell us the rest, Questor."

Questor looked offended. "Rest? What rest? That is the whole of it, thank you—unless you expect technical details on how the magic works, which I am not going to give you, since you would not understand them anyway. I have developed a means to complete the transformation from dog to man and that is that! If you wish me to use the magic, I will! If not, I will dismiss the matter from my mind!"

"Questor . . ." Ben began soothingly.

"Well, really, High Lord! I work hard to discover a difficult and elusive magical process and I am greeted with insults, jeers, and accusations! Am I Court Wizard or not, I ask myself? There certainly seems to be some doubt!"

"I simply asked . . ." Abernathy tried.

"No, no, you need not apologize for the truth of your feelings!" Questor Thews seemed to relish thoroughly the role of martyr. "Throughout history, all great men have been misunderstood. Some have even died for their beliefs."

"Now, look here!" Ben was growing angry.

"That is not to say that I feel my own life is threatened in any way, you understand," Questor added hastily. "I was simply making a point. Ahem! It only remains for me to repeat that the process is complete, the magic is found, and we can use it if you wish. Simply say so. You have all the facts." He stopped suddenly. "Oh. Except one, that is."

There was a collective groan. "Except one?" Ben repeated.

Questor tugged uncomfortably on one ear and cleared his throat. "There is one small matter, High Lord. The magic requires a catalyst for a transformation of this magnitude. I lack such a catalyst."

"I knew it . . ." Abernathy muttered under his breath.

"But there is an alternative," Questor continued hastily, ignoring the other. He paused and took a deep breath. "We could use the medallion."

Ben stared at him blankly. "The medallion? What medallion?"

"Your medallion, High Lord."

"My medallion?"

"But you would have to take it off and give it to Abernathy to wear during the transformation process."

"My medallion?"

Questor looked as if he were waiting for the ceiling to fall in on him. "It would only be for a few moments, you understand—that would be all. Then you could have your medallion back."

"I could have it back. Right."

Ben didn't know whether to laugh or to cry. "Questor, we spent weeks trying to get the damn thing back when it wasn't really gone in the first place, and now you want me to take it off for real? I thought I was *never* supposed to take it off. Isn't that what you yourself have told me on more than one occasion? Isn't it?"

"Well, yes . . ."

"What if something goes wrong and the medallion is damaged or lost? What then?" A dark flush was beginning to creep up Ben's neck. "What if . . . what if, for whatever reason, Abernathy *can't* give it back? Great balls of fire! This is the most half-baked idea I ever heard, Questor! What are you thinking about, anyway?"

Everyone had sort of shrunk away from him during this explosion, and now Ben found himself alone amid the flower boxes with the wizard. Questor was standing fast, but looking none too comfortable.

"If there were another choice in the matter, High Lord . . ."

"Well, find one, confound it!" Ben cut him short. He started to elaborate, then stopped, glancing instead at the others. "How much sense does this make to anyone else? Abernathy? Willow?"

Abernathy did not answer.

"I think you have to consider carefully what is at risk, Ben," Willow said finally.

Ben put his hands on his hips, looked at them each in turn, then gazed out wordlessly into the gardens beyond. So he had to consider what was at risk, did he? Well, what was at risk was the thing that had made him King of Landover and kept him there. It was the medallion that summoned the Paladin, the knight-errant who served as the King's champion and protector—*his* champion and protector on more than one occasion already. And it was the medallion that let him pass back and forth between Landover and other worlds, including the one he had come from. That's what was at risk! Without the medallion, he was in constant danger of winding up as just so much dog meat!

He regretted that last comparison almost immediately. After all, what was also at risk was Abernathy's permanent future as a canine.

He frowned blackly. What had begun as a fairly uneventful day was turning into a quagmire of unpleasant possibilities. His memory tugged at him. Ten months ago, he had been tricked into conveying the old wizard Meeks back into Landover when he had thought his worst enemy safely exiled. Meeks had then used his considerable magic to steal Ben's identity and the throne and—most important of all—to convince Ben that he had lost the medallion. It had almost cost Ben his life—not to mention Willow's—to discover what had been done to him and to defeat the old troublemaker once and for all. Now he was King again, safely ensconced at Sterling Silver, comfortably settled, the reins of kingship firmly in hand, his programs for a better life nicely under way, and here was Questor Thews playing around again with the magic!

Damn!

He stared at the flowers. Gardenias, roses, lilies, hyacinths, daisies, and dozens of variations of other familiar species along with a truckload of ground cover and flowering vines—all spread out before him like a vast patchwork quilt, scented and soft as down. It was so peaceful here. He didn't get to enjoy the garden room that often. This was his first morning in weeks. Why was he being hounded like this?

Because he was the King, of course, he answered himself. Let's not be stupid here. This wasn't a nine-to-five job. This wasn't why he had left his profession as a successful trial lawyer in Chicago, Illinois, to apply for the position of High Lord of Landover, a kingdom of magic and fairy folk that wasn't anywhere near Chicago or anywhere else anyone there had ever heard about. This wasn't why he had chosen to alter his life so completely that he was no longer even recognizable as the person he had been in his old world. He had wanted to change all that; that was why he had come here. He had wanted to escape the purposelessness of being who and what he had become—a bitter and reclusive widower, a disillusioned practitioner of a profession that had lost its character. He had wanted a challenge that would again give meaning to his existence. He had found that here. But the challenge was constant and not circumscribed by time or place, by need or want. It was simply there, always new, always changing; and he understood and relished the fact that he must always be there to meet it.

He sighed. It was just a little difficult sometimes.

He was conscious of the others watching him, waiting to see what he would do. He took a deep breath, inhaled the mix of fragrances that filled the noonday air, and turned to face them. Whatever doubts he'd had were gone. The decision wasn't really all that hard after all. Sometimes he just had to do what felt right.

He smiled. "Sorry to be so touchy," he said. "Questor, if you need the medallion to make the magic work, then you've got it. As Willow said, I have to consider the risks involved, and any risk is worth helping Abernathy get back to himself." He looked directly at his scribe. "How about it, Abernathy? Want to take the chance?"

Abernathy seemed undecided. "Well, I don't know, High Lord." He paused, thought, looked down briefly at his body, shook his head, and looked up again. Then he nodded. "Yes, High Lord, I do."

"Splendid!" Questor Thews exclaimed, promptly coming forward. The others murmured, hissed, and chittered their approval. "Now, this won't take a moment. Abernathy, you stand here, right in the center of the room, and the rest of you stand back a bit behind me." He adjusted them accordingly, beaming all the while. "Now then High Lord, please give the medallion to Abernathy."

Ben reached for the medallion where it rested about his neck and hesitated. "You're certain about this, Questor?"

"Quite certain, High Lord. All will be well."

"I mean, I can't even speak or write Landoverian without the medallion!"

Questor brought his hands up quickly in a gesture of reassurance. "Here, now. A simple spell will solve that problem." He motioned briefly, muttered something, and nodded in satisfaction. "There we are. Go ahead. You can take it off."

Ben sighed, took off the medallion, and handed it to Abernathy. Abernathy slipped it carefully about his shaggy neck. The medallion lay against his tunic front, sunlight dancing off its polished silver surface, detailing the etching of a knight riding out of an island castle at sunrise—the Paladin riding out of Sterling Silver. Ben sighed again and stepped back. He felt Willow come up beside him and take his hand in hers.

"It will be all right," she whispered.

Questor breezed back about Abernathy again, adjusting him first this way and then that, telling him all the while that things would take only a moment. Satisfied at last, he moved directly in front of the scribe and took two careful steps right. He tested the air with a wet finger. "Ah!" he declared mysteriously.

He brought his arms high out of the gray robes, flexed his fingers, and opened his mouth. Then he paused, his nose twitching. One hand dropped quickly to rub at it in irritation. "Dratted sunshine tickles," he muttered. "Pollen does nothing to help, either."

The G'home Gnomes crowded close again, pressing up against the wizard's robes, their ferret faces peering out at Abernathy in anxious anticipation.

"Could you move those creatures back?" the dog snapped and even growled a bit.

Questor glanced down. "Oh. Well, yes, of course. Back now, back with you!" He shooed the gnomes away and resumed his stance. His nose twitched again, and he sniffed. "Quiet, please!"

He began a long incantation. Bizarre gestures accompanied words that brought frowns of puzzlement to the faces of his listeners. They edged forward a pace or two to listen: Ben, a lean, fit man of forty standing firm against the advancement of middle age; Willow, a child in a woman's body, a sylph, half-human, half-fairy; the kobolds Parsnip and Bunion, the first thick and stolid, the second spindle-legged and quick, both with sharp, glittering eyes and teeth that suggested something feral; and the G'home Gnomes Fillip and Sot, furry, unkempt ground creatures that appeared to have just poked their heads up from their earthen dens. They watched and waited and said nothing. Abernathy, the focus of their attention, closed his eyes and prepared for the worst.

Still Questor Thews went on, looking for all the world like some scarecrow escaped from the fields, his recitation seemingly as endless as the complaints of the G'home Gnomes.

Ben was struck suddenly with the incongruity of things. Here he was, until recently a member of a profession that stressed reliance on facts and reason, a modern man, a man from a world where technology governed most aspects of life, a world of space travel, nuclear power, sophisticated telecommunications and a hundred-and-one other marvels—here he was, in a world that was all but devoid of technology, fully expecting a wizard's magic to transform completely the physiological makeup of a living creature in a way that the sciences of his old world had barely dreamed was possible. He almost smiled at the thought. It was just too bizarre.

Questor Thews' hands swooped down suddenly and then up again, and the air was filled with a fine silver dust that sparkled and shimmered as if alive. It floated in breezy swirls all about Questor's hands for a moment, then settled over Abernathy. Abernathy saw none of it, his eyes still tightly closed. Questor continued to murmur, his tone changing, growing sharper, becoming more a chant. The silver dust swirled, the light in the room seemed to brighten, and there was a sudden coldness in the air. Ben felt the G'home Gnomes shrink back behind his legs, muttering guardedly. Willow's hand closed tighter about his own.

"Ezaratz!" Questor cried out suddenly—or something like it—and there was a brilliant flash of light that ricocheted off Ben's medallion and caused them all to flinch away.

When they looked back again, there stood Abernathy—unchanged.

No, wait, thought Ben, his hands are gone! He has paws!

"Oh, oh," Questor said.

Abernathy's eyes blinked open. "Arf!" he barked. Then, in horror, "Arf, arf, arf!"

"Questor, you've turned him completely into a dog!" Ben exclaimed in disbelief. "Do something!"

"Drat!" the wizard muttered. "A moment, a moment!" His hands gestured, and the silver dust flew. He resumed the incantation. Abernathy had discovered paws where his hands had been. His eyes had snapped wide open and his muzzle had begun to quiver.

"Erazaratz!" Questor cried. The light flashed, the medallion flared, and the paws disappeared. Abernathy had his hands back. "Abernathy!" the wizard exulted.

"Wizard, when I get my hands on you . . . !" the scribe howled. Clearly, he had his voice back as well.

"Stand still!" Questor ordered sharply, but Abernathy was already advancing on him, moving out of the ring of silver dust. Questor moved quickly to stop him, brushing at the dust where it formed a screen between them. The dust darted away from him as if alive and flew suddenly into his face.

"Erazzatza!" Questor Thews sneezed suddenly.

A well of light opened up beneath Abernathy, a cloudy brightness that seemed to fasten about the dog's legs with tiny feelers. Slowly, the light began to draw Abernathy down.

"Help!" Abernathy cried.

"Questor!" Ben screamed.

He started forward and tripped over the G'home Gnomes, who had somehow edged in front of him.

"I . . . I have him . . . High Lord!" Questor Thews gasped between sniffles. His hands tried desperately to regain control of the swirling dust.

Abernathy's eyes had opened even wider, if that were possible, and he was struggling to climb free of the pooled light, calling out to them frantically. Ben tried to untangle himself from the G'home Gnomes.

"Be . . . calm!" Questor urged. "Be . . . ca . . . ah, ah, ah . . . ACHOOO!"

He sneezed so hard, he lurched backward into Ben and the others and knocked them all sprawling. The silver dust flew out the windows into the sunlit gardens. Abernathy gave one final cry and was sucked down into the light. The light flared once and disappeared.

Ben pushed himself up on his hands and knees and glared at Questor Thews. "Gesundheit!" he snapped.

Questor Thews turned crimson.

BOTTLE

"Well?" Ben demanded. "Where is he? What's happened to him?"

Questor Thews didn't seem to have a ready answer, so Ben diverted his attention from the flustered wizard long enough to help Willow up, then turned quickly back again. He wasn't angry yet—he was still too shocked—but he was going to be very angry any second. Abernathy had disappeared just as surely as if he had never been—vanished, just like that. And, of course, Ben's medallion, the medallion that protected the kingship and his life, the medallion Questor had assured him would be perfectly safe, had vanished as well.

He changed his mind. He wasn't going to be angry after all. He was going to be sick.

"Questor, where is Abernathy?" he repeated.

"Well, I . . . the fact of the matter is, High Lord, I . . . I am not entirely certain," the wizard managed finally.

Ben seized the front of the wizard's robes. He was going to be angry after all. "Don't tell me that! You've got to get him back, damnit!"

"High Lord." Questor was pale, but composed. He didn't try to draw away. He simply straightened himself and took a deep breath. "I am not sure yet exactly what happened. It will take a little time to understand . . ."

"Well, can't you guess?" Ben shouted, cutting him short.

The owlish face twisted. "I can guess that the magic misfired, of course. I can guess that the sneeze—that wasn't my fault, you know, High Lord, it simply happened—that the sneeze confused the magic in some fashion and changed the result of the incantation. Instead of transforming Abernathy from a dog back into a man, it seems to have *transported* him instead. The two words are quite similar, you see, and the magics likewise are similar. It happens that the results of most incantations are similar where the words are similar . . ."

"Skip all that!" Ben snapped. He started to say something further, then caught himself. He was losing control of the situation. He was behaving like some B-picture gangster. He released the front of the wizard's robes, feeling a bit foolish. "Look, you think that the magic sent him somewhere, right? Where do you think it sent him? Just tell me that."

Questor cleared his throat and thought a moment. "I don't know," he decided.

Ben stared at him, then turned away. "I don't believe this is happening," he muttered. "I just don't believe it."

He glanced momentarily at the others. Willow stood close, her green eyes solemn. The kobolds were picking up a planter that had been knocked over in the struggle. There were dirt and broken flowers scattered in a six-foot circle about them. The G'home Gnomes were whispering together anxiously.

"Perhaps we should . . ." Willow started to say.

And then there was a bright flash of light from the spot where Abernathy had disappeared, a popping sound as if someone had pulled a cork free, and something materialized from out of nowhere, spun wildly about, and came to rest on the floor.

It was a bottle.

Everyone jumped, then stared. The bottle lay there quietly, an oval-shaped container about the size of a magnum of champagne. It was corked and wired tightly shut and it was painted white with red harlequins dancing on its glass surface, all in varying poses of devilish gaiety, all grinning madly.

"What in the world is that?" Ben muttered and reached down to pick it up. He studied it wordlessly for a moment, hefting it, peering into it. "Doesn't appear to be anything inside," he said. "It feels empty."

"High Lord, I have a thought!" Questor said suddenly. "This bottle and Abernathy may have been exchanged—transposed, one for the other! Transpose sounds like transform and transfer, and I think the magics are close enough that it is possible!"

Ben frowned. "Abernathy was exchanged for this bottle? Why?"

Questor started to reply and stopped. "I don't know. But I am quite positive that is what happened."

"Does this help determine where Abernathy is now?" Willow asked.

Questor shook his head. "But it gives me a starting point. If I can trace the source of the bottle, then perhaps . . ." He trailed off thoughtfully. "Odd. This bottle seems familiar."

"You've seen it somewhere before?" Ben wanted to know immediately.

The wizard frowned. "I am not sure. It seems as if I might have and at the same time it seems I must be mistaken. I do not quite understand it."

Along with just about everything else, Ben thought rather unkindly. "Well, I don't give a hoot about this bottle," he declared, "but I do care about Abernathy and the medallion. So let's find a way to get them back. Whatever it takes, Questor, you do it and do it quickly. This mess is your responsibility."

"I realize that, High Lord. You need not remind me. It was not my fault, however, that Abernathy tried to move out of the incantation's sphere of influence, that the dust flew into my face when I tried to stop him, and that I thereupon sneezed. The magic would have worked as it was intended to work if I had not . . ."

Ben impatiently brushed the explanation away with a wave of his hand. "Just find him, Questor. Just find him."

Questor Thews bowed curtly. "Yes, High Lord. I will begin at once!" He turned and started from the room, muttering, "He *might* still be in Landover; I will begin my search here. The Landsview should help. He should be safe for the moment in any event, I imagine—safe even if we do not reach him immediately. Oh! Not that there is any reason he shouldn't be safe, High Lord," he added, turning hastily back. "No, no, we have time." He started away again. "The sneeze was not my fault, drat it! I had the magic perfectly under my control, and . . . oh, what is the point of belaboring the matter, I will simply start looking . . ."

He was almost through the door, when Ben called after him, "Don't you want this bottle?"

"What?" Questor glanced back, then hastily shook his head. "Later, perhaps. I have no immediate need for it. Odd, how familiar . . . I wish my memory were a little bit better on these things. Ah, well, it cannot mean much if I cannot summon even a faint recollection . . ."

He disappeared from view, still muttering—the Don Quixote of Landover, searching for dragons and finding only windmills. Ben watched him go in frustrated silence.

It was difficult to think about anything beyond the lost medallion and the missing Abernathy, but there was nothing to be done about either until Questor reported back. So while Willow went into the gardens to pick fresh flowers for dinner and the kobolds went back to their work about the castle, Ben forced himself to resume consideration of the latest complaint of the G'home Gnomes.

Intriguingly enough, the gnomes were no longer so anxious to pursue the matter.

"Tell me whatever you have left to tell me about the trolls," Ben ordered, resigned to the worst. He settled himself wearily in his chair and waited.

"Such a beautiful bottle, High Lord," said Fillip instead.

"Such a pretty thing," echoed Sot.

"Forget the bottle," Ben advised, remembering for the first time since

Questor had departed that it was still there, sitting where he had put it down on the floor next to him. He glanced at it in irritation. "I'd like to."

"But we have never seen one like it," persisted Fillip.

"Never," agreed Sot.

"Can we touch it, High Lord?" asked Fillip.

"Yes, can we?" pleaded Sot.

Ben glared. "I thought we were here to discuss trolls. You seemed anxious enough to do so earlier. You practically cried to do so. Now you don't care anymore?"

Fillip glanced hastily at Sot. "Oh, we care a great deal, High Lord. The trolls have mistreated us grievously."

"Then let's get on . . ."

"But the trolls are gone for now and cannot be found again immediately in any case, and the bottle is right here, right in front of us, so can we touch it for a moment, Great Lord—just for a moment?"

"Can we, Mighty High Lord?" echoed Sot.

Ben wanted to take the bottle and beat them over the head with it. But instead he simply picked it up and handed it over. It was easier than arguing. "Just be careful," he cautioned.

There really wasn't much to worry about on that count, he realized. The bottle was heavy glass and looked as if it could endure a good deal of mistreatment. Actually, it seemed almost something more than glass—almost a metal of some sort. Must be the paint, he thought.

The G'home Gnomes were fondling and caressing the bottle as if it were their most precious treasure. They stroked it and loved it. They cradled it like a child. Their grimy little paws moved across its surface almost sensuously. Ben was disgusted. He glanced out into the gardens at Willow and thought about joining her. Anything would be better than this.

"How about it, fellas," he said finally. "Let's finish up with the trolls, okay?"

Fillip and Sot stared at him. He beckoned for them to return the bottle, and they reluctantly handed it back. Ben set it down next to him again. The gnomes hesitated, then resumed their complaint against the trolls. But the effort was halfhearted at best. Their eyes kept straying back to the bottle, and finally they gave up on the trolls altogether.

"High Lord, could we have the bottle?" asked Fillip suddenly.

"Oh, yes, could we?" asked Sot.

Ben stared. "Whatever for?"

"It is a precious thing," said Fillip.

"It is a treasure," said Sot.

"So beautiful," said Fillip.

"Yes, beautiful," echoed Sot.

Ben closed his eyes and rubbed them wearily, then looked at the gnomes.

"I would love to be able to give it to you, believe me," he said. "I would love to say, 'Here, take this bottle and don't let me see it ever again.' That's what I would love to do. But I can't. The bottle has some connection with what happened to Abernathy, and I have to know what."

The G'home Gnomes shook their heads solemnly.

"The dog never liked us," muttered Fillip.

"The dog never did," muttered Sot.

"He growled at us."

"And even snapped."

"Nevertheless . . ." Ben insisted.

"We could keep the bottle for you, High Lord," interrupted Fillip.

"We would take good care of it, High Lord," assured Sot.

"Please, please," they implored.

They were so pathetic that Ben could only shake his head in wonder. They were just like little children in a toy store. "What if there were an evil genie in the bottle?" he asked suddenly, leaning forward with a dark frown. "What if the genie ate gnomes for breakfast?" The gnomes looked at him blankly. Obviously they had never heard of such a thing. "Never mind," he said. He sighed and sat back again. "You can't have it, and that's that."

"But you said you would love to give it to us," Fillip pointed out.

"That is what you said," agreed Sot.

"And we would love to have it."

"We would."

"So why not give it to us, High Lord?"

"Yes, why not?"

"Just for a little while, even?"

"Just for a few days?"

Ben lost his temper once again. He snatched up the bottle and brandished it before him. "I wish I had never seen this bottle!" he yelled. "I hate the damn thing! I wish it would disappear! I wish Abernathy and the medallion would reappear! I wish wishes were candy and I could eat them all day long! But they aren't, and I can't, and neither can you! So let's drop the whole subject of the bottle and get back to the trolls before I decide I don't want to listen to you anymore on *anything* and send you on your way!"

He put the bottle down again with a thud and sat back. The gnomes glanced at each other meaningfully.

"He hates the bottle," whispered Fillip.

"He wishes it would disappear," whispered Sot.

"What did you say?" Ben asked. He couldn't quite hear them.

"Nothing, Great High Lord," answered Fillip.

"Nothing, Mighty High Lord," answered Sot.

They went quickly back to their tale of woe about the trolls, a tale which they wrapped up rather quickly. While they were telling it, they never took their eyes off the bottle.

The remainder of the day slipped by rather more quickly than Ben had expected. The gnomes finished their tale and departed for their quarters. Guests were always invited to spend the night, and Fillip and Sot invariably accepted the invitation because they loved Parsnip's cooking. That was all right with Ben so long as they stayed out of trouble. Before they were even through the garden room door, Ben was moving to join Willow. Belatedly, he remembered the bottle, still sitting next to his chair amid the flower boxes. He retraced his steps, picked it up, glanced around for a safe place to put it, and decided on a cabinet that displayed a series of ornate flower pots and vases. He slipped the bottle inside, where it blended quite nicely, and hurried out.

He walked the gardens with Willow for a time, reviewed his agenda for the following day—how in the world was he going to get along without Abernathy to remind him of his appointments and to keep his calendar?—stuck his head in the kitchen to see what Parsnip was preparing, and went for a run.

Running was the one exercise he still practiced faithfully. He kept what he could of his boxer's routine—a holdover from his days as a silver gloves champion and after—but he lacked the sophisticated punching equipment that would let him train as he would in a Chicago gym, so he relied heavily on the running, together with rope work and isometrics. It was enough to keep him fit.

He dressed in his sweats and Nikes, crossed from the island to the mainland in the lake skimmer—his private skiff, a vessel that ran without any power but that of his own thought—climbed the hills beyond, and began to run along the rim of the valley. Fall was in the air, a brief hint of color already beginning to show in the green of the trees. Days were growing short, the nights cold. He ran for almost two hours, trying to work through the day's frustrations and disappointments; when he was sufficiently tired, he crossed back again.

By now the sun was slipping quickly into the west, already partially masked by a screen of forest trees and distant peaks. He watched the dramatic outline of the castle loom up before him as he sat in the skimmer, thinking how much he loved it here. Sterling Silver was the home he had always searched for—even when he didn't know he was searching for it. He remembered how forbidding she had seemed that first time, all worn and discolored from the Tarnish, the loss of magic in the land having sickened her. He remembered how huge and empty she had seemed. That was before he had discovered that she was alive and that she was as capable of feeling as he. He remembered the warmth he had felt in her that first night—a warmth that was real and not imagined. Sterling Silver was a singular bit of magic, a creation of stone and mortar and metal that was nevertheless as human as any creature of flesh and blood. She could extend warmth, she could provide food, she could shelter, she could comfort. She was a wondrous magic, and he never ceased to marvel that she could actually be.

He received word from Willow on his return that Questor had surfaced long enough to report that he had determined that Abernathy definitely wasn't still in Landover. Ben accepted the news stoically. He hadn't really expected things to be that easy.

Willow came to him and washed him in his bath. Her tiny hands were gentle and loving, and she kissed him often. Her long, green hair swept down about her face as she worked, and it made her seem veiled and mysterious.

"You must not be too angry with Questor," she said finally as he was toweling himself dry. "He tried to do what he thought best for Abernathy. He wanted desperately to help."

"I know that," Ben said.

"He holds himself responsible for Abernathy's condition, and such responsibility is a terrible burden." She looked out the window of his bedchamber into the darkening night. "You should understand better than anyone what it can be like to feel responsible for another person."

He did. He had carried the weight of that responsibility more times than he cared to remember. A few times he had carried it when it was not really his to carry. He thought of Annie, his wife, gone now almost four years. He thought of his old law partner and good friend, Miles Bennett. He thought of the people of Landover, of the black unicorn, of his new friends Willow, Abernathy, Bunion, Parsnip, and, of course, Questor.

"I just wish he could manage to control the magic a little better," he said softly. Then he stopped in the middle of what he was doing and looked over at the sylph. "I'm scared to death of losing that medallion, Willow. I remember all too well what it was like when I thought I'd lost it last time. I feel so helpless without it."

Willow came to him and held him. "You will never be helpless, Ben. Not you. And you will never be alone."

He hugged her close and nodded into her hair. "I know. Not while you're around. Anyway, I shouldn't worry. Something will come up."

Something did come up, but it wasn't until dinner was nearly over that it did, and it wasn't what either of them expected. Dinner was a sparsely attended affair. The G'home Gnomes did not show up—an astonishing occurrence—nor did Questor. Bunion dropped by briefly and was off again, and Parsnip stayed in the kitchen. So Ben and Willow sat alone at the great dining hall table, eating dutifully and listening to the silence.

They were just finishing when Questor Thews burst into the room, his owlish face so distraught that Ben was on his feet instantly.

"High Lord!" the wizard gasped. "Where is the bottle?"

"The bottle?" Ben had to think a moment. "In the garden room, in a display case. What's wrong?"

Questor was trying so hard to catch his breath that Ben and Willow felt obliged to help him to a chair. Willow gave him a glass of wine, which he quickly drained. "I remember now where I saw the bottle, High Lord!" he said finally.

"Then you *did* see it before! Where?" Ben pressed.

"Here, High Lord! Right here!"

"But you didn't remember that earlier when you saw it?"

"No, of course not! That was over twenty years ago!"

Ben shook his head. "You're not making any sense, Questor."

The wizard lurched to his feet. "I will explain it all to you as soon as we have that bottle safely in hand! I will not feel comfortable until we do! High Lord, that bottle is extremely dangerous!"

Bunion and Parsnip had appeared as well by now, and the bunch of them hastened down the castle halls toward the garden room. Ben tried to find out more as they went, but Questor refused to elaborate. They reached the garden room in moments and pushed through the closed doors in a knot. The room was dark, but a touch of Ben's hands on the castle walls brought light.

He crossed the room to the display cabinet and peered through its glass doors.

The bottle was gone.

"What, what in . . . ?" He stared in disbelief at the empty space on which the bottle had rested. Then he knew. "Fillip and Sot!" He spit their names out like loose stones. "Those damn gnomes, they couldn't leave well enough alone! They must have stayed behind at the door to see where I put it!"

The others pushed forward, racing past him to the cabinet.

"The G'home Gnomes took the bottle?" Questor asked incredulously.

"Bunion, go search for them," Ben ordered, already fearing the worst. "If they're still here, bring them—quick!"

The kobold was gone instantly and back again just as quickly. His monkey face grimaced and his teeth showed.

"Gone," Ben cried in fury.

Questor looked faint. "High Lord, I am afraid that I have some very bad news for you."

Ben sighed stoically. Somehow, he wasn't surprised.

GRAUM WYTHE

Abernathy came awake with a start. He didn't come awake in the ordinary sense because he had never really been asleep, just wishing he was, his eyes squinched closed, his breath held like a swimmer underwater. It seemed as if he came awake, however, because first the light was there, all around him, so intense he could feel its brightness even with his eyes closed, and then all of a sudden it was gone.

He blinked and looked around. A screen of shadows and half-light masked everything. He took a moment to let his vision clear fully. There were bars in front of his face. He blinked again. There were bars all around! Good heavens, he was in a cage!

He tried to scramble up from the sitting position in which he found himself and discovered that his cage would not permit it. His head was right up against the ceiling. He maneuvered one arm—he could barely move that either—to touch the ceiling experimentally, then the bars . . . Wait, what was this? He touched the bars again. They were set in glass of some sort—and weren't really bars, but some sort of latticework, very ornate, very intricate. And the cage wasn't square, it was hexagonal!

Who ever heard of a hexagonal cage?

He glanced down. A pair of delicate-looking vases were squashed between his legs and the glass, looking for all the world as if they would shatter with his next breath.

Nevertheless, he did breathe, mostly from astonishment. He wasn't in a cage; he was in some sort of display case!

For a moment he was so bewildered that he was at a complete loss as to what to do next. He stared out beyond the case into the shadows and half-light. He was in a massive stone and timber hall filled with cabinets and shelving, cases and pedestals, all displaying various artifacts and art objects. The light was so poor that he could barely make any of it out. A scattering of windows that were small and set high on the walls allowed in what little light there was. Tapestries decorated the walls at various intervals, and a floor of stone flagging was covered with scattered squares of what appeared to be handwoven carpet.

Abernathy scowled. Where in the name of all that was good and decent in the world was he? That confounded Questor Thews! He might still be in Sterling Silver for all he knew, locked away in some half-forgotten room of old art, except . . . He let the thought trail away unfinished. Except that he wasn't, he sensed. His scowl deepened. That muddleheaded wizard! What had he done?

A door opened at one end of the room and closed softly. Abernathy squinted through the gloom. Someone was there, but he couldn't see who. He held his breath and listened. Whoever was there apparently didn't know about him yet. Whoever was there was strolling idly about the room, moving very slowly, stopping from time to time, looking things over. A visitor, Abernathy decided, come to look at the art. The footsteps grew closer, off to his left now. His display case sat rather far out from the wall, and he could not see clearly behind him without turning his head and shoulders. If he did that he was afraid he might break something in the case. He sighed. Well, maybe he should. After all, he couldn't just sit there indefinitely, could he?

The footsteps passed behind him, slowed, came around, and stopped. He looked down. A small girl was looking up. She was very young, he decided, no more than maybe twelve, with a tiny body, a round face and curly honey-blond hair cut short. Her eyes were blue and there was a scattering of freckles on her nose. She was apparently trying to decide what he was. He held his breath momentarily, hoping that she might lose interest and go away. She didn't. He tried to stay perfectly still. Then he blinked in spite of his resolve, and she drew back in surprise.

"Oh, you're alive!" she exclaimed. "You're a real puppy!"

Abernathy sighed. This was turning out about the way he had expected it would—about the same as the rest of his day.

The little girl had come forward again, eyes wide. "You poor thing! Locked in that case like that, no food or water or anything! Poor puppy! Who did this to you?"

"An idiot who fancies himself a wizard," Abernathy replied.

Now her eyes *really* opened wide. "You can talk!" she whispered in a voice of conspiratorial elation. "Puppy, you can talk!"

Abernathy frowned. "Would you mind not calling me 'puppy'?"

"No! I mean, no, I wouldn't mind." She edged closer. "What's your name, puppy? Uh, I'm sorry. What's your name?"

"Abernathy."

"Mine's Elizabeth. Not Beth or Lizzy or Liz or Libby or Liza or Betty or anything else, just Elizabeth. I hate those cute abbreviations. Mothers and fathers just stick you with them without asking you what you think about it, and there they are, yours forever. They're not real names, just half-names. Elizabeth is a real name. Elizabeth was my great-aunt's name." She paused. "How did you learn to talk?"

Abernathy frowned some more. "I learned as you did, I imagine. I went to school."

"You did? They teach dogs how to talk where you're from?"

Abernathy was finding it hard to stay patient. "Of course not. I wasn't a dog, then. I was a man."

Elizabeth was fascinated. "You were?" She hesitated, thinking. "Oh, I see—a wizard did this to you, didn't he? Just like *Beauty and the Beast.* Do you know the story? There was this handsome prince and he was changed into an ugly beast by a wicked spell and couldn't be changed back again until he was truly loved." She stopped. "Is that what happened to you, Abernathy?"

"Well . . ."

"Was the wizard a wicked wizard?"

"Well . . ."

"Why did he change you into a dog? What kind of dog are you, Abernathy?"

Abernathy licked his nose. He was thirsty. "Do you suppose you could open the door to this display case and let me out?" he asked.

Elizabeth hurried forward, curls bouncing. "Oh, sure." She stopped. "It's locked, Abernathy. These cases are always locked. Michel keeps them that way to protect his things. He's very mistrustful." She paused. "Oh, oh. What's happened to the bottle that was in there? There was a white bottle painted with dancing clowns and now it's gone! What's happened to it? Are you sitting on it, Abernathy? Michel will be furious! Is it under you somewhere, maybe?"

Abernathy rolled his eyes. "I have no idea, Elizabeth. I cannot see anything under me because I cannot move out of the way to look. I will probably never see anything under me again if I do not get out of here!"

"I told you, the door's locked," Elizabeth repeated solemnly. "But maybe I can get a key. My father is steward of Graum Wythe. He has keys to everything. He's gone right now, but let me check his room. I'll be right back!" She started away. "Don't worry, Abernathy. Just wait here!"

Then she was gone, out the door like a cat. Abernathy sat quietly in the silence and thought. What bottle was she talking about, who is Michel, where is Graum Wythe? He had known a Michel once. And a Graum Wythe. But that was years ago, and that Michel and that Graum Wythe were best forgotten . . .

He felt a sudden chill steal up his spine as the almost forgotten memories took shape once more. No, it couldn't be, he told himself. It was just a coincidence. Probably he heard wrong. Probably Elizabeth said something else and he misunderstood.

The minutes slipped away, and finally she was back. She appeared noiselessly through the door, crossed to the display case, inserted a long iron key into the lock, and twisted. The glass and iron-mesh door opened, and Abernathy was free. Gingerly, he extricated himself.

"Thank you, Elizabeth," he said.

"You're welcome, Abernathy," she replied. She straightened the upended vases, searched about in vain for the missing bottle, and finally gave up. She closed the display case door and locked it once more. "The bottle isn't there," she announced solemnly.

Abernathy straightened himself and brushed off his clothing. "I give you my word, I know nothing of its whereabouts," he advised her.

"Oh, I believe you," she assured him. "But Michel might not. He isn't very understanding about such things. He doesn't even allow people in this room normally unless he invites them in—and then he stays right there with them. I can get in alone only because my father is steward. I like to come here to look at all the neat things. Do you know that there's a picture on the far wall with people in it that really move? And a music box that will play whatever you ask it to? I don't know what was in the bottle, but it was something special. Michel never let anyone near it."

A picture with people that moved and a music box that played requests? *Magic,* Abernathy thought instantly. "Elizabeth," he interrupted, "where am I?"

Elizabeth looked at him curiously. "In Graum Wythe, of course. Didn't I tell you that before?"

"Yes, but . . . where is Graum Wythe?"

The blue eyes blinked. "In Woodinville."

"And where is Woodinville?"

"North of Seattle. In Washington State. In the United States of America." Elizabeth watched the confusion on Abernathy's face grow. "Doesn't any of this mean anything to you, Abernathy? Don't you know any of these places?"

Abernathy shook his head. "These are not places in my world, I am afraid. I do not know where . . ." Then suddenly he stopped. There was alarm in his voice. "Elizabeth," he said slowly, "have you ever heard of a place called Chicago?"

Elizabeth smiled. "Sure. Chicago is in Illinois. But that's a long way from here. Are you from Chicago, Abernathy?"

Abernathy was beside himself. "No, but the High Lord is—or was! This is a nightmare! I'm not in Landover anymore! I have been sent to the High Lord's world! That fool wizard!" He stopped in horror. "Oh, good heavens—and I have the medallion! The High Lord's medallion!"

He fumbled desperately at the chain and medal that hung about his neck while Elizabeth cried, "Abernathy, it's all right, it's okay, don't be frightened, please! I'll take care of you, really I will, I'll look out for you." And all the while she petted him soothingly.

"Elizabeth, you do not understand! The medallion is the High Lord's talisman! It cannot protect him while I have it in this world! He needs it to be with him in Landover! This is no longer his worl . . . !" Again, he stopped. There was new horror in his eyes. "Oh, for . . . His world! This is his world, his *old* world! Elizabeth! You say this place is called Graum Wythe—and that its master is called Michel. What is his full name, Elizabeth? Quickly, tell me!"

"Abernathy, calm down!" Elizabeth kept trying to pet him. "His name is Michel Ard Rhi."

Abernathy looked as if he were about to have a heart attack. "Michel Ard Rhi!" He breathed the name as if to speak it too loudly would bring on the pending heart attack for sure. He took a deep, calming breath. "Elizabeth, you must hide me!"

"But what's wrong, Abernathy?"

"It is quite simple, Elizabeth. Michel Ard Rhi is my worst enemy."

"But why? What happened to make you enemies?" Elizabeth was full of questions, her blue eyes dancing. "Is he a friend of the wizard who changed you into a dog, Abernathy? Is he a bad . . ."

"Elizabeth!" Abernathy tried to keep the desperation from his voice. "I will tell you everything, I promise—after you hide me! I cannot be found here—not with the medallion, not with . . ."

"Okay, okay," the little girl assured him quickly. "I said I would take care of you, and I will. I always keep my promises." She thought. "You can hide in my room. You won't be found there for a while. No one comes there much except for my dad, and he won't be back for a few days." She paused. "But we have to find a way to get you there first. That might not be easy, you know, because there's always someone wandering about the halls. Let me see . . ."

She studied him critically for a moment, Abernathy wishing he could make himself invisible or something, and then she clapped her hands excitedly.

"I know!" She grinned. "We'll play dress-up!"

It was the low point of Abernathy's life, but he did it because Elizabeth assured him it was necessary. He trusted Elizabeth instinctively, the way you will a child, and did not question that she truly intended to help him. He was frantic to get out of the open and into hiding. The worst thing in any world that could happen to him was to be found again by Michel Ard Rhi.

So he let Elizabeth tie a makeshift collar and leash about his neck, he dropped down on all fours still wearing his silks with their silver clasps, and he walked out of that room like a real dog. It was uncomfortable, disgraceful, and humiliating. He felt like a complete fool, but he did it anyway. He even agreed to sniff at things as he walked and wag his stubby tail.

"Whatever you do, don't talk," Elizabeth cautioned as they stepped through the door into a hallway beyond. The hallway was as shadowed and closed away as the room filled with art, and Abernathy could feel the cold of the stone on his feet and hands. "If anyone sees us, I'll just tell them you're my dog and we're playing dress-up. I don't think they will question it much when they see those clothes you're wearing."

Charming, thought Abernathy, irritated. And exactly what is wrong with my clothes? But he didn't say anything.

They passed down a long series of corridors, all rather poorly lit by a combination of tiny windows and lamps, all constructed of stone and timber. Abernathy had seen enough of Graum Wythe by now to know that it was a castle much like Sterling Silver. That suggested that perhaps Michel Ard Rhi was living out his boyhood fantasies, and that in turn made the scribe curious to know more. But he didn't want to think about Michel just now; he was almost afraid that thinking of him might somehow make the man appear, so he forced the matter from his mind.

Elizabeth had brought him quite some distance through Graum Wythe's halls without encountering anyone when they rounded a corner and found themselves face to face with a pair of men in black uniforms. Elizabeth stopped. Abernathy immediately edged back behind her legs, finding them entirely too skinny to hide behind. He sniffed the floor dutifully and tried to look like a real dog.

"Afternoon, Elizabeth," the men greeted.

"Good afternoon," Elizabeth replied.

"That your dog?" one asked. She nodded. "All dressed up, eh? Bet he doesn't like it much."

"Bet he hates it," the other agreed.

"What's he got on his nose, glasses? Where'd you find those, Elizabeth?"

"Pretty fancy stuff for a dog," the other observed. He started to reach down, and Abernathy growled, almost before he realized what he was doing. The man pulled his hand back quickly. "Not very friendly, is he?"

"He's just frightened," Elizabeth offered. "He doesn't know you yet."

"Yeah, guess I can understand that." The man started on his way again. "Let's go, Bert."

The other hesitated. "Does your father know about this dog, Elizabeth?" he asked. "I thought he told you no pets."

"Oh. Well, he changed his mind," Elizabeth said. Abernathy slipped out from behind her, pulling on the leash. "I have to go now. 'Bye."

"'Bye, Elizabeth," the man said. He started away, then turned back. "Hey, what kind of dog is that anyway?"

"I don't know," Elizabeth called. "Just a mutt."

It was all Abernathy could do to keep from biting her.

"I am not a mutt," he told her when it was safe to talk again. "I happen to be a soft-coated Wheaten Terrier. My bloodlines are probably better than your own."

Elizabeth blushed. "Sorry, Abernathy," she said softly, eyes downcast.

"Oh, well, that's all right," he soothed, trying to make up for his gruffness. "I simply wanted you to know that I possess pedigree despite my condition."

They sat in her room on the edge of her bed, safe for the moment. Her room was bright and sunny in contrast to what they had seen of the rest of the castle, the walls paneled and papered, the floor carpeted, and the furniture soft and feminine with stuffed animals and dolls scattered about. Books lined a case on one wall beside a small writing desk, and pictures of teddy bears and puffins were hung casually about. A poster of something or someone called Bon Jovi was taped to the back of the closed door.

"Tell me about you and Michel," Elizabeth asked, eyes lifting once more.

Abernathy sat back stiffly. "Michel Ard Rhi is part of the reason that I am a dog," he said. He thought for a moment. "Elizabeth, I honestly don't know if I should tell you this or not."

"Why, Abernathy?"

"Well . . . because much of it is going to be very hard for you to believe."

Elizabeth nodded. "Like what you told me about the wizard changing you from a man into a dog? Like you being from another world?" She shook her head and looked very solemn. "I can believe things like that, Abernathy. I can believe there are things most people don't know anything about. Like magic. Like make-believe places that really aren't make-believe. My dad tells me all the time that there are all kinds of things people don't believe just because they don't understand them." She paused. "I don't tell anyone this—except for my best friend Nita—but I think that there are other people living out there somewhere on other worlds. I do."

Abernathy regarded her with new respect. "You happen to be right," he said finally. "This is not my world, Elizabeth. It is not Michel Ard Rhi's world either. We are both from a world called Landover, a kingdom really, not very big, but very far away. It is a crossroads for many worlds besides yours, all leading into the mists where the fairy people live. The mists are the source of all magic. The fairies live entirely in the magic; other worlds and people do not—at least, not for the most part."

He stopped, trying to think how to proceed. Elizabeth was staring at him with amazement, though not disbelief. He reached up and shoved his glasses further back on his nose.

"What happened to me happened more than twenty years ago. Michel's father was King of Landover then. He was in the final year of his life. I was his Court Scribe. Michel was about your age—but other than that, he was nothing like you, of course."

"Was he bad?" Elizabeth wanted to know.

"He was."

"He's not very nice now, either."

"Well, then, he has not changed much from when he was your age." Abernathy sighed. The memories came flooding back, painful images that lingered and refused to go. "I played with Michel while he was growing up. His father asked me to and so I did. He was not a very pleasant child, especially after Meeks took him under his wing. Meeks was the old Court Wizard, a very bad man. He made friends with Michel and taught him bits of magic. Michel liked that. He was always pretending he could do anything he wanted to do. When I played with him, he always pretended he had a castle called Graum Wythe, a fortress stronghold that could stand against a hundred hostile armies and a dozen wizards. He liked the idea of having so much power at his command."

Abernathy shook his head. "He played at this and he played at that, and I went along with it. It was not my place to question what was happening to the boy—or what I thought was happening. The old King did not seem to see it as clearly as I did . . ." He shrugged. "Michel was quite a little monster, I'm afraid."

"Was he mean to you?" Elizabeth asked.

"He was, but he was much meaner to others. I had some protection because I was Court Scribe. Others were not so fortunate. And Michel was really cruel toward animals. He seemed to take great delight in tormenting them. Particularly cats. He really hated cats for some reason. He was always finding strays and throwing them off the castle walls . . ."

"That's horrible!" Elizabeth exclaimed.

Abernathy nodded. "I told him so. Then one day I caught him doing something so unspeakable that even now I cannot bear to talk about it. In any case, that was the end of my patience. I picked up that boy, turned him over my knee, and beat him with a switch until he howled! I did not think about what I was doing, I just did it. When I was finished, he ran screaming from the room, furious at me for what I had done to him."

"Well, he deserved it," Elizabeth announced, certain of it even without knowing what it was he had done.

"Nevertheless, it was a terrible mistake on my part," Abernathy continued. "I should have left well enough alone and simply advised the King on his return. The King was gone, you see, and Michel had been left to the care of Meeks. He went immediately to Meeks, therefore, and demanded that I be punished. He wanted my hand cut off. Meeks, I learned later, laughed and agreed. Meeks never cared much for me, you see. He felt I influenced the old King against him. So Michel summoned his guards and they came looking for me. There was no one to protect me. Meeks was acting regent in the King's absence. I would most certainly have had my hand removed had they found me."

"But they didn't." Elizabeth was anxious to help the story along.

"No. Questor Thews found me first. Questor was Meeks's half-brother, a wizard as well, albeit a lesser talent. He was visiting for the week, hoping the old King would find him a position somewhere or other. We were friends, Questor and I. He did not care much for his half-brother or Michel either, and when he heard what was happening he came to warn me. There was no time for me to escape from the castle and no place to hide within it. Michel knew them all. So I allowed Questor Thews to change me into a dog so I would not be harmed. I wasn't, fortunately, but afterward Questor was unable to change me back again."

"So it wasn't a bad wizard who changed you after all," Elizabeth said.

Abernathy shook his head. "No, Elizabeth—just a poor excuse for one."

Elizabeth nodded solemnly, her freckled face lined with thought. "And you've been a dog all these years? Sorry. A . . . a soft-coated Wheat Terrier?"

"Soft-coated *Wheaten* Terrier. Yes. Except for my fingers and my voice and my thinking, which are still the same as they were when I was a man."

Elizabeth smiled a sort of sad child's smile. "I wish I could help you, Abernathy. Help change you back, I mean."

Abernathy sighed. "Someone tried that already. That's how I ended up here, scrunched up in that display case. Questor Thews again, I'm afraid. He is not any more adept at his art now than he was thirty years ago. He thought he had finally found a way to change me back. Unfortunately, the magic failed him once again, and here I am, trapped in the castle home of my worst enemy."

They were silent for a moment, staring at each other. Afternoon sunshine spilled through the curtained windows and warmed the room. The speckled blue and violet wildflowers in the vase on the dresser smelled of meadows and hills. From somewhere distant, there came the faint sound of laughter and a scraping of boxes or crates. Abernathy was reminded of home.

Elizabeth was speaking. "My father once told me that Michel could be very mean to animals," she was saying. "He said that was why I couldn't have a pet—because something might happen to it. No one at Graum Wythe has a pet. You never see any animals here."

"I don't wonder," Abernathy replied wearily.

She looked at him. "Michel mustn't be allowed to find you."

"No, he certainly mustn't."

"But the watch will say something about my having a dog, I'll bet." She frowned at the thought. "The watch tells him everything. They keep this place guarded just like a prison. Even my father can't go everywhere—and he is chief steward of Graum Wythe. Michel relies on him completely. He runs everything—well, almost everything. He doesn't run the watch. They report directly to Michel."

Abernathy nodded, saying nothing, thinking suddenly of the medallion concealed beneath his tunic, imagining what would happen if he were caught wearing it.

Elizabeth sighed. "I don't like Michel very much—even though he's really never done anything to me. He just isn't very friendly. He always looks so . . . creepy."

Abernathy didn't know what "creepy" meant, but he was sure it was something Michel Ard Rhi could be. "I have to get away from here, Elizabeth. You have to help me."

"But, Abernathy, where will you go?" she asked immediately.

"It really doesn't matter so long as it is far away from here," he advised. He paused, frowning. "I still cannot understand why I am here rather than somewhere else. Here, of all places. How could that happen?" He shook his head.

"I think I should go with you," Elizabeth said suddenly.

"No! No, you cannot do that!" Abernathy replied at once. "No, no, Elizabeth, I have to go alone."

"But you don't even know where you're going!"

"I can find my way, believe me. There is a way back into Landover if you wear the medallion. The High Lord told me something of it once—a place called Virginia. I can find it."

"Virginia is at the other end of the country!" Elizabeth exclaimed, horrified. "How will you get there?"

Abernathy stared at her. He had no idea, of course. "There are ways," he said finally. "But I have to get out of here first. Will you help me?"

Elizabeth sighed. "Of course, I'll help you." She stood up, walked over to the window, and looked out. "I have to think of a way to sneak you through one of the gates. They check everyone going out." She thought. "It's too late today to do anything. Maybe tomorrow. I have to go to school, but I get home by four. Or maybe I'll pretend to be sick and stay home. I can't hide you here for very long." She looked over. "I still think I should go with you."

Abernathy nodded. "I know. But you can't, Elizabeth. You are too young. It would be too dangerous."

Elizabeth frowned, then turned back to the window. "My dad says that sometimes when I ask to do things."

"I suppose he does."

Elizabeth turned back again and looked over with a smile. He saw himself fleetingly in the mirror behind her, saw himself as she saw him, a dog in red and gold silk clothing sitting on her bed, glasses on his furry nose, soulful brown eyes looking back at her. He suddenly thought how ridiculous he must seem to her. He looked away, embarrassed.

But she surprised him. "Are we going to stay good friends, Abernathy," she asked, "even after you're gone?"

He would have smiled if it were possible for dogs to do so. "Yes, Elizabeth, we are."

"Good. I'm really glad that I'm the one who found you, you know."

"I am, too."

"I still wish you would let me come with you."

"I know."

"Why don't you think about it."

"I will."

"Do you promise?"

Abernathy sighed. "Elizabeth?"

"Yes?"

"I could think much better if I had something to eat. And maybe something to drink?"

She bounced out of the room. Abernathy watched her go. He liked Elizabeth. He had to admit that he didn't mind so much being a dog around her after all.

DARKLING

"There is something that lives in the bottle," Questor Thews said.

He sat with Ben, Willow, and the kobolds in the garden room. Night's shadows cloaked everything in shawls of gray and black, save only where a single dimmed light from a smokeless lamp lent muted shades of color to a small circle of space where four listeners sat hunched over in silence, waiting for the wizard to continue. Questor's owlish face was gaunt and craggy with worry, his brow furrowed more deeply than usual, his eyes bits of silver glitter. His hands were folded in his lap, gnarled sticks of deadwood that had become inextricably locked together.

"The thing is called a Darkling. It is a kind of demon."

Like the bottle imp, Ben thought suddenly, remembering the old Robert Louis Stevenson story. Then he remembered what the creature of that story had done to its owners and he experienced a sudden twinge of uneasiness.

"The Darkling is very like the genie of the lamp in the old tales," Questor continued. Ben felt the uneasiness begin to subside. "It serves the holder of its bottle, appearing when summoned, doing its master's bidding. It uses various forms of magic to accomplish this." He sighed. "Unfortunately, the magic it uses is all bad."

"How bad?" Ben asked quietly. The uneasiness was back.

"That depends, High Lord." Questor cleared his throat and rocked back in thought. "You have to understand the nature of the magic the Darkling employs. It isn't a magic that is self-contained; it is a magic that is derivatory."

"Which means what?"

"Which means that the Darkling draws its strength from the holder of the bottle. Its magic is fed by the strength of character of the one who calls upon it—not by what is good and kind in that character, but by what is bad and hurtful. Anger, selfishness, greed, envy, other emotions that you can name as well as I, destructive emotions that lurk within all of us to some degree—the Darkling draws the power for its magic from these."

"It feeds on human failing," Willow observed softly. "I have heard of such creatures, long ago banished from the mists."

"Well, that is not yet the worst of it," Questor went on wearily. His mouth had twisted into a scowl that threatened to pull his nose down into his beard. "I mentioned before that the bottle seemed somehow familiar to me. It is—or was—a very long time ago. It has been more than twenty years since I last saw it. It was only just this evening that I was able to remember where." He cleared his throat nervously. "I last saw it in the hands of my half-brother. The bottle belonged to him."

"Oh, oh," Ben groaned.

"But how did it get here?" Willow asked.

The wizard sighed his deepest sigh yet. "To explain that, I have to go back in time."

"Not too far back, I hope?" Ben pleaded.

"High Lord, I will go no further back than is necessary for the purpose of completing my explanation." Questor was slightly indignant. "You must appreciate the fact that the amount of time either of us might believe necessary is somewhat subjective when one . . ."

"Just do it, Questor—please!" Ben urged helplessly.

Questor hesitated, shrugged, nodded, then rocked back once more. He was seated on a bench that offered no back support at all and appeared at every rock to be in danger of going over altogether. He tugged up his legs beneath his robe as a child would, drawing them close to his chest, and his owlish face assumed a faraway look. His brows knitted, and his lips tightened. He appeared to Ben to be a man who had eaten something disagreeable.

Finally, he was ready. "You will remember that my half-brother was Court Wizard to the old King," he began. They all nodded, the kobolds included. "I was without position at the Court, but I would visit from time to time anyway. The old King often gave me small tasks that took me to other parts of the kingdom—tasks that were of no particular interest to my half-brother. My half-brother had been named tutor to the old King's young son shortly after the boy's eighth year, and the whole of my half-brother's time thereafter was occupied with teaching that boy. Unfortunately, he was teaching the boy all the wrong things. He saw that the old King was weakening, aging more quickly, sick from ailments which could not be cured. He knew that the boy would be King after his father was gone, and he wanted control of the boy. Michel was his name. Michel Ard Rhi."

He cocked his head. "Michel had never demonstrated much character, even before he began spending all his study time with Meeks. But after my half-brother got his hands on him, he became a thoroughly despicable lad in no time at all. He was cruel and mean-spirited. He took great delight in tormenting everyone and everything. He was obsessed with the magic Meeks employed and he begged after it as would a hungry man for food. Meeks used the magic to win the boy over and then finally to subvert him altogether."

"Delightful," Ben observed. "So what has this got to do with the bottle, Questor?"

"Well." Questor had assumed his best professorial look. "One of the toys that Meeks gave to Michel to use was the bottle. Michel was allowed to summon the Darkling and order him about. The demon was extremely dangerous, you understand, but not if one appreciated his uses. My half-brother understood enough to keep the creature under control, and Michel's play presented no real threat to him. Michel used the Darkling in quite frightful ways—often in terrible games with animals. It was during one of these uses that Abernathy lost patience with the boy and thrashed him, and I was then forced to change my good friend from a man to a dog in order that he not be harmed.

"It was shortly after that the old King saw what was happening to the boy and ordered all tutoring to stop. Meeks was forbidden to engage in magic thereafter when the boy was about. All the boy's magic things were ordered destroyed—the bottle, in particular."

"But that didn't happen, obviously," Ben interjected.

Questor shook his head. "The old King was weak, but he was still protected by the Paladin. Meeks was not about to challenge him. My half-brother was content to wait for the old man to die. He was already planning his future with the boy, already planning to abandon Landover for other worlds. Time would eventually give him everything, he believed. On the other hand, he was not about to give up the bottle—certainly not about to let it be destroyed. But he couldn't simply hide it; the old King might learn of his deception. And even if he did, he couldn't convey the magic out of Landover when he left, in any case; the natural law of things would not permit it. What was he to do, then?"

Questor paused as if expecting an answer. When he failed to get one, he bent forward conspiratorially and whispered, "What he did was to order the Darkling to convey himself *and* his bottle out of Landover to a place where both would remain hidden until my half-brother came for them once more. Very ingenious."

Ben frowned impatiently. "Questor, what does all this have to do with the price of apples and oranges?" Questor looked befuddled. "What about the bottle?" Ben snapped.

Questor grimaced and held up his hands imploringly. "My half-brother promised it to the boy. That bottle was the boy's favorite possession. My half-brother assured Michel that his bottle would not be destroyed. He said they would recover it later, after the death of the old King, after they had taken up residence in another land and begun selling kingships to Landover. It was to be their secret." He shrugged. "I would have informed the old King, of course, had I known. But I did not learn of all this until later when the old King was gone. That was when Meeks first chose to tell me about it."

"He *told* you about it?" Ben was appalled.

Questor looked mortified. "Yes, High Lord. There was no reason not to. There was nothing I could do about the matter. My half-brother was quite proud of himself, and his pride insisted that he share his satisfaction in his accomplishments with someone. I was always his first choice when it came time to bestow such honors."

Ben was thinking. Questor glanced at him nervously. "I regret that it took me until now to remember all this, High Lord. I realize I should have remembered sooner. But it has been over twenty years, and the bottle simply didn't recall itself to my memory until . . ."

"Wait a minute!" Ben cut him short. "What *about* the bottle? What happened to it?"

"What happened to it?" Questor repeated.

"Yes. That was the question. What happened to it?"

Questor looked as if he wanted to disappear into himself. "My half-brother retrieved it and gave it back to Michel."

"Gave it back . . ." Ben stopped, horrified.

"Well, there was no reason not to give it back, you see," Questor tried to explain. "My half-brother had made the boy a promise, you remember. There was little danger in keeping it. They were in a new world, and the magic of the bottle was considerably diminished by the fact that not much of anyone in that world believed in or practiced magic. It was relatively harmless there, and . . ."

"Wait a minute!" Ben interrupted. "We're talking about *my* world!"

"Your old world, yes . . ."

"My world! The bottle was in my world! You said . . . ! That means . . . !" Ben was beside himself. He took a quick breath. "Your errant magic worked an exchange, didn't it? That was what you said, wasn't it? And if the magic brought the bottle *here,* it must have sent Abernathy *there*! What in the hell have you done, Questor? You've sent Abernathy to my world! Worse, you've sent him to this nut Michel, haven't you?"

Questor nodded dismally.

"Along with my medallion, damnit, so that now I can't even get back into my world to help him!"

Questor cringed. "Yes, High Lord."

Ben sat back without a word, glanced at Willow, then glanced at the kobolds. No one said anything. The room was still, the sounds of the night distant whispers. Ben wondered why these things always seemed to happen to him.

"We have to get the bottle back," he said finally. He looked at Questor. "And when we do, you had better find a way to exchange it back again for Abernathy!"

The wizard's face screwed into a knot. "I will do my best, High Lord."

Ben shook his head hopelessly. "Whatever." He stood up. "Well, we can't do much until sunrise. It's too dark out there to try to track down those confounded gnomes now. Even Bunion would have trouble. Hardly any light at all—clouded over, no moon. Damn the luck!" He strode to the windows and back again. "At least Fillip and Sot don't know what they've taken. They think of the bottle as a pretty possession. Maybe they won't open it before we find them. Maybe they'll just sit there and look at it."

"Perhaps." Questor looked doubtful.

"But perhaps not?" Ben finished.

"There is a problem."

"Another problem, Questor?"

"Yes, High Lord, I am afraid so." The wizard swallowed. "The Darkling is a very unpredictable creature."

"Meaning?"

"Sometimes it comes out of the bottle on its own."

Not a dozen miles from where Ben Holiday was staring in horror at Questor Thews, Fillip and Sot lay huddled together in the concealing blackness of the night. They had scooped out an abandoned badger den and backed their way in, two chubby, furry bodies disappearing inch by inch into the earth until nothing remained but pointed snouts and glittering eyes. They crouched within their makeshift warren, listening to the sounds that rose about them, as still as the leaves hanging limp from the surrounding trees in the windless, peaceful air.

"Shall we take it out one more time?" asked Sot finally.

"I think we should keep it hidden," replied Fillip.

"But we need only take it out for a moment," argued Sot.

"That might be one moment too long," insisted Fillip.

"But there is no light," persisted Sot.

"Some need no light," declared Fillip.

Then they were quiet again, eyes blinking, noses sniffing. Somewhere distant, a bird cried out sharply.

"Do you think the High Lord will miss it?" asked Sot.

"He said he wished he had never seen it," answered Fillip. "He said he wished it would disappear."

"But he still might miss it," said Sot.

"He has many other bottles and vases and pretty things," said Fillip.

"I think we should take it out one more time."

"I think we should leave it where it is."

"Just to look at the dancing clowns."

"Just to give someone else a chance to steal it."

Sot hunched down irritably, squirming in a way that would leave no doubt in his brother's mind as to how he felt about the matter. Fillip ignored him. Sot squirmed some more, then sighed and stared out again into the night. He was thinking of the tasty meal and the warm bed he had left behind at the castle.

"We should have stayed with the High Lord until morning," he said.

"It was necessary that we leave at once with the bottle," replied Fillip, a tad weary now of the other's talk. His nose wrinkled. "The High Lord was disturbed by the presence of the bottle. It gave him great pain even to look upon it. It reminded him of the dog. The dog was his friend—although I admit I will never understand how anyone can be friends with a dog. Dogs are good to eat, but have no other purpose."

"We should have told him we were taking the bottle," argued Sot.

"That would only have caused him more pain," rebutted Fillip.

"He will be angry with us."

"He will be pleased."

"I think we should look at the bottle again."

"Will you stop . . . ?"

"Just to be certain that it is still all right."

". . . asking that same . . . ?"

"Just to be sure."

Fillip sighed a deep, wheezy sigh that sent dust flying from their burrow entrance. Sot sneezed. Fillip glanced at him and blinked. Sot blinked back.

"Perhaps just for a very, very brief moment," said Fillip finally.

"Yes, just for a moment," agreed Sot.

Their wrinkled, grimy fingers pawed at the cluster of sticks and leaves that concealed a narrow hole they had dug in the earth directly before them. When the clutter was pushed aside, they reached in together and gingerly extracted a cloth-bound bundle. Holding it close, they loosened the wrappings and pulled out the bottle.

Carefully, they set it on the ground in front of their noses, its painted white surface gleaming faintly, its red harlequins at their dance. Two pairs of gnome eyes glittered with excitement.

"Such a pretty thing," whispered Fillip.

"Such a beautiful treasure," echoed Sot.

They stared at it some more. The allotted moment stretched into several and then into many. Still they stared, transfixed.

"I wonder if there is anything inside," mused Fillip.

"I wonder," mused Sot.

Fillip reached out and shook the bottle gently. The harlequins seemed to dance faster. "It seems empty," he said.

Sot shook it as well. "It does," he agreed.

"But it is difficult to tell without looking," said Fillip.

"Yes, difficult," said Sot.

"We might be mistaken," said Fillip.

"We might," said Sot.

They sniffed it and pawed it and studied it in silence for long moments, turning it this way and that, moving it about, trying to learn something more of its contents. Finally Sot began poking at the stopper. Fillip moved the bottle quickly away.

"We agreed to open it later," he pointed out.

"Later is too long," countered Sot.

"We agreed to open it when we were safely home."

"Home is too far away. Besides, we are quite safe right here."

"We agreed."

"We could re-agree."

Fillip felt his resolve begin to slip. He was as anxious as Sot to discover what, if anything, was concealed within their precious bottle. They could open it—just for a moment—then close it again. They could look down its neck, take just a quick peek . . .

But what if whatever was within the bottle spilled out in the dark and was lost?

"No," said Fillip firmly. "We agreed. We will open the bottle when we are home again and not before."

Sot glowered at him, then sighed his defeat. "When we are home and not before," he echoed with measurable dejection.

They lay without talking for a time, staring at the bottle. They blinked their eyes weakly, trying to keep it in focus, their sight so poor that they could barely do so. G'home Gnomes relied almost entirely on their other senses to tell them what was happening about them. Their eyes were practically useless.

The bottle sat there, a vaguely luminescent oval against the dark. When the stopper wiggled experimentally in its seating, they missed it completely.

"I suppose we should put it away," said Fillip finally.

"I suppose," sighed Sot.

They reached for the bottle.

"Hsssstt!"

Fillip looked at Sot. Sot looked at Fillip. Neither had spoken.

"Hsssstt!"

It was the bottle. The hissing sound was coming from the bottle.

"Hsssstt! Set me free, masters!"

Fillip and Sot froze, ferretlike faces twisted into masks of terror. The bottle was talking!

"Masters, open the bottle! Let me come out!"

Fillip and Sot jerked their extended hands back as one and scrunched down into their burrow until nothing showed but the tips of their noses. Had they been able to get further down into the earth, they would have done so gladly.

The voice from the bottle began to whine. "Please, please, masters, let me out? I won't hurt you. I am your friend. I can show you things, masters. Set me free. I can show you wonderful things."

"What sort of wonderful things?" ventured Fillip from his refuge, a disembodied voice in the black. Sot didn't say a word.

"Things of bright magic!" the bottle said. There was a long moment of silence. "I won't hurt you," the bottle repeated.

"What are you?" asked Fillip.

"Why can you talk?" asked Sot.

"Bottles don't talk."

"Bottles *never* talk."

The bottle said, "It isn't the bottle speaking to you, masters. It is I!"

"Who's I?" asked Fillip.

"Yes, who?" echoed Sot.

There was a moment's hesitation from the bottle. "I don't have a name," was the answer.

Fillip inched out of the burrow. "Everyone has a name," he said.

Sot inched out with him. "Yes, everyone," he agreed.

"Not I," the bottle said mournfully. Then it became brighter. "But perhaps you can give me a name. Yes, a name you find fitting for me. Why don't you let me out so you can name me?"

Fillip and Sot hesitated, but their fear was already giving way to curiosity. Their marvelous treasure was not just a pretty thing; it was a talking thing as well!

"If we let you out, will you be good?" asked Fillip.

"Will you promise not to hurt us?" asked Sot.

"Hurt you? Oh, no!" The bottle was shocked. "You are the masters! I must never hurt the masters of the bottle. I must do as they bid me. I must do as I am told."

Fillip and Sot hesitated further. Then Fillip reached out his hand tentatively and touched the bottle. It felt warm. Sot did the same. They looked at each other and blinked.

"I can show you wonderful things," the bottle promised. "I can show you things of bright magic!"

Fillip looked at Sot. "Should we open the bottle?" he asked in a whisper.

Sot looked back at him. "I don't know," he replied.

"I can give you pretty things," the bottle promised. "I can give you treasures!"

That was good enough for the G'home Gnomes. Fillip and Sot reached for the bottle as one, fastened their hands about its neck, and pulled the stopper free. There was a puff of reddish smoke that glittered with bits of green light, then a popping sound, and something small, black, and hairy crawled out of the bottle. Fillip and Sot jerked their hands back at once. The thing crawling from the bottle looked like an oversized spider.

"Ahhhh!" The thing on the lip of the bottle sighed contentedly. It perched there and looked down at them. It was barely a foot tall. Red eyes blinked like those of a cat. It looked less like a spider now. It had four limbs, all seemingly the same, a rat's tail that switched and jerked, an arched back with a spine of bristling black hair, whitish hands and fingers like those of a sickly child, and a face that was thick with hair and blunted—as if it had been pushed in once and never came back again to its original shape. Pointed ears pricked up and listened to the night sounds. A mouth crooked with teeth and wrinkled skin smiled in something close to a grimace.

"Masters!" the creature soothed. The fingers of one limb picked at its body as if there were something irritating hidden in all that black hair.

"What are you?" asked Fillip in a whisper. Sot just stared.

"I am what I am!" the creature said. The grimace broadened. "A wondrous child of magic and wizardry! A being far better than those who gave me life!"

"A demon!" whispered Sot suddenly in terror.

The creature winced. "A Darkling, masters—a poor unfortunate made prisoner to this repulsive body by . . . chance. But keeper of the bottle, too, masters—keeper of all its wonders and delights!"

Fillip and Sot were barely allowing themselves to breathe. "What . . . what wonders do you keep in the bottle?" Fillip ventured finally, unable nevertheless to keep his voice from shaking.

"Ahhhh!" the Darkling breathed.

"Why . . . are they kept there?" asked Sot. "Why not in your pocket?"

"Ahhhh!" the Darkling said again.

"Why do you live in the bottle?" asked Fillip.

"Yes, why?" echoed Sot.

The spiderlike body arched and turned on the lip of the bottle like some feeding insect. "Because . . . I am bound!" The Darkling's voice was an excited hiss. "Because it is my need! Would you like it to be yours, too, perhaps? Would you like to feel its touch? Little masters, would you dare? Would you dare to see how it shapes and molds and reworks life?"

Fillip and Sot were inching further back down into their burrow with every word, trying to make themselves disappear altogether. They were wishing they had kept the bottle closed as they had agreed they would. They were wishing they had never opened it up.

"Ohhhhh! Are you frightened?" the Darkling asked suddenly, whining the words, teasing with them. "Are you frightened of me? Oh, no, you mustn't be frightened. You are the masters; I am but your servant. Command me, masters! Ask for something and let me show you what I can do!"

Fillip and Sot just stared at him wordlessly.

"A word, masters!" the Darkling pleaded. "Command me!"

Fillip swallowed the dryness in his throat. "Show us something pretty," he ventured tentatively.

"Something bright," added Sot.

"But that is such a simple task!" the Darkling pouted. "Ah, well. Something pretty, masters, something bright. Here, then!"

It rose from a half-crouch and seemed to swell slightly in size. Fingers flicked this way and that, and tiny bits of green light sparked. All about it flying insects caught fire, turning into brilliant bits of rainbow color. The insects darted madly as the flames consumed them, tiny trailers of brightness as they swept past the astonished gnomes to form intricate patterns against the night.

"Ohhhh!" breathed Fillip and Sot as one, transfixed by the kaleidoscope of color, only vaguely disturbed after the first insect or two by a sense of repulsion.

The Darkling smiled a crooked smile and laughed gleefully. "Here, masters! More colors for you!"

Skeletal white fingers flicked the night air once more, and the bits of green light flew higher this time, exploding with showers of brightness that flared and rainbowed out. A night bird had been set aflame, its cry quick and final as it perished. Others joined it, flaming rainbows of wondrous, terrible color in the dark, stars falling from the heavens. The gnomes watched, their delight growing strangely more demanding as the birds died, their sense of what was being lost gradually becoming submerged in some distant, darkened place within them.

When the birds had been consumed as well, the Darkling turned back to Fillip and Sot. Its eyes glittered a smoky red. That same light was reflected now—just a touch—in the eyes of the gnomes.

"You can see many such things, masters," the Darkling whispered, its voice a low hiss of promise. "The magic of the bottle can give you all you wish—all the delights and wonders of your imagination and beyond! Do you wish these, masters? Do you wish to enjoy them?"

"Yes!" breathed Fillip rapturously.

"Yes!" sighed Sot.

The Darkling hunched over, black hair bristling out, a thing of perverse shape and fawning gestures. "Such good masters," it whispered. "Why don't you touch me?"

Fillip and Sot nodded obediently. Already they were reaching out their hands.

The Darkling's eyes closed in satisfaction.

SPELLBOUND

Ben Holiday slept poorly that night, troubled by dreams of the bottle and the demon that lived within it. He dreamed that the demon came out of the bottle on its own—just as Questor had warned it might—a huge, gargoyle monster that could swallow men whole. It did that with Fillip and Sot, did it with half a dozen others, and was in close pursuit of Ben when he mercifully came awake.

The day was gray and rainy, not an auspicious omen. They had delayed their search for the missing G'home Gnomes until morning to assure favorable tracking conditions and had merely ended up swapping darkness for rain. Ben glanced out the windows as he dressed, watching the rain fall in sheets. The ground was puddled and glistening; it must have been raining for some time. Ben sighed heavily. It would be difficult finding any trail at all in this weather.

Nevertheless, Bunion, whose job it was to track the gnomes, seemed unperturbed by the situation. Ben came downstairs to the dining hall to have breakfast with the others before leaving and found the kobold engaged in earnest conversation with Questor Thews on just that subject. Ben was able to follow most of the conversation, having spent enough time with the kobold to pick up a good deal of his difficult, guttural language, and Bunion was indicating that despite the rain he felt he would have no difficulty. Ben nodded in satisfaction and ate more of the breakfast than he thought he would.

When the meal was finished, he adjourned with Questor and Bunion to the front court. Willow was already there, supervising the selection of the horses they would ride and overseeing the loading of the pack animals. Ben was always surprised at how organized the sylph was, taking on duties that weren't necessarily hers, wanting to make certain of the thoroughness of the work. She smiled and kissed him, the rain trailing off her hooded cloak onto her nose and mouth. Ben hadn't particularly wanted her to accompany him, always worried for her safety, but she had insisted. Now he was glad she was doing so. He kissed her back and gave her a reassuring hug.

They ferried the animals across to the mainland, and by midmorning they were under way. Ben rode Jurisdiction, his favorite mount, a bay gelding, Questor sat atop an elderly gray with one white sock, and Willow had chosen a blue roan. The kobolds, as usual, walked, having little use for horses and vice versa. Ben liked to joke that wherever he went on horseback, he always had Jurisdiction. He said it again this morning, but it sounded flat. Everyone was bundled up in their rain gear, heads lowered against the wet and the wind, bodies hunched up against the morning chill, and they were not particularly interested in jokes. They were mostly interested in trying to ignore their discomfort.

Bunion went quickly on ahead, leaving the others to follow at a slower pace. There wasn't much question in Ben's mind where the G'home Gnomes would go; they were fairly predictable creatures. With a treasure of the sort that they believed the bottle to be, they would head directly for the safety of their burrow home. That meant they would travel north out of the forestlands of Sterling Silver through the western borders of the Greensward and finally to the hill country beyond to their gnome community. They would not travel fast; they were slow creatures under the best of circumstances and they were preoccupied with the bottle. Ben was half-convinced that the little guys really didn't view what they were doing as theft in any event and would not be concerned with anyone following. That meant they would not be running, and Bunion might find them—rain or no rain—before the day was out.

So they meandered north, picking their way through the raindrops and puddles, waiting patiently for Bunion to return with the news that he had found them. Bunion would find them, of course. Nothing could escape a kobold once he made up his mind to track it. The kobolds were fairy creatures who could move from place to place almost swifter than the eye could follow. Bunion would catch up to the gnomes in nothing flat once he came across their trail, and Bunion had seemed certain he would do so quickly. Ben hoped so. He was worried about this demon.

A Darkling, Questor had called it. Ben tried to envision it as he rode and failed to find a satisfactory image. Questor had not seen the creature for better than twenty years, and his memory as usual was a bit hazy. Sometimes it was little and sometimes it was big, Questor had said. Ben shook his head, remembering the wizard's confusion. Big help. What mattered most, in any case, was the magic the Darkling wielded—magic that was always bad news for whoever came up against it. But maybe Fillip and Sot had not yet opened the bottle and let the Darkling free. Maybe they could manage to stifle their curiosity long enough for him to catch them before they gave in to it.

He sighed, shifting uncomfortably atop Jurisdiction as the rain blew into his face on a sudden gust of wind. Maybe the sun would come out if he clapped his hands, too.

"I think it might be clearing a bit, High Lord," Questor called out suddenly from just behind him.

Ben nodded wordlessly, never believing it for a moment. It was probably going to rain like this for forty days and forty nights, and they ought to be out building an ark instead of chasing around the countryside after those pin-headed gnomes. It had been almost a full day now since Abernathy had disappeared into the light with his medallion, and he was beginning to despair. How was Abernathy going to take care of himself in Ben's world? Even if he did somehow manage to elude Michel Ard Rhi, where could he go? He didn't know anyone. He didn't know the first thing about the geography of Ben's world. And the minute he opened his mouth to ask someone . . .

Ben quickly blocked the rest of that scenario from his mind. There was no point in dwelling on Abernathy or the medallion. He had to concentrate his energy on getting the bottle back from Fillip and Sot. Even without the services of the Paladin, he felt confident he could do that. Bunion and Parsnip were more than a match for the gnomes, Darkling or no, and Questor Thews ought to be able to use his own magic to counteract that of the demon if it should become necessary to do so. If they were quick enough, they would get the bottle back again before Fillip and Sot even knew what had happened.

Still, it would have been nice to be able to rely on the Paladin, he thought—as frightening as his alter ego was to him. Ben could still remember the times he had been transformed into the knight-errant—armor closing him about, straps and buckles clinking into place, the smell of fighting and the memories of battle filling his senses. It was both terrifying and exhilarating, and he was repelled and drawn to it at the same time. He breathed the wet, cold air and pictured it again in his mind. Sometimes, when he let himself consider the possibility, he was afraid that, with enough exposure, the experience of becoming the Paladin could become an addiction . . .

He shrugged the thought away. Such thoughts didn't matter just now. Without the medallion, there could be no transformation. Without the medallion, the Paladin was just a dream.

Morning stretched into midday, and they paused long enough to consume a cold lunch within the shelter of a stand of crimson maple. There was still no sign of Bunion. No one spoke of the matter, but all were concerned. Time was quickly slipping away. They rode out again after a short rest, edging now into the Greensward. Long, grassy stretches of flatland spread away before them east and north. The rain had begun to diminish, fulfilling Questor's expectations, and the air warmed slightly. Daylight was gray and hazy through a vast blanket of gauzy, rumpled clouds.

A short time later, Bunion appeared. He appeared not from the north as expected, but from directly west. He came up to them so swiftly that he was almost on top of them before they saw him, his wiry body skittering and dancing through the damp. His eyes were bright, and he was grinning like a delighted child, all his sharp teeth in evidence. He had found Fillip and Sot. The G'home Gnomes were not on their way north after all. As a matter of fact, they did not appear to be on their way to much of anywhere. They were scarcely two miles distant, engrossed in watching raindrops fall from trees and turn into brightly colored gemstones.

"What?" Ben exclaimed in disbelief, certain he had heard wrong.

Questor hastily said something to Bunion, listened to the kobold's reply, and turned back to Ben. "They have opened the bottle, High Lord. They have set the Darkling free."

"And the Darkling is turning raindrops into gems?"

"Yes, High Lord." Questor looked decidedly uneasy. "Apparently it amuses the gnomes."

"I'll bet it does, those little ferret-faced bozos!" Ben scowled. Why wasn't anything ever easy? "Well, so much for getting the bottle back unopened. Now what, Questor? Will the Darkling try to stop us from putting it back in the bottle?"

Questor shook his head doubtfully. "That depends on Fillip and Sot, High Lord. Whoever holds the bottle controls the demon."

"So the real question is, will Fillip and Sot refuse to give the bottle back to us?"

"The magic is a powerful lure, High Lord."

Ben nodded. "Then we need a plan."

The plan he came up with was fairly simple. They would ride over to a place just out of sight of the gnomes. Parsnip would remain with the horses while the others went forward afoot. Ben, Questor, and Willow would approach from the front, openly. Bunion would sneak around behind. If Ben was unable to persuade the gnomes to return the bottle willingly, Bunion would snatch it away before they could do anything to stop him.

"Remember, Bunion, if you see me rub my chin with my hand, that's your signal," Ben finished. "You get in there as fast as you can and you get that bottle!"

The kobold grinned wolfishly.

They turned west, Bunion showing the way, Parsnip trailing with the pack animals, and rode the short distance to where the G'home Gnomes were at play with their treasure. They pulled into a stand of fir behind a low ridge while still hidden from view, dismounted, gave the horses over to Parsnip, sent Bunion on ahead to get into place, and began walking up the ridge. When they reached its crest, they stopped short.

Fillip and Sot sat beneath a massive old willow, legs tucked up underneath, hands outstretched, laughing gleefully. The old willow's boughs were heavy with rain, and as the droplets slipped free they became sparkling gemstones. The gnomes tried to catch those that fell close, but most tumbled earthward out of reach and collected in shimmering piles. There were gemstones everywhere, heaps of them, flashing rainbow colors through the afternoon gray and damp, a seeming mirage come to life.

The bottle sat upon the ground between the G'home Gnomes, forgotten. An ugly, spiderlike creature danced upon the bottle's rim where the stopper had been pulled and flicked bits of green fire at the raindrops. Each bit of fire changed another droplet into a gemstone.

It was the weirdest scene Ben Holiday had ever witnessed. Fillip and Sot looked as if they had gone nuts.

"All right! That's enough!" he yelled sharply.

The G'home Gnomes froze, shrinking down against the earth like wilted flowers. The Darkling crouched catlike on the lip of the bottle, eyes glittering. Ben waited a moment to be certain that he had their attention, then started down the slope of the ridge, Questor and Willow in tow. When he reached the outer curtain of the willow's broad canopy—not more than a dozen yards from the gnomes—he stopped.

"What do you think you're doing, guys?" he asked quietly.

Fillip and Sot looked terrified. "Leave us alone!" they cried. "Let us be!" The words all jumbled together as they spoke them, and Ben couldn't tell who was saying what.

"There is a small problem that needs solving first," he said evenly. "You have something that belongs to me."

"No, no," whined Fillip.

"Nothing," whined Sot.

"How about the bottle?" he asked.

The moment he said the word "bottle" the gnomes had their hands on it, snatching it back away from him. The Darkling stayed perched on the open lip, clinging to the glass as if it had suction cups on its fingers. Ben had a clear view of the creature now; it was an ugly little thing. The red eyes glittered hatefully, and Ben looked quickly away.

"Fillip. Sot." He tried to keep his voice calm. "You have to give the bottle back. It doesn't belong to you. You took it without permission."

"You said you wished you had never seen it!" insisted Fillip.

"You said you wished it would disappear!" added Sot.

"You put it away!"

"You didn't want it!"

"Great High Lord!"

"Mighty High Lord!"

Ben held up his hands quickly to silence them. "You have to give it back, fellas. That's all there is to it. Close it up and hand it over—right now."

The gnomes pulled the bottle closer still. Their eyes narrowed, and something of the look he had seen in the Darkling's eyes reflected suddenly in their own. Fillip's muzzle was drawing back to show teeth. Sot was stroking the demon's arched spine.

"The bottle belongs to us!" snapped Fillip.

"The bottle is ours!" grated Sot.

The terror was still evident in their eyes, but Ben had mistaken completely its source. He had thought them frightened of him; in truth, they were frightened, not of him, but of losing the bottle.

"Nuts!" he muttered and looked at Questor.

The wizard stepped forward. His scarecrow form straightened. "Fillip and Sot, you are hereby charged with theft of royal property and flight to avoid return of same!" He cleared his throat officiously. "Return the property now—the bottle, that is—and all charges will be dropped. Otherwise, you will be arrested and placed in the castle dungeons." He paused hopefully. "You don't want that, do you?"

The G'home Gnomes cringed. Then suddenly they leaned down to the bottle as the Darkling whispered something up to them. When they looked back again, the defiance was evident.

"You lie to us!" declared Fillip.

"You wish to hurt us!" declared Sot.

"You want the bottle for yourselves!"

"You want its treasures for your own use!"

"You try to trick us!"

"You play hateful games!"

They were on their feet now, holding the bottle between them, backing slowly toward the base of the tree. Ben was appalled. He had never seen the gnomes like this; they were actually ready to fight!

"What's happening here?" he whispered urgently.

"It is the demon, High Lord!" Questor whispered back. "It poisons everyone it touches!"

Ben was already regretting that he had even bothered trying to talk the gnomes out of the bottle. It would have been smarter just to send Bunion in to steal the damn thing and be done with it.

Willow appeared suddenly at his other side. "Fillip!" she called out. "Sot! Please, do not do this to the High Lord! Remember how he came to you when no one else would? Remember how he helped you?" Her voice softened. "He has always helped you when you needed it; you owe him much. Return the bottle to him. He needs the bottle to help find Abernathy and bring him safely back. Do not obstruct him like this. Listen to what is inside of you. Give him back the bottle."

For just a moment, Ben thought they would. They seemed to respond better to Willow; they looked sheepish and guilty. They started forward a step or two, tenuous shufflings, muttering something unintelligible, appearing themselves once more. Then the Darkling darted from the bottle onto first Fillip's shoulder and then Sot's, hissing wickedly, then dropped back again, dancing as if maddened. Fillip and Sot stopped abruptly and began retreating once more. The look of fear and defiance returned.

That was enough for Ben. It was time to call on Bunion. He brought his hand up to his chin and rubbed it as if thinking matters over.

Bunion shot out of nowhere, a blur of darkness against the gray haze of the rain. Fillip and Sot never saw him. He was on them before they realized what was happening. But, by then, the attempt to regain possession of the bottle had already failed. One instant Bunion seemed to have his hands on the bottle; in the next he was flung back, thrown by an invisible force. Incredibly, the Darkling had taken matters into its own hands. The demon hissed, spit like a cat, and threw a massive bolt of green fire at the kobold. Bunion was picked up again and hurtled backward through the air to disappear completely from view.

Ben was already rushing forward, but he was not nearly quick enough. The G'home Gnomes screamed in warning, and the Darkling was quick to respond. It whirled on Ben, fingers flicking at the air. Raindrops turned to knives and whistled toward the High Lord in a lethal barrage. Ben had no chance to dodge them.

Fortunately, he didn't have to. For once, Questor Thews got the magic to work right the first time, and the knives were turned aside at the last possible moment. Ben blinked, shied away out of reflex, came around again when he realized he wasn't a pincushion after all, and yelled for Questor and Willow to run. Already the Darkling was lashing out again, this time with a bewildering array of rocks and loose stone, thrown from the earth as if scooped by some giant's hand. Questor's shield held firm, however, and the three friends backed quickly away, crouching down against the strange assault as it hammered toward them.

Then the stones were obscured in a gust of hailstones and winter sleet that suddenly took shape out of the falling rain and came at them with frightening purpose. Questor cried out sharply, threw out his hands, and a flash of blinding light obscured everything. But the protective shield was beginning to give and the hailstones to break through. They struck with stinging, painful blows, and Ben staggered back, trying to protect Willow as they edged toward the summit of the ridge.

"Get down, High Lord!" he heard Questor yell frantically.

Pulling Willow close, he stumbled over the summit and down the far slope. Questor's shield gave way completely. Hail and sleet were all about, a blinding flurry of white, striking at them. Ben fell to the ground and rolled, Willow going down with him, tumbling wildly through scrub and bare earth.

Then, miraculously, the sleet and hail were gone. Rain fell softly once more, the day gray and empty and still. Ben let his eyes slip open, met Willow's as they lifted to find him, then caught a glimpse of Questor over her shoulder as he struggled up woodenly and brushed himself off.

There was no sign of the gnomes or the demon.

Ben was shaking. He was frightened and angry and grateful to be alive. The Darkling had very nearly killed them. He reached over impulsively and hugged Willow close.

They found Bunion snarled in some brush several hundred yards off, bruised and battered, but conscious. He should have been dead, considering the beating he had taken, but kobolds were very tough creatures. Willow worked over him carefully for a time, using the healing powers common to the once-upon-a-time fairy people of the lake country, touching him gently, taking away the worst of the hurt. After less than half an hour, Bunion was back on his feet, stiff and sore, but grinning wickedly. The kobold hissed a few words of unmistakable meaning at Questor. He wanted another crack at the demon.

But the Darkling had disappeared along with the bottle and Fillip and Sot, and there was no trace of where they might have gone. Ben and company searched for a time, scouring the surrounding countryside for a trail. They found nothing. Apparently the demon had used his magic to conceal their tracks.

"Or maybe they simply flew out of here, High Lord," Questor advised solemnly. "The Darkling has such power."

"Are there any limits to what this thing can do?" Ben asked.

"The only limits imposed on it are those imposed by the character of the holder of the bottle. The worse the character, the stronger the demon." Questor sighed. "Fillip and Sot are not really bad creatures. The strength the Darkling can draw from them should exhaust itself quickly."

"I feel sorry for them, Ben," Willow said quietly. "For Fillip and Sot."

He looked at her in surprise, then nodded wearily. "I suppose I do, too. I don't imagine they even know what's happened to them." He turned. "Parsnip, bring the horses!"

The kobold hurried away. Ben glanced skyward momentarily, thinking. The rain was ending, the day edging quickly toward dusk. There wasn't enough time left to accomplish much of anything before nightfall.

"What do we do now, High Lord?" Questor asked him. The others crowded close.

Ben's jaw tightened. "I'll tell you what we do, Questor. We wait until morning. Then we go after Fillip and Sot. We hunt for them until we find them, and when we find them we get the bottle back and shut the Darkling away once and for all!"

He glanced over at a grinning Bunion. "And next time we'll be ready for the little monster!"

MICHEL ARD RHI

Abernathy spent his first full day in Ben's world shut away in Elizabeth's room, discovering how much trouble he was really in. Elizabeth had considered the possibility of staying home sick from school in order to be with him, but had discarded the idea when she realized being sick would bring the housekeeper on a determined crusade of mercy and Abernathy would likely be discovered in the process. Besides, she hadn't come up with a plan to sneak him out of Graum Wythe yet, so she needed the day to think the matter over.

So off she went to school while Abernathy stayed hidden in her room, reading old magazines and newspapers. He asked her for the reading material, and she brought it to him from her father's study before she left. Abernathy was Court Historian as well as Court Scribe in Landover and he knew something of the histories of other worlds as well as his own. He had made it a point to study the history of Ben's world when Meeks moved over there and began recruiting men willing to pay for Landover's throne. It had been pretty frightening stuff. Most of what Abernathy remembered had to do with machines and sciences and any number of wars. Since he was wearing the medallion, he could read and speak the language of any world he was in, so learning what Ben's world was like wouldn't be difficult. But it would be necessary if he was to find a way back to his own.

So he picked through the stack of magazines and newspapers, propped up on Elizabeth's bed amid stuffed animals and dolls, a scattering of pillows at his back, and tried to figure out how things worked. Most of his reading was superfluous. There were an abnormally large number of stories about wars and killing, most the result of politics and economics, many having no rational purpose. There were a number of stories having to do with investigations of one sort or another as well. Abernathy read a few and gave up, concluding that he was trapped in a world full of crooks and thieves. Some of the magazines offered stories of romance and adventure, but Abernathy skipped those. He read more closely the advertisements—that's what they were called, he discovered—and learned most of what was useful from them.

The advertisements told him what was for sale in the way of goods and services, and that let him discover several things. It let him discover that no one traveled by horse or carriage; everyone rode or even flew in machines developed by the world's sciences. It let him discover that in order to use these machines, he had to pay for the privilege with money or something called credit, and he, of course, had neither. Finally, it let him discover—forgetting for the moment the fact that he was a talking dog—that no one dressed anything like the way he did, talked anything like the way he did, or shared much of anything else in the way of a common social, economic, or cultural background. Once beyond the walls of Graum Wythe, he would stand out from everyone else as clearly as day from night.

One of the magazines included a map of the United States, which he quickly realized was Ben's country. He found the state of Washington, where he was, and the state of Virginia, where he had to go. The topography of the country between was clearly delineated on the map. A legend advised him of the distance he would have to travel. Elizabeth had been right—it was a long, *long* way from here to there. He might walk it, but it looked as if the walk could take him forever.

After a time, he put down the newspapers and the magazines, got off the bed, walked over to the twin latticework windows that opened to the south, and looked out. The countryside immediately surrounding the castle was planted with vineyards. There were a few small patches of open space, a tiny stream that meandered about, and several distant houses that dotted the landscape, but not much of anything else. The houses intrigued Abernathy. He had seen pictures of such houses in the magazines, and neither those nor these were anything at all like the houses in Landover. Graum Wythe seemed sorely out of place amid such structures, as if it had been picked up and plunked down without thought to whether it belonged or not. Abernathy assumed it was here solely because it was the prideful re-creation of Michel Ard Rhi's imaginary fortress from his childhood—the place he had occupied in his mind most of his life. There was a moat about it, guardhouses at either end of the drawbridge leading over, a low stone wall farther out with wire and sharp barbs atop it, and a gate. Abernathy shook his head. Michel hadn't changed.

Elizabeth had prepared a sandwich and something called potato chips for Abernathy's lunch, and he ate them at midday before settling back down to read further from the magazines and newspapers. He hadn't been at it for more than a few minutes when he heard footsteps come up to the bedroom door, saw the door handle turn, and watched in horror as it swung open.

There wasn't time to hide. There wasn't time to do anything but drop down amid the newspapers and magazines and play dead. So that was what Abernathy did.

A woman came into the room carrying an armful of what appeared to be cleaning supplies. Abernathy could see this through slitted eyes. She was humming to herself, unaware yet that there was anyone else in the room. Abernathy had curled himself into a ball, trying hard to blend in with the stuffed animals. Was this the dreaded housekeeper Elizabeth had thought to avoid by going on to school instead of playing sick? Why hadn't Elizabeth warned him that she might come into the room to clean anyway? He tried hard not to breathe. Maybe she wouldn't notice him. Maybe she would leave if he just . . .

She turned around and looked right at him. She stiffened in surprise and put her hands on her hips. "Well, what's this? What are you doing here? There's not supposed to be any dogs in here! That Elizabeth!"

She smiled then and laughed—a private joke of some sort, Abernathy decided. There was nothing for him to do now but to play along. He lay there and thumped his stubby tail as best he could, trying to appear like a normal dog.

"Well, well, well! You are a cute thing! All dressed up like a little doll!" The cleaning lady came right up to him, reached down, and gave him a suffocating hug. She was rather stout to begin with, and Abernathy felt the breath leave his body in a rush. "Now what am I supposed to do with you?" she went on, stepping back, giving him an appraising look. "I'll bet no one else knows you're here, do they?"

Abernathy kept thumping his tail, trying to appear cute.

"You've sure made a mess of this room—look at these magazines and newspapers!" The woman bustled about, picking up, straightening up. "Did you eat this sandwich, too? Where'd you get that? I tell you, that Elizabeth!" She laughed some more.

Abernathy lay patiently waiting as she finished moving about, then looked up expectantly as she came back to give him a pat on the head. "None of my business," she muttered and patted him some more. "Tell you what," she said conspiratorially. "You stay right here, don't move. I'll clean the room like I'm supposed to and be on my way. It's not up to me to worry about you. I'll leave you to Elizabeth. Okay?"

Abernathy thumped his tail some more, wishing it were longer. The cleaning lady put a cord in the wall and ran a rather noisy machine about the floor and rugs for a time, ran a cloth over the furniture, picked and straightened up some more, and was done.

She came back over. "Now you be good," she admonished, ruffling his ears. "Don't let anyone know you're here. I'll keep your secret if you will, okay? Now give me a kiss. Right here." She bent down, offering her cheek. "C'mon, just a little kiss."

Abernathy licked her dutifully on the cheek.

"Good dog!" She patted him on the head and rubbed his muzzle. Then she picked up her cleaning gear and headed out the door. "'Bye, old boy," she called back.

The door closed softly and the footsteps moved away.

Abernathy wished he had something to wash out his mouth.

Elizabeth returned around mid-afternoon, unremittingly cheerful. "Hi, Abernathy!" she greeted, pushing through the door and closing it tightly behind her. "How was your day?"

"It would have been better," Abernathy replied archly, "if you had thought to warn me that the housekeeper might clean!"

"Oh, that's right, it's Monday!" Elizabeth groaned and dropped her books on the writing desk with a thud. "Sorry about that. Did she see you?"

"She did. But she thought I was a pet and said I was your responsibility and not hers. I don't think she plans to tell anyone."

Elizabeth nodded solemnly. "Mrs. Allen is my friend. When she gives her word, she keeps it. Not like some I know." She frowned menacingly. "Nita Coles used to be my friend, but she isn't anymore. Know why? Because she told everyone I like Tommy Samuelson. I don't know why she did that. He isn't even my boyfriend or anything, I just said I sort of liked him. He is cute. Anyway, she told Donna Helms, and Donna tells everyone everything, so the first thing you know, the whole school is talking about me and Tommy Samuelson, and I am embarrassed beyond tears! I bet even Mr. Mack, my teacher, knows! I told Eva Richards, my other friend, that if Nita doesn't take it all back and right now, I won't . . ."

"Elizabeth!" Abernathy cut her short with something very much like a bark. "Elizabeth," he said her name again, this time more gently. She stared at him. "Have you come up with a way to get me out of here?"

"Sure." She said it matter-of-factly, as if there had never been any question about it. She dropped herself down on the bed next to him. "A real good way, Abernathy."

"How, Elizabeth?"

She grinned. "We'll send you out with the laundry!" The look on Abernathy's face sent the grin scurrying for cover. "Look, it's simple, really. A truck from the cleaners picks up the laundry every Tuesday. That's tomorrow. Several big canvas hampers go out, full of sheets and stuff. You can hide in one. The guards never check the laundry. You ride out in the back of the truck and when it stops to unload, out you jump. By then, you'll be miles away." She grinned again. "What do you think?"

Abernathy thought. "I think it might work. But what about when they load me in the truck? Won't they think the laundry is a bit heavy?"

Elizabeth shook her head firmly. "No way. The towels and stuff go out wet all the time. They weigh a ton. I've heard Mr. Abbott say so. He's the driver. He won't think anything about it when he puts you in the truck. He'll just think you're a load of wet towels or something."

"I see." Abernathy was undecided.

"Believe me, it'll work," Elizabeth assured him. "All you have to do is sneak down to the laundry early in the morning. I'll go with you. If we go early enough, we won't run into anyone. I can set my alarm. On the clock," she added, pointing.

Abernathy looked at the time-telling device doubtfully, then back at the little girl. He sighed. "Can you give me a good map of the country to take with me, Elizabeth—something that will help me find my way to Virginia?"

Elizabeth immediately shook her head no. "I have an idea about that, too, Abernathy. You can't go trekking across the country on foot all the way to Virginia. It's just too far. There are mountains between here and there, and it's almost winter. You might freeze!"

She reached over and put her hand on his head. "I've got some money saved. I want to give it to you. I'll have to make up something for Dad, but I can do it. I'll give you the money, and here's what you do. You wrap yourself all up in bandages so no one can see what you look like. They'll think you're all burned or something. Then you go to the airport and buy a standby ticket to Virginia. They're real cheap—I'll show you how to do it. You can fly back in a couple of hours. You'll still have to walk a bit when you get there, but not nearly so far as from here—maybe a hundred miles or so. And it will still be warm there; you won't freeze."

Abernathy didn't know what to say. He just stared at her for a moment. "Elizabeth, I cannot take your money . . ."

"Shhhh, shhhh!" She cut him short with a hiss. "Don't say that. Of course you can. You have to. I can't sleep thinking about you out there wandering across the country. I have to know that you're all right. Really, I should go with you. But since you won't let me, you at least have to take the money." She paused. "You can pay me back later, if you want—sometime."

Abernathy was overwhelmed. "Thank you, Elizabeth," he said quietly.

Elizabeth reached over and gave him a big hug. It was a much better hug than the one he had received from Mrs. Allen.

Abernathy stayed in Elizabeth's room when she went down to eat dinner, waiting patiently for her to bring something edible back for him. He passed the time reading idly through something called *TV Guide,* which he didn't understand. He expected Elizabeth to return in short order, just as she had the previous night, but the minutes slipped by and she failed to show. He began listening at the door for her and even risked a quick look down the empty hall. No Elizabeth.

When she finally appeared, she was ghost white and visibly distressed.

"Abernathy!" she exclaimed with a hiss, closing the door quickly behind her. "You've got to get out of here immediately! Michel knows about you!"

Abernathy went cold. "How did he find out?"

Elizabeth shook her head in anguish, tears starting down her cheeks. "It was all my fault, Abernathy," she sobbed. "I told him! I had to!"

"Now, now," he soothed, kneeling down in front of her, paws coming up to rest on her shoulders reassuringly. He wanted nothing so much as to run from that room as quickly as he could, but first he needed to know what he was up against. "Just tell me what happened," he said, trying to sound calm.

Elizabeth sniffed back her tears and sobs and faced him. "The watch told Michel about you, just as I was afraid they would. They came up to us just after dinner to make their report and happened to mention it to him. They remembered it because they saw me standing there, and one of them asked if I still had the dog. He mentioned the odd clothes you were wearing and the way your paws didn't quite look like paws. He described you. Michel got this funny look on his face and started asking me questions. He asked me where I found you, and I . . . Well, I couldn't lie to him, Abernathy, I couldn't! He has this way of looking at you, kind of mean, like he can see everything . . ."

She broke into sobs again, and Abernathy quickly hugged her against him, holding her until the tears began to subside. "Go on," he urged.

"Well, I told him I found you near the art room. I didn't tell him you were in it or anything, but it didn't matter. He went right to the art room, telling me to stay where I was, and when he came back he was furious! He wanted to know what had happened to his bottle. I said I didn't know. He wanted to know what had happened to *you*! I said I didn't know that, either. I started crying, telling him I just wanted someone to play dress-up with and that when I found you, you were wandering about in these old clothes, so I just put you on a leash and took you for a walk, and . . . Then he wanted to know if you *said* anything to me! He seemed to know you could talk, Abernathy!"

Abernathy felt as if the walls were closing in on him. "Hurry up, Elizabeth," he urged. "Tell me the rest as quick as you can!"

She took a deep, steadying breath. "Well, as I told you, I couldn't lie—not completely, not to him. So I said, 'Yeah, he did!'—as if I was real surprised he knew. I said that was why I sent you away, because I was afraid of you. I just turned you loose and you ran off. I said I hadn't seen you since. I said I hadn't said anything to anyone because I was afraid they wouldn't believe me. I said I was waiting to tell my father when he came back Wednesday." She took hold of him with her hands. "He believed me, I think. He just told me to go to my room and wait there for him. He ordered the watch to start a search. But he was yelling at them like he was crazy, Abernathy! You have to get out of here!"

Abernathy nodded wearily. "How do I do that, Elizabeth?"

The little girl's hands tightened on his arms. "Just the way I said you would—except that you have to go down to the laundry room right now!"

"Elizabeth, you just said they were searching for me!"

"No, no, Abernathy—listen!" Her roundish face bent close, brow furrowed with determination. Her nose freckles seemed to dance. "They've already searched the laundry room. That's where they started. I told them that was where I let you go. So no one's there anymore. They're looking around everywhere else. The laundry room is down the hall, around the corner to the right, on the ground floor—not far. If you go out the window . . . listen to me . . . if you go out the window and down the vines, you can slip around the corner and through the window!"

"Elizabeth, I can't climb down . . ."

"The catch is off, Abernathy! I took it off over the weekend when I was playing hide-and-seek with Mrs. Allen! You can slip right through the window into one of the hampers and wait! If not, just wait in the bushes; I'll come down and open it as soon as I can! Oh, I'm so sorry, Abernathy! This is all my fault! But you have to go! You have to hurry! If they find you here, they'll know I lied, that I helped you . . ."

There was the sound of voices and footsteps in the hall beyond, rapidly approaching.

"Abernathy!" Elizabeth whispered fearfully.

Abernathy was already moving for the windows. He released the catch, pushed open the twin latticework frames, and peered down. It was dark, but he could just make out a thick tangle of trailing vines. They appeared strong enough to hold him.

He turned back to Elizabeth. "Good-bye, Elizabeth," he whispered. "Thank you for your help."

"It's the fifth window around the corner!" she whispered back. Then she put her hands to her mouth in horror. "Abernathy, I haven't given you the money for the airplane ticket!"

"Never mind that," he said, already swinging carefully out the window, testing his weight on the vines. His fingered paws gripped poorly. He would be lucky if he didn't break his neck.

"No, you have to have the money!" she insisted, practically beside herself. "I know! Meet me tomorrow at noon at the school—Franklin Elementary! I'll have it then!"

There was a knock at the door. "Elizabeth? Open the door."

Abernathy recognized the voice immediately. "Good-bye, Elizabeth!" he whispered again.

"Good-bye!" she whispered back.

The latticework windows swung silently shut above him, and he was left hanging in the dark.

It seemed to Abernathy that it took him an impossible amount of time to get down. He was terrified of being caught out there, but he was equally terrified of falling. He compromised his fears by making his way at something of a snail's pace, taking time to find each handgrip and foothold as he inched downward through the vines, pressed as close as he could get to the stone block. Lights had come on in the courtyard below, electric lamps—he had read about them—and the darkness was no longer quite so concealing. He felt like a fly waiting for the swat that would end its purposeless life.

But the swat didn't come, and he finally felt the reassuring firmness of the ground touch his feet. He crouched down instantly, eyes sweeping the yard, searching for movement. There was none. Quickly, he made his way along the wall, staying close against its dark shadow, out of the illumination of the lamps. A door opened from somewhere behind, and he heard voices. He scurried along faster, reaching the bend in the wall that would take him to the promised laundry window. It was darker here, the wall turning back into a deep, shadowed alcove. He slipped along silently, counting windows as he went. The fifth window, Elizabeth had said. One, two . . .

Behind him, a beam of light shot across the dark, sweeping the courtyard to the low outer wall and the moat and back again. A flashlight, Abernathy thought. He had read about those, too. A flashlight meant that someone was out there on foot, searching the grounds. He practically ran now, counting three, four . . . five!

He skidded to a stop, almost passing by number five without seeing it because it was partially concealed in a clump of bushes. He looked at it. It was smaller than the previous four—smaller, too, than the ones that followed. Was this the right window? Or was he not supposed to count this one? There was light inside, but there was light in the next one as well. He began to panic. He bent close and listened. Did he hear voices in there? He glanced back frantically. The flashlight was coming closer in the dark, the sound of voices back there as well.

He looked forlornly at the window. There was nothing to do but chance it, he decided. If he stayed where he was, he was certain to be found. He reached down to the window and pushed carefully inward. The window gave easily at his touch. He caught a glimpse of linens in a basket. Relief flooded through him. He knelt down quickly and started to crawl in.

Several pairs of hands reached up to help him.

"We found him sneaking in through the laundry room window," said a guard, one of three from the watch that had captured Abernathy. They held him firmly by the arms. "It was lucky we went back or we would have missed him. We'd searched there first and hadn't found a thing. But Jeff here says he thinks maybe one of the windows was left unlatched, that we ought to check it. We did, and that's when we found him, crawling in."

They stood in a study, a room filled with books and files, desks and cabinets—Abernathy and his captors and Michel Ard Rhi.

The guard speaking paused and glanced uncertainly at Abernathy. "Exactly what sort of creature is he, Mr. Ard Rhi?"

Michel Ard Rhi ignored him, the whole of his attention centered on Abernathy. He was a tall, rawboned man with a shock of black hair and a narrow, pinched face that suggested he had just eaten something sour. He looked older than he was, his brow lined, his skin sallow. He had dark, unfriendly eyes that registered immediate disapproval with everything in view. He stood ramrod straight, affecting an air of complete superiority.

"Abernathy," he whispered almost soundlessly, as if in answer to the guard's question.

He took a moment longer to study his captive, then said to the guards without bothering to look at them, "Wait outside."

The guards left, closing the study door softly behind them. Michel Ard Rhi left Abernathy standing where he was and moved over to sit behind a huge, polished oak desk littered with paperwork. "Abernathy," he said again, as if not yet convinced of it. "What are you doing here?"

Abernathy was no longer shaking. When the guards had captured him he had been so terrified that he could barely stand. Now he accepted his situation with the weary resignation of the condemned, and his acceptance gave him a small dose of renewed strength. He tried to keep his voice calm. "Questor Thews sent me here by mistake. He was trying something with the magic."

"Oh?" Michel seemed interested. "What was the old fool trying this time?"

Abernathy showed nothing. "He was trying to change me back into a man."

Michel Ard Rhi looked at him appraisingly and then laughed. "Remember how he changed you into a dog in the first place, Abernathy? Remember how he botched it? I'm surprised you let him come near you." He shook his head hopelessly. "Questor Thews never could manage to do anything right, could he?"

He made it a statement of fact, not a question. Abernathy said nothing. He was thinking of the High Lord's medallion, still concealed beneath his tunic. He was thinking that whatever else happened, Michel Ard Rhi must not be allowed to discover he wore it.

Michel seemed to know what he was thinking. "Well," he mused, drawing the word out. "Here you are, you say, delivered to me by your inept protector. Such irony. But you know what, Abernathy? Something isn't right about all this. No one human—or dog—crosses through the fairy mists without the medallion. Do they, Abernathy?"

He waited. Abernathy shook his head carefully. "The magic . . ."

"The magic?" Michel interrupted at once. "The magic of Questor Thews? You want me to believe that the magic was the cause of your passage out of Landover into this world? How . . . incredible!" He thought a moment and smiled unpleasantly. "I don't believe it. Why don't you prove it to me? Why don't you satisfy my curiosity? Open your tunic."

Abernathy went cold. "I have told you . . ."

"Your tunic. Open your tunic."

Abernathy gave it up. Slowly he unclasped the tunic front. Michel leaned forward as the silver medallion came into view. "So," he said, his voice a slow hiss. "It *was* the medallion."

He got up and walked out from behind the desk, coming to a stop directly in front of Abernathy. He was still smiling, a smile without warmth. "Where is my bottle?" he asked softly.

Abernathy held his ground, fighting down the urge to step back. "What bottle are you talking about, Michel?"

"The bottle in the case, Abernathy—where is it? You know where it is and you're going to tell me. I don't believe for a moment that you just happened to appear in my castle. I don't believe that this is all just the result of errant magic. What sort of fool do you think I am? The medallion brought you here from Landover. You came to Graum Wythe to steal the bottle, and that's what you've done. It only remains for me to discover where you have hidden it." He paused thoughtfully. "Maybe it's in Elizabeth's room. Is that where it is, Abernathy? Is Elizabeth your accomplice in all this?"

Abernathy tried to keep any trace of fear for Elizabeth from his voice. "The little girl? She just happened to stumble on me, and I had to pretend with her for a bit. If you want, search her room, Michel." He tried to sound disinterested.

Michel watched him like a hawk. He leaned forward a bit. "Do you know what I am going to do with you?"

Abernathy stiffened slightly. "I am sure you will tell me," he replied.

"I am going to put you in a cage, Abernathy. I am going to put you in a cage just as I would with any stray animal. You'll be given dog food and water and a pad to sleep on. And that is where you will stay, Abernathy." The smile was gone completely now. "Until you tell me where the bottle is. And . . ." He paused. "Until you take off the medallion and give it to me."

He bent closer still, his breath strong in Abernathy's nostrils. "I know the law of the medallion. I cannot take it from you; you must give it to me. It must be given freely, or the magic is useless. You will do that, Abernathy. You will give me the medallion of your own choice. I grow tired of this world. I think perhaps I might return to Landover for a time. I think I might *like* being King now."

He stared into Abernathy's eyes for a moment, searching for the fear concealed there, found it, and stepped back again in satisfaction. "If you don't give me the bottle and the medallion, Abernathy, you will be left in that cage until you rot." He paused. "And that could take a very long time."

Abernathy didn't say a word. He simply stood there, paralyzed.

"Guard!" Michel Ard Rhi called. The men without reappeared. "Take him down to the cellar and put him in a cage. Give him water and dog food twice a day and nothing else. Don't let anyone near him."

Abernathy was dragged roughly through the door. Behind him, he heard Michel call out in a singsong, taunting voice, "You should never have come here, Abernathy!"

Abernathy was inclined to agree.

SLIGHT MISCALCULATION

Fillip and Sot fled north with the bottle, intent on putting as much distance between themselves and the High Lord as was possible. They had escaped in the first place because the Darkling had transported them from the site of battle to a point some miles north, enveloping them in a shroud of smoke and brightly colored lights and whisking them off with all the ease that true magic allows. They had no idea what had become of the High Lord and his companions and they frankly didn't want to know. They didn't even want to think about it.

They ended up thinking about it anyway, of course. All the while they fled north, they thought about it, even without speaking to each other about it, even without acknowledging by covert glances or gestures what they were doing. They couldn't help it. They had committed the most unpardonable, treasonable act imaginable—they had defied their beloved High Lord. Worse, they had actually attacked him! Not directly, of course, since it was the Darkling who had done the attacking, but it was all at their behest and that was the same thing as if they had struck the blows. They couldn't imagine why they had done such a thing. They couldn't conceive of how they had allowed it to happen. They had never even dreamed of challenging the wishes of the High Lord before. Such a thing was unthinkable!

Nevertheless, it had happened, and there was no turning back from it now. They were fleeing because they didn't know what else to do. They knew the High Lord would come after them. He would be furious at what they had done and he would hunt them down and punish them. Their only hope, they sensed, was in flight and, eventually, in hiding.

But where to run and where to hide?

They hadn't resolved the dilemma by the time nightfall and exhaustion made further flight impossible, and they were forced to stop. They wormed their way down into an abandoned badger nest and lay there in the dark listening to the pounding of their hearts and the whisper of their consciences. The bottle was open before them, the Darkling perched on its rim, playing with a pair of frantic moths it had captured and secured with long strands of gossamer webbing. Moon and stars were hidden behind a bank of low-hanging clouds, and night sounds were strangely muted and distant.

Fillip and Sot held hands and waited for the fear to go away. It refused to budge.

"I wish we were home!" Sot whined over and over to Fillip, and Fillip nodded each time without speaking.

They huddled close, too frightened even to think of eating, though they were hungry, or sleeping, though they were tired. They could do nothing but crouch there and think on the misfortune that had befallen them. They watched the Darkling cavort about the bottle, flying the moths like tiny kites, turning them this way and that as the mood struck. They watched, but it was different from what it had been the night before. They no longer found the demon or the bottle so wonderful a treasure.

"I think we did a terrible thing," ventured Fillip finally, his voice a cautious, frightened whisper.

Sot looked at him. "I think so, too."

"I think we made a very bad mistake," Fillip went on.

"I think so, too," said Sot again.

"I think we should never have taken the bottle," finished Fillip.

Sot just nodded this time.

They glanced over at the Darkling, who had stopped playing with the moths and was looking intently at them.

"It might not be too late to give the bottle back to the High Lord," suggested Fillip tentatively.

"No, it might not," agreed Sot.

The Darkling's eyes flared bright red in the dark, blinked once, and fixed on them.

"The High Lord might forgive us if we return the bottle," said Fillip.

"The High Lord might be grateful," said Sot.

"We could explain that we did not understand what we were doing," said Fillip.

"We could tell him how sorry we were," said Sot.

They were both sniffling a bit, wiping at their eyes and noses. The Darkling pointed once at the moths and turned them to bits of blue fire that flared and were gone.

"I do not want the High Lord to hate us," said Fillip softly.

"Nor I," said Sot.

"He is our friend," said Fillip.

"Our friend," echoed Sot.

The Darkling spun suddenly about the lip of the bottle, throwing bits of colored light all about the darkness, the light sparking and exploding in brilliant streamers. Strange images formed and faded and formed again. The G'home Gnomes watched, intrigued anew. The demon laughed and danced, and there were jewels raining down about them as flying moths crystalized and tumbled from flight.

"The bottle is so pretty," said Fillip in awe.

"The magic is so wondrous," sighed Sot.

"Perhaps we could keep the bottle just a bit longer," ventured Fillip.

"Perhaps for just a day or two," agreed Sot.

"What could it hurt?"

"What harm could there be?"

"Perhaps . . ."

"Maybe . . ."

They began and stopped talking at the same moment, turning suddenly to each other, seeing the red glare of the demon's bright eyes reflected in their own and recoiling from it. They tightened their clasped hands and blinked with dazed incomprehension.

"I'm frightened," said Sot, tears in his eyes.

Fillip's voice was a wary hiss. "I don't like the bottle anymore," he said. "I don't like how it makes me feel!"

Sot nodded voicelessly. The Darkling was watching them, the lights and colors and images gone back into the night. The demon hunched down on the lip of the bottle and its red eyes were slits.

"Let's put it back in the bottle," suggested Fillip quietly.

"Let's," agreed Sot.

The demon curled down into a ball and spit suddenly.

"Go away!" said Fillip bravely, making shooing motions with one hand.

"Yes, go away!" echoed Sot.

The demon hissed sharply. "Where would you have me go, masters?" it asked, a bit of a whine in its voice.

"Back into the bottle!" answered Fillip.

"Yes, into the bottle!" agreed Sot.

The demon studied them a moment longer, and then the strange spider-like body skittered back into the bottle and was gone. Fillip and Sot reached up as one, grabbed the bottle almost frantically, and jammed the stopper back into place.

Their hands were shaking.

After a moment, they set the bottle back down again, just in front of them, hidden in leaves and twigs at the forefront of their little den. They watched it silently for a time, and then their eyes began to droop, and sleep began to steal through them.

"Tomorrow we will return the bottle to the High Lord," murmured Fillip.

"Give it back to the High Lord," yawned Sot.

They were asleep in moments, reassured that all would be well. Soon, their snores grew steady and their breathing deep.

Immediately, a dull red glare began to emanate from the bottle.

Sot dreamed of brightly shining jewels. He dreamed that they were falling all about him like raindrops, shimmering as they tumbled down from clouds of rainbow-lined fleece and skies of depthless blue. He sat upon a hill of fragrant grasses and wildflowers and watched them gather all about him in mounds. Sunshine shone from somewhere, warming him, and there was a sense of endless peace.

Beside him sat the bottle—his precious, wondrous bottle. It was the bottle and the Darkling locked within that made the jewels fall.

"Set me free, little master!" the Darkling pleaded suddenly, a small, frightened voice. "Please, master!"

Sot stirred within his dream, and he knew somehow that if he did as the demon had asked that the jewels that fell about him would increase in number and beauty beyond anything he could imagine. He knew that if he obeyed, the demon would give him precious things beyond all comprehension.

It all seemed so easy and right.

He reached over, still asleep, still in his dream, it seemed, and he pulled the stopper free . . .

It was raining when Fillip and Sot came awake again, the skies leaden and clouded over. The rain fell in great, heavy drops that splattered noisily as they struck the earth. Puddles and streams were already forming, mirrors of silver and trickles of gray. It was barely dawn, and everything in the haze of damp and new light was a shimmer of vague images and phantoms.

Coarse, gnarled hands wrenched Fillip and Sot from their slumber and dragged them roughly to their feet. The G'home Gnomes stood shivering with the cold, their weak eyes blinking in bewilderment. Bulky, dark shapes encircled them, a ring of grotesque shadows that lacked clear definition. Fillip and Sot squirmed and wriggled, trying to break free, but the hands held them fast.

One of the shapes detached itself from the ring. It bent close, a body consisting of heavy limbs, bent spine, and matted, dark hair, with a face that was almost featureless under a covering of skin like rough hide.

"Good morning, little gnomes," the troll greeted in his rough, guttural language.

Fillip and Sot shrank back, and trolls all about them laughed with delight.

"Can't you talk?" the speaker asked, feigning sadness.

"Let us go!" pleaded the gnomes in unison.

"But we just found you!" the other said, aggrieved now. "Must you run off so quickly? Have you somewhere to go?" A meaningful pause. "Might you be running from someone, perhaps?"

Fillip and Sot both shook their heads vigorously.

"From someone looking for this?" the troll asked slyly.

He held forth one massive hand. In that hand was their precious bottle, unstoppered once more, the Darkling dancing along its rim, withered child's hands clapping merrily.

"The bottle is ours!" cried Fillip angrily.

"Give it back to us!" wailed Sot.

"Give it back?" the troll said in disbelief. "A thing as wonderful as this? Oh, I think not!"

Fillip and Sot kicked and fought like trapped animals, but the trolls holding them just tightened their grip. The speaker was bigger than the others and obviously in charge. He reached out suddenly with his free hand and thumped them hard on their heads to quiet them down. The force of the blows knocked them to their knees.

"It appears to me that you've been thieving again," the troll continued thoughtfully. "Stealing what doesn't belong to you." The gnomes managed to shake their heads once more in denial, but the troll ignored them. "I think this bottle cannot belong to you. I think it must belong to someone else, and whoever that someone is, he has clearly suffered a great misfortune because of you." He brightened. "Still, another's misfortune need not necessarily be passed on. One man's loss is another man's gain, as the old saying goes. We cannot be certain whom the bottle formerly belonged to. So it seems best that it now belong to me!"

Fillip and Sot looked at each other. These trolls were scavengers, common thieves! They looked quickly to the Darkling where it danced along the neck of their precious bottle.

"Don't let them do this!" pleaded Fillip desperately.

"Make them give you back to us!" begged Sot.

"Stop them, stop them!" they cried together.

The demon did handstands and backflips and watched them through slitted eyes that glittered redly in the haze. A bit of multicolored fire spurted to life at the end of the fingers of one hand, and it blew the fire toward them in a shower of sparks that flared, died, and turned to ashes that caused them to choke and cough and go silent again.

The troll who held the bottle looked down at the Darkling. "Do you belong to these gnomes, tiny fellow?" he asked solicitously.

The Darkling went still. "No, master. I belong only to the holder of the bottle. I belong only to you!"

"No, no!" wailed Fillip and Sot. "You belong to us!"

The other trolls laughed with glee, the sound as chill as the rain that fell all about them.

The speaker bent close. "Nothing belongs to a G'home Gnome, foolish ones! Nothing ever has and nothing ever will! You haven't learned how to keep your possessions safe! How do you think we found you? Who do you think brought us here? Why, gnomes, it was this very creature you now call upon for help! It showered the skies with its brightly colored fire! It *asked* that we take it from you! It *asked* that it not be left your prisoner!"

The G'home Gnomes stared wordlessly, their last shred of hope gone. The Darkling—their friend, their maker of wondrous magic—had deliberately betrayed them. It had given them over to their worst enemies.

"Ho, hum," the speaker said with a yawn. "Time to dispose of you, I think."

The other trolls growled their assent and stamped their feet impatiently. They were growing bored with this game. Fillip and Sot struggled anew.

"What shall we do with them?" the speaker mused. He glanced about at the others. "Cut their throats and spike their heads? Pull off their fingers and toes? Bury them alive?"

Roars of approval sounded from all about, and the G'home Gnomes cringed down into small puddles of despair.

The troll leader shook his head. "No, no, I think we can do better than that!" He looked down at the cavorting demon. "Little fellow, what do you say should be done with these gnomes?"

The Darkling danced and balanced on fingers and toes, a wicked spiderlike shape clinging to the bottle's slick surface. "They might make good feeding for the animals of the forest," it teased.

"Ah!" the troll leader exclaimed. The others joined in a chorus of raucous approval, and the early morning stillness was filled with the sound.

So it was that Fillip and Sot were thrown to the ground, bound hand and foot with cord, hoisted feet first from a line slung over a low branch of a nearby hickory, and left to dangle with their down-turned heads some four feet above the ground.

"Not so close as to drown you in a rain wash and not so far as to prevent the scavengers from reaching you," the speaker advised as the trolls turned away north. "Farewell, little gnomes. Keep your chins up!"

The pack laughed and shoved playfully at one another as they departed. The Darkling sat upon the speaker's broad shoulder and looked back, eyes a blood-red glitter of satisfaction.

In moments, Fillip and Sot were left alone, hanging upside down from the hickory. They swayed gently in the wind and rain and cried.

ONE-WAY TICKET

It was raining and blowing on Ben Holiday as well as he began his day some twenty miles south of where the G'home Gnomes had been strung up by their heels. He unwrapped himself from the warmth of Willow and his sleeping gear and shivered with the early morning chill as he dressed. They were encamped within a sheltering stand of giant fir that sat back against a rocky bluff, but the damp seemed to penetrate even there. The kobolds were already up and moving about, Bunion making ready to begin scouting ahead for the fleeing gnomes. Questor staggered about sleepily, attempted to make breakfast with his magic, and succeeded in producing five live chickens that flapped about madly and a cow that scattered Parsnip's cooking gear. Within minutes, wizard and kobold were yelling at each other irritably, and Ben was wishing he were back at Sterling Silver in the comfort and seclusion of his own bedchamber.

But there wasn't much point in wishing for what he couldn't have, so he consumed a stalk of Bonnie Blue and a little water, mounted Jurisdiction and set off with the others in tow. Bunion quickly went on ahead, disappearing into the shadows and half-light like some aberrant wraith. The others rode after in a line, Ben leading, Willow and Questor following, Parsnip bringing up the rear on foot with the pack animals.

They traveled in silence. It was cold, rainy, and dark, and no one felt much like talking. It was the kind of day that you wished on your enemies or, at the very worst, on yourself when you knew you were going to be comfortably settled indoors before a warm fire. It was not the kind of day in which you traveled. Ben sat atop Jurisdiction and wondered why things had to be like this. He was thoroughly discomforted within minutes of setting out. The rain gear kept the water off his body, but the damp and the chill permeated everything. His toes were numb through his boots, his fingers through his gloves.

What good thoughts he might have started out with trickled away with the speed of the puddles and streams that passed underfoot.

He began brooding about his life.

Oh, sure, he liked his life well enough. He liked being King of Landover, High Lord of a fantasy realm in which mythical creatures were real and magic was a fact of existence. He liked the challenge of what he did, the diversity of its demands, the constant ebb and flow of the feelings it generated. He liked his friends, even at their worst. They were good and loyal, and they genuinely cared for one another and for him. He liked the world in which he had placed himself and would not have traded it back again for the world he had left, even in the darkest of times.

What disturbed him was how little he felt like what he was supposed to be—a King.

Jurisdiction snorted and shook his head lazily, and a shower of water flew into Ben's face. Ben brushed it away and kicked the horse reproachfully with his boots. Jurisdiction ignored him, plodding ahead at his own pace, blinking against the rain.

Ben sighed. He just didn't feel as if he really was a King, he told himself gloomily, picking up his train of thought. He felt that he was just playing at it, that he was filling in for the real King, someone who had been called away unexpectedly, but who would return and prove infinitely more capable than he. It wasn't that he didn't try to do the job right; he did. It wasn't that he couldn't understand its demands; he could. It was more a question of not ever being quite in control. He seemed to spend all his time trying to extract himself from situations he should have avoided in the first place. After all, look at this latest mess—Abernathy dispatched to God-knew-where, his medallion gone the same way, and now the G'home Gnomes run off with the bottle. What sort of King allowed these things to happen? He could excuse matters by arguing that events beyond his control were responsible for everything that had happened, but wasn't it a bit ridiculous for him to try to blame everything on a sneeze?

He sighed again. Well, it most certainly was. He had to accept whatever responsibility needed accepting; that was what Kings were for, after all. But the minute he did that, he was confronted once again with that nagging sense of inadequacy—that sense that he really didn't have a handle on things and never would.

Willow saved him from further self-degradation by riding up next to him and offering a quick smile. "You seem so alone up here," she said.

"Alone with my thoughts." He smiled back. "This day is depressing me."

"You mustn't let it," she said. "You must keep its unpleasantness from you and make it serve your own needs. Think of how good the sunshine will feel after the rain has gone away. Think of how much better its warmth will seem."

He rocked back slightly in his saddle, stretching. "I know. I just wish some of that sunshine and warmth would hurry up and appear."

She looked away for a moment, then back again. "Are you worried about the gnomes and the bottle?"

He nodded. "That, Abernathy, the medallion, and a dozen other things—mostly the fact that I don't feel like I'm doing much of a job as King. I can't seem to get it right, Willow. I just sort of muddle around, trying things out, trying to get out of trouble I shouldn't have gotten into in the first place."

"Did you think it would be different from this?" Her face was shadowed and distant beneath her riding hood.

He shrugged. "I don't know what I thought. No, that's not so. I knew what it would be like—at least, I knew once I was here. That's not the problem. The problem is that things keep happening that I don't seem to have any control over. If I were a real King, an honest-to-God true King, that wouldn't be the case, would it? Wouldn't I be able to anticipate and prevent a few of these things from happening? Wouldn't I be better at this?"

"Ben." She said his name quietly and for a moment didn't say anything more, simply riding there next to him, looking over. Then she said, "How long do you think Questor Thews has been trying to get the magic right?"

He stared at her. "What do you mean?"

"I mean that you have been a King for a much shorter time than Questor has been a wizard. Should you expect so much of yourself when you see how hard it still is for him? The truths of what we undertake in our lives are never quickly mastered. No one is born with those truths; they must always be learned." She reached over and touched him briefly on the cheek. "Besides, was there ever a time in your life when events you could neither anticipate nor control did not intrude on your plans and disrupt them? Why should it be different now?"

He felt suddenly foolish. "It shouldn't, I suppose. And I shouldn't be moping about like this, I know. But it just seems that I'm not really what everyone thinks I am. I'm just . . . me."

She smiled again. "That is what we all are, Ben. But it doesn't stop others from expecting us to be more."

He smiled back. "People should be more considerate."

They rode on in silence, and he consigned his brooding to the back burner, concentrating instead on formulating a plan for getting the bottle back from Fillip and Sot. Morning passed steadily away, and it was nearing midday when Bunion reappeared from out of the mist.

"He has found the gnomes, High Lord," Questor advised hurriedly after a brief conference with the tracker. "It appears that they are in some sort of trouble!"

They spurred their horses ahead and rode at a fast canter through the gloom, the rain and wind blowing into their faces as they sought to keep the elusive Bunion in sight. They passed along a ridge line and down a wash to a grassy hillock beyond. Bunion stopped them at its base and pointed.

There, halfway up, suspended head downward from an aging hickory, were Fillip and Sot. The G'home Gnomes dangled in the wind like a pair of rather bizarre pods.

"What the heck's going on here?" demanded Ben.

He urged Jurisdiction forward, slowly, cautiously, the others following. When he was several dozen yards away, he dismounted and looked guardedly about.

"Bunion says they are alone," Questor offered over one shoulder, his owlish face poking out of his rain cloak's hood. "The bottle and the Darkling appear to be gone."

"Great High Lord!" called out Fillip weakly.

"Mighty High Lord!" echoed Sot.

They sounded as if they were just about all done in, their voices a faint gurgle of rainwater and exhaustion. They were sodden and muddied and presented the most pathetic spectacle Ben had ever witnessed.

"I should just leave them there," he muttered half to himself, thinking of the missing bottle.

It was as if they had heard him. "Don't leave us, High Lord, please don't leave us!" they implored as one, whining like beaten pups.

Ben was disgusted. He shook his head hopelessly, then looked at Bunion. "All right, Bunion. Cut them down."

The kobold skittered forward, climbed the hickory, and cut the ropes suspending the gnomes. Fillip and Sot dropped headfirst into the muck. Serves them right, Ben thought darkly.

Willow hastened forward, rolled them out of the mud and water, and cut the bonds that secured their hands and feet. Gently, she helped them sit up, rubbing their wrists and ankles to help restore the circulation. The gnomes were crying like babies.

"We are so sorry, Great High Lord," whimpered Fillip.

"We meant no harm, Mighty High Lord," whimpered Sot.

"It was the bottle—it was so beautiful."

"It was the creature—it could do wondrous magic things!"

"But it heard us say we would return it."

"It made us free it in our sleep!"

"Then it brought the trolls, High Lord!"

"It used magic lights to guide them!"

"And they captured us!"

"And tied us like dogs!"

"And hung . . . !"

"And left . . . !"

Ben put his hands up quickly. "Whoa, stop! I can't follow any of this! Just tell me what happened, all right—but slowly, please. Just tell me where the bottle is now!"

The G'home Gnomes told him everything. They dissolved into tears of repentance numerous times, but they finally got through it. Ben listened patiently, glancing once or twice at Questor and Willow, wondering for what must have been the hundredth time in the past few days why these things always seemed to happen to him.

When the gnomes were finished and lapsing once more into tears, Questor said something to Bunion, who moved away for a few moments and then returned. He spoke with the wizard, who turned to Ben.

"The trolls left several hours ago, it seems. But it is unclear where they have gone. Their tracks appear to lead off in several different directions." Questor paused uneasily. "Apparently, the Darkling knows we are following and is using its magic to confuse us."

Ben nodded. Hardly a surprise, he thought. Murphy's Law was kicking into high gear. He asked Willow to do what she could to help the shaken gnomes recover, then stood up and walked away to look out into the gloom and think.

What to do?

He felt a sudden resurgence of the insecurities that had plagued him earlier. Damn! He was just not getting anywhere! The longer he spent traipsing around the countryside in search of the bottle, the farther away it seemed to get! Not to mention Abernathy and the medallion, he reminded himself bitterly. God only knew what had happened to them by this time, sent into a world where animals were simply pets and magic medallions were scorned as tools of the devil. How long could they last before something happened to them, something for which he would have to hold himself forever accountable?

He breathed the chill air to clear his thoughts and lifted his face to let the rain cool it. It was no use berating himself. It was pointless to stand there and wish that things were different, that he were more a King, or that he had a better sense of what to do about things. Just shove the insecurities and doubts back into their cubicles and keep them there, he admonished himself. Just decide what to do and do it!

"High Lord?" Questor inquired anxiously from somewhere behind him.

"In a minute," Ben answered.

He had already decided that he was going about matters in the wrong way, that he had reversed his priorities. It was more important that he retrieve Abernathy and his medallion than it was that he retrieve the stolen bottle. It was going to take time to track down that demon and force it back into the bottle, and Abernathy simply didn't have that kind of time. Besides, it was going to take either luck or magic to subdue the Darkling, and Ben didn't feel he could rely on the former. He needed his medallion back.

So the problem then became, how did he get Abernathy and the medallion back without being able to switch the bottle for them?

"Questor," he called suddenly, turning to where the others huddled in a knot beneath the hickory. He saw that Willow had gotten Fillip and Sot back to their feet and had stopped their crying. She was talking to them in a low, quiet voice, her eyes straying momentarily to find him as she heard him call.

Questor Thews shambled over quickly, tall form stooped against the wind, rainwater dripping off his hooked nose. "High Lord?"

Ben looked at him critically. "Have you sufficient magic to send me back after Abernathy? Could you employ something of the same sort of magic you used on him to send me back to wherever he is now? Or do we have to have the medallion? Is the medallion the only way?"

"High Lord . . ."

"Is the medallion necessary, Questor? Yes or no."

Questor shook his head. "No. The medallion was needed only for the purpose of interacting with the magic to separate out the animal from the man in Abernathy. That was the difficult part of the incantation. Simply sending one somewhere is a relatively easy magic."

Ben grimaced. "Please don't say that. It always worries me when you say something involving the magic is easy. Just tell me that you can send me back after Abernathy, okay? Can you do that? No sneezing, no mistakes—just send me back in one piece, right to where he is?"

The wizard hesitated. "High Lord, I do not think this a good . . ."

"No editorials, Questor," Ben interrupted quickly. "No arguments. Just answer the question."

Questor rubbed his rain-drenched beard, tugged his ear, and sighed. "The answer is yes, High Lord."

"Good. That's what I wanted to hear."

"But . . ."

"But?"

"But I can only send you there; I cannot bring you back again." Questor shrugged helplessly. "That is all I have been able to learn of that particular magic. After all, if I knew more, I could simply bring Abernathy and the medallion back myself, couldn't I?"

True enough, Ben thought dismally. Well, you take your chances in this world, just like you do in any other.

"High Lord, I really wish you would think this . . ."

Ben brought his finger up quickly and made a hushing sound. "Just give me a moment to consider this, Questor. Please?"

He glanced away into the gloom once more. If he did this thing, it meant that he couldn't come back again unless he regained the medallion. He would have to stay in his old world, whatever happened, until he could locate it. This all presumed, of course, that Questor could get the magic right this time and actually send him where he was supposed to go and not to some other place and point in time.

He looked back at the wizard, studying the owlish face. Questor Thews. Wizard at large. He would have to leave Questor in control of Landover's affairs. That was a pretty scary proposition all by itself. He had allowed Questor to act in his place once before when he had been forced to return to his old world, but he had only been gone three days. He was likely to be gone much longer this time out. Maybe forever.

On the other hand, who else could he trust to assume the duties of the throne? Not Kallendbor or any of the other Lords of the Greensward. Not the River Master and his lake country fairies. Certainly not Nightshade, the witch of the Deep Fell. Willow, perhaps? He thought about that a moment. Willow would defer to Questor, he decided. Besides, Questor's confidence in himself would be shattered if he were not named ruler in Ben's absence. The Court Wizard was supposed to be the second most powerful figure in the monarchical structure.

Supposed to be. Those were the operative words, of course, Ben thought wryly. The truth of the matter might be something else altogether.

Well, Questor Thews had been a friend to him when he had no others. Questor had stood by him when it seemed foolish for anyone to do so. Questor had done everything asked of him and more. Maybe it was time to repay his loyalty with a little trust.

He brought his hands up to the narrow shoulders and gripped them firmly. "I've decided," he said quietly. "I want you to do it, Questor. I want you to send me back."

He kept the other's gaze locked onto his own, waiting. Questor Thews hesitated once more, then nodded. "Yes, High Lord. If you wish."

Ben walked him back to where the others waited and gathered them about. Fillip and Sot started to sob again, but he quickly quieted them with assurances that all was forgiven. Bunion and Parsnip hunched down against the trunk of the old hickory, their gnarled bodies glistening wetly. Willow stood apart, an uneasy look to her. She had seen something she didn't like in Ben's eyes.

"I have asked Questor to use the magic to send me after Abernathy," Ben announced brusquely. "He has agreed to do so." He avoided Willow's startled eyes. "I have to do what I can to help Abernathy and to regain possession of the medallion. When I have done that, I'll come back to you."

"Oh, Great High Lord!" cried Fillip dismally.

"Mighty High Lord!" sobbed Sot.

"We are so sorry, High Lord!"

"Oh, yes, we are!"

Ben patted them on the head. "Questor will assume the duties of the throne in my absence. I want you all to do your best to help him." He paused and looked directly at his Court Wizard. "Questor, I want you to continue to try to find a way to get the Darkling back into the bottle. That little monster is too dangerous to be allowed to remain loose. See if Kallendbor or the River Master will agree to help you. But be careful."

Questor nodded wordlessly. The others continued to stare at him, waiting.

"I guess that's all I have to say," he finished.

Willow came right up to him then, the determination in her face unmistakable. "I am going with you, Ben."

"Oh, no." Ben shook his head quickly. "That would be much too dangerous. I could be trapped over there, Willow. I might never get back. If you were with me, you would be trapped there as well."

"Which is why I must go with you, Ben. I cannot risk that you might be separated from me forever. What happens to you happens to me as well. We are one person, Ben. It was foretold by the weaving of the flowers in the garden where I was conceived. Even the Earth Mother knows of it." She took his hand in her own. "Do you remember her admonishment to you? Do you remember what she said?" She waited until he nodded yes. He had forgotten about the Earth Mother—that strange elemental who aided them in their search for the black unicorn. Willow's hand tightened suddenly. "You are to be my protector; that was what she said. But, Ben, I must be your protector as well. I must be because if I am not, then my love for you is meaningless. There is no argument that you can offer that will dissuade me. I am going with you."

He stared at her, so in love with her in that instant that he could scarcely believe it. She was so much a part of him. It had happened almost without his realizing it, a gradual strengthening of ties, a binding of feelings and emotions, a joining of their lives. He recognized the truth of it and marveled in his recognition that such a thing could be.

"Willow, I . . ."

"No, Ben." She put a finger to his lips, and her beautiful, flawless face lifted to kiss his own. "It is decided."

Ben kissed her back and held her. He guessed it was.

He decided that they would depart at once.

He had Questor use the magic to outfit them both in jogging suits and Nikes, giving Willow a sweatband to hold back her long hair and sunglasses to help mask her startling eyes. There was nothing he could do about her green complexion; he wouldn't risk allowing Questor to try anything with magic. They would simply have to make something up if there were questions. He had the wizard conjure up some folding money so he could pay whatever expenses he might incur while trying to find Abernathy. He hoped there wouldn't be any, of course. He hoped he would find his missing scribe and the medallion right off the bat. But he doubted that he would be that lucky. He hadn't been very lucky so far in trying to straighten out this mess.

Questor did a superior job of suiting them up in the sweats and running shoes, right down to the appropriate logos. He did yeoman work on the money as well; it felt like the real thing. It was fortunate, Ben thought, that he had shown the wizard some samples on earlier occasions. He gave the money a hasty glance and shoved it down into his pocket.

"And, Questor, you'd better spell Willow to speak English when we get there," he added.

Willow came over to stand next to him, her slim arms wrapping about his waist to hold him. He wanted to ask her once more if she was still certain about going with him, but he didn't. Such a question was pointless now.

"Ready, Questor," he announced. He glanced doubtfully at the gloom and damp that surrounded them, a gray and misty haze. He looked down through the wash to the grasslands beyond, to the hills and forests. He wished he could see it all in a better light, in sunshine, in bright color. He wanted to remember it all. He was afraid he would never see it again.

Questor Thews moved the others behind him, back against the trunk of the hickory. The kobolds were grinning fiercely, the gnomes whining as if they were about to be strung up again. Questor shoved back the sleeves of his robes and lifted his hands.

"Be careful," Ben said quietly, his arms tightening about Willow.

The wizard nodded. "Good luck to you, High Lord."

He began the incantation, the magic words spilling out in a steady stream of meaningless rhetoric. Then came the gestures, the appearance of the silver dust, and the coming of the light. Rain and gloom faded, taking with them the kobolds and the gnomes, then Questor Thews as well. Ben and Willow were alone, holding each other close.

"I love you, Ben," he heard the sylph say.

Then everything disappeared in a flash of light, and they closed their eyes tight against its brilliance.

They drifted for a time, a long, slow drifting that lacked direction or focus, the sort of drifting one sometimes experiences when sleep grows into gradual wakening. Then the light grew less intense, the drifting stopped, and the world about them grew distinct again.

They were standing on a street corner in a city, the air filled with the sounds of cars and people. Willow clung to Ben, burying her face in his shoulder, clearly frightened. Ben looked quickly about, shaken himself by the sudden rush of noise.

Good heavens, it was hot! It was as if it were the middle of summer instead of fall! But that couldn't be . . .

"Holy mackerel!" he breathed.

He knew exactly where he was. He would have known whatever the circumstances of his being there.

He was right in the middle of the Las Vegas strip.

CASTLES AND CAGES

Questor Thews stared thoughtfully at the empty space that had been occupied by Ben Holiday and Willow only seconds before, then rubbed his hands together in satisfaction and said, "Well, I believe they are safely on their way."

Bunion and Parsnip came forward, peered at the emptiness, and hissed their agreement. Their teeth showed and their yellow eyes blinked like signal lamps.

"Great High Lord," whimpered Fillip from somewhere in the shadows behind them.

"Mighty High Lord," whimpered Sot.

"Come, come! The High Lord is safe and sound," Questor assured them, wondering briefly if he had remembered correctly all the words and gestures to the part of the incantation having to do with the place to which he had sent them. Yes, he was certain that he had. Reasonably certain, at any rate.

"Got to concentrate on dealing with matters here," he announced, mostly to himself. "Hmmmmmm. Let me see."

He straightened himself beneath his robes, tugged on his beard, and peered out into the gloom. It was still raining heavily, the drops spattering into ever-widening puddles and streams that interlocked across the whole of the landscape as far as he could see. Clouds hung low against the horizon, and the day seemed to be growing darker. The haze of mist that had shrouded the valley since dawn was thickening.

Questor frowned. It would be a perfectly reasonable decision to return to Sterling Silver here and now and forget about chasing after that confounded demon.

On the other hand, there was nothing waiting at Sterling Silver that wouldn't keep a few days more—and he had promised the High Lord that he would do his best to retrieve the bottle. Although he didn't care to dwell on it, he knew he was at least partially responsible for the bottle being in Landover in the first place; therefore, he should do his best to set matters right again—especially since the High Lord had placed such great trust in him.

"I think, perhaps, that we should continue our hunt," he declared. "Bunion? Parsnip? Shall we keep after the Darkling a little while longer?"

The kobolds glanced at each other and hissed their approval.

"Excellent!" Questor turned to the G'home Gnomes. "I should be less charitable with you than was the High Lord, Fillip and Sot, if the choice were mine. Still, all was forgiven, so you are free to go."

Fillip and Sot stopped whimpering and shivering long enough to glance about at the gray, empty landscape and then at each other. Their eyes were wide and frightened.

"Good and kind Questor Thews!" said Fillip.

"Wondrous wizard!" declared Sot.

"We will stay with you!"

"We will give you our help!"

"Please let us stay?"

"Please?"

Questor Thews looked down at them with undisguised suspicion. The gnomes were asking to stay only because they were afraid of being left alone come nightfall with the Darkling still on the loose. He hesitated, then shrugged. Well, after all, what could you expect of G'home Gnomes?

"Just be sure you stay out of the way if we come across the trolls and that bottle," he admonished sternly.

The gnomes could not agree quickly enough, falling all over each other in their efforts to assure him that such would be the case. Questor had to smile in spite of himself. He was quite certain they were telling the truth on this occasion.

So they struck out north through the weather, Bunion sweeping the land ahead in an effort to pick up some true sign of the trolls' passing, Questor and the others trailing after at a slower pace. Questor rode his old gray, letting Parsnip and the gnomes follow afoot, with Parsnip leading Jurisdiction, Willow's mount, and the pack animals. The rain continued to fall steadily, its gray haze mingling with the mist to wrap the land in ribbons of shadow. Daylight faded as nightfall approached, and still there was no sign of the trolls.

Bunion returned at sunset, and the company made camp within a gathering of rain-drenched cyprus along a river whose swollen waters churned by in sluggish, monotonous cadence. It was relatively dry beneath the great, hanging limbs, and Questor was able to produce a small, cheerful fire by using his magic. Parsnip cooked a delightful dinner which was quickly consumed. Then, buoyed by his earlier success, Questor employed the magic once more to produce blankets and pillows. He would have done better to let well enough alone, but he decided to try one last incantation, a spell that would have produced an enclosed, heated, waterproof shelter complete with bath. The effort failed abysmally. One of the trees actually toppled over on the spot, allowing the rain to douse the fire and leaving the entire company exposed to the weather. They were forced to move their camp farther back within the remaining trees, salvaging what they could of the now-dampened blankets and pillows, and that was that.

Questor apologized profusely, but the damage was nevertheless done and couldn't be undone. It was most embarrassing. While the others slept, Questor Thews lay awake within his blankets and thought long and hard about the vicissitudes of a wizard's life. Teaching oneself reliable use of the magic was not an easy task, he lamented. Nevertheless, he must do so. After all, he stood now in the shoes of the High Lord and he was responsible for the well-being of all Landover.

Daybreak brought more rain. The dawn was iron gray and thick with mist stirred by sluggish winds and a mix of cool air and warm earth. The little company ate breakfast and struck out once more across the grasslands of the Greensward. Bunion roamed ahead, still searching for some sign of the trolls, while the rest followed at a slower pace. Everyone was soaked through and thoroughly discomforted. Questor thought briefly to dry them off with the magic, then decided against it. He had resolved during the night not to employ the magic again except when he could be certain of its results or in time of desperate need. He would conserve himself; he would focus his concentration on specific and limited conjuring. That way, he felt, he would be at his best.

Midday came and went. They were well into the grasslands by now, far north and east of Sterling Silver, deep in the country of the Lords of the Greensward. Plowed fields decorated the landscape in checkerboard fashion, most of the crops taken from them now, the earth black and hard looking. Farm buildings and cottages were scattered about, brightened by gardens and hedgerows blooming with flowers of all colors and shapes, rainbow streaks across the rain-swept, gray land.

Questor's eyes surveyed the misted countryside. Less than a dozen miles distant was Rhyndweir, the fortress castle of Kallendbor, the most powerful of the Lords of the Greensward. The wizard permitted himself a small sigh of expectation. Tonight, he promised himself, they would sleep beneath a dry roof, in dry beds, with steaming baths to remove all memory of the damp and the chill.

It was nearing midafternoon when Bunion abruptly appeared from out of the haze, his hard, dark body glistening with the wet. He approached at something very close to a run—unusual for him—and spoke hurriedly to Questor, his breath hissing from between his sharp teeth, his eyes narrowed and furtive.

The wizard caught his breath. Bunion had found the trolls—but not as any of them had imagined.

The company pressed at a quicker pace, Questor saying nothing to the others yet, still stunned by what Bunion had told him. They passed across a series of fields and a small, quick-flowing stream into a stretch of timber.

The trolls lay in a clearing, amid a close gathering of pine, dead to a man. They were sprawled on the rain-drenched earth in grotesque positions, throats cut, bodies stabbed, tangled together in an orgy of death. The G'home Gnomes took one look and shrank back behind the pack animals, whining in fear. Even Parsnip shied away. Questor went forward with Bunion because it was expected. Bunion whispered again what he had whispered earlier. This tragedy had not been caused by some third party. The trolls had evidently set upon themselves. They had killed one another.

Questor listened patiently and said nothing, but he knew what had happened. He had seen the Darkling's work before. The chill of the day worked into him more deeply. He was suddenly very frightened.

Bunion pointed ahead into the gloom. One of the trolls had escaped the massacre. One had survived, wounded, and staggered ahead into the woods. That one had taken the bottle.

"Oh, dear," Questor Thews murmured.

The wounded troll was heading directly for Rhyndweir.

"Abernathy!"

The scribe lifted his head from the straw matting on which he lay to peer into the near-blackness beyond. "Elizabeth?"

She appeared out of the shadows of an alcove set into the far wall, slipping through a break in the stone that he could have sworn hadn't been there a moment before. She crossed the dungeon passageway on tiptoe and put her face up against the bars of his cage. Abernathy, unable to stand erect in the small enclosure, crawled over on all fours to greet her. He could just make out the roundish face with its scattering of nose freckles.

"Sorry I couldn't come sooner," she whispered, glancing left and right cautiously. "I couldn't chance trying. I couldn't let my dad or Michel know I cared about what happened to you or they might have been suspicious. I think Michel already is."

Abernathy nodded, grateful that she had come at all. "How did you get in here, Elizabeth?"

"Through a secret passage!" She grinned. "Right there!" She pointed behind her to the break in the wall, a seam of light still faintly visible against the black. "I found it months ago when I was exploring. I doubt anyone else even knows that it's there. It leads all up and down the south wall." She hesitated. "I didn't know how to get to you at first. I didn't even know where you'd be. I just found out this afternoon."

"This afternoon? Is it night, then?" Abernathy asked. He had lost all track of time.

"Yep. Almost bedtime, so I have to hurry. Here, I brought you something to eat."

He saw then that she was carrying a paper bag. She reached into it and produced several sandwiches, some raw vegetables, fresh fruit, a bag of potato chips, and a small container of cold milk.

"Elizabeth!" he breathed gratefully.

She passed the items through, and he tucked them into the straw to hide them—all but the first sandwich, which he began to devour hungrily. He hadn't been given anything to eat but stale dog food and a little water in almost three days now, the time that he had been imprisoned there. He had been shut away in the bowels of Graum Wythe, ignored except for periodic visits from his uncommunicative jailers, who either came to make certain he was still there or to give him his rations. He hadn't seen sunlight the entire time. He hadn't seen Michel Ard Rhi, either.

"How are you, Abernathy?" Elizabeth asked as he ate. "Are you all right? They didn't hurt you, did they?"

He shook his head and continued to chew. Ham and cheese—one of his favorites.

"I talked to my father about you a little bit," she ventured after a moment. Then she added hastily, "I didn't tell him about you and me, though. I just told him that I had found you wandering about and Michel didn't seem to like you and I was worried about you. I told him I thought it was wrong. He agreed, but he said he couldn't do anything. He said I knew better than to get involved with strays in the first place, that I knew how Michel was. I said sometimes you had to get involved."

She hunched down thoughtfully. "I know you aren't being given any food. I found out from one of the guards, a sort of friend." She bit her lip. "Why is Michel doing this to you, Abernathy? Why is he being so mean? Does he still hate you so much?"

Abernathy stopped chewing, swallowed, and lowered what remained of the sandwich. He couldn't have eaten it at all if he hadn't been so hungry. His cage smelled of sick animals and excrement, and the walls were dark with mold.

"It's simple, really—he wants something from me." He decided it couldn't hurt to tell her the truth now. "He wants this medallion I am wearing. But he cannot take it from me. I have to give it to him. So he has locked me away down here until I agree to give it up." He brushed some straw from his muzzle with one paw. "But the medallion isn't his; it isn't even mine. It was just loaned to me, and I have to return it to its owner."

He thought, for the first time in quite a while now, about the High Lord and thc problems he faced in Landover without the medallion to protect him. Then he sighed and began eating again.

Elizabeth looked at him a moment, then nodded slowly. "I talked to Nita Coles about you today. We're friends again, see. She explained all about Tommy Samuelson and said she was sorry. Anyway, I told her about you, 'cause we tell each other everything. But we keep it all secret. Most of the time, anyway. This was a sworn, double-locked finger secret, so neither of us can tell *anyone* or we'll have seven years bad luck and Tad Russell for a husband for life! She says you can't be real, of course, but I told her you were and that you needed us to help. So she said she would think about it, and I said I'd think about it, too."

She paused. "We've got to get you out of here, Abernathy."

Abernathy pushed the last of the sandwich into his mouth and shook his head vehemently. "No, no, Elizabeth, it's gotten much too dangerous for you to try to help me anymore. If Michel finds out . . ."

"I know, I know," she interrupted. "But I can't keep sneaking food down to you like this. Michel is going to figure out that you're not starving or anything, that someone's feeding you. And how will you get out of here if I don't help you?"

Abernathy sighed. "I'll find a way," he insisted stubbornly.

"No, you won't," Elizabeth declared, just as stubborn. "You'll just be down here in this cage forever!"

There was a sudden barking from somewhere down the hallway through a closed door. Abernathy and Elizabeth both turned to look, freezing into motionless statues. The barking lasted only a few seconds and died away.

"Real dogs," Abernathy whispered after a moment. "Michel keeps them locked away down here, poor things. I don't even want to speculate why. I hear them cry out sometimes, calling. I can understand something of what they are saying . . ."

He trailed off, distracted. Then he looked quickly back at the girl. "You have to stay out of this, Elizabeth," he insisted. "Michel Ard Rhi is very dangerous. He would hurt you if he knew what you were doing—even if he suspected! It wouldn't make any difference to him that you were a little girl. He would hurt you anyway—maybe your father, too, for that matter."

There was immediate concern reflected in her eyes when he mentioned the danger to her father. He felt bad about suggesting such a thing, but he had to make certain that she did not take any further chances on his account. He knew what Michel Ard Rhi could be like.

Elizabeth was studying him intently. "Why do you try to scare me like that, Abernathy?" she asked suddenly, almost as if she could read his mind. "You are trying to scare me, aren't you?"

She made it a statement of fact. "Yes, of course I am, Elizabeth," he answered immediately. "And you should be scared. This isn't a game for children!"

"Just for dogs and wizards, I suppose!" she snapped back angrily.

"Elizabeth . . ."

"Don't try to make up to me!" There was hurt now in her eyes. "I am not a child, Abernathy! You shouldn't call me one!"

"I was just trying to make a point. I think you would . . ."

"How are you going to get out of here without me?" she demanded again, cutting him short.

"There are certainly ways that . . ."

"There are? How? Name one. Just one. Tell me how you're going to get out. Go on, tell me!"

He took a deep breath, his strength deserting him. "I don't know," he admitted wearily.

She nodded in satisfaction. "Do you still like me, Abernathy?"

"Yes, of course I do, Elizabeth."

"And would you help me if I needed helping, no matter what?"

"Yes, of course."

She bent forward against the bars of the cage until her nose was only inches from his. "Well, that's how I feel about you, too! That's why I can't just leave you here!"

The dogs began barking again, more insistent this time, and someone yelled at them to shut up. Elizabeth began backing away toward the alcove.

"Finish your food so you'll stay strong, Abernathy!" she whispered hurriedly. "Shhh, shhhh!" she cautioned when he tried to speak. "Just be patient! I'll find a way to get you out!"

She paused halfway through the break in the wall, a slight shadow in the half-light. "Don't worry, Abernathy! It'll be all right!"

Then she was gone, the break disappearing once more into blackness.

The barking down the hall was punctuated by several sharp yelps and then faded slowly into silence. Abernathy listened for a time, then pulled out the medallion from beneath his tunic, and studied it silently.

He was scared to death for Elizabeth. He wished he knew what to do about her. He wished he could find some way to protect her.

After a time, he put the medallion back in place again. Then he uncovered the rest of his food and slowly began to eat.

CHARADES

Ben Holiday squinted through the glare of the hot Nevada sun in total disbelief. Massive hotel and casino signs lined the street in both directions, jutting up against the cloudless desert horizon like some bizarre, twentieth-century Druidic Stonehenge, garish even without the dance of the bright, flashy lighting that would come with nightfall. The Sands. Caesar's Palace. The Flamingo.

"Las Vegas," he whispered. "For crying out loud, what are we doing in Las Vegas?"

His mind raced. He had assumed that when he was transported from Landover into his old world, he would emerge just as he always did when coming out of the fairy mists into the Blue Ridge Mountains of Virginia. He had assumed, quite reasonably he thought, that Abernathy must have been dispatched to that same point when the magic went awry. But now, it seemed, he had been wrong on both counts. The magic must have gone sufficiently bonkers to send them both to the other end of the country!

Unless . . .

Oh, no, Ben thought. Unless Questor had messed up yet again and sent Abernathy to one place and Willow and him to another!

He caught himself. He wasn't thinking this through clearly. The magic had exchanged Abernathy and the medallion for the bottle and the Darkling. Abernathy would have been sent to wherever the bottle was being kept by Michel Ard Rhi—assuming Michel still had the bottle. In any case, Abernathy would have been sent to *whomever* it was that had the bottle. And Ben had asked Questor to send him to wherever Abernathy was. So maybe Las Vegas was exactly the place he was supposed to be.

Willow still had her body turned into him protectively, but she brought her face up from his shoulder long enough to whisper, "Ben, I don't like all this noise!"

The strip was jammed with cars even at midday, the air filled with the sounds of engines, horns, brakes and tires, and shouts from everywhere. Cabs zipped past and a descending airliner passed overhead with a frightening roar.

Ben glanced around once more, still confused. Passersby and motorists were beginning to rubberneck in his direction. Must be the jogging suits, he thought at first, then realized it was nothing of the sort. It was Willow. It was a girl with emerald green hair that tumbled to her waist and flawless sea-green skin. Even in Las Vegas, Willow was an oddity.

"Let's go," he said abruptly and started walking her south up the street. Las Vegas Boulevard, the sign said. He tried to remember something useful about Las Vegas and couldn't remember a thing. He had only been there once or twice in his life, and that had been for only a day or two and on business at that. He had visited a few casinos and recalled nothing about any of them.

They reached the intersection of Las Vegas Boulevard and Flamingo Road. Caesar's Palace was on the left, the Flamingo on the right. He hurried Willow across, pushing through a knot of people going the other way.

"Far out, honey!" one called back and whistled.

"You been to the Emerald City?" another asked.

Great, thought Ben. This is all I need.

He swept Willow on, ignoring the voices, and they faded behind him. He had to come up with a plan, he thought, irritated at how matters had worked out. He couldn't just wander about the city indefinitely. He glanced at the two massive hotels bracketing the boulevard on the south side of the intersection. The Dunes and Bally's. Too big, he thought. Too many people, too much going on, too . . . everything.

"Where's the circus, doll?" he heard someone else shout.

"Ben," Willow whispered urgently, clutching at him tighter.

Questor, Questor! You better be right about this! Ben walked faster, sheltering Willow as best he could, moving her to the inside of the street traffic, hurrying her past the crush of people coming and going through the entrance to Bally's. The Shangri-La loomed ahead, then the Aladdin and the Tropicana. He had to pick one of them, he admonished angrily. They had to spend the night somewhere—had to get their bearings, decide where to begin their search for Abernathy. Maybe it would be better if he *did* choose one of the larger hotels. They might be less noticeable there, blend in a bit easier with all the other bizarre sorts . . .

He turned Willow about abruptly and walked her through the entrance of the Shangri-La.

The lobby was jammed. The casino beyond was jammed. There were people everywhere, the sounds of cards and dice and roulette wheels and one-armed bandits a steady, low-level din mixed with the excited voices of the game players. Ben took Willow through it all, ignoring the stares that followed them, and went directly to the registration desk.

"Reservation for . . ." He hesitated. "Bennett, please. Miles Bennett."

The clerk looked up perfunctorily, looked down, looked up again quickly on seeing Willow, then nodded and said, "Yes, sir, Mr. Bennett."

Willow, confused about the name, said, "Ben, I don't understand . . ."

"Shhhh," he cautioned softly.

The clerk checked his reservations sheet and looked up again. "I'm sorry, sir, I don't have a reservation for you."

Ben straightened. "No? Perhaps you'll find it under Fisher then. Miss Caroline Fisher? A suite?"

He took a deep breath while the registration clerk looked again. Naturally, the result was the same. "Sorry, Mr. Bennett, I don't find a reservation under Miss Fisher's name, either."

He smiled apologetically at Willow and for a very long moment was unable to look away from her.

Ben stiffened in feigned irritation. "We have had that reservation for months!" He lifted his voice just loud enough to draw attention. A small scattering of people slowed and began to gather to see what was happening. "How can you not have any record of it? It was confirmed only last week, for God's sake! We have a shooting schedule that begins at five o'clock in the morning, and I cannot afford to waste time on this!"

"Yes, sir, I understand," the clerk said, understanding only that something had gone wrong for which he was not to blame.

Ben pulled out the wad of bills Questor had given him and began to thumb through them absently. "Well, our luggage will be here from the airport shortly, so I see no point in arguing about the matter. Please arrange whatever you can for us, and I'll speak with the manager later."

The clerk nodded, looked back at the reservation sheet, looked next at the bookings on the computer, then said, "Excuse me just a moment, Mr. Bennett."

He went out while Ben, Willow, and the small crowd gathered behind them waited expectantly. He was back quickly, another man in tow. Someone with more authority, Ben hoped.

He was not disappointed. "Mr. Bennett, I'm Winston Allison, Assistant Manager. I understand that there has been some sort of mix-up in the reservations you booked? I'm sorry about that. We do have rooms available for you and Miss Fisher." He smiled broadly at Willow, clearly assessing her potential for star status. "Would you still like a suite?"

"Yes, Mr. Allison," Ben replied, "Miss Fisher and I would like that very much."

"Well, then." Allison spoke quietly to the clerk, who nodded. "For how long will you need the suite, Mr. Bennett?" he asked.

"A week at the outside." Ben smiled. "Our shooting schedule only calls for three, possibly four days."

The clerk began writing, then passed Ben the registration forms. Ben filled them out quickly, using a bogus studio reference for a business name, still playing his role to the hilt, and passed the forms back. The crowd behind them began to disperse again, moving on to find some new attraction.

"I hope you enjoy your stay with us, Mr. Bennett, Miss Fisher," Allison said, smiled once more, and went back to wherever he had come from.

"The rate for the suite is four hundred and fifty dollars a night, Mr. Bennett," the clerk advised, consulting the registration forms officiously. "How will you be paying for this?"

"Cash," Ben answered nonchalantly and began thumbing through the roll of bills. "Is one thousand dollars a sufficient deposit?"

The clerk nodded, stealing another quick glance at Willow, smiling warmly when she noticed him looking.

Ben proceeded to count out the sum of five hundred dollars in fifties, then noticed something odd about one of the bills. He paused, slowly worked a new bill free of the roll as if the bills were sticking, and looked closely at its face.

Ulysses S. Grant's picture wasn't on the bill. His was.

He surreptitiously checked another bill and another. His picture was on every one, bigger than life, and looking not a thing like Grant's. He felt his heart drop. Questor had messed up again!

The clerk was looking at him now, sensing that everything was not quite right. Ben hesitated; then, unable to think of anything else, lurched forward suddenly against the counter, hands clutching at the bills, his breath coming in gasps.

"Mr. Bennett!" the clerk exclaimed, reaching out to catch him.

Willow's hands clutched at him as well. "Ben!" she cried before he could do anything to stop her.

"No, no, I'm quite all right," he assured them both, praying the clerk hadn't noticed that she had used a different name. "I wonder . . . could I go directly to my room and lie down a bit? Finish this later, perhaps? The sun was a bit too much, I think."

"Certainly, Mr. Bennett," the clerk agreed hastily, summoning a bellhop instantly. "Are you certain you don't need medical help? We have someone on staff if . . ."

"No, I'll be fine . . . once I've rested a bit. I have my medicine. Thank you again for your help."

He smiled weakly, pocketed the bills once more, and gave a silent sigh of relief. With Willow and the bellhop both holding tightly onto him, he moved off through the crowded lobby. Another silver bullet dodged, he thought gratefully.

He prayed that Abernathy was having the same sort of good fortune.

"All right, students, quiet down now! Everyone find a seat! Let's have your attention, please!"

The energetic young principal of Franklin Elementary in Woodinville, Washington, walked to the center of the gymnasium floor, microphone in one hand, other hand held high and signaling for order, voice booming out over the loudspeaker system. The K through sixth graders slowly settled down on their bleacher seats, the din of their voices dying into a rustle of anticipation. Elizabeth sat six rows back with Eva Richards. She watched the principal glance at a man who stood to one side, his lanky frame slouched, a smile on his bearded face. The man reached down and scratched the ears of a small black poodle who sat obediently beside him.

"We have a special treat for you this afternoon, something many of you have enjoyed before," the principal announced, looking around with a broad grin. "How many of you like dogs?"

Hands shot up everywhere. The man with the dog smiled some more and waved hello to a section of students close at hand. They waved back eagerly.

"Well, we've got some special dogs for you this afternoon, some dogs who can do things that even some of you can't do!" A titter of laughter sounded. Elizabeth grimaced. "I want you to watch closely and listen to what our guest has to say. Students, please welcome Mr. Davis Whitsell and his *Canine Review*!"

Applause and whistles sounded as Davis Whitsell took the floor, accepting the microphone from the departing principal. He waved and pretended not to notice that the little black poodle was trailing after.

"Good afternoon, everyone!" he greeted. "Such an enthusiastic group! I am delighted to have you all here, happy you came—even if you had to come, this being one of those required assemblies." He made a face and there were hoots of laughter. "But maybe we can have some fun together. I'm here to tell you about dogs—that's right, dogs! And since your parents don't want you going to the dogs, I'm bringing the dogs to you!"

He raised his hands and everyone clapped in response.

"Now, I want you to listen up, because I have to tell you something important. I have to tell you . . ."

He paused, acting as if he had just noticed Sophie tugging dutifully at his pants leg. "Hey, hey, what's this? Let go now, Sophie, let go!"

The little black poodle released her grip and sat back, watching.

"Now, as I was saying, I have something to tell you that . . ."

Sophie began tugging at him again. Elizabeth laughed with the others. Davis Whitsell looked down, distracted once more from his speech.

"Sophie, what is it? You want to say something first?" Sophie barked. "Well, why didn't you say so? Oh, you just did, didn't you? Well, I don't think the kids heard. Maybe you better say it again." Sophie barked once more. "What, you want to show them how smart you are?" Sophie barked. "How smart *all* dogs like you are?" He looked up at the bleachers. "What do you say, kids? You want to see how smart Sophie is?"

They all yelled that they did, of course. He gave an exaggerated shrug. "Okay. Let's see what you can do, Sophie. Can you jump?" Sophie jumped. "Can you jump higher?" Sophie jumped almost to his shoulder. "Whoa! Bet you can't do a back flip." Sophie did a back flip. "Hey, how about that, kids? That's not bad, is it? Now, how about . . ."

He took Sophie through one trick after another, jumps through hoops and over hurdles, more flips, retrieving and carrying off, and a dozen-and-one other marvelous stunts. When she was finished, the students gave her a tumultuous round of applause, and Davis Whitsell sent her off. Then he began to talk about the need for proper pet care. He gave a few statistics, talked about the good work of the ASPCA, stressed the ways a little love and understanding could affect the lives of animals, and pointed out the need for every student there to involve himself or herself in this ongoing project.

Elizabeth listened intently.

Then, back came Sophie. She appeared from the edge of the floor leading a big tan boxer by the leash about his neck. Davis Whitsell expressed surprise, then went through the whole routine all over again, asking Sophie what she was doing there with Bruno, pretending he understood what she was saying when she barked, carrying on a conversation with her just as if she were human.

Elizabeth began to think.

Then came a whole new repertoire of stunts involving Sophie and Bruno, the former riding the latter, the two of them jumping through hoops and over hurdles, racing about in leaps and bounds, playing tag, and conducting contests of skill and daring.

The program closed with a reminder of the need for responsibility where animals were concerned and a wish for a good school year for all of them. Whitsell went off with a wave to the cheers and applause, Sophie and Bruno in tow. The principal shook his hand, took back the mike, thanked him publicly, then dismissed the students to their classes.

Elizabeth made up her mind.

As the other students filed out, one after the other, Elizabeth hung back. Eva Richards tried to stay with her, but Elizabeth told her to go on ahead. Davis Whitsell was watching as the students passed by, returning their smiles.

Elizabeth waited patiently. The principal came up and thanked Whitsell once more, saying he hoped he'd be back next year. Whitsell replied that he would.

Then the principal moved off as well, and Davis Whitsell was alone.

Elizabeth took a deep breath and walked up to him. When he looked down at her, she said, "Mr. Whitsell, do you think you could do something to help a friend of mine?"

The bearded man grinned. "Depends, I guess. Who's your friend?"

"His name is Abernathy. He's a dog."

"Oh, a dog. Well, sure. What's his problem?"

"He needs to go to Virginia."

The grin broadened. "He does? Hey, what's your name?"

"Elizabeth."

"Well, look, Elizabeth." Whitsell put his hands on his knees and bent forward confidentially. "Maybe he doesn't really need to go to Virginia. Maybe he just needs to get used to living in Washington, you know? Tell me something. Are you planning to go back to Virginia with him? Did you used to live there, too, maybe?"

Elizabeth shook her head firmly. "No, no, Mr. Whitsell, you don't understand. I didn't even know Abernathy until about a week ago. And he's not really a dog, in any case. He's a man who was turned into a dog. By magic."

Davis Whitsell was staring at her open-mouthed. She hurried on. "He can talk, Mr. Whitsell. He really can. He's a prisoner right now in this . . ."

"Whoa, back up!" the other interrupted quickly. He shifted into a crouch. "What are you trying to tell me? That this dog can talk? Really talk?"

Elizabeth backed off a step, beginning to wonder if she had done the right thing coming to this man. "Yes. Just like you and me."

The bearded man cocked his head thoughtfully. "That's some imagination you've got there, Elizabeth."

Elizabeth felt stupid. "I'm not making this up, Mr. Whitsell. Abernathy really can talk. It's just that he needs to get to Virginia, and he doesn't know how. I thought maybe you could help him. I was listening to what you said, about how dogs need proper care and how all of us should involve ourselves in helping. Well, Abernathy is my friend, and I want to be sure that he's taken care of, even if he isn't a real dog, and I thought . . ."

Davis Whitsell raised one hand quickly, and she went still. He stood up and glanced around the gymnasium, and Elizabeth glanced with him. The last few students were filing out. "I have to go," she said quietly. "Can you help Abernathy?"

He seemed to consider. "Tell you what," he said suddenly. He took out a wrinkled card that bore an imprint of his name and address. "You bring me a talking dog—a genuine talking dog, now—and I'll help him for sure. I'll take him anywhere he wants to go. Okay?"

Elizabeth beamed. “Do you promise?”

Whitsell shrugged. “Sure.”

Elizabeth beamed some more. “Thanks, Mr. Whitsell! Thanks a lot!” She clutched her books tightly to her chest and hurried off.

The minute her back was turned, Davis Whitsell dismissed the matter with a shake of his head.

Miles Bennett, lawyer-for-hire, sat in the study of his suburban Chicago home amid a clutter of *Northeast Reporters* and *ALR*s and seriously considered having a drink. He had been working on this damn corporate tax assessment case since Monday a week ago, and he wasn’t any closer to a resolution of its multiple legal dilemmas now than he had been when he had first picked it up. He had been working on it day and night, at the office and at home, living it, sleeping it, eating it, and he was sick of it, both figuratively and literally. Yesterday, he had caught the flu, the unpleasant kind that attacks you from both ends, and he was just now beginning to shake its effects. He had spent the afternoon in no small amount of discomfort tramping around the subject properties, a vast office complex in Oak Brook, and he had brought his notes home with him in an effort to decipher them while everything was still fresh in his mind.

If it was possible that *anything* could be fresh in his mind at this point, he thought dismally.

He leaned back in his leather desk chair, his heavy frame sagging. He was a big man with thick dark hair and a mustache that seemed to have been tacked on as an afterthought to a face that in happier times was almost cherubic. Eyes perpetually lidded at half-mast peered out with a mix of weary resignation and sardonic humor on a world that viewed even hardworking, conscientious lawyers such as himself with unrelenting suspicion. Still, that was all right with him. It was just part of the price you paid to do something you really loved.

His sudden smile was ironic. Of course, sometimes you loved it more than others.

That made him think unexpectedly of Ben Holiday, formerly of Holiday & Bennett, Ltd., their old law partnership, of when it was Ben and him against the world. His smile tightened. Ben Holiday had loved the law—knew how to practice it, too. Doc Holiday, courtroom gunfighter. He shook his head. Now Doc was God-knew-where, off fighting dragons and rescuing damsels in some make-believe world that probably existed only in his own mind . . .

Or maybe for real. Miles wrinkled his brow thoughtfully. He had never been quite sure. Maybe never would be.

He brushed the extraneous thoughts from his mind and bent back over the law books and yellow pads. He blinked his eyes wearily. His notes were beginning to blur. He needed to get this done and get to bed.

The phone rang. He glanced over at it, sitting on the end table next to his reading chair. He let it ring a second time. Marge was at bridge and the kids were up the block at the Wilson house. No one home but him. The phone rang a third time.

"Damnit all, anyway!" he swore, lifting himself heavily out of the desk chair. Phone was never for him, always for the kids or Marge; even if it was for him, it was always some ditsy client who didn't have sense enough not to bother him at home with questions that could just as easily wait until morning.

The phone rang a final time as he lifted the receiver. "Hello, Bennett's," he rumbled.

"Miles, it's Ben Holiday."

Miles stiffened in surprise. "Doc? Is that you? I was just thinking about you, for God's sake! How are you? *Where* are you?"

"Las Vegas."

"Las Vegas?"

"I tried to reach you at the office, but they said you were out for the day."

"Yeah, tramping all over hell and gone."

"Listen, Miles, I need a big favor." Ben's voice crackled on the connection. "You'll probably have to drop everything you're doing for the rest of the week, but it's important or I wouldn't ask."

Miles found himself grinning. Same old Doc. "Yeah, yeah, butter me up so you can toss me into the frying pan. What do you need?"

"Money, to begin with. I'm staying at the Shangri-La with a friend, but I don't have any money to pay for it."

Miles was laughing openly now. "For Christ's sake, Doc, you're a millionaire! What do you mean you don't have any money?"

"I mean I don't have any here! So you have to wire me several thousand first thing in the morning. But listen, you have to send it to yourself, to Miles Bennett. That's how I'm registered."

"What? You're using *my* name?"

"I couldn't think of another on the spur of the moment, and I didn't want to use my own. Don't worry, you're not in any trouble."

"Not yet, anyway, you mean."

"Just send it to the hotel directly to my account—your account, that is. Can you do it?"

"Yeah, sure, no problem." Miles shook his head in amusement, settling down comfortably now into the reading chair. "Is that the big favor you needed, money?"

"Partly." Ben sounded subdued and distant. "Miles, you remember how you always wanted to know something about what happened to me when I left the practice? Well, you're going to get your chance. A friend of mine, another friend, not the one with me now, is in trouble here, somewhere in the United States, I think—maybe not, though, we have to find out. I want you to call up one of our investigating agencies and have them find out anything they can about a man named Michel Ard Rhi." He spelled it out and Miles hastily wrote the name down. "I think he lives in the U.S., but, again, I can't be certain. He should be pretty wealthy, probably somewhat reclusive. Likes to use his money, though. Have you got all that?"

"Yeah, Doc, I got it." Miles was frowning.

"Okay. Now here's the rest—and don't argue. I want you to check to see if there is any news—anything at all, rumors, gossip, anything, anywhere—about a dog who talks."

"What?"

"A dog who talks, Miles. I know this sounds ridiculous, but that's the other friend I'm looking for. His name is Abernathy. He's a soft-coated Wheaten Terrier, and he talks. Did you write that down?"

Miles did so hastily, shaking his head. "Doc, I hope you're not putting me on about this."

"I'm dead serious. Abernathy was a man who was turned into a dog. I'll explain it all later. Get what you can on either subject and catch a plane out here as quickly as possible. Bring me whatever sort of file the investigators can put together. And tell them you need it right away, no delays. First of the week at the latest." He paused. "I know this won't be easy, but do what you can, Miles. It really is important."

Miles shifted himself, chuckling. "The part that's going to be hard about this is finding a way to tell the investigators that we're looking for a talking dog! Christ, Doc!"

"Just pick up whatever bits of information there are about any sort of dog that's supposed to talk. It's a long shot, but we might get lucky. Can you break away to fly out?"

"Sure. It'll be good for me, actually. I've been working on a tax assessment case, and it's about to bury me in a sea of mathematics. So you're at the Shangri-La? Who's with you?"

There was a pause. "You wouldn't believe me if I told you, Miles. Just show up and see, okay? And don't forget to wire the money! Room service is the only thing keeping us alive!"

"Don't worry, I won't forget. Hey!" Miles hesitated, listening to the static in the line. "Are you all right, Doc? I mean, other than this thing? You okay?"

There was a pause at the other end. "I'm fine, Miles. I really am. We'll talk soon, okay? You can reach me here if you need me. Just remember to ask for yourself—don't get confused."

Miles roared. "How could I possibly be any more confused than I am now, Doc?"

"I suppose. Take care, Miles. And thanks."

"See you soon, Doc."

The line went dead. Miles placed the receiver back on its cradle and stood up. How about that? he thought, grinning. How about *that*?

Humming cheerfully, he went over to the cupboard and took out a bottle of the Glenlivet scotch Ben Holiday liked so much. Damned if he wasn't going to have that drink after all!

BUTTON, BUTTON

Abernathy lay in his darkened cage and dreamed fitfully of Landover's sunshine and green meadows. He hadn't been feeling very well the past day or so, a condition he attributed to a combination of his confinement and the food—mostly the lack thereof. He half suspected that something in the environment of this land in general was having a debilitating effect on his system, something apart from his present circumstances, but there was no way to test his theory. In any case, he spent most of his time dozing, finding what small refuge he could in his dreams of better times and places.

Elizabeth hadn't been to see him in more than two days now. He noticed that the guards had been checking on him more frequently, and he assumed that her failure to appear was due in part at least to fear of discovery. Michel Ard Rhi had come once. That, too, had been at least two days ago. He had looked at his prisoner quite dispassionately, asked him once if he had anything to give him, then left without another word when Abernathy advised him in no uncertain terms that he was wasting his time.

No one else had come at all.

Abernathy was beginning to grow frightened. He was beginning to believe that he actually was going to be left there to die.

The thought stirred him from his sleep, his dreams faded away, and the reality of his situation intruded once more. He grappled momentarily with the prospect of dying. It might not be so frightening if he were to confront it directly, he decided. He considered his choices in the matter of Michel Ard Rhi and the medallion. There were none. He certainly could not relinquish the medallion; his conscience and his duty would not allow it. Such a powerful magic must not be allowed to pass into the hands of so evil a man. Even death was preferable to that.

Of course, once he was dead, what was to prevent Michel from just taking the medallion off his lifeless body?

He was despondent all over again, thinking of that possibility, and he closed his eyes once more in an effort to escape back into his dreams.

"Hsssst! Abernathy! Wake up!"

Abernathy's eyes slowly opened and he found Elizabeth standing outside his cage. She was gesturing impatiently. "Come on, Abernathy, wake up!"

Abernathy rose stiffly, straightened his soiled clothing, fumbled in his waistcoat pocket for his spectacles, and slipped them over his nose. "I am awake, Elizabeth," he insisted sleepily, shoving the spectacles carefully into place.

"Good!" she whispered, fumbling now with the cage door. "Because we're getting you out of here right now!"

Abernathy watched in befuddlement as the little girl located the lock, inserted a key, twisted it, and pulled. The cage door swung open. "How about that?" she murmured in satisfaction.

"Elizabeth . . ."

"I took the key off the rack in the guard room where they keep the spares. They won't miss it right away! I'll have it back before they know it's gone. Don't worry. No one saw me."

"Elizabeth . . ."

"Come on, Abernathy! What are you waiting for?"

Abernathy couldn't seem to think, staring vacantly at the open cage door. "This seems awfully dangerous for you to . . ."

"Do you want out of here or not?" she demanded, a trace of irritation in her voice.

From down the hall, beyond the passageway door, the imprisoned dogs suddenly began barking, yelps and howls of dismay. "Yes, I do," Abernathy answered quickly and crawled through the open door.

He stood erect in the passageway beyond for the first time since his imprisonment, feeling immediately better. Elizabeth closed the cage door once more and locked it. "This way, Abernathy! Hurry!"

He followed her across the passageway and through the break in the wall to a stairway beyond. Elizabeth turned and pushed the hidden door in the wall section closed. The sounds of the barking dogs died away into silence.

They stood there in the blackness a moment until Elizabeth clicked on a flashlight. Abernathy was pleasantly surprised to discover that he still retained sufficient faculties to remember reading about flashlights in one of the little girl's magazines that first afternoon he had hidden out in her room. He guessed he wasn't as debilitated as he had imagined.

Elizabeth led the way up the stairs, Abernathy dutifully following. "We don't have much time," she was saying. "The Coles are already here to take me to the school chorus program. You remember my friend Nita? They're her parents. They're visiting with my dad while I finish dressing." Abernathy noticed she was wearing a ruffled pink and white dress. "That's what I'm supposed to be doing now. Nita's up there in my room, keeping watch, pretending she's helping me. When we get back, she'll go down and tell her parents and my dad that I'll be right there. While she's doing that, I'll sneak you downstairs the back way to a door that leads out to the yard. The Coles' car is parked there and we can hide you in the trunk. The release is on the dash. It's perfect! The guards won't bother to check the Coles—not with my dad with them."

Abernathy started. "An automobile, one of those mechanical . . . ?"

"Shhhh! Yes, yes, an automobile! Just listen, will you?" Elizabeth had no time for interruptions. "Once at the school, we'll all go in to get ready, but I'll tell the Coles I have to go back out for my purse, which I'll leave in the car. When I come out, I'll open the trunk and let you out. Okay?"

Abernathy was shaking his head doubtfully. "What if you cannot get me out? Will I be able to breathe in there? What if I . . . ?"

"Abernathy!" Elizabeth turned, exasperated. "Don't worry, all right? I'll get you out. And you can breathe just fine in a car trunk. Now, listen! I found someone to help you get to Virginia."

They had reached a landing where the stairs stopped at a door. Elizabeth turned, eyes bright. "His name is Mr. Whitsell. He's a dog trainer. He goes around to the schools and talks about animal care and things. He said if I brought you to him, he would help you. Now wait here."

She pushed open the door on the landing, handed the flashlight to Abernathy, disappeared through the opening, and pushed the door shut again. Abernathy stood there pointing the flashlight at the wall and waiting. Things were happening much too rapidly to suit him, but there was nothing to be done about it. If there was even the slightest chance that he might escape Graum Wythe and Michel Ard Rhi, he had to take it.

Elizabeth was back almost at once, bundled in a coat, scarf, and gloves. "Put this on," she instructed, handing him an old topcoat and brimmed hat. "I took them from the storage closets where they keep the old stuff."

She took the flashlight from him while he struggled into the hat and coat. The coat felt like a tent on him, and the hat wouldn't stay in place. Elizabeth looked at him and giggled. "You look like a spy!"

She led him through the wall opening into a closet filled with brooms, mops, and buckets. She paused, peered through the door leading out, then beckoned him after her. They slipped quickly down a hallway to a back stairs that wound downward to the ground floor and a set of double doors that opened onto the back yard.

Abernathy peered through a glass panel in the door over Elizabeth's shoulder. An automobile was parked close against the castle wall. Lights bathed the yard in their muted yellow glow, but no one was about.

"Ready?" she asked, turning to look up at him.

"Ready," he answered.

She pulled open the double doors and rushed for the automobile. Abernathy followed. She had the driver's door open and the trunk release pulled by the time he reached her. "Hurry!" she whispered and helped him climb hastily inside. "Don't worry!" she said when he was safely settled, pausing momentarily with her hands on the lid. "I'll be back to get you out when we reach the school! Just be patient!"

Then the lid slammed down and she was gone.

Abernathy lay hidden in the automobile for only a few minutes before he heard voices approach, the passenger doors open and close again, and the engine start up. Then the automobile began to move, jouncing and bumping him all over the place as it twisted and wound down the roadway and steadily picked up speed. The trunk was carpeted, but there wasn't much padding underneath, and Abernathy was thoroughly knocked about. He tried to find something to hold on to, but there wasn't anything to grasp, and he had to settle for bracing himself against the top and sides.

The ride seemed to go on interminably. To make matters worse, the automobile gave off a rather noxious odor that quickly upset Abernathy's stomach and gave him a headache. He began to wonder if he was going to survive the experience.

Then, finally, the automobile slowed and stopped, the doors opened and closed, the voices faded away, and all went still except for the muffled and somewhat distant sounds of other doors opening and closing and other voices calling out. Abernathy waited patiently, letting cramped muscles relax again, rubbing strained ligaments and bruised bones. He promised himself faithfully that if he could just get safely back to Landover, he would never, under any circumstances, even think of riding in another of these horrendous, mechanical monsters.

Time slipped away. Elizabeth did not come. Abernathy lay in the dark and listened for her, thinking that the worst had happened, that she had been prevented somehow from returning, and that now he was trapped there indefinitely. He began to doze. He was almost asleep when he heard the sound of footsteps.

The car door opened, the trunk latch was sprung, the lid popped up, and there was Elizabeth. She was gasping for breath. "Hurry, Abernathy, I have to get back right away!" She helped him from the trunk. "I'm sorry it took so long, but my dad wanted to come with me and I had to wait until he . . . Are you all right? You look all bent over! Oh, I'm sorry about this, really I am!"

Abernathy shook his head quickly. "No, no! No need to be sorry about anything. I am just fine, Elizabeth." A few latecomers were passing in the distance, and he pulled the topcoat close about him and adjusted the brimmed hat. He bent down to her. "Thank you, Elizabeth," he said softly. "Thank you for everything."

She put her arms about him and hugged him, then stepped quickly back. "Mr. Whitsell lives a couple of miles north. Follow this road out here." She pointed. "When you reach a road with a sign that says Forest Park, turn right and count the numbers until you find 2986. It'll be on the left. Oh, Abernathy!"

She hugged him again, and he hugged her back. "Don't worry. I will find it, Elizabeth," he assured her.

"I have to go," she said and started away. Then she turned and hurried back. "I almost forgot. Take this." She thrust an envelope into his paw.

"What is it?"

"The money I promised, for an airplane ticket or whatever. It's okay to keep it," she added hastily as he tried to give it back. "You might need it. If you don't, you can give it back when we see each other again."

"Elizabeth . . ."

"No, you keep it!" she insisted, turning and starting quickly away. "Good-bye, Abernathy! I'll miss you!"

She ran toward the school building and was gone.

"I'll miss you, too," Abernathy whispered after her.

It was approaching midnight by the time Abernathy turned up the walk to 2986 Forest Park, still wearing the brimmed hat and the trench coat. He had made a wrong turn some distance back and had been forced to retrace his steps. As he approached the little house with the shuttered windows and flower boxes, he could see a man dozing in a chair through the partially drawn blinds of the front window. The light next to him was the only light burning in the house.

Abernathy went up to the door cautiously and knocked. When there was no response, he knocked again.

"Yeah, what is it?" a voice growled.

Abernathy didn't know what to say, so he waited. After a moment, the voice said, "Okay, just a minute, I'm coming."

Footsteps approached. The front door opened, and the man from the chair stood there, bearded and sleepy-eyed, wearing jeans and a work shirt open to the waist over a sleeveless undershirt. A tiny black poodle stood next to him, sniffing. "Are you Mr. Whitsell?" Abernathy asked.

Davis Whitsell stared, his mouth dropping open. "Uh . . . yeah," he said finally.

Abernathy glanced around uneasily. "My name is Abernathy. Do you suppose that . . ."

The other man started; then he seemed to understand and managed a slight smile. "The little girl at Franklin!" he exclaimed. "You're the one she told me about! You're the one she said was locked up somewhere, right? Sure, you're the talking dog!"

"I'm a man who was turned into a dog," Abernathy said rather stiffly.

"Sure, sure, she told me about that!" Whitsell backed off a step or two. "Well, come in, come on in . . . Abernathy! Sophie, get back. Here, let me take that coat from you. Way too big, anyway. Hat doesn't do a thing for you either. Here, sit down."

"Who is it, Davis?" a woman's voice called from somewhere down the hall.

"Uh, no one, Alice—just a friend," Whitsell replied hurriedly. "Go back to sleep." He leaned close. "My wife, Alice," he whispered.

He took Abernathy's coat and hat and beckoned him across the living room to the couch. Sophie wagged her tail and whined softly, sniffing at Abernathy with dismaying enthusiasm. Abernathy nudged her away.

The TV was on. Whitsell turned the volume down carefully, then seated himself across from Abernathy. He leaned forward eagerly, his voice hushed. "Well, tell you the truth, I thought the little girl was kidding me. I thought she was making all this up. But . . ." He stopped, as if trying to gather his thoughts. "So, you were changed into a dog, were you? Terrier breed, right? Uh, English breed, I'd guess."

"Soft-coated Wheaten Terrier," Abernathy advised, looking around doubtfully.

"Sure, that's it." Whitsell got up again. "You look all done in, you know that? Would you like something to eat, drink maybe? Uh, real food, right—you being human and all? Come on into the kitchen, I'll fix you something."

They walked from the living room to a kitchen that looked out into the back yard. Whitsell poked through the refrigerator and came up with some cold ham, potato salad, and milk. He made Abernathy a sandwich, commenting over and over again on how amazing he was. God almighty, he said, a real live talking dog! He must have said it a dozen times. Abernathy was offended, but he kept it to himself. Finally Whitsell finished, carried the food to a small folding table with four chairs, made Abernathy sit down, grabbed a beer for himself, and sat down as well.

"Look, the little girl . . . uh, what's her name?"

"Elizabeth."

"Yeah, Elizabeth said you had to get to Virginia. That right?"

Abernathy nodded, his mouth full of sandwich. He was starved.

"What do you have to go to Virginia for?"

Abernathy considered his answer. "I have friends there," he said finally.

"Well, can't we just call them up?" the other asked. "I mean, if you need help, why not just give them a call?"

Abernathy was confused. "A call?"

"Sure, by phone."

"Oh, telephone." He remembered now what that was. "They don't have a telephone."

Davis Whitsell smiled. "That so?" He sipped at his beer and watched while Abernathy finished his food. The dog could feel him thinking.

"Well, it won't be easy getting you all the way to Virginia," he ventured after a moment.

Abernathy looked up, hesitated, then said, "I have some money to pay my way."

Whitsell shrugged. "Maybe so, but we can't just put you on an airplane or a train and ship you out. There would be all sorts of questions about who or what you were. Uh, pardon me for saying that, but you got to understand that people aren't used to seeing dogs who dress up and walk about and talk like you do."

He cleared his throat. "Other thing is, the little girl said something about you being held prisoner. That right?"

Abernathy nodded. "Elizabeth helped me escape."

"Then this might be dangerous business, me helping you. Someone's going to be pretty unhappy once they find you gone. Someone's liable to be coming after you. That means we have to be extra careful, don't it? 'Cause you're pretty special, you know. Don't find dogs like you every day. Sorry. Men like you, I mean. So best to get in quick, get out quick. Make what we can off this, eh?" He seemed to be thinking his way through the matter. "Won't be easy. You'll have to do exactly what I tell you."

Abernathy nodded. "I understand." He drank the last of his milk. "Can you help at all?"

"Sure! You bet I can!" Whitsell rubbed his hands briskly. "Best thing for now, though, is to get some sleep, then we'll talk about it in the morning, come up with something. Okay? Got the spare room down the hall you can use. Bed's all made up. Alice won't like it, doesn't like anything she can't understand, but I'll handle her, don't you worry. Come on with me."

He took Abernathy down the hall to the spare room, showed him the bed and the bath, provided him with a set of towels, and got him settled in. All the while he was thinking out loud, talking about missed opportunities and once-in-a-lifetime chances. If he could just figure out a way to make things work, he kept saying.

Abernathy pulled off his clothes, climbed into bed, and lay back. He was vaguely bothered by what he was hearing, but he was too exhausted to give the matter proper consideration. He closed his eyes wearily. Whitsell switched off the light, stepped outside, and pulled the door shut behind him.

The house was very still. Just outside, the branches of a tree brushed against the window like claws.

Abernathy listened for only a moment. Then he was asleep.

JERICHO

It was approaching nightfall when Questor Thews, the kobolds, and the G'home Gnomes arrived at Rhyndweir. The sky was hazy blue-gray with tiny strips of pink where the sun still lingered as it fled from the encroaching darkness. Mist clung to the Greensward in gauzy strips, turning the land to shadows and blurred images. Rain still fell, a thin veil of damp that seemed to hang on the air. Sounds were muted and displaced in the murkiness, and it was as if life had lost all substance and drifted bodiless.

Bunion led the way cautiously as they crossed the bridge spanning the juncture of the rivers that fronted the towering plateau on which the fortress castle of Lord Kallendbor had been built. The town beneath was closing down for the day, a jumbled mix of grunting men and animals, of clanging iron and creaking wood, and of weariness and sweat. The little company passed down the roadway through the shops and cottages; the buildings were dim, squat mounds in the mist, from which slivers of candlelight peeked out warily. The roadway was rutted and muddied from the rain, a morass that sucked at their boots and the horses' hoofs. Heads turned to watch them pass, evidenced momentary interest, then turned quickly away again.

"I'm hungry!" whined Fillip.

"My feet hurt!" added Sot.

But Parsnip hissed softly in warning, and the gnomes went still again.

Then Rhyndweir materialized before them out of the mist and rain. Walls and parapets, towers and battlements, the whole of the great castle slowly took shape, a monstrous ghost hunkered down against the night. It was a massive thing, lifting skyward over a hundred feet, its uppermost spires lost in the low-hanging clouds. Flags hung limply from standards, torches flickered dimly from within their lamps, and dozens of sodden guards kept watch upon the walls. The outer gates yawned open, huge wooden and ironbound jaws fronting a lowered portcullis. The inner gates stood closed. It was a forbidding sight, and the little company approached with mixed feelings of wariness and trepidation.

The gate watch stopped them, asked them to state their business, and then moved them into the shelter of an alcove in the shadow of the wall while a message was carried to the Lord Kallendbor. Time dragged slowly past as they stood shivering and weary in the gloom and the damp. Questor was not pleased; a King's emissary was not to be kept waiting. When their escort finally arrived, a pair of lesser nobles dispatched directly from Kallendbor with perfunctory apologies for the delay, the wizard was quick to voice his displeasure at their treatment. They were representatives of the King, he pointed out coldly—not supplicants. The escort merely apologized once again, no more concerned about the matter than before, and beckoned them inside.

Leaving the horses and pack animals, they circumvented the portcullis and inner gates by slipping through a series of hidden passages in the walls, crossed the main courtyard to the castle proper, entered an all but invisible side door which first had to be unlocked, and then passed down several corridors until they reached a great hall dominated by a huge fireplace at its far end. Logs burned brightly in the hearth, the heat almost suffocating. Questor winced away and squinted into the light.

The Lord Kallendbor turned from where he stood before the blaze—so close to the fire, it seemed to Questor, that he must be scorched. Kallendbor was a big man, tall and heavily muscled, his face and body scarred from countless battles. He wore chain mail tonight beneath his robes, armored boots, and a brace of daggers. His brilliant red hair and beard gave him a striking appearance—more so against the flames of the hearth. When he came forward, it was as if he brought the fire with him.

He dismissed the lesser nobles with a brief nod. "Well met, Questor Thews," he rumbled, extending one callused hand.

Questor accepted the hand and held it. "Better met, my Lord, if I had not been kept waiting so long in the cold and the wet!"

The kobolds hissed softly in agreement, while the G'home Gnomes shrank back behind Questor's legs, their eyes like dinner plates. Kallendbor took them all in at a glance and dismissed them just as quickly.

"My apologies," he offered Questor, withdrawing his hand. "Things have been a bit uncertain of late. I must be cautious these days."

Questor brushed the loose water from his cloak, owlish face twisting into a frown. "Cautious? More than that, I would guess, my Lord. I saw the deployment of your watch, the guards at all the entrances, the portcullis down, and the inner gates closed. I see the armor you wear, even in your own home. You behave as if you are at siege."

Kallendbor rubbed his hands briskly and looked back at the fire. "Perhaps

I am." He seemed distracted. "What brings you to Rhyndweir, Questor Thews? Some further bidding of the High Lord? What does he require now? That I battle demons with him? That I chase after that black unicorn again? What does he wish now? Tell me."

Questor hesitated. There was something in the way Kallendbor asked his questions that suggested he already knew the answers. "Something has been stolen from the High Lord," he said finally.

"Ah?" Kallendbor kept his eyes on the blaze. "What might that be? A bottle, perhaps?"

The room went still. Questor held his breath.

"A bottle with dancing clowns painted on it?" Kallendbor added softly.

"You have the bottle in your possession, then." Questor made the question a statement of fact.

Kallendbor turned now, smiling as wickedly as the kobolds ever thought of doing. "Yes, Questor Thews, I have it. A troll gave it to me—a miserable, thieving troll. He thought to sell it to me, actually, this thief. He had stolen it from some other trolls after they had quarreled among themselves. He survived the quarrel, wounded, and came to me. He would not have done so—come to me, that is—if he had been thinking clearly, if he had not been so badly hurt . . ."

The big man trailed off, shaking his head. "He told me there was magic in the bottle, a little creature, a demon, a Darkling he said, who could give the holder of the bottle anything he wished. I laughed at him, Questor Thews. You can understand. I have never had much faith in magic; only in strength of arms. Why would you want to sell anything so dear, I asked this troll? Then I saw the fear in his eyes and I knew why. He was frightened of the bottle. Its power was too great. He wanted to be rid of the bottle—but there was enough greed left in him to wish something in return."

Kallendbor looked away. "I think he believed the bottle was responsible somehow for the destruction of his companions—that in some way this creature that lives within caused it."

Questor said nothing, waiting. He wasn't sure yet where this was leading and he wanted to find out.

Kallendbor sighed. "So I paid him the price he asked, and then I had his head cut off and spiked on the gateway. Did you see it when you entered? No? Well, I put it there to remind anyone who needs reminding that I have no use for thieves and swindlers."

Fillip and Sot were shivering against Questor's legs. Questor reached down surreptitiously and slapped them. He straightened again as Kallendbor looked around.

"You claim the bottle belongs to the High Lord, Questor Thews, but the bottle does not bear the mark of the throne." Kallendbor shrugged. "The bottle could belong to anyone."

Questor bristled. "Nevertheless . . ."

"Nevertheless," the big man cut in quickly, "I shall give the bottle back to you." He paused. "After I am finished with it."

The flames in the hearth crackled loudly in the silence as they consumed the wood. Questor was buffeted by a mix of emotions. "What are you saying?" he asked.

"That I have a use for this bottle, Questor Thews," the other said quietly. "That I intend to give the magic a chance."

There was something in the big man's eyes that Questor could not identify—something that wasn't anger or determination or anything else he had ever seen there before. "You must reconsider," he advised quickly.

"Reconsider? Why, Questor Thews? Because you say so?"

"Because the magic of the bottle is too dangerous!"

Kallendbor laughed. "Magic doesn't frighten me!"

"Would you challenge the High Lord on this?" Questor was angry now.

The big man's face went hard. "The High Lord isn't here, Questor Thews. Only you."

"As his representative!"

"In my home!" Kallendbor was livid. "Let the matter rest!"

Questor nodded slowly. He recognized now what was reflected in Kallendbor's eyes. It was an almost desperate need. For what, he wondered? What was it that he wanted the bottle to give him?

He cleared his throat. "There is no reason for us to argue, my Lord," he said soothingly. "Tell me—to what use will you put the magic?"

But the big man shook his head. "Not tonight, Questor Thews. Time enough to talk about it tomorrow." He clapped his hands and a scattering of servants appeared. "A hot bath, some dry clothes, and a good meal for our guests," he instructed. "Then to bed."

Questor bowed reluctantly, turned to go, then hesitated. "I still think . . ."

"And I think," Kallendbor interrupted pointedly, "that you should rest now, Questor Thews."

He stood there, armor glinting in the firelight, eyes flat and hard. Questor saw there was nothing more to be accomplished at this meeting. He must bide his time.

"Very well, my Lord," he said finally. "Good night to you."

He bowed and departed the room with the kobolds and gnomes in tow.

Later that night, when his companions were sleeping and the castle was at rest, Questor Thews went back. He slipped down the empty corridors, hiding himself with small touches of magic from the few guards he encountered, moving on cat's feet through the stillness. His purpose was rather vague, even in his own mind. He supposed he needed to satisfy himself about Kallendbor and the bottle—that matters were as Rhyndweir's Lord had declared them to be and not as Questor feared.

He reached the great hall without being seen, bypassed its entrance and the sentries standing watch in favor of a connecting anteroom, eased the anteroom door open, then closed it softly behind him. He stood there in the darkness for a moment, letting his eyes adjust. He knew this castle as he knew all the castles of Landover. This one, like most of the others, was a maze of connecting halls and rooms, some known, some secret. He'd learned much that he wasn't necessarily intended to learn while carrying messages in the service of the old King.

When his sight grew sharp enough to permit it, he moved across the room to a shadowed nook, touched a wooden peg in the wall, and pushed gently on the panel it secured. The panel swung back, giving him a clear view of what lay beyond.

Kallendbor sat in a great chair facing the hearth, the bottle with its painted clowns resting loosely in his lap. His face was flushed and his smile an odd grimace. The Darkling skittered about the room, going first to this, then to that, eyes as bright as the flames blazing in the hearth, but infinitely more wicked. Questor found he could not stare into those eyes comfortably for more than an instant.

Kallendbor called, and the Darkling scampered up his arm and rubbed itself against him like a cat. "Master, great master, such strength as I feel in you!" it purred.

Kallendbor laughed, then said to it, "Leave me, creature! Go play!"

The Darkling dropped down again, skittered across the stone floor to the open hearth, and leaped into the fire. Dancing about, the creature played with the flames as if they were cool water.

"Black thing!" Kallendbor hissed. Questor saw him raise an ale mug rather unsteadily, the contents splashing down his front. Kallendbor was drunk.

Questor Thews thought seriously then of stealing the bottle and its loathsome inhabitant from the Lord of Rhyndweir and ending this nonsense once and for all. There would be little risk to himself. He could simply wait until the man tired of his game and returned the bottle to its hiding place, then nip the treasure for himself, collect the Kobolds and the G'home Gnomes, and disappear.

It was a most tempting thought.

But he decided against it. First, everyone who had stolen the bottle had come to a bad end. Second, Questor had never been a thief and did not relish the thought of starting now. Finally, Kallendbor had said he would return the bottle after he finished with it and he deserved the benefit of the doubt. He had always been—despite his other obvious failings—a man of his word.

Reluctantly, Questor set the thought aside.

He risked a final look into the room. Kallendbor sat slumped in his chair, staring at the hearth. Within its flames, the Darkling was laughing and dancing gleefully.

Questor let the wall panel swing shut again, shook his grizzled head doubtfully, and departed for his room.

Dawn brought an end to the rains, with skies swept clear of clouds and gloom and colored once more a vast, depthless blue. Sunshine flooded the valley, and even the dark, catacombed recesses of Rhyndweir seemed bright and new.

Questor and his companions were awakened at first light by a knock on their bedchamber door and a message from Kallendbor. They were to dress and join him for breakfast, the young page announced. After that, they would be going for a ride.

The G'home Gnomes had long since had enough of Kallendbor and begged Questor to be allowed to stay in their rooms where they could draw the window coverings closed again and snuggle safely in the darkness. Questor shrugged and agreed, inwardly relieved that he would not have to contend with their constant whining while dealing with the problem of how to get the bottle back from Kallendbor before he caused any mischief with it. He assigned Parsnip to keep watch over them and arranged for breakfast to be delivered to their rooms. Then, with Bunion in tow, he hurried out to join Rhyndweir's Lord.

Breakfast was almost completed, however, before Kallendbor appeared, armored head to foot and bristling with weapons. In one gloved hand he carried a sack containing an object that was almost certainly the bottle. He greeted Questor perfunctorily and beckoned him to follow.

They went down to the main courtyard. Several hundred knights in full battle dress waited with their mounts. Kallendbor called for his own horse, saw to it that Questor was provided with his gray, mounted, and wheeled the knights into formation. Questor had to hurry to keep up. The gates opened, the portcullis rose with a screech of metal, and out the column rode.

Questor Thews was brought to the forefront to ride directly beside Kallendbor. Bunion raced off on his own, on foot as always, anxious to keep himself clear of the dust and noise of the horsemen. Questor looked once or twice to find him, but the kobold was as invisible as air. The wizard quickly gave up searching and directed his efforts instead to the task of discovering what Kallendbor was up to.

The Lord of Rhyndweir appeared to have no intention of disclosing that information, all but ignoring Questor as he led his men down the rutted roadway through the town. People appeared in the doors and windows of the shops and cottages, and a few halfhearted calls and whistles trailed after. No one in the town had any idea what Kallendbor was about, or cared much, for that matter. They wanted to be kept safe—that was all that really mattered to them. Kallendbor had never been a popular ruler—just a strong one. Twenty Lords ruled the Greensward, but Kallendbor was the most powerful and his people knew it. He was the one Lord to whom the others all deferred. He was the Lord no one dared challenge.

Until now, it seemed.

"I am betrayed, Questor Thews!" Kallendbor was suddenly telling him. "I am beset at every turn in a way I would never have believed possible! Betrayed, mind you, not by my enemies, but by my fellow Lords! Stosyth, Harrandye, Wilse! Lords I thought I could trust—Lords who, at least, were too cowed to act if I did not approve!" Kallendbor's face was scarlet. "But Strehan is the one who surprised and disappointed me most, Questor Thews—Strehan, the closest of them all to me! Like an ungrateful child who bites its father's tending hand!"

He spit into the dirt as they rode, the column winding down across the bridge and out into the grasslands. Leather battle harnesses creaked, metal fastenings clanked, horses snorted and nickered, and men called out. Questor tried to picture the tall, shambling, dour Strehan as a child of any sort, ungrateful or otherwise, and found the task beyond him.

"They have built this . . . this tower, Questor Thews!" Kallendbor snapped in fury. "The four of them! Built it at the falls of the Syr, at the juncture of my lands! They tell me it is an outpost, nothing more. They apparently take me for a fool! It stands taller than the walls of Rhyndweir, and its battlements shadow the whole of my eastern borders! If they should choose, they could close off the river itself and dam up the waters that feed my fields! This tower offends me, wizard! It hurts me in ways I would not have thought I could be hurt!"

He bent close as they rode. "I would have destroyed it the moment I discovered it but for the fact that the combined armies of these four dogs guard it as one! I have not the strength to break them without so decimating my own armies as to leave me weakened and vulnerable to all! So I have been forced to endure this . . . this aberration!"

He jerked upright again, eyes bits of ice. "But no more!"

Questor saw it all instantly. "My Lord, the magic of the bottle is too dangerous . . ."

"Dangerous!" Kallendbor cut him short with a vicious chop of one hand. "Nothing is more dangerous than this tower! Nothing! It must be destroyed! If the magic can serve my needs, then I will chance whatever danger it poses and gladly!"

He wheeled ahead, and Questor was left with a mouthful of dust and a feeling of helplessness in the face of what was surely to come.

They rode northeast toward the Melchor through the remainder of the morning until at last, as the midday approached, the falls of the Syr came into view. There was the tower, a massive, stone-block fortress situated on the bluff at the edge of the falls where they spilled down into the valley. It was indeed a monstrous thing, all black and bristling with battlements and repelling devices. Armed men stalked its parapets, and riders patrolled its causeways. Trumpets and shouts sounded at the approach of Kallendbor's knights, and the tower stirred to life as if a sluggish giant.

The Lord of Rhyndweir signaled for a halt, and the column pulled up at the river's edge some several hundred yards beyond the base of the bluff and the fortress tower. Kallendbor sat looking at the tower for a moment, then called forward one of his knights.

"Tell those in the tower that they have until midday to leave," he instructed. "Say to them, at midday the tower will be destroyed. Now, go."

The knight rode off and Kallendbor had the column stand down. They waited. Questor considered once again saying something to Kallendbor about the danger of using the bottle's magic, but decided against it. It was pointless to argue the matter further; Kallendbor's mind was made up. The wiser course of action was to allow Rhyndweir's Lord to have his way for the moment, but to get the bottle back from him immediately after this business was finished. Questor Thews was not happy with the prospect, but it seemed to him that he had no other reasonable choice.

He stood next to his gray, his tall frame stooped beneath his patchwork robes as he stared off into the distance and thought suddenly of the High Lord and of Abernathy. Thinking of them distressed him further. He certainly had not done much to help either of them in this matter so far, he thought dismally.

The messenger returned. The men in the tower would not be leaving, he reported. They had simply laughed at the ultimatum. They had suggested that Kallendbor leave instead. Kallendbor grinned like a wolf when he heard the messenger's report, fixed his gaze on the tower, and did not look away again as he awaited the arrival of midday.

When it came, Rhyndweir's Lord grunted in satisfaction, climbed back aboard his mount, and said, "Come with me, Questor Thews."

Together, they rode forward along the river's edge for about a hundred yards, then stopped and dismounted. Kallendbor stood so that the horses blocked what he was doing from his waiting men. Then he brought out the sack from a saddle pouch and produced the brightly painted bottle.

"Now, we shall see," he whispered softly, cradling his treasure.

He pulled free the stopper and out climbed the Darkling, squinting its reddened eyes against the sunlight. "Master!" it hissed softly, stroking its hands along Kallendbor's gloved fingers. "What is it you wish?"

Kallendbor pointed. "Destroy that tower!" He paused, glancing briefly at Questor. "If your magic is strong enough, that is!" he added in challenge.

"Master, my magic is as strong as your life!" The demon spit the words out with a curl of its lip.

It climbed down from the bottle and skittered off across the ground, over the river's waters as if they were nothing more than a walkway, and out into the plains directly below the bluff where the fortress stood. There it stopped. It did nothing for a moment, gazing upward. Then it seemed to jump and whirl, to dance about in a sudden profusion of colored light, and a monstrous horn appeared out of nowhere. The demon darted away to a point another hundred yards along the base of the bluff, and a second horn appeared. It darted away again, and a third appeared.

The demon stood back then and pointed, and the horns began to sound—a long, deep, mournful howl like the wailing of some great wind through an empty canyon.

"See!" Kallendbor whispered in delight.

The wailing was causing the whole of the land about them to quake, but nowhere more so than atop the bluff where the offending tower sat. The tower shuddered as if it were a stricken beast. Cracks began to appear along its seams, and stone blocks began to loosen. Kallendbor and Questor Thews braced. The sound of the horns rose, and now the horses were stamping and rearing, and Kallendbor had to seize the reins of both and hold them fast to keep them from fleeing.

"Demon spawn!" the Lord of Rhyndweir cried with a howl.

The horns reached a new pitch, and the land split apart all about them in deep cracks and crevices. The bluff was shattered, and the tower was turned into an avalanche of crumbling rock. Men screamed from within. The walls exploded into rubble in an instant's time, and the whole of the tower collapsed. Down it tumbled to the plains and the river's waters and was gone.

Then the horns disappeared, and the sound of their wailing faded into silence. The land was still again, empty save for the awestruck men of Rhyndweir and the cloud of dust and silt that rose above the rubble of the shattered tower.

The Darkling skittered back across the river and bounded up once more onto the lip of the bottle, its grin wicked and sharp. "Done, master!" it hissed. "Done at your command!"

Kallendbor's face was alive with excitement. "Yes, demon! Such power!"

"Your power!" the Darkling soothed. "Yours only, master!"

Questor Thews did not care one bit for the look that crossed Kallendbor's face when he heard that. "Kallendbor . . ." he started to say.

But the big man waved him into silence. "Back into the bottle, little one," he commanded.

The Darkling slipped obediently from view, and Kallendbor replaced the stopper.

"Remember your promise," Questor tried again, stepping forward to claim the bottle.

But Kallendbor snatched it away. "Yes, yes, Questor Thews!" he snapped. "But only when I am finished! Only then. I may have . . . other uses yet."

Without waiting for the wizard's response, he mounted his horse and rode quickly away. Questor Thews stood there, staring after him. He turned back one final time to gaze up at the empty space where only moments earlier the tower had stood. All those men dead, he thought suddenly. And Kallendbor barely gave them a thought.

He shook his head worriedly and pulled himself back up on his frightened gray.

He knew already that Kallendbor was never going to return the bottle to him. He was going to have to take it back.

He returned to Rhyndweir lost in thought, the day slipping into evening almost before he knew it. He ate dinner in his room with the gnomes and Parsnip. Kallendbor left him there willingly, making no effort to insist on his presence in the dining hall. Kallendbor did not attend himself. There were clearly other matters of more pressing concern for the Lord of Rhyndweir.

Questor was halfway through his meal when he realized that Bunion had failed to return. He had no idea what had become of the little kobold. No one had seen anything of him since early morning.

When dinner was finished, Questor took a walk to clear his thoughts, found that they were too murky to do so, and returned to his bedchamber to sleep. He went to bed still wondering what had become of Bunion.

It was after midnight when the bedchamber door burst open and Kallendbor stalked through. "Where is it, Questor Thews?" he shouted in fury.

Questor looked up from his pillow, sleepy-eyed, and tried to figure out what was happening. Parsnip was already between him and the Lord of Rhyndweir, hissing in warning, teeth gleaming brightly. The G'home Gnomes were cowering under the bed. Torchlight cast a harsh glare from the hallway beyond and there were armed men milling about uncertainly.

Kallendbor loomed over him, an angry giant. "You will return it to me at once, old man!"

Questor rose, indignant now. "I haven't the faintest idea what you . . ."

"The bottle, Questor Thews—what have you done with the bottle?"

"The bottle?"

"It is missing, wizard!" Kallendbor was livid. "Stolen from a room locked all around and guarded at every entrance! No ordinary man could have accomplished that! It would have required someone who could enter and leave without being seen—someone like yourself!"

Bunion! thought Questor instantly. A kobold could go where others could not and not be seen doing it! Bunion must have . . .

Kallendbor reached for Questor, and only the sight of Parsnip's bared teeth kept him from seizing the wizard's thin neck. "Give it to me, Questor Thews, or I'll have you . . . !"

"I do not have the bottle, my Lord!" Questor snapped in reply, pushing forward bravely to confront the other. Kallendbor was as big as a wall.

"If you do not have it, then you know where it is!" the other rasped in fury. "Tell me!"

Questor took a deep breath. "My word is known to be good everywhere, my Lord," he said evenly. "You know that to be so. I do not lie. The truth is exactly as I have told you. I do not have the bottle nor do I know where it is. I have seen nothing of it since this morning when you took it away." He cleared his throat. "I warned you that the magic was dangerous and that—"

"Enough!" Kallendbor wheeled away and stalked back to the open door. When he reached it, he wheeled back again. "You will stay as my guest a few days more, Questor Thews!" he said. "I think you would do well to pray that the bottle reappears in that time—one way or the other!"

He walked out, slamming the door behind him. Questor could hear the locks snapping into place and the sound of men taking up watch.

"We are being made prisoners!" he exclaimed in disbelief.

He started across the room, stopped, started forward again, stopped again, thought angrily of what the High Lord would do when he learned that his representatives were being held against their will by a land baron, and then remembered that the High Lord would do nothing because Ben Holiday wasn't even in Landover anymore and wouldn't know a thing about any of this.

In short, Questor realized dismally, he was on his own.

It was several hours later that Bunion reappeared. He did not come through the door, being no fool, but through the window of the tower wall. He tapped softly on the shutter until Questor opened it in curiosity and found him perched there on the window ledge. Below, it was a straight drop of at least sixty feet to the battlement wall.

The little kobold was grinning broadly, his teeth flashing. In one hand was a length of knotted rope. Questor peered out. Somehow Bunion must have scaled the castle wall to reach them.

"Come to rescue us, I see!" Questor whispered in excitement and smiled back. "You were right to do so!"

Bunion, it happened, had been as suspicious of Kallendbor's intentions as

Questor and had decided to keep an eye on things from a distance after witnessing the destruction of the tower. Kobolds, of course, could do that; you couldn't see them if they didn't want you to. That was the way of things with true fairy creatures. Bunion understood all too well the awesome power of the magic wielded by the Darkling and he did not think Kallendbor strong enough to resist its lure. Better that he remain hidden, he had decided, until he could be certain that Questor and the others would not become victims of Kallendbor's misguided ambition. It was fortunate he had done so.

Questor helped the kobold crawl inside, and together they began tying one end of the knotted rope about a wall hook. The others were awake now as well, and Questor was quick to hush the gnomes into silence. The last thing he needed was for Fillip and Sot to start whining. They worked quickly and quietly, and the rope was firmly fastened in minutes. Then out the window they all went, one after the other, hand over hand down the castle wall. It was easy going for the kobolds and the gnomes, and only Questor was forced to work a bit at it.

Once safely down, they followed Bunion along the castle wall to a stairway and down that to a passage leading to an iron door that opened to the outside. Slipping through the dark, keeping within the shadows, they crossed to the back of the town and arrived at a shed where waited the horses and pack animals Bunion had somehow managed to retrieve.

Questor mounted his gray, put Fillip and Sot together on Jurisdiction, left the remaining animals to Parsnip's care, and signaled for Bunion to lead them out. Slowly, cautiously, they made their way through the sleeping town, crossed the bridge, and disappeared into the night.

"Farewell and good riddance, Lord Kallendbor!" Questor shouted back once they were safely into the grasslands.

He was feeling considerably better about things. He had extracted himself and his friends from a difficult situation before any harm had been done to them. He neatly sidestepped the fact that it was Bunion who had actually rescued them by telling himself that it was his leadership that had made it all possible. He was free now to resume his duties and to carry out the responsibilities that had been given him. He would prove his worth to the High Lord yet!

There was only one problem. Bunion, it turned out, didn't have the missing bottle after all. Someone else had stolen it—someone who, like Bunion, could get in and out of a heavily guarded room without being seen.

Questor Thews knotted his owlish face in thought.

Now who could that someone be?

SHOW TIME

When the phone finally rang, Ben Holiday almost broke his leg falling over a chair in his eagerness to catch the call.

"Damn! Hello?"

"Doc? I'm here, finally," Miles Bennett said through the receiver. "I'm downstairs in the lobby."

Ben breathed a long, audible sigh of relief. "Thank God!"

"You want me to come up?"

"Immediately."

He hung up the phone, collapsed onto the nearby sofa, and rubbed his sore leg ruefully. Salvation, at last! He had been waiting four days for Miles to arrive with the information on Michel Ard Rhi and Abernathy—four long, endless days of being cooped up in the opulent confines of the Shangri-La. Miles had wired the promised money, so at least he had been able to avoid starvation and eviction. But it hadn't been possible to leave the room for more than an hour or two each day—always late at night or early in the morning. Willow simply drew too much attention.

Besides, the sylph had not been feeling well ever since their arrival from Landover.

He glanced over to where she sat naked in a pool of sunlight on the balcony just outside the sliding glass doors that opened off the living room of their suite. She sat there every day, sometimes for hours, staring out into the desert, face lifted toward the sun, perfectly still. It seemed to help her to be exposed like that, so he left her alone. He figured that it had something to do with her amorphous physiology, that the sunlight was good for both the animal and plant parts of her. Nevertheless, she seemed listless and wan, her coloring not quite right, her energy mysteriously depleted. At times, she appeared disoriented. He was very worried about her. He was beginning to believe that something either present or lacking in the environment of his world was causing the problem. He wanted to finish this business with Abernathy and the missing medallion and get Willow safely back to Landover.

He got up, walked into the bathroom, and splashed some cold water on his face. He hadn't slept well these past few days, too keyed up, too anxious to do something and end this waiting. He toweled his face dry and gazed at himself in the mirror. He looked healthy enough, he decided, except for his eyes. His eyes were tiny roadmaps. That came from lack of sleep and reading two or three paperback novels a day to keep from going stir crazy.

A knock sounded on the door. He tossed aside the towel, crossed the room, and squinted into the peephole. It was Miles. He released the latch and pulled open the door.

"Hiya, Doc," Miles greeted, extending his hand.

Ben took it and pumped it vigorously. Miles hadn't changed a bit—still the big, baby-faced teddy bear with the rumpled suit and the winning smile. He was carrying a leather briefcase under one arm. "You look good, Miles," he said and meant it.

"You look like a damn yuppie," Miles replied. "Running suit and Nikes, camped out in the Shangri-La, waiting for nightfall and the lights of the city. Except you're too old. Can I come in?"

"Yeah, sure you can." He stepped aside to let his old friend into the room, checked both ways down the outside hall, then closed the door behind them. "Find a comfortable seat, why don't you?"

Miles moved across the room, admiring the furnishings, whistling softly at the fully stocked bar, and then suddenly stopped dead in his tracks. "For Christ's sake, Doc!"

He was staring through the sliding glass doors at Willow.

"Nuts!" Ben exclaimed in dismay. He had forgotten all about Willow.

He went into the bedroom, took down a bathrobe, and went out onto the balcony. He placed the robe gently around Willow's slender shoulders. She looked up at him questioningly, her eyes distant and haunted.

"Miles is here," he told her quietly.

She nodded and rose to join him. They walked back into the living room to confront the still-paralyzed man who was clutching his briefcase like a shield. "Miles, this is Willow," he said.

Miles seemed to remember himself. "Oh, yeah, pleased to meet you . . . Willow," he stammered.

"Willow is from Landover, Miles," Ben explained. "From where I live now. She's a sylph."

Miles looked at him. "A what?"

"A sylph. A mix of wood nymph and water sprite."

"Sure." Miles smiled uneasily. "She's green, Doc."

"That's just her coloring." Ben was suddenly uncomfortable. "Look, why don't we sit down on the sofa and have a look at what you brought, Miles."

Miles nodded, his eyes still on Willow. The sylph smiled briefly, then turned and moved off into the bedroom. "You know, it's a good thing I'm standing here having this conversation with you, Doc, and actually seeing this girl, rather than hearing about her over the phone," Miles said quietly. "Otherwise, I'd be tempted to write you off as a certified nut case."

Ben smiled. "I don't blame you." He dropped onto the sofa and motioned Miles to join him.

"A sylph, huh?" Miles shook his head. "So all that stuff about a world of magic with dragons and fairy creatures was real after all. That right, Doc? Was it all real?"

Ben sighed. "Some of it, anyway."

"My God." Miles slowly sat down beside him, a stunned look on his face. "You aren't kidding me, are you? It really exists? Yeah, it does, doesn't it? I can see it in your face. And that girl . . . she's, well, she's beautiful, different, something like you'd imagine would live in a fairy world. Damn, Doc!"

Ben nodded. "We can talk about it some more later, Miles. But what about the information I asked you to get? Any luck?"

Miles was staring at Willow through the bedroom door as she undraped the bathrobe and stepped off into the shower. "Uh, yeah," he said finally. He unsnapped his briefcase and pulled out an orange-colored file. "Here's what the investigators got on this Michel Ard Rhi character. And, believe me, he's a character with a capital C."

Ben accepted the file, opened it, and quickly began to scan its contents. The first page offered general history. Michel Ard Rhi. Birthplace, parents, age, early history all unknown. A financier, mostly through private concerns. Net worth estimated at two hundred twenty-five million dollars. Lived outside Woodinville, Washington—Washington?—in a castle purchased and then shipped, block by block, from Great Britain. Unmarried. No hobbies, no clubs, no organizations.

"Not much here," he remarked.

"Keep reading," Miles said.

He did. On the second page, it began to get interesting. Michel Ard Rhi kept his own private army. He had helped finance several revolutions in foreign countries. He owned pieces of banking institutions, major arms corporations, even a few foreign government–subsidized industries. There was a suggestion that he might be involved in a good deal more, but there was no hard evidence. He had been charged with various criminal acts, mostly fraud related to SEC violations, although there was something about animal cruelty, but he had never been convicted. He traveled extensively, always with bodyguards, always by private transport.

Ben closed the file. "Washington, huh? I don't get it. I was sure Las Vegas was where we would find . . ."

"Wait a minute, Doc," Miles interrupted quickly. "There's something more, something that just turned up yesterday. It's pretty farfetched, but it might tie in somehow with this guy being up there in Washington."

He dug through his briefcase and extracted a single sheet of typed paper. "Here we go. The investigators threw this in after I told them I wanted anything they could find on a talking dog. Seems one of them has some contacts in the scandal sheet business. Listen to this. Some fellow living in Woodinville, Washington—same place, right—tried to make a deal with *Hollywood Eye* for a hundred thousand dollars cash on delivery for an exclusive interview and photo session with a genuine talking dog!"

"Abernathy!" Ben exclaimed immediately.

Miles shrugged. "Could be."

"Did they give his name? The dog's?"

"Nope. Just the man's. Davis Whitsell. He's a dog trainer and showman. But he lives right there in Woodinville, same place this Ard Rhi keeps his walled tower. What do you think?"

Ben sat forward, his mind racing. "I think it's an awfully big coincidence, if that's all it is. But, if not, what's Abernathy doing with this Whitsell character instead of Ard Rhi? And what are Willow and I doing here? Could be Questor messed up with the magic and sent us to Nevada instead of to Washington. Damn! I suppose I should be grateful he didn't deposit us in the Pacific Ocean!" He was thinking out loud to himself now, and Miles was staring at him. He smiled. "Don't worry, I'm just trying to sort all this out. You did a heck of a job, Miles. Thanks."

Miles shrugged. "You're welcome. Now are you going to tell me what's going on here?"

Ben studied his old friend a moment, then nodded. "I'm going to try. You deserve that much. You want a Glenlivet while we talk?"

Miles had his scotch, then another, then a third as Ben tried to explain the story behind Abernathy and the missing medallion. This, of course, necessarily involved some minimal description of Landover, and that, in turn, took them off on a variety of side trips. Ben didn't tell Miles everything, particularly where it involved anything dangerous, because he knew it would only worry Miles. Willow appeared from the shower, and Ben sent down for dinner. Miles seemed to grow more comfortable in the sylph's presence after a time, and she in his, and they began to talk with each other like real people. Much of what Miles had to say to Willow left her mystified, and much of what she had to say to him left him speechless—but they got along. The evening wore on, the questions mostly got answered, and the lights of the strip began to brighten the casinos and lounges against the night skies.

Finally, Willow drifted off to bed, and Miles and Ben were left alone. Ben poured them a brandy from the bar stock, and they sat together staring out the window.

"You have a place to stay?" Ben said after a time. "I never thought to check."

Miles nodded, his gaze distant. "Down a floor or two. Down with the commoners. I booked it with the plane tickets."

"That reminds me." Ben was on his feet. "I have to call the airport right now for a flight out tomorrow."

"Washington?"

Ben nodded. "Where the heck is Woodinville?" he called back as he crossed to the phone.

"North of Seattle." Miles stretched. "Make sure you make reservations for three."

Ben stopped. "Wait a minute, you're not going."

Miles sighed. "Sure, I'm going. What do you think, Doc? That I'm leaving just when this is getting interesting? Besides, you might need me. You don't have all the connections you used to. I do—not to mention credit cards and money."

Ben shook his head. "I don't know. This could be dangerous, Miles. Who knows what we're up against with Michel Ard Rhi. I don't like the idea—"

"Doc!" Miles cut him short. "I'm going. Make the call."

Ben gave up arguing, made the reservations on an early morning PSA flight, and returned to the sofa. Miles was staring out the window again.

"Remember when we were kids and we did all that pretending? Remember how we created all those make-believe worlds to play in? I was thinking about how lucky you were to find one for real, Doc. Everyone else has to live with the world they've got." He shook his head. "Not you. You get to live what others can only wish for."

Ben didn't say anything. He was thinking about how differently they looked at things. It was the difference in their realities. Landover was his reality; Miles had only this world. He remembered how desperately he had wished for exactly what he had now just two short years ago. He had forgotten about that. It was good to remember it again.

"I am pretty lucky," he said finally.

Miles did not reply.

They sat together in silence, sipping brandy and letting their private dreams take shape in the playground of their thoughts.

Their flight out of Las Vegas was at 7:58 A.M. on PSA flight 726, a smaller jet making a single stopover in Reno on its way north to Seattle. They arrived early at the airport, camped out in an empty terminal until boarding, and took seats at the rear of the airplane to avoid drawing any more attention than was necessary. Ben had bound up Willow's hair in a head scarf, covered her face with skin-toned foundation cream, and clothed her head to foot to hide her skin, but she looked like a walking sideshow nevertheless. Worse, she was more listless than ever. Her strength seemed to be simply draining away from her.

When they had taken off the second time out of Reno and Miles was dozing, she leaned over to Ben and whispered, "I know what troubles me, Ben. I need to nourish in the soil. I need to make the change. I think that is why I am so weak. I'm sorry."

He nodded and hugged her close. He had forgotten about her need to transform from human to tree every twenty days. Perhaps he had simply blocked it away when he had agreed to bring her on this journey in the misguided hope that it wouldn't prove to be a problem. But the twenty-day cycle had obviously come around again. She would have to be allowed to change.

But what would the elements in the soil of this world do to her body systems?

He didn't like to think about it. It made him feel helpless. They were trapped here now, trapped until he found Abernathy and retrieved his medallion.

He took a deep breath, gripped Willow's gloved hand tightly in his own, and leaned back in his seat. Just one more day, he promised silently. By tonight, he would be on Davis Whitsell's doorstep, and his search would be over.

The phone rang in the living room, and Davis Whitsell pushed back his bowl of Wheaties, got up from the breakfast table, and hurried to answer it. Abernathy watched him through a crack in the bedroom door. They were alone in the house. Alice Whitsell had gone to visit her mother three days ago. Show dogs were one thing, she had said on leaving—talking dogs were something else. She would be back when the dog—if that's what it really was in the first place—was gone.

Probably just as well, Davis had insisted afterward. It was easier to concentrate on things when Alice wasn't running the TV or her mouth.

Abernathy didn't know what he meant. What he did know was that as far as he could determine he was no closer to reaching Virginia than before. Despite his host's repeated assurances that everything would be fine, he was beginning to grow suspicious.

He listened as Davis picked up the receiver. "Davis Whitsell." There was a pause. "Yes, Mr. Stern, how are you? Uh, huh. Sure thing." He sounded very eager. "Don't worry, I'll be there!"

Davis placed the receiver back on its cradle, rubbed his hands together briskly, cast a quick look down the hall in the direction of Abernathy's bedroom, then picked up the phone again and dialed. Abernathy continued to stand at the door and listen.

"Blanche?" Whitsell said into the receiver. His voice was hushed. "Let me talk to Alice. Yeah." He waited. "Alice? Listen, I only got a moment. I just got a call from the *Hollywood Eye*! Yeah, how about that? *The Hollywood Eye*! You thought I was nuts, didn't you? One hundred thousand dollars for the interview, a few pictures, and out the door! When it's done, I put the dog on the plane, wish him luck, and we get on with our lives—a hell of a lot richer and a hell of a lot better known. The *Eye* will have the exclusive, but the other magazines will pick up the story afterward. I'll have more business than I know what to do with. We're gonna be in the big bucks, girl! No more scratching and scrimping for us!" There was a brief pause. "Sure, it's safe! Look, I gotta go. See you in a few days, okay?"

He hung up and went back into the kitchen. Abernathy watched him rinse the dishes and put them in the sink, then start down the hall toward the bedrooms. Abernathy hesitated, then moved back from the door to the bed and lay down, trying to look as if he were just waking.

Whitsell stuck his head through the door. "I'm going out for a bit," he advised. "That guy I told you about, the one who's going to provide the rest of the money we need to get you back to Virginia, is down at the motel waiting to talk to me. Then we'll be coming back here for the interview. If you check out, we're all set. So maybe you'd better get yourself ready."

Abernathy blinked and sat up. "Are you sure all this is necessary, Mr. Whitsell? I feel rather uncomfortable with the idea of talking about myself and having pictures taken. I doubt that the High Lord . . . uh, my friend, would approve."

"There you go with that 'High Lord' business again," Whitsell snapped. "Who is this guy, anyway?" He shook his head wearily when Abernathy just stared at him. "Look, if we don't talk to the man with the money and let him take your picture, we don't get the money. And if we don't get the money, we can't get you back to Virginia. As I told you before, the money Elizabeth gave you just isn't enough."

Abernathy nodded doubtfully. He wasn't sure he believed that anymore. "How much longer until I can go?"

Whitsell shrugged. "Day, maybe two. Just be patient."

Abernathy thought he had been patient long enough, but he decided not to say so. Instead, he stood up and started for the bathroom. "I will be ready when you return," he promised.

Whitsell left him there, passed back through the living room, pausing to scratch Sophie's ears affectionately, went out the side door into the carport, and got into his old pickup. Abernathy watched him go. He knew he was being used, but there was no help for it. He had no one else he could turn to and nowhere else he could go. The best he could do was hope that Whitsell would keep his word.

He walked into the living room and peered out the window long enough to see the pickup back out the driveway and turn up the street.

He paid no attention at all to the black van parked across the way.

Somewhere down the hall, the old clock ticked methodically in the stillness. Abernathy stood in front of the bathroom mirror and looked at himself. Four days were gone since he had escaped Michel Ard Rhi and Graum Wythe, and Landover seemed as far away as ever. He sighed and licked his nose, rethinking his options. If this business of the interview and the pictures didn't produce results, he guessed he was simply going to have to bid Davis Whitsell good-bye and strike out on his own. What other choice did he have? Time was running out on him. He had to find a way to get the medallion safely back to the High Lord.

He cleaned his teeth, brushed his fur, and studied himself some more in the mirror. He was looking much better than he had on his arrival, he decided. Eating and sleeping like a regular person did wonders for one.

He toweled his paws absently. Too bad Mrs. Whitsell had felt it necessary to leave. He couldn't understand why she had been so upset . . .

He thought he heard something and started to turn.

That was when the immobilizing spray hit him in the face. He staggered back, choking. A cord wound about his muzzle and a sack came over his head. He was lifted off his feet and carried out. He struggled weakly, but the hands that held him were strong and practiced. He could hear voices, hushed and hurried, and through a small tear in the sack he caught a glimpse of a black van with its rear doors open. He was tossed inside and the doors slammed shut.

Then something sharp jabbed into his backside, and he was engulfed in blackness.

LOVE SONG

Day slipped away into evening in the country of the River Master, and the fairy folk of Elderew put aside their work and began to light the lamps of the tree lanes and pathways in preparation for the coming of night. All through the massive old trees which cradled their city, they darted—along limbs and branches, up and down gnarled trunks, through steadily lengthening shadows and thickening mist. Sprites, nymphs, kelpies, naiads, pixies, elementals of all forms and shapes, they were the creatures of the fairy world that surrounded the valley of Landover, creatures who were exiled or had fled from lives in which they had found no pleasure, though such lives had lasted an eternity.

The River Master stood at the edge of a park fronting his hidden forest city and mused on dreams of paradise lost. He was a tall, lean man, dressed in robes of forest green, a sprite with grainy, silver skin, gills at the side of his neck that fluttered gently as he breathed, hair that grew thick and black on his head and forearms, and an odd, chiseled face with eyes that were flat and penetrating. He had come into Landover at the time of its inception, bringing his people with him, exiled forever by choice from the mists of fairy. Mortal now, in a sense he had never appreciated in his old life, he lived in the seclusion of the lake country and worked to keep its earth, water, air, and life forms clean and safe. He was a healer sprite, capable of giving back life where it had been stolen. But some wounds refused to heal, and the irretrievable loss of his birth home was a scar that would always be with him.

He walked a few steps closer to the city, conscious of the guards who trailed at a respectful distance to allow him his privacy. Five of eight moons glimmered full in the night sky, colors bright against the black—mauve, peach, jade, burnt rose, and white.

"Paradise lost," he whispered, thinking still of the haunting dreams of the fairy mists. He looked around. "But paradise gained, too."

He loved the lake country. It was the heart and soul of his people, the exiles and the wanderers who had banded with him to begin anew, to discover and build for themselves and their children a world of beginnings and ends, a world of no absolutes—a world they could not find within the mists. Elderew lay hidden within marshlands, deep within a sprawling maze of forests and lakes, so well concealed that no one could find a way in or out without the help of its denizens. Those who tried simply disappeared in the mire. Elderew was a haven from the madness of those in the valley that could not appreciate the value of life—the land barons of the Greensward, the trolls and gnomes of the mountains, the monsters driven from fairy who still survived after a millennium of war. Destruction and misuse of the land was the trademark of such beings. But here, in the sanctuary of the River Master, there was peace.

He watched a dance procession begin to form at the edge of the park before him, a line of children draped in flowers and bright cloth and bearing candles. They sang and wound their way along the paths, over the waterway bridges, and through the gardens and hedgerows. He smiled as he watched them, content.

It was better now in the lands beyond the lake country, he reflected, than it had been before the coming of Ben Holiday. The High Lord of Landover had done much to heal the breach that existed between the disparate peoples of the valley; he had done much to encourage preservation and conservation of the land and its life. Holiday judged rightly—as the River Master did—that all life was inextricably bound together and that if one tie was cut, others were endangered as well.

Willow had gone with the High Lord, Willow his child—chosen, she claimed, in the manner of the sylphs of old, by fates that were woven in the grasses on which her parents lay at her conception. Willow believed in Ben Holiday. The River Master found her belief enviable.

He breathed deeply the night air. Not that his opinions mattered much these days with the High Lord. Holiday was still angry with him for attempting to trap the black unicorn and harness its powers some months back. Holiday had never been able to accept the fact that fairy power belonged only to fairy creatures because they, alone, understood its use.

He shook his head. Ben Holiday had been good for Landover, but he still had much to learn.

There was a small disturbance off to his left, and it brought him about. Onlookers to the dancing of the children had moved rapidly aside as a pair of his marsh sentries stalked out of the gloom of the lowlands mist with a singularly frightening creature between them. Hardened veterans, their grainy wood faces as fixed as stone, the wood nymphs nevertheless kept a fair amount of distance between themselves and their charge. The River Master's guards started to close about him instantly, but he quickly waved them back. It would serve no purpose to show fear. He stood his ground and let the creature approach.

The creature was called a shadow wight. It was a form of elemental whose physical self had been ravaged at some point in its existence for an unspeakable deed or misuse so that, while it did not die, all that remained of it was its spirit. That poor life was consigned to an eternity of nonbeing. It could sustain itself only within shadows and dark spots, never within light. It had been denied its body and so had no real presence. What presence it possessed it was forced to construct from the debris of its haunts and the remains of its victims. A succubus, it stole life from others so that it, in turn, could survive, thieving and robbing from the lost and dying as a scavenger would. There were few of these horrors left in the valley now, most having perished with the passing of the ages.

This one, the River Master thought darkly, was particularly loathsome.

The shadow wight came to him on spindly, warped legs that might have belonged to an aged troll. Its arms were the limbs of some animal; its body was human. It possessed gnome hands and feet, a human child's fingers, and a face that was a mix of ravaged parts.

It bore in one hand an old woven sack.

It smiled, and its mouth seemed to twist in a silent scream. "Lord River Master," it said, its voice an echo of empty caverns. It bowed crookedly.

"It came to us without being brought," one of the sentries informed the River Master pointedly.

The Lord of the lake country people nodded. "Why have you come?" he asked the wight.

The shadow wight straightened unsteadily. Light passed through its misshapen body at the ragged joining of its bones. "To offer a gift—and to ask one."

"You found your way in; find your way out again." The River Master's face was as hard as stone. "Life will be my gift to you; ridding yourself from my presence will be your gift to me."

"Death would be a better gift," the shadow wight whispered, and its empty eyes reflected the distant candlelight. It turned to where the children still danced, wetting its lips with its tongue. "Look at me, Lord River Master. What creature that lived in all the worlds of all the times that are or ever were is more pathetic than I?"

The River Master did not respond, waiting. The wight's empty gaze shifted again. "I will tell you a story and ask that you listen, nothing more. A few quick moments that might be of interest, Lord River Master. Will you hear me?"

The River Master almost said no. He was so repulsed by the creature that he had barely been able to tolerate its presence this long. Then something caused him to relent. "Speak," he commanded wearily.

"Two years now have I lived within the crawl spaces and dark spots of the castle of Rhyndweir," the shadow wight said, edging a step closer, its voice so low that only the River Master could hear. "I lived on the wretches the Lord of that castle cast into its keep and on those poor creatures who strayed too far from the light. I watched and learned much. Then, this past night gone, a ruined troll brought to Rhyndweir's Lord a treasure to sell, a treasure of such wondrous possibilities that it surpassed anything I had ever seen! The Lord of Rhyndweir took the treasure from the troll and had him killed. I, in turn, took it from the Lord of Rhyndweir."

"Kallendbor," said the River Master distastefully. He bore no great affection for any of the Lords of the Greensward, Kallendbor least of all.

"I stole it from his sanctuary while he slept, stole it from beneath the noses of his watch because, after all, Lord River Master, they are only men. I stole it, and I brought it to you—my gift for a gift in return!"

The River Master fought back the wave of revulsion that passed through him as the shadow wight laughed hollowly. "What is this gift?"

"This!" the wight said and pulled from the sack it carried in its withered pink hand a white bottle with red dancing clowns.

"Ah, no!" the River Master cried in recognition. "I know this gift well, shadow wight—and it is no gift at all! It is a curse! It is the bottle of the Darkling!"

"It calls itself so," the other said, coming closer still, so close its breath was warm against the River Master's skin. "But it is indeed a gift! It can give the bearer of the bottle . . ."

"Anything!" finished the River Master, shying away despite his resolve. "But the magic it employs is evil beyond all words!"

"I care nothing for good or evil," the wight said. "I care only for one thing. Listen to me, Lord River Master. I stole the bottle and I brought it to you. What you do with it now is of no concern to me. Destroy it, if you wish. But first use it to help me!" Its voice was a hiss of despair. "I want myself back again!"

The River Master stared. "Back again? That which you once were?"

"That! Only that! Look at me! I cannot bear myself longer, Lord River Master! I have lived an eternity of nonbeing, of shadowlife, of scavenging and horror beyond all words because I have had no choice! I have stolen lives from every quarter, thieved them from every being that is or was! No more! I want myself back; I want my life again!"

The River Master frowned. "What is it that you expect me to do?"

"Use the bottle to help me!"

"Use the bottle? Why not use it yourself, shadow wight? Haven't you already said that the bottle can give the bearer anything?"

The wight was trying to cry, but there were no tears in its ruined body. "Lord River Master, I—can—give—myself—nothing! I cannot use the bottle! I have no being and cannot invoke the magic! I am . . . only barely here! I am only a shadow! All the magic in the world is useless to me! Look at me! I am helpless!"

The River Master stared at the shadow wight with newfound horror, seeing for the first time the truth of what its existence must be like.

"Please!" it begged, dropping to its knees. "Help me!"

The River Master hesitated, then took the sack from the creature's extended hand. "I will consider it," he said. He signaled back the watch. "Wait here for a time while I do so. And be careful you work no harm on any of my people, or the choice will be made for me."

He moved away a bit, holding the sack loosely, slowed, and looked back. The shadow wight was crouched upon the earth, huddled like a broken thing, watching him. He had not the power to heal such a being, he thought wearily. And if the bottle's magic should give him such power, had he even the right to try?

He turned sharply and walked away. He passed from the park into the city, passed by the dancers and the merrymakers, walked down pathways and along garden rows, lost in the barren landscape of his thoughts. He knew the power of the Darkling. He had known of its power for years, as he knew of the power of most magics. He remembered the uses to which it had been put by the old King's careless son and the dark wizard Meeks. He understood the way such magic wove brightly colored ribbons about its holder and then turned them suddenly to chains.

The greater the power, the greater the risk, he reminded himself.

And power such as this could do almost anything.

He reached the edge of the city before realizing where he was. He stopped, looked back momentarily for his guards, found them trailing at a respectful distance as always, and promptly dismissed them. He needed to be by himself. The guards hesitated, then were gone.

The River Master walked on alone. What should he do? The bottle was his if he chose to help the shadow wight. It never occurred to him simply to keep the bottle and send the wight packing; he was not that sort. Either he would keep the bottle and help the wight as it had asked, or he would give the bottle back and dismiss the unfortunate creature from his life. If he chose the latter, there was nothing more to consider. If he chose the former, he must decide whether he could use the magic to aid the wight—and perhaps even himself in some way—without falling victim to its power.

Could he do that, he wondered?

Could anyone?

He stopped within a clearing of Bonnie Blues that rose twenty feet above him and screened the night skies in a webbing of deep azure silk. The sounds of the city trailed after him, faint now and distant—laughter, singing, the music and dancing of the children. The old pines were close at hand, the grove in which the wood nymphs danced at midnight, the place where he had first met Willow's mother . . .

The thought trailed away in a wash of bitter memories. How long had it been? How long since he had seen her? He could still see her so clearly, even though he had been with her only that one night and lain with her only that once. She was the muse that tortured his soul still, a wondrous, nameless creature, a wood nymph so wild that he could never hope to possess her, not even for a single night more . . .

And then it came to him, a design so dark that it engulfed him as if he had been submerged in ice water.

"No!" he whispered in horror.

But why not? He stared down suddenly at the sack that contained the magic bottle—the bottle that could give him anything.

Why not?

The bottle needed testing. He must know if he could control it. He must know if he could help the shadow wight as it had asked him or if the magic was too strong to control. What harm, then, in indulging himself just this little bit, just this once.

Why not ask the Darkling to bring him Willow's mother?

He went hot and cold at the same time, warmed by the thought of her presence after so long an absence, chilled by the prospect of using the magic thus. Ah, but the heat was so much stronger! He longed for the nymph as he had longed for nothing in his life. It had been seemingly forever! Nothing was so missing from his life as what she could bring to him . . .

"I must try!" he whispered suddenly. "I must!"

He walked swiftly through the woodlands, through the great, silent trees where only the night sounds could reach him, until at last he stood within the grove of old pines. The stillness there was pervasive, and it was only in his mind that he could hear the children's laughter and see Willow's mother dance once more.

He would not ask much, he told himself suddenly. He would only ask to see her dance for him—just dance.

The need to have her there again burned through him like a fever. He set the sack upon the earth and lifted out the brightly colored bottle. Red harlequins gleamed like blood drawings in the moonlight.

Quickly, he pulled free the stopper.

The Darkling crawled into the light like some loathsome insect. "Oh, sweet are your dreams, master!" it hissed and began to writhe about the lip of the bottle as if possessed. "Sweet longings that need to be fulfilled!"

"You can read my thoughts?" the River Master asked, sudden apprehension flooding through him.

"I can read your very soul, master," the black thing whispered. "I can see the depth and height of your passion! Let me satisfy it, master! I can give you what you wish!"

The River Master hesitated. The gills at his neck fluttered almost uncontrollably, and his breathing was harsh in his ears. This was wrong, he thought suddenly. This was a mistake! The magic was too much . . .

Then the demon sprang upright on the bottle and wove its fingers through the air, conjuring from out of nowhere a vision of Willow's mother. She danced in miniature in a cloud of silver, her face as lovely as it had ever been in the River Master's memories, her dance a magic that transcended reason or restraint. She spun, whirled, and was gone.

The Darkling's laughter was low and anxious. "Would you have her whole?" it asked softly. "In flesh and blood form?"

The River Master stood transfixed. "Yes!" he whispered finally. "Bring her! Let me see her dance!"

The Darkling sped from sight as if one of night's shadows fleeing daylight. The River Master stood alone in the grove of old pines and stared after him, hearing again the music of the children, the bright, mesmerizing sounds of the dance. His silver skin glistened, and his hard, flat eyes were suddenly alive with expectation.

To see her dance again, to see her dance just once more . . .

Then, with the speed of thought, the Darkling was back again. It skittered through the ring of pines into the clearing, its laughter high and quick. It held in its hands lines of red fire that did not seem to burn, tugging on them in the manner of a handler.

The lines were secured at their other end to Willow's mother.

She came into the light as if a dog at its master's bidding, the lines of red fire fastened about her wrists and ankles, her slender form shaking as if from a chill. She was lovely, so small and airy, so much more alive than the pale vision the River Master still guarded deep within his memory. Silver hair fell waist-length and shimmered with every movement of her tiny limbs. Her skin was pale green like Willow's, her face childlike. A gown of white gauze clothed her body, and a silver ribbon cinched her waist. She stood there, staring at him, her eyes filled with fear.

The River Master saw nothing of the fear. He saw only the beauty he had dreamed of all these many years, come finally to life. "Let her dance!" he whispered.

The Darkling hissed and jerked on the lines, but the frightened wood nymph simply crouched down against the earth, her face buried in her arms. She began to keen, a low, terrified cry that was almost birdlike.

"No!" the River Master shouted angrily. "I want her to dance, not cry as if stricken!"

"Yes, master!" the Darkling said. "She requires only a love song!"

The demon hissed once again, then began to sing—if singing it could be called. His voice was a harsh, rasping wail that caused the River Master to flinch from the sound and Willow's mother to jerk upright as if possessed. The lines of red fire fell away, and the wood nymph stood free once more. Yet she was not truly free, for the voice of the demon bound her as surely as iron chains. It picked her up and moved her about like a puppet, forcing her to dance, compelling her to move to the music. All about the clearing, she whirled and spun, a seemingly lifeless, if perfectly formed bit of workmanship. She danced, yet the dance was not a dance of beauty, but only of forced motion. She danced, and while she danced, tears ran in streams down her child's face.

The River Master was horrified. "Let her dance free!" he shouted in fury.

The Darkling glared at him with blood-red eyes, hissed in loathing, and changed the shape and form of its song to something so unmentionable that the River Master dropped to his knees at the sound. Willow's mother danced faster, her speed of movement disguising now her lack of control. She was a blur of white gauze and silver hair as she spun recklessly, helplessly through the night.

She was destroying herself, the River Master realized suddenly! The dance was killing her!

Still she danced on, and the River Master watched, helpless to act. It was as if the magic bound him, too. He was caught up in its feel, a peculiar satisfaction welling up within him at the power it released. He recognized the horror of what was happening, yet could not break free. He wanted the dance to continue. He wanted the vision stayed.

Then suddenly he was screaming without knowing how or why, "Enough! Enough!"

The Darkling abruptly ceased its song, and Willow's mother collapsed on the forest earth. The River Master dropped the bottle, rushed to where she lay, lifted her gently in his arms, and cringed as he saw the ravaged look on her face. She was no longer the vision he remembered; she was like some beaten thing.

He whirled on the Darkling. "You said a love song, demon!"

The Darkling skittered to the discarded bottle and perched there. "I sang the love song that was in your heart, master!" it whispered.

The River Master froze. He knew it was the truth. It was his song the

Darkling had sung, a song born of selfishness and disregard, a song that lacked any semblance of real love. His impassive face tried to twist in on itself as he felt the pain well up from within. He turned to hide what he was feeling.

Willow's mother stirred in his arms, her eyes fluttered and opened, and the fear returned to them instantly. "Hush," he said quickly. "There will be no more harm done to you. You will be allowed to go."

He hesitated, then impulsively he hugged her close. "I'm sorry," he whispered.

His need for her in that moment was so great that he could barely bring himself to speak the words that would free her, but his horror at what he had done compelled him to. He saw the fear lessen perceptibly and the tears come again to her eyes. He stroked her gently, waited while her strength returned, then helped her to her feet. She stood there momentarily looking at him, glanced past him once in anguish at the creature who crouched upon the bottle's lip, then whirled and fled into the forest like a frightened deer.

The River Master stared after her, seeing only the trees and the shadows, feeling the emptiness of the night all about him. He had lost her forever this time, he sensed.

He turned. "Back into the bottle," he said softly to the demon.

The Darkling climbed obediently from view, and the River Master replaced the stopper. He stood there momentarily staring at the bottle and found that he was shaking. He jammed the bottle into the sack and stalked from the clearing back through the forest to the city. The sounds of the music and the dancing grew distinct again as he approached, but the feeling of joy they had given him earlier was completely gone.

He crossed torchlit bridges and wound down paths and garden walks, feeling the weight of the sack and its contents as if it were the burden of his guilt. Finally, he re-entered the park.

The shadow wight crouched where he had left it on the grass, dead eyes fixed on nothing. It rose at the approach of the River Master, impatience apparent in its movements. Poor soul, the River Master thought and suddenly wondered how much of his pity was meant for the wight.

He came up to the shadow wight and stood there for a moment, studying the creature. Then he handed back the sack with the bottle. "I cannot help you," he said softly. "I cannot use this magic."

"Cannot?"

"It is too dangerous—for me, for anyone."

"Lord River Master, please . . ." the wight wailed.

"Listen to me," the River Master interrupted gently. "Take this sack and drop it into the deepest pit of mire in the marshland you can find. Lose it where it can never be found. When you have done that, come back to me, and I will do what I can for you, using the healing powers of the lake country people."

The shadow wight flinched. "But can you make me what I was?" it cried out sharply. "Can you do that with your powers?"

The River Master shook his head. "I think not. Not completely. I think no one can."

The shadow wight shrieked as if bitten, snatched the sack with the bottle from his hands, and fled wordlessly into the night.

The River Master thought momentarily to pursue it, then changed his mind. As much as he disliked risking the possibility that the bottle might fall into other, less wise hands, he hadn't the right to interfere. After all, the shadow wight had come to him freely; it must be let go the same way. There was nowhere for it to run in any case, if not to him. There was no one else who would wish to help it. Other creatures would be terrified of it. And it couldn't use the magic of the bottle itself, so the bottle was useless to it. It would probably think the matter through and do as he had suggested. It would drop the bottle and its demon into the mire.

Distracted by thoughts of what he had done that night, haunted by memories of Willow's mother in that clearing, he pushed the matter of the shadow wight from his mind.

He would regret later that he hadn't been thinking more clearly.

The shadow wight fled north all that night, escaping from the marshland forests of the lake country into the wooded hills surrounding Sterling Silver and continuing on toward the wall of the mountains. It ran first without purpose, fleeing the intangibles of disappointment and despair, then discovered quite unexpectedly the purpose it had lacked and ran toward its promise. It sped from one end of the valley to the other, south from the lake country, north to the Melchor. It was as quick as thought, the shadow wight, as quicksilver as a kobold like Bunion, and it could be anywhere in almost no time.

As dawn approached, it found itself at the rim of the Deep Fell. "Mistress Nightshade will help me," it whispered to the dark.

It started down the wall of the hollows, picking its way swiftly through undergrowth and over rock, the sack with the precious bottle held firmly in one hand. Light began to creep from behind the rim of the mountains, silver shards of brightness that lengthened and chased the shadows. The shadow wight pushed on.

When at last it reached the floor of the hollows, deep within the tangle of trees, scrub, marsh, and weeds, Nightshade was waiting. She materialized before him out of nothing, her tall, forbidding figure rising up from the shadows like a wraith's, black robes stark against her white skin, the streak of white that parted her raven hair almost silver.

Green eyes studied the shadow wight dispassionately. "What brings you to me, shadow wight?" the witch of the Deep Fell asked.

"Lady, I bring a gift in exchange for a gift," the wight whimpered, falling to its knees. "I bring a magic that . . ."

"Give it to me," she commanded softly.

It handed the sack over obediently, unable to question or resist her voice. She took it, opened it, and lifted out the bottle. "Yessss!" she breathed in recognition, her voice a serpent's hiss.

She cradled the bottle lovingly for a moment, then glanced back again at the shadow wight. "What gift would you have of me?" she asked it.

"Give me back my real self!" the wight exclaimed quickly. "Let me be as I was before!"

Nightshade smiled, her ageless face sharp and cunning. "Why, shadow wight, you ask so simple a gift. What you were before was what we all were once." She bent down and touched him softly on his face. "Nothing."

There was a flash of red light and the shadow wight disappeared. In its place was a huge dragonfly. The dragonfly buzzed and looped away as if maddened. It sped frantically across a bit of marshy swamp. Then something huge snapped at it from out of the mire, and it was gone.

Nightshade's smile broadened. "Such a foolish gift," she whispered.

Her gaze shifted. Sunlight streamed from out of the eastern skies overhead. The new day was beginning.

She turned with the bottle cradled in her arms and prepared to welcome it.

LOST AND FOUND

Ben Holiday turned the rental car into the drive of 2986 Forest Park, brought it to a stop, shut down the engine, and set the brake. He glanced briefly at Miles, who looked a little like what Bear Bryant used to on the sidelines, and then at Willow, who smiled at him through a mask of weariness and pain. Ben smiled back. It was becoming increasingly difficult to do so.

They left the car and walked to the front stoop of the small, well-kept ranch home and knocked on the door. Ben could hear the sound of his pulse in his ears and he shifted his feet anxiously.

The door opened, and a lanky, bearded man with hollow eyes and a guarded look stood facing them. He was holding a can of beer in one hand. "Yeah?" His eyes fastened on Willow.

"Davis Whitsell?" Ben asked.

"Yeah?" Whitsell's voice was a mix of fear and mistrust. He couldn't stop staring at the sylph.

"Are you the man who has the talking dog?"

Whitsell continued to stare.

"The one who called *Hollywood Eye*?" Ben persisted.

Willow smiled. Davis Whitsell forced his eyes away. "You from the *Eye*?" he asked cautiously.

Miles shook his head. "Hardly, Mr. Whitsell. We're from . . ."

"We represent another concern," Ben interrupted quickly. He glanced about the empty neighborhood momentarily. "Do you suppose we could step inside and talk?"

Whitsell hesitated. "I don't think . . ."

"You could finish your beer that way," Ben interjected. "You could let the lady rest a moment, too. She's not feeling very well."

"I don't have the dog anymore," the other said suddenly.

Ben glanced at his companions. The uncertainty and concern mirrored in their faces was undisguised. "Could we come inside anyway, Mr. Whitsell?" he asked quietly.

Ben thought he was going to say no. He seemed right on the verge of saying it, closing the door, and putting them out of his life. Then something changed his mind. He nodded wordlessly and stepped aside.

When they were inside, he closed the door behind them and went over to sit in a well-worn easy chair. The house was dark and still, the blinds drawn, and the ticking of the old clock at the head of the hall the only sound. Ben and his companions sat together on the sofa. Whitsell took a long pull at his beer and looked at them. "I told you the dog was gone," he repeated.

Ben exchanged a quick glance with Miles. "Where did he go?" he asked.

Whitsell shrugged, trying hard to be nonchalant. "I don't know."

"You don't know? You mean he just left?"

"Sorta. What difference does it make?" Whitsell leaned forward. "Who are you, anyway? Who do you represent? The *Inquirer* or something?"

Ben took a deep breath. "Before I tell you that, Mr. Whitsell, I have to know something from you. I have to know if we're both talking about the same dog. We happen to be looking for a very particular dog—a dog that really does talk. Did this dog really talk, Mr. Whitsell? I mean, really talk?"

Whitsell suddenly looked very frightened. "I don't think we should continue this," he said abruptly. "I think you should go."

None of them moved. Willow wasn't even paying attention to him. She was making a strange, birdlike sound—a sound Ben had never heard before. It brought a tiny black poodle out from under the couch with a whine and into her lap as if they had been friends all their lives. The dog nuzzled the girl and licked her hand, and the girl stroked the animal fondly.

"She's been badly frightened," Willow said softly, to no one in particular.

Whitsell started to get up, then sat back again. "Why should I tell you anything?" he muttered. "How do I know what you want?"

Miles was drumming his fingers on his knee impatiently. "What we want is a little cooperation, Mr. Whitsell."

They stared at each other for a moment. "You from the police?" Whitsell asked finally. "Some special branch, maybe? Is that what this is all about?" He seemed to think better of the question almost before he had finished asking it. "What am I thinking here? Police don't use girls with green hair, for Pete's sake!"

"No, we're not police." Ben stood up suddenly and walked about for a minute. How much should he tell this man? Whitsell had his eyes fixed on Willow again, watching the little dog nuzzle into the girl as she continued to pet it.

Ben made his decision. "Was the dog's name Abernathy?"

He stopped walking and looked directly at Whitsell. The other man blinked in surprise. "Yeah, it was," he said. "How did you know that?"

Ben came back and sat down again. "My name is Ben. This is Miles and Willow." He pointed to the other two. "Abernathy is our friend, Mr. Whitsell. That's how we know. He's our friend, and we've come to take him home."

There was a long moment of silence as they studied each other wordlessly, and then Davis Whitsell nodded. "I believe you. Don't know why, exactly, but I do. I just wish I could help you." He sighed. "But the dog's . . . but Abernathy's gone."

"Did you sell him, Mr. Whitsell?" Miles asked.

"No, hell, no!" the other snapped angrily. "I never planned anything like that! I was just gonna make a few bucks off that interview with the *Eye,* then send him to Virginia, the way he wanted. Wasn't no harm gonna come to him. But it was the chance I'd waited for all my life, don't you see, the chance to get a little recognition, get off the circuit, maybe, and . . ."

He had leaned forward in the chair, but now he trailed off, spent, and slumped back again. "It doesn't matter now, I guess. The point is, he's gone. Someone took him."

He took another long pull on his beer and put it down carefully on the table beside him, back into a glistening ring of condensation that the bottom of the can had formed earlier. "You're really who you say you are?" he asked. "You're really friends of Abernathy?"

Ben nodded. "Are you?"

"Yeah, though maybe you wouldn't know it from all that's happened."

"Why don't you tell us about it?"

Whitsell did. He started at the beginning, telling them about how he had gone to Franklin Elementary to do his show, how the little girl Elizabeth—hell, he didn't even know her last name—had come up to him, asked his help. He told them about the dog, about Abernathy, coming to his door that night, a genuine talking dog walking upright like a man, saying the little girl sent him, that he needed to get back to Virginia for some reason or other, and that he couldn't use a phone because there wasn't any. Whitsell hadn't believed a word of it. But he had agreed to help anyway, hiding Abernathy out in his home, packing Alice off to her mother's, then trying to line up that interview with the *Hollywood Eye* so he could raise enough money to pay the cost of sending the dog to Virginia and maybe make a few bucks for himself in the bargain.

"But I got fooled," he admitted sourly. "I was tricked out of the house. When I got back, Abernathy was gone, and poor old Sophie was stuffed in the freezer, half froze!" His gaze shifted momentarily to Willow. "That's why she's so skittish, Miss. She's a very sensitive animal." He looked back then at Ben. "I can't prove it, of course, but I know sure as I sit here that the same fellow that had your friend caged up in the first place found out about what I was doing and took him back again! Trouble is, I don't even know who he is. Not sure I want to, man like that."

Then he seemed to realize how that sounded and reddened. He shook his head. "Sorry. Fact is, I could find out about him from the school, find out the little girl's last name, where she lives. She'd know the man's name. Hell, I'll do it right now, mister, if you think it'll help that dog! I feel terrible about this whole business!"

"Thanks anyway, but I think we already know the name of the man," Ben said quietly. "I think we know where he is, too."

Whitsell hesitated, surprised.

"Is there anything else you can tell us?"

Whitsell frowned. "No, I guess not. You think you can do something to help the dog—uh, Abernathy?"

Ben stood up without answering, and the others followed suit. Sophie jumped down from Willow's lap and nuzzled her legs through her dress. The hem lifted slightly, and Whitsell caught a brief glimpse of silky emerald hair on the back of the sylph's slender ankle.

"Thanks for your help, Mr. Whitsell," Miles was saying.

"Look, you want me to go with you, maybe help out?" the other offered suddenly, surprising them. "This seems like pretty dangerous stuff, but I want to do my part . . ."

"No, I don't think so," Ben said. They moved toward the door.

Davis Whitsell followed. "I'd be worried about that little girl, too, if I were you," he added. Sophie had returned to his side now, and he picked her up. "She might have been found out."

"We'll look into it. She'll be all right." Ben was already thinking about what to do next.

Whitsell saw them to the door and outside. The late afternoon sun was sinking rapidly below the horizon, the dusk turning the light silver. Shadows from shade trees and utility poles dappled and ribbed the neighborhood houses. A man with an insurance sign pasted on the side of his car was just pulling into a driveway down the block, the crunch of his tires on the gravel sharp in the stillness.

"I'm sorry about all this," Davis Whitsell told them. He hesitated, then reached out to shake hands with the men, as if needing some small reassurance that they believed him. "Look, I don't know who you are or where you're from or what all this is about. But I do know this much. I never wanted anything bad to happen to Abernathy. Tell him that, will you? The little girl, too."

Ben nodded. "I'll tell them, Mr. Whitsell."

He was hoping as he said it that he would have the chance.

In the country of Landover, the wizard Questor Thews was hoping much the same thing. He was not, however, optimistic.

Following their escape from the castle fortress of Rhyndweir, Questor, the kobolds Bunion and Parsnip, and the G'home Gnomes Fillip and Sot had journeyed south and east once more to the sanctuary of Sterling Silver. Questor and the kobolds had gone home because there really didn't seem to be any alternative now that the trail of the missing bottle had come to an end. Questor still hadn't been able to fathom who might have stolen the bottle from Kallendbor; until he could figure that out, he really hadn't any idea where he ought to start looking again. Besides, affairs of state had been left alone for several days now and needed looking after in the High Lord's absence.

The G'home Gnomes tagged along because they were still too frightened after their ordeal with the band of trolls to do anything else.

A message from the Lord Kallendbor in the form of a threat of immediate reprisal for the imagined theft of the bottle almost beat Questor back to the castle, but the wizard was undaunted. Kallendbor was hardly likely to challenge the power of the High Lord—unless, of course, he was to discover that Holiday was missing, heaven forbid!—however irritated he was about losing the bottle. Questor penned off a strongly worded reply on realm stationery repeating once again that he was in no way responsible for the theft of the bottle, nor were any of those in his company, and that any hostile response would be dealt with severely. He stamped it with the High Lord's seal and dispatched it. Enough was enough.

During the next twenty-four hours, he met with a delegation of other Lords from the Greensward to address their grievances, including Strehan's concerning the destruction of his tower by Kallendbor, advised the newly formed judicial council on establishment of courts to enforce the King's Rule, studied irrigation charts that would enable farmers to cultivate portions of the arid eastern expanses of the valley, and heard ambassadors and others from all parts of the realm. He did this as representative of and advisor to the High Lord, assuring all that the King would give immediate attention to their concerns. No one questioned his word. Everyone still assumed that Holiday was somewhere in the valley, and Questor was not about to suggest otherwise. Everything went smoothly, and that first day expired without incident.

The first signs of trouble appeared with the next. Reports began to drift in of disturbances from all corners of the valley, a random scattering of raindrops that quickly grew into a downpour. Crag Trolls were suddenly, unexplainably skirmishing, not only with G'home Gnomes, but also with outlying residents of the Greensward, with kobolds and sprites, and even with each other. The lake country claimed it was being inundated with fouled water from the Greensward and infested by plant-eating rats. The Greensward complained that it was under siege from a flurry of small dragons that were burning crops and livestock alike. Fairy folk and humans were setting on one another as if fighting were a newly discovered form of recreation. As fast as Questor read one report, two more came in. He went to bed that night exhausted.

The third day was even worse. The reports had accumulated overnight, and on waking he was deluged. Everyone seemed to be at odds with everyone else. No one knew exactly why. There was hostility at every turn. No one knew what was causing it. Dissatisfaction quickly grew into a demand for action. Where was the High Lord? Why wasn't he dealing with this mess personally?

Questor Thews began to smell a rat. He had already begun to suspect that the Darkling was somehow behind all this sudden unrest, and now he was beginning to suspect that the demon was serving the interests of someone whose primary concern was getting back at Ben Holiday. It seemed obvious to the wizard that the one clear purpose of all these unrelated incidents was to focus everyone's anger on the High Lord. Excluding Kallendbor, who had already lost the bottle once and was unlikely to have gotten it back again so fast, the two who most wanted revenge on Holiday were the dragon Strabo and the witch Nightshade.

Questor considered the two.

Strabo was hardly likely to bother himself with magic where Holiday was concerned; he was more apt simply to try to flatten him.

Nightshade was another matter.

Questor left messengers and ambassadors alike to cool their heels in the reception rooms and ascended Sterling Silver's high tower to where the Landsview was kept. He stepped onto the platform, fastened his hands on the polished railing, and willed himself out into the valley. Castle walls and towers disappeared, and Questor Thews was flying through space, swept away by the magic. He took himself directly across the valley to the Deep Fell and down within. Safe, because he was only seeing what was there and was not himself present, the wizard began to search for the witch. He didn't find her. He took himself out of the hollows and crisscrossed the valley, end to end. He still didn't find her.

He returned to Sterling Silver, went back down to the various reception rooms, addressed another spate of grievances, went back up to the Landsview, and went out again. He repeated this procedure four additional times that day, growing increasingly frustrated and concerned as the valley's problems mounted, the outcry for an appearance by the High Lord grew, and his own efforts went unrewarded. He began to wonder if he was mistaken.

Finally, on his fifth trip out, he found the witch. He discovered her at the far north corner of the hollows, almost into the lower peaks of the Melchor, situated where her view of the valley was unobstructed.

She was holding the missing bottle, and the Darkling was rubbing its small, twisted, bristling dark form lovingly along one thin, white hand.

Questor returned to Sterling Silver, dismissed everyone for the day, and sat down to try to figure out what to do.

He couldn't escape the fact that this whole mess was his fault. He was the one who had insisted on trying the magic that would have changed Abernathy back into a man. He was the one who had persuaded the High Lord to give his precious medallion to the dog so that it might act as a catalyst. He was the one who had then permitted the magic to go awry. He cringed at that admission. He was the one who had dispatched the poor scribe into Holiday's old world and brought the bottle and the Darkling into his. He was the one who had allowed the bottle to sit unattended so that it might be stolen by the G'home Gnomes, the troll thieves, Kallendbor, and in the end some final unknown so that now it was in the hands of Nightshade.

He sat alone in the shadows and silence of his private chambers and faced truths he would have preferred to leave alone. He was a poor wizard at best; he might as well admit it. Sometimes he could control the magic—what little he had learned—but, more often than not, it seemed to control him. He had enjoyed a few successes, but suffered many failures. He was an apprentice of an art that defied his staunchest efforts to master it. Perhaps he was not meant to be a wizard. Perhaps he should simply accept the fact of it.

He rubbed his chin and screwed up his owlish face in distaste. Never! He would sooner be a toad!

He stood up, paced about the darkened chamber for a time, and sat down again. There was no point in bemoaning his life's condition. True wizard or no, he was going to have to do something about Nightshade. The problem, of course, was that he didn't know what. He could go down into the Deep Fell and confront the witch, demand the bottle back, and threaten her with his magic. Unfortunately, that would likely be the end of him. He was no match for Nightshade in her own domain, especially with the bottle and its demon in her service. She would gobble him up like a sweetmeat.

He saw again in his mind the witch and the Darkling at the hollows rim, a match if ever there was one, darkest evil and her favorite child.

He clasped his hands before him, frowning so hard the ends of his mouth almost disappeared below his chin. The Paladin was the only one who could master the witch—but the Paladin would only appear if the High Lord summoned him, and the High Lord was trapped in his old world until he could find the missing Abernathy, regain his medallion, and get back again.

Questor Thews gave a great sigh of disgust. It had all gotten so complicated!

"Well!" he snapped, coming abruptly to his feet. "We shall have to uncomplicate things!"

Brave words, he thought darkly. Uncomplicating things meant finding Holiday, Abernathy, and the medallion and getting all three safely back into Landover to deal with Nightshade and the Darkling. He hadn't the magic to do that. He'd told Holiday as much when he had sent him back.

There was another way, however.

A rather unlikely way.

He was chilled suddenly at the thought of what he had to do. He wrapped his gray robes with their bright-colored silk patches close about him for momentary warmth, then released them again to tug restlessly at his ear. Well, either he was Court Wizard or he wasn't! Better learn the truth of matters right here and now!

"No point in waiting, either," he whispered.

Determined, he went out the door and down the hall to find Bunion. He would leave tonight.

GAMBIT

"I'm telling you, it won't work," Miles Bennett insisted. "I don't know why I let you talk me into these things, Doc."

Ben Holiday leaned forward wearily. "You keep saying that. Why don't you try being more positive about things."

"I am being positive! I'm positive it won't work!"

Ben sighed, leaned back again, and stretched his legs out comfortably in front of him. "It'll work," he said.

They were speeding through the countryside north of Woodinville on 522 in a black stretch limousine, Miles driving, Ben sitting alone in the back seat. Miles wore a chauffeur's cap and coat at least one size too small, which was unfortunate because the whole scenario would have played better if the driver had been as immaculately dressed as his passenger. But there hadn't been time to shop for Miles—and even if there had, they probably wouldn't have been able to find a clothing store with chauffeur uniforms for rent or sale in any case—so they'd had to settle for what the original driver was wearing. Ben looked considerably better. There'd been time to shop for him. He wore a five hundred dollar three-piece dark blue suit with just a hint of pinstriping, a pale blue silk shirt, and a deep mauve silk tie with a scattering of blues and lavenders woven in. A matching scarf was tucked neatly into his breast pocket. He glanced surreptitiously at himself in the rearview mirror. Just your average millionaire businessman, he thought—with just a touch of the wheeler-dealer in evidence. Sitting in his stretch limo with his chauffeur and his fine clothes, he looked every bit the successful entrepreneur.

Which was the way he was supposed to look, of course.

"What if he's seen your picture somewhere?" Miles asked suddenly. "What if he recognizes who you really are?"

"Then I'm in big trouble," Ben admitted. "But he won't. He's had no reason to track down a picture of me. Meeks always handled the Landover sales by himself. Michel Ard Rhi was content to collect the money and let matters take care of themselves. He had his own interests to look after."

"Like running guns and overthrowing foreign governments." Miles shook his head. "This plan is too risky, Doc."

Ben stared out into the darkness. "True. But it's the only plan we've got."

He watched the dark shapes of the trees on either side of the highway rush past and disappear like frozen giants, the land sullen and empty, the night skies overcast and impenetrable. It was always smart to have a plan, he told himself. Too bad it couldn't always be a good one.

They had left Davis Whitsell knowing that Abernathy was again in the hands of Michel Ard Rhi. It didn't matter that Whitsell hadn't seen Abernathy's abductors. They were as certain as the trainer that it had been Michel Ard Rhi who had taken him. Abernathy was imprisoned somewhere in Ard Rhi's castle fortress, and it was up to them to rescue him—quickly. There was no telling what Ard Rhi would do to the dog now. There was no telling what he would do to that little girl either, once he found her out. He might even use the little girl as a weapon against the dog. Abernathy still had the medallion; Whitsell had mentioned seeing it. They had to assume that Ard Rhi knew about the medallion and was trying to get it back. If not, he would have done away with Abernathy long ago. He couldn't take the medallion by force, of course, but he could put an awful lot of pressure on the dog to persuade him to part with it willingly. The little girl would provide just the sort of pressure Ard Rhi would be apt to use.

That being the case, there simply wasn't any time to come up with the sort of elaborate, foolproof plan they might otherwise have envisioned. Abernathy and the little girl were in immediate danger. Willow was growing steadily sicker from the environment into which she had willingly placed herself in order not to be separated from Ben. God only knew what was happening back in Landover with the Darkling still on the loose and Questor Thews trying to govern. Ben seized hold of the first reasonable plan that came to mind.

It was going to take an awful lot of luck to make it work.

"Don't forget about Willow," he reminded Miles suddenly.

"I won't. But I don't see how she's going to have any better luck than you." He glanced quickly back over his shoulder. "There's bound to be lights all over the place, Doc."

Ben nodded. He was worried about that, too. How effective would Willow's magic be when she needed it? What if it failed her entirely? Under normal circumstances, he wouldn't have thought twice about it; he knew that, like all the fairy folk, the sylph could move about freely without being seen. But that was in Landover and that was when she was well. Willow was so weak, so drained by the attack on her system! She desperately needed the nurturing soil and air of her own world. She needed to make the transformation. But she couldn't do it here in this world. She had already told him so. Too many of the chemicals in the soil and air were toxins to her system. She was trapped in her present form until Ben could find a way to get her back to Landover again.

He tightened the muscles of his jaw. It was pointless to dwell on it. There would be no help for her until he regained the medallion—no help for any of them.

He turned his attention to the plan. It had been a fairly simple matter to have the rented limo and driver sent north out of Seattle to the little motel in Bothell that they had quickly made their base of operations. It had been equally simple to bribe the driver to part with the limo and his coat and cap for a few hours while he waited in the motel room and watched TV. After all, five hundred dollars was a lot of money. And it hadn't been too tough to track down the clothes Ben needed.

Finding Michel Ard Rhi had been easier yet. "Oh, sure, that nut that lives out in the castle!" the manager of the motel had eagerly volunteered when Ben asked. "Gramma White or some such, it's called. Looks like something out of King Arthur. Sits back in there behind the winery off 522. Can't even see it from the road. Guy runs it like a prison. Doesn't allow anyone close. As I said, a nut case! Who else would live in a castle in the middle of nowhere?" Then he had drawn Ben a map.

Finding the nut case was one thing; arranging to see him on short notice and at night was something else. Ben had made the call. He had spoken with a man whose sole position with Ard Rhi, it appeared, was to prevent people like Ben from disturbing his boss. Ben had explained that he was only in Seattle that one night. He had explained that the timing was quite important. He had even suggested that he was used to doing business at night. Nothing helped. Ben had talked money, opportunity, ambition, everything he could think of to persuade the man. The man was a stone. He had left the phone twice, presumably to confer with his boss, but each time he had returned as implacable as before. Perhaps tomorrow. Perhaps another day. Definitely not tonight. Mr. Ard Rhi never meets with anyone at night.

Finally, Ben had used Abernathy's name and alluded none too subtly to his own strong connection with certain government agencies. If he were not permitted to speak to Mr. Ard Rhi and speak with him now, personally, this night, he would have to consider turning the matter over to one of those agencies, and Mr. Ard Rhi might not find it so easy to refuse them.

That did the job. Grudgingly, the secretary had advised him that he would have his appointment. But must it be at night? It must, Ben insisted. There had been a pause, more background conversation, heated words. Very well, a few minutes only, nine o'clock sharp at Graum Wythe. The phone had gone dead.

At the close of things, the secretary's voice had sounded very dangerous indeed. But that hadn't mattered to Ben. His meeting with Michel Ard Rhi had to take place at night, or the entire plan was out the window.

Miles slowed the limo abruptly, distracting Ben from his thoughts, wheeled left at a pair of stone block pillars with globe lights, and proceeded down a narrow, single-lane road that disappeared back into the trees. What little light there was from the headlamps of other cars, from the distant windows of solitary houses, and from the reflection of ground light off the clouded skies disappeared. The lights of the limo were lonely beacons in the gloom.

They drove on, a long, solitary journey through the night. The woods gave way to the vineyards, acres of small, gnarled vines planted in endless rows. The minutes slipped away.

Ben thought of Willow, hidden in the trunk of the car, carefully wrapped in blankets. He wished he could check on her, make certain she was all right. But they had agreed. No chances were to be taken. Once they had left Bothell, there was to be no stopping until . . .

Ben blinked.

Lights flared ahead from beyond the wooded hill they climbed—triggered, it seemed, by their approach. As they topped the rise, the spires of Graum Wythe lifted starkly before them. Though still far distant, they could see the castle clearly. Flags and pennants blew sharply in the night wind, their insignia unidentifiable in the shadows. A drawbridge had already begun to lower across a moat, and a portcullis was being raised. Breastworks and spiked fences crisscrossed the open countryside surrounding the castle, dark scars on the grassland. The limo crawled down the roadway toward a set of massive iron gates that opened through a long, low stone wall that ran for miles in either direction.

Ben took a deep breath and shivered in spite of himself. How grotesque the castle seemed!

The iron gates swung open soundlessly to admit them, and Miles eased the limo through. He had quit talking, rigid in the driver's seat. Ben could imagine what he was thinking.

The roadway wound snakelike toward the castle, brightly lit and flanked by deep culverts. That's probably so nobody wanders off by mistake, Ben thought darkly. For the first time since he had conceived this venture, he began to have doubts. Graum Wythe hunkered down before him like some huge beast, all alone in the empty countryside with its towers, parapets, guards, spotlights, and sharp wire. It looked less like a castle than a prison. He was going into that prison and he was going in unprotected.

The full realization of where he was struck him suddenly, a frightening and certain truth that left him shaken. He was such a fool! He thought of himself as still being in a world of glass high-rises and jetliners. But Graum

Wythe wasn't part of that world; it was part of another. It was part of a life he had bought into when he had purchased his kingship nearly two years ago. There wasn't anything from the modern world out here. He could dress in suits and ride in limos and know that cities and highways were all around him, and it wouldn't make one bit of difference. This was Landover! But the Paladin was not here to rescue him. Questor Thews was not here to advise him. He had no magic to aid him. If anything went wrong, he was probably finished.

The car reached the end of the winding roadway and pulled onto the lowered drawbridge. They passed over the moat, under the portcullis, and into a courtyard with a turn-around drive that looped ahead to the main entry. Manicured lawns and flower gardens failed to make up for the towering stoneblock walls and iron-grated windows.

"Charming," Miles whispered from the front.

Ben sat quietly. He was calm now, quite composed. It was like old times, he told himself. It was like it had been when he was a lawyer. He was simply going into trial court one more time.

Miles pulled the limo to a stop at the top of the drive, got out, and walked around to open the door for Ben. Ben stepped out and glanced around. The walls and towers of Graum Wythe loomed all about him, casting their shadows against the blaze of lights that flooded the yard. Too many lights, Ben thought. Guards patrolled the entries and the walls, faceless, black-garbed figures in the night. Too many of them as well.

A doorman appeared through the heavy brass and oak doors of the main entry and stood waiting. Miles closed the car door firmly and leaned close.

"Good luck, Doc," he whispered.

Ben nodded. Then he went up the steps and disappeared into the castle.

The minutes slipped past. Miles waited by the back door of the limo for a time, then walked around to the driver's door, stopped, and glanced casually about. The castle doors were closed again and the doorman gone. The courtyard was deserted—discounting, of course, the spotlights that lit it up bright as day and guards that patrolled the walls all around it. Miles shook his head. He reached in the car under the dash and popped the trunk, trying hard not to think about what he was doing, trying to appear nonchalant. He walked back to the trunk, lifted the lid, reached in, and took out a polishing cloth. He barely glanced at the blanketed, huddled shape in one corner. Leaving the trunk open, he moved to the front of the car and began wiping down the windshield.

A pair of black-uniformed guards walked out of the shadows from one corner of the building and stopped, watching him. He kept polishing. The guards carried automatic weapons.

Willow will never make it, he thought dismally.

The guards strolled on. Miles was sweating. He released the hood latch, then moved to the front of the car and looked in, fiddling with nothing. He had never felt so entirely alone and at the same time so completely observed. He could feel eyes on him everywhere. He glanced surreptitiously from beneath the hood. Who knew how many of those eyes would catch Willow trying to sneak past?

He finished with the phony engine inspection and dropped the hood back in place. There hadn't been a sign of movement anywhere. What was she waiting for? His cherubic face grimaced. What did he think she was waiting for, for God's sake? She was waiting for a power outage!

That damn Doc and his harebrained schemes!

He walked back around the car to the trunk, half-determined to find a way to call the whole thing off, certain the whole plan was already shot to hell. He was utterly astonished when he glanced in the trunk and found Willow gone.

Standing inside the front entry, the doorman patted Ben down for weapons and, presumably, wires. There weren't any to be found. Neither man said a word.

When the search was finished, Ben followed the doorman along a cavernous, vaulted corridor past suits of armor, tapestries, marble statues, and oil paintings in gilt-edged frames to a pair of dark oak doors that opened into a study. A genuine study, mind you, Ben thought—not a little room with a few shelves and bookcases and a reading chair, but a full-blown English-style study with dozens of huge, stuffed leather reading chairs and companion tables of the sort you saw in those old Sherlock Holmes movies in mansions where the characters retired to take brandy and cigars and talk murder. A fire blazed in a floor-to-ceiling fireplace, the embers of charred logs smoldering redly beneath the iron grate. A pair of latticed windows looked out into gardens that featured sculpted hedges and wrought-iron benches and were disturbingly deep.

The doorman stepped aside to let Ben enter, pulled the study doors closed behind him, and was gone.

Michel Ard Rhi was already on his feet, materializing from out of one of the huge stuffed chairs as if he had miraculously taken form from its leather. He was dressed entirely in the stuff, a sort of charcoal jumpsuit complete with low boots, and he looked as if he were trying to do Hamlet. But there was nothing funny about the way he looked at Ben. He stood there, a tall, rawboned figure, his shock of black hair and his dark eyes shadowing the whole of his face, his features pinched with displeasure. He did not come forward to offer his hand. He did not invite Ben in. He simply viewed him.

"I do not appreciate being threatened, Mr. Squires," he said softly. Squires was the phony name Ben had given over the phone. "Not by anyone, but especially not by someone looking to do business with me."

Ben kept his poise. "It was necessary that I see you, Mr. Ard Rhi," he replied calmly. "Tonight. It was obvious that I was not going to be able to do so unless I found a way to change your mind."

Michel Ard Rhi studied him, apparently considering whether to pursue the matter. Then he said, "You have your meeting. What do you want?"

Ben moved forward until he was less than a dozen paces from the other. There was anger in the sharp eyes, but no sign of recognition. "I want Abernathy," he said.

Ard Rhi shrugged. "So you said, but I don't know what you are talking about."

"Let me save both of us a little valuable time," Ben continued smoothly. "I know all about Abernathy. I know what he is and what he can do. I know about Davis Whitsell. I know about *Hollywood Eye.* I know most of what there is to know about this matter. I don't know what your interest is in this creature, but it doesn't matter as long as it doesn't conflict with mine. My interest is paramount, Mr. Ard Rhi, and immediate. I don't have time to wait for sideshows and the like."

The other man studied him, a hint of shrewdness displacing the anger. "And your interest is . . . ?"

"Scientific." Ben smiled conspiratorially. "I operate a specialized business, Mr. Ard Rhi—one that investigates the functioning of life forms and explores ways to make them better. My business operates somewhat covertly. You'll not have heard of either its name or mine. Uncle Sam aids in funding, and we exchange favors from time to time. Do you understand?"

A nod. "Experiments?"

"Among other things." Another smile. "Could we sit down now and talk like businessmen?"

Michel Ard Rhi did not smile back, but indicated a chair and sat down across from Ben. "This is all very interesting, Mr. Squires. But I can't help you. There isn't any Abernathy. The whole business is a lie."

Ben shrugged as if he expected as much. "Whatever you say." He leaned back comfortably. "But if there were an Abernathy, and if he became available, then he would be a most valuable commodity—to a number of interested parties. I would be prepared to make a substantial offer for him."

The other man's expression did not change. "Really."

"If he were undamaged."

"He doesn't exist."

"Supposing."

"Supposing doesn't make it so."

"He would be worth twenty-five million dollars."

Michel Ard Rhi stared. "Twenty-five million dollars?" he repeated.

Ben nodded. He didn't have twenty-five million dollars to spend on Abernathy, of course. He didn't have twenty-five million dollars, period. But then he didn't really expect that any amount of money could purchase his friend—not before Michel Ard Rhi had his hands on the medallion.

What he was doing was buying time.

So far, it hadn't cost him much.

Willow slipped noiselessly along the dimly lit passageways of Graum Wythe, little more than another of night's shadows. She was tired, the use of the magic that kept her concealed a drain on her already diminished strength. She felt sick inside, a pervasive queasiness that would not be banished. At times she was so stricken she was forced to stop, leaning back in dark corners and waiting for her strength to return. She knew what was wrong with her. She was dying. It was happening a little at a time, a little each day, but she recognized the signs. She could not survive outside of her own world for more than a short time—especially not here, not in an environment where the soil and the air were unclean and poisoned with waste.

She had not told Ben. She did not intend to. Ben had enough to concern him, and there was nothing he could do for her, in any case. Besides, she had known the risk when she had decided to come with him. Any fault was her own.

She breathed the close air of the castle, nauseated by its taste and smell. Her skin was pale and damp with perspiration. She forced herself from her hiding place and continued swiftly on. She was on the second floor and close to where she needed to go now. She could sense it. She must hurry, though. Ben could give her only a few minutes.

She reached a single door at the bend in the hall and pressed her ear against it, listening. There was breathing within.

It was the little girl, Elizabeth.

She placed her hand on the latch. It was for this reason that they had come to Graum Wythe at night—so that they could be certain the little girl would be there.

She pressed down on the latch until it gave, pushed the door open, and slipped inside. Elizabeth was in her nightdress, propped up in her bed on one elbow, reading a book. She started when Willow appeared, her eyes going wide.

"Who are you?" she breathed. "Oh! You're all green!"

Willow smiled, closed the door behind her, and held a finger to her lips. "Shhh, Elizabeth. It is all right. My name is Willow. I am a friend of Abernathy's."

Elizabeth sat bolt upright in the bed. "Abernathy? You are?" She pushed the covers back and scrambled out of the bed. "Are you a fairy? A fairy princess, maybe? You look like one, you're so beautiful! Can you do magic? Can you . . ."

Willow moved her finger to the little girl's lips. "Shhhhh," she repeated softly. "We do not have much time."

Elizabeth frowned. "I don't understand. What's wrong? Oh, I bet you don't know! Abernathy's gone! He's not here anymore! Michel had him locked in a cage in the cellars, but I sneaked him out and sent him . . ."

"Elizabeth," Willow interrupted gently. She knelt down next to the little girl and took her hands. "I have to tell you something. I am afraid Abernathy did not escape after all. Michel found him and brought him back."

"Oh, poor Abernathy!" Elizabeth's face tightened into a knot of anguish. "Michel will hurt him, I know he will! He was starving to death when I helped him escape! Now Michel will really hurt him. That's how he is! He'll really hurt him!"

Willow turned her toward the bed and sat with her on its edge. "We have to find another way to help him escape from here, Elizabeth," she said. "Is there anyone you can think of who could help us?"

Elizabeth looked doubtful. "My father, maybe. But he's gone."

"When does you father return?"

"Next week, Wednesday." Elizabeth's face knotted further. "It's not soon enough, is it, Willow? Michel was looking funny at me at dinner tonight—as if he knew something. He kept talking about dogs, and then he would smile, a mean smile. He knows I helped, I'll bet. He's just teasing me with it. He's going to hurt Abernathy, isn't he?"

Willow squeezed the small hands. "We will not let him. I have friends with me. We are going to take Abernathy away."

"You are?" Elizabeth was immediately excited. "Maybe I can help!"

Willow shook her head firmly. "Not this time."

"But I want to help!" Elizabeth said firmly. "Michel already knows I helped once, so I can't be in any worse trouble! Maybe you can take me, too! I don't want to stay here anymore!"

Willow frowned slightly. "Elizabeth, I . . ."

"Michel's already said I can't leave my room! I have to stay up here all the time until he says different. He has to know! Tomorrow is Halloween, and I don't even get to go trick-or-treating! I practically had to beg to get permission to go to the school party tomorrow night. I even had to get Nita Coles to get her parents to call up and offer me a ride! With my dad gone, Michel wasn't going to let me go. But I told him everyone would wonder if I wasn't at the party because the whole school was going—so he gave in." She was crying. "I guess going to the party doesn't matter much now, not with Abernathy locked up again. Oh, I thought he was safe!"

Suddenly she stopped crying and her head jerked up sharply. "Willow, I know a way to get Abernathy out! If Michel's got him locked up again in the cellar, I know how to get him out!"

Willow touched the little girl's tear-streaked face. "How, Elizabeth?"

"The same way I got him out before—through the passageway in the wall! Michel doesn't know about that yet! I know because I was in it again after Abernathy got away, and it wasn't closed off or anything! And I could get a key to those cages again if I had to—I know I could!" She was excited now, her breathing rapid, her face flushed. "Willow, we could get him out tonight!"

For just an instant, Willow considered it. Then she shook her head. "No, Elizabeth, not tonight. Soon, though. And perhaps you can help. In fact, you already have. You have told me of a way to reach Abernathy. That was one reason I came to you—to see if there was a way. But we must be very careful, Elizabeth. We must not make any mistakes. Do you understand?"

Elizabeth was crestfallen, but managed a grudging nod.

Willow tried a wan smile. She had already stayed beyond her allotted time and she was growing dangerously weak from the effort. "You must not say anything about seeing me, Elizabeth. You must pretend I never came. You must act as if you know nothing about Abernathy. Can you do that?"

The little girl nodded. "I can pretend better than anyone."

"Good." Willow rose and started for the door, one of Elizabeth's hands still clinging to her. She turned. "Be patient, Elizabeth. We all want Abernathy safe again. Perhaps tomorrow . . ."

"I love Abernathy," Elizabeth said suddenly.

Willow turned, looked at the little girl's face, and then hugged her close. "I do, too, Elizabeth."

They held each other for a long time.

"Twenty-five million dollars is a lot of money, Mr. Squires," Michel Ard Rhi was saying.

Ben smiled. "We try not to put limits on the price of our research, Mr. Ard Rhi."

Still seated in the stuffed leather chairs, they studied each other in the silence and shadows of the study. No sound reached them from without.

"The subject of our discussion would have to be in good condition, of course," Ben repeated. "A damaged specimen would be useless."

The other said nothing.

"I would need to make an inspection."

Still nothing.

"I would need assurances that Abernathy . . ."

"There is no Abernathy, Mr. Squires—remember?" Michel Ard Rhi said suddenly. Ben waited. "Even if there were . . . I would have to think about your offer."

Ben nodded. He had expected that. It was too much to hope that he would have a chance to see Abernathy right away. "Perhaps if I were to arrange to stay a bit longer than planned, Mr. Ard Rhi, we might continue this discussion tomorrow?"

The other man shrugged. He touched something beneath the table beside him and rose. "I will decide the time and the place of any future meetings, Mr. Squires. Is that understood?"

Ben smiled companionably. "As long as it's soon, Mr. Ard Rhi."

Surprisingly, Michel Ard Rhi smiled back. "Let me give you some advice, Mr. Squires," he said, coming forward a few paces. "You should be more careful with your demands. This is a place of some danger, you know. That is its history. People have disappeared in these walls. They were never seen again. There is magic here—some of it very bad."

Ben was suddenly cold. He knows, he thought in horror.

"A life or two snuffed out, what does it matter? Even important lives—like your own—can be swallowed up and disappear. The magic does that, Mr. Squires. It simply swallows you up."

Ben heard the door behind him open.

"Be careful after this," the other warned softly, eyes hard with the promise that the threat was real. "I don't like you."

The doorman stepped into view and Michel Ard Rhi turned abruptly away. Ben walked quickly from the study, daring to breathe again, feeling the chill in his spine begin to fade. He passed back down the empty corridor to the front entry and went out, the doorman showing the way. As he stepped into the night, he thought he felt something brush against him. He looked but there was nothing there.

The door closed behind him. Miles was standing by the rear door, holding it open. Ben climbed into the car and sat back wordlessly. He watched Miles walk around the rear of the limo to the driver's door. The trunk was already closed. There was no sign of Willow.

"Willow?" he whispered urgently.

"I'm here, Ben," she replied, a disembodied voice from out of the pool of shadows at his feet, so close to him that he jumped.

Miles got in and started the car. Within minutes they were back through the portcullis, over the drawbridge, up the winding roadway, and out the iron gates. Willow sat up in the seat then next to Ben and related everything Elizabeth had told her. When she was finished, no one said anything for a time. The car's engine hummed in the silence as they passed back out onto 522 and turned south toward Woodinville.

When Miles turned up the heater, no one complained.

SNATCH

October 31 was a gray, cloudy, drizzly day where the wind blew in sharp gusts, and the rain spit and chilled the air, as the whole western half of Washington State experienced a forewarning of winter's coming. It was a gloomy day of shadows and strange sounds, the kind of day when people think about curling up next to a warm fire with a glass of something hot and a good book. It was a day when they found themselves listening to the sounds of the weather and to things that weren't even there. It was, in short, a perfect day for an Allhallows Eve.

Elizabeth was eating lunch in the school cafeteria when she got the message that a telephone call from home was waiting for her in the office. She hurried to get it, leaving Nita Coles to guard her double-chocolate-chip cookie; when she returned, she was so excited she didn't bother to eat it. Later, when they were at recess, she told Nita that she didn't need a ride to the Halloween party that night after all—although she might need one home. Nita said okay and told Elizabeth she thought she was acting weird.

Ben Holiday spent the better part of that blustery day south of Woodinville and Bothell in greater Seattle visiting costume shops. It took him a long time to find the costume he was looking for. Even then, he had to spend several hours afterward, back in the motel room, altering its appearance until it met with his approval.

Willow spent the day in bed, resting. She was growing steadily weaker and she was having trouble breathing. She tried to hide it from Ben, but it wasn't something she could hide. He was good about it, though, not saying anything, letting her sleep, forcing himself to concentrate on his preparations for that night. She saw that and loved him the more for it.

Miles Bennett visited several private airports until he found one with a suitable plane and pilot that could be chartered for a flight out that night. He told the pilot that there would be four of them and they would be flying to Virginia.

They all went about their business, right along with the rest of the world, but for them, it seemed, Friday was an endless wait . . .

Finally, dusk found Ben, Miles, and Willow back once more on 522 headed north out of Woodinville toward Graum Wythe. They were in the rental car this time, the limo long since dispatched back to Seattle. Ben was driving, Willow was beside him in the passenger seat, and Miles sat in back. The wind whistled and the weaving shadows of branches played along the car's dark shell like devil's fingers. The skies were slate gray, turning black as the final twinge of daylight slipped rapidly away.

"Doc, this isn't going to work," Miles said suddenly, breaking what had been a seemingly interminable stretch of silence.

It was like a replay of yesterday. Ben grinned, though Miles couldn't see it. "Why not, Miles?"

"Because there are too many things that can go wrong, that's why. I know I said the same thing about last night's plan and you still got away with it, but that was different. This plan is a hell of a lot more dangerous! You realize, of course, that we don't even know if Abernathy is down there in those dungeons or cages or whatever! What if he's not there? What if he's there, but you can't get to him? What if they've changed the locks or hidden the keys, for God's sake? What do we do then?"

"Come back tomorrow and try again."

"Oh, sure! Halloween will be over! What are we supposed to do? Wait for Thanksgiving and go in as turkeys? Or maybe Christmas and go down the chimney like Santa and his elves?"

Ben glanced around. Miles looked pretty funny sitting there in that gorilla suit. But, then, he looked pretty funny himself in the shaggy dog outfit that made him look somewhat like Abernathy. "Relax, Miles," he said.

"Relax?" Ben could practically see him turning red inside the heavy suit. "What if they count heads, Doc? If they count heads, we're dead!"

"I told you how to handle that. It will work just the way we want it to. By the time they figure out what's happened, we'll be long gone."

They rode on in silence until they reached the stone pillars with the lighted globes and Ben wheeled the car left down the wooded, private road. Then Willow said, "I wish we didn't have to take Elizabeth with us."

Ben nodded. "I know. But we can't leave her behind—not after this. Michel Ard Rhi will know she was involved. She's better off out of there. Her father will understand after Miles has talked to him. They'll be well looked after."

"Humphhh!" Miles grunted. "You're crazy, Doc, you know that? No wonder you like living in fairyland!"

Willow slumped back in the seat and closed her eyes again. Her breathing was ragged. "Are you sure you can do this?" Ben asked quietly. The sylph nodded without replying.

They drove through the vineyards and finally the electric sensor that triggered the floodlights. When they reached the low stone wall, the iron gates were open and Graum Wythe's drawbridge and portcullis were already in operation. The castle looked massive and forbidding against the mix of low-hanging clouds and distant mountains, the outline of its towers and parapets hazy with the mist and rain. The wipers of the car clicked back and forth, blurring and clearing in brief intervals the sweep of the land ahead. Ben eased the rental car down the winding roadway, unable to escape the feeling that he had somehow managed to forget something.

They crossed the drawbridge, the tires thumping on the timbers, passed through the maw of the castle gates, and pulled around the drive. Lights blazed through the mist and gloom, but the guards they had seen the previous night were not in evidence. Doesn't mean that they're not out there, though, Ben thought and swung the car in close to the entry.

They stepped out quickly and hastened into the shelter of the front entryway, Ben holding Willow close to keep her from slipping. They knocked and waited. The door opened almost at once, and the doorman was there to greet them. He blinked in surprise.

What he saw was a gorilla, a shaggy dog, and a young woman dyed green from head to foot.

"Evening," Ben greeted through the dog suit. "We're here to pick up Elizabeth for her Halloween party at the grade school. I'm Mr. Barker, this is my wife Helen, and this is Mr. Campbell." He made the introductions quickly so the names wouldn't register, and they didn't.

"Oh." The doorman was not a conversationalist. He beckoned them inside, however, and they gladly went. They stood in the entryway, brushing off stray drops of rain and looking guardedly about. The doorman studied them momentarily, then went to a phone and called someone. Ben held his breath. The doorman put the phone down and returned.

"Miss Elizabeth asked if one of you could help her with her costume," he said.

"Yes, I can help," Willow offered, right on cue. "I know the way, thank you."

She disappeared up the winding stairway and was gone. Ben and Miles sat down on a bench in the entryway, oversized bookends from a curio shop. The doorman studied them some more, probably trying to figure out how any sane adult could be talked into dressing up like that, then turned down the hall and disappeared from view.

Ben felt the heat of the two costumes he was wearing turn his back and underarms damp.

So far, so good, he thought.

Willow tapped lightly on Elizabeth's bedroom door and waited. Almost immediately, the door was opened by a small clown with frizzy orange hair, a white face, and an enormous red nose. "Oh, Willow!" Elizabeth whispered, grasping her hand and pulling her urgently inside. "It's all going wrong!"

Willow took her shoulders gently. "What's going wrong, Elizabeth?"

"Abernathy! He's all . . . strange! I went down to the cellars this afternoon after school to see if he was all right—you know, to make certain he was still there. I know I probably shouldn't have, but I was worried, Willow!" The words practically tumbled over one another. "I sneaked out of my room. I made sure no one saw me, then went down through the passage in the walls to the cellars. Abernathy was there, locked in one of those cages, all chained up! Oh, Willow, he looked so sad! He looked all ragged and dirty. I whispered to him, called to him, but he didn't seem to know who I was. He just . . . he sounded like he couldn't talk right! He said a bunch of stuff that didn't make any sense and he couldn't seem to sit up or move or anything!"

The blue eyes glistened with tears. "Willow, he's so sick! I don't know if he can even walk!"

Willow felt a mix of fear and uncertainty wash through her, but she forced it quickly away. "Do not be afraid, Elizabeth," she said firmly. "Show me where he is. It will be all right."

They slipped from the room into the empty hall, the tiny clown and the emerald fairy. An old clock ticked in the silence from one end, and the sound of very distant voices echoed faintly. Elizabeth took Willow to a cluttered broom closet. Closing the door behind them, she produced a flashlight, then spent a few seconds pushing at the back wall until a section of it swung open. Silently, they went down the stairs that lay beyond, navigating through several twists and turns, two landings, and one short tunnel, until at last they reached another section of wall, this one with a rusted iron handle fixed to it.

"He's right through here!" Elizabeth whispered.

She took hold of the handle and pulled. The wall eased back, and the rush of stale, fetid air caused Willow to gasp. Nausea washed through her, but she swallowed against it and waited for the feeling to pass.

"Willow, are you all right?" Elizabeth asked urgently, her brightly colored clown's face bent close.

"Yes, Elizabeth," Willow whispered. She couldn't give in now. Just a little longer, she promised herself. Just a little.

She peered through the opening in the wall. Cages lined a passageway, shadowed cells of rock and iron bars. There was movement in one. Something lay there twitching.

"That's Abernathy!" Elizabeth confirmed in a small, frightened voice.

Willow took a moment longer to check the corridor beyond for other signs of movement. There were none. "Are there guards?" she asked softly.

Elizabeth pointed. "Down there, beyond that door. Just one, usually."

Willow pushed her way out into the cellar passage, feeling the nausea and weakness surge through her once more. She went to the cage that held Abernathy and peered in. The dog lay on a pile of straw, his fur matted and soiled, his clothes torn. He had been sick, and the discharge clung to him. He smelled awful. There was a chain fastened about his neck.

The medallion hung there as well.

Abernathy was mumbling incoherently. He was talking about everything and nothing all at once, his speech slurred, his words fragments of witless chatter. He has been drugged, Willow thought.

Elizabeth was handing her something. "This is the key to the cage door, Willow," she whispered. She looked very frightened. "I don't know if it fits the chain on his neck!"

Her clown nose fell off, and she picked it up hurriedly and pushed it back into place. Willow took the key from her and started to insert it into the cage door lock.

It was at that same moment that they heard the latch on the door at the end of the corridor begin to turn.

Michel Ard Rhi came down the front hallway past the entry and paused momentarily as he saw the gorilla and the shaggy dog sitting there on the waiting bench. It was apparent that he wasn't sure what to make of them. He looked at them, and they looked back. No one said anything.

Ben held his breath and waited. He could feel Miles go rigid beside him. Suddenly, Michel seemed to realize what they were doing there. "Oh, yes," he said. "The Halloween party at the school. You must be here for Elizabeth."

A phone rang somewhere down the hall.

Michel hesitated, as if he might say something more, then turned and walked away quickly to answer it. The shaggy dog and the gorilla glanced at each other in silent relief.

The guard pushed his way wearily through the cellar door and came down the corridor of iron cages, boots clumping heavily on the stone block. He was dressed in black and wore an automatic weapon and a ring of keys at his belt. Elizabeth shrank further into the darkness behind the hidden section of wall where she was concealed, peering out through the tiny crack she had left open.

Willow was still out there in the corridor. But where? Why couldn't she see her?

She watched the guard pause at Abernathy's cage, check the door perfunctorily to make certain it was locked, then turn and walk back again the way he had come. As he passed her hiding place, the keys at his belt suddenly came free. Elizabeth blinked in disbelief. The snap that held them seemed to loosen of its own accord and all at once the keys were gone. The guard completed his walk down the corridor, pushed back through the metal door, and disappeared.

Elizabeth slipped quickly from her hiding place. "Willow!" she called in a muffled hiss.

The sylph appeared out of nowhere at her side, the ring of keys in one hand. "Hurry, now," she whispered. "We do not have much time."

They went back to Abernathy's cage, and Willow opened the door with the key Elizabeth had given her earlier. They hastened inside, moving to the incoherent dog and kneeling beside him. Willow bent close. The scribe's eyes were dilated and his breathing was rapid. When she tried to lift him, he sagged helplessly against her.

A moment of panic seized her. He was far too heavy for her to carry—far too heavy even if Elizabeth helped. She had to find a way to bring him out of his stupor.

"Try these until you find one that fits," she told Elizabeth, handing her the key ring.

Elizabeth went to work with the keys, trying one after another in the lock of the neck chain. Willow rubbed Abernathy's paws, then his head. Nothing seemed to help. Her panic deepened. She had to bring Ben down. But she knew, even as she considered the idea, that it wasn't possible. The plan wouldn't work with Ben down here. Besides, there simply wasn't time.

Finally, she did the only thing she could think to do to help the dog. She used her fairy magic. She was so weak that she had little to command, but she called up what she had. She placed her hands on Abernathy's head, closed her eyes in concentration, and drew the poison out of his system and into her own. It entered her in a rush, a vile fluid, and she worked desperately to negate its effects on her own body. She was not strong enough. It was too much for her. Some of it broke through her defenses and began to sicken further her already weakened system. Nausea mingled with pain. She shuddered and wrenched herself away, vomiting into the straw.

"Willow, Willow!" she heard Elizabeth cry out in fear. "Please, don't be sick!"

The little clown's face was pressed up against her own, whispering urgently, crying. Willow blinked. The red nose was gone again, she thought, distracted. She couldn't seem to organize her thoughts. Everything was drifting.

Then suddenly, miraculously, she heard Abernathy say, "Willow? What are you doing here?" And she knew it was going to be all right.

It was only after they were back in the passageway, safely clear of the cages, that Elizabeth rubbed her face where the clown's nose should have been and realized she had lost it. Panic gripped her. She must have dropped it while they were freeing Abernathy. It would certainly be found. She thought about stopping, then decided not to. It was too late to do anything now. Willow was too weak to go back and would never let Elizabeth return alone. She bit her tongue and concentrated on the task at hand, shining the flashlight's thin beam on the stairs ahead as they climbed toward the broom closet. Willow and Abernathy followed a few steps behind, hanging on to each other for support, both of them looking as if they would collapse with every step.

"Just a little farther," Elizabeth kept whispering to encourage them, but neither replied.

They reached the landing to the broom closet, worked the wall section open, and pushed inside. Willow's pale face was bright with perspiration, and she seemed to be having trouble focusing. "It is all right, Elizabeth," she assured the little girl, seeing the look of worry in her eyes, but Elizabeth was no fool and could clearly see that it was definitely not all right.

When they were finally back inside Elizabeth's room, the little girl and Willow worked hurriedly on Abernathy, combing his matted fur, cleaning him up as best they could. They tried to strip off his ruined clothes, but he protested so vehemently about being left naked that they finally agreed to let him keep the half pants and boots. It wasn't what Ben had wanted, but Willow was too tired to argue. She could feel herself withering a bit more with the passing of every second.

She surprised herself though. She wasn't as frightened of dying as she had imagined she would be.

The hall phone rang for what seemed to Ben and Miles an interminable length of time before the doorman appeared to answer it. There was a brief conversation, and then the doorman hung up and said to them, "Miss Elizabeth said to tell you that she would be right down."

"Finally!" Miles breathed in a hushed voice.

The doorman lingered a moment, then walked away again.

"I'm going out now," Ben whispered. "Remember what to do."

He rose and disappeared silently through the front door. He went down the front steps and got into the car. There, he stripped away the dog suit, straightened the costume beneath, and slipped a new mask into place. Then he got out again and went back inside.

The doorman was just returning. He frowned on seeing the gorilla now sitting in the company of a skeleton. "This is Mr. Andrews," Miles said quickly. "He was waiting in the car, but he got tired. Mr. Barker went upstairs to help his wife with Elizabeth."

The doorman nodded absently, still staring at Ben. He appeared to be on the verge of saying something when Elizabeth, the green lady, and the shaggy dog came down the stairway. The green lady did not look well at all.

"All set, John," Elizabeth said brightly to the doorman. She was carrying a small overnight bag. "We have to hurry. By the way, I forgot. I'm spending the night with Nita Coles. Tell Michel, will you? 'Bye."

The doorman smiled faintly and said good-bye. The bunch of them, the gorilla, the skeleton, the green lady, the shaggy dog, and Elizabeth went out the door quickly and were gone.

The doorman stared after them thoughtfully. Had the shaggy dog been wearing pants when he came in?

By the time Ben Holiday pulled the rental car into the parking lot of Franklin Elementary, there were miniature witches, werewolves, ghosts, devils, punk rockers, and assorted other horrors arriving from everywhere, all dashing from their cars to the shelter of the lighted school as if truly possessed. The rain was still falling heavily. There were going to be more than a few disappointed trick-or-treaters this night.

Ben turned the wheel into the curb and put the gearshift into park. He looked over at Elizabeth seated next to him. "Time to go, kiddo."

Elizabeth nodded, somehow managing to look sad even with the painted happy face. "I wish I could go with you."

"Not this time, honey," Ben smiled. "You know what to do now, don't you—after the party?"

"Sure. I go home with Nita and her parents and stay there until my dad comes for me." She sounded sad, too.

"Right. Mr. Bennett will see to it that he finds out what has happened to you. Whatever happens, don't go back to the castle. Okay?"

"Okay. Good-bye, Ben. Good-bye, Willow." She turned to Willow, seated next to her, and gave the sylph a long hug and kiss on the cheek. Willow kissed her back and smiled, saying nothing. She was so sick it was hard for her to talk. "Will you be okay?" Elizabeth wanted to know, asking the question hesitantly.

"Yes, Elizabeth." Willow managed another quick kiss and opened the door. Ben had never seen her this bad, not even when she had been prevented from making the transformation into her namesake that first time she was taken into Abaddon. His patience slipped a notch.

"'Bye, Abernathy," Elizabeth said to the dog, who was seated with Miles in the back. She started to say something, stopped, and then said, "I'll miss you."

Abernathy nodded. "I will miss you, too, Elizabeth."

Then she was out the door and dashing for the school. Ben waited until she was safely inside, then wheeled the car out of the parking lot and sped quickly back through Woodinville to 522 and turned west.

"High Lord, I cannot thank you enough for coming to rescue me," Abernathy was saying. "I had given myself up for lost."

Ben was thinking of Willow and trying hard to keep the car within the speed limit. "I'm sorry this had to happen, Abernathy. Questor is sorry, too. He really is."

"I find that hard to believe," the dog declared, sounding very much like his old self. The effect of the drugs had pretty much worn off, and the scribe was more tired than anything. It was Willow who was in trouble now.

Ben eased the speed of the rental car up a notch.

"He was trying to help you, don't forget," he said.

"He scarcely understands the meaning of the word!" Abernathy huffed. He was quiet a moment. "By the way—here." He took the chain with the medallion from his own neck, reached across the seatback, and placed it carefully about Ben's. "I feel much better knowing you have this safely back."

Ben didn't say so, but he felt much better, too.

He reached Interstate 5 twenty minutes later and turned the car south. The rain diminished somewhat and it appeared to be clearing ahead. The airport was less than half an hour's drive.

Willow's hand stretched across the seat and found his. He squeezed it gently and tried to will some of the strength from his body into hers.

A car passed them in the left lane and a woman in the passenger seat stared over. What she saw was a skeleton driving a gorilla, a shaggy dog, and a lady dyed green. The woman said something to the driver and the car moved on.

Ben had forgotten about their costumes. He thought momentarily about removing them, then decided against it. There wasn't time. Besides, this was Halloween. Lots of people would be out in costumes tonight, going one place or another, trick-or-treating, attending parties, having fun. It was like that in Seattle; he'd read as much in this morning's newspaper. Halloween was a big deal.

He was feeling better about things by the time the lights of the city came into view. The rain had practically disappeared, and they were only moments from their destination. He watched the skyscrapers brighten the night skies and spread away before him in vertical lines. He took a deep breath and allowed himself the luxury of thinking they were almost safely home.

That was when he saw the lights of the state patrol car coming up behind him. "Oh, oh," he muttered.

The patrol car closed quickly, and he eased the rental car over onto the freeway shoulder by a bridge abutment. The patrol car pulled in behind.

"Doc, what's he stopping you for?" Miles demanded. "Were you speeding or something?"

Ben had a sick feeling in his stomach. "I don't think so," he said quietly.

He watched in the rearview mirror. The trooper was on the radio a moment, and another patrol car pulled up behind the first. The trooper in the first car got out then, walked up to Ben's window, and looked in. His face was inscrutable. "Can I see your license, sir?"

Ben reached for his billfold and belatedly remembered he didn't have it. Miles had signed for the car on his license. "Officer, I don't have it with me, but I can give you the number. It is a valid license. And the car is registered with Mr. Bennett."

He indicated the gorilla. Miles was trying to take off the head, but it was stuck. The trooper nodded. "Do you have some proof of identification?" he asked.

"Uh, Mr. Bennett has," Ben said.

"I do, officer," Miles hastily confirmed. "Here, right inside this damn suit if I can just . . ." He trailed off, struggling to get it free.

The trooper looked at Willow and Abernathy. Then he looked back at Ben. "I'm afraid I'll have to ask you to come with me, sir," he said. "Please pull your vehicle out behind mine and follow me downtown. The other patrol car will follow you."

Ben went cold. Something had gone terribly wrong. "I'm a lawyer," he said impulsively. "Are we being charged with something?"

The trooper shook his head. "Not by me, you aren't. Except maybe I'll issue you a warning ticket for driving a vehicle without carrying your license—assuming you have a license like you say. I'll want to check the registration on this vehicle as well."

"But . . . ?"

"There is apparently another matter that needs clearing up. Please follow me, sir." He turned away without further explanation and walked back to his car.

Ben slumped back and heard Miles say softly in his ear, "We've been made, Doc. What do we do now?"

He shook his head wearily. He didn't have the slightest idea.

ITCH

It took Questor Thews the better part of three days to travel by horseback from Sterling Silver to the eastern edge of the Wastelands. He went alone, slipping from the castle before dawn of the first day, departing while the bothersome G'home Gnomes and all those annoyingly insistent ambassadors, couriers, and supplicants from one place or another still slept. Affairs of state would simply have to wait, he had decided, whether it was convenient or not. Bunion and Parsnip were there to see him off, anxious that they be allowed to accompany him, distressed at his insistence on going alone. Questor would not be swayed by the toothy grins and the furtive looks. This was something he must do by himself. Neither of them could help. It was best that they stay at the castle and look after things in his absence. He mounted his old gray and rode out, Don Quixote without his Sancho Panza, a scarecrow searching for his field of need. He went north through the wooded hill country of Sterling Silver, northeast across the fields and pastures of the Greensward, and finally east into the Wastelands.

It was nearing sunset on that third day when he finally sighted the distant glow of the Fire Springs.

"Come along, now," he urged his old gray, who had caught the scent of what lay ahead and was beginning to balk.

Questor Thews was a man who bore a very large burden of guilt. He knew that things would not be right again in the Kingdom of Landover until the High Lord was returned. Nightshade would continue her campaign of disruption and anarchy until someone found a way to deal with that bottle and its demon. Questor was not, unfortunately, the one who could do that. The High Lord was. But the High Lord was trapped in his old world and would not be able to come back again until he recovered his lost medallion—and even then would likely not come back if he could not bring Willow and the missing

Abernathy with him. All of this was the fault of one Questor Thews, of course, and the wizard could not afford to stand by longer and allow matters to assume their own course when the course they assumed might well be the wrong one.

Therefore, he had come up with a plan to put things back the way they were. It was a very straightforward, if somewhat minimally developed plan—but a plan nevertheless. He would enlist the aid of the dragon Strabo to bring Holiday and the others back.

It was all quite simple, really, and he was surprised that he hadn't thought of it earlier. No one could journey in or out of the valley of Landover without passing through the mists of fairy, and no one could pass out of Landover and back in again through the mists of fairy without the magic of Holiday's missing medallion—no one, that is, except Strabo. Dragons could still go pretty much where they chose. Oh, they couldn't go deep into the fairy mists, of course, because dragons had been banished from there long ago. But they could go most places. The magic that allowed them passage through the mists was their own. That was why dragons were apt to pop up almost anywhere. Strabo was no exception. He had already taken Ben Holiday down into the netherworld of Abaddon for the purpose of rescuing Questor, Willow, Abernathy, and the kobolds from the demons. He could certainly make a second trip now to rescue Holiday.

Questor's face knotted. Strabo *could,* to be sure—but whether or not he *would* was another matter entirely. After all, the Abaddon trip had been made under extreme duress, and the dragon had made it quite clear on a number of occasions since that he would rather choke on his own smoke than lift a claw to help Ben Holiday again.

So while the plan's conception was indeed quite simple, its execution probably would not be.

"Ah, well," he sighed resignedly. "*Something* has to be tried."

He guided the gray to the edge of the hills that ringed the Fire Springs, dismounted, stripped saddle and bridle from the old horse, slapped him on the rump, and sent him home. No point in worrying about keeping the horse, he thought. If he couldn't persuade Strabo to help, he wouldn't be needing a horse.

He tugged at one long ear. How *was* he going to persuade Strabo to help anyway?

He thought about it a moment, then shrugged away his worry and began to make his way up the slope through the heavy scrub. Twilight descended gradually over the valley in darkening patches of blue and gray, and the sun diminished to a thin silver slash above the treeline along the western rim, then disappeared altogether. Questor glanced up. A bank of low-hanging clouds hung directly overhead, and its underside shimmered orange and red from the glow of the Springs. The wizard breathed in smoke and ash and sneezed. A sneeze, he thought irritably! That was how this whole mess had begun! He shoved ahead doggedly, heedless of the brambles and scrub that caught his robes and tore through fabric and skin. The explosions were audible now, short, booming coughs that lifted into the night like giant hiccups before subsiding into gurgles of discontent. The heat grew intense, and Questor began sweating freely.

At last he topped a rise and stopped, hands settling firmly on his hips. The Fire Springs were spread out below him, a series of jagged craters in which a blue and yellow liquid bubbled and sizzled. Periodically, a crater would erupt in a geyser of flame, then settle back again discontentedly. The air was sulfurous and hot, its stench a mix of the burning liquid and the blackened bones of animals the resident dragon had devoured.

The dragon was eating now, it happened. He lay wrapped about one of the smaller craters at the north end of the Springs, busily gnawing on what appeared to Questor to be the remains of an unfortunate cow. Bones snapped and crackled loudly within the monstrous jaws, black teeth grinding contentedly. Questor wrinkled his nose in distaste. Strabo's eating habits had always annoyed him.

"Dragon, dragon," he murmured softly to himself.

Strabo seared a section of the cow with his fire, then tore it from the carcass and chewed loudly.

Questor Thews came forward to the very edge of the rise so that he was plainly visible. "Old dragon!" he called out. "I need a word with you!"

Strabo stopped chewing a moment and looked up. "Who's there?" he snapped irritably. He squinted. "Questor Thews, is that you?"

"It is."

"I thought so. How boring." The dragon's teeth snapped the air for emphasis. "And who are you calling 'old'? You're practically a fossil yourself!"

"I need a word with you."

"So you said. I heard you quite clearly. It comes as no surprise, Questor Thews. You always want a word with someone. You seem to delight in talking. I sometimes think that if you could manage to transform your unending conversation into magic, you would indeed be a formidable wizard."

Questor's brow furrowed. "This is quite important!"

"Not to me. I have a dinner to finish."

The dragon went back to work on the cow, gnawing a new portion free and chewing contentedly. He seemed oblivious of anything else.

"Reduced to stealing cows again, are you?" Questor asked suddenly, coming forward another few steps. "Tch, tch. How sad. Practically a charity case, aren't you?"

Strabo stopped eating in mid-bite and swung his crusted, scaled head slowly about to face the wizard. "This cow is a stray that wandered in and stayed for dinner," he said, grinning. "Rather like yourself."

"I would make a poor meal for you."

"Then perhaps you would make a decent dessert!" The dragon seemed to consider the idea. "No, I suppose not. There's not enough of you even for that."

"Not for a stomach the size of yours!"

"On the other hand, eating you would at least silence you."

Questor shook his head. "Why don't you just hear what I have to tell you?"

"I told you, wizard, I am eating!"

Questor hunkered down on his heels, smoothing his patched robes. "Very well. I shall wait until you are finished."

"Do anything you please, so long as you keep silent!"

Strabo returned to his meal, searing the flesh with quick bursts of fire, tearing off great chunks of meat and bone, and chewing ferociously. His long tail twisted and snapped as he ate, as if it were the impatient recipient of food that was too long in reaching it. Questor watched. Out of the corner of one eye, Strabo watched back.

Finally, the dragon discarded the carcass of the cow by spitting it into the mouth of the crater he was wrapped about and wheeled sharply once more toward the wizard. "Enough of this, Questor Thews! How can I eat with you sitting there and staring at me as if you were some harbinger of doom? You ruin my appetite! What is it that you want?"

Questor climbed gingerly to his feet, rubbing at his cramped legs. "I want your help."

The dragon snaked his way through the craters, his monstrous, cumbersome body impervious to the ash and fire, his tail and wings shaking off drops of liquid flame as he went. When he reached Questor's end of the Springs, he lifted himself up on his hind legs and licked his jaws hungrily with a long, split tongue.

"Questor Thews, I find it impossible to think of a single reason why I would want to help you! And do not, please, give me that tired old recitation about the close ties of dragons and wizards, how we have shared so much of history, and how we must do what we can for each other in times of need. You tried that last time, if you recall. It was nonsense then and it is nonsense now. Helping you in any way, frankly, is abhorrent!"

"Your help is not for me," Questor finally managed to get in. "Your help is for the High Lord."

The dragon stared at him as if he were mad. "Holiday? You want me to help Holiday? Why ever in the world would I agree to do that?"

"Because he is your High Lord as well as mine," Questor said. "It is time to acknowledge the fact, Strabo. Like it or not, Ben Holiday is High Lord of Landover, and so long as you live within the valley you are subject to his laws. That means that you are required to give aid to your King when he needs it!"

Strabo was in stitches. He was laughing so hard he could no longer hold himself upright; he collapsed in one of the craters, showering flames everywhere. Questor ducked a scattering and straightened. "There is nothing to laugh about here!"

"There is everything!" the dragon howled. He choked and gasped and belched smoke and fire. "Questor Thews, you are truly astounding. I think you even believe yourself sometimes. How droll!"

"Will you help or not?" Questor demanded indignantly.

"I should say not!" The dragon rose up once more. "I am not a subject of this land or its High Lord! I live where I choose and obey my own laws! I am certainly not required to give aid to anyone—least of all Holiday! What utter nonsense!"

Questor was not surprised to hear Strabo speak like this, knowing perfectly well that the dragon had never willingly done anything to help anyone in his entire life. But it had been worth the try.

"What of the pretty sylph, Willow?" he asked. "She is in need of your help as well. You saved her life once before, remember? She has sung to you and given you dreams to muse on. Surely, you would help Holiday if it meant helping her."

"Not a chance," the dragon sniffed.

Questor thought. "Very well," he said. "Then you must help Holiday for your own sake."

"My own sake?" Strabo licked his teeth. "What clever argument will you conjure up now, wizard?"

"An argument that even a dragon can understand," Questor Thews replied. "Nightshade has gained control of a magic that threatens everyone in the valley. She has already begun to employ it, turning humans and the fairy folk against each other and causing disorder everywhere. If she is allowed to continue, she will destroy them all."

The dragon sneered. "What do I care?"

Questor shrugged. "Sooner or later she will get around to you, Strabo. Next to Holiday, you are her worst enemy. What do you imagine will happen to you then?"

"Bah! I am a match for any magic the witch might command!"

Questor rubbed his chin thoughtfully. "I wish I could say the same. This is a different magic, Strabo—a magic as old as your own. It comes in the form of a demon that lives in a bottle. The demon draws its strength from the holder of the bottle and can employ that strength in any way it chooses. You would agree, wouldn't you, that Nightshade's strength is formidable?"

"I agree to nothing!" The dragon was irritated. "Get out of here, Questor Thews! I tire of you!"

"As much as you hate Holiday, his is the only magic that can withstand the demon. Landover's High Lord commands the Paladin, and the Paladin can withstand anything."

"Begone, wizard!"

"If you do not agree to help Holiday, Strabo, there will be no Paladin to stand against Nightshade and the demon. If you do not agree to help, we are all doomed."

"Begone!"

The dragon breathed a stream of fire that seared the whole of the slope below where Questor Thews was standing and left the air smoking and filled with ash. Questor choked and gasped and retreated from the heat. When the air cleared, he saw the dragon turning sullenly away. "I care nothing for Nightshade, her demon, Holiday, you, or anyone else in this valley!" he muttered. "I barely care anything for myself! Now, go!"

Questor Thews frowned his deepest frown. Well, he had tried. No one could say that he hadn't. He had done his best to reason with the dragon and he had failed. The dragon was simply being his normal, intractable self. If he continued to press the matter now, it would mean a fight.

He sighed wearily. That was the way it was between dragons and wizards. That was the way it had always been.

He strode forward to the edge of the rise again and stopped. "Strabo!" The dragon's crusted head swung about. "Old dragon, it appears that we shall have to do this the hard way. I had hoped that common sense would prevail over innate stubbornness, but it now appears clear that will not be possible. It is necessary that you agree to help the High Lord, and if you will not do so willingly, then you shall do so nevertheless!"

Strabo stared at Questor in genuine amazement. "Good heavens, Questor Thews, are you threatening me?"

Questor drew himself up to his full height. "If threatening you is what it takes to gain your cooperation, then I will threaten you and worse."

"Really?" The dragon took a long moment to study the wizard, then slapped his tail in a crater of fire with a loud whack and sent the burning liquid flying everywhere. "Go on home, silly old wizard!" he snapped and started to turn away.

Questor brought his hands up in a broad sweep, fire gathering at his fingertips as he did so. With a lunge, he sent the fire hurtling at the dragon. It struck Strabo full along the length of his great body, lifted him from the earth, and sent him flying over several of the bubbling craters to land in a tangled heap. Rock and flames scattered everywhere, and the dragon gave an audible grunt.

"Dear me!" Questor whispered, surprised that he could muster such magic.

Strabo picked himself up slowly, shook himself head to tail, coughed, spit, and turned slowly back to the wizard. "Where did you learn to do *that*?" he asked, a hint of admiration in his voice.

"I have learned much you do not yet know about," Questor bluffed. "Best that you simply agree now to do as I have asked."

Strabo replied with a sheet of flame that lanced at Questor and sent him cartwheeling head over heels into a patch of brush. A second rush of fire followed, but Questor was tumbling back down the hillside by that time, out of sight, and the fire merely fried the landscape until it was black.

"Bah, come back here, Questor Thews!" the dragon called after him from the other side of the rise. "This fight hasn't even started yet and already you're running for home!"

Questor picked himself up gingerly and started back up the slope. This was going to require a considerable effort on his part, he decided grimly.

For the next twenty minutes, wizard and dragon attacked each other with a ferocity that was terrifying. They twisted and dodged and skipped about, hurdling craters that spit smoke and steam and flame, turning the whole of the Fire Springs into a blackened battleground. Blow for blow they traded, Questor employing every conceivable form of magic against the dragon, conjuring up spells he didn't even know he knew, Strabo answering back with bursts of flame. Back and forth they swung, pushing and shoving like fighters in a ring, and when the twenty minutes drew to a close, they were both gasping for breath and lurching like drunks.

"Wizard . . . you continually astonish me!" Strabo panted, slowly curling himself into a ball at the center of the Springs.

"Have you . . . given further consideration to . . . my request?" Questor demanded in reply.

"Most . . . certainly," Strabo said and sent a fireball hurtling at the wizard.

They resumed their struggle wordlessly, and only their grunts and cries and the occasional booming coughs of the craters broke the evening stillness. The clouds dispersed, and a scattering of stars and several of Landover's moons broke through the cover. The wind died, and the air warmed. Twilight passed away, and night descended.

Questor sent a swarm of gnats at the dragon, clogging his nose, eyes, and mouth. Strabo choked and gasped and breathed fire everywhere, thrashing as if chained. He began to swear, using words Questor had never heard before. Then he lifted free of the earth, launched himself at the wizard, and attempted to flatten him. Questor conjured a hole in the earth and dropped into it just before the dragon landed with a *whump* where previously he had been standing. Strabo sat there, looking about for him, not seeing him, so angry at his apparent miss he didn't realize what had happened. Then a six-foot bee stinger shoved at him from underneath and sent him lurching skyward again with a howl. Questor appeared from the hole, throwing fire; the dragon threw fire back; and both of them fell apart again, singed and smoking.

"Wizard, we are . . . too old for this!" Strabo gasped, licking away bits of ash that were crusted on his nose. "Give it up!"

"I will give it up . . . when you say 'yes'—not before!" Questor answered.

Strabo shook his blackened head. "Whatever . . . it is you wish, it cannot possibly . . . be worth all this!"

Questor wondered. He was black from head to foot with ash and burns, his robes were tattered and soiled beyond repair, his hair was standing straight out from his head, and the muscles and joints of his body felt as if they would never be right again. He had tried every magic he knew and then some, and nothing had fazed the dragon. He was alive, he thought, only by a series of flukes unparalleled in the history of wizardry. Much of the magic he had tried had misfired—as usual—and much of what he might like to do was beyond him. The only thing that was keeping him on his feet was the knowledge that if he failed now, he might as well forget about ever calling himself a wizard again. This was his last chance, his one opportunity to prove to himself—even if to no one else—that he really was the wizard he had always claimed to be.

He took a deep breath. "Are you . . . ready to listen?" he asked.

Strabo opened his maw as far as it would open and showed Questor all of his considerable teeth. "Step . . . inside, why don't you, Questor Thews . . . so you can better hear my answer!"

Questor sent a flurry of canker sores into the dragon's mouth, but the hide was so tough they couldn't even begin to settle before they were dispatched. Strabo responded with a blast that sent the wizard tumbling head over heels and burned off his boots. They traded fireballs for a moment, then Questor pinwheeled his arms until it seemed they might fly off and sent a ferocious ice storm at the dragon. Sleet and frigid wind beat against the dragon as he sought refuge in the fire of one of the larger craters. But the storm was so fierce it suffocated the flames and turned the liquid in the crater to ice. Strabo was trapped in the resulting block, the ice hammering off his head as he howled in rage.

Finally, the magic gave out and the storm subsided. A foot of snow covered the dragon, but it was already melting from the heat of the other craters. Strabo poked his head out from beneath the covering and shook off the last of the flakes irritably. Then he heaved upward with a roar, and the ice shattered into cubes. The dragon was free once more, steam pouring from his nostrils as he swung about to face Questor Thews.

Questor stiffened. What would it take to overcome the beast, he wondered in frustration. What did he have to do?

He dodged another rush of flame, then another, and threw up a shield of magic against a third. Strabo was simply too strong. He wasn't going to win a test of strength against the dragon. He had to find another way.

He waited for Strabo to pause for breath, then sent an itch.

The itch started inside the dragon's left hind foot, but when he lifted the foot to scratch, the itch moved up to his thigh, then to his back, his neck, his ear, his nose, and back down to his right foot. Strabo twisted and grunted, flailing madly as the itch worked its way up one side and down the other, as elusive as buttered sausage, slipping and sliding away from him as he sought to relieve it. He howled and he roared, he writhed and he lurched, and nothing helped. He forgot about Questor Thews, working his serpentine body over the sharp edges of the craters, dousing himself in the liquid fire, trying desperately to scratch.

When at last Questor Thews made a quick motion with his hands and took back the itch, Strabo was a limp noodle. He lay gasping at the center of the Fire Springs, his strength momentarily spent, his tongue hanging out on the ground. His eyes rolled wearily until they settled at last on the wizard.

"All right, all right!" he said, panting like an old dog. "I have had enough! What is it that you want, Questor Thews? Just tell me and let's get it over with!"

Questor Thews puffed up a bit and permitted himself a smile of satisfaction.

"Well, old dragon, it is really quite simple," he began.

HALLOWEEN CRAZIES

Chief Deputy Pick Wilson of the King County Sheriff's Department leaned forward cautiously across his paper-laden work desk and said to Ben Holiday, "So you and your friends were just on your way to a Halloween party at . . . What hotel was that again?"

Ben looked thoughtful. "I think it was the Sheraton. I'm not sure. The invitation should be in the car somewhere."

"Uh-huh. So you were on your way to this party, in a rental car, your suitcases packed in the trunk . . ."

"We were leaving right afterward for the airport," Ben interjected. The room smelled of new paint and disinfectant and was suffocatingly hot.

"With no identification, not even your driver's license?" Wilson paused, looking mildly baffled.

"I explained all that, Deputy." Ben was having trouble concealing his irritation. "Mr. Bennett has identification. Mine was left behind by accident."

"Along with that of Mr. Abernathy and the young lady," Wilson finished. "Yes, so you explained."

He eased himself back again in his chair, looking from the skeleton to the gorilla to the shaggy dog to the pale green lady and back again. None of them had taken off their costumes yet, although Ben had long ago removed his death's mask and Miles had finally gotten rid of the troublesome gorilla head. They sat there in that sterile, functional, bare-walled office somewhere in the bowels of the King County Courts Building, where the Washington State Police had deposited them nearly an hour ago, looking for all the world like candidates for "Let's Make A Deal." Wilson continued to look at them, and Ben could tell exactly what he was thinking.

The deputy cleared his throat, glancing down at some papers before him. "And the shaggy dog costume we found in the back seat . . . ?"

"Was an extra. It didn't fit right." Ben leaned forward. "We've been over this ground before. If you have a charge to make, please make it. You've seen our card, deputy. Mr. Bennett and I are both lawyers, and we are prepared to defend ourselves and our friends, if that should prove necessary. But we are growing very tired of just sitting here. Are there any more questions?"

Wilson smiled faintly. "Just a few. Uh, wouldn't Mr. Abernathy be more comfortable with his mask off?"

"No, he would not," Ben snapped irritably. He glanced sideways at Abernathy. "It took considerable effort to get it on him in the first place, believe me. And we still hope to make that party, deputy. So another five minutes and that's it. You'll *have* to charge us."

He was bluffing, but he had to do something to move matters along. He still didn't know exactly what Wilson knew or what sort of trouble they were in. Just a mix-up of some sort, the deputy had assured them. Just a matter of straightening it all out. But when it came right down to doing any straightening, they just seemed to continue running about in circles.

Willow sat next to him in something that resembled a trance. Her eyes were half-closed, and her breathing extremely shallow. Wilson had watched her with growing suspicion. Ben had explained to the deputy that she was just a little under the weather, but he knew Wilson didn't believe him. Wilson believed she was on drugs.

"Your lady friend doesn't appear to be doing so well, Mr. Holiday," the Chief Deputy said, as if reading Ben's mind. "Would she like to lie down?"

"I don't want to leave you, Ben," Willow said quietly, eyes flickering open briefly before closing again.

Wilson hesitated, then shrugged. Ben moved his chair closer to Willow and put his arm around her, trying to make it look as much as possible as if he were simply comforting her rather than holding her upright. She sagged against him weakly.

"I'm going to call local counsel, Deputy Wilson," announced Miles suddenly. He stood up. "Is there a phone I can use?"

Wilson nodded. "Next office. Dial 9 to get an outside line."

Miles glanced meaningfully at Ben, then exited the room. As he went out, one of several clerks working in the reception area outside stuck her head through the door and told Wilson he was wanted on the phone. Wilson got up and walked over. Ben could hear a couple of the deputies lounging outside talking about how the whole city was overrun like this every Halloween. Witches, goblins, ghosts, and God-knew-what, one said. Zoo animals everywhere, the other said. It was hard enough keeping the peace on normal nights, the first said. Impossible on Halloween, the other said. Bunch of nuts, the first said. Bunch of crazies, the other said.

Wilson finished his conversation with the clerk. "Excuse me a moment, Mr. Holiday," he said and went out. The door closed behind him.

Abernathy looked over worriedly. "What's going to happen to us, High Lord?" he asked in a whisper. He hadn't said a word since they got there because Ben had warned him not to. It was hard enough keeping up this charade about a Halloween party without trying to explain how the mouth in a dog mask could move so much like the real thing.

Ben smiled, trying to look reassuring. "Nothing's going to happen. We'll be out of here soon enough."

"I don't understand why they keep asking if I want to take off my mask, High Lord. Why don't I just tell them the truth?"

"Because they can't handle the truth, that's why!" Ben sighed, irritated with himself. There was no point in snapping at the faithful scribe. "I'm sorry, Abernathy. I wish we could just tell the truth. I wish it were that simple."

Abernathy nodded doubtfully, glanced at Willow, then leaned forward and whispered, "I know you came back for me and I am deeply grateful. But I think that, if we are not allowed to go soon, you must forget about me. You must cross back into Landover and help those whose needs are more pressing." His eyes flickered briefly to Willow and away again. Willow appeared to be asleep.

Ben shook his head wearily. "Too late for that, Abernathy. I'm as much a prisoner now as you. No, we'll all go back together. All of us."

Abernathy kept his brown eyes locked on Ben's. "I don't know if that's going to be possible, High Lord," he said quietly.

Ben didn't reply. He couldn't. He watched as Miles reappeared through the door and closed it again.

"Help's on the way," he said. "I reached Winston Sack, senior partner with the firm of Sack, Saul, and McQuinn. We did some business with them a few years back in that Seafirst case. He said he'd send someone right over."

Ben nodded. "I hope whoever it is hurries."

Wilson came back into the room, all business. "Mr. Holiday, do you know a man named Michel Ard Rhi?"

Ben had been ready for that question from the beginning. There couldn't be any other reason that they would be detained like this. He pretended to think a moment, then shook his head. "No, I don't think so."

"Well, it appears that Mr. Ard Rhi has accused you and your friends of stealing something from him. Some sort of medallion."

The room got very quiet. "That's ridiculous," Ben said.

"Mr. Ard Rhi has given a description of the medallion to us. The description is quite thorough. The medallion is silver and engraved with some sort of knight and a castle." He paused. "Do you have a medallion like that, Mr. Holiday?"

Ben felt his throat constrict. "Let's wait for the attorney that Mr. Bennett contacted to arrive before we answer any more questions. Okay?"

Wilson shrugged. "Up to you. Mr. Ard Rhi has contacted someone in the Attorney General's office. That's why you're here. Mr. Ard Rhi's coming down from up around Woodinville, I gather. Should be here in just a bit. The Attorney General's office already has a man in the building." He got up. "Maybe when everyone gets here, we can clear all this up."

He went out again, closing the door softly behind him. There was a moment of silence while he moved away, then Miles snapped, "Damnit, Doc, all he has to do is search you to find . . ."

"Miles!" Ben cut him short with a hiss. "What was I *supposed* to do? Tell him I had it? If he finds out I have it, we'll be charged for sure and the medallion confiscated in the bargain! I can't allow that to happen!"

"Well, I don't see how you can prevent it! They'll find it anyway the moment they search you!"

"Listen up, will you? He's not going to search me! He can't do that without probable cause, and he hasn't got any! Besides, it won't come to that!"

Miles' round face tightened. "With all due respect, Doc, you are not a criminal lawyer! You're a hell of trial lawyer, but your specialty is civil litigation! How do you know if he's got probable cause or not? Ard Rhi is going to say you took it, and that sounds like probable cause for a search to me!"

Ben felt trapped. He knew Miles was right. But if he admitted to having the medallion, they would be there in that Courts Building for the rest of their lives, or at least long enough to make it seem that way. He looked from Miles to Abernathy to Willow. Miles was beside himself with worry, Abernathy was within an inch of doing something that would blow his cover, and Willow was so sick she could no longer even sit upright without help. Landover was looking farther and farther away with the passing of every moment. His plan of escape was coming apart at the seams. He could not afford any further complications. He had to find a way to get them out of there right now.

He got up, walked to the door, and opened it. "Wilson," he called quietly, and the Chief Deputy left what he was doing to wander over. "I've been thinking," Ben said. "Why not put this whole matter over until tomorrow—or even until the first of the week. This isn't anything that won't keep. Willow seems to be getting worse. I want her to get some rest, maybe see a doctor. When that's done, I'll be happy to answer any questions you want. How about it?"

He meant it. He would come back, from Landover if necessary, and set things straight once and for all. He had already decided that he didn't care for the idea of Michel Ard Rhi running around loose in his old world after all.

But Wilson was already shaking his head. "Sorry, Mr. Holiday, but I can't do that. I might consider it if it were just me making the decision. But the order to hold you came right from the Attorney General's office. I can't release you until they say so. You're a lawyer; you understand."

Ben nodded wordlessly. He understood, all right. Somewhere along the line, Michel Ard Rhi had greased some political wheels. He should have expected as much. He thanked Wilson anyway and went back inside the office, closing the door once more. He sat down again beside Willow and cradled her against him.

"Well, you tried, Doc," Miles offered quietly.

Willow's head lifted momentarily from his shoulder. "It will be all right, Ben," she whispered. "Don't worry."

He did worry, though. He worried that time was slipping away. He worried that all the doors out of this mess were closing one after the other, and he wasn't going to be able to do a thing about it.

He was still worrying twenty minutes later when there was a brief knock, the door opened, and a young man in a neatly pressed, three-piece suit and carrying a briefcase appeared, spoke momentarily over his shoulder to Wilson, and stepped inside. This had better be the cavalry, Ben thought. The young man stopped. He was not prepared for what greeted him.

"Mr. Bennett?" he asked, looking doubtfully at the skeleton, gorilla, shaggy dog, and pale green lady facing him. Miles stuck out his hand and the young man shook it. "Lloyd Willoughby, Mr. Bennett, from Sack, Saul, and McQuinn. Mr. Sack called me and asked me to come over."

"We appreciate it, Mr. Willoughby," Miles said and proceeded to introduce the others. Ben shook his hand. Abernathy and Willow just looked at him, and he in turn looked back at them. Ben thought he looked awfully young—and that meant awfully green. You could tell from the way he was looking at them that he was thinking much the same thing Chief Deputy Wilson had been thinking a short time earlier.

Willoughby put his briefcase on Wilson's desk and rubbed his hands together nervously. "Now, then, what seems to be the problem?"

"The problem is simple," Ben offered, taking charge. "We are being held on a bogus theft charge—a charge made by a Mr. Ard Rhi. This man apparently has some clout in the Attorney General's office, because that's where the order to hold us originated. What we want—and right now—is to be allowed to go home and worry about this another time. Willow is quite ill and needs to be put to bed."

"Well, I understood that there was a possible theft charge pending," Willoughby said, looking increasingly nervous. "Some sort of medallion? What can you tell me about that?"

"I can tell you that I have it and that it is mine," Ben answered, seeing no purpose in pretending otherwise. "Mr. Ard Rhi has no basis for his charge that I stole it."

"Have you told this to the Chief Deputy?"

"No, Mr. Willoughby, because if I did, he would want to take the medallion, and I have no intention of giving it up."

Willoughby now looked as if he were waist deep in alligators. He managed a faint smile. "Certainly, Mr. Holiday, I understand. But, do you have the medallion on you? Because from what I understand, if they choose to charge you, they might search you, find the medallion, and take it from you anyway."

Ben fumed. "What about probable cause? Isn't it Ard Rhi's word against ours? That's not enough for probable cause, is it?"

Willoughby looked perplexed. "Actually, Mr. Holiday, I'm not sure. The truth is, criminal law is only a sideline in our firm's practice. I handle a small amount to satisfy those of our clients who want one of us to represent them, but I don't do much otherwise." He smiled weakly. "Mr. Sack always calls me to cover for him on these nighttime matters."

Green as new wood, Ben thought. We're doomed.

"You mean you're not even a criminal attorney?" Miles began, coming to his feet as if he might actually be the gorilla he was dressed as. Willoughby took a quick step back, and Ben restrained Miles with a hand on his shoulder, pushing him back down again into his seat with a quick warning glance in the general direction of the door that separated them from Wilson.

He turned back to Willoughby. "I don't want them to search me, Mr. Willoughby. It is as simple as that. Can you prevent it?" Willoughby looked doubtful. "Tell you what, then," Ben followed up quickly. "Let's play it by ear. You be local counsel, but I'll call the shots. Just follow my lead, okay?"

Willoughby looked as if he were considering whether or not he was being asked to do anything unethical. His brows were knit and his smooth, young face was deeply intense. Ben knew he would be useless if push came to shove. But there was no time to bring in anyone else.

The door opened to re-admit Wilson. "Mr. Martin of the Attorney General's office has asked me to bring you up to Three Court for a short meeting, Mr. Holiday. All of you, please. Maybe now you can go home."

When cows fly, Ben thought dismally.

They took the elevator up several floors and got off in a carpeted waiting area. The Chief Deputy led them down a short hall to a pair of paneled doors and from there into an empty courtroom. They stood at the head of an aisle that led down through a dozen rows of a viewing gallery to a gate that opened onto the trial floor and the judge's bench. The jury box and the witness stand sat to the left, the reporters' stand to the right. Further right, a bank of windows that ran the length of the wall opened out onto the lights of the city. Shadows lay over the room, broken only by a pair of recessed ceiling lamps that spotlighted the counsel tables situated directly in front of the gate.

A man with glasses and graying hair rose from one of the tables and said,

"Chief Deputy, would you bring Mr. Holiday and his friends down here, please?"

Willoughby stepped to the forefront on their arrival, sticking out his hand and announcing, "Lloyd Willoughby of Sack, Saul, and McQuinn, Mr. Martin. I have been asked to represent Mr. Holiday."

Martin shook his hand perfunctorily and promptly forgot him. "It's late, Mr. Holiday, and I'm tired. I know who you are. I've even followed a case or two you've tried. We've both been around the block, so let me get right to the point. The complainant, Mr. Ard Rhi, says you took a medallion from him. He wants it returned. I don't know what the dispute is, but I have Mr. Ard Rhi's word that if the medallion is returned, the whole matter will be forgotten. No charges will be filed. What do you say?"

Ben shrugged. "I say Mr. Ard Rhi is nuts. Is that why we're being detained—because someone says we stole a medallion? What kind of nonsense is this, anyway?"

Martin shook his head. "Frankly, I don't know. A lot of what happens anymore is beyond me. At any rate, you better think it over because if the medallion doesn't show up and Mr. Ard Rhi does—he's supposed to be on his way—you are likely to be charged, Mr. Holiday."

"On one man's word?"

"Afraid so."

Ben came right against him. "As you said, Mr. Martin, I'm a lawyer who's been around the block. So is Mr. Bennett. Our word ought to count for something. Who is this Ard Rhi? Why should you take his word? That's all you have, isn't it?"

Martin was unruffled. He stood his ground. "The only word I get, Mr. Holiday, is from my boss, who keeps me employed, and he says to charge you if Mr. Ard Rhi—whoever he is and whatever he does—signs a complaint. My guess is that if he doesn't get the medallion back, he'll sign. What do you think?"

Ben couldn't say what he was thinking without getting in worse trouble than he already was. "Okay, detain me, Mr. Martin. But how about letting the others go? Apparently I'm the one who's to be charged."

Martin shook his head. "No such luck. Your friends are to be charged as accomplices. Look, I've just finished a long, hard day in court. I lost the case I was trying, I missed my kid's Halloween party, and now I'm stuck down here with you people. I don't like this any better than you do, but that's the way life works sometimes. So let's just have a seat here while we wait for Mr. Ard Rhi. And maybe I can finish some of this paperwork I'm too damned tired to haul back to my office." He motioned to the gallery. "Give me a break, huh? Talk it over. I don't want to mess with this thing."

He trooped wearily back to the counsel table and sat down, bending over a legal pad and notes. Willoughby motioned them all solicitously toward the gallery seats, where they sat in a row.

Martin looked up again. "Chief Deputy? Your people got orders to bring Mr. Ard Rhi up here when he arrives?" Martin waited for the affirming nod, then went back to his notes. Wilson drifted back up the aisle to the courtroom doors and stayed there.

Willoughby eased his way down the line to Ben and bent down. "Maybe you really should reconsider your decision not to give up the medallion, Mr. Holiday," he whispered, sounding as if perhaps Ben should realize that this would be best for all concerned.

Ben gave him a look that caused him to move quickly away. Willow's voice was a whisper in his ear. "Don't . . . give them the medallion, Ben." She sounded so weak it made his throat constrict. "If you must," she said, "leave me. Promise you will."

"Me as well, High Lord," Abernathy said, bending close. "Whatever happens to us, at least you must get back to Landover!"

Ben closed his eyes. There was that choice. He had the medallion back again. Alone, he could undoubtedly find a way to slip out. But it would mean abandoning his friends, and he wasn't about to do that, no matter what. Miles would probably be all right, but Willow wouldn't last the night. And what would become of Abernathy? He shook his head. There had to be another way out of this.

Miles leaned over. "Maybe you better think about hiding the medallion, Doc. Just for tonight. You can come back for it tomorrow. You can't let them find it on you!"

Ben didn't answer. He didn't have an answer. Hello, choice number two. He knew Miles was right, but he also knew that he didn't want to part with the medallion again for any reason. Twice now he had lost it, once before when Meeks had tricked him into thinking he had given it up when in fact he hadn't, and this time when he had given it to Abernathy in Questor's ill-fated effort to change the dog back into a man. Both times he had managed to retrieve it, but only after considerable difficulty. He was not anxious to risk a third mishap. The medallion had become an integral part of him since he had crossed into Landover, and while he didn't yet fully understand how it had happened, he knew that he could no longer function without it. It gave him the magic that made him King. It gave him power over the Paladin. And while he was reluctant to admit it, it gave him his identity.

He sat in the near-dark courtroom and thought about the medallion and all that he had become since it had been given to him. He looked at the trappings of the courtroom, symbols of his old life as a member of the bar, shards of the person he had been, and thought about how far he had gone away from them. Democracy to monarchy. Trial and error to trial by combat. A jury of his peers to a jury of one. No law but his. It had all been made possible by his acquisition of the medallion. His hand drifted to his tunic front. His smile was ironic. The trappings of his old life might be gone, but hadn't he simply exchanged them for new ones?

The doors pushed open and another deputy appeared. He spoke briefly with Wilson, and Wilson walked down to Martin. They in turn conversed, and then Martin got up and walked back up the aisle with the Chief Deputy. All three men pushed through the doors and disappeared.

Ben felt the hair on the back of his neck begin to prickle. Something was up.

A few moments later, they were back. Martin walked down the aisle to stand before Ben. "Mr. Ard Rhi is here, Mr. Holiday. He says you came to his house last night posing as a Mr. Squires in an attempt to buy the medallion. When he wouldn't sell, you came back tonight with your friends and stole it. Apparently, the daughter of his steward helped you. He says she's admitted her part in the matter." He looked toward the courtroom doors. "Chief Deputy?"

Wilson and the other deputy pushed open the doors and said something to someone outside. Michel Ard Rhi stepped into view, his face impassive, but his eyes dark with anger. Behind him appeared two members of Graum Wythe's watch.

Elizabeth stood disconsolately between them. Her eyes were downcast and tears streaked her freckled face.

Ben felt sick. They had found Elizabeth. There was no telling what they had threatened her with to force her to confess to stealing the medallion. And there was no telling what they would do to her if Ard Rhi didn't get it now.

"Do any of you know the little girl?" Martin asked quietly.

No one said anything. No one had to.

"How about it, Mr. Holiday?" Martin pressed. "If you return the medallion, this whole matter can be dropped right here and now. Otherwise, I have to charge you."

Ben didn't answer. He couldn't. There seemed no way out.

Martin sighed. "Mr. Holiday?"

Ben leaned forward, just to shift positions while he tried to stall, but Abernathy misinterpreted the move, thinking he had decided to give up the medallion, and hurriedly brought up a paw to restrain him.

"No, High Lord, you cannot!" he exclaimed.

Martin stared at the dog. Ben could see in the man's eyes what he was thinking. He was thinking, how can the mouth on a dog costume move like that? How come he has teeth and a tongue? How come he seems so real?

Then a ball of crimson fire exploded outside the bank of courtroom windows, a black hole opened through the night, and out of the hole flew Strabo the dragon and Questor Thews.

DRAGON AT THE BAR

It was one of those rare moments in life when everything seems to come to a halt, where movement is suspended, and everyone is trapped in a sort of three-dimensional still life. It was one of those moments that imprints itself in the memory, so that years later everyone still remembers exactly what it was like—what the feelings were, the smells, the tastes, the colors, and the lines and angles of everything around; and most of all, the way everything that happened just before and just after seemed focused on that moment like sunlight reflected off still water in colored threads.

It was like that for Ben Holiday. For that one moment, he saw everything as if it were captured in a photograph. He was half-turned in his seat in the front row of that courtroom gallery, Willow on one side, slumped down against his shoulder, Abernathy on the other, eyes shining, and Miles further left, still in his gorilla outfit, his cherubic face a mix of astonishment and dismay. Martin and Willoughby stood just in front of them on the other side of the gate, two generations of three-piece suits, their entire lives given over to a belief in the value of reason and common sense, the former looking as if he had just witnessed Armageddon, the latter looking as if he had caused it. Behind and to the rear, just visible in Ben's peripheral vision, were Chief Deputy Wilson and his brothers-at-arms, minions of the law, bent in half crouches that gave them the appearance of startled cats poised to run either way. Michel Ard Rhi had black hatred etched on his face, and his men were white with fear. Only Elizabeth radiated the pure wonder that was captured, too, somewhere in Ben.

Outside, pinned against the backdrop of the lights of the city of Seattle, was Strabo. His bulk seemed to hang in the air, wings outspread like a monstrous hang glider's, his black, crusted, serpentine form framed in the windows of the courtroom like an image projected on a screen. His yellow-lamp eyes blinked, and smoke trailed in streamers from his nostrils and mouth. Questor Thews sat astride him, patchwork gray robes so tattered they seemed to hang in strips, white hair and beard streaked with ash and flying in the wind. There was wonder mirrored in the wizard's face as well.

Ben wanted to howl with the exhilaration he was feeling.

Then Martin whispered, "Good God!" his voice like a small child's, and the moment was gone.

Everyone began moving and shouting at once. Wilson and the second deputy came down the aisle still crouched, slipping their guns from their holsters, yelling at everyone to get down. Ben yelled back, telling them not to shoot, glancing once over his shoulder to where Questor Thews was already making a quick circling motion with his fingers, then back again to see the astonished deputies staring at fistfuls of daisies where the guns had been. The hallway outside had become an impassable jungle, floor-to-ceiling deepest Africa, and Michel Ard Rhi and his men, trying desperately to flee, found their exit blocked. Elizabeth had broken free of them and was running down the aisle to greet Abernathy, crying and saying something about a clown nose and Michel and how sorry she was. Willoughby was pulling and tugging on Miles as if somehow Miles might get him out of this nightmare, and Miles was trying in vain to shove the other man away.

Then, suddenly, Strabo shifted positions outside the window, and his huge tail swung about like a wrecking ball and hammered into the bank of windows with an explosion that shattered glass, wooden frames, and half the wall. The city night rushed in, wind and cold, the sounds of cars from the streets and ships from the docks, and the lights of the adjacent high rises which now seemed magnified a hundredfold.

Ben went to the floor, Miles was thrown back into the gallery seats, and Abernathy and Elizabeth came together in a rush.

"Strabo!" Michel Ard Rhi screamed in recognition.

The dragon flew in through the opening like a dirigible and settled onto the courtroom floor, flattening counsel benches, the reporters' stand, and part of the gate.

"Holiday!" he hissed, and his tongue licked out from between the blackened spikes of his teeth. "What an ugly world you come from!"

Martin, Willoughby, Wilson, the second deputy, Michel Ard Rhi, and his men were climbing all over one another in an effort to get out of the way of the dragon, but they couldn't break through the wall of foliage that blocked the courtroom doors. Strabo glanced at them; his maw opened, and a jet of steam shot out at the five, who screamed in terror and dove for the cover of the gallery seats. The dragon laughed and clicked his jaws at them.

"Enough of that nonsense!" Questor Thews snapped. The wizard began climbing down from the dragon's back.

"You drag me here against my will, force me to rescue a man I despise, a man who is nothing less than what he deserves to be—the victim of his own foolhardiness—and now you would deprive me of the tiny bit of pleasure this pointless venture affords!" Strabo huffed and snapped his tail, taking out another row of gallery seats. "You are so tiresome, Questor Thews!"

Questor ignored him. "High Lord!" The wizard came forward and embraced Ben warmly. "Are you well?"

"Questor, I have never been better!" Ben exclaimed, pounding the other on the back so hard he almost knocked him over. "And I have never been happier to see anyone in all my life! Not ever!"

"I could not tolerate even the thought of you being here another moment, High Lord," Questor declared solemnly. He straightened. "Let me make my confession here and now. This entire mishap has been my fault. I am the one who made a mess out of things and I am the one who must put them right again."

He turned, his eyes settling on Abernathy. "Old friend!" he called over. "I have done you a grave disservice. I am sorry for what I did. I hope you will forgive me."

Abernathy wrinkled his nose with distaste. "Cat's whiskers, Questor Thews! There is no time for this nonsense!" Questor assumed a pained look. "Oh, for the . . . Very well! I forgive you! You knew I would! Now, get us out of here, confound it!"

But Questor had caught sight of Michel Ard Rhi. "Ah, hello, Michel!" he called up the aisle to where the other was crouched behind a line of benches. He smiled brightly, then whispered out of the corner of his mouth to Ben, "What is going on here, anyway?"

Quickly, Ben filled him in. He told him what Michel had done to Abernathy and tried to do to them.

Questor was understandably appalled. "Michel hasn't changed a bit, it seems. He remains the same detestable fellow he always was. Landover is well rid of him." He shrugged. "Well, this is all great fun, but I am afraid we must be going, High Lord. I suspect the magic I employed to close off this room won't last very long. Magic has never enjoyed much success in this world." He took a moment to survey his handiwork at the courtroom door, then sighed. "That's a much better than average forest wall I conjured, don't you think? I am quite proud of it. I have always been rather good at growing things, you know."

"A regular green thumb," Ben acknowledged. He had his eyes fixed on Michel Ard Rhi. "Listen, Questor, as far as I'm concerned, the quicker you get us out of here, the better. But we have to take Michel with us. I know," he added hastily, seeing the look of horror on the other's face, "you think I'm nuts. But what about Elizabeth if we leave him? What happens to her?"

Questor frowned. Clearly, he hadn't considered that. "Oh, dear," he said.

Elizabeth, a dozen feet up the aisle, was clearly thinking much the same thing. "Abernathy!" she begged, tugging on his sleeve. When he looked down, her eyes were huge. "Please don't leave me behind! I don't want to stay here anymore. I want to come with you."

Abernathy shook his head. "Elizabeth, no . . ."

"Yes, Abernathy, please! I want to! I want to learn magic, and fly dragons and play with you and Willow and see the castle where . . ."

"Elizabeth . . ."

". . . Ben is King and the fairy world and all the strange creatures, everything, but I don't want to stay here, not with Michel, not even if my father said it would be all right, because it wouldn't, not ever . . ."

"But I can't take you!"

They stared at each other in anguish. Then Abernathy bent down impulsively, hugged the little girl close, and felt her hug him back. "Oh, Elizabeth!" he whispered.

Outside the window, still in the distance, sirens sounded. Miles grabbed Ben. "You have to get out of here now, Doc— or you're liable not to get out at all." He shook his head. "I still think this whole thing is just a crazy dream. Green fairies and talking dogs and now dragons! I think I'm going to wake up tomorrow and wonder what I had to drink tonight!" Then he grinned. "Doesn't matter, though." He glanced at the dragon, who was chewing on a section of the judge's bench. "I wouldn't have missed a minute of it!"

Ben smiled. "Thanks, Miles. Thanks for sticking with me. I know it wasn't easy—especially with so many weird things happening all at once. But someday you'll understand. Someday I'll come back and tell you everything."

Miles put a big hand on his shoulder. "I'll hold you to that, Doc. Now get going. And don't worry about things here. I'll do what I can for the little girl. I'll find a way to straighten it all out, I promise."

Questor had been studying Elizabeth and Abernathy while Miles was speaking, but now suddenly he started. "Straighten things out!" he exclaimed. "That gives me an idea!" He wheeled and hurried up the aisle to where Michel Ard Rhi and the others still crouched behind the gallery seats. "Let me see," the wizard muttered to himself. "I think I still remember how this works. Ah!"

He muttered a few quick words, added a few curt gestures, and pointed, one after the other, to Chief Deputy Wilson, to the second deputy, to Michel's two henchmen, to Martin, and finally to Lloyd Willoughby of Sack, Saul, and McQuinn. All immediately assumed a rather blissful look and settled to the floor sound asleep.

"There!" Questor rubbed his hands together briskly. "When they wake up, they will have had a very pleasant rest and all this will seem a rather vague dream!" He beamed at Miles. "That should make your task somewhat easier!"

Ben glanced at Miles, who was studying the vacant look on Willoughby's face suspiciously. The sirens had settled underneath the Courts Building, and a spotlight was playing about the ragged opening in the wall.

"Questor, we have to get out of here!" Ben called sharply. He picked up Willow and cradled her in his arms. "Bring Michel and let's go!"

"Oh, no, High Lord!" Questor shook his head adamantly. "We can't have Michel Ard Rhi running about Landover again! He was much too much trouble the last time he was there. I believe he will do better here, in your world."

Ben started to object, but Questor was already approaching Michel, who was on his feet again and backed up against the courtroom wall. "Stay away from me, Questor Thews," he was snarling. "I'm not afraid of you!"

"Michel, Michel, Michel!" Questor sighed wearily. "You were always such a pathetic excuse for a Prince, and it seems you have not changed. You appear determined to bring unpleasantness into the lives of everyone around you. I simply don't understand it. In any case, you are going to have to change—even if I have to help you."

Michel crouched. "Don't come near me, you old fool. You play tricks with your magic that might fool others, but not me! You always were a charlatan, a pretend wizard who couldn't *begin* to do real magic, a ridiculous clown everyone . . ."

Questor made a short chopping motion, and the words ceased to come out of Michel Ard Rhi's mouth, even though he continued trying to speak. When he realized what had been done to him, he reeled back in horror.

"We can all improve ourselves in this life, Michel," Questor whispered. "You just never learned how."

He made a series of intricate motions and spoke softly. There was a wisp of golden dust that flew from his fingers and settled onto Michel Ard Rhi. The exiled Prince of Landover shrank back, then stiffened, and his eyes seemed to catch sight of something very far away, something that none of the others could see. He relaxed, and there was a strange mix of horror and understanding mirrored in his face.

Questor turned away and started back down the aisle. "Should have done that a long time ago," he muttered. "Simple sort of magic, best kind there is. Strong enough to last, too, even in this barbaric world of nonbelievers."

He stopped momentarily as he reached Abernathy and Elizabeth, and he put his gnarled hands on the little girl's shoulders. "I am sorry, Elizabeth, but Abernathy is right. You cannot come with us. You belong here, with your father and your friends. This is your home, not Landover. And there is a reason for that, just as there is a reason for most of what happens in life. I won't pretend that I understand all of what that reason is, but I understand a bit of it. You believe in the magic, don't you? Well, that is surely part of why you are here. Every world needs someone who believes in the magic—to make certain that it isn't forgotten by those who don't."

He bent to kiss her forehead. "See what you can do, will you?"

He continued down the aisle past Ben. "Do not worry, High Lord. She will have no further problem with Michel Ard Rhi, I assure you."

"How do you know that?" Ben asked. "What did you do to him?"

But the wizard was already through the gate and climbing back up on the dragon. "I'll explain later, High Lord. We really have to be going now. Right this instant, I think."

He motioned back up the aisle, and Ben could see that the wall of foliage blocking the courtroom entry was beginning to fade. In moments, the entry would be clear again.

"Get out of here, Doc!" Miles whispered roughly. "Good luck!"

Ben clutched the other's arm for a moment, then released him and carried Willow through the courtroom debris to where Strabo had swung about to face the opening in the wall. The dragon eyed Ben malevolently, hissed, and showed all of his teeth. "Ride me, Holiday," he invited menacingly. "It will be the last chance you will ever have to do so."

"Strabo. I would never have believed it," Ben marveled.

"I care nothing for what you believe," the dragon snarled. "Quit wasting my time!"

Ben cradled Willow tightly against him and started to mount. "It must have taken a small miracle for Questor to . . ." He stopped at the sudden sound of approaching helicopters, their rotors whipping through the night.

Strabo's lips curled back. "What is that I hear?" he hissed.

"Trouble," Ben answered, and hitched his way up quickly behind Questor. Willow opened her eyes briefly and closed them again. Ben squeezed her shoulders and pulled her close. "Hurry up, Abernathy!"

Elizabeth was hugging the dog once more. "I still want to go with you!" she whispered fiercely. "I still do!"

"I know," he whispered back, then broke free roughly. "I'm sorry, Elizabeth. Good-bye."

The others were calling out to him. He was halfway through the shattered gallery gate to join them when he heard Elizabeth call frantically, "Abernathy!" He turned at once. "Come back? Please? Someday?"

He paused, then nodded. "I promise, Elizabeth."

"Don't forget about me!"

"I won't. Not ever."

"I love you, Abernathy," she said.

He smiled, tried to respond, then simply licked at his nose and hurried away. He was crying when he pulled himself up behind Ben. "Sorry, High Lord," he said softly.

"Home, dragon!" Questor Thews cried.

Strabo hissed in response and lifted clear of the shattered courtroom.

Wind blew and dust swirled with the beating of the great beast's wings; the lights that remained flickered and went out, and the dragon seemed to fill the whole of the night. A thing out of legend and bedtime tales, he was real for yet another instant to the man and the child who watched. Then he flew through the opening in the wall and was gone.

Miles walked back up the aisle to where Elizabeth was staring out into the dark. He stood there with her in silence, smiling as he felt her hand come up to take his own.

Strabo burst through the opening in the wall of the Courts Building five stories up and nearly collided with a helicopter. Machine and beast veered away from each other, slicing through the chill night air and the narrow beams of several spotlights situated in the streets below. Neither was sure of what the other had encountered, each a dark shape against the city, and the confusion was evident. The helicopter disappeared skyward with a roar of its engine. Strabo dropped down between the buildings, flattening out.

There were screams from the people in the streets.

"Climb, dragon!" Questor Thews cried frantically.

Strabo soared skyward once more, arcing between a pair of tall buildings, steam rolling off his scaled hide. Ben and his companions clung to him for dear life despite the fact that Questor's magic strapped them all securely in place. The helicopter roared back around the corner of a building, lights searching. A second ship followed. Strabo shrieked.

"Tell him not to use his fire on them!" Ben cried to Questor in warning, picturing flaming ships and buildings and Miles and Elizabeth in jail.

"He can't!" Questor shouted back, head bent close. "His magic is as limited in this world as my own! He has only a little fire and he must save it if we are to make the crossover!"

Ben had forgotten. Strabo needed his fire to open a passage back into Landover. That was how he had brought them out of Abaddon when the demons had trapped them there.

They dodged and twisted, but the helicopters followed. Strabo rounded the corner of a building and shot out toward the bay. Wharfs, piers and jettys, shipyards with their dry docks and containers of freight, giant cranes that looked like goose-necked dinosaurs, and a kaleidoscope of vessels of all sizes and shapes passed away underneath. Ahead, far beyond, loomed a massive range of mountains. Below, the lights of the city winked and flashed.

A ship whistle sounded with a shriek, frightening them all with its closeness. Strabo shuddered, twisted left, and began to climb. Ben squinted. Something huge loomed close behind, dropping rapidly, small red and green lights blinking.

"A jet!" he cried in frantic warning. "Look out, Questor!"

Questor screamed something to Strabo, and the dragon whipped aside, just as the huge airplane dropped past on its path of descent. Engines roared, the wind screamed, and every other sound disappeared into white silence.

Strabo came around again and started back for the city, blackened teeth showing.

"No!" Questor howled. "Climb, dragon—take us home!"

But Strabo was too infuriated. He wanted someone or something to fight. Steam blew in jets from his nostrils and there were strange, frightening sounds emanating from his throat.

He passed back over the harbor and spotted the helicopters. He roared in challenge, and now fire burned redly from his jaws.

Ben was wild. "Turn him, Questor! If he uses up all his fire, we'll be trapped here!"

Questor Thews shouted in warning at the dragon, but Strabo ignored him. He went straight for the helicopters, slashed between them so that they were forced to veer frantically aside to avoid a collision, then sped back into the midst of the city buildings. Spotlights whipped across the sky in search of them. Ben was certain he could hear people screaming. He was certain he could hear gunfire. Strabo, heaven help them, was flying blind.

Then, just when it appeared that matters were completely out of control, the dragon seemed to remember himself. With a shriek that froze the entire night into stillness, Strabo suddenly shot skyward. Ben, Questor, Abernathy, and Willow were thrust back viciously. Wind whipped and tore at them, threatening to unseat them, chilling them to the bone. Sound and sight disappeared in a vortex of motion. Ben held his breath and waited for them all to disintegrate. That was how this chase was going to end, he decided. They were simply going to come apart. There wasn't any doubt of it.

He was wrong. Strabo shrieked a second time and suddenly breathed out a rush of fire. The air seemed to melt and the sky to open. A jagged hole appeared, black and empty, and they flew into it.

The blackness swallowed them. There was a flare of light and a surge of heat. Ben closed his eyes, then slowly opened them again.

A scattering of colored moons and solemn, twinkling stars brightened the night like a child's picture book. Mountain walls rose all about and trailers of mist played hide-and-seek through craggy peaks and great, silent trees.

Ben Holiday let his breath escape in a slow hiss of relief.

They were home.

STOPPER

The little company spent the remainder of that night on the western slope of the valley just north of the Heart. They settled themselves in a grove of fruit trees mixed with a scattering of crimson-leaved maples, the smell of berries and apples mingling with hardwood bark and new sap in the cool night air. Cicadas hummed, crickets chirped, night birds called from near and far, and the whole of the valley whispered in the softest cadence that all was well. Sleep was an old and valued friend on such a night. For all but one of the worn and harried members of the little company, it came easily.

Ben Holiday alone remained awake. Even Strabo slept, curled up some distance off within the shelter of a low ravine, but Ben stayed awake. Sleep would not come for him. He leaned back against Willow and waited for the dawn, troubled and anxious. Willow was a tree now. She had made the transformation moments after they had eased her down off the back of the dragon, barely conscious. She had tried to reassure Ben with a quick squeeze of one hand and a momentary smile, and then she was changing. Ben remained unconvinced. He stayed awake next to her, wishing that it was not just in his imagination that he could seem to hear the sound of her breathing grow steadily stronger, smoother, deeper in tone. He knew she believed the transformation was necessary, that whatever the nature of the illness that had ravaged her in his world, whatever the form of the poison that attacked her, the soil of her own world would heal her. Maybe yes, maybe no, Ben thought. He had seen it work before, but that was before. He continued to keep an uneasy watch.

Even so, he tried several times to snatch a bit of sleep, tried to close his eyes and let it embrace him, but his thoughts were dark and filled with the promise of terrifying dreams. He could not shake the memory of how close they had all come to not making it back. He could not forget the sense of helplessness he had experienced there in that empty courtroom when all his options had been stripped from him, a trial lawyer whose arguments and appeals had finally been exhausted. He could not forgive himself for so completely losing control.

Questions whispered to him from the night. How far away from himself had he come in giving up his old life for his new? How much had he sacrificed to regenerate his sense of purpose? Too much, perhaps—so much that he was in very real danger of losing his identity.

He drifted in and out of a sort of half sleep, through uneven bouts of self-recrimination and second-guessing, plagued by demons of his own making. He knew he should dismiss them, yet he could not find the means. He grappled with them helplessly, each encounter provoking new pain and doubt. He was too vulnerable, and he could not seem to protect himself. He simply drifted.

When dawn's light did begin at last to creep into the dark recesses of his consciousness, the eastern sky lightening and the night fading west, he found he had slept somehow, if only briefly. He jolted awake from a fitful doze, his eyes searching quickly for Willow, finding her asleep beside him, her color strong again, her life miraculously restored. There were tears in his eyes, and he brushed at them, smiling. Then, finally, the demons began to slip away, and he could feel again some small measure of hope that he might yet make sense out of who and what he was and take back into his own hands the lines that measured out his life.

He confronted then, for the first time, something he had carefully avoided that entire night—the prospect of dealing with Nightshade and the Darkling. The specter of such an encounter had been lurking at the edge of his subconscious ever since Questor had told him after landing what had become of the bottle, kept just back of where he would be forced to think about it. But now he must think of it, he knew. He could put it off no longer. Everything that had gone before in his long search for the medallion and Abernathy would be rendered pointless if he did not find a way, once and for all, to dispose of that damnable bottle. That meant he must face Nightshade. And that could easily cost him his life.

He sat in the gradually brightening clearing, feeling the pulse of the morning begin to quicken and the sluggishness of its night sleep begin to fade. He let his hand drift down to Willow's face and his fingers brush her skin softly. She stirred, but did not waken. How was he to do what must be done? he wondered. How was he to retrieve the bottle from Nightshade so that the demon could be put back inside? The doubts and fears had left him now, their needles withdrawn. He was able to think in clear, pragmatic terms. He must become the Paladin again, he realized, the knight-errant that was the alter ego of the Kings of Landover, that frightening iron juggernaut that seemed to claim a bit more of his soul each time he called upon its services. He shuddered involuntarily at the surge of ambivalent emotions that were stirred within him. He would need the Paladin's strength to withstand Nightshade's magic, not to mention the demon's. Questor Thews would help, of course. Questor would lend his own magic to the cause. The real question was, would the two of them be enough? Even forgetting Nightshade for the moment, how could they overcome the Darkling? How could anyone overcome a creature whose power was apparently limitless?

Ben Holiday sat alone in the brightening dawn and pondered this puzzle. He was still pondering it when the others came awake, the solution he sought as elusive as summer frost.

He was pleasantly surprised, therefore, when halfway through a breakfast in which he was principally concerned with assuring himself that Willow was well again, the answer came to him.

He was surprised, too, when, following breakfast, Strabo offered to carry them all north to the Deep Fell. He needn't have been. The dragon didn't make the offer because he felt an obligation to do anything further to help, or because he felt Questor had any further hold over him either. He had no sense of responsibility or concern for the success of their endeavors. He made it because he was anxious to let Holiday and Nightshade have at each other and he wanted to be there to enjoy the show. Someone's spilled blood was necessary to satisfy his irritation at having been dragged into this conflict in the first place, and he could only hope that witch and King would both bleed freely in the battle that was to follow.

"You owe me, Holiday!" the dragon announced with a venomous hiss on making the offer to convey Ben to his own funeral. "This makes twice now that I have saved your worthless skin and twice now that you have given me nothing in return! If Nightshade dispatches you, I will consider the debt paid—but not otherwise! Think of what I have suffered for you! I was attacked, Holiday—chased and hounded by metal flying things, hunted with lights, screamed at and threatened by others like yourself, my system fouled by poisons I can only guess at, and my equanimity thoughtlessly disrupted!" He took a long, careful breath. "Let me put it another way. I find you the most annoying, bothersome creature I have ever had the misfortune of encountering and I *long* for the day you are finally no more!"

Having said that, he knelt down so that the object of his derision might mount him. Ben glanced at Questor, who shrugged and said, "What else can you expect from a dragon?"

Willow and Abernathy gave him fits as well by insisting that they should accompany him. When he had the temerity to suggest that he didn't think this was such a good idea, given the extent of the danger Questor and he would likely be facing from the witch and the bottle demon, both immediately suggested that perhaps he had better think again.

"I did not survive the acute discomforts of Graum Wythe's dungeons and the vicissitudes of Michel Ard Rhi's personality to be left behind now!" his scribe announced rather irritably. "I intend to see this matter through to its proper conclusion! Besides," he huffed, "you need someone to keep an eye on the wizard!"

"Nor do I intend to be left behind, either," Willow hastened to add. "I am well now, and you may have need of me. I have told you before, Ben Holiday—what happens to you happens to me."

Ben was hardly convinced by either argument; neither appeared to him to have fully recovered from the hardships of the journey over and back and neither would be of much help in dealing with Nightshade and the Darkling. But he knew there wasn't anything he could say that would change their minds and he decided it would be easier to take them than to try to force them to remain behind. He shook his head. Things never seemed to work out quite the way he wanted them to.

So they lifted skyward aboard the dragon, departing the grove of fruit and maple trees that had been their night's camp, leaving behind the Heart with its rows of flags, stanchions, and polished oak benches and the distant, tiny island where rested castle Sterling Silver, and passing finally out of the hill country of the south into the plains and grasslands of the north. They flew until the Greensward was behind them and the wall of the Melchor rose ahead. Then Strabo dipped earthward, sailing lazily across the dark, misted bowl of the Deep Fell, presumably so that Nightshade couldn't miss seeing them, settling at last on a small scrap of grassland a short distance from the hollows' edge.

Ben and his companions eased themselves down from the dragon's back, casting furtive glances toward the rim of the witch's home. Mist swirled sluggishly in the windless midday air as if stirred by some invisible hand, and silence masked all signs of whatever life waited below. The air was sultry and fetid, and the clouds were gathered thick across this stretch of the mountains. East, sunlight brightened the land; here, gray haze cloaked everything.

Signs of the wilt that had marked the land at the time of Ben's arrival in Landover were evident again. Leaves were withered and sick-looking; whole stands of trees and patches of scrub were black. The devastation spread outward from the Deep Fell for as far as the eye could see—almost as if some sickness had crawled out of the hollows and begun devouring what lay beyond in ever-widening circles.

"A fitting place for your demise, Holiday!" sneered the dragon, bending close. "Why don't you get on with it?"

He spread his wings and soared off into the mountains, settling comfortably upon an outcropping of rock that overlooked the hollows and gave him a clear view of everything below.

"I find him quite intolerable these days," Questor Thews said quietly.

"I find it hard to believe he was ever anything else," Ben said.

He positioned Willow and Abernathy in a broken stand of Bonnie Blues some distance back, pleading with them to stay out of sight until matters with the witch and the demon were resolved. He had no real expectation that his entreaties would be heeded, but he at least had to make the effort.

He returned to Questor and spoke quietly with him then, explaining for the first time his plan for dealing with the Darkling. Questor was thoughtful for a moment, then announced, "High Lord, I think you may have found the answer."

Ben's smile was faint. "Finding the answer is one thing; applying it is another. You know what I mean, don't you? This will be tricky, Questor. It has to be done just so. Much depends on you."

Questor's owlish face was solemn. "I understand, High Lord. I won't let you down."

Ben nodded. "Just don't let yourself down. Are you ready?"

"Ready, High Lord."

Ben turned to face the Deep Fell and called out sharply, "Nightshade!" The name echoed and slowly died away. Ben waited, then called again. "Nightshade!" Again, the name echoed into silence. Nightshade did not appear. Beside him, Questor shifted his booted feet uneasily.

Then a swirl of black mist lifted out of the hollows, churning and seething as it settled on the parched grasses at its rim, and Nightshade appeared at last. She stood there against the mist, robes and hair black, face and hands white, a stark and forbidding vision. One hand clutched the familiar bottle, its painted surface luminescent in the gray air.

"Play-King!" she whispered with a hiss. With her free hand, she pulled the stopper on the bottle. The Darkling crept forth, wizened spider's body dark, sticklike, and covered with hair. Red eyes gleamed and fingers curled on the bottle's edge. "See, precious one?" the witch asked softly and pointed. "See what comes to amuse us?"

Neither Ben nor Questor moved. They became statues, waiting to see what would happen next. The Darkling crept about the lip of its bottle like an anxious cat, searching here and there, whispering and hissing words that no one but the witch could hear. "Yes, yes," she soothed, over and over, bent down now. "Yes, little demon, they are the ones!"

Finally, she looked up again. Her free hand slipped the stopper into her robes, and her fingers stroked the fawning demon. "Come play with us, High Lord and Court Wizard!" she called over. "Come play! We have games for you! Such games! Come closer!"

Ben and Questor held their ground. "Give us the bottle, Nightshade," ordered Ben quietly. "It doesn't belong to you."

"Anything I wish belongs to me!" Nightshade screeched.

"Not the bottle."

"Especially the bottle!"

"I will bring the Paladin, if I must," Ben threatened, his voice still quiet.

"Bring whomever you like." Nightshade's smile was slow and wicked. Then she whispered, "Play-King, you are such a fool!"

The Darkling shrieked suddenly, leaped upward, and thrust its tiny crooked fingers toward them. Fire and shards of iron flew at them with the blink of an eye, slicing through the hazy afternoon air. But Questor's magic was already in place, and the fire and shards of iron passed harmlessly by. Ben's hand was about the medallion, his fingers closed upon its metal surface, the heat beginning to surge through him. Light flared less than a dozen yards off, and the Paladin appeared, white knight on white charger, a ghost come out of time. Fire burned in the medallion, then surged outward through mist and gray to where the ghost took form. Ben felt himself ride the light, borne on its stinging brightness as if a mote of dust, carried from his body as if weightless. Then he was inside the iron shell, and the transformation had begun. A second more and it was completed. Iron plates closed about, clasps, straps, and buckles tightened, and the harness latched in place. Ben Holiday's memories faded and were replaced by those of the Paladin—memories of countless battles fought and won, of struggles unimaginable, of blood and iron, of screams and cries, and of the testing of courage and strength-of-arms on distant fields of combat. There was that strange mix of exhilaration and horror—the Paladin's sharpened expectation of another fight, Ben Holiday's repulsion at the thought of killing.

Then there was only the feel of iron and leather, muscle and bone, the horse beneath, and the weapons strapped close—the Paladin's body and soul.

The King's champion surged toward Nightshade and the Darkling.

The lance of white oak dropped into place.

But the witch and the demon were already fusing hatred and dark magic to produce something they believed not even the Paladin could withstand. It climbed out of the hollows behind them, born of green fire and steam, clawing free of the mists and the haze, a huge, lumbering thing as white as the Paladin himself.

It was a second Paladin—of sorts.

From behind the shield of his magic, Questor Thews blinked and stared. He had never seen anything quite like this monster. It was a perversion—a joining of what appeared to be a huge, squat, lizardlike creature and an armored rider twice the size of the knight-errant, all twisted and sprouting weapons of bone and iron. It was as if some impossibly warped mirror had produced a distorted image of the Paladin, as if that image had been reflected in the most loathsome way possible and given life.

The monstrous creature—a single being—wheeled from the hollows' rim and lumbered to meet the charge of the Paladin.

They came together with a thunderclap of sound, white oak and bone shattering, iron scraping and clanging, beasts grunting and shrieking their pain and anger. They slid off each other and passed by, dust and debris flying. Back around came the Paladin, discarding the remains of his lance, reaching down for the battle axe. The creature of the witch and demon slowed, turned, and seemed to swell in size, growing as if fed by the force of the conflict, lifting until it towered over everything.

All eyes were fixed at that moment on the creature.

Questor Thews made a slight motion with his hands. He seemed to shimmer, disappear, then reappear looking vaguely translucent. No one noticed.

The Paladin attacked, battle axe swinging. Nightshade and the Darkling fed their combined magics into their creation, shrieking with delight as it swelled even further, then lifted on its hindlegs and waited. It was as big as a house now, a mass of sluglike flesh. The Paladin rushed it, and the creature surged forward, trying to crush its attacker. The earth shook with the force of its weight as it struck. The Paladin just managed to slip past, the battle axe ripping along the beast's thick hide. But the wound closed over almost at once. Magic gave the creature life, and magic was not subject to the laws of man and nature.

Back came the Paladin, broadsword drawn now, the gleaming blade cutting and hacking with tremendous fury, carving lines of red along the length of the beast. But the wounds closed as quickly as they were made, and the creature kept lunging for the knight, waiting for its chance. Nightshade and the Darkling urged the monster on. The witch's face was rapt with pleasure. The demon's tiny body was stretched taut. Magic surged from both of them, feeding their creature, keeping it strong. They could see that the beast's lunges were getting closer now to the attacking knight. It would not be long now, they knew.

From within the cover of the decimated Bonnie Blues, Abernathy and Willow watched silently. They, too, could see how this fight was going and could tell how it was going to end.

Then something strange happened.

The creature suddenly lurched upward and began to shrink.

It shuddered as if stricken with a poison. The Darkling saw it first. The demon shrieked with anger and disbelief, raced down Nightshade's black robes, and thrust its spider arms out to feed its pet more magic. But the creature failed to respond. It continued to shrink, flinching back now from the blows of the broadsword struck by the Paladin, stumbling and tottering away as it felt its life drain from it.

Nightshade saw it now, too, screamed in fury, then made her own determination of the cause and wheeled suddenly on Questor Thews. Fire as dark as pitch flew from her outstretched hands and enveloped the wizard. Questor Thews erupted in a pillar of smoke and ash. Willow and Abernathy gasped in horror. The wizard had disappeared completely.

But the creature was still shrinking. And now something was happening to the Darkling as well. It was doubled over, writhing on the ground at Nightshade's feet, twisting as if the same poison that had infected its creature had infected it as well. It was shrieking something at Nightshade, who bent quickly to listen.

"The bottle, mistress!" it was saying. "The bottle has been sealed! I cannot find the magic! I cannot live!"

Nightshade still had the bottle in one hand. She stared at it uncomprehendingly, finding it unchanged, undamaged, the stopper pulled, the neck open. What was the demon screaming about? She was mystified.

A short distance away, the creature of the witch and demon's magic had breathed its last, crumbling completely into dust. The Paladin ground it beneath his charger's hooves and wheeled about once more. Nightshade looked up from the bottle in confusion. The Paladin was coming now at her.

Only then did she think to reach down to test the bottle's opening. Blue wizard fire sparked and bit at her, and she jerked her fingers back. *"Questor Thews!"* Willow heard her shriek in fury. The Darkling was barely moving, clinging to one sleeve. The witch snarled, clasped the bottle by its throat, and prepared to send her own magic surging into its blocked opening.

She was too late.

The Paladin was almost on top of her.

Then Questor Thews seemed to explode out of nowhere right in front of the witch, seizing the bottle before she could think to react, snatching it quickly away. Nightshade shrieked once and lunged for the wizard just as the Paladin reached her.

Fire seemed to erupt from everywhere at the point of impact.

No longer within the concealment of the Bonnie Blues, but running to reach Questor Thews and Ben, Willow and Abernathy drew up short, wincing from the sound and the heat. Fire flared, seemingly of all colors and shapes, exploding into the mist and gray like a geyser out of the earth.

Then the debris settled, and Nightshade and the Paladin were gone. Questor Thews was on his knees, both hands clutched tightly over the top of the bottle, watching stonefaced as the Darkling writhed on the scorched earth and turned to lifeless dust.

Ben Holiday returned to himself, lightheaded and dazed, with the medallion still warm against his chest. He started to sway and topple over, but then Willow was there, holding him upright, and Abernathy was beside her, and he managed to smile and say, "It's okay now. It's over."

The four friends sat quietly at the site of battle and talked about what had happened.

Nightshade was gone. Whether she had been destroyed by the Paladin or escaped to trouble them another day, none of them knew. They could recall the moment of impact—a flare of light and a glimpse of the witch's face. That was all. They were not willing to bet that they had seen the last of her.

Strabo was gone, too. He had lifted into the sky almost immediately at the battle's conclusion, winging his way east without a backward glance. They could only imagine his thoughts. They were certain they had not seen the last of the dragon.

The Darkling, they hoped, was gone for good.

So, with any immediate danger dispelled, Ben was able—with occasional interjections from Questor—to explain to Willow and Abernathy how the puzzle of the Darkling had been solved.

"The secret was the bottle," Ben said. "The Darkling lived in the bottle and never left it completely for long, even when freed from it, so there had to be some logical tie between them. Otherwise, the demon, who was always so anxious to be let out, would have simply abandoned its prison and gone its way. I thought, what if it can't leave the bottle? What if that's where it gets its power? What if the magic comes from the bottle, not the demon, and the demon stays with the bottle because it has to, if it wants to continue to use the magic? The more I thought about it, the more sense it made."

"So the High Lord suggested to me," Questor broke in eagerly, "that if the magic came from the bottle, then shutting off the bottle would cut off the Darkling's power."

"The trick was in doing that without letting Nightshade know what was happening—and then getting the bottle back before she could do anything about it." Ben regained control of his explanation. "So while the Paladin was engaged in battle with the Darkling and Nightshade, Questor used the magic to shrink himself down and slip over to hide in the bottle's neck. He became its stopper. He left an image of himself so that Nightshade wouldn't know what he was up to. What Nightshade ended up destroying, when she guessed that Questor was behind the loss of magic, was just the image."

"You might have alerted us to that much, at least!" Abernathy interrupted heatedly. "You scared us to death with that trick! We thought the old . . . Well, we thought he had been fried!"

"Questor sealed off the bottle," Ben continued, ignoring his scribe's outburst. "That shut off the source of the Darkling's power and rendered Nightshade's own magic, which was focused on the bottle's, useless. It all worked exactly the way we had thought. By the time Nightshade figured out what had happened, it was too late. The creature was done, the demon was too weak to help, and the Paladin was bearing down. Questor surprised Nightshade by jumping out at her the way he did, full-size again, and snatching back the bottle. She couldn't do anything."

"What we hadn't anticipated, of course, was the extent of the effect that sealing off the bottle would have on the Darkling," Questor cut in again. "The demon drew not only its magic from the bottle, but its life as well. Once it was shut outside, it could not survive."

The four glanced as one at the small pile of dust some dozen feet away. A fresh breeze had come up. Already, the flakes were beginning to scatter.

HOMECOMINGS

It was Monday morning in Seattle, nearing noon. Miles Bennett sat in one of the waiting areas of the United Airlines Annex at SeaTac Airport waiting for the arrival of Flight 159 out of Chicago O'Hare. Elizabeth's father would be on that flight. It had taken Miles most of the weekend to track him down and arrange for his return. When he landed, they would drive out to Graum Wythe and begin making the necessary arrangements to dispose of Michel Ard Rhi's estate.

Miles stared out the Annex windows momentarily into the gray, overcast day. It was funny how things worked out.

Elizabeth was seated beside him, reading something called *Rabble Starkey.* She was wearing a black and yellow knit skirt and blouse, and her jeans jacket was draped over the back of the seat next to her. She was immersed in the book and unaware that he was watching. He smiled.

Copies of the *Seattle Times* and the *Post Intelligencer* rested on his lap, and he began leafing through them idly. He had read the headlines and their various trailers a dozen times already, but each time it seemed he found something new. The events of Halloween night were far enough behind him already that he could hardly believe he had been a part of them. It was almost as if he were reading about something that had happened to someone else. It was as if it were one of those foreign affairs reports that he never quite felt had anything to do with him.

But that wasn't true, of course—not with foreign affairs and certainly not with this.

The headlines were all very much the same. "Halloween Goblins Invade Seattle." "Seattle Spirits Trick-Or-Treat City Hall." "Spook Wars Over Elliott Bay."

The subheadings referred to the mysterious collapse of a portion of the

Courts Building, the sightings by policemen, firemen, various city officials, and the ubiquitous man on the street of some form of unexplained phenomenon, and the strange state in which a number of lawyers and members of the sheriff's department had been found in a courtroom that looked as if World War III had been fought in it.

The stories beneath related the details, at least insofar as anyone was able to relate them, given what little there was to work with. The municipal police and fire departments had been summoned on Friday night, Halloween, to the Courts Building in downtown Seattle, following a report of an explosion. Upon arrival, they found a hole apparently blown out of the side of the building on the fifth floor. Attempts to reach that floor from inside were unsuccessful. There were varying accounts as to why. Several stories referred with tongue in cheek to the reports of vast jungles of growth that later disappeared entirely. Helicopters were summoned. Firefighters eventually broke through and found most of one courtroom in ruins, with an outside wall gone entirely. A number of people working in the building were found "in a dazed condition" but no one was seriously injured.

Farther down the page and often farther into the paper, there were stories about the sightings. A dragon, some indicated quite positively. A flying saucer, others said. A return of Satan's hordes, some swore. Yes, there was something, agreed the helicopter pilots who had chased and been chased by whatever it was. They didn't know what. Could have been some form of sophisticated aircraft playing games, one city official theorized. Sure, and maybe it was one of those close encounters that have their origins in Friday night taverns, another quipped. Come Christmas, we'll be getting sightings on Santa Claus.

Ho, ho, ho, Miles thought.

There were stories in which scientists, theologians, lay ministers, government officials, and one or two channelers were interviewed and asked for their opinions, which all were only too happy to give.

No one was even close, of course.

Miles finished with those stories and turned to the single column report on the front page of the *Northwest* section of Sunday's *Times*. There was a picture of Graum Wythe and a headline that read: "Millionaire Gives Castle To State."

Underneath, the accompanying story began:

> Millionaire businessman Michel Ard Rhi announced at a news conference today that he was donating his castle home and surrounding lands to the state of Washington as a park and recreation area. A fund will be set aside to maintain and improve the facilities, and the balance of Ard Rhi's estate, conservatively estimated at three hundred million dollars, will be donated to various organizations throughout the world

for humanitarian and charitable causes. Ard Rhi announced that the castle, Graum Wythe, will become a museum for pieces of art he has collected over the years and will be open to the public. Arrangements for readying the facilities will be handled by his private steward, whose name was not released.

Ard Rhi, a reclusive businessman who is thought to have made the bulk of his fortune in real estate and foreign trade, advised newsmen that he plans to retire to the Oregon coast to write or work on other projects. A small trust will be set aside for his support.

The story went on for several more paragraphs, relating Michel Ard Rhi's personal history and the reaction of a number of local and national notables. Miles read the story twice and shook his head. What *had* Questor Thews done to the man?

He put the papers aside, stretched, and sighed. Too bad Doc wasn't still around. There were just too many unanswered questions.

Beside him, Elizabeth looked up suddenly from her book, blue eyes intense. She seemed to read his mind. "Do you think they're all right?" she asked.

He looked down at her and nodded. "Yep, Elizabeth," he said. "Matter of fact, I'm sure of it."

She smiled. "Me, too, I guess."

"That doesn't mean we can't worry about them, though."

"Or miss them. I miss them a lot."

Miles looked out the windows again, across the broad expanse of the runways and taxi lanes, into the distant gray mix of clouds and mountains and sky. "Well, they'll be back," he said finally. "Someday."

Elizabeth nodded, but didn't reply.

A moment later, the arrival of Flight 159 was announced. Miles and Elizabeth got up from their seats and walked over to the windows to watch it come in.

Several weeks later, Ben Holiday and Willow were married. They would have been married sooner, but there was protocol to be observed in a wedding such as theirs, and it took awhile even to figure out what the protocol was, let alone to implement it. After all, hardly anyone alive could even remember a marriage of a High Lord of Landover. So Abernathy dug out his histories, and Questor Thews consulted a few of the valley's elders, and between them they finally figured out what had to be done.

Ben frankly wasn't interested in the formalities. All he knew was that it had taken him an impossibly long time to realize what Willow had known from the very first—that they should be together, joined as one, husband and wife, High Lord and Queen, and that whatever it took to get the job done, they should do it. Once, not so very long ago, he would never have allowed himself to feel that way; he would have considered such feelings a betrayal of his love for Annie. But Annie had been dead almost five years, and he had managed finally to lay her ghost to rest. Willow was his life now. He loved Willow, had known he loved her almost from the first, had heard her speak countless times of the foretelling of her destiny at the moment of her conception, and had learned from her the Earth Mother's prediction that one day she would bear him children.

Still he had hesitated to believe and to commit himself. He had been afraid, mostly. He had been afraid of a lot of things—that he still didn't belong, that he was somehow inadequate to be Landover's King, and that one day he would simply be gone, back again in the world he had wanted so badly to escape. The realization of the dream was greater than his expectations, and he had feared that he hadn't enough to give.

He was still afraid. Fears such as these lingered in the subconscious and would not be banished.

But it was another fear altogether that decided him on Willow. It was his fear that he was going to lose her.

He had almost lost her twice now.

It was not almost losing her the first time, when he had just come into Landover, that decided him. It was all too new then, and he had not yet put Annie behind him.

It was almost losing her this second time, when she had come back with him into his old world and he was forced to face the fact that she had come, not because she had to, but because she loved him enough to die for him. She had known that such a journey would endanger her and ignored the risk to herself because she knew that he might have need of her.

That was what decided him. She loved him that much. Didn't he love her just as much? Did he want to risk losing her before they had even tried to discover what sort of life they might have as husband and wife? At least he had shared that much with Annie. Didn't he want to share it with Willow as well?

Any fool could have given the right answers to those questions. And Ben Holiday was no fool.

So there was nothing more to say, nothing more to be decided. The marriage took place at the Heart. Everyone came: The River Master, uneasy as always in the presence of his child, still reminded too much of her mother by what he saw in her, and still searching for a way to reconcile the mix of feelings she generated within him; the fairy folk of the lake country, some almost human, some no more than faint shadows flitting through the trees; the Lords of the Greensward, Kallendbor, Strehan, and the rest, with their retainers and followers, an unsettled group that trusted no one, each other least of all, but who arrived and encamped together for the sake of appearances; the trolls and kobolds from the mountains far north and south; the G'home Gnomes, Fillip and Sot in the vanguard, proud of their part—the story varied as to what it was—in the making of this marriage; and common folk from cottages and farms, shops and villages—farmers, merchants, hunters, trappers, traders, peddlers, artisans, and workers of all sorts.

Even Strabo put in an appearance, flying overhead during the feast that followed the marriage ceremony, breathing fire across the sky and presumably taking some small satisfaction from the fact that women and children still ran shrieking at the sight of him.

The marriage was simple and direct. Ben and Willow stood at the center of the Heart on the dais of the Kings of Landover and told each other and those gathered that they loved each other, would be kind and good to each other, and would always be there for each other when needed. Questor Thews recited a few archaic vows of joining that High Lords and Queens might possibly have repeated years ago, and the ceremony was concluded.

The guests feasted and drank all that day and night and into the next, and all behaved themselves relatively well. Quarrels were kept to a minimum and quickly settled. Those from the Greensward and those from the lake country sat side by side and talked of renewed efforts at cooperation. The reclusive trolls and kobolds exchanged gifts. Even the G'home Gnomes took only a few dogs when they left.

Ben and Willow thought it all went pretty well.

It wasn't until several days later, when things had settled back down to normal, that Ben thought once again to ask Questor about what he had done to Michel Ard Rhi. They were seated in the chamber at Sterling Silver that housed the histories of Landover, a cavernous study that always smelled musty and close, trying to interpret some ancient rules on land ownership. Just the two of them were there, it was late at night, and the day's work was completed. Ben was sipping at a glass of wine and thinking about all that had happened the past few weeks; then his thoughts drifted to Michel, and he suddenly remembered that Questor had never finished his explanation.

"What *did* you do to him, Questor?" he pressed, after asking the question once and getting only a shrug for a response. "Come on, tell me. What did you do? I mean, how did you even know what kind of magic to use? I seem to remember you telling me that use of the magic was pretty uncertain over there."

"Well . . . most kinds of magic," Questor agreed.

"But not the kind you used on Michel?"

"Oh, well, that magic was mostly for effect. Not much real magic was necessary."

Ben was floored. "How can you say that? He was . . . he was . . ."

"Basically misguided, if you recall the story," Questor finished. "Remember, my half-brother was primarily responsible for making him into the disagreeable kind of person he was."

Ben frowned. "So what did you do?"

Questor shrugged once more. "He just needed his values rearranged, High Lord."

"Questor!"

"Very well." The wizard sighed. "I gave him back his conscience."

"You what?"

"I let the poor thing out from where Michel had locked it away. I used the magic to enlarge it and to give it a primary place of importance in Michel's thoughts." Questor smiled. "The guilt he felt must have been intolerable!" He smiled some more. "Oh. I did do one other little thing. I planted a small suggestion in his subconscious."

He arched an eyebrow, looking like the cat who had eaten the canary.

"I suggested that in order to atone for his guilt, he should give everything away immediately. That way, you see, if the magic gives out before his conscience has a chance to take hold permanently, it will be too late for him to do anything to reverse matters."

Ben grinned broadly. "Questor Thews. Sometimes you really amaze me."

The wizard's owlish face crinkled. They regarded each other with amusement for a moment, sharing the joke.

Then suddenly Questor jumped up. "Goodness! I almost forgot! I have some news that will amaze you indeed, High Lord." He forced himself to sit down again, clearly excited. "What if I were to tell you that I have found a way to change Abernathy back again? I mean, *really* change him back!"

He studied Ben eagerly, waiting. "Are you serious?" Ben asked finally.

"Certainly, High Lord."

"Change him back? Into a man?"

"Yes, High Lord."

"Like before?"

"Oh, no, not like before."

"But with magic?"

"Of course, with magic!"

"Have you tested it? This magic?"

"Well . . ."

"On anything?"

"Well . . ."

"So this is still just a theory?"

"A well-reasoned theory, High Lord. It should work."

Ben leaned forward until their heads were almost touching. "It should, should it? Have you told Abernathy about this?"

The wizard shook his head. "No, High Lord. I thought . . . uh, perhaps you might?"

There was a long silence. Then Ben whispered, "I don't think either of us should tell him just yet. Do you? Not until you've spent a little more time on it."

Questor frowned, then squinched up his owlish face thoughtfully. "Wellll . . . perhaps not."

Ben stood up and put a hand on his shoulder. "Good night, Questor," he said. Then he turned and walked from the room.

Here is an excerpt from

A PRINCESS OF LANDOVER

A new adventure in the
Magic Kingdom of Landover series!

Mistaya continued to climb until even the thinning winter trees hid all traces of the highway behind a screen of dark trunks and limbs and a thickening curtain of mist. The little falls had been left behind, and even the trickling sounds of its waters had faded. Ahead, the mist was growing more impenetrable, swirling and twisting like a living thing, climbing into the tree-tops and filling in the gaps that opened to the sky.

Had she not known what to expect, all this would have frightened her. But she had traveled between worlds before, and so she knew how it worked. The mists marked the entry into Landover, and once she passed through them, she would be on her way home. Others who found their way into these woods and encountered the mists would be turned around without realizing it and sent back the way they had come. Only she would be shown the way through.

Assuming she didn't get careless and stray from the path, she reminded herself. If she did that, things could get complicated. Even for her.

She pulled the collar of her coat tighter, her breath clouding the air as she trudged ahead, still following the path that had taken her up. When at last the path ended, she kept going anyway, knowing instinctively where to go, aware of how she must travel.

A wall of ancient oak trees rose before her, huge monsters casting dark shadows in the failing light. Mist swirled through them, but at their center they parted to form a tunnel, its black interior running back into the forest until the light gave out. Trailers of mist wove their way through the trunks and branches, sinuous tendrils that moved like huge gray snakes. She moved toward them and entered the tunnel. Ahead, there was only blackness and a screen of mist. She kept walking, but for the first time she felt a ripple of uncertainty. It wasn't altogether impossible that she could have made a mistake. There wasn't any real way of knowing.

The consequences of a mistake, however, were enormous. One misstep here, and you were in the land of the fairies.

She pressed on, watching the mist and the darkness recede before her at a pace that matched her own. She hugged herself against the chills that ran up and down her spine. Whispers nudged her from within the trees to either side, the voices of invisible beings. She knew those voices, knew their source and their purpose. Fairies, teasing travelers who passed through their domain. They were insidious, unpredictable creatures, and even she, who was born in part of their soil and therefore a part of their world, was not immune to their magic. Partly their child, partly an earth child, and partly a child of Landover—that was her heritage and that was what had determined who and what she was.

Her mother, Willow, had told her the story many times when she was small. Her mother was a sylph, an Elfish creature who transformed periodically into the tree for which she was named to take root and nourish in the earth. She had done so in order to give birth to Mistaya. In preparation, she had collected a mix of soils—from a place in Ben's world called Greenwich and from the old pines in the lake country and from the fairy mists in her world. But she had unexpectedly gone into labor and been forced to take root in a hurried mix of the soils she carried while she was still down in the dark confines of the Deep Fell, the home of the witch Nightshade. The consequences were unimaginable, and while Mistaya had been born without incident, she had also been born the only one of her kind.

You couldn't be more different than that.

But being different only got you so far. For one thing, you were never exactly like anyone else and so you never completely fit in. It was so here. Being part fairy was not enough to guarantee safe passage. Staying on the path and keeping your head was what would protect you.

So she did as she knew she must, even though the temptation to step away, to follow those intriguing voices, to try to find even one of the speakers, played on her curious mind. She pushed ahead very deliberately, waiting for the dark and the mist to fade, for the trees to open before her, for the passing between worlds to end.

Which, finally, it did.

Quickly, smoothly, without warning of any sort, the trees thinned and the curtains of mist lifted. She walked out of the darkened forest into a bright, sunlit day filled with sweet scents and warm breezes. She paused in spite of herself, drinking it in, letting it infuse her with good feelings.

Home.

She had entered at the west end of Landover, and the sweep of the valley spread away before her. Close by, just below, lay the broad, open grasslands of the Greensward; south, the lake country that was her mother's home; north, the Melchor Mountains where the Trolls lived; and east, beyond the

Greensward, the wastelands and the fire springs where Strabo, last of the dragons, made his home. She couldn't see it all; the distance was too great, and when you reached the ring of mountains that encircled the valley, the mists cloaked everything.

As she scanned the familiar countryside, enjoying the good feelings that coming home generated, her eyes passed over and then returned to the dark smudge below the Melchor that marked the Deep Fell. Memories she did not care to relive surfaced anew, and she felt a twinge of regret. The Deep Fell was her real birthplace, dark and terrible, and though she would have wished it otherwise, it was a part of her. Nightshade had told her so. Nightshade, who had wanted her for her own child. For a while, she had wanted that, too. Treachery and deception had marked that period in her life, when she was only eleven years old. But that was finished now. Nightshade was gone, and she wouldn't be coming back.

She shifted her gaze, fixing it instead on the place where she knew Sterling Silver waited, not too far away now, less than a day's walk if she hurried.

She started ahead at once, moving deliberately down from the foothills into the valley, choosing her path almost without thinking about it. She breathed deeply of the scents of the valley as she descended into it, marking each of them in turn, identifying each one, able to separate them out and match them to their names. She had learned to do that a long time ago while studying under the able tutelage of Questor Thews, the court magician. Questor, ancient and amusing, held a special place in her heart. It wasn't just because he was so funny, frequently mixing up his spells and causing all sorts of minor catastrophes. It wasn't because he had always treated her like an adult and never a child, better attuned to who and what she was than her father. It wasn't even because he was the dearest friend she had, aside from her parents.

It was because he had saved her life and almost lost his own by doing so. It was because he had done so impetuously and without a second thought for the consequences. It was because he had dared to go up against a much stronger sorcerer in Nightshade, the Witch of the Deep Fell.

Mistaya had used her own magic to save him, a combination of newfound talent acquired from studying with the witch and her natural talent. Enraged upon discovering she had been deceived into using both to attack her father, she had lashed out at Nightshade in a red-hot fury. The two had gone toe-to-toe in a battle of sorceries that might have seen both destroyed if not for the timely intervention of Haltwhistle. Her spell had turned back upon herself, and Nightshade had disappeared in an explosion of green witch fire. Afterward, Mistaya had used her talent and determination to nurse Questor back to health. When he was well again, he became her teacher and constant companion.

Until her father had sent her away to Carrington where, he insisted, she would learn new and necessary things.

To his credit, Questor hadn't argued. He had agreed with her father who, after all, was King and had the final word on almost everything. He had told her that her father was right, that she needed to see something of another world, and her father's world was the obvious choice. He would be waiting when she returned, and they would pick up right where they left off on their study of the flora and fauna, of the creatures and their habits, of the world that really mattered to her.

Remembering his promise, she was suddenly anxious for that to happen.

Abruptly, a huge black shadow fell across her, a dark stain that spread wide in all directions, as something massive and winged swept overhead in soundless flight. She gasped and dropped into a protective crouch, preparing to defend herself. A beating of great, leathery wings churned the sleepy air into a howling wind that threatened to flatten her, and Strabo hove into view. Body extended, the dragon banked into a glide that brought it about and down into a smooth landing directly in front of her.

She straightened tentatively and faced the dragon as it towered over her. "Good day, dragon!" she greeted bravely.

"Good day, Princess," the dragon replied in a voice that sounded like metal being scraped with a saw's sharp teeth.

She wasn't sure where this was going but decided it was best to find out sooner rather than later. "You seem as if you have a purpose in coming upon me like this. Is there a reason for your being here? Are you here to welcome me home?"

"Welcome home," he said.

She waited for more, but the dragon simply sat there, blocking her way. It was a massive beast, its weight something in the area of four or five tons, its body sheathed in leathery skin and armored with bony plating, its spine ridged with spikes, its triangular head encrusted with horns, and its legs as big as tree trunks. One yellowish eye fixed on her with determined intent while the other closed with languid disinterest. Neat trick, she thought, and wondered if she could learn how to do it.

"We have a small problem, Princess," Strabo rumbled after a long few minutes. "You have engaged in behavior that is forbidden to you. Are you aware of what that behavior might be?"

"I am not," she declared, wondering suddenly if it had something to do with Rhonda Masterson.

"You used your magic to create an image of me to frighten someone," the dragon said, confirming her suspicion. "This is not allowed. This is never allowed. No one is ever, ever, ever allowed to use an image of me, in any form whatsoever, for any purpose whatsoever, without my permission. Perhaps you did not know this?"

She took a deep breath. "I did not. I thought it was a perfectly acceptable usage."

"Think again. More to the point, don't do it again. I don't know what kind of manners they teach you at the castle, or what sort of behavior you have been led to believe is acceptable, but labeling all dragons as scary beasts is way out of line. Consider this fair warning. If you ever create an image of me again without my permission, you shall hear from me much more quickly than this and you will be made to answer for your foolishness. Am I clear?"

She tightened her lower lip to keep it from trembling as the dragon bent over her like a collapsing rock wall and she got a clear whiff of its incredibly rancid breath. "You are very clear," she managed.

"Good," he declared. When he straightened he was as tall as a three-story building and with his wings spread he was twice as wide. "I shan't keep you longer. It is good to see you again, and I wish you well. I have always liked and admired you and your mother; your father, of course, is a different story. Please do yourself a favor and don't take after him. Now, farewell. Take care to remember my warning."

Huge wings flapping with enough force to knock her sprawling, Strabo rose into the sky and soared away, flying east until he was little more than a dwindling black speck against the horizon. Mistaya stared after him from where she sat sprawled on the ground, aware of how close she had come to finding out a whole lot more about dragon breath than she cared to.

ABOUT THE AUTHOR

TERRY BROOKS is the *New York Times* bestselling author of more than twenty-five books, including the Genesis of Shannara trilogy: *Armageddon's Children*, *The Elves of Cintra,* and *The Gypsy Morph; The Sword of Shannara;* the Voyage of the Jerle Shannara trilogy: *Ilse Witch, Antrax,* and *Morgawr;* the High Druid of Shannara trilogy: *Jarka Ruus, Tanequil,* and *Straken;* the nonfiction book *Sometimes the Magic Works: Lessons from a Writing Life;* and the novel based upon the screenplay and story by George Lucas, *Star Wars®: Episode I The Phantom Menace.*™ His novels *Running with the Demon* and *A Knight of the Word* were selected by the *Rocky Mountain News* as two of the best science fiction/fantasy novels of the twentieth century. The author was a practicing attorney for many years but now writes full-time. He lives with his wife, Judine, in the Pacific Northwest.

www.shannara.com
Terrybrooks.net